The Owl Hoot Trail:
Book Two

The Withlacoochee Renegades

by

T.H. Bear

The contents of this book regarding the accuracy of events, people, and places depicted; permissions to use all previously published materials; opinions expressed; all are the sole responsibility of the author, who assumes all liability for the contents of this book and indemnifies the publisher against any claims stemming from publication of this book.

International Standard Book Number 13: 978-1-60452-039-2
International Standard Book Number 10: 1-60452-039-6

Library of Congress Control Number: 2010909981

BluewaterPress LLC
52 Tuscan Way Ste 202-309
Saint Augustine Florida 32092
http://bluewaterpress.com

This book may be purchased online at -

http://bluewaterpress.com/renegades

The Owl Hoot Trail

This trilogy, we call the *Owl Hoot Trail*, is the story of a man, not unlike many of this very day, who leave their home and everyone they love to serve their country in the time of war. This man was a soldier, like all good soldiers, who did not question the politicians or their motives, rather he devoted his all in serving to protect his nation from an invader, only to return and find almost everything he had loved had been swept away and his home land in the hands of corrupt officials and an occupational army. How different were the feelings of the people of Belgium, France, and Poland between 1940 and 1945 and the people of Alabama, Florida, and Georgia between 1863 and 1873?

These books were named 'The Owl Hoot Trail' because in those times, a person who was considered a criminal fugitive was often referred to as an Owl Hoot and the roads they took to ply their trade and evade their pursuers was known as 'The Owl Hoot Trail.' It is upon this trail our returning soldier must travel until he can clear his name of an uncommitted crime.

Book One: *Gold in the Red Desert* tells us how, in a vain effort to protect his family, Clifford Brown, was unjustly accused of murder and thrust upon the owl hoot trail, and finding this trail leading him to the gold fields in and around South Pass City in the Territory of Wyoming. There he witnessed a murder and as a result became entangled in a struggle to right this wrong. There also he found the only woman he would ever love.

Book Two: *The Withlacoochee Renegades* reveals his return to his native state of Georgia during the infamous Reconstruction Period, and of his forming a band of brothers, who like vigilantes everywhere throughout time, were created only by desperate souls in desperate times when legal authority either failed or was too corrupt to protect the people.

Book Three: *The Long Trail* allows us to ride with Cliff Brown in pursuit of the almost mythical villain who was responsible for the murder of several members of his family. A pursuit that takes him almost six years, on a 3500 mile journey through seven states, where in every corner he must struggle with the evils of greedy people and the revenge burning fiercely within himself, each begging, often commanding an inner peace that would be denied him for over seventeen years.

Acknowledgements

The Single Action Shooting Society (SASS) requires all members to have an alias that most closely identifies them to the nineteenth century character they wish to be while attending any club function. A proper dress code is also a requirement, proper meaning nineteenth century, zeroing in on the last forty years of that century. The Withlacoochee Renegades Hunt Club is both NRA and SASS sanctioned and observes their rules and regulations.

In this novel, I have, by permission, used several aliases from members of this club, and have entitled the story from their name, or was it vice-versa?

I also have tried to employ many historical events that took place in and around this area during the time period of the story into the novel as well.

I, too, have entered some of the events my grandmother told me about when I was a lad. Her father and grandfather and many uncles served during that great struggle we have come to call the American Civil War, and more so endured and witnessed the tremendous hardships that were placed upon the civilian population who had supported their home state during that war. Several of the murders and other ghastly deeds recorded herein came to me from her lips as she related her remembrances of those hard times. I will never forget her saying over and over, "You must listen and remember what I tell you because the Yankee historians did not tell the truth very often." We all know one of the spoils enjoyed by the victors is being able to record their side as the right side of any given struggle and therefore, I tend to give much credence to what she had to say.

I would like to point out one fact; the 103rd Colored Troops were stationed in Valdosta shortly after the end of the war. They did not remain as long as this story would lead one to believe and I have no knowledge that they committed any specific crimes against the civilian population other than the murder of Dick Force and their involvement with the Holliday shooting. However often such crimes, like those recorded herein, did occur to southern families during the so-called Reconstruction Period and to save confusion, I have taken the liberty of assigning many of these truths to this military unit.

There is no question that Ruffus Bullock was the Governor of Georgia and history indeed tells us that he fled the state to avoid impeachment and possible severe punishment for the corruption of his office. He did return several years later and was acquitted of his crimes. There is a strong feeling, with not a little evidence, this trial outcome had been agreed upon before he returned, considering the politics of the times.

Also, history has given us one John Henry Holliday who lived most of his early life in Valdosta, Georgia. It is also generally accepted locally, that he left the state for dental college because of a shooting incident with one or more colored troops at the swimming hole on The Withlacoochee River. I have taken this incident and incorporated it into my story with some liberties. Being an admirer of Doc and the colorful life we think he lived, has always inspired his image to me. From what I have been able to find out, he was not at all like Kirk Douglas, Stacy Keach, Val Kilmer or any of the many other movie and TV actors who have played his character; rather he was somewhat short and quite frail and having been infected with tuberculosis as a young man led even more so to his lack of physical strength. His mother and older step-brother also succumbed to this same disease. I have tried to portray him as truthfully as I can imagine he might have been, a gentleman for certain, an educated and talented artist true, and a man who, even as a teenager would not be ordered about, most certainly. His family was very well-respected in the area and his father, 'The Major,' was at least twice elected Mayor of Valdosta. Even though Doc is not a main character in this tale, he does add a spark of color and I hope you enjoy meeting him.

It would also be a true negligence were I to fail to mention the fact that one of the minor characters who walks through this story was a real and true hero to the people who lived in these parts in the early 1870's, that being John J. Inglis. A man who returned from being a POW to a devastated homeland and through hard work and honesty became one of the most predominate leaders this area has ever known. Some of his descendents still live in the area to this day and are proud to say their forefather was one of the most respected and loved in their family and perhaps Madison's favorite citizen of all time.

As in Book One of this trilogy, the main characters are purely images cultivated from my imagination and, with the exception of what is recorded above, the incidents are also.

Appreciation

Some of the illustrations contained in this book are taken from my personal photos and from the website, "Wyoming Tales & Trails." It is to this site we give credit and appreciation. Were it not for the enormous labor and endless hours of devotion in preserving the pictorial history of The Great State of Wyoming by Geoff Dobson so much would not be available to the reader. Thank you Geoff.

Additional thanks and application must go to The Treasures of Madison County for their generosity in allowing the use of photographs of John Inglis and his store found herein.

The Florida Archives in Tallahassee provided the photograph of Sheriff David Montgomery.

The photograph of John Henry Holliday is by courtesy of Miss Caroline Manley, a descendant of the Hollidays.

The picture of The Valdosta Institute is by courtesy of The Lowndes County Historical Society and to whom I am sincerely grateful.

The photograph on the rear cover depicting the Madison Train Station is used by permission of The Madison County Genealogy Society.

Special thanks goes to Danny Hart who furnished the information of his ancestor Richard S. Force's murder by the 103rd Troops in Valdosta in 1866 as well as his photograph.

My appreciation goes out to Sonya Webb and Jim Gillis in their assistance with the editing of this book and to Joe and Ardis Clark of BluewaterPress LLC who offered so much help in the correct arranging of the photographs.

Also many thanks must be given to the members of The Withlacoochee Renegades Hunt Club, for it is from their SASS aliases that many of the names found in this book were taken. The reader might also enjoy knowing that it is from this story, as it lay festering in my mind, that this SASS club received its name. One could not proceed without mentioning Horton Photography in Tallahassee, known to us as Hoss, who helped so much with some of the photographs herein. As well as to The State of Wyoming, Division of State parks and Cultural Resources Division of Cultural Resources, State Archives.

I also want here to relate something that I feel is most important in making this work complete, and I feel this is best explained by telling you a true story. You see, I think a book has different purposes to different people. Some read to kill time, a simple means to occupy one's mind for a few hours, others read to learn and these hunger for education, then you find those who read for the pure and genuine pleasure of the tale, and also there are those whose greatest enjoyment in reading a manuscript is to find fault, usually in spelling and grammar. These people tend to be English majors or masters of the perfect sentence. This last group used to be a thorn in my side but I had an Ohio Yankee, who had several books already in print, explain something he had learned. He told me he purposely left a few words misspelled and a few sentences grammatically incorrect, even on occasion having less than the perfect paragraph, just so these readers will find something gratifying in his work. This made sense to me therefore I have taken his advice; so when you come upon a misspelled word or a comma where a period should be or even that less than perfect paragraph, just smile and continue, knowing it was intentionally left uncorrected to please the Grammar Troopers. That way I hope all who read my work find something in the story that brings them pleasure.

I also have another dear friend who is constantly on me about not being politically correct. I try to tell him that I go through a great deal of research to find what was politically correct at the time and place of the story, and really don't give a rat's ass about what is politically correct today. The jargon of the twenty-first century would have been so out of place in the deep south of the 1870's, and that is when and where this story takes place. So there.

Cover Information

Front Cover
The Withlacoochee River

The head waters of The Withlacoochee River lie some three miles southwest of Sylvester Georgia at Hardy Mill Creek and terminates at the junction with the Suwannee at Ellaville in Madison County Florida, or Suwannee County depending on which side of this black-water stream you are standing. The distance a crow would travel between its headwaters and its termination is near 90 miles but the Withlacoochee does not travel the route a crow would fly, it meanders and curves and runs and drags creating a water flow some ten times that distance.

The word Withlacoochee is a Creek Indian word meaning Great River and when they lived in this part of North America, they found it to be a great river. Later, when they were driven into Central Florida, they found another great river and so called it, only the white man did not understand much of the Creek language thus he named a second river the Withlacoochee, near Green Swamp in Polk County. So Florida now has two separate rivers with the same name.

The Great River we are concerned with here is the original stream to carry the name Withlacoochee in the halls of the white man's history.

The picture on the front cover of this book is of The Withlacoochee River near where Bass' Ferry once was, looking north towards Sam's crossing, very close to the original site of Belleville.

Rear Cover
The Train Depot

The picture on the rear cover is of the Madison Florida train Depot taken in the 1920's. It is offered courtesy of The Madison County Genealogical Society.

The Withlacoochee Renegades

Book Two

Of The Trilogy:

The Owl Hoot Trail

Is dedicated to the men & women who make up the SASS Club: "The Withlacoochee Renegades," who meet at *Estherbrook* Stage Stop on the south bank of the Withlacoochee River the last Saturday of every month to do battle with The Dreaded Carpetbaggers & The Hated Scallywags.

Introduction

The reader found in Book One of *The Owl Hoot Trail: Gold in the Red Desert,* Clifford Brown had fled his home state of Georgia ahead of a murder warrant concerning a man who had actually been killed by a corrupt appointed official.

His travels allowed him to be in the right place at the right time to witness another murder, also by corrupt men in power, although this second killing took place on the great plains of Wyoming Territory.

During the following year, he is the one person mainly responsible for the righting of this wrong and the returning of stolen property to its rightful owner. There also, he falls in love with a beautiful raven-haired woman who becomes his wife.

Book Two is the story of their return to Georgia during times many considered more horrible than the war itself, 'The Unholy Reconstruction Period,' where corruption outnumbered Christianity in the Occupational Government

A telegram had been received telling of the murder of one of his brothers and the threat of the same to his other brother and father. Clifford Brown and his bride arrive to find the worst, and not only to his family but to almost all of 'the home folk' in South Georgia.

He soon forms and leads a vigilante group which the local newspaper names The Withlacoochee Renegades, until most of the corruption is cleaned from the area and many of those responsible for their cruel deeds are either dead, arrested, or have fled the state. The cost of this cleaning is so great that one wonders where a man finds the strength to bear it.

Preface

The Withlacoochee Renegades

Louis Brown had been the son of a farmer who had settled in what became Grayson County, Kentucky, when the Red Coats were occupying most of Virginia. William Swift was the farmer's given name, but because of his refusal to join up with the Continental Army, everyone he knew had turned from him, not only refusing to speak, also refusing to do any business with him. It's mighty hard on a farmer when nary a soul will sell you a thing with which to farm. So he up and moved west.

There in Kan-tuck,' nobody had any knowledge of him, and he figured to shun off any trouble that might show its ugly head down the road by changing his name as well as his residence.

The folks in this wilderness where he chose to stop knew him as Willie Brown. He chose Brown because he admired a man named Brown back in Jamestown.

Willie Brown married a local woman who bore him five sons before the fever took her and their two oldest. Louis had been her fourth and grew up a hard working lad who seemed always unable to please his father. Some felt Willie resented Louis for not dying with the others.

On his twenty-first birthday, in the summer of '35, Louis Brown saw a poster on the up-right at Cidney's Store in Caneyville that said there was work to be had with 'The Kentucky Boat Works' at the mouth of the Tennessee River near Paducah. The next day, Louis loaded what possessions he had on a gray horse and rode south away from his abusive father.

In order to avoid more conflicts with his father, earlier that same year, Louis had bought and paid for a quarter section piece of bottomland on the Rough River several miles from his father and the home where he had grown up. When he left, he asked his brother, Everett, to keep an eye on his land. Nine months later, when he returned with enough money to begin farming, he found Everett had sold his land, taken the money, and bought himself a farm adjoining their father's land. Everett's only explanation was, "I didn't think you'd be coming back."

Louis knew he could take his brother to the law and win, but such was against the scriptures, and what great thorn it would place in his side for doing such to a blood family member. Everett offered to share with him the new land, but what did he want with a farm that wasn't half as good as the one he had on the river, besides it being next door to his father's place? It was, after all, the differences he and his father had with one another that had caused him to move in the first place.

In the summer of 1839 he married Addie and they headed first to Louisville[1], and then south. They did not stop until they reached South Georgia where he started a business of supplying cut lumber from the cypress swamps to the folks that were building a town called Troupville.

Only weeks after their arrival, Louis, a relatively unknown resident to the area, distinguished himself while fighting with General Scott at Brushy Creek against the Red Stick Creek Indians. After that, the people of Lowndes County knew him. In fact, he soon became one of their most talked about residents.

Louis and Addie's first-born was a girl child who died six days after she came to this earth. A son, Samuel, came two years later; then in the bitter winter of 1843, Clifford James was born. A third son, John, blessed the Brown couple in 1846, and by then Louis had built himself a fine sawmill and secured title to a section of land some ten miles north of the Florida line.

He did well raising hogs and a small herd of scrub cattle. He did not like cotton and instead farmed food crops that he could sell to

---

[1] An overnight stop south of Louisville at what would become known as The Tucker House, see the book by T.H. Bear *The Big Open*, Chapter One.

the less fortunate at reasonable prices, for it was cypress lumber that had become his main source of income. By the time Valdosta became the new county seat in 1860, Louis had accumulated a rightly sum of United States currency, both in gold and silver coin.

A year later, when Georgia seceded, a call went out for her faithful sons to come, Louis and his two oldest went right away leaving Addie and fifteen year old Johnny Boy, as everyone called him, home to take care of business.

"Mrs. Brown, we'll be back in six weeks," he paused and then corrected, "six months, tops," he said, and leaning from the dapple gray he kissed Addie square on the lips. It was the first time any of her sons had seen anything like that from their parents.

He was true to his word. Six months later, he came home with a shattered left wrist and a piece of steel in his hip. For the rest of his life he would find it most painful to sit a horse and walking was out of the question, if any distance was involved.

For the remainder of the struggle, he and Johnny Boy cut and shipped lumber north for the cause, gladly accepting Confederate notes for the work and goods.

Louis Brown had never owned a slave. He didn't think much of the Negro race as a whole, although he would admit he had seen some that were hard workers and trustworthy, but he was always quick to point out, they were the exception.

Instead of slaves, he employed twenty to thirty white men who for one reason or another were down on their luck and needed the work. "You can leave most white men unsupervised and he will produce for you, the same as if you were standing there a looking at 'im but take your eyes off' a nigger and he'll go lazy on you in half a second," was one of Louis' often expressed opinions.

Not once did he consider that he, or anyone else he knew were fighting for slavery. Georgia had seceded from the Union and joined the Confederate States of America and thereby was no longer a part of those United States of America.

The United States was now a separate nation from his, and when that nation invaded his nation he did as almost everyone else and fought the invader with all his resources.

During the war years, Brown's Mill employed boys too young to fight and yet it still produced as much lumber as before the war.

With the collapse of the Confederacy, Louis Brown found himself a man rich in worthless paper money and penniless in the kind that suddenly counted.

In 1866, the carpetbaggers arrived in strength even in the little towns of South Georgia and Middle Florida.

A Civilian Division of Reconstruction was set up in many districts to oversee the new Freedman's Bureau. Georgia's South Central District Office was located in Valdosta and John M. Tidwell was appointed commissioner of the division. He immediately imposed a War Tax on all secessionists' properties. Brown's Mill was seized and turned over to a freedman named B. T. Polk, who was brought in from somewhere in Arkansas to take over the business.

Louis accepted this defeat as he had accepted the defeat of his nation and began to earnestly farm his land and increase the size of his animal herds.

Clifford James Brown had served in "The Army of Tennessee" under N. B. Forrest and was reluctant to come home and become a farmer, but he knew with the loss of the family fortune, he was needed and come home is just what he did, by returning to South Georgia and hiring out as a teamster at "The South Lowndes Saw Mill," the very mill his father had built and run for so many years.

With what Cliff earned and what crops his father and brothers could grow they began to see light at the end of the tunnel; that is, until Mr. Tidwell sent troops out with a notice that the farm also was in arrears on war taxes. With no place to obtain the money, he decided to burglarize his father's old sawmill to obtain the tax funds and save the farm. Unfortunately, Tidwell and Polk arrived and a shootout ensued that left Polk with one of Tidwell's poorly aimed revolver balls in his back. The Commissioner immediately had a murder warrant issued on Clifford Brown and the lad fled the state ahead of a hangman's noose.

Drifting from one place to another he eventually arrived in the Sweetwater Region of Wyoming Territory during the gold rush. There he would find an unknown treasure, beyond his wildest dreams. However, with the arrival of a wire from his mother beckoning him home, we find Clifford Brown, "Bound for Dixie" very shortly thereafter.

CHAPTER ONE

Bound for Dixie

Mr. and Mrs. Clifford Brown spent their wedding night under a cloudless sky; lit only by the twinkling of a million stars, beneath a roof made of branches from the grove of cottonwood trees, while being serenaded by the rushing of the Sweetwater River over a thousand small round granite rocks. It was not the elegant wedding suite that Nadine dreamed of as a child, but it was more special than any other place she had ever known.

There was another thing, more special than she had ever experienced before, that took place that night in August on the high plains. The sex they shared was the first she had ever really enjoyed. Not that it never had been physically pleasurable, on the contrary; but having had hundreds of men since she was first taken as a young teenager, through her first marriage and then the awful years whoring, she had found sex to be an act of survival. Sometimes it was good, sometimes bad, but it had always been a necessity of life, as it was for most women of her financial status in the west, not unlike the drinking of water or eating one's meals.

There under the stars, listening to the sounds of the night and the rushing of the water, lying on woolen blankets placed there by a special hand, over hard clay, softened only by riverbed turf; she had experienced her first true orgasm. A screaming, biting, scratching, mad explosion from within her deepest emotions; an experience she never dreamed could exist. An experience she desperately hoped would show its wonderful head often throughout the rest of her life.

She never really knew when she had fallen in love with Reb Brown. She did know, after the first time she had sat beside him and shared a drink of good whiskey, that anytime he would suddenly appear, her world would brighten and a blanket of security would seem to fall around her, and she would feel warm and safe. She knew too, there were times when she didn't see him for several days, she would worry about his safety and her life would seem sharp and almost mechanical. She had never experienced love before, not love of a man. It was not until she learned he was leaving, and the thought of her never seeing him again was suddenly ripping at her insides, did she realize she was in love with him. She of course knew she was attracted to him, but as a friend. He was a good friend and good man. A man she admired, yes; but she didn't realize how much she had become dependent on his friendship, his strength, and his presence, until that awful moment when she thought she may never see him again.

She never dreamed he was in love with her. He had never paid for her; he had not even taken her when she offered it for free. Even at the very spot where they had spent this night, he had not taken her the first time they were there; even when she had peeled down to her drawers and jumped into the freezing water, just so he would see her naked body through the thin white cotton of her undergarments. She had been positive he would not be able to resist her, but he had.

From that day onward she also had been sure that he thought of her as a whore; his friend, the whore; and little more, right up to the moment he had told her to wash her face so they could be married.

Now as they rode southward, she was still astonished at how her life had so suddenly changed, and also the fact that the tall handsome man riding beside her was her husband.

They took a late lunch at the Big Sandy Crossing and then once more headed south to spend another night wrapped in each other's limbs under the stars.

An hour before noon, on the third day of their marriage, they rode past the shingle that read "Green River, Wyoming."

She waited with their mounts while he went into the depot to arrange for the horses and the tickets that would start them on their journey to Dixie.

"Everything alright?" she asked when he returned.

"Sure, I had a little trouble about the horses. They didn't have a car scheduled for animals on the eastbound until day after tomorrow, but I convinced him to get one."

"Really, how on earth did you do that?" she asked, looking up at him.

"I laid a ten-dollar bill on the counter and he slipped it into his vest pocket and suddenly the car was scheduled for today."

"Oh, I should have guessed," she replied a little relieved. She had first thought he had threatened the man somehow. There were times when her new husband's stare alone could intimidate some to do his bidding.

They lunched at Swain's Restaurant which was only a short walk from the tracks and then Cliff took her to Leonard Brannen's Gun Shop and bought her two pistols.

"I really don't think I need a gun now that I have a husband to protect me," she said as he was looking over the little stock there.

"It's for you to protect me with," he said in reply and in a strong enough voice that she decided not to protest anymore.

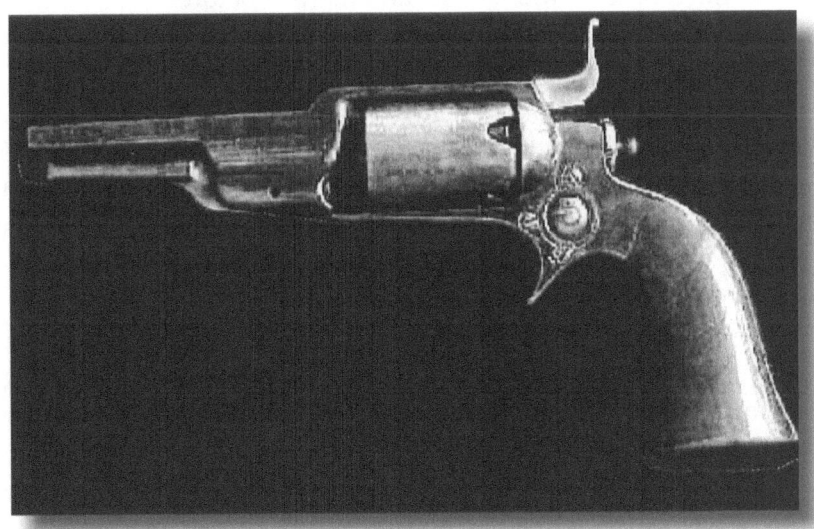

A Colt Root Side-Hammer Revolver

He found a Root pocket pistol with a three and a half inch barrel that had been converted to use the 32 self-contained cartridges. Cliff was partial to cartridge conversion guns since his 44 Richards Conversion had proven itself so well, and this little guy fit in her hand bag much better than his Navy Colt.

Once before, when he was in Green River City, he had Brannen shorten the barrel on the Navy for him, but the butt stock was much larger than what was on the Root and besides it was still a percussion gun. So he traded the Navy for the Root. He also bought her a four barrel Sharps derringer that was chambered for the twenty-two brass case that Smith & Wesson had made so popular. Cliff told her it was the same as the one with which Darla Kimball had tried to kill Cinch DeMoss.[2]

As they were walking from the store Cliff said, "Put the little Sharps somewhere on your person and out of sight."

"So no one will find it?" she replied.

"Exactly."

"What about you?" she teased.

"Oh, I plan to look everywhere. I'll find it."

"That sounds delicious," she snickered.

Next they went to The Green River Bank, the same bank where he had interrupted a robbery several months before.

There they closed her account and took red-backs on the Bank of San Francisco for their stake.

Afterwards, the lovers walked over to The R. L. Livery where Cliff had arranged for their animals to be given grain and water. He paid the tall, balding man and then they mounted and rode back to the Union Pacific depot to await the east bound. Just as they were arriving, she noticed an animal car being pulled up on the tracks next to the switching post and she smiled.

The lonely call of the arriving coal burner could just be heard drifting in with the wind and a rush of excitement swept through her body as she once more realized all this was really happening, and to her.

Cliff put her on the train, but he did not board with her. He waited until he was satisfied that Red and Treasure had been properly taken care of, and then he came forward and sat beside her.

---

[2] See The Owl Hoot Trail Book One., *Gold in the Red Desert*.

Union Pacific Train Arriving At Green River Station

"Are they all right?" she asked knowing the answer before she spoke.

"Yeah, they will be all right. It's just two cars back. I'll go back and check on them every now and again," he said as he slid down and let his hat tilt forward blocking the afternoon sun that was now entering the car's window.

Nadine slid her hand around his powerful bicep and squeezed it trying to let a little of the love she had bursting inside her slip through her grasp into him. The feel of her so close pleased him and he smiled, but she didn't see it.

The train stopped about every forty minutes to take on water and it was during such a stop, at a place called Rock Creek, that Cliff stood and stretched.

"Nadine, I think I'll mosey back and check on our children."

"Alright," she said back, "Don't be long."

He winked at her just before he adjusted his hat. Then he was gone out the door of the car.

She leaned over, placing her head out of the window, and there she could see the man standing on the short platform that was constructed around the huge round water barrel. He was talking to someone who apparently was atop the engine but she could not see that man. Suddenly the large black spout was jerked upward by a spring and the man on the platform swung it to the side away from the train. It all seemed so interesting to her at the time.

She was just pulling herself back inside when she noticed a group of men walking from the water tank towards the rear of the train. There were half a dozen and most were dressed in checkered or plaid shirts and were wearing dirty brown chaps.

'Cowboys,' she thought. Nadine had come to know them very well while working the saloons. Most were pretty good fellows, once the liquor had worn off. They seemed a lonely clan of boys. *'And boys they are, seldom over twenty-five years of age and often homesick,'* she thought, as her mind slipped back to less happy days.

Then suddenly, she saw him; Tom Joiner. His pals had called him Hap. She seemed to remember he worked for an outfit up north, somewhere near Platte Bridge Crossing, but what she remembered most was he had taken a liking to her and had started to tell everyone that she was his gal. He once started a fight in the Monia[3] that ended in a mess, and with him being pitched out on his bottom. Fights among drunks were nothing to especially remember; only Hap had started this one because a miner was paying attention to her, and Hap, being six and a half feet tall and strong as an ox, had hurt the man badly.

Hap Joiner was one of the last people on earth she wanted to meet up with now.

Nadine turned her head back hoping the darkness in the interior of the car would hide her when he walked past, but she heard one of the other cowboys say, "Hey Hap, don't you go a-poking every whore in Medicine Bow while you're there."

'Just what I need,' she thought.

When Cliff returned, he immediately saw her mood had changed.

"What's the matter, Hon?" he asked.

"Nothing, what makes you think there is something the matter?" she snapped back.

He could see she had her feathers up about something, and he had learned enough about women from his mother to know when they had their feathers up, a man would be wise to keep away, or

---

[3] Monia: A Saloon and whore house. See Book One *Gold in the Red Desert*.

if he couldn't do that, keep quiet. Lowering his hat over his eyes he slumped down in his seat and acted like he was going to sleep.

The train lunged forward and then backward and then forward again and the sparks and black smoke began slipping in the window. Cliff rose, leaned across her, and closed the window.

"I hope you are not planning to stay the night in Medicine Bow," she spat out.

"Well, as a matter of fact that is just what I had planned. It's not good for the horses to be locked up in a train car for too long a time and they need to be let out and walked some."

"I knew you would pay more attention to the horses than what I wanted."

"Honey, our tickets call for us to stay over at Medicine Bow and catch the 8:10 out in the morning. This animal car wasn't even supposed to go out today. They have other horses that will be coming on the train in the morning and this car will go back tonight to Green River for them," he explained.

"Just what I am looking forward to, a night in wonderful Medicine Bow."

"Hell, Medicine Bow ain't all that bad."

"For men and horses, I guess."

Cliff again pulled the brim of his hat down. *'I reckon she is jealous of the horses,'* he thought.

Medicine Bow was really not much of a town as far as towns go; but there were few in Wyoming that were much better, except maybe South Pass City and Cheyenne.

There was the depot, and the hotel, and the large stock pens, and loading ramps, a store for general goods, a livery, and three saloons; one of these was in the hotel.

The Army was building a small post there, but on this day there were no soldiers around, except the construction crew, and the woodcutters, and teamsters who were to bring in the timber. South of Medicine Bow, some ten miles, a growth of cottonwoods had been found along a bend in the river which served this purpose well. The location of Medicine Bow itself had not seen a tree since the last ice age.

The Depot was not really a depot; just a little four-by-four wooden building where the Union Pacific attendant kept his lanterns and

Mud Wagon in front of the Medicine Bow Hotel

a telegraph switch, but a body could purchase tickets for the train there, so most folks called it "The Depot."

The Hotel was a two-story affair made of cut wooden planks some people had started calling slap boards. It was not painted but it was tight, and that helped keep out the ever-present wind, blistering hot in August and bitter cold the remainder of the year.

Cliff stayed at the train and oversaw the unloading of their horses but Nadine hurried off.

She had just signed for a room at The Medicine Bow Hotel when she saw two cowboys coming up the steps out front.

Their room was on the second floor and she hurried up and quickly closed the door behind her.

Hap Joiner would be housed in the room across the hall, but she did not realize this at the time.

Cliff had saddled Red and with a bridle on Treasure, he rode around a few minutes leading her for exercise before taking them to The Shirley Livery for grain and stalls.

"Come on, Nadine. Let's go and get some supper," he said when he came in and sat beside her on the bed, while removing his spurs.

"I'm not hungry."

"Come on. I'm hungry. It's likely we won't get another thing afore we get to Cheyenne."

"Well, you go then, but I'm staying here."

"What's come over you?"

She turned her head away and spoke to the wall "Nothing, I just ain't hungry, that's all."

"Look, Honey, I got a' take care of the horses. We're gon'a need them before we get to Georgia."

"Of course you must take care of the horses. What kind of fool statement is that?"

"Look Nadine, I don't know what burr you got under your saddle, but I ain't one to fuss with a woman. I'll be back and I'll bring you something when I come."

Cliff got up and reached for this gun belt.

"What are you taking that for?" she asked startled.

"I might run into a passel a' Indians for all I know. For God's sake Nadine, this is Wyoming."

She bit her bottom lip a little and then said in a softer, kinder voice, "Of course, you should take your Colt. I'm just a little tired from it all. You know a week ago I was just a whore in a saloon and now I'm headed to a strange land with my husband. It's all so overwhelming, I just need to rest a little, that's all."

Nadine had removed her prairie dress and was lying on the blanket in her bloomers and camisole. When he started out, she jumped up and ran over and gave him a kiss. "Hurry back."

"I will," he promised.

Before he closed the door, the one across the hall opened and she quickly turned and headed back to the bed.

"Howdy" Cliff said to the big man who stepped out into the hall.

"Howdy" the man said back and the two began walking toward the stairs in tandem.

Hap stood at the bar and sipped on a whiskey until he saw Cliff was seated and had ordered food, and then he turned and headed back upstairs.

Knocking on the door, he waited. There was no answer and he knocked again, louder.

Finally when no answer came he spoke loudly into the wooden plank door.

"Nadine, I saw you. I know you're in there, and I ain't leaving until you let me in."

Still there was no answer.

Finally Hap almost shouted, "Nadine if I have to, I'll go downstairs and stomp that skinny little runt you wus kissing on to a pulp."

"You get away from here, you hear!" she said through the door.

"I ain't going nowhere until you go with me. Now you just as well open up or I mean what I said about whipping up on your suitor. Hell, I'll give him back his money."

He waited, but she made no sound.

"Nadine, you know I ain't putting up with no other fellow poking you while I'm around."

"You ain't gon'a have to go downstairs to find me, Mister," Cliff said standing in the hall just up from the stairwell.

Hap whirled around at his words.

Looking closely at the shorter man, he suddenly noticed the hardness of his eyes and the looseness in the way his hand hung beside the ivory grip on his revolver.

"Hey man, I ain't wanting no real trouble with you. It's just that whore you got in there, well, she is my best girl and I aim to party with her tonight."

"That so?"

"Yeah, now if you want, I'll give you back your money, so you won't be out nothing, but if'n that don't suit you, I'll just bust your teeth in and kick this here door down and take her anyway. Now, that be what you want?"

"No, I don't want you to bust out my teeth, and I don't want you to kick in my door, as I aim to sleep there tonight," Cliff said and then he moved his hand up a little so it almost was touching the grip. "And I don't think you could pay me enough," Cliff paused a moment and took a deep breath and let it out with a hissing sound.

"I do suppose you are able to bust my teeth out though; so I guess the only thing to do is shoot you where you stand."

"Now, don't get me wrong, Mister," Hap said studying his foe. "I ain't no gun hawk and I don't see no reason we can't work this out. Say, I take her half the night and you can have her when I'm finished."

"You don't seem to understand," Cliff said back very sternly, "I am a gun hawk and I know you are big enough to whip me, like you said; but you ain't fast enough to get the chance."

"Mister, I don't intend to go for my gun."

"Don't matter none. When the Deputy comes, I'll say you did, and since everybody in the hotel has heard you call my wife a whore, not a soul will question me."

"Your wife?"

"Yep, Mrs. Clifford Brown."

"Mister, I didn't know___I just___I er'___"

"You were probably thinking of Miss Tipper, the whore that used to work over to the diggings."

"Yeah, that is who I was thinking of; Nadine Tipper. She a', she worked at Monia City."

"I remember her too, though I never had her. She was a looker all right, but not as pretty as my wife."

"I guess you're right," Hap said, trying to keep his hands as low and as far away from his pistol as he could. "I think I'll just go," he said looking quickly at the door of his room, "Go to bed. Er' in there. It's my room."

"Yes, I know. I saw you come out of it," Cliff replied still not moving from his obvious 'at ready' stance.

"Alright?"

"Go ahead."

Hap Joiner shot for the door to his left and closed it with a bang.

Cliff walked on to his own door and called through.

"Honey, I ordered you a beef steak. Would you like to accompany me to the dining room?"

The door opened and she had her arms around his neck before he could move. "I'm so sorry," she sobbed.

Stepping inside he said, "I had rather eat with you, than alone."

"Oh, Cliff, I saw Hap board the train and knew if he saw me what he would do." She sobbed, "I'm so sorry you had to be so humiliated."

"Nadine, you're my wife. What you were in another life is past; I don't hold that agin you. You were doing the best you could. Now you are in a new life and I am proud to call you my wife and I will tell that to any fool what wants to know. Now get dressed and accompany me to dinner."

"Are you sure?"

"I'm sure."

Nadine again put on her plain yellow prairie dress and a straw bonnet. Other than her striking face and obvious figure, no one would have thought of her to be anything other than a pretty frontier wife.

The dining room and saloon were for all practical purposes the same room. Only the eating tables were each covered with a red and white checkered oil cloth.

The men there all glanced up as the couple came in, but quickly looked away so as not to offend.

Both Nadine and Cliff knew these men had heard most of what Hap Joiner had been yelling but no one showed anything but respect to them as they walked past to the table where Cliff had first sat. On the table were two pewter plates, each containing a large beef steak smothered in broth.

"I have been so afraid that something like this would happen," she said after taking a sip from her birdseye cup.

"Not to worry," he replied.

"But what if your mother finds out what I've been?"

"Georgia is a long way from Wyoming and anyway, you are my wife. Mother will accept you as such."

"I'm not so sure," she replied with a worried voice.

The next night they stayed over in Cheyenne before taking another U. P. to Omaha. There they boarded the sternwheeler, *"The Far West,"* and enjoyed several days and nights before reaching Saint Louis.

In Saint Louis they exchanged more of the dust for folding money and three days later boarded *"The Natchez"* for the trip down the Mississippi.

At Vicksburg, Cliff had the animals unloaded and before they departed for Jackson on horseback, he bought a strong mule to use as a pack animal.

The Steamer *'The Far West'*

CHAPTER TWO

Magnolias and Spanish Moss

It had been almost three weeks since they had left the high barren plains of the Red Desert in western Wyoming. The ever-present winds of the prairie were no longer whipping at their necks and the days were warm for late September.

Cliff had taken the 66 carbine and placed it in a scabbard on Treasure, and kept the Henry with him on Red. She liked to have the butt-stock pointed up and slightly forward of her right hand but he preferred to have his mounted with the stock to the back and the barrel riding under his right fender, so he mounted each accordingly.

Using the rifle, he had made a lucky shot and put a ball in the base of a hen turkey's neck late one afternoon just before they made camp along the banks of a creek in Covington County, Mississippi. The grass was still green and thick for the animals and the creek water was good; once you let the red settle to the bottom of the cup. Frogs and crickets were singing a full chorus as Nadine lay back on the blanket with her head against his arm pit.

The old fear of him not desiring her because of her former occupation, was no longer alert in her mind. They had enjoyed each other's body almost every evening since they were married. This night had been no different. Cliff was now asleep and breathing heavily, having spent himself with her a few minutes before. They had enjoyed the turkey roasted over a small fire and even taken a nip of some good corn and she felt so incredibly warm lying beside him while he slept.

Earlier the previous day, some twenty five miles south of Jackson, they had come across a fellow by the name of Hiram O'Hara. Mr. O'Hara said he was a traveling shoemaker. However, they soon found out he had more jugs in his wagon than shoes or leather, and Cliff bartered to him a prime badger pelt for the shine. It was much better tasting than what she had experienced at South Pass, and now she was glowing warm and feeling safe as she watched gray shadows move slowly across the dark sky between the branches of the big magnolia under which they had camped.

She had wanted to go back by Clay County when they came through Missouri to see her old home place, but she knew it was out of the way. And too, he was in somewhat of a rush to get home with the trouble his family was having; so she had never mentioned it to him. Still, as she lay there in the last moments before sleep swept over her, she regretted not having gone back. *'I will someday, I'll ask him to take me after this trouble is over down in Georgia.'*

Red was the first to notice the pair of dark figures creeping along the creek bank, and he blew a little air through his big nostrils. Treasure, then alerted, made a similar noise, though not so forceful. Nadine was now deep in sleep and heard nothing. Cliff however, had heard Red and was searching the shadows for what had disturbed his horse; at the same time he was reaching for his Colt.

The dying embers of their campfire made a dull glow on the water, and the outlines of the two men crouching low beside a mayhaw bush could be dimly seen directly across the narrow stream.

Faintly he heard one say, "They look asleep ta' me."

"Maybe so, maybe not. Let's watch a few more minutes."

"I'll club him while you go for the animals."

"Listen, Ruben, you leave that woman be. She's mine. I be the one what come up with the idee."

"Sure, Hiram. You can have her first. Just don't wear her out."

Cliff wished now he had not encouraged Nadine to sleep naked as he always did, when weather permitted.

There was no possible way he could remove his arm from beneath her head without disturbing her and possibly alerting them to the fact that he was awake; which was the last thing he wanted to do. Cliff had learned in the war the best thing to do with trouble was give it a wide birth when you could; but when it was upon you, never flee from it. Do so, and it would most likely stalk you and come on you again, when you least expected it.

Nonetheless, he wished he could reach the Winchester, which was cradled just above her head. The Henry was leaning against a tree behind him where he had left it after a complete cleaning.

The two men were now in the water, moving slowly across the knee-deep creek.

Cliff could see the husky man carried something long in his hands. *'Is it a rifle; or maybe a limb?'*

At first, the tall thin man appeared to have his hands free of anything; then the shiny blade of a large knife reflected a sliver of light the moon gave to the scene, and he knew where the real danger was.

The men split when they reached the coals, the man with the knife moved around his left, heading for the horses. The other man headed straight for the young couple. At that moment, Nadine moved and the blanket slipped from her chest exposing one of her large breasts.

Cliff heard the man catch his breath when he saw her mound, white and bare in the moonlight. He lowered his club and reached for the blanket that covered her. Lifting it ever so slowly until he had exposed most of her body, he stood upright and ingested the sight.

Red suddenly snorted and reared. It was then that Cliff squeezed the trigger of the Colt.

Spinning clear of her as fast as he could, he raced up to the grassy knoll.

The blast of the revolver, Nadine's scream, the painful bellow of the man as the ball entered his stomach just below his heart and the rearing of Red, had all taken place in less than a second, and the thin man was in a state of bewilderment for a moment. He turned away from the horses and looked towards the sound of the shot but when he did, Red struck at him with powerful front hoofs and caught him on the left forearm; breaking it like a stick of peppermint candy. The knife still in his right hand was swung at the horse's legs. He never saw the man or the flash of burning powder. The 44 conical struck him behind the left ear and his life was gone in a split second.

Now Nadine was running up towards Cliff. She was sobbing a little. When she reached him, she threw her arms around him and questioned. "What happened?"

"A couple a' white trash bent on robbing us."

"Who are they? Where did they come from?"

"My guess is they are from up near Braxton way."

"You know them?" she asked looking at the dead man lying in front of Red.

"Not this one," he replied turning and starting back.

When he reached the little camp he slid his hand into his saddle bags and retrieved a short yellow candle. Taking it to the coals he held the wick in them and blew. Shortly it lit.

Moving back, he rolled the chubby man over and holding the Colt under his chin, brought the light over his face with the other hand.

"Why, it's Mr. O'Hara!" she exclaimed.

"Yeah, that's who I thought."

"Why, that no account son-of-a-bitch," she said sharply.

Cliff snickered a little at her statement then walked over to their poke. Unrolling the lean-to tarp he removed a coal oil lantern and lit it and started towards the creek.

"Where are you going?"

"To get back my badger skin," he said.

"You going to leave me here with them?"

"O'Hara is about spent. If he moves, shoot him with the Winchester. The t'other one is dead as a pole cat. He won't hurt you none."

When he had crossed the creek he looked back at her standing there, stark naked, pointing his Yellowboy at the dying man.

"You might want ta get dressed. We need to be moving out real soon."

She looked across at her husband who was carrying the lantern, clothed only in his gun belt and hat. "You are someone to be talking."

When he returned, she was dressed and had the camp packed and laying beside the mule. Her saddle was on Treasure.

"Red wouldn't let me put the saddle on him," she said then turning and pointing the gun barrel at the shot man added "He's still alive."

Cliff brought the lantern over and looked closely at the man. He judged him to be in his fifties. His hair and beard was mostly gray and he was missing some teeth in the front. The blood was spouting from his large stomach at a goodly rate and Cliff knew it was not long before he would be gone.

"O'Hara, you are a dying man. Is there anybody you want me to notify about where you can be found?"

"I got a wife. Who's gon'a take care a' her?"

"Your kin I suppose," Cliff replied then asked "Where is she?"

"I ain't got no kin; here abouts anyway," he said back, before he began coughing.

"Where is your wife?" Cliff asked again.

"New York. She only just got here from Ireland," he said and groaned deeply then added, "That wus why we meant to rob you. I needed the money to send fur her."

"Sounded to me like you were more interested in my wife than yours," Cliff said back and then the man knew his lie had not been believed.

Cliff dressed and then told Nadine to keep an eye on O'Hara as he saddled Red and loaded the pack mule.

When he returned, O'Hara's soul had departed.

"You going to bury them?" she asked.

**1866 Winchester Carbine Affectionately
Called The Yellowboy**

"Nope, wolves got to eat too," he said, taking her by the arm and leading her away from the dead man.

They traveled south riding in the creek for three miles before he moved up the bank and turned due west.

"Ain't we going the wrong way?" she asked. "Or am I turned around?"

"No, two times," he said back.

"Never know what locals will think about that back there. Could be they wus known no accounts, and then again could be they was well liked by some. We don't even know who the t'other fellow was; maybe has kin here abouts."

"You think someone will blame us?" she asked.

"Doubt it, but no need to take chances. We'll head west until we come to a good place to turn back," he said pulling up on the reins and crossing one leg over the horn. "I reckon we can stop for a spell though, but don't dismount."

"Gee, I really could go to the bushes," she replied.

"Not here; don't want to leave your boot tracks here."

"My boot tracks are all over the camp," she said back.

"Not anymore," Cliff said removing his hat and wiping his brow with his shirt sleeve.

"How did you do that?"

"Well, I found their wagon half a mile back up the creek. My pelt wasn't there so he has stopped someplace since we traded with him yesterday. I did find a pair of brogans in the wagon with a hole worn near through one sole. When I came back, I covered your prints with tracks made by those shoes. Got us another jug, also."

Nadine just smiled and appreciated him for being the man he was; a man who always seemed to be on top of everything, a man she loved very much.

They came upon a large green piece of land just at sunrise. There were three horses and a dozen cows in the two hundred acre field enclosed by a flat rock fence.

Cliff stopped along the fence and looked it over for several minutes before he spoke. "Let's see if we can find a place to get in there, mingle our tracks up with the other stock, then we can head out towards Georgia again."

Two days later found the newlyweds riding in swamp water stirrup high as they approached the Mobile River. Cliff was not well acquainted with the area, having been there only once before when he was a teenager.

In the fall of 1855, he had gone with his father and older brother to Mobile Bay to see about the purchase of thirty thousand acres of timber that lined the bay on both sides. The deal never went through. His father had decided that there weren't enough trees close to the water to warrant the building of another saw mill. Sometime later, Cliff had overheard his mother say that when his father learned the owner was a rich investor from Philadelphia, he had told her he wanted no part of dealing with Yankees. Cliff thought it was the latter that had really stopped the move as he saw plenty of suitable trees, and there were others in the Bay Area that were doing well at sawmilling.

"Do you know where we are?" she asked as she watched a fat black snake swim away from them and disappear among some cypress knees.

"Well, plus or minus," he replied "We are north of Mobile, maybe thirty miles. There is a place here som'ers where a body can cross one river and a little swamp and not have to tackle the t'other one."

"What other one?"

"This here is the outer limits of the Mobile River. Over yonder a spell is the Tensaw River. If I can find it, there is a place along here where we won't have to cross the Tensaw. Kind a' a land bridge, it wus whar my Pa intended to build a sawmill some years back."

His answer didn't soothe her worries much, but she questioned him no more on it.

A short time after the sun passed overhead, they came to a hut of sorts; a shack made of wood and looked to her as if it had been painted silver. The sun shone on it and the glare hurt her eyes if she looked directly at it.

'Why would anyone paint a shack like that silver?' she thought as they neared the building.

Upon riding up onto the little sand bar where the hut was located, she realized that it was not painted at all but made of some kind of silver wood.

"What kind of wood is that?" she asked.

"Cypress," he replied.

"I seen them cypress trees and they ain't silver."

"Well, they turn silver when you strip 'em of their bark," he explained to her.

"Think I'd get a different wood."

"No you wouldn't," he said as he dismounted. "Not once you learned cypress don't never rot and the woodeaters don't like it much either."

"Woodeaters?" she questioned, looking around for some strange animal that might come out of this awful swamp at any moment and begin eating away at the trees.

"Yeah, you know them little bugs that come out of the ground and eat up wooden houses."

"Oh," she replied feeling a little embarrassed and a little relieved at the same time.

Now that they were close, she could see that the hut was really some kind of store. A sign crudely painted with 'Nanna Lubba Trading Post' hung from the roof.

"Come on and let's stretch our legs and give the animals a rest," he said as he lifted his arms to assist her in dismounting.

Nadine had not worn a dress since they left the boat in Vicksburg. While there, she had bought two pair of boys' overalls and a couple shirts. The overalls were baggy on her, but covered her legs well while they were riding; but the shirts were too small and failed to hide her large breasts. Cliff had thought that perhaps these tight shirts that strained at their shell buttons might have been the cause of O'Hara's decision to come after them. He planned to buy her some larger ones when they had the chance, but he fancied the peeks he got from time to time when one or more buttons would simply pop open with her bouncing about as she rode along, and he finally made up his mind to wait until they got closer to home; he would surely have to then. There was no way his mother would approve of her showing off such a fine figure in public. Not Addie Brown. She was Hard Shell through and through and he had wondered how he and his siblings had ever been born, for there was no way that woman would have gotten naked around any man, even his father.

The little hut was perhaps twenty-by-twenty and mostly dark inside. The only light was from the open door and where the sun showed through the walls, because the vertical boards did not fit tightly to one another. These openings gave off a strange setting and reminded her of the pictures of a striped horse she had seen. She couldn't remember where the striped horse was from, but she had always wanted a horse like that, ever since she saw that picture.

"Howdy," Cliff said after a few moments inside.

"Howdy," came an answer.

Her eyes had not yet become accustomed to the darkness and she was surprised at the reply. Focusing at the sound of his voice, a man slowly began to materialize from the east side of the building.

"Need some supplies," Cliff said.

"Going fishing? We got night crawlers."

"No, not today," her husband replied to the man. "Need an ax."

"I got 'em, over thar," the man said lifting a white shirted arm and pointing at a barrel with several wooden handles protruding from its top.

The drawl of this man was slower and stronger than any she had ever heard before and she wondered if he might be part Indian. His skin was quite dark, what she could see of it on his hand and under the old black floppy hat he wore.

"Obliged," Cliff returned and walked to the wooden barrel.

Picking a double-bitted one from the bunch, he asked without looking at the man, "How much?"

"Half-a-dollar," was his answer then, "Only Yankee; don't take Confederate no more," was added.

"We don't have Confederate," Cliff said and paused a split second before he added, "no more. Wish we did." The last was more of a thought than a statement.

"Ain't no good no more; 'round here no ways. Used mine to cover the cracks in th' out building round back."

Cliff just nodded his head.

The man then continued his statement. "Might be good up to Momgumry.' That there is the capital, you know."

"The capital of Alabama?" Nadine asked.

"The Confederacy, Ma'am. The Confederacy," the man replied as if she had said something stupid.

Cliff shook his head quickly at her and she realized he meant for her to say no more on the subject. Instead she spoke softly to him. "I need to go."

"Your out building; 'round back, you say?" Cliff directed this as much a question as a statement.

"Sho-'nuff, just go back out the door you come in and go 'round the boardwalk to the back. Nice one, too, and I don't charge nutton fur it."

Cliff nodded his head to her to go ahead and she turned and exited back into the sunlight.

The little walk was made of round sticks about three inches in diameter; also of cypress, she guessed. When she rounded the back of the hut she realized that it was built between two live trees that were growing in the water. A small slap board enclosure about the size of a closet was there. Upon entering, she saw through the hole in the seat board, that there was nothing but the river below.

She could hear Cliff and the man talking but she couldn't understand what was being said. She did understand the bay of a mule displaying his displeasure with the strange horses out front.

Upon returning she decided to stay out with their animals, feeling she had seen enough of the insides of that place.

Finally, Cliff came out with the ax and a slab of white meat that looked to be five or more pounds in weight. The man followed him out.

Now, in the sunlight she could see he was not an Indian at all, just a dirty old man with a dark beard and filthy blood-stained hands.

"Obliged fur the information," Cliff said mounting Red and pulling on the right rein.

"Just you follow the river here. Come six, seven mile you'll see the ferry boat. You just tell 'em Cooter sent ya'."

"There is a ferry?" she asked as they moved away.

"So the man says," Cliff answered with a frown on his face.

They had ridden southward along the edge of the swamp keeping the river in sight for most of the way.

Suddenly he pulled up and raised his hand signaling for her to do the same.

"What?"

He lifted his hand to his mouth and whispered, "Shhh."

She turned her head and looked to her right as he was doing.

Yes, she could hear something; but it was very faint.

A moment or two later, she noticed he was slowly shaking his head as in disagreement with something.

"What is it?" she whispered.

Finally he said, "Not sure, but I heard something yonder a ways off."

"Yes, I heard it too but I couldn't make out what it was."

"Yeah," was his only answer.

A minute passed before he spoke again. Then he said, "Let's rest the animals a few minutes. I want to go take a look over there." He nodded with his head towards where the sound had come from, "Stay here and stay close to that Winchester."

Cliff removed the Henry from its scabbard and slipped off into the timber without waiting for her to answer.

He was out of her sight in a few seconds. The underbrush was very thick along the edge of the swamp, more so than she had ever seen before from Missouri to Wyoming.

There were also strange sounds coming from the swamp. Sounds of living creatures she realized; nonetheless, they were strange to her, as she had never been around such places before, and everything seemed a little frightening. The longer he was gone the more frightening they became.

Nadine tied the animals; then removing the Winchester she eased back up against a large tree and crouched so she was hidden by a good size bush growing between the trail and the tree.

All over the ground around the tree were spiny balls the size of a small hen's egg and she surmised they had fallen from the tree as seed. She had never seen seeds like this before and as she carefully examined one of the balls in her hand, Nadine wondered what type of tree it was. Unable to come to a satisfying answer, she finally slipped the ball into one of the pockets in her overalls with intent to ask Cliff about it when he returned.

Another ten minutes of stressful wait passed before she saw Red lift his ears and look in the direction Cliff had gone.

Shortly she could hear the sound of something moving there in the brush and she quietly cocked the hammer on the Yellowboy and held her breath.

"Easy boy," she finally heard her husband say to the big horse and she let out a sigh of relief before standing.

Cliff saw her rise from the hiding place and asked, "Any trouble?"

"No, just you were gone so long."

"You did good to hide. Makes me feel I can do what I must without unnecessary worry about you."

His words were like warm milk on a cold night and filled her with pride and a rush of love. "You can count on me," she said back.

Lowering the hammer she stepped forward before asking, "Did you find out anything?"

"I found a road that parallels the river yonder half a mile. Must come from Mt. Vernon or we'd a crossed it as we came down."

"Why didn't Mr. Cooter tell us about it?"

"I think that noise we heard was a wagon passing on the road. I found fresh sign; one came along pulled by a mule from up there; lightly loaded or not loaded at all, and moving as fast as a mule will pull," he said then paused before adding, "You notice how Cooter said 'whoss' instead of house? That ain't no way for a man from 'Bama to talk. I heard a bluebelly we captured once call a house a 'whoss'. He were with the Ninth Pennsylvania."

"I don't know, I never in my life heard a man with more of a drawl than he had," she disagreed.

"Could be he has a put-on drawl."

"For what reason?"

"I ain't sure but I'd bet you a gold piece, he ain't from these parts."

"I still don't see why he would put-on?"

"Just like you said, why didn't he tell us about the road?" Cliff offered and then added, "And that stuff about Confederate money might be good at Montgomery. Hell everybody knows Confederate money ain't no good here, in Montgomery, or in Richmond, for that matter."

"I don't know," she agreed and then she added her own evidence, "The walls of his outhouse were covered with Confederate money. He even had some there for sanitary paper."

"Let's move up and take the road and see where it leads us," he said as he was mounting. "We might not be taking that ferry after all, if there even is one."

Nadine followed his example and they rode into the thick brush and soon were climbing a slight grade.

Seeing it, she could tell the road was well-traveled and the tracks of the wagon were easy to spot. It was then she remembered the baying of the mule she had heard while using the outhouse. "Cliff, I heard a mule back there. At the trading post."

"He must'a been in a corral som'ers," Cliff replied still not looking at her, rather keeping a keen eye out for unnatural happenings.

They had traveled three miles down the road when it turned sharply to the east. Moments before they were to make the turn they both heard sounds off to their left.

"What was that?" she asked.

"Sounds like people to me," he said. "Wait here while I check."

Cliff was off Red in a fluid like motion, with the Henry coming out of the scabbard as part of the motion giving her the feeling her husband and the rifle were attached, even though she knew better.

Again he was gone from sight in a matter of moments and that uneasy feeling swept over her once more, but before she became too nervous, he returned and mounted.

"There is a ferry there and the river trail does come out there just like Cooter said."

"Well that is a relief," she said easing the tension out of her back and shoulders.

"Trouble is, Cooter and another fellow are there with long guns laying in ambush for whoever comes down that trail."

"Waiting on us?" She took a deep breath and let it out harshly, "What are we gon'a do?"

"I bought this here ax to cut us a raft and that is the sensible thing to do," he said, "especially with you along," nodding his head in agreement with his statement.

Then he started slowly, shaking his head in disagreement. "It just rubs me wrong to let that damn Yankee go on with his scheme. No telling how many folk he has robbed an' thrown in the river just like he was planning to do us."

Nadine swallowed hard at his statement. She knew he was right and this man or men should be stopped, but she didn't want any more shooting. She was married less than a month and she didn't want to become a widow again.

"Reb, are you sure?"

It was the first time she had called him that since they were married, and he knew she was worried.

"Dismount and stay with the animals," he told her. "This won't take long."

He took a couple steps and then turned back to her and smiled before saying, "Besides, I never did make friends with no axe. We'll use the ferry."

"Reb, be careful."

He just smiled and turned and headed around the bend in the road.

She did as told for a while, and then couldn't stand it any longer.

Once again she secured the animals, and taking the Winchester she followed him.

Nadine had just gotten far enough down the road to see the ferry, when she heard someone shout.

She couldn't tell what was said but it didn't really matter, for less than a second later the report of the Henry drowned out the sound of human voices, and then came a louder boom from a shotgun, followed by two more shots from the Henry, and then silence.

She waited and stared into the thick undergrowth from where the shots had come but couldn't see anything.

Her next thought was to go back to the horses like he had told her, before he found out she had disobeyed; but then she knew she couldn't go back until she was assured he was all right, so she moved forward slowly down the clay road towards where her husband had to be.

When she was fifty yards from where the ferry boat was tied up, she was startled as Cliff suddenly appeared from out of the brush.

Nadine lowered the Winchester and let a flood of relief flow over her face when she saw he was unharmed. "Oh, thank God," she said then realizing his face looked strange. At first she thought he was mad and she was about to get a bawling out for not staying with the horses, then she jumped straight up as the hard muzzle of the revolver was pushed into her back.

A second later, a hairy arm came around and wrenched the Winchester from her hands effortlessly.

"Now, I guess you'll be sorry fur what you just done, you Rebel trash," the man said as he pushed the barrel hard into her back. The pain was sharp and she lunged forward to escape it, stopping beside Cliff.

She dared not look at his face; she knew she had made a huge mistake by not doing as she had been instructed. He might have been able to deal with this fellow, if he did not have her to worry about, and she was afraid to see his expression. Instead she looked up at the man standing in front of them.

"Well now, ain't you a real beauty. I ain't seen hair that dark since we freed New Orleans," he said with a disgusting grin on his face. "You one a' them Cajun Queens?"

He was wearing dirty blue trousers with a dark blue stripe down each pant leg. His shirt was a checkered pattern of small red and white squares and his hat was very much the same black floppy affair that the man wore at the trading post. He too had a dark beard but this one was streaked with gray. Around his waist was a leather belt that held two holsters worn backward, in the manner that was customary to the military. From the one on the right she could see the butt of a revolver exposed, the other was empty, as this revolver was easily seen to be in his hand. When his grin became wider, tobacco stained teeth appeared.

"Come over here, little girly," he said.

She didn't move.

"You wan'a see him shot dead right now?" he yelled quite loudly. "You better get over here."

"It don't matter, Nadine. He aims to shoot me anyway," Cliff said, trying to get the man's attention off of her.

"You's right about that, buster. Just when I do that, is up to her."

Nadine moved over and stood in front of him trying to block his view of Cliff, but he was too tall and kept glancing from her to her husband.

"Come on closer," he said, beckoning her on with the fingers of his left hand.

When she was within arm's reach he stretched forth his hand and cupped one of her breasts and then squeezed hard. "Nice tits, you got there, Girly," he said just before he clenched her shirt and ripped it upward.

Cliff saw most of the shirt tear loose exposing her left breast, and she felt it pull with his grasp and then fall back, and she prayed the man had not seen it.

'*The gold chain must be exposed now*', she thought but dared not look down.

Cliff's rifle was lying on the ground beside him. When he moved toward it, the man pushed her aside and again yelled, pointing the Remington at him, "Good way to die sooner."

This was all she needed and in an instant, she had the Sharps from between her breasts and as she shoved it into his ear, the chain broke.

He felt the cold steel but didn't realize what it was.

He never heard the hammer fall or the cartridge discharge. The tiny 22 caliber bullet destroyed the ear drum before entering his brain.

He spun around and reached for his head with his left hand as the big Remington fell from his other, but he never screamed out.

Nadine's eyes focused on the black powder burn on his ear as his knees buckled and he slumped to the yellow clay road. Soon thereafter, his right leg began to kick in a steady, non-threatening, rhythmic manner, and the hobnail heel of his boot began to dig a small trench in the clay.

Cliff was beside her in an instant and pulled her away so she was no longer looking at the dead man whose leg refused to give up.

He squeezed her hard to him and then pushed her back to arm's length and smiled. "I knew that little Sharps would come in handy someday," he said then he kissed her hard on the lips.

"You're not mad at me? I mean, I didn't do like you said," she said almost sobbing.

"Hell, you just saved our lives, kid. How could I be mad? Now, reload that thing and try to get your big beautiful bosom covered, and then go get our horses," he said releasing her from his grip.

"I'll see if I can get everything loaded on the ferry."

She turned and opened the little gun as she walked back towards the animals. '*This man amazes me more every day I'm with him*', she thought. '*Brady[4] would have been furious at me for not doing as he said.*'

While she was gone, he went over the area and picked up the spent cases from the Henry and put them in his pocket.

When she returned leading the horses, he saw she had discarded her torn shirt and was now wearing the other one.

She looked at the bodies he had loaded on the ferry raft. Two lay face down; the man called Cooter was tied standing upright to one of the posts that secured the tow rope for the ferry. On his chest was a piece of yellow paper on which Cliff had penciled something.

While he was loading the horses she lifted the top of the paper and read what was written there:

> Here stands the body of a Bushwhacking
> Carpetbagger who'll Murder no more

She let the top of the paper fall over again and thought of her approval as she stepped on the log ferry.

Joel Nielson was born on a British Man-of-War off the coast of Jamaica fifty-eight years and one day earlier. His mother had been the wife of the third mate and as such, was given the unofficial right to sail with her husband.

---

[4] Brady Tipper was Nadine's first husband

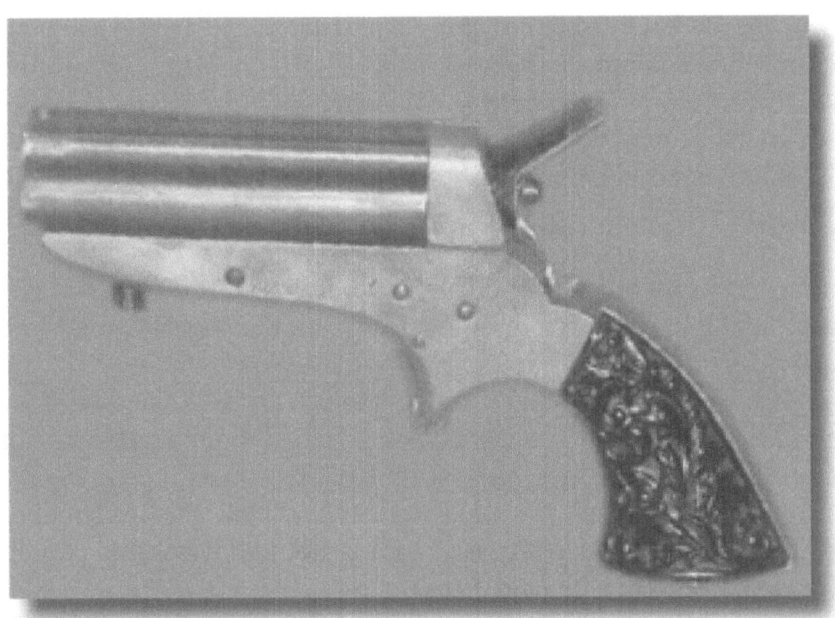

A Sharps 4 Barreled Derringer In 22 S&W

His father had fallen and struck his head on the third day out of Birmingham. He never regained consciousness and was buried at sea. As a result, Ruby Nielson had no husband to provide for her; she had been given a choice of being put ashore at the first available island or harbor, or become helper to the ship's cook. She chose the latter. This, of course presented her with the unfortunate condition of having no man to protect her. The other wives onboard shunned her and soon she realized the only possible means of survival was to share her favors with the strongest men on board whether their strength came from brute force, or power of rank.

A little over a month later Joel was born.

Having wives on board was a common occurrence; though The Admiralty denied it ever occurred. Unattached women were another thing altogether, and a suckling babe was out of the question. The first port reached after the child came was New York, and it was there Ruby and her son were put ashore and there the boy learned to survive.

In the summer of 1864 he was chosen to attend training for the job of 'Land Acquisitioner' that was being financed by Congressman Thad Stevens. Stealing had been Joel's specialty from the time he could walk. *'So, how can I go wrong now that they are going to pay me to do it?'* he wondered.

Joel arrived in Selma three days after N. B. Forrest left, and set up his office in Grace Hall on Lauderdale Street. Now seven years later, he had been appointed Sheriff of Baldwin County by Governor William Smith.

The fact of finding the three bodies at the ferry crossing had occurred in Mobile County never entered Joel Nielson's mind. The note left on his brother's body, made it plain this had been the work of a Copperhead,[5] and he aimed to see the shooter hung.

Cliff and Nadine had worked their way east to Latham by sundown and he found a thick oak hammock about a mile south of town. There they made a camp for the night.

"I think I will go up to the settlement and pick up some supplies before we head on east. We need some coffee and beans and I might find some hen eggs fur sale there."

"Wait, I'll go with you," she said, standing from the bed roll she had just finished spreading.

"Honey, I think it best that I go alone this time."

"Why?" she asked.

He could tell her feelings had somehow been hurt, which was not his intention at all.

"Well, we left tracks back there at the river of two people, a man and a woman or small boy, two horses and a mule. Should there be anyone looking into the shootings, which I doubt, two strangers suddenly appearing in these parts might bring suspicion down on us."

"I see," she replied.

He knew his explanation made sense to her, but also knew she was not satisfied with it either.

He saddled Red again, which did not meet with good humor from the big animal. Just before he mounted he kissed her and said, "Stay close. When full dark comes, light the lantern; but keep it as low as you can and don't build a fire until I get back."

She nodded her head and looked off in obvious disapproval of his going alone.

She didn't really believe he was going to see a woman. Although he had been very popular with several in the two years they had

---

[5] Copperhead: Slang name used by northerners towards those who supported succession from the Federal government.

known each other before their marriage, and there was no doubt he was attractive to any woman that dared to look at him; still she felt a little twinge of jealousy sweep over her as he disappeared among the tall oaks. '*He did say he was here before with his father,*' she thought.

Latham was little more than a spot in the road. There was a store run by a man called Taggart; and in this store, sitting in a small circle around an unlit pot bellied stove were four older men. On the table in front of two of them was a board of checkers and a tan jug.

The other two men seemed content on letting nothing interrupt their concentration on the game. The players were much less concerned with the activities. Taggart, a big man with a mustache and goatee wore a large brimmed straw hat with a rattlesnake-skin band. His drawl was much more believable than Cooter's had been. "You passing through?" he spoke softly as Cliff approached the counter.

"New here; looking fur a job," was the answer he got.

"I see," the store-keep replied. "What can I do fur ya'?"

"Need some coffee, and beans, maybe a few hen eggs if you got them."

"I got coffee and beans. Not cold enough yet to be keeping eggs."

"I'll take what you got," he replied. "Any salt pork?"

"Where ya' headed mister?" one of the checker players asked loudly.

"He's looking fur work," Taggart replied to the man, as he cut off a slab of pork.

"What kind a' work you looking fur?"

"Most any honest work," Cliff replied.

"Well, you better be careful; wandering about these days, ain't safe."

"That so?" Cliff replied not looking at him.

"Yeah, it's plum dangerous. Sheriff Nielson was in an hour or so back, looking fur a couple road agents what done murdered half a dozen men back at the ferry crossing," the man said before he spit into a tin can sitting beside his chair, then he added, "Come this way too, he said."

"I'll be looking out," Cliff said back, still not turning towards the man.

"Some say it were homeboys that done the killing," Taggart said just above a whisper. "Some say they needed killing."

"What do you say?" Cliff asked back.

"I say them that got kilt were carpetbaggers just like that damn Sheriff Nielson."

Cliff nodded his head slightly in acknowledgment but offered no more.

"Sheriff seems to think they went on east towards Atwater."

Again Cliff just nodded his head slightly, before asking, "You got any cartridges for a Henry Rifle?"

"I do. Order them fur the Sheriff, he'-self," Taggart replied and then walked down the counter a few feet and picked up two tan boxes. "Anything else?"

"Could use some chocolates if you have 'em."

"No chocolate. Peppermint?"

"All right, give me two peppermints."

Taggart wrapped his goods in a brown paper and tied a string around it before setting it on the counter. "Let's see, that comes to two dollars and forty cents."

Cliff reached for one of the ten-dollar red backs he had taken in exchange at the bank in Green River and laid it on the counter.

Taggart whistled softly as he picked up the bill. "First one of these I ever see'd."

"It's good money," Cliff returned.

"I ain't doubting ya' mister. It's just I ain't see'd no folding money this size on a white man since 'afore the war. That's all."

Taggart moved around from one jar to another until he had found enough to make change. "Mister, a man could get killed in these parts for less money than your change."

"By carpetbaggers or home folk?"

"Could be both, I 'speck."

"I'll keep that in mind as I head for Atwater," Cliff replied loud enough for the others to hear.

"You be careful going to Atwater," the checker player yelled out. "That's whar them killers are headed."

Cliff left and pointed Red down the road towards the southeast. Passing the blacksmith's shop he raised his hand in greeting to the workman there, who returned the gesture. A mile further south he left the road and cut west across a field until he came to a creek. There he moved down the bank and headed south for another mile and then when he came upon a place where the bank was three feet high and the creek quite narrow, he forced Red up the steep bank.

From there he moved out west again only to turn around and with a kick of his heels, the big horse jumped the creek effortlessly and finally they were moving back towards the clay road. When he found the right bend he entered the road and started north back towards Latham. As soon as he could see the tops of the oak hammock again, he kicked Red and the big horse jumped clear of the road without leaving tracks along its edge.

He found Nadine waiting by the lantern, as he had told her.

After making a small fire and cooking some bacon and boiling the coffee, he drenched the fire and sat next to her.

"Something go wrong in town?" she asked.

"No, I just learned a bit. That's all."

"Tell me."

Cliff told her what he had learned, and that night was the first night, since their camp on the Sweetwater, they did not have sex.

Sheriff Nielson was intent on getting the men who had killed his brother and cousins. He had been the one who had sent for Scott Nielson and Aunt Lucy's sons, Jason and Wheeler. He had set Cooter up in the old trading post when Nanna failed to meet his taxes. A day later the old man had fallen into a slough where an 'ole gator was raisin' her young. Some said Nanna never fell into that slough.

The boys had turned a good profit in the last three years, and not only was the sheriff likely to lose that revenue now, but there too, was the family honor to be avenged.

Nielson outfitted five loyal men with Army issue repeaters, that he had requisitioned while acting as the Land and Tax Assayer of the district, and soon they had the road to Atwater covered. He was sure the murderers were not ahead of him and he would be waiting when they arrived.

Before first light Cliff had slipped from the little camp out to where he could watch movement on the road. By sunup he had seen none. Finally satisfied, he returned to her.

Nadine was dressed and had coffee boiling when he returned. He immediately felt her anger as he reached for the pot.

"I'll do that," she spat at him.

"Alright."

"A body would think I was nothing but the hired help; why shouldn't I get you coffee."

"Nadine, what's the matter?"

"Nothing," she replied looking away.

"Alright," he replied knowing she would get around to telling him in her own good time.

"You wouldn't be interested, anyway."

"Alright, what is it?"

"Nothing."

He drank the coffee and then picked up the frying pan she had set out and put it back into the saddle bag.

This motion again brought on several non-understandable comments. She mumbled as she walked to where the paint pony was hobbled.

When he had the camp packed and on the mule, he said to her, "Listen, I don't know what burr you got under your bustle this morning, but we got to make some miles today and I don't hanker to do them with you feudin' like this."

"I ain't feuding."

"Well, I don't know what you call it, but whatever it is, it's got to stop right now."

She turned away for several seconds and then turning back and looking him straight in the eye she spoke, "Don't much take to waking up with my husband gone and me not knowing where he is."

"I was watching the road."

"You could 'a told me where you were going."

"You were asleep."

"I'd rather you have woke me up than just slipping off in the night."

Cliff could see he had no way of winning this so he just said, "I was wrong. I should have woke you and told you where I was going."

"Now, before you mount, put on a dress."

"What!"

"Put on a dress," he said, "That sheriff is looking for two men and I want everyone who might see us to know you are a woman."

"You could a' told me before I got dressed."

"Yes, I could have, only I was out watching the road when the idea came upon me, and when I got back you were already dressed."

"Well, hell," she exclaimed as she pushed the suspenders from her shoulders.

They skirted Latham and headed north. Passing through

Tensaw without stopping, they continued on coming upon Blackshear's Mill just before eleven o'clock. She needed to take a relief, so he stopped at the saw mill and asked for drinking water.

The sight of her walking to the outhouse stopped the workers still and it took a command from the pusher to get them back to their task.

"I ain't never seen a woman ride a horse like that 'afor," the foreman said to Cliff.

"Yeah, well, my wife would rather use a side-saddle, but we can't afford one, me being out of work and all."

"If'n you need work we could maybe put ya' to work as a saw-man," he said then scratching his beard added, "Maybe even give the lady some work a' cooking."

"Well now, I do thank you for that kind offer but you see we are headed fur Nashville. My Ma is ailing and I need to get there as soon as I can," Cliff offered hoping he could remember all the tales he was telling, and to whom.

"Alright, I understand, but be careful, don't go east towards Red Hill."

"Why's that?"

"It's Injun land, Creeks, 'tween here and there," the man replied. "Never know about them people. One day they's Christian, the next they's Injun," he said back just before he spat a huge stream of tobacco juice onto an ant hill. Then he snickered as he watched the tiny red creatures run franticly about the small mound. Finally, he took the toe of his boot and kicked the mound hard, destroying it for the moment.

"The same with Hedapeada. It be mostly a Creek Hamlet."

When she came out and walked back to the horses, once again the work came to a halt and stayed that way until they were a quarter mile up the road.

Glancing back off and on until Cliff was sure they were out of sight of the mill he turned east again and headed towards Red Hill, but soon cut southeast across a large open area that looked to have been under cultivation a year or two back.

Before long they came upon the village of Hedapeada and skirted it also. However, just before they were out of sight, they met an old man and a boy in an old two-wheel cart; both were obviously of the red race.

Each spoke to the other in gesture without words, but Cliff didn't like the idea of them being seen after they were once again headed generally south. He decided they would travel on this trail until they came to a crossing and then turn another direction, hopefully east.

What he found was not a crossroad, rather a railroad. It obviously had been well used several years before, but where they crossed, the rails were now rusty and did not show signs of having a train on them in recent times. Here they turned east and followed the tracks a few miles until they came upon another village that was even smaller than Hedapeada. In fact, he decided it was only an abandoned station along the railroad where a few families had taken up residence. He decided to avoid this too and finding a game trail that led off to their right, they once again were traveling south.

In less than twenty minutes this trail cut a road and soon they could see the steeple of a church. Nadine felt a sense of relief upon seeing it and as they approached, she read the small sign that declared it to be The Dry Springs Holiness Church. It was a log structure and the only building in town that had paint on it.

As they passed, a man and woman both dressed in black were hoeing a small patch of sweet potatoes next to a little cemetery. Cliff touched the front of his brim in a gesture of greeting. The Parson spoke, "Howdy neighbors."

"Howdy," Nadine said back but they did not stop the slow walking of the animals.

The woman looked at her as she rode off and spat at the ground, "Disgraceful," she said resentfully. "No decent woman would ride astride a horse in public."

"Judge not," her husband said, returning to his work.

Still she stared at them until they had passed the big white oak at the bend of the road where its huge trunk and low hanging branches hid them from her view. Looking back at the up-turned earth so recently disturbed by her hoe, she spat before digging into the yellow earth again.

It was nearly dusk when they rode into the single dirty street. Here she saw a shingle "Miss Mary's Pies and Good Food."

"Oh, Cliff, could we stop? I'm so tired of sitting here and my insides are sticking together."

He looked at her and then smiled, '*She has come a long way today with little to say*', he thought, '*Guess she has earned a cooked meal.*'

"Sure," he replied and turned Red towards the hitching post in front of Mary's.

Miss Mary's was a small building about twenty-five feet square. The kitchen was in a smaller detached building out back.

"Howdy, folks," The little woman in her late forties said as they came in. "You looking fur some pie or wanting some supper?"

"Well, we are mighty hungry. What you got?" Cliff asked.

"Got some good collards and a tasty coon stew with real carrots in it and a rutabaga, too."

"Sounds good to me," he replied looking at Nadine.

She looked at the woman with a blank look and then finally said, "Yeah, I'll have some, too."

After the woman had gone she looked at him and asked, "What are collards?"

He snickered a little and then said, "Greens, like turnip tops."

"Oh," she replied and then added, "And rutabaga?"

"Well, it's kind 'a like the root of turnips, only tastier."

"Oh," she said back, nodding her head slightly.

"Don't worry, Hon, you'll get to love vittles cooked the right way," he paused and then added, "in no time at all."

When they had finished, the lady came up and said, "My specialty here is pies. I cook them for all the men what work the mills and them that fish the river. You folks want some?"

"What do you have?" Cliff asked.

"I got apple, and peach, and some wild berry."

"Got any mincemeat?" Nadine asked.

"Not here, Ma'am. This here is the south."

"Oh," Nadine replied not realizing she had exposed herself as an immigrant. "I'll have apple," she said.

"Peach for me," Cliff replied.

Just as they are being served the pies, a group of men rode into town. Most of them went directly to Milton's Store across the street where a large sign announced beverages were available, among other goods.

Cliff gritted his teeth when he saw one of the men head their way. After tying his horse beside their animals, he walked around each of them looking them over carefully, checking her carbine in the scabbard. He even lifted the fender on Treasure looking for any sign of identification. When he got to Red, he pulled the Henry from its boot far enough to identify it's make and then he shoved it back in its scabbard, but when he reached for this saddle fender Red began to protest by dancing about and jerking his head as high as he could without pulling the reins loose from the hitching post. He even attempted to kick the man, and that was enough to deter future action, and the investigator quickly moved from between the two animals and walked over to the mule and looked him over carefully before he came inside.

The big man touched the brim of his hat when he spoke, "Afternoon, Miss Mary."

"You know full well it ain't Miss, Joel Nielson. It's Mrs.," she said back obviously having been insulted by the man's addressing of her.

"Yes, Mary, we all know you wus married and we all know you're no account husband left you, two year past."

"My husband were a God-fearing man, just as Christian as any, and you got no right to talk poorly a' him."

"Yeah, he were God-fearing; when he didn't have his head stuck in a jug. Only we both know that weren't too often, now don't we Mary?"

"He lost his leg, Joel, you forget that? A man loses a lot when he loses a leg."

"Well, the way I hear tell it, he just up and got him a peg and signed on one of them steamers out of Mobile."

"Ain't no such, and you know it. He never would 'a left me, were he alive."

"Well, it don't make much matter, how he left. He left you and that be the facts, but I didn't come in here to discuss your love life, I come in here to have me a talk with 'em what owns 'em fine animals outside," the man said and turned to the table where Cliff and Nadine sat. "That 'a be you, I 'spect."

"The three in front there are ours," Cliff replied.

"Yeah, where you from?"

"Who's asking?"

"Oh, excuse me; I should a' introduced Joel Nielson, the sheriff of Baldwin County, Alabama," Mary said in a disgusted voice.

"Sheriff, oh, I am sure glad to see this wilderness has law," Cliff answered.

"That's a mighty good attitude stranger. Now, who are you and where you from?" the big man said back with a smile on his face, but sternness in his voice.

"I'm Clifford Burris and this is Mrs. Burris. We come from up in Tennessee. Been down to Pensacola on our honeymoon but got word my Ma's sick and had to cut it short. We are on our way back to Nashville."

"Headed north, huh?" he questioned.

"That's right Sheriff, we're Tennessee bound," Cliff replied trying to look as not guilty as he could.

"You sure do fit the description of a couple what were seen near noon up to Blackshear's Mill."

Cliff knew their story had holes clear through it and now needed some explanation as to why they were twenty miles south of where they had been seen a few hours ago. "That's right; we were there some before noon. Not long after we left there we came upon these two fellows, Indians I do believe, although they were sure 'a wearing white man's clothes. We came upon 'em at a river crossing. They told us they was headed to Repton and knew a shortcut, so we followed them. They's seemed like nice fellows, but just a few miles back them two varmints up and stole our money and took off yonder way. If'n one didn't have a repeater, I might 'a tried 'em, but there just weren't no way, not with the Misses here with me," Cliff replied and then seeing the disbelief in the Sheriff's expression he added, "I wonder where Indians would get repeaters in these parts."

"I see you are carrying repeaters yous-self."

"Shor 'nuff, I bought us each one a' for we left Nashville. You know a body just can't be too careful these days."

"Mighty strange to see so many strangers with repeaters all of a sudden. How 'bout 22's, you two carrying any of them little guns?"

Suddenly she felt a sickness rush into her stomach. *'Why would he ask about a 22?'* she wondered.

"22, naw," Cliff replied, "We have only 44's. I had me one when I was a kid though, made a good squirrel rifle."

"Only 44's, huh, nothing else?"

"Well now, my wife does carry a little Root Side-hammer in her purse, but it ain't no 22.

"I'd be obliged to see it," the big man said.

Cliff watched the sheriff's hand slid slowly and easily over to where it rested on his belt only an inch from the butt-stock of the heavy revolver that he carried in an old cut-down army holster.

Looking over at Nadine, Cliff could see the frightened expression on her face. "Sure. Honey, show the sheriff your Root," he said and reached forward and squeezed her shaking hand.

Nadine dropped the fork she was holding in her other hand and it struck the table and then slid off onto the floor. Immediately she turned her gaze to her husband.

'She looks like she is about to scream.' Cliff thought.

"Now look a' here. All this talk about them two robbers has done got the little woman scared plum to death. It's alright; show the sheriff your hideout," Cliff said and nodded his head to her.

"Well, we are mighty glad to meet up with you sheriff, now you can go get our money back," Nadine suddenly said as she reached into her handbag and carefully pulled the Root out and laid it on the table.

The sheriff reached down and picked up the small revolver and looked it over. Satisfied it was a 32 he dropped it back on the table, a move that irritated Cliff.

"Lady, I'm on the trail of some murderers, not no common thieves. You will have to get you own money back."

"Now, that don't seem right, maybe the murderers you are after and the men what stole our money are the same hombres," Cliff said back. When the lawman seemed not to consider that a possibility Cliff asked, "Why are you looking fur a 22, Sheriff?"

" 'Cause two fellows used a 22 to murder my brother."

"A 22, that do seem strange," Cliff said back. "You sure it were a 22?"

"I'm sure," he replied and reaching into the pocket of his dirty black vest he retrieved a spent shell and dropped it on the table.

Nadine froze. She couldn't for the life of her remember what she did with the spent round she had removed when she reloaded her Sharps.

Cliff reached forward and picked it up. Looking at the head he saw the slanted dent in the rim that was unquestionably made by a Sharps derringer. He just hoped the sheriff did not know enough about guns to realize why the firing pin that had struck this cartridge was not straight.

"Yeah, this here is a 22 alright," he said rolling the small case around between his thumb and his forefinger.

Nielson reached down and took the case from his hand and returned it to his pocket. "This here is evidence. The gun what fired this has a twisted firing pin and when I find that gun, I'll have my murderer."

"Honey, you remember that gun the little man was carrying? The one with the skeleton stock?" Cliff asked Nadine looking her straight in the eyes.

She didn't reply and she didn't change her panicky expression; in fact she did not look like she had even heard him.

"You know sheriff, that little rifle he were carrying could a' been a 22, sure could a' been," Cliff said looking back up at the lawman.

Nielson shook his head and looked out the window to the store across the street. His thoughts were of the whiskey his posse was putting down while he stood here arguing with these pilgrims. Finally he asked, "Just where did you last see 'em?"

"Not three miles up the road. I'm sure you can see where we parted company, if you go look," Cliff said. "They headed northeast."

"Three miles is in Florida, I'm a' Alabama Sheriff, can't do nothing about no stealing what took place in Florida."

"You mean, we are back in Florida? Why, we left Florida this morning, didn't we honey?" Cliff said with a surprised expression looking over at Nadine.

"That's right Joel Nielson, you are in Florida and you got no business questioning folks here," Mary said.

"I got the right when I'm hot on the trail of murderers," he spat back.

"I do believe the trail is getting colder every minute you let them no account thieving Indians travel on with our money. It's bound to be the same ones you are looking for," Cliff said. Then turning to the woman he asked, "Is there a place where my wife and I can stay the night?"

"Well, there ain't no hotel or nothing like that, but I do have a spare room I could let you have fur a dollar," she said back.

"That would be just wonderful," Nadine said.

At that very moment, a shot was heard coming from across the street.

"What now?" Nielson said looking at the store and shaking his head.

In a second or two, one of the men who had ridden into town

with him came charging out of the store and ran towards them yelling, "Sheriff! Sheriff!"

"Shit," was all Nielson said in reply.

When the man came rushing in he exclaimed, "Sheriff, Derry done got himself shot."

"What? How did that happen?"

"He wus fooling with that little O'Brien girl, and her Pa done up an' put a load a bird-shot in his ass."

"For God's sake, how bad off is he?"

"He ain't gon'a die or nothing but he's hurtin' a plenty."

"Shit," the Sheriff said again and then slapped his hat against his leg and started for the door but before he left he turned and pointing a finger straight at Cliff he said, "It's good you are staying over here tonight, I'll want to talk to you a' for you leave in the morning."

"Sure, Sheriff, we'll be right here," Cliff said nodding his head.

They did rent the room from Mary Stewart that night, but by the time her clock chimed three bells, they were mounted and headed east through a huge forest of long leaf pine that stretched for miles.

Cliff had retraced their route of the day before until they came to the church and there he led them across the upturned earth of the Pastor's garden leaving a trail a six year old boy could find. Anyone looking could easily see they were headed north.

The pine forest was a God-sent blessing and he didn't fail to grasp the opportunity it gave them. Traveling through this timber, on the carpet of fallen pine needles beneath them, would greatly slow any pursuers because the ground was so thickly covered with the needles, their animals left little or no trace.

The wind had been up when they left Mary's and they had not been in the forest over an hour, when a strong storm came rushing up from the south. It didn't last more than ten minutes but it did leave them drenched to the bone.

After the rain, the night air became colder and he knew Nadine was chilled, but he dared not stop or build a fire. He wanted to be as far away from Sheriff Nielson as they could be when he found out they had left in the night.

Finally just as the eastern sky was beginning to show signs of purple, Red drew up short and lifting his head he shot his ears forward. Cliff knew the sign and quickly raised his arm for her to also stop.

They waited there in the almost darkness for two minutes before he heard a rooster crow off in the distance.

He waited still for another minute or more before he loosened his grip on the reins and Red once again moved forward toward the sounds.

They were almost upon the log structure before either of them saw it. In fact, it was the sound of a horse and Red's snorting reply that brought his focus on a barn and then the house off to its right some twenty yards. Again he stopped and waited.

The night was ever so slowly giving up its control over the earth, and before long the vague outline of a stagecoach appeared in front of the house.

At first he intended to skirt this place and he would have, had he been alone, but when he thought of Nadine and knew she was soaked and very cold, he decided to risk it and moved forward toward the house.

Just as they were within ten yards of the coach, an older colored man came from out of the darkness and seeing them, jumped straight in the air as he let out a "Yelp!" not unlike a dog would make when hit with a thrown rock.

"Howdy," Cliff said.

"Laud above, f'om whar does cow person's com' dis time ob' a' mornin'?"

"Didn't mean to startle ya'. The Missis and I got drenched in the storm and was hoping to warm up and dry off some."

The old man looked closely at Nadine and then said, "Laudy, Laudy, it do be a lady."

Immediately he turned and heading for the front porch he began to yell, "Marster Wiggins, Marster Wiggins," and then he disappeared through the front door.

Shortly they could see the brightness of a lamp being lit inside and a lot of commotion that could not be understood from where they sat.

Cliff reached forward and pulled one of the Colts from his pommel holsters and laid his hand over the saddle horn. Turning his head so he could speak to her without taking his eyes off the house he said, "Be ready to depart in an instant, if this don't work out so good."

When she tried to reply, she broke out in harsh raspy coughing that almost took away her breath and consciousness.

Now he turned and looked at her. What he saw was a surprise. She was gasping for air and her head was high and her eyes rolled back.

Forgetting all about the possible danger from inside the house he jumped from his horse and grabbing her by the arms pulled her from the saddle.

She tried to smile but a fit of coughing again took control of her and she passed out in his arms.

Cliff didn't know when the man had come to his side, but he appreciated the concerned expression on his face when he looked at Nadine.

Cliff had her in his arms still holding the Colt, and seeing this the man said, "Bring her inside, and you won't need that."

"Pookie, get your wife. This lady is bad off sick," Wiggins said to the tall thin man who had just sat down at the long table with a cup of hot coffee.

"Peekon," he called out to the kitchen.

"Oui?"

"The femee est malade venez vite, Peekon."

Suddenly a dark, very thin woman came rushing through a door. Cliff thought at first she was a negress but when he saw her long straight hair he realized she was Creole.

This woman looked at Nadine and placed her hand on her forehead and then exclaimed, "Chambre a coucher Vilain une fievre prendre elle."

Cliff looked at her not understanding a word she had said, and yet he was sure she had just given him a command.

Looking up at him realizing his confusion she added, "Quick you skinny mullet le fram' you take no'?"

Cliff just shook his head at her totally at a loss.

She nodded her head to him and then said, "My man Pookie, will take, no'?"

The lanky man came over and took Nadine from him and carried her through a door into another room. Cliff started after them but the woman placed her hand on his chest and stopped him and said as she closed the door. "Peekon nurse, you Boo will be fine."

Cliff stepped back not really knowing what else to do and waited.

Less than a minute later he heard the woman cry out "Drawz ste'pin conson no."

He had no idea what she had said but it sounded frightening and he started for the door but before he reached it, it flew open and the man came out almost in a run.

"What is it? Is she alright?"

"Oui, she will be fine. My wife is a good nurse. She saved my life after doctors give up. The lady has a very bad fievre much weakened," he nodded his head and then again said, "My woman, good nurse."

The Cajun, Pookie Pitre, had married Wiggin's sister Lacy before the war and took her back to his native state, but she did not survive the occupation of General Butler's troops.

Pitre himself served in Company B, 26th Louisiana Infantry Regiment under Captain Sanders, until he was severely wounded near Vicksburg where he hid out in the swamps until found and slowly nursed back to health by a Cajun wench named Peekon Lefleur. At war's end he returned to New Orleans only to learn of the death of his wife. A couple of months later he sought out and married Peekon. Two years after that he moved back to Florida to work for his former brother-in-law.

"He is right. Peekon is the best doctor in these parts. She knows about herbs and roots and other things that most doctors have no idea of. Your lady is in good hands," Wiggins assured Cliff.

They stayed there for two weeks before Nadine was well enough to travel. Cliff helped them when the stages came in and worked with Pookie and the other hands tapping some of the trees and hanging the drip pots for the turpentine.

When they were ready to leave, Nadine gave Peekon a long and hard hug and kissed her man on the cheek before she mounted Treasure. Cliff didn't really know what to say that could express his feeling of gratitude and he just hoped when Mr. Wiggins and Peekon each found the small bags under their pillows they would understand the meaning of why they were left there.

Three miles down the stage road she turned to him and asked, "What is Mr. Wiggins' first name?"

Cliff thought for a minute before answering, "I don't rightly know," he shook his head and then added, "I never ask 'im."

CHAPTER THREE

West Florida

Late that afternoon when they came over the hill and the gray waters of the Gulf of Mexico were seen ahead, Cliff felt for the first time in several weeks, a load lift from his shoulders.

The bay at Pensacola was the first time she had seen so large a body of water and it was mind-boggling to a girl who had been raised in Missouri.

Nadine[6] took a deep breath inhaling the salty air and felt a little weak as its richness filled her lungs.

The adventure she and her new husband had undertaken had not been without stressful days and nights interrupted by moments of stark terror. At times, only the love and respect she held for this man had kept her spirits so high; in addition to the fact that a new life, no matter how dangerous, was better than the one from which he had rescued her.

In the month of October, when the nights at South Pass City were already dropping near zero with snow often littering the strong west winds, here she was enjoying eighty-degree temperatures and

---

[6] Nadine: Described in Chapter One of *Gold in the Red Desert*; A beautiful intruder, her hair was as black as a crow's wing in the Georgia sun and her skin almost as white as new snow. The valley between her breasts was very visible and her mounds moved independent of one another when she moved. Her smile revealed straight white teeth and a small dimple on her left cheek.

a pleasant breeze from the Gulf of Mexico. It was with ease she let the worries of the past few weeks slip away, being only forgotten memories, at least for a time.

Cliff too, enjoyed the smell of the salt air, though not for the first time by any means. However, it was not so hypnotizing to him. Instead of a feeling of tranquility sweeping over him as the couple entered the age-old city, the cold bitterness of Union Blue tunics appearing at almost every turn of the head, was biting at his gut.

An occupational army, no matter how well behaved, is a nagging sore in the hearts of home folk in any country anywhere in the world; and it was certainly no different during the Reconstruction Period to those who had been raised in the South.

Another sore that began to bleed was the sight of Freedmen walking the streets, smoking big cigars and deliberately bumping into or throwing slurred remarks at any white man or woman with a southern drawl, hoping to enrage them into a confrontation; an act that would almost surely result in the white being arrested and any and all of his property being confiscated by the courts. Many of the judges were appointed; but even those who had been created by an election were tainted with the corruption of having only Freedmen and immigrants who had come in the post war years being allowed to seek office or cast a vote. It was even a crime for a former Confederate to be an elder or deacon in a church.

Cliff had taken a room for them at "Trader's Hotel" not far from the docks. The choice was not at random, but with purpose. He had stayed there with his father in the late fifties and knew it to be a place of sympathy to the cause, and too, it was near the railroad spur that ran to the off loading ramps on the docks.

While signing the register book as C. Burris, he asked if Tom Trader was there. The clerk shot him a sharp glance before replying, "No."

He had planned to stay there a couple of days before they ventured on eastward, but when they came down for supper, Cliff overheard one of the soldiers talking to a short, balding man who sported a strong northeastern accent. The intoxicated sergeant loudly referred to the Yankee as "Trader" and Cliff knew things had changed substantially since he had last spent a night here.

A man sitting at the table next to them, though obviously from his speech was no northerner, was nonetheless vulgar to the point Cliff stood to challenge him on the matter.

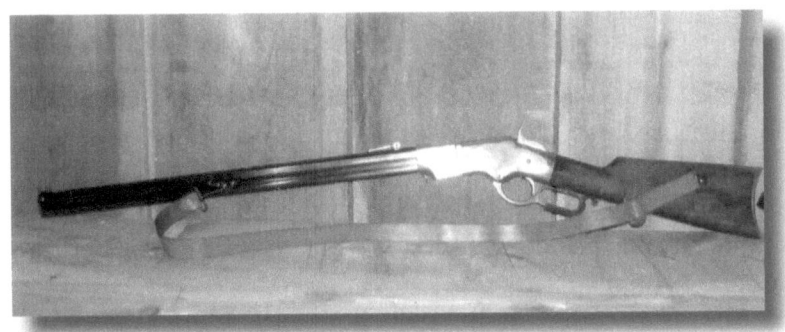

**Henry Rifle Used by Both Union and Confederate Troops
During the War Between the States
Held 16 Self-Contained 44 Caliber Rim Fire Copper Cartridges**

Nadine grabbed his arm and pulled him away and out of the room before he pursued the matter.

'*This here Pensacola sure ain't the way I left it,*' he thought as they headed for the stairs.

Cliff stopped at the hotel desk just long enough to inquire of the man's name from the clerk.

"Oh, he's Mr. Edgar Watson[7]," The clerk replied. "A bad one from down at Tater Hill Bluff[8]."

"Whar's that?" Cliff asked.

"Manatee County," the little man whispered then added, "He is said to be a back shooter, hires out his gun to anybody with enough money."

Cliff nodded to him before taking Nadine's elbow and walking her upstairs.

An hour later, there was a soft knock on their door.

"Who's there?"

"Me. Wesley Barber, the clerk from downstairs."

"What do you want?" Cliff asked.

The voice outside was barely above a whisper, and Cliff, looking to see she was not exposed, reached for his Colt and then cracked the door. "What do you want?"

---

[7] Edgar Watson, was the prime suspect in the ambush murder of Belle Starr some eighteen years later in Indian Territory. He was never convicted and returned to Florida. There he is credited with 57 killings, and suspected of many more, finally being ambushed himself at Chokoloskee Island.

[8] Tater Hill Bluff: Now known as Arcadia Florida

"That man, Watson, he was asking about you."

"What did he ask?"

Barber looked around first over one shoulder and then the other and Cliff could see he was greatly troubled about something. "I don't want to be overheard."

Cliff glanced back at Nadine and seeing she was dressed only in pantaloons, he nodded for her to move over behind the dressing screen.

"All right, come on in, but be quick," Cliff said obviously aggravated by the sudden appearance of the clerk.

"I'm sorry Mr. Burris, but I thought you should know."

"Know what?" Cliff asked then added when the man was slow about answering, "Be quick man, my wife was preparing for bed."

"I know, but that Watson said he has a paper on you."

"What kind a' paper?"

"A wanted paper, issued by the Occupational Government for murder."

"That's ridiculous. We just got here today."

"This paper is from Alabama," Barber told him. "He told the Sergeant here he's been after you for several days now. Claims you kilt a deputy sheriff up there."

"Why you telling me this?"

" 'Cause you're homefolk, I can tell. 'Sides, you asked about Mr. Trader, may he rest in peace, and the way you look at them Bluebellies, I knows you hate them as much as I do," the boy replied.

"Where are you from, Wesley?" Nadine asked as she stepped from behind the screen now covered in a white corduroy robe she had bought that very day.

"Columbia County, Ma'am," he answered.

The lad appeared to be around 18 or 19 years of age and a little on the puny side to her, "Where is that?"

"Lake City," he answered, "They's call it Lake City now, but when I was a wee-tot we called it Alligator's Town."

'You still look pretty young to me', she thought.

"East of here, maybe three hundred mile by rail," Cliff injected.

"How did you get way out here at so young an age?" she asked the boy.

"I'm older than I look," he said "I'm twenty."

"Oh," she replied not daring to smile, although that was just what she was fighting.

"I know I look young, but I wus in the army. I fit in the war with the Yankees," he said then added. "I was a drummer boy with General Lee in Virginia. I was in the Marian Rifle Guards, Fourth Florida Infantry. I got this here bad leg at Cold Harbor," the boy said almost in a plea for her to accept him as what he claimed to be.

Nadine looked at the left leg that he was pointing to, but admitted to herself she had not realized he favored it until he brought to her attention. "I'm sure it took a great deal of courage to walk into battle armed with only a drum," she replied softly.

"Thank you, Ma'am. Some don't consider it much."

"Well I do."

"I do, too," Cliff said. "I always had a horse under me, to get me out of it when it got too bad."

"Mighty kind of you folks to say such."

"Tell me Wesley, what happened to Tom Trader?"

"He's dead. Shot right in the face. It were me what found 'im, downstairs there beside the bar. It were a sight to see," the boy said and Nadine noticed the expression on his face turn sour, and for a moment she thought he might be sick.

"I called out fur help, but them Bluebellies are all the law we got here and one a' them sergeants said it must a' been a robbery," the boy added and shook his head. "T'weren't though," again he slowly shook his head. "The very day I found him, they done had a Yankee here to take over and he done took on the name a' Trader." Still shaking his head, he finished with "It were murder; they done it to steal this here hotel, 'cause he wouldn't sell and he had the gold to pay their taxes."

Wanting to change the subject for the lad's sake, Cliff asked, "Where did this Watson go?"

"He went off with Sergeant Tinsley to find his commanding officer, but they won't find him cause Colonel Faux is upstairs with a whore passed out drunk," the boy said then suddenly looked at Nadine and added, "Oh, I'm sorry Ma'am, I didn't mean to be vulgar."

"If the lady is a whore Wesley, it may not be by her choosing. You never know who might become a whore, given bad circumstances. I don't judge them," she said back.

"That's real understanding, Ma'am. Most ladies don't know them truths."

"Is Watson staying here?"

"No, he tried to get a room, but we wus all filled up a' for he come in tonight."

Cliff reached into his vest pocket and retrieved a five dollar gold coin, placing it into the boy's hand. "Come by here early in the morning and I will give you a paper to get our mounts out of the livery, down on River Street," Cliff said then added, "You think you can do that?"

"I think so," he replied nodding his head, "But you don't need to give me nut'in. I was doing it fur you and da' lady."

"I know that Wesley, but you would honor me by taking this."

"But Mr. Burris, it's too much. I don't make that much in half a year."

"If you save us from Watson and the military, it is not near enough," Nadine said and closed his hand by wrapping hers around his. When she did, she noticed how much larger her hand was than his.

When he was gone, she turned to Cliff and said, "We never killed no deputy sheriff."

"No, I don't think so, but we did kill the sheriff's brother. He might a' been some kind a' deputy, I suppose."

"Great," she replied shaking her head.

Neither got a lot of sleep that night, and both were up and dressed before first light.

Cliff listened to the big clock in the lobby beat out five strong gongs only moments before footsteps were heard on the wooden floor of the hall outside their room.

He lifted the Colt from its leather and turned to see Nadine with Winchester in hand, near the screen.

There were moments of heavy heartbeats before a short knock was followed quickly by Wesley's whisper.

Cliff opened the door and pulled the boy inside.

"You gave me a fright," the boy gasped.

"We were a little concerned about who was out there, too," Cliff replied.

"Morning, Ma'am."

"Good morning, Wesley," she said smiling at the boy.

"I see'd Watson already. I don't think he ever went to sleep."

"Where is he?"

"I see'd him downstairs on the front porch. He's just sitting there in one of the chairs looking at the docks," Barber replied. "He didn't see me though. I made sure a' that."

"Good. Here's what I want you to do. Go to the livery and get our horses and gear. Here's two dollars and a note to the hostler saying to let you have them," Cliff said handing him a folded piece of brown paper. "Pay what we owe and bring them to the street just north of the railroad depot. You know where that is?"

"Sure, it's Lee Street; well they calls it Cannon Street now, but it used to be Lee."

"All right, bring them there," Cliff said again and then took a deep breath before adding, "You won't have no trouble with the Pinto but the big sorrel might be another thing. Ole' Red is a quarrelsome creature at times. I'm afraid we had better leave the mule here."

"Don't you worry none, Mr. Burris. Animals take to me," Wesley replied quite confident of his abilities.

"Alright then, the train leaves at seven, if it's on time. I need for you and the horses to be there at seven. Can you do that?"

"You becha', Mr. Burris."

They were out the back door of Trader's before sunup, and were moving towards the railroad depot without being seen by Watson or anyone else.

A small yellow building near the tracks had a shingle painted 'Restaurant' hanging above the front door and the flicker of a coal oil lamp inside gave hope the place was open for business.

Nadine entered first while Cliff stayed back in the shadows and watched for signs of a follower. After three minutes and none was seen, he too went in.

His bride was seated near the wall facing the front door. A blue birds-eye cup was in her hand. The small swirl of smoke told the tale of hot coffee for them, if nothing else. Cliff walked up and took a chair at the table next to hers saluting with his hat to her in gentlemanly fashion before he removed it and sat down, "Morning, Ma'am."

"Good morning, sir," she replied without really looking at him.

Soon a black boy came from the rear of the building and asked "You's wont som'in' to 'et, Misser?"

"No, just coffee," Cliff replied.

"Ober dar din," he said nodding to a pot sitting on a pot belly stove in the corner.

Cliff was still not used to being told what to do and where to go by darkies and his hand went quickly to a fist, but just as quickly he nodded and got up and moved to the coffee.

"Dat be a nickel."

Cliff flipped a coin at him making sure it fell short and he had to pick it up. The boy recognized the gesture for just what it was, but he smiled when he picked it up knowing he still had the white man's money.

At five minutes to seven, Cliff got up and left. Two minutes later, she followed.

He bought two tickets to Jacksonville, and they sat only three seats apart in the last of the passenger cars. Most of the other passengers were soldiers, save a few men who looked like they were making a business trip.

Just as the train began to roll, someone called out something about a fire and everyone looked back down the street towards the docks. A man running by on the street was heard yelling something about Trader's Hotel being afire.

No one let the man and woman, who quickly disembarked, interfere with their looking out of the windows at the smoke coming from the rear of the hotel three blocks away.

As promised, Wesley Barber was there with their two horses along with a strange buckskin pony. "I guess I'd better be riding on myself," he said "My room caught afire and old man Trader will surely blame me when he gets it put out. 'Sides, with this here five dollars I can get back home."

Cliff nodded his head in approval and Nadine gave him a large smile, now understanding the source of the blaze.

The three moved on through Pensacola and out the east side of town while most of the population was just beginning their day.

The ferry, alongside the railroad bridge crossing the Escambia River, was run by an older man with no left limb below the knee. He smoked an old wooden pipe that gave off the worst odor Nadine ever remembered smelling.

He was dressed in coveralls, not unlike what she usually wore, but old and torn. He had no shoes or shirt, and his slouch hat was dirty and sweat-stained. Some would have said it was black, others a very dark brown, but Cliff knew it had once been butternut and there on the front of the crown, ever so faint, was the evidence; crossed cannons had once been pinned there.

When they were mid-stream, Cliff moved over closer to the man and without looking at him and speaking in a strong and knowing voice said, "I reckon that old hat tells the tale."

The man looked up at him from his little perch at the side of the barge. "What tale a' that be?"

"Tells me the man who wore it proudly was a' Art Man."

The old man rolled his eyes and looked him over for several seconds then visibly moved his tongue between his front teeth and his bottom lip, as if he were cleaning the channel there before he spat into the blue water. "That mean somunt' to you? Don't most, these days."

"How did you lose your leg?"

"Yankee Sharpshooter, up in a tall sweet gum. Had 'im one of em' globe sighted Sharps," he said a little disgusted, then a change came to him and with pride shinning in his voice he continued. "I wus on Lt. Rambo's gun, Milton Light Artillery. It were mounted on a railroad flat car and we wus a giving um' hell, but then nigh on a thousand colored troops being led by white officers located our position and they come a-charging at us. They were too close to bring the gun down on 'em by the time we see'd 'em, and with that Sharpshooter up thar a-cutting into us, we wus about to be in a bad way. Suddenly one 'a 'em Georgia Boys spotted him, and send 'em to hell in a heartbeat, and then 'em boys cut into those colored troops and dropped 'em in their tracks. 'Em Georgia Boys are shooters, I want you to know."

"Where was that?" Cliff asked, seeing it was doing the old man good to remember.

"Olustee." There was a short pause and then he said, "It were worth it though, losing this leg I mean. Them rotten Bluebellies were a-coming down on us all over the country. 'The General' was being pushed back in Virginnie; Hood was retreating in Tennessee; Shelby lost Vicksburg; even Little Joe Johnson had been replaced, but not us. We whipped 'em damn Yankees right out a' Florida. Cut 'um down like they wus blow flies on a pile a' rotten mullet," catching his breath he finished, "We shor whooped 'um at Olustee."

Cliff could see, for a while, the old man had not really been with him at all, rather back in another time, in another place. *'A time when a body could tell his enemies by the color of their clothes and the accents of their voices, not like these times,'* he thought remembering Watson.

"You?" the old man asked, bringing him back to reality.

"I wus with General Forrest's Cavalry, in Tennessee," Cliff paused thinking back himself, "Tennessee, Mississippi, Alabama, Carolina, and finally back to Tennessee, where I wus captured."

"Um," was all the reply he got other than a slight nod of the head.

The mule team that had pulled the barge across the river was standing with heads down as Wesley led his buckskin and Treasure off the log ferry. Nadine had jumped clear herself and Cliff took the reins of Red to lead him ashore but stopped just before he departed and spoke, without looking at the man, "There most likely will be some come looking for us. Mee'be wearing blue, mee'be not. I'd be obliged if 'n you never saw us."

"Yanks?"

Cliff nodded his head, "Yanks and a no good scalawag named Watson."

"Got no use fur invaders, nor them what work fur invaders," the old man said.

Nadine was wiping some of the mud from her button up shoes before mounting. "Where do we go from here?" she asked.

"Well, we got a' get across this bog," Cliff replied as he looked at the muddy road ahead. "After that we'll try to catch another train."

Travel was slow for a few miles then the black mud began to slowly turn red as clay materialized, showing the keen-eyed traveler a change in soil was taking place.

When she noticed the sun was on her left, Nadine realized they were headed northeast. An hour before sundown, she could make out a few buildings ahead.

"What is this place?"

"Campton Junction," Cliff answered "I hope."

"I just hope it has a' outhouse," she said back.

They were able to get a room for the night at the stage stop there. Wesley stayed in the livery with the horses. He had said that there he could have them saddled in a flash if the need be; but Cliff knew he was too much a gentleman or too embarrassed to stay in the room with them, and too, the boy really didn't want to spend the money for a room.

They both appreciated the solitude as it was much too early in their married life for the lust of each other's body not to play a most important role in their minds, nightly.

Before sunup the next morning, Cliff went to the Pensacola & Georgia Railroad shack and arranged to have the train stop there to pick them up. The agent had telegraphed to Pensacola and found that the army had an animal car already scheduled, so Cliff again bought tickets to Jacksonville for them.

Wesley and Nadine boarded together. Cliff boarded just as the train was moving out, having satisfied himself the horses were properly taken care of.

When he sat down, it was across the aisle from them and facing the back of the car.

The train stopped every fifteen miles to take on water and sometimes wood. Even though at times it could obtain speeds of thirty miles an hour, the stops cut their average time to nearly half that. The sun was already down and the horizon a golden orange glow when they pulled into Tallahassee.

Nadine asked the conductor if it were possible for her and her little brother to stay overnight there and visit a sick aunt, then continue on in a day or two. He, being a man in his early forties, could not refuse such an attractive woman, and he exchanged her tickets for new ones dated for October 20, 1870.

That night Nadine enjoyed her first taste of gator tail. It had been battered and fried in hog fat just enough to cook without allowing the heat to toughen it.

Before her first bite she looked deep into Cliff's eyes and said, "You know I trust you very much or I wouldn't be doing this."

Ten minutes later she was trying to decide if gator tail or buffalo hump was the finest tasting meat she had ever eaten.

Later, while walking past the State Capitol Building, Cliff explained that Tallahassee will always have a special place in the hearts of all true Rebels, as it was the only Confederate Capital east of the Mississippi that was not taken by the invading armies during the war.

The rising sun was again to her right as they headed out the next morning.

Wesley continued east having another hundred miles to go to Lake City, but Cliff took the trail to Thomasville. The parting was sad as they all had come to feel so close to one another in the short time they had been together. In some ways, Nadine felt they might owe the boy their lives. They both knew had it not been for him warning them and starting the fire that allowed them to slip out of Pensacola undetected, their escape might not have been so satisfying; but still she knew how badly Cliff wanted to get home and she was sure

Wesley felt the same for his family, so with a slight tear in her eye, she waved to the little lad as they rode north.

Within two hours, Cliff felt his heart grow warm when the blood red clay assured him he was back in Georgia after more than four years.

Cliff dismounted and tossed his left fender over the saddle seat before he began pulling his cinch strap tighter.

"See that?" he said to her, nodding at the ground below his boots.

"What?"

"That red earth."

"Yeah," she said back not sure what he meant.

"That is Georgia clay," he said, and she suddenly could sense, somewhat, the feeling he was enjoying at that moment.

"I want to see a sweet gum tree then."

"What?"

"I have heard you talk so much about sweet gum trees, I want to see one."

"Alright," he replied and looked around quickly spying his target. "There, that big one with the spiny balls hanging from it."

She dismounted too and spotting the seeds on the ground she bent over and picked one up in her gloved hand, "That's a sweet gum?"

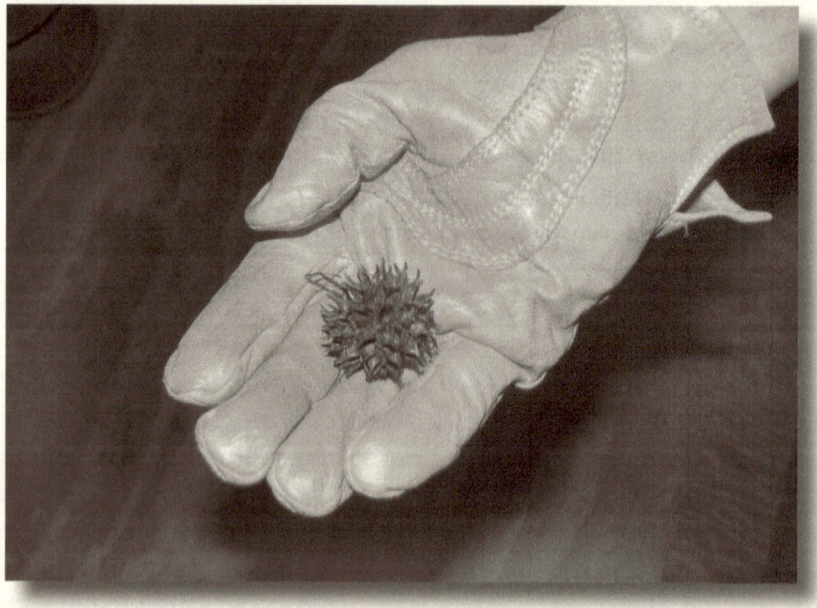

The Spiny Seed of a Sweet Gum Tree

"Yes, that's a sweet gum."

"Hell, I saw one of them back in Alabama."

"No doubt; they're all over the south."

"I thought they could only be found in Georgia, the way you bragged about them."

Cliff just shook his head.

She reached up and pulled some Spanish Moss from the low hanging tree limb and it was then he warned her about red bugs.

"What are red bugs?"

"Little critters that live in the moss and bite the hell out of you; make sores that stay on you for weeks."

Quickly she tossed the moss away and began looking for bugs but saw none.

"I bet you're just telling one," she finally said.

"Just you wait. If them little bastards are on you, Mama will make you sleep outside."

Again she examined her arms where the moss had touched her skin and found nothing.

Before they reached another settlement, he turned east and they rode into the sun until nearly noon then they came to another intersection. There he stopped and they dismounted. A wet creek flowed beside the road and he let the horses drink while he refilled their canteens.

"This, me darling, is the old Coffee Road. It'll take us clear to Lowndes County."

"Where is Lowins County?"

"Not Lowins County, Lowndes County. Valdosta just happens to be the county seat."

"Hallelujah," she said somewhat relieved their journey was nearly over.

That night they stayed at the stage station just down from the Okapilco Methodist Church.

Late the next day after crossing a lazy river on a ferry, they rode south bypassing the town a couple miles and cut across Mr. Dasher's west pasture, before turning due south on a sandy trail around a large cypress swamp. There he let the animals drink but did not dismount. Nadine saw a large, black snake swim away from the shore and dive into the dark water.

"Come on," he finally said pulling on Red's reins.

Two miles further, they came around a bend where the road had given way to an oak hammock and there, just over a little rise, was an old wagon with a stump where the right rear wheel should have been, and immediately behind it a house stood. She thought she could see traces of paint, but if so, it had long since been weathered away.

On the front porch sitting in a rocking chair was a very thin, gray-haired old woman. She was shelling peas and dropping the pods into a porcelain pot. Looking up at the two intruders, she held one hand over her eyes, shading the glare of the late afternoon sun.

"Hello, Mama," Cliff said in a tone of voice Nadine had never heard from him before.

"Praise the Lord, it's Clifford James," she replied as she stood, spilling her peas.

He dismounted and walked to her, and as gentle as could be, he lifted her well off her feet as he hugged her.

"Put me down, you big brute," she said to him, not as a rebuke but rather showing some embarrassment.

When he did, she straightened her apron and put her hand to her hair as if she were looking for strands that had been squeezed out of place.

"Who is this you brung with you?" she asked in a soft voice.

"My wife, Nadine. Didn't you get my letter?"

"Wife?" she said sharply back and then looking strongly at the other rider she added. "Ain't got no mail for nigh on a year now. Yankees won't let 'em bring it. Them carpetbaggers what run the post office, steals all the letters intended fur home folk. They used to read it and if there weren't nut'en in it that they's interested in, they'd give it to Mr. Ousley to deliver, but after what happened with your brothers and Pa and all," she paused a moment before continuing, "they just throw it away after reading it, I reckon."

She suddenly remembered what he had said, and she looked up quickly at Nadine. "Wife you say?"

"Yes, wife. I wrote you last summer."

"Well, like I said, ain't got no mail," she answered still staring at Nadine, "What's she doing riding astride that animal?"

"It's alright, Ma. She's from the west. They don't have side-saddles in Wyoming."

"Well, she ain't in Wyoming no more," Addie said flatly and turned around and walked inside.

The house was a two room affair with a hallway or breezeway between the two rooms.[9] Nadine noticed the room to the right was obviously a bedroom and the one to the left contained a good size table and a rocking chair in front of the fireplace. Several straight back chairs were scattered loosely around the table.

The older woman walked on through and out the back door onto a small porch where she sat the little pot down on a shelf, beside a pitcher pump.

There was also a second house some twenty feet directly behind the main house that gave off odors of food cooking inside.

"Got some collards biling and a couple chickens; were planning on doing a Pileau[10] fur Sunday supper. Guess I'll have to go on with it now."

**Typical 1870'S Cracker House
with Spanish Moss Hanging from the Limbs
of a Live Oak Tree**

---

9 This type of cracker house was often called a dog trot.
10 Pileau: African word meaning cooked with rice. Any boiled meat like chicken, pork, squirrel, coon, possum and rice with onion and celery all mixed together and served as a main course. Pronounced Per-lo'.

Nadine knew she had not been accepted by Cliff's mother. She hoped it was because of the sudden news rather than something about her personally, but she still worried about it. *'Could she sense I was a whore?'* she wondered.

Cliff too was disappointed and embarrassed by his mother's actions, but knew some things take time and it usually was best not to bring sores to a head before they had time to heal.

"Come on," he said to Nadine putting his arm around her and walking behind his mother to the kitchen house.

Inside, Nadine saw an iron stove that looked too big for the room and a high back sink with no source for water. There were windows in the center of each wall save the front, where the door was located. A slight but comforting breeze entered from the north and carried out most of the heat as it exited through the south window.

"You like collards, girl?" the woman asked.

"I, I don't know what collards are," Nadine replied quite embarrassed.

"They's greens, kind 'a like turnips or mustards, you know."

"Well, I like turnip greens. My ma often cooked them back home."

"Where was that?"

"Missouri, Clay County, Missouri."

"I thought Clifford James said you's from Wyoming."

"Wyoming was where I was living when we met," Nadine replied as politely as she could.

"Get me that thar pot yonder," she said pointing at a good size black kettle sitting on the floor at the back wall.

Nadine reached for the cast iron pot, but Cliff stepped up and picked it up for her and sat it on the stove.

"I see you ain't lost all your up-bringing while you wus wandering all over the country," his mother said without looking at either of them.

"Nadine, you've had collards."

"I have?"

"Yeah, don't you remember, at Miss Mary's just out a' Alabama? We was eating collards when that sheriff came in looking for the Indians with the 22."

"Oh," she said and gave him a mean look for even bringing that up.

Cliff realized he had touched on a sour spot and quickly changed the subject. "Where's Pa?"

"No telling," his mother replied "Wandering around som'ers, I 'spec. His mind is gone, mostly, after Johnny Boy___," she stopped as if she was trying to find the right words then added "After Johnny Boy left. He usually gathers up some food most e'ry morning a'for he sets off."

"Where's Johnny Boy?"

"Who knows? Dead most likely," she said taking her apron and wiping her brow.

"Why do you say that?" Cliff shot back quickly "What happened?"

"One night, two, three months back we heard riders come up; they said they had papers on him fur murder and had to arrest him. Your Pa tried to tell them Johnny Boy was to home the night that nigger wus killed and that they already took Sammy fur that, but it didn't do no good. They took him off into the night and we never see'd him again," she paused before adding, "Your Pa took it hard. He loved that boy like life itself."

"Didn't nobody look for him?"

"Sure, your Pa and me went over to Mr. Dasher's come light and he went to town with us, but that Yankee Commander, who is in charge of Valdosta said Johnny Boy escaped into a cypress swamp and they couldn't find him in the dark. Bunch 'a lies, nothing but Yankee lies."

"Well, Mama, you know Johnny Boy was a good horseman and he knew these swamps better'n any Bluebelly; he might be over to Waycross at Uncle Virgil's."

"No, Son, your Pa went over there looking fur him. You just don't know how bad it's been."

The old woman stopped what she was doing at the stove and looked off. If someone was watching her at the moment they would have said she was staring at the wall but in reality she was looking far beyond the wall. "It wus the same with Sammy. He went to work one morning and never came back. They said he was arrested fur shooting a nigger, but he didn't have no gun. It were all just a put-up, to get rid of him. They found his body no more'n a mile from where he wus took from, just riddled with pistol balls." She stopped for a few more seconds and finally seemed to return to the little kitchen house and looked around at them, "It were bad when you left, but it got worse, much worse. Home folk are disappearing all the time," she said, shaking her head slowly as she spoke.

Nadine could tell she had tears building in her eyes and she wanted to get out of there and let the old woman have her cry in the privacy of her own kitchen, but she wasn't sure that it might be somehow offensive if she were to leave, so she just turned and looked out of the window at a gray squirrel digging in the leaves close by. Soon she excused herself and went to the little house to the rear of the kitchen, as much as an avenue of escape as the call of nature.

An hour after dark as they were sitting down to supper on the back porch, she heard the front door open and heavy footsteps in the hall. The sounds also told her someone had placed a hat to the wall and removed some upper garment and tossed it into the bedroom. Suddenly a man walked into the room. He was much shorter than Cliff and thin as could be. She was so surprised at his size, because his steps sounded heavy and large.

"Who is that there?" he said in a voice that was some broken but not rough at all.

"It's me, Pa."

"Johnny Boy, you ain't dead after all," the old man cried out.

"No, Pa, it's Clifford. I come home from the west."

"Clifford?" the man repeated "Clifford James? That ain't you, Johnny Boy?"

"No, Mr. Brown, it's your second son, Clifford James," the old woman said to him sternly.

"Clifford James," he repeated as if trying to focus on the name. "Clifford James come home? Why?"

"Because I wrote him to come home," his mother said. "I told you I did last spring."

"Boy, don't you know they got papers on you fur murdering that nigger?"

"Yes, Pa, I knowed it. That's why I left in the first place. Don't you remember?" Cliff said back, walking up closer to him. "You helped me get away."

"Then why did you come back?"

"Mama said you needed me."

"Them Bluebellies will kill you sure, boy; just like they done all your brothers."

"Maybe not, Pa," Cliff answered and then to change the subject he placed both hands on his father's arms and turned him towards Nadine. "Look, Pa, I got me a wife."

"A wife?" the man repeated in amazement.

"Yeah Pa, a wife," he said back with pride in his voice. "I done settled down and took me a wife."

"Damn sure is a purty thing, Son," the little old man said, squinting his eyes as he stared at her.

"None of your vulgarity in this house Mr. Brown," his wife shot at him quickly.

"Still is a purty thing. You done good boy, real good."

"Yes, I think so too, Pa," Cliff said with pride and confidence.

Nadine had to admit the collards were better than she had remembered and she felt a little better after the way Mr. Brown had carried on about her. Still she was uncomfortable about the obvious dislike her mother-in-law had shown for her.

The next morning was Sunday and Nadine could hear the two arguing in the other room.

"Sunday or no, that thar buckboard ain't got but three wheels and no three wheel wagon is gon'a be drove to church."

Cliff stood and slipped on his pants, "I had better get out there and put that wheel back on before she clobbers him with a stick a' lighter."

"Augh, she wouldn't do that," Nadine said back to him as she watched him dress.

"You don't know Mama when it comes to going to church; she's a Campbellite[11] and a headstrong one, too."

An hour later they had loaded the Pileau into a buckboard now sporting four wheels and were driving to the Corinth Church of Christ a few miles up the road. Mr. & Mrs. Brown sat straight as statues beside Nadine on the spring seat as the little wagon moved along the canopy road. Cliff rode Red a hundred yards behind them.

The church house was so much like a hundred she had seen in the last six months. Tall and small and whitewashed with a tin roof, only this one had no steeple as most did. A dozen animals were

---

[11] Campbellite: Followers of Alexander Campbell, who broke away from the Baptist claiming to be the restorers of "Primitive Christianity." Campbell was disenchanted with the Baptist introducing instrumental music like the Catholics and Methodist had, as well as other new doctrine.

around the building, mostly hitched to wagons or buggies, but some with saddles loosely cinched.

When the Brown family arrived, everyone in front of the building seemed to be watching a group of men sitting on horses a hundred yards to the south atop a small knoll, in full view of the building. The horsemen did not venture closer while the families were gathered around the front of the church building, but after the congregation went inside as a group, the riders slowly eased closer and looked over the animals tied outside.

The voices inside were drumming out *"When The Roll Is Called Up Yonder"* as the black soldiers inspected the brands. A large corporal patted the left hip of Red searching for the mark. Red cut his eyes back and lowered his ears just before he kicked.

His left rear hoof caught the corporal in the upper thigh, six inches above the knee. The snapping of the bone could be heard inside the church building just as the hymn stopped, as could his screams shortly thereafter.

Cliff rose as did the Gaston boy across the room. Slowly opening the door, Cliff peered out.

Two of the soldiers were trying to give aid to the fallen man as a sergeant with an extremely black face reached for his reversed draw holster and lifted the flap.

Cliff had his Colt up and pointed at the man's head before the soldier had a good grip on the stock.

"No need to get violent on a beautiful Lord's day," he said as he cocked the hammer back.

The uniformed men all turned at the sound.

'Nothing is quite as loud as the sound of hammer sears clicking on a Colt trigger,' Cliff remembered, and smiled inside.

They all now were staring at him, even the injured corporal.

"What business you got here?" Cliff asked.

"This here horse nigh on killed my corporal," the sergeant said.

"A man can't get kicked if 'n' he ain't too close," the shorter man now standing beside Cliff said.

This was the first time Cliff had realized the man was there beside him.

"We be jus lookin' to sees if 'n da' be stolen stock here."

"Well, you now know there ain't; so best you pick up your man there and move on."

"Who be you?"

"He's my brother, not that it's any a' your business," the man standing with Cliff said, as he also lifted a revolver of his own.

One of the men said, "No CSA brands among these."

"You be hearing from us," the sergeant said to them, then gave the order to help the injured up and onto his mount.

There was considerable screams of pain in the process but when it was done, they rode away.

"I'm obliged to ya." Cliff said extending his open left hand to the shorter man. His offer was clasped as the man returned the Griswold to its hidden home inside his coat with his other hand.

The two then returned through the door to the congregation.

Shortly after the song of invitation was sung, Nadine noticed two teenage boys ease out a side door and disappear into a stand of pines growing close by.

The small group of men gathered around the front of the building for several minutes talking and shaking hands while the women folk began placing the fried chicken, stewed pork, and several bowls of vegetables, along with a heap of corn pone out for the noon dinner.

Cliff was quite proud of the attention his bride was stirring among the members there. The men looked at her with envy and the women with jealousy, but all kept proper appearances and were very friendly to her.

Cliff approached the shorter man and spoke, "I want to thank you again for standing with me."

"I consider it a privilege to stand beside Reb Brown," the young man said.

"You know me, then."

"I do, and you know me too."

Cliff narrowed his eyes and looked sharply at the small man. He felt a strong feeling but no real recollection.

"I'm John Gaston, Emmett's boy."

Nodding his head Cliff finally began to remember a smaller than average lad running behind him, here at the church, before the war had come. Johnny was only thirteen or fourteen back then and often sickly.

"I do remember you, Johnny. How is your folks? I didn't see them here today."

"My Pa is dead. The Carpetbaggers came and run us off the farm and put us to living in the swamp. Pa just couldn't stand it. He just up and died one day. He had walked back to the home place and was standing there, looking at the house he had build twenty years 'afore, watching the darkies, who the Occupational Government had given it to, trashing the place, and he just up and fell over dead, right there by the split rail fence," John said, then he turned and kicked his boot toe into the clay before he continued, "Mama is over to a home for widows in Madison, Florida. It's mostly run by a few of the women whose husbands came down here from the north. I reckon all Yankees ain't bad as most."

"I reckon," Cliff said remembering Bruce Whitticar back at South Pass City. "Sorry to hear about your troubles, Johnny. You might have brought on a whole new mess a' them today."

"No matter, I stay a half-step ahead a' trouble anyways."

Nadine walked up then and Cliff introduced her.

"It be a powerful pleasure to meet you, Ma'am," he said.

She smiled at the man noting he was perhaps two inches shorter than she. "Just call me Nadine. Ma'am is a little new to me."

Cliff quickly picked up before Gaston could get the wrong impression. "My wife is from the west. Most folk out there don't know proper etiquette when speaking to a lady."

"Well, Miss Nadine, it is a pure pleasure, just the same," the boy said.

"Johnny stood beside me today when them darkies started to shoot Red," Cliff told her.

"Well now, that was very brave of you, Mr. Gaston."

"Tweren't nutten' and please call me Johnny."

"Johnny it is," she said smiling and extending her hand.

He hesitated a moment[12], finally he took her hand, gently shook it, then quickly let go.

Several quilts were spread under the shade of nearby trees as the congregation ate what had been brought by its members for their dinner. Nadine delighted in all that she tried, but especially found Mrs. Brown's pileau to be the tastiest.

When all were filled, the ladies gathered their bowls and any leftovers, and began returning them to their vehicles; then set about engaging in the latest news.

Nadine was beginning to wonder why they were staying so

---

[12] It was rare for a lady in the south to offer her hand without a glove to cover it.

long after the meal had ended, but before she could ask Cliff, the two boys she had seen leave the building earlier, returned from opposite directions at almost the same time. They went straight to the preacher and spoke to him shaking their heads, one at a time as he apparently asked them several questions. Finally satisfied, he began moving about the couples and speaking to each. When he got to the Brown family he said "The Horne boys said the road is clear for five miles in both directions. I think it is safe to go home now. Don't forget the meeting south a' the Crossroads Store Thursday night around seven."

Cliff nodded and shook the man's hand as his father asked, "What meeting?"

"Oh, Mr. Brown, it's a meeting the young men of the congregation are putting on in preparation for the Thanksgiving holiday coming up in a few weeks."

"Ain't much to be giving thanks fur," he said back turning and heading for the buckboard.

"We got our number-two son back. Now, that's something to be thankful for," Addie said to him.

"Guess you're right, Mrs. Brown," he replied without a change in the tone of his voice. "Guess you're right 'bout that."

Two days later, while they were still eating breakfast Cliff heard Red give his warning whinny and he slowly rose from the table and reached for the Henry that he had hung over the door to the hallway.

"Where ya' headed son?" his father asked.

"Thought I heard a turkey out there, Pa," he said; placing his hat on his head he added, "I won't be long. Nadine, stay close," and then he was out of the room.

She knew what stay close meant, and immediately rose too. "I think I will get some fresh water for another pot a' coffee," she said, and immediately went into their room and took the Winchester from over the door.

Cliff had removed both of his father's old muzzleloaders from where they hung and replaced them with the repeaters the first night they were home. He had taken the double-barrel to the kitchen house and made hangers by heating and bending a couple of discarded horseshoes and hung it there over the door. The Fayetteville Rifle his father had brought home from the war was loaded and placed in the armoire uncapped. Now any room they might be in had a least one long gun.

Cliff slipped out of the back door and around the kitchen house just as a rider was seen coming out of the fog at the bend in the road.

Nadine watched as a rider approached. He made no attempt to detour or hide his intended destination, swinging from the little clay road and into the front yard of the Brown homesite.

"Helloo, the house," he called out in deep drawl.

Cliff heard his mother's voice next, but he couldn't tell what she was saying. The voice did not sound angry or alarmed, so he moved around the house and eased out where he could see the front yard.

The man had dismounted, but the chestnut mare was between them, and Cliff still could not see his face.

"Dwayne, you come right on up here and join us. My new daughter is fixin' some fresh coffee right now," Addie Brown said.

When the man came forward, Cliff saw him to be Dwayne Zipper. He had fought with Georgia's 50th Regiment under Major Pendleton and received a head wound at Sharpsburg. This brought about a medical furlough and he returned home soon afterward. Cliff had heard that Dwayne still had a piece of steel from a Yankee shell embedded in his skull. His thinking and actions were as good as the next man, but he could not speak well after being wounded. His brain would muster up a sentence but his mouth would often leave out words and you had to pay close attention to what he was trying to say to understand him. Few now remembered him as anything but Dwayne, but his name in reality was Robert Millington Zipper.

"That's mighty kindly, Mrs. Brown, but I don't___I 'et several hen___over to Lawyer Dasher's already."

Stepping around the house Cliff injected, "Come on Dwayne, you don't want to hurt Ma's feelings, now do you."

"Why Reb, I heard you___. I'm mighty proud to see___. No, I don't mean to be___ thankful but, I'll guess I will at that."

"Good," Cliff said patting the man on the back and guiding him toward the front porch.

"I see'd you're alert, Reb. That's good, mighty good. D'em dirty Yankees and their nigger soldiers is bad business these days," he said as they entered the house. "That's what I come to tell ya' about. Mr. Dasher said I should warn you that ___ heard you are back and has sent men to ___. I looked close coming but I ne'r see none. They be here soon I 'spec."

Nadine replaced the carbine and stepped into the hall as they came inside, the men following Addie.

"Nadine, you go ahead with that fresh pot a' coffee," she said in more of an order than request.

"Yes, Ma'am," Nadine replied as polite as could be.

"Wait, Honey, I want you to meet Dwayne Zipper, a good Georgia Boy."

"I'm glad to meet you, Mr. Zipper," she said extending her hand.

Dwayne, like John Gaston, was hesitant to touch the uncovered hand of a lady, but she held it there and he had no recourse but to take it; as before, the shake was very gentle and very quick.

Nadine had a hard time understanding Dwayne, as he relayed his message while they sat around the table, but it was obvious somehow the authorities knew or suspected Cliff was home.

'That will mean they will be after him for the old murder warrant.' she thought, *'I was so in hopes he would be able to get that cleared up.'*

"I don't see why we can't get Colonel Pendleton to run something in *The Times* about this barbarism," Cliff said.

"Colonel Pendleton is dead," his father said. "Not long after you left, Clifford James."

"How?"

"It was reported as a buggy accident."

"Colonel Pendleton! Why he was as sure with a vehicle as he was with a horse."

"Surprised everybody here, too."

"Well what about Phil?"

"He's dead, too," Dwayne said.

"Phil Junior took over 'The Times' after his father's death, but only a few months later he, too, turned up dead," Addie added.

"Well, who runs 'The South Georgia Times' then?" Cliff asked.

"Yankees," Dwayne said, "And it are now called 'The South Georgia Pioneer.'

"W.F. tried to run it after Phil Junior's death, but soon after he and Danbridge left the country, sold out completely. In fact, it ain't even the same paper. This here 'South Georgia Pioneer' was printing lies before 'The Times' shut down," Addie said.

"Damn," Cliff said.

"There a' be no vulgarity in this house, Clifford James Brown," Addie spat at him.

Cliff just nodded his head at her statement.

They sat around talking for some time after the women cleared the dishes from the table.

"Thursday night," were the last words Dwayne said as he went down the front steps.

After he had gone, she asked Cliff what all had he said.

"Well, with Dwayne, no one is ever sure, but the gist of it was Colonel Northrop, who is the commanding officer of the 103rd US Colored Mounted Infantry, has received information I am back in the area and has sent men out to spy on the farm. I'll have to stay out of sight during the daylight hours, at least for a spell."

"How did they find that out?"

"Doe'no, maybe some suspected it from the trouble at church Sunday."

"Maybe there's a rat among you. It happened to some friends of mine in Missouri."

"That kind a' unloyalty might take place in a border state, but never in Georgia," Addie Brown said sternly.

Nadine took the cut to her home state without reply, but Cliff could see the redness begin to show on the back of her neck and he went over and placed his arm around her shoulders. "Easy now," he softly said.

Nadine was getting anxious for the evening to arrive all day Thursday in anticipation of the meeting they were going to, until she found out it would be a "men only" meeting; then she began to steam. The kiss he received as he slipped out the backdoor was less than affectionate and he knew she was hot, but there was nothing he could do about it. No one would talk freely with any stranger there, let alone a member of the weaker sex who had the reputation of breaking down and spilling everything to save a loved one.

Cliff of course knew she was tough as any of them, but they didn't know that and he did not want them to find out how she had gotten that way; so he figured he would take the wrath of her anger, which surely wouldn't last too long, he hoped.

Mr. Brown left before sundown, but Cliff waited until full dark before he walked into the little hammock where a small corral had been constructed from laurel oak saplings.

Red gave him an 'about time' look as he came into view. The big sorrel did not like being closed up in the thicket after having spent so many years in the open plains of the western desert, but he was getting older and was not as forceful with displaying his displeasures as he had once been.

The twelve miles to Yeoman's 'Crossroads Store', which was built on the southeast corner of the intersection of the Valdosta and Nankin roads, would take almost three hours in a buckboard and he overtook his father just as he reached the intersection. Cliff noticed a small dim light mostly hidden by closed curtains when they passed the 'Crossroads Store' before turning south towards the river. *'I wonder if Lynch Yeoman will be at the meeting?'* he asked himself.

They traveled nearly three miles more before reaching Gunter's Store.

Lynch Yeoman built his store mainly as a service to the men who worked for the Clyatt brothers' sawmill, which was almost directly across from him.

Martin and J. M. had inherited The Gunter General Store from their father and it had been operating since long before the war. They catered more to the farmers in the area than did Yeoman. Old Jacob Munroe Gunter thought Yeoman was nuts for building so far from the river where he couldn't have a grits mill, but the business from the Clyatt's workers proved him wrong and he became quite irritated at Yeoman "For cutting into my business" as he often said; but the boys never felt that way and after their father passed on, the two families assisted each other whenever the need arose.

Gunter's was a typical building for the times, mostly made of cypress logs with a tall tin roof; only it was wider than deep. At least it started out that way, but as Jacob's family grew he found the need to add another room on the back where they lived.

Upon entering, Cliff saw a woman behind the counter near a coal oil lantern that hung from a wire at the ceiling; he judged her to be in her late thirties or early forties.

"Evening," he said touching the brim of his hat.

"My, my, it's true," she said as he stepped closer. "I heard you were home, Reb, but I didn't know if'n I should believe it or not."

Cliff looked at her with squinted eyes, not recognizing who was speaking to him.

"It's him all right, Mrs. Gunter, Clifford James he-self," his father said.

"Yes, it is," she agreed, "And don't he look fine."

Suddenly, he realized who she was. "Mary Annette, is that you?"

"Every bit of me," she replied touching the ball of red hair she had wound tightly on the back of her head.

Cliff had sparked her before the war and had always figured he was her first lover. When he had gone away she had promised to be waiting for him to return, but he knew her need for attention and guessed that might not be the case, and a letter from his mother in the summer of '63 had proven him right. There was a short sentence among other news mentioning Mary Annette had married one of the Griffin boys.

"Did I hear Mrs. Gunter?" he asked.

"Yes, Pauly, ah Paul Griffin, my first husband, died in a prison somewhere in New York and Marty and I were married Christmas of '67."

"That's great, Martin always wus a good worker," he said to her.

"I hate to interrupt, but I don't see nobody else here, Mrs. Gunter," his father said.

"J. M. decided to hold the meeting over to the grits mill, in case spies were watching the store," she told them.

Cliff touched his hat again and turned with his father for the door.

"No, don't go that way, come through here," she said lifting a blanket that served as an entrance door between the store and an attached room in the back.

"Go out through here, there's a path to the left of the shed yonder. It's a good path."

As Cliff followed his father out the back door she touched his arm with her hand.

"It's good to see you again, Reb."

"You too, Mary Ann," he said and then hurried on into the darkness.

The moon was just beginning to rise behind them and they easily found the path she had directed them to. The trail wandered through oak and pine for nearly a quarter of a mile before they could hear the rushing of water and knew the river was now close. A sharp turn to the right around a huge red oak brought them directly to the grits mill; its unpainted cypress sides shining silver in the moonlight.

A voice from the darkness challenged them at that moment. "Who be you?"

"Louis Brown," his father said back stopping suddenly in his tracks.

"Who be with you?" the voice asked.

Cliff knew the man was ahead and to his right somewhere but he couldn't locate him.

"My son, Johnny Boy."

"Cliff," He reminded his father.

"I mean Clifford James."

There was a long pause and then a man suddenly stepped into the moonlight.

"Reb, is it really you?"

"It's me, Jerry," Cliff replied.

"Hot damn, it does a body good to see you again. There wus talk you be dead."

"That'll be the day," Cliff answered and extended his hand as the man appeared from the darkness.

Jerry Chamblin had been a childhood friend of his, but he had not seen him since they left for the war. He was a well-built man a couple years younger than Cliff and maybe four inches shorter. His sandy hair looked strange in the moonlight.

"Go on in; most are already here. Take the stairs at the back wall, meeting's in the little room up top, but be careful, the wheel is turning the gears there." He pointed then added as they moved past him into the dark mill, "Good to see you, Reb."

"You too, Jerry."

The stairs were steep and Cliff could hear his father's heavy breathing as he followed behind him.

Once inside he saw ten or more men there, some sitting, and several more standing, or more accurately, leaning against the walls. One man who he didn't know was pulling back a dark croaker sack that served as a window curtain and peering out. A single barreled shotgun was cradled in the crook of his arm, and Cliff noticed under the hammer was a shiny new cap.

"Come in if 'n you can find room," a familiar voice said.

Looking at the man who had welcomed them, Cliff recognized Marty Gunter. He also noticed Marty was somewhat heavier than he remembered him and his head was bald, save a row of black hair thick as a hedgerow that ran around the back of his head from ear to ear.

"I want you all to see my son, Johnny Boy, is back," Cliff's father said.

The place immediately went silent.

"No, Pa, I'm Cliff."

"Oh, that's what I meant to say. Clifford James is back."

"Hello, Reb," several said in a warm greeting.

He knew most of the men there from before the war. John Gaston moved around a seated man and came over and stood beside Cliff. "Glad you made it, Reb," he said.

Two more men came in shortly after the Browns and then Marty spoke. "Well, it's past seven; let's get started."

The Georgia State flag that had been out of sight until now, was unfurled and brought forward. John Gaston reached over to lend a helping hand to Israel Henley who was holding the crude staff, to which it was attached.

"Well, I think we all are here, and we all know why we are here. So, let's get to it," Marty said. He then added, "During the last six months, twelve of our local men have either been kilt, or have simply disappeared. We all know it's the work of them damn carpetbaggers Governor Bullock sent here, and mostly it was done by the darkies in Bullock's army. That's what we do know; what we don't know is what we aim to do about it."

Georgia State Flag of 1870

"I say, get our guns and make a raid on downtown Valdosta," John Gaston said strongly. "That a' teach 'em."

His suggestion was well received by some; in fact this line of talk continued for several minutes with the main theme being the killing and burning of anything that appeared black or blue, but Gunter stopped the murmuring with, "That'll surely stir up a mess all right, a hornet's nest. What we need is to work at getting Bullock out of office."

"How we gon'a do that, when the Yankee Congress took away our right to vote?" Stan May asked.

Finally he had heard enough and stepping forward into better light Cliff said, "Organize."

A hush swept over the room for a few seconds as everyone digested the word from the strong deep voice. Finally, Israel Henley said. "Hell, Reb, we are already organized or we wouldn't be here."

"We are together, yes, but we are not organized. We need to become a fighting force, something to be dealt with. Not necessarily one of violence but rather of strength; not unlike a military company. With everyone giving his oath to stand by the group no matter what and no one ever revealing a name of another member. We need to appoint leaders, and for the others to obey the orders of the leaders; no matter what. We need a set of internal laws that all know and know well, and all swear to, just as we did to the Confederacy. I remember Miss Zimms teaching us in school, to most of us standing here tonight, what Ben Franklin once said to the other members of a group who had gathered, not so much different than we are doing right now, only these men were about to start a revolution. Franklin said, 'We must hang together or surely we will hang separately,' and I think that should be our motto," Cliff said. The room went silent for a moment or two. Finally John Gaston spoke, "Reb is right. We got a' stand together. We got a' organize."

There was some murmuring again among the men, finally Marty Gunter stood and said "I think everyone should go home and think this over well," he paused and let it sink in, "before anyone takes an oath to such a cause. This is not something to be taken lightly. Search your souls and decide are you truly ready to rebel as a vigilante group, for that is exactly what we are talking about."

"That's good thinking," Danny Faux said.

"What's there to think about? I say we organize tonight," Johnny argued.

"No, Marty is right, we need to think on this carefully, because I say the first rule of the group is, if anyone turns in another member to the authorities, it will be the duty of every member, to seek out that scalawag and put him to death," Cliff added.

Again the room fell silent. Finally Marty broke it with "Alright, let's move out of here one or two at a time. Meet here again next Thursday night, same time."

"I think anyone who still wants to go with this idea should also be thinking of what rules he deems necessary and bring them up then. If this does go, we need to be acting soon," Cliff added.

With that thought lying heavy on them, the men began heading down the stairs.

Louis wanted to buy Addie some coffee so they stopped back at the store on the way. When Cliff and his father started out of the store, Mary Ann stepped close so Cliff could not pass through the front door without his arm brushing her breast. Instantly he felt a stirring in his groin. "I am really glad you are home, Reb," she said softly. "Come back again, real soon."

Cliff smiled and touched the brim of his hat.

Johnny Gaston rode beside him as he followed the buckboard. Johnny was talking along at a steady pace but Cliff's mind was back to the summer of '59. He remembered vividly the day he and Mary Ann had gone down to the spring on the Withlacoochee River. They were supposed to meet two other young couples there for a picnic, but no one else arrived. Finally he talked her into going skinny-dipping in the spring and he could still see the goose bumps caused by the cold water on her large breasts as he held them in his hands. They had enjoyed each other's body there in the water; that day and several times afterward, until he went away to school in Tennessee the following year.

He remembered how surprised he had been when he saw the red hair of her triangle. For some reason, he had thought everyone had black hair down there, no matter what color it was on their head, and this memory caused him to smile at his youthfulness. Finally, it was John's laughing that brought him back to the present.

The moon was high by the time they passed Yeoman's store, and turning east into the open country it lit the road well, now that it was not canopied by the trees. It was at just such a place further on towards home, he saw the moon's reflection on something ahead.

Cliff pulled up so suddenly that Johnny's horse moved on ahead a couple lengths before he could stop him.

"What is it?"

"Doe-no," Cliff answered. "Something ahead."

"What, I don't see nut'in'."

"I don't now, but I did," Cliff replied and strained his eyes, but saw nothing.

Finally, he said, "You ride on with Pa. I'll lay back and watch."

"Sure, Reb."

"Johnny," he paused before adding, "be careful."

"Sure, Reb."

He watched the younger man trot his mare up close beside the wagon, and could hear them talking but they were too far away for him to understand what was being said.

When the buckboard disappeared over a small rise, he eased Red off the road and turned due north heeling him into a trot as fast as he dared on uncharted ground in poor light.

They came over the hill a quarter mile to the left of the road.

The lay of the land was such that a small depression had formed from rain runoff where two short hills met. It was there he saw the buckboard stopped on the road, with four additional riders circling it.

Cliff pulled the Henry from its scabbard and eased Red forward until he was less than 100 feet from the voices that were now behind the hill and hidden from view.

The night was cool and still and the conversation was as clear as the air.

"I know your son came home, now where is he?"

"My son disappeared last year and you bastards know it."

"He was at the Corinth Church last Sunday and he threatened officers of the law."

"That was my brother," John spat back "and they ain't officers. They is hired bullies."

"They are the men of the Occupational Government and as long as you secessionist's won't heed to the laws of the land, they will be here," the man said strongly. He then added, "We both know you went to some gathering with him tonight; you was seen right here on this road."

"What your spies saw, was me riding with Mr. Brown. We were just checking out my trot lines down to the river," Johnny said.

"You don't go wallowing around the river banks dressed like you two are," the voice of the stranger replied.

"Well, that is still what we did," Cliff heard Johnny yell back at him.

"That boy a' yours has a murder charge on his head and I aim to see him behind bars for it."

"You took my boy off last spring and we ain't never seen him since."

"That was your youngest and he escaped. Where he went after he escaped, I can't say, I'm now talking about the one known as Reb Brown."

Cliff thought he had heard the voice before, but couldn't remember where.

Finally with more exchanges of a similar nature, the four men rode west at a fast pace.

Cliff returned his Henry to the scabbard and waited a couple minutes before easing over the hill and quickly catching up to the wagon.

"Hold up," he said.

Stopping the horse, his father turned and said to him "That damn John Tidwell said your brother was back. We had better get home and see if it's true."

"No, Pa, he meant me. He meant I was home, not Johnny Boy," Cliff said. Then he rubbed his chin and added, "So, John M. Tidwell is still around."

"Still around!" Gaston exclaimed "He don't only run the bank, he also is the Civilian Representative to Colonel Northrop for this whole district."

"No fooling?"

"They call it the Civilian Division of The Freedman's Bureau."

"Sounds like something he would be involved in."

"You remember him then?"

"Remember him? Hell, he's the one who shot Bugger-T Polk."

John thought a few seconds and then said, "I do remember that name but can't rightly place it."

"He's the darkey I am supposed to have murdered," Cliff said back bitterly, "John M. Tidwell is who really shot him, I saw him do it, but he claimed I did, and that's the reason I had to leave Georgia to begin with."

"Well, I'll be," Johnny replied, "No wonder he's so set on you getting caught."

"Yeah, he sure would like to see me hanging from the limb of a sweet gum tree."

"Don't kid yourself. If he catches you, you won't hang; you will disappear while trying to escape," John Gaston offered.

"Just like my little brother."

"Yeah, just like your brother."

"We had better be getting on home. That man said my son was home," Louis Brown said as he gently dropped the whip on the back of his horse.

A mile from the Brown house both Cliff and Johnny stopped and let the buckboard go on ahead.

"This is where I turn off," Johnny said, "Whatever you decide, Reb, I will be with you."

"Thanks, Johnny. I knew I could count on you."

Cliff then eased into the timber and worked his way to their hidden corral.

Nadine came out to meet him just as he was placing the saddle on a top rail. His father's wagon still had the horse harnessed and he began taking care of it also.

"How did the "Men's Only" meeting go?" she asked.

"I'm sorry about that, Honey. There are customs in the west that we don't even think of here, and this just happens to be one in these parts. Men make the decisions and women folk don't worry their purty little heads about such."

"Well, this one does; and I guess I'll just have to show you southern gentlemen a thing or two."

"I bet you could at that," he said.

When he had finished with the horses he grabbed her and held her close. The feeling of her body pressing against his as they kissed caused his blood to begin stirring for the second time that night, only this time he intended to do something about it.

After they had enjoyed a poke in the hay, she laid back looking at the slivers of moon light leaking down through the heavy branches. She smiled as she spoke, "You know, it's so much better out here. Out here, I don't have to bite my lip trying to keep your folks from hearing me scream when we do it."

"What makes you think they didn't hear you tonight?" Cliff asked laughingly.

She slapped his bare chest with an open palm.

"Reb," she began, then stopped and changed what she had intended to say. "Why do they call you Reb? I always thought it was because you were in the Rebel Army but it sounds like these folks have called you Reb all your life."

"Yeah, seems so," he agreed.

"Why is that?"

"When I was knee high to a grasshopper I just didn't want to do anything I was told, especially in school. The teacher, Mrs. Zimms, called me a rebel one day right out in class and the kids started calling me Reb after that. I guess it kind a' stuck."

"I like it. "Reb," yeah it does fit you."

"I'm glad you approve, Mrs. Brown."

"That's something else. Why do your folks not use their first names?"

"I never knew," he said shaking his head. "In all my life I never heard them say anything but Mr. Brown or Mrs. Brown. I guess they were proud of the relationship and wanted everybody to know they were married."

"That's kind a' romantic," she said placing a strand of straw between her teeth.

"You know, you look just like a naked farm girl with that straw in your mouth."

"So?"

"So, I like poking naked farm girls," he said and rolled over on top of her again. This time, they took their time and the coupling was intense.

It was over an hour after she had gone out to meet him before they slipped back into the house.

Louis Brown could be heard snoring in the living room where they usually slept, and when Cliff turned up the lamp, he was seen asleep in a chair with his head back and his face pointed straight up.

"Come on, Pa; I'll help you get to bed," Cliff said as he lifted the drowsy older man.

"I wus waiting on Johnny Boy to come in," he said, "The man down the road said he was home."

"Come on to bed now, Pa. I'll watch for him," Cliff said as he guided him into the other room.

"You call me now, Son, when your brother comes in. I need to scold him for being out so late."

"I will, Pa."

"Poor man," Nadine said softly with no one to hear.

When Cliff returned, she lay close beside him; after having lain naked so long in the cool night air she wanted to feel the warmth of his body.

Being fully awake staring at the black ceiling, she finally asked, "What happened at the meeting?"

He, on the other hand was more than ready to get some sleep, and replied, "I'll tell you all about it in the morning."

"Oh, no!" she said strongly. "I kept my place and stayed home, now you tell me all about it or I wake everybody up."

"Alright, but it weren't so much."

Cliff roughly told her about the thought of organizing a vigilante group and also of the encounter with Tidwell on the way home. He left out any mention of Mary Ann Gunter.

Saturday, near noon, Cliff was out making repairs to the corral fence where Red had kicked a pole clean off, when he heard the sounds of a horse approaching. He never went anywhere without a gun and this time he had the Henry leaning up beside the small makeshift shed were they kept the hay.

Picking it up, he walked towards the house, remaining in the cover of the trees.

He could not see who had ridden up, but soon Nadine came out of the back door of the house and called to him. "Reb, your Mama said to fetch you."

"Who is it?"

"I don't know. Someone I ain't never seen before."

When he went in the backdoor he saw Robert Maycomber standing in the hall with his old brown slouch hat in hand. Robert had moved to Lowndes County as a refugee from Albany after the war. In May of '65 Elder Maycomber's harness business was taken over for unpaid taxes; soonafter, he disappeared as he was making his way home and was never heard of again.

When Robert himself made it home from the hostilities, he found his mother living with a sister in a small one room shack that had been slave quarters on one of the big plantations before the war. Robert gathered what was left of his family and moved south.

He had been in the Terrell Light Artillery at the second battle of Murfreesboro and he and Cliff had spent the better part of New Years

Day talking about Georgia while they waited for Rosecran[13] to decide when to begin the attack. Cliff had not seen him before or since; until the past Thursday when Robert had come up as they were leaving the meeting and introduced himself to Cliff and his father.

"Hello, Robert," he said extending his hand, "This is my wife, Nadine."

"Miss Nadine," the man said nodding his head.

"What brings you here?"

"It's Bob May, Stan's brother," he said lowering his head. "He's been killed."

"What!" Cliff replied.

"Oh, the poor boy," Addie said.

"How did it happen?"

"Well, the way I hear it, Bob," he paused, "you knew he was teaching school over to Pelham, didn't you?"

"Naw, I saw him last Thursday, but I barely spoke to him after the meeting."

"Well, he was the teacher over thar and yesterday some troops came and took him right from his class. The kids said he had been arrested for teaching rebellion. Anyway, they sent word to Stan this morning that he had jumped one of the soldiers and took his gun and they had to shoot him, to defend themselves."

"Bob May!" Cliff exclaimed, "Not a chance. He was as gentle as a lamb."

"Well, he has been a little more aggressive since his wife was killed."

"I don't know about that, when wus this?"

"Oh, a year or so, she was driving home from Valdosta and her horse ran away and she was thrown from the buggy. Hit her head on a rock or something."

"Just like Colonel Pendleton," Cliff said.

"Yeah, I never thought of that," Robert replied, "Anyway, Stan wanted you should know."

"Thanks, Robert," he said. "If you see Stan before I do, give him my sympathies, will you?"

"Sure, Reb," the tall man said and placing his hat back on, he turned and started for the door.

---

[13] Rosecran: Commander of the Federal Forces at the Battle of Murfreesboro, Tennessee

"Wait, Robert," Addie said. "You must be hungry; I'll fetch you some dinner."

"No, Ma'am, thank you. I 'et before I started out, I'm obliged though," he said as he pulled gently on the front brim of his hat.

"See you Thursday, Reb," and then nodding to Nadine he added, "Pleased to make your acquaintance, Ma'am."

"It just don't seem right," his mother said, "Poor Bob sure had his troubles."

"I'm beginning to see what we're up against," Nadine said to no one in particular.

"Well, we'll face it head-on," Cliff replied.

"Yes, we will," she agreed.

"Not us," his mother said. "We women must stay out of it, let the men folk take care of trouble. It's not lady-like."

"No disrespect, Ma'am," Nadine said, "but I ain't one not to be beside my man when he is in trouble."

Addie who was bending over wiping the table, shot upright straight as an arrow, but said nothing in return.

That Sunday, Cliff thought it best not to go to services. "I'm sure the Bluebellies will have spies watching the Corinth Church," he said to his parents.

Nadine elected not to go either, which did not set well with Addie and it showed. Even so, Nadine remained behind when they drove away.

It also gave her and Cliff some time alone without ears in the next room and they put the privacy to good use.

While still in bed after a morning romp, the sound of horses approaching slipped in through the cracks in the wooden window cover.

Cliff quickly jumped into his trousers and grabbed his gun belt with one hand and the Henry with the other and went into the hall.

Three riders were stopped outside.

One called out, but neither he nor Nadine answered.

Nadine slipped on her overalls, which she had not worn since his mother had looked down on her so about them, but they were the only thing she could get into fast. Hurrying back to the bedroom she reached for the Yellowboy, then followed him into the hall.

"Do you know them?"

"No," he answered. "Come on."

After his encounter with the black soldiers at the church, Cliff had cut a trap door in the floor of the room they slept in and hinged it with a pair of discarded boot soles. Lifting it, he dropped to the ground, below the house.

Looking back up at her he whispered. "Ask them what they want."

She went back to the hall and called out through the front door, "What do you want?"

All three had started approaching the house but with the sound of her voice they stopped where they were and looked at each other, obviously not expecting anyone to be home, especially a woman.

"Ah, Ma'am, ah, we need to water our horses," the tallest one said.

"Well, go ahead. You see the water trough."

"Could we talk to you?"

"You are talking to me."

"Ah, well there was an accident over to the church house and your husband was hurt, the parson sent us to fetch you."

"My husband was killed nigh on four years ago by a Yankee gambler," Nadine said back.

"Oh, I thought I wus talking to Mrs. Brown."

"You are talking to Mrs. Brown."

He didn't reply; rather turned to the man on his left and nodded his head. Both of the other two then turned and started back for their horses. Cliff was on his knees in the darkness under the house unseen by them, but with a perfect view of their actions through the lattice works and when he saw one of the men take a gallon can that hung on a small rope from the saddle horn, Cliff immediately knew what was in the making and he took careful aim at the man's back.

The other arsonist had picked up two small limbs that had fallen from a nearby oak, and after wrapping rags tightly around their ends, brought them over to the man with the can.

When these two had returned beside the talker he continued, "Alright, Mrs. Brown, or whoever you are, come on out and do it now."

"And if I don't?" Nadine yelled back.

"Oh, you will. You can come on out now, or wait and get a little burned; but you will come out. That old shack is built a' heart pine and it will go up like lightning struck it."

She smiled at his ignorance of Southern wood, but only replied,

"Oh, you brave men are planning on burning down my house around me, are you?"

"No more talking. Come out or get singed," he said striking a Lucifer against his saddle and setting both limbs ablaze.

The talker now advanced with one of the torches, as did the second of the men. The third man returned to the horse with the can of coal oil. Cliff noticed this and figured they had other stops planned this fine Lord's Day morning.

Just as the talker pulled back to toss the torch on the roof, Cliff squeezed the trigger. The conical bullet struck him an inch left of his heart and caused him to stagger backward two steps before dropping to his knees with an expression of wonderment on his face. The second man threw his torch and it landed on the front porch but before he could turn, a 44 slug hit him in the stomach and doubled him over, squealing. The third man mounted and kicked his horse into a quick gallop back down the road. Cliff tried to get off a shot but the other animals were between him and the fleeing horseman. He began to crawl forward as fast as he could, and kicked a section of lattice away in order to get out from under the house so he could stand, before the rider could get around the bend in the road.

Just before he was clear of the porch floor, he heard the carbine fire above him and saw the man's arms fly high into the air and then he and horse were out of sight around the bend.

As soon as he could stand, Cliff turned and saw Nadine with the Winchester in one hand and a burning torch in the other.

"I think I hit him."

"I know you hit him, but I'm not sure how bad. We can't let him get to help and tell who shot him," Cliff said, dashing off towards the horses that were now milling around in the front yard. As he passed the man with the stomach wound, using his rifle butt, he clubbed him with an uppercut to the face, then he grabbed the reins of the first mount he came to, and swung on its back in a smooth sweep that some would say was a jump and others a roll. Then with a snatch of the reins he was off chasing the fleeing bandit, with only one foot in a stirrup and his left hand on the horn. Within seconds, the shirtless pursuer was also out of her sight.

She leaned the carbine against the wall and took the burning stick out into the front yard and dropped it on the ground, then rolled it with her foot until the fire was little more than a smoldering rag.

She then went back, retrieved the gun, and went inside to dress. She had scarcely gotten her overalls off, when she again heard a horse outside. Peeking through the window, she saw Cliff approaching leading the third horse, a body draped over the saddle.

As soon as she was presentable, she went outside.

"I see you got him," she said.

"No, you got him. He was laying dead just around the corner yonder," he said pointing generally in the direction of the road. "But I liked to never have caught his horse. That creature had a mind to run all the way to Valdosta."

"What are we going to do?" she asked.

"I aim to put on a shirt and my boots and take them to Loch Laurel Swamp."

"Where's that?"

"West a' here, three, four miles, at the headwaters of Brown's Lake. There used to be some big ole gators there. These here boys look like gator bait if I ever saw any," he said tying the reins to the hitching rail by the water trough.

"I want to go with you," she said.

"Guess you earned it, but I'd not go barefooted were I you," he said nodding at her small feet sticking from under her day dress.

"I can take care of that," she said and snickered, then added, "I'll even put something on under the dress too, if you want me to."

"It's your bare bottom that will be sitting on the saddle."

"Well, since you put it that way," she said and went back inside.

When she returned, he had the three bodies tied to their saddles and was walking up to the porch. She had his tall brown boots in hand with a pair of clean butternut socks.

"How long do we have before someone starts looking for them?"

"Probably not till tomorrow," he said stamping his foot into the boot then sitting back down for the other one. "Your man was careful to put that can of coal oil back in his saddle bag, so my guess is they had plans to visit others this morning while folks were in church. Johnny Gaston's place is only a mile or so away. Good bet they would a hit it next." Standing, he stepped off the porch as he continued talking, "They never planned on nobody being to home here. That was plain enough. We kind a' messed up their plans, didn't we, Honey."

"Glad you brought me along, ain't ya?" she said.

"More'n you'll ever know," Cliff replied, looking at her with deep affection in his eyes.

Coming to a place where the road topped a little hill, he reined up sharply. She did likewise. "What is it?"

"A lot a' dust ahead, yonder," he said pointing to the next rise in the terrain ahead.

"Come on, let's get to some cover. "I don't want to try explaining these three."

They led the horses into a hammock a half mile from the road.

Soon seven or eight horsemen appeared riding at a good pace east bound.

"Cavalry," Cliff said.

"How can you tell from this distance?"

"When you have hid from as much Yankee Cavalry as I have, you will be able to tell, too."

She did not question him again on it.

They stayed hidden another twenty minutes giving the horses a rest; then moved on, passing a field of cotton that had been left to rot on the stalks, before turning back to the road.

The swamp was larger than she had seen since they had left the lowlands near Pensacola. It was perhaps two miles across and a mile north-to-south. Cypress trees were scattered about everywhere, and their knees growing above the surface proved this was not a deep body of water. Dark turtles with striped green necks were seen in large numbers along the banks and on anything large enough for them to sit out in the lake itself.

"Funny looking turtles," she said.

"Cooter. Good to eat," he replied looking up at what she was pointing to.

Nadine raised the corner of her upper lip in protest. "I don't know."

"You will after you eat one."

"Maybe so, I do like gator."

"Tail," he corrected.

"What?"

"You liked gator tail. It's the good part. The rest of that old lizard is a might tougher."

"Alright, I like tail," she said with a quick nod of her chin.

Cliff looked at her well rounded hips and said back, "So do I."

High in the sky, heavy clouds pushed southward, powered by a much cooler north wind. The thick clouds soon blocked the sun; and the pesky mosquitoes that had been a plague in the early evenings, were not to be seen this afternoon.

She rubbed her hands over her blouse sleeves, warming her arms. "It's turning cold, Cliff."

"Yeah, a norther is blowing in. I didn't expect it to take us this long. That cavalry set us behind. Should a' left the folks a note. Ma will be worried."

"I did."

"Did what?"

"Left her a note."

"What did you say? In the note I mean," he quickly asked worried that friends of these men might come by.

"I said, we have gone for a picnic, be back around dark, and signed it, Your loving daughter-in-law."

"Well, that should cover it, I guess."

"I guess it will," she agreed feeling proud she had thought of it.

"Too bad it's so cool. I've a mind to go skinny-dipping," she said.

Immediately he thought of Mary Ann but his only reply was, "Them gators would love that."

"Oh, forgot about them," she said smiling at him.

"Forget about gators around these swamps and he will be likely eating your tail, instead a' you eating his."

"Well, don't know much about taste, but my tail is prettier than any old gator's."

"Yes Ma'am, it surely is that," he said feeling that stirring in his groin again.

Cliff left the dead men's horses at the swamp's edge fully saddled with all gear, except their weapons; knowing most animals when abandoned will return home, if they aren't too far away. He also realized there were several bogs around that might claim them. *'And too, these jaspers might have been from somewhere else, brought in to do paid work.'* Anyway, he decided to leave the horses and let them fend for themselves or be found; either way, there would be no sign of what happened to the riders and he was sure some old she-gator would have their no account bodies buried in a day or so.

They stopped by Gaston's on the way home and Cliff told Johnny what had happened. He also gave him the two Remington Army revolvers he had found in one of the saddle bags of the arsonist.

"I reckon, once again, I'm obliged to you, Reb. Them yeller varmints would a' burned me out, for sure."

"I see it that away, Johnny," Cliff agreed.

"These low-downs are getting mighty brave to come burning in broad daylight." Then lifting his head so he could look the taller man in the eye he asked, "Wus they niggers?"

"No, white trash, maybe hired from som'ers. They 'spected to find us all in church," Cliff said. "We shor' surprised 'em."

"Yes, sir, you did," Gaston agreed "and I, I thank you again. Won't you come on in and sit a spell? I got some coffee biling."

"No, Johnny, we best be moseying on home; the folks will be worried as it is."

"I understand, Reb. Thank you both," the man said nodding his head.

It was long after dark when they walked into the house.

"I hope you two took enough with you on that picnic to get you through the night," his mother said hatefully when they came in.

"Well, as a matter of fact, we ain't 'et nothing," Cliff said back.

"That's just too bad, 'cause I didn't save no supper fur ya'," she replied turning and walking into the hall. "Down right disgraceful, the very idea a' going on a picnic when ya' should a' been in church. It's the devil's work I tell ya'," she said looking at Nadine.

"Yes, Ma'am, you're more than right. It was the devil's work that took us away today," Nadine replied staring right back at her.

"Mama!" Cliff said in a tone of voice he had never used before to her, "You come back in here. It is important you know why we were gone today."

Addie recognized there was no nonsense in the tone of his voice and she obeyed him for the first time in her life, but not the last.

His father was sitting in his chair at the table and she sat down beside him.

"Today three men came here and tried to burn down the house, full well knowing Nadine was inside when they were doing the dirty deed."

Addie remembered seeing the scorched spot on the front porch. She had planned to scold him for it; instead she sat in silence.

"We had to kill 'em to stop 'em. I shot two and Nadine, the third as he was going for help. We found evidence they were on a burning spree and our home was only one of several they intended to destroy. We took their bodies away and put them where it is doubtful they will ever be found," he said then looking at them he added, "Were it not for Nadine, we surely would now be without a home, perhaps all dead; for had that man escaped he would have brought others of the same breed to finish what they failed to accomplish." He paused long enough for what he had said to sink in then continued, "Today was no picnic."

Addie sat there silently for a while then asked "Why did you say you were going on a picnic? You surely knew it would anger me."

Nadine spoke then, softly but surely, "You really don't think I should have left you a note saying we were off to rid ourselves of three bodies we had just killed, do you? What would have become of us if such a note had fallen into the wrong hands?"

Again Addie sat there quietly for several seconds and then she stood and said, "I'll fetch you something to eat." In a flash she was gone.

Louis turned to his son and asked, "Where did you take them?"

"To a swamp," Cliff replied, not wanting to give the exact location for fear his father might let it slip unknowingly.

"Did you see your brother there?"

"No, Pa. I didn't see him."

The old man nodded his head and then bowed it and went to sleep.

The next day they heard that Jerry Strange's house had been burned and all the stock killed, while he was at church.

Jerry's little farm was east of the Brown's on the other side of the lake, by three miles.

"Too bad they didn't come here first," Cliff said upon hearing the news.

When Thursday came around, Addie killed a hen and fried it and put it into a paper sack and sat it on the eating table. "Here's a little fur you two to 'et, should you get hungry along the way."

"That's kindly of ya' Mama, but Pa and I will get a bite before we leave."

"Your Pa ain't well enough to be out in the night air. He's likely to catch his death a' cold," She said looking at a piece of cloth she had cut to sew on the quilt she was making.

"Well I don't need____."

She cut him short. "You take Nadine with you. It's time she met some ladies her own age. Mary Annette Griffin married Martin Gunter some years back and she'll likely be som'ers around the store. You introduce Nadine to her. They can get acquainted while you men folk are making your plans. Besides, if you were to run into trouble, Nadine might be a help to you. Something I doubt your Pa can do anymore," his mother stood and started to leave the room before the two shocked youngsters could reply, but she hesitated just before she cleared the door and added "Maybe Mary Annette and Nadine can compare notes." Then she was gone out the back door before Cliff could respond.

'So, I'm about to meet Reb's old girlfriend, am I?' Nadine thought, but made no indication she had even heard the statement.

"Well, I'll be," Cliff said. "I do believe she is coming around."

"Think so?" Nadine asked.

They stopped by Gaston's and he followed the buckboard on horseback.

"Your Pa sick?"

"No, Mama thought Nadine should meet Mary Ann."

"Oh," was all John said in return and in the darkness neither saw him roll his eyes.

Johnny usually was quite talkative but for some reason he couldn't find anything that needed saying with Miss Nadine there and rode the whole way without starting a single sentence.

They had agreed before they left, should they run into marauding troops they would say they were Johnny's brother and sister-in-law, but there was no need; they arrived at Gunter's store without seeing anyone except Jason and Chase Hufsterler who rode the last two miles with them.

As they approached Gunter's store, they saw the figures of two women sitting in rockers on the front porch.

Johnny quickly said, "I'll take my horse on around back so as not to give any alarm."

Cliff nodded his approval to the younger man.

Pulling up in front, he stopped the buckboard and stepped down without looking at either of the women. He came around and helped Nadine down and taking her arm in his hand walked with her up the four steps to the porch. "Ladies, may I present my wife, Nadine. Honey, this is Mrs. R. M. Gunter, 'Tillie,' and this is Mrs. Martin Gunter, 'Mary Annette.' "

The women each looked the other over with smiles on their faces, and stern inspections on their minds.

"Mama suggested I bring Nadine over so she could meet some of the ladies her own age."

"Oh, how nice," Tillie said.

"Yes, how nice," Mary Ann agreed before adding, "Reb failed to tell us he had a wife when he was here last Thursday night."

Nadine was well pleased with what she saw.

Mary Ann was a pretty woman and her breasts were as large as her own but that is where the similarities ended. Mary Ann was a little shorter than Nadine, and at least forty pounds heavier.

Tillie, on the other hand, was three inches taller than she, but was shaped like a barrel weighing well over two hundred pounds and the Lord had not been kind to her when he was giving out faces either.

'No, there is nothing here I need to worry about.' she thought and immediately began to open up and talk with them.

She found Tillie to be the friendliest woman she had ever met since she had become a woman herself, and before the night was over, she decided Tillie needed to be so large; otherwise there wouldn't be enough room inside for all of her heart.

Mary Ann, on the other hand, was not so pleasant. Not unpleasant, just not the open loving person Tillie was.

"Tell me, Mrs. Brown, how did you and Reb meet?" Mary Ann asked.

"Please call me Nadine," she replied then added, "I was working for the Local Judge in South Pass City at the time, and he had some business to do with a gentleman named Colt there, and one day he asked me to go on a picnic with him."

"Oh, how romantic, where is this South Pass City?" Tillie asked.

"In Wyoming Territory."

"Oh my goodness, they still have wild Indians out there."

She was looking at Tillie when she realized the opportunity that had just been given her, "Yes, they do. As a matter of fact, we shot four while on that picnic. Reb got three and," she paused and turning her head so she was looking straight into the blue eyes of his former lover she finished, "I only killed one."

"Oh how adventurous; you must tell us about it," Tillie squealed.

"Yes," Mary Ann agreed, although obviously stunned by the statement made by Reb's wife, "Sometime, you must tell us all about it."

"Oh, it would be better if Reb were to tell you; he's such a good story teller," Nadine said back, smiling at them.

Just after full dark, three children came into the store from the back. One was a girl about ten or twelve; the other two were about half her age; a boy, Tillie called Buckshot; and a little girl with fiery red hair she called Freckles.

Nadine learned that Buckshot and the older girl, Sissy, were Tillie's children while Freckles was one of Mary Ann's three offspring.

The room inside the store where the men had gathered became totally silent when Stan May walked in, and finally Marty spoke, "Stan we sure are sorry about your brother."

The man nodded his head, "I thank you. I sure am a-missing him."

"We all will miss him," Marty said back. Then in a different tone began, "And it's just such goings-on that has brought us here to begin with, so let us get on with it."

With this, Nadine watched the men head out the back door and disappear into the black air.

When everyone was in the loft, John Gaston went over and brought out the state flag. "This is what it's all about," he said, "It should be out for all to see and think on while we make our decision here tonight." He then stood the old limb next to a stool where the flag could be seen by any who cared to look.

"We all know last week, right here in this very room, Bob May stood among us; today he is gone," Marty began. "It's these kind a' happenings that has made us come to such a meeting. I don't doubt fur one minute if 'n they knew we wus meeting here tonight we all would be shaking hands with Bob within a very few days." He paused and let his last statements sink in. "The question we are here for tonight is, are we going to allow such to continue, or are we going to put a stop to it?" Again he paused, "Last week Reb Brown made a suggestion that we organize and fight fire with fire. Sunday past, someone burned out Jerry Strange's home and kilt or run off all his pigs and other stock. No one knows who done it, but we got our suspicions."

Johnny looked over at Cliff and gave him a slight smile, but said nothing.

Marty continued, "Are we to go and burn out someone who has come here after the war and settled from some whar up north?"

"Yeah, that's just what we should do," Jason said.

"I ain't so sure. All folks from the north ain't evil."

"Who says so?" Jason asked.

Marty countered with, "I do, a body can't help whar' his folks wus, when he wus bornt. It's what he does with his life that we should be concerning ourselves with. I served with Con Hathaway during the war, and he was from New York City; if there wus a better fighter for the cause, I never saw him."

"I agree with Marty," Cliff said. "If we do this, we must be very selective as to who we bring retaliation upon. Let one innocent person, Yankee or Homefolk, be hurt and we will be hunted down like dogs, and rightly so."

Cliff continued, "There is something I think we all should understand and this is touching on it right now. The only way we will win," he paused and looked slowly around at all the faces turned in his direction, "is if homefolk believe in us. We will need complete cooperation from them, or the Federals will find us very soon, and we will be hung or shot. There is sure to be a price put on us. A reward for each and every one of us, and in these awful hard times it will be mighty tempting to even those who are our friends not to turn us in for Yankee gold. So, if we are to survive we must have one hundred percent backing of homefolk and that means no harassing of them, even by accident. If we are able to come by some money, and in the line of work we are talking about here tonight, that is possible, we will keep only what we need to survive and continue our cause. All the rest will be given to those who need it here abouts. If the homefolk know we share with them they will be less likely to be tempted by rewards."

"What Reb says makes good sense," Jerry Chamblin said. "I know a Yankee family over to Brooks County what is downright decent folk."

"Oh, Jerry you just like the looks a' their daughter. We know whar' you're heart is," someone called out.

"They do have a mighty fine-looking daughter," Jerry admitted, "but that ain't the point. We got 'a know who we are after, and go after no one else. That's the trouble with the Kuk-Lux[14]. They started out just like we's talking here tonight, but they's got now to the point it ain't safe fur no nigger to walk the roads a' Thomas County after dark."

"I say we should contact the Kuk-Lux and ask for their help on this," Danny Faux said.

"No, I disagree," Cliff interrupted. "The Kuk-Lux is a Klan out to

---

[14] Kuk-Lux: The original name of the Ku Klux Klan

mostly get darkies, and here the darkies that give us the most trouble is in the 103rd, Company G. There are a lot a' good darkies what has been with us before the war, some slaves and some were already free. Don't forget 80,000 darkies wore gray just like we did. We got no quarrels with none a' them. It's the soldiers and the Freedman who is living off a' other's land that we need to tend to."

The meeting went on for another hour with many exchanges of opinion. Finally Marty asked for a show of hands. "Those what is willing to give their oath to this cause raise your hands."

It looked as if the whole room was in agreement, but to be sure he added, "Anyone not wanting to take the oath should make themselves known now and nothing will be held against them."

Danny Faux and Jay Shaw raised their hands.

"Alright boys, we understand, but you should leave now and there will be no hard feeling agin' you, but if you ever reveal anything you have learned here, it will be the duty of every man here to hunt you down, even to the wilds a' Canada, and kill you," Marty said.

After the two had left, he again spoke.

"It's time to take the oath. Raise your right hands," he said and then began, "I do solemnly swear. I give my loyalty to the cause we have met here for. I fully understand I will be hunted down and killed should I ever reveal any information that would help the authorities, or identify any other member of this cause, so help me God."

"Wait a minute," Cliff said. Let's add, "And faithfully follow orders given me by the leaders of this cause."

Everyone repeated the oath including Cliff's amendment.

"Good, next we need to appoint these leaders," Marty said.

John immediately said, "Reb Brown is the best man for this job."

There were several who agreed with him but it was Cliff himself who stopped it.

"I will do whatever I can, but I think Marty is who we need to lead us." There were still those who held out for Reb, and some agreed that Marty would be a good leader, and the sides were pretty much even on the dispute. Finally Cliff said, "If all will agree, I will be second in command to Marty."

That was what finalized the deal, and that night twelve men came to the same agreement.

They also all agreed to meet and make strategies once each

month, but anyone would be able to call an emergency meeting at anytime for cause.

Additionally, they decided that they would change their meeting night, just in case one of those who did not take the oath was to let a word slip. No one would be there on Thursday nights should a raid come. The last Saturday of every month was then chosen.

The first order of business would be to take the payroll coming in for the 103rd for the month of November. Wayne Flanders, who had a job at the depot near the courthouse in the city of Valdosta, agreed to gather information on it and report back to Marty within a week.

"We also need plenty of ammunition," Cliff said.

"We have plenty of lead in the store," Marty replied, "but powder and caps___," he paused and then added "caps are down to a couple hundred and maybe we got two kegs a' gun powder."

"Wayne, if you can, see if there's any information on such," Cliff suggested.

The lanky boy nodded his head before putting on his black hat.

When they left, Mary Ann was not as friendly as she had been the week before.

The night was quite dark with little moon and mostly overcast skies, and it took the better part of three hours to reach the fork in the road that led to the Gaston cabin.

Pulling up, the horses stopped and the buckboard came to a rest.

"Johnny, you seem distant. Are you worried about what we have done tonight?"

"No, Reb, I wus just thinking about the land here," Johnny said with moist eyes, "My Pa used to own all this," he said swinging his arm to the right. "Over two thousand acres of prime farm land. Now, I have half an acre and a little cabin. Just don't seem fair that the government can come and take away a man's inheritance."

"No, it don't. That's what we are going to try and stop."

After he disappeared into the darkness, Nadine asked about the meeting. She had not mentioned it before, as she knew sometimes things were best not explained, especially in front of others. Now she wanted to know what her husband was getting himself into, getting them both into.

"We agreed to organize as a secret group and cause the Occupational Government as much pain as they have given us."

"That sounds like a rebellion, like you are going to war."

"I guess in our small way that is what we are going to do, but only to those who make war on homefolk."

"I can't say I like it, but I knew when we left Wyoming Territory, we were coming back because your brother was in trouble___, so I reckon I have to say, I will support you all the way."

"Honey, I never doubted you would support me, but it is good to hear you say it," Cliff replied turning to look at her. Just at that moment a sliver of moonlight shot from breaks in the cloud cover and her raven hair shone brightly against her white face, the loveliest face he had ever seen.

"By the way, did you like the Gunter Ladies?"

"Oh yes, I do; especially Tillie. She seems so genuine," she said and then added, "And Mary is quite pretty, for a chunky woman."

A week passed and nothing happened to anyone they knew. At least they heard nothing in the nature of bad news until the following Friday near noon when Jerry Chamblin rode up at a fast pace.

"Get down, Jerry," Mrs. Brown said when she recognized him. "Come in and sit a spell. I got some coffee biling in the kitchen house."

"Thank ya', Ma'am. I do believe I could stand a cup. Is Reb around?"

"Som'ers," she answered, then called out, "Nadine, fetch Clifford."

Nadine came out to the hallway from their room where she had been darning socks. "Hello, Mr. Chamblin," she said.

He immediately replied, "Please, Ma'am, I feel like a stranger if 'n called Mister."

"Alright then, Jerry, you must call me Nadine."

Cliff's mother cleared her throat showing her disapproval of such familiarity between a married woman and a single man.

Jerry had lived in Lowndes County since before the war. He had been raised across the state line in Madison County, Florida, but he had married a woman whose father worked for the Atlantic & Gulf Railroad and was stationed in Valdosta. Unfortunately, she had not been one to tolerate being left alone for the three long years he was away fighting for his state and she had taken up with more than one man who happened to be available and willing to ease her loneliness. When Jerry did return and times were so bad, the hardship of poverty was not something she could handle any better, and she began to see one of the officers on Colonel Northrop's staff when he came to town. Eventually, Jerry found out about it and he shot the man. There had been several witnesses that had seen the confrontation; one of them, a Lieutenant Placid, also on the Colonel's staff. Placid had a special dislike for the deceased Captain Ogletree, and it was his testimony that Ogletree had seduced the wife, had started the fight, and that Chamblin was only defending himself, that kept Jerry from a hanging.

Jerry now worked in a woodshop that made ornamental furniture for clipper ships. His skill with his hands had been appreciated by Major Day, a well-to-do businessman, who had come to Valdosta in the summer of '68 and taken over Mr. Wise's 'Wood Knot Shop'.

The Major, who was from Providence, Rhode Island, had bought the property from the government after Jefferson Wise had not been able to come up with the tax money for the years of 1860 through 1865. The fact that he had paid his taxes in 66 and 67 made no difference. Governor Bullock had signed into law a bill that required all land owners of Georgia to pay taxes for the years of secession. He said it was necessary to help cover the Federal Government's war debt that Georgia secessionists had caused.

Major Day was able to obtain a contract to manufacture the Captain's quarters on several of the new steam powered ships the Navy was building as replacements for the older sailing clippers, as well as for two new ironclad battle wagons. He was proud to have the skilled hands of Jerry Chamblin on his payroll.

"Come on, Jerry," Nadine said, "Reb is out back cutting some wood for the stoves; I'll take you to where he is."

The man followed her at two steps, as was the custom.

Entering the oak hammock she called out, "Reb, we have a visitor." She knew he had surely heard the hoofbeats of Jerry's horse and would be on the lookout for an intruder.

Cliff was bare-chested when they approached. Even though it was now November, the weather was still often in the eighties during the heat of the day and with his swinging the ax, he had worked up a sweat. The beads of moisture seen between the curls of dark hair on his muscular chest gave her a stirring of her own.

"Hello, Jerry, what brings you out on a work day?" he said replacing the Colt to its holster, that hung nearby on a short limb.

"I told 'em I wus coming down with the crud. The Major's scared stiff of catching sump'in and he sent me home. Works every time."

"I guess that's good to know."

"Well, what I really came for wus to tell you, a couple a' squads a' them Colored Soldiers raided Gunter's Mill last night. They surrounded the place and then came charging in from all sides. When they didn't find nobody they roughed up Marty purty bad. One a' them clubbed him with a rifle butt and Miss Mary Ann said he's been out 'most ever since."

"Will he be all right?" Nadine asked.

"I don't rightly know, Ma'am."

"Anyways, I aim to find out which squad it were and let the boys know."

"Damn, that's a bad thing to happen right now," Cliff stated to no one in particular.

"You sure wus right about moving the meeting night Reb," Jerry said.

"What bothers me is, was I right about someone talking?"

"You mean Faux and Shaw?"

"Well, they are sure suspects, but it's possible someone followed us to the mill the last two weeks and figured out we were meeting there every Thursday night," Cliff said back. "We did run into John Tidwell on the way home, a week back."

"That is sump'in we'll have to figure out."

"Yes we will."

"I reckon this puts you in charge, until Marty gets back on his feet," Jerry said.

"I reckon it do," Cliff agreed raising his eyebrows. "I'll send word of a special meeting in a day or so. Be ready."

"I'll be ready."

"And let me know if you find out anything about who were the ones who done this."

"Will do," Jerry said back and then touched his hat brim and added, "Miss Nadine," before he turned and headed back down the dim path.

When he was gone she said, "Well, 'One-in-charge', what do you think?"

"I think I wish I was not the 'One-in-charge'," he replied, sinking the ax deep into the stump of a water oak.

He and Nadine had decided, until the troubles were over, they would not be seen in public. As a result they again had not attended the services Sunday morning. When his parents returned, Johnny Gaston rode in with them.

He brought news. "In the last two weeks, everyone who was at the meetings over to the mill, have been visited by somebody from the Occupational Government, except you and me," John said. "First it was Marty and then his brother. Monday or Tuesday Stan Mays house was raided and his wife scared out a' her wits. Chase and Jason's place was burned on Wednesday. I just heard about it today and both a' them are in jail. Loren Renfoe was stopped on his way home from work and beaten badly. He's being taken care of over to the Widow Jones'. Now Billy Fouracres' spread was raided last night and he was shot. I don't know if 'n he's gon'a make it," the young man stopped and shook his head and spit on the ground and then took his boot heel and ground the moisture into the clay causing the small spot to turn blood red. "I reckon we'll be next."

"What about Jerry?" Nadine asked.

"I do' know. He's the one what told me about t'others."

"Huh', that do seem funny," Cliff said not looking at them.

Their conversation was suddenly interrupted, "I smell smoke," Nadine said.

"Yeah, wood smoke."

Moving away from the house where they could see to the west, a tall column of black smoke was clearly visible.

"That's my place," Johnny said.

"Yes, it surely is," Cliff agreed.

John ran for his horse but, Cliff stopped him. "Wait! From the looks a' that smoke you ain't gonna save it. You go rushing in and you might be running head on into a' ambush."

The young man stopped and thought a moment or two and then said "I got a' try. I might save somp'in."

"Wait," Nadine said, "I'll go. You two come through the woods. They won't be expecting that, if they are still there."

"Alright," Johnny agreed.

"I'll go with you," Cliff's mother said and she ran for the buckboard. "They won't dare bother two women."

His father was inside the house asleep when they pulled out.

Nadine used the thin whip urging the horse to travel faster.

"He can't do no better," Addie said, "This here is a two-horse vehicle and he was broke to pull with Richmond Augusta. Now that he's all alone and old, he just can't do no better."

When they turned into the dim road that lead to Gaston's cabin, it was plain the log structure was fully engulfed.

Just as they arrived at the slab rail fence in front of Johnny's home, three soldiers came running out of the woods and grabbed the horse's bridle. "You's women can't do nut'in," a large soldier said, with a smirk on his face.

"You black trash, you let go a' my horse," Addie yelled.

One of the men holding to the bit let go and walked back to the other man who had first addressed them. "You knows, Jackson, I bech'a dat' dar' young un' would be mighty juicy. Enough dar' fa' me and yous'. Wha' you tink?"

"I tink' we let Washington has da' old one and we tries da' purty 'n' ourselves," he replied smiling at Nadine.

She immediately cut his cheek to the bone with the whip and he screamed loudly.

"White bitch!" was the next words from his mouth as he charged her.

Again she beat him back with the whip, but finally he wrapped the small end of the latigo around his arm and pulled hard.

She had the leather thong around her wrist and was pulled forward and off the wagon.

Addie began to scream as the second man approached her side of the rig.

Cliff and Johnny were by now not far away, but even when they heard the screams of his mother, Cliff held to John's arm and shook his head, then whispered, "Take your time from here on. They may have a trap set."

John looked at him almost in disbelief. *'How can he remain so calm when he is hearing the screams of his women folk?'* he wondered, but he did as told and followed closely behind. They were now only a few hundred feet from the clearing where the burning cabin was plainly seen through the timber. Luckily the north wind was blowing the smoke and embers away from them.

It was then they heard the report of a small caliber gun being fired and Cliff immediately knew what it meant.

Fortunately for them, others nearby had heard it too and moved out from their cover to better see what was happening.

Cliff caught the movement on his flank and reached back with his right arm for Johnny.

The boy stopped and looked at him.

Cliff had been carrying the Henry in his left hand and now brought it around where the butt plate was against his shoulder and pointed the long barrel.

Following the aim, Johnny saw the men who had been hidden in the thick brush fifty feet to their right and he dropped to one knee immediately as he reached for one of the 44 caliber Remingtons that Cliff had given him a few days before.

Slowly the forms of four soldiers moving forward came into focus, and he took careful aim at the one in the rear and began tracking him. Fully aware the Remington revolvers were sighted in for seventy five yards, Johnny placed the front bead on the man's pants just where the legs separated.

Cliff carefully moved a little to his left.

From where he now stood he had these men in sight and also could see the buckboard, still he waited.

Addie had been pulled from the wagon by her assailant, but he had let her go when the gun fired and was now facing Nadine.

She had the Root cocked and pointed at the face of one of the colored soldiers who had been attacking her.

Still, Cliff waited as he watched the four men move slowly forward. Finally, they all stepped into the clearing and the one with large inverted chevrons raised his Spencer and took aim.

It was then Cliff centered the sights on the left ear of the corporal and squeezed the trigger of his Henry.

The unexpected sound of the rifle report brought about three things that followed one another almost within a second. The men who were following the sergeant turned to see where the shot had come from, Johnny dropped the hammer on his 44 and sent a round ball into the chest of the closest soldier, and Nadine jerked off another 32 round from the Root. This struck her target to the left of his wide nose, breaking his cheek bone; then following the esophagus down into his stomach where spent, it stopped. The man screamed and fell grabbing first his face and then his middle and began kicking his left leg and squealing like a wounded pig sometimes will do when shot and not immediately killed.

The expression of total surprise was on the faces of the other men in front of Johnny as he cocked the big revolver with his left thumb.

The sound of the Henry again firing was all it took and he squeezed off a second shot dropping the last of the ambushers.

When they entered the clearing, they saw one uninjured man on his knees with the woman who's dress had been torn to the point that her legs were exposed to the upper thigh when she moved; pointing the short revolver at his head. She could not see his face as he was bending over and praying loudly. The kepi that had covered his gray kinky hair moments before, lay at the toe of his hob nailed boots.

"Prepare to meet your maker, you black son-of-a-bitch," she said just short of a shout.

Cliff could see his mother lying on the ground beside the old horse dead or unconsciousness; which, he did not know, as he walked up beside his wife and clasped his large hand around hers and gently took the gun from her.

"We won't shoot this one," he said.

She looked at him in disbelief.

"They was trying to rape us, me and your mother."

"I know, but shooting him in the top of the head won't make up for that."

"Well, just what will?" she yelled at him with a quivering voice.

"We'll hang 'im, slow," Cliff said back.

"Oh Laud," the older colored Sergeant said loudly when he heard Cliff's words, but he did not raise his face to see the people he had attacked a few short minutes before.

"See to Mama, Nadine," Cliff said as he walked over to the man who was still kicking and squealing, though not as loud as before.

Satisfied he was no threat, Cliff turned to Johnny and said, "See if you can find their horses."

The younger man immediately headed back into the hammock in the direction from which the ambushers had appeared.

When he returned leading the seven horses, he saw Mrs. Brown lying in the back of the wagon talking to Nadine.

The uninjured man was dragging the last of the dead soldiers over to where the others were laid out in a reasonable neat row.

Cliff had a coil of hemp rope that he was sectioning into proper lengths.

When Johnny tied the horses to the fence, he turned to Cliff as if to await further instruction.

"Nadine," Cliff called.

"Yes," she answered looking up from the wagon bed at him.

He motioned her over with his head, still working with the rope.

"Yes," she again said when she was close.

"I want you to drive Mama home. This is not something she should see or even know about."

"I want to see that bastard die!" she exclaimed.

Johnny was surprised at her language and looked away.

"I'll tell you all about it, but please do as I say and take Mama back home."

"If you insist," she said showing her displeasure.

"Thank you."

At that moment the old darkie began to sob again.

"I hope it takes you a long time to die," she said as she walked by him.

When the buckboard was out of sight, Cliff slipped a noose around each of the heads of the dead men and after tossing the rope over a low limb of a big magnolia tree, he attached the other end to the back of a horse's McClellan saddle and led the animal forward until the man's feet were off the ground by a yard or so; then he removed the rope from the saddle and tied it off before going back for another body. Once all the dead men were hanging side by side he slid a noose around the neck of the wounded man who did not realize what was happening. This man kicked only a few seconds before his body went limp.

Then Cliff took a piece of yellow paper from his vest pocket, and with a lead pencil wrote something on it and pinned it to the shirt of the last man, who once again fell to his knees sobbing openly and begging for mercy.

Cliff totally ignored his pleas and slipped the noose around his neck, having already thrown it over the limb and tied it to the horse.

"Oh! Mister, please. I didn't do nut'en myself."

"You were the one who knocked my mother down. You will die slowly."

With that, Cliff took the big bay horse that he had been working and led him forward.

Cliff had not tied the man's hands and he started to struggle as the coarse hairs began to tighten around his throat. He pulled at the knot unsuccessfully and then tried to lift his weight upward by pulling on the rope above the knot and was successful at this for a few seconds but his lack of fresh oxygen was making him grow weak and finally he had to release his grip. At that point his legs began to kick furiously trying to find the ground that was just out of his reach. After some four minutes he stopped thrashing about.

Johnny had watched this for awhile, but could not stomach it to the finish and had turned away. When he heard no more noise coming from the man, he turned back just in time to see Cliff reach up and rip the Sergeant Major chevrons from the dead man's sleeves and stuffed them into his shirt.

"You are a hard man, Reb Brown. You got the right to be, but you are surely a hard man," he said and then he walked forward and looked at the paper pinned there and wondered what had been written on it.

Very soon after, they heard the sound of a wagon approaching fast. Both quickly stepped into the cover of the brush.

When Nadine turned the buckboard into the trail to Johnny's, Cliff suddenly became angry and yelled, "I told you to take Mama home."

"I did, only there ain't no home left," she shouted back. "They burned your place, too, and I think your father was inside," she said almost hysterically.

Cliff could see Henry Roosevelt was winded and almost ready to fall so he told her to follow at a slow pace and save the horse if she could. With that, he turned to Johnny and yelled, "You come with the women and see they are not attacked again." Then he mounted one of the soldier's horses and headed out at a gallop towards his home.

When he arrived it was totally engulfed. As he dismounted he saw a blue uniformed pair of legs protruding from what had been the front porch. Approaching nearer the blaze, he could see a second body that still held a double barreled shotgun, but before he was able to do anything more, the sounds of gunfire came from the hammock in the direction of the corral.

Running in that direction he had to side-step as Red came charging past him. Close behind was a black soldier with a revolver in his hand.

Cliff sent him to his maker with a quick shot from the Henry to his forehead and then he hurried forward towards the sounds of more gunfire and laughter. When he was within a few yards, he could hear Treasure emitting cries of great pain and then another gunshot and all was quiet, save the sound of human voices.

A quick look at the loading sleeve follower revealed to him the Henry was either empty or down to a single round in the chamber, so he pulled his Colt and advanced slowly.

The voices now could be heard and he knew there was at least one white man with the coloreds and they were coming back down the trail towards him. When the line appeared, he saw two were packing his and Nadine's saddles and he waited just off the trail behind a large red oak until they were very close before he stepped out into the path; the expression on the lead man's face was that of total surprise. Recovering his composure, the soldier reached for his holstered revolver, but was much too slow.

The man who was suddenly next in line after his comrade fell forward, already had his revolver out and took a quick aim at Cliff and almost surely would have gotten in a strong hit, as Cliff could see the hole in the barrel's muzzle, had he not already spent his rounds killing Treasure.

The sickening sound of a hammer striking a spent cap was his last earthly memory.

Cliff's bullet caught him center between the breastbones and he was dead when he hit the ground.

The next soldier still had Nadine's saddle over his right shoulder and had just stopped and was standing there with his mouth open. Cliff sent a 44 slug into his upper body and side-stepped him looking for the next man, but only saw his own saddle being flung in his direction.

He knew he was too far away for it to hit him, and he shot at the man who now was running away; but the lead stopped in the saddle's cantle.

Cliff followed the thin man wearing a black frock coat into the woods and caught several quick glimpses of him, but never got a clear shot. Finally he decided to go back and try and catch Red and use him to chase the man down, when he eventually emerged from the thick woods.

When he got back to what had been his home, the fire was dying some and he saw the buckboard was there.

Nadine was standing beside Red and patting him on the neck.

Cliff quickly headed towards him with his saddle, but she looked up and shook her head.

"He's hurt too bad to ride," she said.

Cliff stopped and dropped the saddle, then walked slowly forward.

He now could see there was a torn hole in his paunch where some of his intestines were protruding a few inches. Another hole on his left side, where the shoulder muscle could be seen under the skin, was shooting large amounts of blood every time his big heart beat. Tears filling Cliff's eyes kept him from seeing the other bullet hole farther back just forward of the left hip.

All Cliff could think of was the many years and countless miles they had traveled together, the many battles when the big sorrel had carried him through the thickest of fighting, and galloped him away to safety. He walked up and with one arm around the big neck, squeezed him with a loving grasp and said, "Ole Red, I love you", and then he placed the long barrel behind the left ear and pulled the trigger. The big animal fell like a rock, kicking only once and then lay still.

Cliff felt faint and thought for a moment he was going to pass out, but regained his strength and with tears still rolling down his cheeks he spoke. "Johnny, if you would, go back and get the other horses we left at your place and bring them. We're gon' a need them."

He was able to drag his father's body from the fire and soon he buried him. He dared not take time to dig graves for the two horses they had lost, even though that was just what he wanted to do.

He knew well the white man who had escaped would be bringing a posse, and they needed to be gone when the bluecoats arrived.

That night the four homeless people stayed in an old shack Johnny had used before the war when he fished Brown's Lake southeast of his father's plantation. It was not nearly far enough away to be a place of permanent hiding, but it was hard to find and would serve for a day or two.

Two nights later, Cliff returned to the homesite and placed a marker he had carved at the head of his father's grave. He was pleased to see the large mound of dirt where neighbors, who knew of what had happened, had buried the horses. A chore he had not desired, but had come prepared to do. The thought of Red's body being picked clean by buzzards was more than he could stomach at the time, and he was sincerely grateful to whoever had shown him so much respect.

The marker he erected read:

Louis Henry Brown
Born Virginia September 1801
Murdered by Arsonists and
Horse Killers November 12, 1870

When finished at the grave site, he dug up the remaining cash he had buried behind the corral, and slipped away into the night.

CHAPTER FOUR

The Third Letter

"The last Saturday of this month will fall on the 25th," Cliff said to his friend. "Johnny, do you think you can get word to the others that we will hold a meeting in Ben Jordan's old barn? There is a substantial stock of cotton bales in it and this will cover any light that might otherwise be seen. I wus over there last night and it did not look like anybody had been around it for a month or two."

"I'll slip out at dusk and ride all night if I have to," Johnny replied nodding his head.

"You might have to, if you contact everybody; we are so scattered out around the county," Cliff agreed then added, "And Johnny, don't fail to go by and let Marty know what we are doing."

"He's hurt so bad, I doubt he can come."

"I still want him to know."

"Sure thing, Reb."

"And Johnny, be sure you stress to all the importance of not telling anyone when or where we are meeting."

"Sure, Reb."

Cotton balls were compressed into one hundred pound bundles and wrapped with burlap cloth to keep the integrity of the bale. Thus, burlap rolls were in abundance in the large barn.

Friday night before the meeting, Cliff and Nadine spent over two hours hanging the long runs of burlap on the interior walls of the loft, to hide any light from the lanterns that might otherwise shine through the cracks.

When sundown came the next day, he was cinching up his saddle on the bay horse that had supplied the power to hang the arsonists at Johnny's a couple weeks before.

"You will be careful," she said knowing it was a silly statement, yet one that needed to be said.

"Not to worry. I'll be home 'for you know it."

Mounted on the McClellan he leaned over and kissed her and gave her his wicked little smile and a half wink, then pulled on the right rein and touched his heel to the bay's side; the horse responded immediately.

Cliff knew the US brand on his mount's left hip would be a death warrant should he be caught riding him, but at the time he had no other choice.

He was the first to arrive, and after lighting a lantern inside he went back out and walked up to the top of the hill about three hundred yards away and there he sat down. The moon was just rising over a stand of tall pines and the glow of its fat crescent body was beginning to light the terrain around the area.

From where he sat, he could see for a mile or more in any direction. This had been a huge cotton field before the war, a clearing of three square miles, perhaps more. The only reason the barn was not destroyed when the Federal troops came in '65 was a darkie family that had belonged to Mr. Jordan's nephew was living there and their orders were not to burn any slave quarters.

Cliff had found a pair of field glasses in the saddle bags of one of the horses they had taken from Johnny's house and he now used them to survey the area.

About one third of the clearing had been in cotton this year; the rest was left unplanted and wild grass had grown freely. Several deer could be seen browsing on the last of the leaves on the small brush that had taken growth here and there competing with the native wiregrass for the moisture and nutrients in the soil.

Cliff loved to watch deer. They were so alert to everything

about them and so graceful when they hastily bounded away from suspected danger. It was just such a happening that brought his attention to a rider approaching from the northwest. After careful study, he concluded it to be Jerry Chamblin.

He watched him in the glasses until he tied up his buckskin and entered the backdoor of the barn.

Ten minutes later, Stan May followed almost the same tracks Jerry had left in the grass, a hundred yards behind him was Wayne Flanders.

'That's everybody from the north. Any more riders coming from that way will not have been invited,' he thought.

Scanning the clearing, he saw two more coming from the southwest. It was not hard to recognize Johnny, they had spent so much time together in the last month, but he was not sure who rode beside him.

Then, from due south on the trail he had come, were two more horses slowly moving north. He recognized them as Dwayne Zipper and Sam Brooks.

Cliff had always admired Sam's horse. It, like Red, was a sorrel with a flaxen mane and tail, only not as large a horse as Red had been.

Suddenly, from the trees to the east appeared two more riders. When they were near the barn he recognized Aaron Smith Jr. and Israel Henley.

Finally, he saw the tall lanky frame of Robert Maycomber on his white horse just as he entered the clearing. There was no misguessing that shape and horse combination.

'All nine made it,' Cliff thought with some relief. Still he remained for another fifteen minutes. He knew the horse he had left at the barn would be recognized by Johnny and the lad would make sure everyone waited.

Finally, Cliff walked down the hill and entered the back door of the barn.

Stepping inside, he heard Wayne saying in his slow and deliberate manner, "I know he's coming. I just want to get this show on the road. It's a fur piece home and I don't relish the ride."

Climbing to the top of the ladder, Cliff called out, "Keep your britches on Wayne, I'm here," he nodded his head as a greeting to all present and then he asked, "Johnny, will you take these?" He handed the field glasses to him, "and go up to the top of the hill and keep a look-see."

He could tell his friend was somewhat disappointed that he would not be a part of this first meeting under Reb's leadership, but he made no protest; taking the glasses and picking up the Spencer he had taken from the dead soldier at his burned out home, he started down the ladder.

"Alright let's get this thing rolling," Cliff said. "Wayne, what have you got to report?"

"Well, as I told Marty, it appears the payroll comes in around the first of the month, leastwise that's when them nigger soldiers are rootin' and tootin' in the bars. It comes by train from Savannah. That's all I know right now."

"So, we've already missed November's opportunity. Let's work on December."

"Wayne you done good, but we need more precise information. We need to know which train will be carrying it."

"Well now, that will be a might harder."

"Harder or not, that's what we need," Cliff said sternly and then before Wayne could complain more, he turned to Jerry and asked the same question, "Jerry, what can you tell us?"

"I found out that Mr. John Griffiss has ordered a load of powder from the DuPont Company, up north som'ers. Griffiss said he had the contract to furnish it to the Army. It is supposed to be delivered before Christmas as they plan to have a big celebration and will be shooting off their big cannon during the parade."

"That's good news. See if you can find out if there will be any percussion caps in that order," Cliff said.

Aaron Smith then spoke. "My daughter, Jean, is studying to be a doctor over to the Military Headquarters at the old prison in Savannah. I could take a trip over there and see what I could find out about the payroll shipments."

"If you will do that it will be a big help, but I don't think it would be a good idea to board the train in Valdosta. In fact, I'm afraid for any of us being seen too much. We must face the facts, somebody has given out our names to the authorities and we are being singled out," Cliff said.

"They stop at Stockton to take on wood and water," Aaron said. "I'll board the train there."

"That will be good. Just be careful."

The meeting continued on with small items being discussed and finally Israel said, "I need to wring out my rag."

Cliff said, "Israel how 'bout relieving Johnny up on the hill so he can get in his two-cents worth?"

"Sure, Reb," the young man replied before heading for the ladder.

The first words from Johnny's mouth when he arrived was, "What have I missed?"

"Nothing much. Wayne found out the payroll comes in around the first of the month and Jerry found out about some powder coming into Griffiss' store soon. J. M. gave us a report on his brother, and Robert reported he had heard about some new mounts being brought up from Florida for the company a' cavalry up in Albany. That's about all," Cliff said. "What can you tell us?"

"Not much more, I reckon 'cept my granddaddy Horne owned a big spread a' land down on the state line. I run into Lily Keeling, my Granny on that side a' the family, and she said we could use that place as headquarters if 'n we need to. There's a good size barn there, 'hit ain't two-story like this one but it is good size and it ain't being used none now and there ain't no roads nearby that folks travel. It's this side a' the state line, I reckon, but t'other side a' the river."

"That might be to our advantage when the authorities come looking fur us," Cliff said. "How many a' you know where this is?"

"J. M. does," Johnny said, "and so does Jerry."

"It's only six mile or so from the mill," J. M. added. "There be a nice piece a pasture there too. Be good fur grazing horses or cattle."

"I like the sound of it," Cliff said, "Before we meet again I'll take a look at it."

"Anything else?" he offered and seeing no response he continued, "Alright, Dwayne, will you go up to where Israel is and make sure it's all clear before we move out?" Cliff asked, and then said to the others, "Make sure when you leave to scatter. If possible take a different trail than the one you came on."

The next morning, Cliff and Johnny were up early and headed for the Horne/Keeling pasture.

The Withlacoochee River was low for the lack of recent rain in the area, and a place to cross was found a mile or so east of Gunter's Mill.

On the south bank, near the river was a stand of natural growth pines but no road, and they had to use the sun as a direction finder anytime they ventured far from the stream due to the thickness of the timber.

After traveling about half an hour Johnny said, "Thar's the spring yonder," pointing to the far side of the river.

**'Thunder', Granny Keeling's Black Stallion
in front of her House**

Cliff would have not known it was a spring, except for being told so, but he did notice the river was a foot or so higher from there on.

Shortly after they had passed it, Johnny cut south until they came upon a dim road right at a sharp turn. It continued south as far as Cliff could see but it was to the east Johnny lead him. A mile later, they came to an old cracker house that Cliff would have thought to be abandoned had it not been for a thin trail of smoke rising as straight as a pine from the stick chimney.

"Granny is to home," Johnny said and he reined into the front yard. "That there stallion belongs to her, only she can't ride him no more and he's a might wild."

Cliff looked at the magnificent Black and wondered what a woman old enough to be Johnny's grandmother needed with such a fine animal.

"Granny Keeling, Granny Keeling," Johnny called out.

Finally, an old woman that Cliff judged to be in her eighties, came to the door and peered out. "Who it be?" she called out.

"Me, Johnny Gaston, your grandson."

"Who?"

"Emmett's boy. John."

"John Boy. I knew you wus a-coming," she said through a toothless mouth. "Where you been? I wus looking fur you this morning."

"It's still morning, Granny," he said back as he dismounted.

"It is?"

"Who'd you brung with you?" she asked.

"This is the man I wus telling you about, Reb Brown, he wus a hero during the war, Granny."

"You killed a mess a' them invaders, did you?"

"I killed some," Cliff acknowledged.

"God bless ya, and you's' welcome to Granny's house," She replied nodding her head in approval of his statement.

"Thank you, Ma'am," Cliff answered.

Cliff looked at the porch that was slanting substantially. The flat rocks that held the east end were intact but those that had held up the west end were scattered some and the edge of the wood frame sat lower to the earth. This caused the roof to dip some too. A tall lone pine stood between the trail and the old structure near where a split-rail fence once protected her home from unwelcome intruders, but most of it was now gone. A couple of chairs could be seen on the porch but the whole affair looked like it might fall were he to put his 180 pounds on it.

"You boys want some coffee?"

"No, Ma'am, not right now," Cliff said quickly as he figured Johnny would agree and he just wasn't sure he wanted to go inside.

"I guess not, Granny. Not right now, but we'll stop on our way back," her grandson said. "We need to take another look at the old hay barn."

"You do that, and I'll get some rutabagas on a' frying so you boys don't starve slap to death."

Cliff watched the old woman turn and enter her home and he thought, *'She's as skinny as a split-rail fence post.'*

The little trail now looked a lot more like it was once a well-constructed road. It was wide enough for a wagon but it obviously had not been used very much for many years. Thorn vines rose right up from the ground for several feet until they were able to grab onto one of the overhanging limbs, and he was fully aware they were murder on bare skin. The trees were so close together along each side, their inter-locking limbs blocked the sun from view much of the time.

In a little less than a mile along the winding trail they came to a large, treeless clearing. Wild grass and broom sage stood four foot tall throughout the clearing.

Johnny turned his horse along the edge of the woods heading back towards the river. A quarter mile into the hammock that lined the west side of the field, they came upon a little cove almost surrounded by live oak trees, and there Cliff saw the barn. He was surprised at the condition of the log structure.

Its silver color testified it was constructed of well-aged cypress which will never rot and is a distasteful meal for the ever-present termite that inhabits every square inch of soil in this part of the world. Even the roof looked to be cypress slabs. The building was perhaps a two thousand square foot rectangle, being only a little wider than it was long. Although it had no loft, the roof was quite high and he realized an abundance of hay or other material could be stored there with a little work.

Granny Keeling's Barn

"What do you think?" John asked.

"I like it," Cliff said back never taking his eyes away from the building.

They spent several minutes inspecting it and finally Johnny said, "Come on. I want to show you something else."

"Just leave the horses and let 'em graze and we'll walk," he added and reached for the Spencer.

Cliff likewise removed his repeater and laid the barrel over his shoulder and followed the younger man.

They walked a quarter mile northward into a pine thicket and then in another hundred yards they came to the river.

At this point the river was twenty-five feet below the banks and made a horseshoe bend in front of them; by doing so a small white sandy beach had formed. Cliff was amazed. *'This spot is simply beautiful,'* he thought looking at the black water river moving lazily by, carrying a willow leaf along with it. "I believe this is the most peaceful spot I have seen in years," he said to his friend.

"Good swimming hole there," Johnny said. "And I have caught some big ole' catfish, yonder, and the Withlacoochee Queen right from this beach."

"The Withlacoochee Queen?" Cliff questioned.

"Yeah, a 12 pound bass, from yonder, she was bedding just beyond 'em cypress knees. I see'd the King he' self too, only I had the queen on my pole and by the time I landed her, he done slipped off into deeper water."

"Your Grandma own all this?"

"Yeah, it were Grand Pa Horne's, but he's gone now. He wus really my Great Grand Pa but, we all call him Grand Pa Horne. Now, it's Granny Keeling's."

"This clearing must be three hundred acres."

"I'd say 'bout that," Johnny agreed. "Use ta' grow hay and sell it to the Rebel army but then when the war came crashing down, it laid dormant fur a couple years and then Uncle John planted it in hemp for a season, and then corn one year, and two years back we got a contract for hay fur the Yankee troops up to Valdosta, but last year nothing was growed here."

"Well, let's go back and see what it will take to get it for our use."

"You tell her we's fighting the Yankees again and she won't charge you nut'in," Johnny said.

"I pay my way," Cliff said. "Pay folks well and they will remember you when necessary or maybe not remember you, as the need be."

"You are right about that," Johnny agreed.

When they arrived back at her old home they both removed the saddles from their horses, to give them a chance to rest while their masters negotiated the terms of the deal with Granny Keeling.

Cliff moved slowly and carefully as he stepped onto the old porch before following John inside her house.

"Granny Keeling, we're a-coming in."

The old woman called from the kitchen house out back, "Make yourselves to home. Dinner is a-smokin' good."

Cliff noticed an old single barrel shotgun over the fireplace mantel and being a lover of weapons came closer for a better look. It was then he also noticed a black and tan hound asleep in the corner of the room.

'I don't believe he even knows we are here.' Cliff thought as he watched the long-nosed dog's deep breathing.

John began to tell him about his Great Grandfather coming to Georgia from South Carolina, which Cliff found interesting, but before he finished his tale, a call was heard from the kitchen house beckoning them for a light dinner.

The rutabagas had been fried in hog fat and mashed. There was a thick layer of sautéed onions lying over the red vegetable and the smell was tremendously delicious. When Cliff had finished his second helping he pushed away from the small table that had been made by splitting a good size log in half and sawing it to the length needed for the tiny room.

"That's mighty fine eating, Ma'am," Cliff said and he could see the pride swell in her expression when she heard it.

"My boys always liked their rutabagas fried," she said.

"Mrs. Keeling, I'd like to buy that piece a' land where the barn is. I can pay cash money, either gold or folding dollars. I'll pay a fair price."

"I don't know. I ain't never sold to nobody that weren't family a' for," she said.

"I need the land. I'm in a fight with the Occupational Government up in Valdosta and they done burned out my folk's home the same day they burned Johnny's."

"What you gon' a do about it?" she asked.

"I aim to fight 'em," he answered strongly.

"That's just what you ought a do, too, but that might mean they's come down here and burn me out fur selling to ya."

"I can't say that won't happen, but I also aim to keep it a close guarded secret as to where we are staying, just fur that reason."

"You's married with young'uns'?"

"Married, no young'uns'."

"There's some over three hundred acres in what we call the clearin' and the barn's worth a might too."

"Yes, Ma'am. It's a good one too."

"Yep, it is."

"I'll sell fur a dollar a' acre and twenty-five fur the barn. Yankee dollars and not one penny less."

"You have a deal Mrs. Keeling," Cliff said. "I'll bring the money tomorrow."

"You bring the money when you bring your Missis. I want to meet the woman what captured you," she said with a sly expression.

"That will be tomorrow, too."

"Good, then it's tomorrow."

Returning to the property, they rode completely around the outer perimeter before criss-crossing the clearing. He was pleased the barn could only be seen from directly in front of it, and then if one did not know it was there it might be missed.

"The first thing will be to build an outhouse," he said to John. "Women folk don't cotton to squatting much."

Johnny laughed a little, but Cliff could tell he was embarrassed at the statement.

On the way back they searched the river for a closer place to cross but found no real suitable crossing south of the spring.

Johnny offered, "There is a good crossing yonder a few miles, at Rocky Ford. Wagons can cross easy there, when the river ain't high."

The next day Cliff had his mother and what belongings they still possessed in the buckboard, while Nadine and Johnny rode the other horses behind her. Cliff led the way staying a few hundred yards in front.

Again on this day, his mother seemed to be in a bad mood and he figured it to be because she was leaving the gravesite of her husband; but she said nothing and he knew questioning her would prove fruitless.

Everything went well until they were nearing the road that came from Valdosta to Gunter's Store and there he saw a small dust cloud rising and he motioned for them to clear the road while he checked on it.

The intersection of the two roads where the Yeoman's lived was nearly three miles north of Gunter's store and when he got close to that point, he left the road and slipped through the timber.

Soon he could see the front porch of Gunter's store and there were seven horses tied to the hitching rail out front.

They all sported McClellan saddles and had dark blue blankets with light blue piping.

He waited.

After several minutes, the soldiers came out of the store and mounted. Each had an orange in their hands. When they left, they took the east turn off, the direction Cliff and his family had just come.

'Good thing we saw their dust,' Cliff thought as he watched them disappear over the hill a mile away.

When he went back to where the others were hiding he said, "Yankee troops."

Nadine nodded her head, "We saw them heading east."

"We'll stop at Gunter's store and make sure everything is alright there. Mama, you stop out front. The rest of us will go around back and keep these horses out of sight."

"You think it's alright to stop?" Addie asked showing her disapproval.

"Mama, I need to check on them, and it will be a good place to give the horses a rest. Henry Roosevelt will need all his strength to pull this wagon up the river bank."

"Well, I don't like it," she said just above a whisper but loud enough that she was sure he heard her.

Upon entering the store front, Addie looked at the two women who were standing close to one another. A red-headed child, perhaps four years old, was standing behind Mary Ann grasping her leg tightly.

"Oh thank the Lord it's you, Miss Addie. We thought those terrible nigger soldiers were coming back."

"Did they harm you?"

"Not really," Tillie said.

"Not really! I can't believe you said that," Mary Ann replied to her sister-in-law. "Look at my arm," she added but of course no one could see her arm as it was covered with her dress sleeve.

"Yes, he grabbed you and threatened you, but you ain't hurt. Not really hurt."

"Well, he didn't grab you."

"That's because I didn't call him a stinking nigger right to his face."

"Well, he was bragging about the beating they gave to Marty."

The others came in through the back of the store and the little red-headed girl began to scream when she saw them, which caused her mother to scream out also.

"It's all right. It's just us," Nadine said to the little girl who stopped screaming, but continued to cry loudly and wrapped her arms around her mother's leg and buried her face in the long dress and apron.

"Did they hurt you?" Cliff asked.

"They grabbed Mary Ann and shoved her a bit, but no one was hurt. They were here asking questions about you, though," Tillie said.

"What kind of questions?"

"About where you were and when did we last see you."

"They know your name too," Mary Ann added, "They called you Reb Brown!"

"Yeah, there's a spy in the woodpile. I'm sure of it," he said.

"Not one of our boys," Addie said sternly.

Cliff just looked at her and raised one eyebrow but, said nothing.

"How is your husband, Mary?" Nadine asked.

"Not good at all. Doc Rambo said he may lose his eye."

"Oh! How awful," Nadine said back showing true concern, but no surprise. She had seen similar happenings in Missouri during the war. A man on either side who refused to give the requested information would often be beaten senseless or even to death. Then she added, "At least he's alive. That's more than Mrs. Brown can say about her husband."

It was not meant as a put-down of Mary Ann, but rather as sympathy for her mother-in-law, but Mary Ann took it as an insult.

"Just you wait until your husband is injured or killed," Mary shot back. "You won't be so free with your talk then."

"I'm sorry, Mary, if I offended you. It was not my intention, and I do know how you feel. You see, I have already buried one husband that I loved very much."

Immediately, Addie turned her head and looked at her daughter-in-law. She had no knowledge that Nadine had been married before.

Cliff had gone into the living quarters of the store to see Marty while this exchange was taking place and knew nothing of it. When he returned he recognized a strained air was in the room.

"We lost everything in the fire," he said to Tillie. "We will be needing to set up house all over again. Will you order the things that you would want to get settled if you were in our place, and we will pick them up in a week or so."

"I'll do what I can. These days, most everything comes from Savannah or Tallahassee."

"Well, do the best you can," he said to her and then turning to her sister-in-law he tipped his hat and said, "Mary Ann." Which, she answered with a slight smile.

"Come on, ladies," Cliff then said to his family and escorted them out the front.

"Nadine, will you drive Mom on down to the river? I'll bring the other horse."

"Sure."

"I can drive."

"No one is questioning that you can drive but I want sharper eyes driving as we near the river. It's time to let us take care of you for a spell," he said and after helping them both onto the spring seat he handed the traces to Nadine and then left before any more argument could be brought.

The crossing started well but the tired old horse simply did not have the stamina to pull the wagon up the steep bank on the south side.

Cliff and Johnny each looped a rope over the shafts and tied them to their saddles and helped the old boy up the bank. As soon as they were able, they moved into the woods and stopped for a rest.

Less than an hour later, they were pulling onto their new property.

Nadine was all eyes; as soon as she stopped the wagon she jumped clear and began moving around in circles like a child might do. "Oh! This is a wonderful piece of land and look at that barn; it's built like a fortress."

Addie Brown was less enthused. She could see it was a good piece of land. It was mostly cleared but still had some stands of timber. She knew the value of good wood. Wood was always needed. In fact there was really nothing, she could put her foot on, that was wrong with it except, it was theirs and not her's. That was something she had not had to contend with since she was a child. Even when they had lost the big farm after the war, the little cracker house they had moved into had been on their property for years. Now it was all gone. She had no husband, no house, no property, no youth. She owned nothing other than the clothes on her back; a terribly depressing situation, with so little hope of it ever changing.

Cliff worked from daylight to dark for three days digging the deep hole and then constructing the little house over it. Finally, the ladies had an outhouse and he was proud of it.

Next would come a well. He had bought a pitcher pump at Gunter's Store but the water table was too deep for it to draw, so he had to dig a hole and line it with something. The small branches of the numerous oaks would do to begin with, but before they rotted he would have to find brick and line it with them. Buying the brick was not the problem. The real problem with new brick was who might be watching for new homesteaders picking up such items from the stores.

It was one week to the day after they arrived at the new place that Johnny came by with news. "I stopped in Marty's Store tonight and Miss Tillie said to tell you they had news."

Cliff immediately began gathering the essentials for a trip across the river.

They had come to the feeling that the river was a boundary that kept them safe. Evil lived north of the Withlacoochee, but somehow was not allowed to cross it; a feeling of security they needed and appreciated, as thin as it might have been.

The two young men moved out when the moon was high and headed west to the crossing.

They both had gone to considerable pains erasing all signs of a wagon having crossed there and even had constructed a false trail that led north and then west from there. The false trail eventually ended up back at the river a mile or two up stream.

Every time they used the crossing they would take the false trail back and forth until it looked to be traveled regularly. They had likewise taken pains to conceal the real trail that in reality turned east.

Cliff had some experience hiding trails from the war years, when not only your life depended on the enemy not being able to follow you, but perhaps the lives of your whole troop.

Johnny, too, had lived in the woods much of his life, preferring that to the fields, when his father had fields, and he knew a trick or two himself that aided in the concealment.

The nine o'clock hour had just stopped gonging on Mary Ann's mantel clock when the two men approached the back door of the store. A short knock was followed by two more quick ones.

They had not made agreement of such a signal but Cliff knew they would recognize it as something rather than an intrusion from men of authority.

Cliff could see through a crack in the door the light of a coal oil lamp moving from the living quarters to the back of the store.

"Who is it?" a female voice called out.

"Reb."

"Oh, thank God," Mary said as she quickly opened the door. She threw her arms around his neck and pressed her body tightly against him and began to sob slightly. Cliff could feel her nipples becoming hard, through the thin cotton gown she wore, and he knew he needed to do something very quickly.

"Nothing to worry about Mary Ann, Johnny and I will take care of whatever is the trouble."

Immediately, she shot back from her embrace and looked at the shorter man who stood behind Cliff.

"I, I am just so afraid. Marty is so much worse. I think he may die. I'm sorry I fell upon you like that."

"There was no harm, Mary Ann. You have a right to feel relieved to see old friends in a time of need."

"Yes," she said turning back into the store, "I am in need."

The statement meant nothing to Johnny but its meaning was not lost on Cliff.

Taking a few steps back into the room she said, "Please come in."

It was then Johnny said, "Miss Tillie told me to bring Reb here, there was news for him, important news."

"I see you came because Tillie sent for you, and I was thinking you came to see about my husband's condition."

"We came because we were sent for, but we are certainly concerned about Marty. How bad has he gotten?" Cliff asked.

Mary Ann gave him a harsh look and replied, "None better," before she turned and went to the shelves where they stocked canned goods and set the lamp on the counter, then reached up to a higher shelf and pulled out a can of peaches, set it down, then looking over her shoulder as if someone might be spying on them, she took the can behind the outer one, and handed it to Cliff.

Johnny could not help but notice that the outline of her naked body could be easily seen through the thin gown, when the light was on the other side of her, and he turned quickly so no one could see the bulge that suddenly sprang to life in his overalls.

Cliff reached into the open-topped can and retrieved a piece of paper and then moved past her and picked up the light with one hand as he held the note with the other. When finished reading, he looked off at nothing in particular before setting the lamp back down and then slid the edge of the paper into its chimney until it caught fire. He held it as long as possible and then laid the remaining piece on the tin top of a candy container and watched it destroy itself.

"Well, you certainly made sure I would not ever know its

contents. It must have been a very special note," she said hatefully.

Cliff had little doubt but what she had already read the paper herself but instead of pointing that out he simply replied, "It is better if no one knows intelligence we receive, Mary Ann. Should you be questioned by the Authorities, you have nothing to lie about," he said and then added, "I would like to see Marty now, if I may."

"Come this way," she said picking up the lamp.

Both men followed her.

"Hello, Marty. Mary Ann has been telling us you are not getting any better."

"Oh, hell, she tells that to the crows every morning just to bore them into leaving the area. I'm much better, except for my eye. I can't see a blame thing out a' it," he replied lifting the bandage to show them.

Cliff could see the eye was ruined. It had turned a pale yellow and there was only a dark spot where the pupil had been. "Well, a man only needs two eyes when he's chasing women and you done all that you are gon' a' do many years ago."

"Yeah, that's true," he said smiling. "A man don't need more of a woman than Mary Ann."

"What are you here for, Reb?"

"Got a message from Jerry," Cliff said but added no more.

Marty realized he didn't want to talk about it in front of noncombatants and he nodded his head. "I'll be in good enough shape soon, and I'll go with you when you ride."

"You just keep a good picture in your mind of the ones who did this to you, and when you can ride we will look them up."

"I'm looking forward to that ride," Marty said. Then he fell back on the small cot.

"Guess my strength ain't as good as I thought."

"Time, Marty, give it time. You lost a lot of blood and it takes quite a spell for broken bones to mend."

"Yeah, I guess so."

"Good to see you, Johnny," he said to the short man when Cliff turned to go.

"You too, Marty. Get well soon and we'll get 'em Yanks fur sure."

"You bet we will," the injured man said.

When the trio were back in the storefront Mary turned the lamp down so it gave only the slightest glow and opened the door.

Johnny said, "I'll slip out and take a look."

Cliff wished he had not, but didn't say anything.

Mary then moved close to him and pressed her body tightly against his back and whispered, "Oh, Reb, I need you so bad."

"Mary Ann," he said turning, "You are a very purty woman, and I can't say I'm not real tempted to tear that gown from you and take you right here on the floor, but I ain't gon' a do it. You got a husband in there, and a good one too, what loves you and needs you. He has provided for you and your kids well, during some mighty hard times, too. You need to think on those things."

"I'm still young, I have needs, too."

"Well, then, he can help you use one of these," he said, and he took her wrist and guided the hand down to her crotch.

"Oh, I never," she said, "I'm shocked that you would suggest such a thing. I never."

"Oh, yes you have and will again," he said, and then stepped into the darkness before she could reply.

Her slamming of the door sounded unusually loud in the stillness of the dark night.

When he reached the horses Johnny asked, "What made that banging noise?"

"Oh, I think Mary Ann had trouble getting the door to close properly," Cliff answered, then added, "Come on, we got 'a go on to Chamblin's."

The younger man mounted without question and followed him onto the clay road.

They had gone perhaps a mile when Cliff said in a low tone. "Jerry's found out about some horses coming this way."

Their friend lived a mile out of town on the Coffee Road in a small Cracker House that had belonged to his great uncle, years before. After the war, when his mother lost their Florida land, she moved to Lowndes county so she could be closer to her family. Now these days Jerry lived with her, since they only had each other.

Cliff knew there was a good chance all the boys that had attended those first meetings were being watched, so he and Johnny tied their horses half a mile from the house and slipped up on foot.

When they were close, Cliff could see a hound sleeping on the front porch and dared not go closer for fear of awakening the dog and he alerting any spies that might be around.

Looking about, he saw a small stone on the ground and he

tossed it at the windowpane on that side of the house. It missed the window but struck the slab board next to it and woke the dog who jumped up and howled once, and then lay back down and went back to sleep.

Cliff saw Jerry pull back the sack that served as a curtain over the window and look out. A minute later he walked out onto the small back porch and lit his pipe.

Cliff whistled like a whippoorwill once and Jerry knocked the burned filling out of his pipe on his trouser leg and then walked to the outhouse a few yards away.

Cliff said to Johnny, "Wait here and keep watch."

The lad knew he need not answer, and he watched Cliff disappear into the darkness of the woods only to reappear behind the outhouse and then dash to its rear wall. He stayed there for three or four minutes and then ran back into the woods. Shortly thereafter, Jerry came out and again, lit his pipe, and walked around the house and up on the front porch. He patted the dog and then sat down in a straight back chair and leaned back against the front wall of the house and began puffing on the pipe.

"Come on let's get out of here while they are watching him," Cliff said quietly.

When the two reached the horses, Johnny asked, "You think they were watching?"

"Jerry thought so. Said he had seen two men slip into the woods across from the house right at dark."

"Bastards!" Johnny replied.

On the way home, they stopped by Sam Brooks' and Aaron Smith's, and told them of a meeting to be held the next night. Each had another person he was to tell and so on.

They agreed to meet at the Methodist Church on Central Avenue in downtown Valdosta at seven o'clock. It being a Wednesday, prayer meeting would bring out the congregation and Jerry had gotten permission from Pastor Ousley to use the basement for a special meeting of some of "God's Chosen Children" while the Bible study was taking place in the meeting hall upstairs. It looked like a good cover.

Cliff had considered having the meeting at his new home, but he was not sure yet about the loyalty of everyone, so he was pleased with Jerry's arrangement.

Wednesday night, while the old piano beat out the notes to

"Amazing Grace," Jerry told the group what he had stumbled across.

"First, Captain Stone came into Mr. Day's office yesterday and asked about having us do an ornamental canopy bed for him. Seems his wife will be joining him for Christmas. Mr. Day told him it was out of the question with so little time and the navy contracts and all, but Stone offered him $100 if he would do it; and Day never missing a chance for an extra $100 agreed, provided Stone would pay up front. Well, Stone told him he would have it by next Friday morning. So, I wandered down to the train station and had Wayne check."

Wayne Flanders then spoke, "Sure enough, a special Military Train is scheduled to arrive 2:15 p.m. on Thursday next."

"So, that will give the good Captain time enough to get his pay Thursday afternoon or early Friday morning and get it to Day on time," Jerry added.

He took a deep breath and then said, "And second, there is a man named Barber from Columbia County, Florida that has a contract to deliver forty green broke horses to the 103rd, one day next week. They are to break them into Cavalry mounts and then ship them to Albany."

"We could use them horses," Robert said.

"Yes, we could," Cliff agreed.

"I have one other thing that might be useful," Wayne said.

"Shoot."

"Today we unloaded several crates of supplies for the Army. Two or three of them had been damaged by water somewhere along the way and Lt. Nash refused to accept them saying the railroad was responsible to deliver goods undamaged," he said and then stopped.

Finally, when he said nothing else, J. M. asked, "Well, Wayne, are you going to tell what that has to do with us?"

"Oh, well, they was full of Yankee uniforms, that's all."

"Uniforms?" Cliff questioned.

"Yeah, both trousers and tunics. One crate a' each."

"What has happened to them?"

"I doe-no' guess they is still in the back a' the storeroom at the depot."

"All right, first Wayne and Robert, right now, go over there and see if they are there, and if so, get them out and hide them somewhere where they won't be found," Cliff said.

As soon as the two had left, he turned to the others and asked,

"Is there any one of you that can't ride out right now?"

"Well, most of us have jobs. What will happen to them?" Jerry questioned.

"Let me rephrase this. Who can ride at a moment's notice?"

Johnny stood up, as did Israel Henley and Dwayne and Sam.

"I know Wayne needs to stay on the job and we need him there, as we do you, Jerry," Cliff said. "I'm not sure about Robert."

"He works for a pulpwood plant, what makes some kind a' paper," Israel offered.

"Well, we'll see when he gets back," Cliff said. "All right, those of you who can jump when we call, wait here, the rest of you move on out," Cliff said, and then he added, "I want you all to understand that I am sending you home without you knowing any of the plans on purpose, not because I don't trust you, but rather because it is best that you don't know anything you don't need to. That way should you be picked up, you have nothing to tell them and you can be honest about it."

This helped ease a little hurt feelings on Jerry's part, as he had not liked being dismissed so abruptly. *'After all, it was my information that brought this meeting on to begin with,'* he reasoned.

The piano was playing *"Bless Be the Ties That Bind"* when Robert and Wayne returned.

"You find them?" Cliff asked.

"Got them outside," Robert said.

Cliff frowned in disbelief.

"There was a one horse team tied up in front of the Holton Hotel and we borrowed it."

"Who does it belong to?"

"Hell, how should I know," Wayne answered. "I didn't go in and ask who owns the wagon I'm about to steal."

"The thing is Wayne, we don't want to, in any way, cause hardship on any homefolk. If we do, it will be real hard to have them cover for us when we need them."

"Yeah, I forgot."

"We'll, take it back," Robert said.

"What about the uniforms?" Wayne asked.

"Unload them and bring them down here first, then take the wagon back," Cliff ordered.

"All right, all right, don't get in a stew," Wayne said as he started up the stairs.

Looking over the uniforms, Cliff was well satisfied. They were soiled all right but not any more than those that had been worn by a man on horseback for a week or two.

"Here, find what you need that will fit, take it with you and be at the water tower at Stockton tomorrow morning at sunrise," he said to the others.

When he had found trousers and tunic for himself, he rolled them in a piece of canvas he found there in the basement and headed upstairs.

"Brother Ousley," Cliff called out as the man was walking out the front door beside a very thin young man. The two stopped and turned back around.

"I have a small contribution to make for your congregation," Cliff said and handed the minister a roll of bills tied with hemp twine. "It was good of you to oblige us so."

The man unrolled the bills and counted out forty dollars. "My, so much!" he responded.

"I could tell, even though the good sister, whoever she was, did her best, you need a new piano," Cliff said.

"Mr. Brown, I want you to meet John Henry," he said indicating the young man beside him.

Cliff offered his left hand to the man who he judged to be ten or more years younger than he. "John Henry," he said as a greeting.

"John Henry Holliday," the young man said. "Better known in some circles as the good sister who plays the piano."

Cliff looked surprised and then laughed, "I guess the joke is on me."

"Yes, we stole John from our brothers over at The First Presbyterian congregation on Hill Street. I heard him playing at a funeral that turned out to be for his brother Francisco. I was so impressed that I agreed to help him get into The Valdosta Institute, if he would come and play for us," the man said and placed his arm around the very thin lad.

"You made a good deal."

"I think so."

Their conversation was interrupted by the report of a large caliber weapon being discharged and shortly thereafter some men running by.

"What has happened?" the minister called out to one of them.

The man called back as he ran, "We're after a thief who was driving a stole' wagon and we shot him."

"Did you hit him?" Cliff yelled.

"Don't know; he ran this way," he man said as he continued into the darkness.

"Excuse me, Brethren," Cliff said. "I need to get with my people before they all go home."

"What were they doing here?" John asked when Cliff had disappeared around the building.

"Masons," Nathan Ousley said back. "They are Masons and they held a meeting in the basement tonight."

"Oh," the younger man said as he stepped from the front porch and walked around the house in the direction Cliff had disappeared.

"I think it is Wayne they are shooting at," Holliday overheard Cliff saying to the other men there, and he stepped into the shadow made by the tall chimney.

"We'll spread out and see if we can find him," Johnny Gaston said.

"No," Cliff replied. "We can't afford to have any of you caught, too. If Wayne is all right he will know to stay hidden. It's best for us to slip out of here as soon as we can, they might start a house-to-house search."

John Henry listened, but did not make his presence known to them. When they were gone he stepped out from his place of concealment and rubbed his chin with his palm. *'I do not believe these men are of the Masonic Order,'* he thought to himself.

Wayne Flanders made it back to the railroad depot, but once inside he collapsed. The mini ball had hit him in the lower back two inches in from his side and passed through the right kidney before busting out of his body and striking a wooden barrel, practically filled with nails in front of Crawford's Store. Spent, it rested there on top of the nails.

"Damn that Reb Brown. If 'n he hadn't made me take that wagon back this would never have happened," were the last words he said before he passed out.

The next morning "The South Georgia Pioneer" ran a small column, on the front page:

Railroad Clerk Found Dead At His Station

It is believed clerk Wayne Flanders interrupted a burglary and the men who had broken into the depot killed him before they stole a wagon, to haul away goods also stolen from the depot. Unfortunately, they escaped despite a vigilant search by the Military Authority and a citizens group led by young John Henry Holliday and others of the N.E. Methodist Church. Mr. Holliday was quoted as having said, "We followed a trio of coloreds across the tracks and into the quarters. We first saw them when they fled past the back of the church grounds. Two were carrying a long crate," he also informed the *Pioneer*.

Cliff and his six men were at the water tower in Stockton before dawn the next morning. Each was dressed in Union Blue over their regular clothes.

Everything was going as planned, but a few things were bothering Cliff. He realized they had all fought in the war, but none had fought with him. There were courageous men on both sides and some that were near yellow, too. He had no way of knowing how these men would act when the chips were down. Another thing that bothered him was, none had forage hats or issue leather and all spoke with heavy southern drawls. Still he knew their loyalty was to the homefolk and he hoped that would be enough.

When engine "Number 7" pulled up to the woodpile at Stockton, the uniformed men climbed aboard from the left side. The engineer saw them but assumed they were part of the guard that had stepped off to relieve themselves while they were stopped.

The train consisted of the engine, two passenger cars, an animal car, and a heavy mail car painted black.

Reb was sure the payroll would be in the mail car. He also was relieved there was no caboose.

The terrain between Stockton and Valdosta is mostly low rolling country with a lot of swamp land for the first one third of the trip, especially at the Alapaha River[13] bridge and it was there Cliff wanted to take the mail car but Robert could not get the hitch pin to

---

13 Alapaha River: A small tributary of the Suwannee

release, so they waited. The next good spot would be much nearer Valdosta, where a fair sized sand hill rises a couple hundred feet then slopes back into the five mile run into downtown Valdosta. As they approached this location, he and Robert both pulled on the pin until it was free thereby disconnecting the passenger cars from the animal car moments before they topped the hill.

"Robert, as soon as we stop rolling, drop the loading gate and get all the horses out. Saddle up seven, and if there is more than seven have them bridled so we can take them with us. There might be one or two men in that car so be ready when you enter it but wait until we are inside the mail car. I don't want you to alert those back there with a gunshot."

"Can do," he replied and then followed Cliff back up the ladder to the top of the car where the other men waited.

"Dwayne, go with Robert in case he needs help," Cliff said and then he turned to the task at hand and knocked on the door of the mail car with the stock grip of his Colt.

"Open up, it's Captain Brown."

"Sorry, Captain, we ain't supposed to open until we get to the depot."

"Don't you think I know that?" Cliff replied. "But the animal car has taken on some smoldering soot down into the hay and unless we get you uncoupled soon you're going to burn to death with it," he paused and then added. "The train is almost stopped now and we need to get uncoupled before it stops completely and I can't do it by myself."

The three men inside tried to look outside but could see nothing of what was ahead as the tracks are straight as an arrow at this point.

"I don't see no smoke," Harp said to the other men, "but the train is stopping and I don't plan to burn."

"All right," Corporal Kelly agreed and he pulled back on the heavy dead bolt that secured the thick door. As soon as the door cracked Cliff and Johnny hit it with their shoulders and caused it to knock the Corporal down.

"You ain't no Captain," one of the soldiers said.

"Not in your army," Cliff replied as he stuck the barrel very close to the mouth of Harp. "Now remove your leather and tunics and drop those hats."

The train was now traveling about ten miles an hour and he told Israel to help Sam get the side door open.

When the sliding door was fully open, he ordered the soldiers to jump.

"We could break our legs!" Harp protested.

"You could stay here and then they would bury you with two good legs and a hole in your head," Cliff said.

Harp jumped first and was soon followed by the other two.

The cars came to a stop within another two minutes and Cliff saw the big door drop from the animal car. Two blue clad men came down the ramp followed by Dwayne who held a nice new looking Remington revolver on them.

"Have them drop their leathers and hats and then send them down the tracks to meet up with their buddies who should be about a mile back."

"You bet, Reb," Dwayne answered and right then Cliff realized a huge flaw in his plan.

"Get these animals out as soon as you can. You never know when that engineer will realize he has lost half his load."

There were nine horses in all and Robert had them all saddled and ready.

"Bring three back here," Cliff said and then turned his attention inside. "And how are you coming?"

"We found a strong box. I reckon that's it," Johnny said. "Want I should shoot the lock open and have a look-see?"

"No, here be some keys!" J. M. yelled.

"See if you have the right one," Cliff said to him.

The third key he tried opened the padlock and after removing the heavy chain that circled the box, they lifted the lid.

"Ye-haw hi!" Johnny yelled at the sight of the greenbacks.

"Lock it back and bring it with us; be easier to carry it that way," Cliff said.

"Shit!" Kelly said and spit at the ground as the five men watched the robbers ride north into the timbered countryside.

Number 7 pulled into the depot on time and it was not until Captain Ford stepped onto the rear platform that anyone realized they only had half the train they started out with.

Ivan Poe, the engineer, said he noticed they picked up speed a few miles back but figured it was the downhill slope that caused it. A week later Poe was out of a job and enroute back to Ohio.

After riding north for two miles, Cliff turned east and paralleled the railroad tracks until they came to a big swamp. Entering this, they released the extra horses and crossed back to the tracks and then continued east on the railroad bed until they came to the river. There they moved into the shallow water and followed the Alapaha in its meandering course to the southwest. A few miles later they climbed the east bank and entered cleared land. The farmer was only a few yards from the location where they came into his field, and a contact was unavoidable.

"Damn Yankee troops ain't welcome here," Allen Carter said raising his hoe in a threatening gesture.

"Hold on there, Mister," Cliff said. "Despite what we may look like, we ain't no Yankee soldiers."

"Well then, what are ya?"

"We're a group a' homefolk that borrowed these here uniforms fur a spell, but there might be some, who wear these blues on a regular basis, following us."

"I reckon you don't sound like no Yank at that," the young man replied. "Come on over past the house and mix in with my cows yonder," he said pointing to ten scrub cattle that were in another field just west of a cypress swamp. "If 'n you travel through thar I'll move the cattle around a bit and it will cover up your tracks. Make it a might harder fur anyone to follow."

Cliff could see the tall trees of a good size swamp beyond the field where the cattle were and welcomed the help.

When they rode past a small cracker house, a young woman, perhaps in her late teens, came to the door and placed her hand above her eyes to shade the sun in an attempt to get a better look at the trespassers. Cliff touched the front brim of his forage hat as he passed and she thought the gesture strange, coming from a Yankee officer, none the less she spit off the porch in his direction showing her disapproval of Occupational Troops crossing her land.

Entering the swamp they cut sharply south and then back west into the river and again south another two miles before coming out and heading west.

'If anybody is able to track us this far, it will take them half a day and by then we will be long gone,' he thought.

When they hit the road to Statenville, Cliff pulled up and said to them, "We are east of Lawyer Dasher's land and I am inviting you all to come home with me, and let's us celebrate; but it's up to you."

Israel, who lived only a few miles from J. M., decided to go home. J. M. said he wanted to check on Marty but would be on down around dark. Sam also wanted to go home and check on his wife but said if all was well he, too, would be down. Dwayne, Robert, and Johnny chose to go on with Cliff. He gave directions for the two to follow him and the others split off at this point.

Cliff went due south for another six miles and then turned west until he hit the road to Belleville. Following it a ways they cut back into the timber, skirting the small village, and headed straight for the Withlacoochee which runs almost due south at this point. From there they followed the river until they found a place where deer had created a crossing and they moved over to the other side and then followed it back to where the river bends once again westward. A mile further they came to his new land.

"Let's remove these blue coats before Nadine spots us and sends lead our way," he said to the others.

She had indeed seen the riders but they were far enough away she couldn't make out anything about them so she took the Winchester and slipped into the hammock behind the barn. Addie stayed inside and prayed.

When they finally rode up Nadine came out of the woods with the Yellow Boy over her shoulder. "Howdy boys, new in town?" she said jokingly.

"Depends," Cliff replied "on how much you charge?"

"How much you got big boy?"

"A bunch," he said to her and dropped the heavy chest to the ground.

"Yee haw!" she yelled. "How much is in there?"

"I don't know, but I betch-ya', it's a bunch," he said sliding off the horse.

"By the way boys, this purty rifle-toting woman is my bride."

"Ma'am," they said at nearly the same time, except Johnny who felt he was almost family, just slowly nodded.

"Come on inside and let's count it," Cliff said as he picked up the box with one hand and wrapped his other arm around his wife. The box was heavy enough that he had to use his thigh to help carry it along and each time he moved that leg forward it pained him a little, a pain he enjoyed.

Once inside he introduced everyone to his mother and then got down to some serious work.

"By the way, Honey, I've invited everyone who went with us today to come by and celebrate tonight. I think J. M. will be here later and also Sam Brooks and his wife.

"Oh, great, so now I have to go to work cooking," she said jokingly.

"Not just yet, first we count."

They arranged the greenbacks into nine stacks, each containing fifty twenty-dollar bills.

Also in the chest were some papers marked:

Colonel Northrop
Private Do Not Open.

Cliff laid out eleven stacks, each containing five bills. The remainder he had put back into the strong box and locked it once more.

Then he opened the first letter. It contained instructions for Col. Northrop to meet Rex Barber at the old Micco Town site. Cliff knew it was near the state line on the road to the Jennings Station. The rendezvous was to take place the morning of December the fourth, upon which he was to purchase 40 horses at a price of not greater than $12 a head, and then only if they met his approval.

The second letter concerned the Colonel's wife being sick with yellow fever in Jacksonville; and the last one contained the military records of the men who had sworn the oath that night in Gunter's Mill, along with a letter of authority to apprehend and hang each of the men. It was signed by General Sheridan, Commander of the Army.

Cliff folded it and placed it with the money stacks.

Johnny asked, "What's in the letters?"

"I'll share them all when the others arrive."

Addie at first took the news of company as an unwelcome chore, but soon was busying herself about making bread and two pies from a large can of peaches Cliff had bought at Gunter's Store a few days before.

Nadine had taken the buckboard over and bought two chickens from Granny Keeling, who promised to come to the party if her grandson would come and pick her up. When Nadine returned, she wrung the heads off the hens and gave them to Johnny to pluck, while she put on a large pot to boil.

Sam and his wife, Esther, arrived just before dark in a Doctor's buggy he had borrowed from Mr. Mose Smith, a man he had once worked for.

They built a large bonfire in a sandy area in front of the barn, and just after dark they heard the sound of human voices followed shortly by the cry of a child. In a minute or less all could see a wagon coming up from the trail. When it arrived, Cliff recognized the whole Gunter family, J. M. and Tillie and their two children and Mary Ann and her three, and in the back on a moss mattress lay Marty.

"You don't know how good it is to see you, Marty," Cliff said.

"You don't know how good it is to be clear a' that store," he said back, grinning.

Soon the women were busying themselves around with the cooking and the gossiping, while the men gathered out around the Gunter wagon where J. M. produced a jug.

The kids were running and playing without anyone paying much attention to them except when one would get hurt and start to cry, and then Mary Ann would take a switch to whoever was the culprit and then there would be two of them crying. However, there was too much fun to be had this night to waste time on crying, and all too soon they would be back in the thick of it again.

The women had put together a good big pot of Pileau and everyone filled their stomachs, and then added more.

Finally, the men went inside. Mary Ann put the children to bed on blankets in the back of the barn and then joined the other women outside to clean the dishes and get in on the talk.

"Here's the deal, boys," Cliff stated. "I counted the money and found nine thousand, two hundred and twenty dollars in the money box."

J. M. whistled at the news.

"I have divided it up like this, there are twelve stacks, each contains

$100, one stack for each of us who took the oath. The rest we'll keep for operating money. Does that sound all right to you, Marty?"

"That's good thinking, Reb. Too much cash will only bring suspicion on us."

"That wus my reasoning and we'll talk about that some more in a few minutes," Cliff replied then he walked over to the box and opened it.

"There was also three letters in the box addressed to Colonel Northrop."

"One is personal, concerning his wife's failing health. I would like to get this to him, but just can't figure out how to do that without him finding out we have the other two."

"The second one is concerning that herd of horses Jerry told us about. It gives locations and dates, so I think we will intercept them. It will give us fresh unbranded mounts when we need 'em, and now we can get rid of any we have with US brands," he said then, taking a deep breath first, he read the third letter. When he had finished, he waited.

After a long time, Robert broke the silence, "Where did they get our military records?"

"I'm sure the Federals gathered everything when they took Richmond. This just goes to show you how little privacy we have anymore," J. M. said.

"I want a' see mine," Sam said.

Cliff handed him the sheet. After reading it he replied, "Well it's purty accurate."

Cliff then handed each the sheet containing the record with their name on it.

Again a silence fell over the group.

Finally, Sam, who was the oldest man there, spoke. "Well, I guess it's kind a' shocking to ya' to find out your country wants to kill you because you disagree with their right to steal. It sure is to me."

Israel, the youngest, spoke next, "Hell, I weren't in the army but six months and then the war ended. I never even fired a shot at nobody."

Dwayne was the next to speak, "I tell ya' what this says to me and that's somebody done up and___and that's the gospel___a' it"

Cliff, feeling sure he was following Dwayne's line of thought, picked up on it and added. "Dwayne is right. There is or wus a spy among us, and we need to find that individual and eliminate him."

A murmuring among the men began.

Cliff stopped this by continuing "There is no possible way they would have gotten everyone's name exactly right without someone who was there that first night, giving it to them."

"Reb's right and I want to be the one what cuts Danny Faux's throat," Johnny said.

"If it turns out to be Danny, you can have the privilege but what about Jay Shaw. He wus there, too," Marty reminded them.

"You know this puts me to mind of what happened to Dick Force." Sam said "You remember him, Reb?"

"Sure, he was that little kid that run off and joined the 9th Georgia when he was just 13 or 14. What about him, where is he anyway?" Cliff asked, "I haven't seen him since I got back."

"Dead, been dead since right after you left."

"What happened?"

Sam moved over a little closer so he wouldn't have to speak too loud and still everyone could hear him correctly as he didn't relish telling this tale twice. "It were back in '66 alright. Dick and his sister wus in Valdosta fur something and___."

"It were his step-sister, Thannie." Israel said.

"Sister, half-sister, step-sister, what the hell difference do it make now." Johnny murmured just above a whisper but Israel heard him and lowered his head embarrassed.

"Maybe J.M. should tell it, being Thannie is his niece." Sam said.

"Well, again it don't make no difference, but she is Tillie's niece on the Smith side, not mine; but no Sam you go ahead, you tell things clearer than me anyway."

Several of the men nodded their heads.

"Well alright, it seems Dick and Thannie were in Valdosta fur something and a smart ass nigger bumped into Thannie, kind a' vulgar like."

"You remember Reb, Thannie's got a fine set a' lungs and that Darkey done up and took a feelly a' one a' them." Johnny injected.

"Sam's telling this." Israel said suddenly getting back at Johnny for his earlier comment.

Johnny just nodded his head and looked hard at the younger man.

"Well, anyway, Dick grabbed the Darkey by the throat and whispered something in his ear real polite like about showing respect for his sister. About that time, a colored Sergeant what some call the Black Dutchman, bowed up and it almost came to fist-a-cuffs there for a minute between him and Dick. I reckon the only thing what saved it wus Doc Parramore's steppin' in and ushering Dick Force and Thannie on into his office which they wus in front of, and everybody thought it were all over, but not so. The next day, they come and arrested Dick saying he assaulted a Freedman and took him away and locked him up in Mr. Griffin's store, it wus what they were using as a stockade at the time, but as they were taking him in, Peggy Griffin saw him and asked what he was being arrested fur, and Dick told her, "They said I choked a Darkey, so here I am." Well, Peggy is a feisty little thing and she said loud enough fur everybody around to hear, that she wus going to choke three or four of them black buzzards, and if they tried to arrest her she would have her Daddy put all of them out, on account it was his building they were using as their stockade. This just riled a big Sergeant they call Bacon, I don't rightly know if'n that's his real name or they call him that on account a' his big belly. Anyway he had his men put her out at bayonet point. When word a' this got around it riled a lot a folk, and since it were Mr. Griffin's building, he knew of a' old door that wus mostly growed over with wait-a-minute vines, what lead into the root-cellar under the very room they were holding Dick, and a couple a' nights later they sprung him and had Rex, his favorite horse there, and he made his liberty right out of the county."

"The state, he went down to Little Cat Creek in Madison County." Johnny added.

"Well I didn't know where he went but he did get free, only they put out a reward on his head. Then a few months later after it had quieted down, Thannie decided to have a private birthday party fur Dick and sent word fur him to come home on his birthday and kick up his heels for a few hours.

"He should a' stayed in Florida." Johnny said.

"Sam's telling this." Israel said again and once more Johnny cut a sharp stare at him but said no more.

"That's the truth of it, Johnny, he should a done just that, 'cause right in the middle a' the party while they wus playing the Virginia Reel the house was surrounded by the Black Dutchman and a passel of his Colored Troops and they ordered him to come out or they was going 'a fire the house. Dick knew if he didn't do it a lot of his family and friends might get hurt so he walked out the front door with his hands high, but he didn't get ten feet from the porch when one of them blasted him with a revolver and Dick fell gut shot. Doc Parramore and even the Federal surgeon tended to him during the next few months, but it weren't no good, there wus too much poison on that 44 ball. He lay up suffering for nigh on six months 'afore the Angel a' Mercy came and took him home."

"Pure cold-blooded murder." J. M. added.

Richard Sam Force
1847 - 1866

"It were fur shor." Israel agreed. "Poor Richard weren't but 19 year old at the time they buried him."

"Who is this Black Dutchman?" Cliff asked.

"He ain't here no more, they sent him back up north, soon afterwards, and all them what wus involved." Sam explained.

"Sounds like them," Cliff replied. He then asked, "Who all knew about that party?"

"None but those what wus there."

"In that case there had to be a scalawag in the party," Cliff said twisting his head to the left as he spoke.

"There were one there, Danny Faux." Johnny said strongly.

"How do you know that?" Israel questioned the short man.

"On account I was there myself. I come with Dick, we rode in together from down at Granny Keeling's."

"That do put a shade on Faux, I admit." Cliff offered.

"Reb's right and I want to be the one what cuts Danny Faux's throat." Johnny said.

"As I said before, if it turns out to be Danny, you can have the privilege but what about Jay Shaw, wus he there too?" Marty asked.

"Yeah, I reckon he wus at that." Johnny admitted.

"And he wus at th' meeting at the mill, too." Marty reminded them.

Several of the men nodded their heads.

"There's one more possibility," Cliff said.

They all looked to him waiting for his thought.

"The scalawag may be on this here list. Put there to throw us off, should this paper ever fall into our hands."

This time it became so quiet they could hear the women talking outside by the fire.

"One thing is for sure. It ain't safe for any of us to be seen in Valdosta no more." Cliff said. "In fact I don't think you should even go to your homes." He paused and spit before continuing, "I bought this land here and there's plenty a room for everybody to come and build them a home, right here. We can start us a new community. Change our names and just drop out of sight as far as the Federals are concerned, except when we hit them, and then we'll disappear again."

"What about my grits mill and Marty's store? We can't just up and walk away from all that," J. M. said.

"Better to lose your goods than your life," Cliff said.

"I don't know." J. M. said still shaking his head.

His brother then spoke up after clearing his throat, "I'm in no condition to do much a' anything, but if you fellows will help me, you know I will help you all I can."

"I'll help you, Marty; what is it you want us to do?" Israel said immediately.

"I want you to go back to the store tonight and bring every blame thing you can get in my wagon and then we will make another run tomorrow night. We'll leave the women there to keep it open as long as we can, so as not to give away what we are doing, but I'm taking Reb up on his offer."

"Marty, we will take some of the money we got today and buy all your stock and put it up here. Then everyone will be welcome to whatever they need, when they need it. It will be a community store and you can run it, only instead of charging us, you just keep a tab," Cliff said.

"I think we need to let the women folk in on what we're doing," Sam said.

"Of course, you're right," Cliff agreed. "Go get them, will you, Sam?"

When the women were all inside the barn, Cliff read them the third letter.

"Oh, my God," Mary exclaimed placing the back of her hand in front of her mouth.

"Be quiet, woman," Marty scolded, and then he took the lead and told them what had been decided.

Mary Ann began to bring up reasons why it would not work and finally Marty again said strongly. "This ain't put ta' ya' fur no asking. We brung ya' in here to tell ya' what had been decided; now stop your bellyaching and put your minds to work on how you can best help the cause."

"Well!" was all Mary Ann said in reply to her husband's rebuking.

The next morning, Cliff asked Johnny, "Do you think you can find that farm over near Statenville whar' we cut across his pasture?"

"I reckon so."

"Good, I want you to take this to him and tell him we are obliged for his help the other day," Cliff said handing him one of the greenback bills he had taken from the strong box. "Tell him to be careful where he spends it though."

Cliff had learned that John Henry Holliday's father, "The Major," was living north of Troupville near the Bemiss Plantation and he arranged for Israel to give one of the same to John Henry.

Monday morning found Cliff and six of his men again dressed in Union uniforms waiting in a patch of pine to the south of Micco Town on the Jennings Station road.

Cliff was pretty sure they were in Florida, and thereby would be less likely to run into troops from Valdosta, had the information on the horses arrived there by some secondary means.

It was near the ten o'clock hour when the sound of many hoofs pounding on the sandy road came drifting in from the south.

Cliff sent Johnny back north a half mile to keep a watch on their backside, while he intervened with the wranglers.

Moving south in a column of twos, the blue clad soldiers headed out.

Just around a bend in the road less than a mile away, the herd could be seen emerging through the dust cloud.

Looking over the men approaching, Cliff spotted a large man who seemed to be giving the orders to the others and turned his mount towards him.

"Good morning! Mr. Barber, I presume," he said saluting the man.

"That's me, Yankee boy," was the reply he received.

"I have a letter here as introduction," Cliff said handing him the letter addressed to Colonel Northrop. "The Colonel authorized me to give you scrip for the horses; you can get it changed into cash at any federal post office."

"Not a chance," Barber replied, just as Cliff had thought he would. "I'll not take the word a' any Yankee officer. It'll be gold or hard cash or these horses will be headed back for Columbia County."

"Well, all right," Cliff said and they began to look over the animals. When satisfied, Cliff paid him in greenbacks and the two parties headed in opposite directions.

Barber leaned close to one of his fellow riders and said as they were riding south, "That there Lieutenant, must be a scalawag, he's got a Georgia accent if 'n I err' heard one. Can't stand a man who'd turn on his own state like that." The man shook his head and spit before he added, "I'm glad to be rid a' the likes a him."

They moved the horses into the Alapaha River, and continued north. All the rivers in the area were quite shallow due to the lack of recent rain, and for most of the way the water was never over the horses' knees. At times it was dry altogether, but finally Cliff found a place where the bank was not too high and other animals had made it a crossing, and it was there he took them out.

Cutting out ten head, he had the boys run them back into the river and up the other bank, across a field and then into a shallow swamp, then turned them around and headed them back again regrouping with the main herd.

He knew this would not stop a good tracker, but it would slow down most, and he didn't figure the Colored troops from Valdosta had any good trackers. He was wrong.

They arrived back at the home place an hour before sundown and let the tired horses enjoy the tall grass of the cleared land.

It gave Cliff pleasure to think of paying for the Yankee mounts with the money that had been taken from the Yankee payroll.

The next day he asked Sam and Dwayne to herd four of the horses that they had taken from the train back to the river crossing and turn them loose there, as a possible cause of the tracks one might find at that location.

Sunday morning, the eleventh of December, found Addie Brown and Granny Keeling in the buckboard on their way to the Church at Mt. Horeb Crossroads some four miles down the road. Tillie and Mary were following in their wagon with all the children.

Nadine and Esther had stayed to make the food for the men who were putting the roof on a house for J. M. and Tillie.

The first home to have been built at the new location was for Marty and Mary; they had moved into it earlier in the week. When finished with this roof, they planned to begin construction on a cabin for Sam and Esther.

Johnny was living with his grandmother down the road a mile, and Israel had chosen to stay at home with his folks, believing their need for him to be home was greater than the threat of arrest, a decision he would later regret.

Although Mt. Horeb Baptist Church only met on the second Sunday of the month when the parson could make it, there were six regular families who attended the services there faithfully, all related to Granny Keeling in one fashion or another, and with the coming of these new folks, the church congregation doubled in size.

Cliff had not thought it a good idea for others to know of their being in the area but there would be no keeping his mother from church, and with her went the other women. He eventually could see the futility of his argument, and accepted this as a matter of fact. He and Marty may command the men, but no one truly commanded the women.

It was pointed out to him that between their new home and Madison, some fifteen miles away, there was not one living being that had not supported the cause during the war, save some Freedmen, and every reason to believe the home folk would still be supportive of anyone who opposed the occupational governments and the hated carpetbaggers. Cliff did appreciate their reassurances.

Later that afternoon, Nadine accompanied Esther to her old house to pick up some items she had left behind when they moved away so suddenly a few weeks before.

The Brooks' house was located about three miles east of where they now had settled but on the other side of the river, just a little south of Belleville.

They planned to drive up to a place Esther knew of that was near the cabin and then wade across the river to the house, that way no one in the village of Belleville would see them.

The trail they were following had at one time been a stage road, but after that run had been stopped, it was mostly abandoned, except when Sam and Esther used it as a cut over to Granny Keeling's. It had also been the route the men had used when bringing the horses in earlier in the week and was now well defined.

They parked the buckboard a quarter of a mile off the road along the riverbank almost directly across from the Brooks' house. Both cried out a little as the cool water covered their feet and legs when they first stepped into it, and then began to giggle. Once inside the old house, the two women looked over several small personal things that Esther wanted to have with her, and gathered those in their aprons.

It was just as they were getting back to the buckboard and trying to dry off their feet and legs, when Nadine noticed the old horse pick up his ears and begin staring in the direction of the road. She placed her hand on Esther's forearm to stop her from talking. Both women suddenly froze when they saw, there on the old Belleville Stage Road, several horsemen following a man who was walking.

Taking a deep breath, Esther asked, "Can you tell who they are?"

"I can't see them well enough, but from the noise they're making they got a' be military," she replied. "That one a' walking must be a tracker."

"Oh my God," Esther exclaimed. "They're tracking the horse herd. The men won't have a chance in hell a' seeing them coming. They're all up there working on that roof back in the hammock."

"Come on," Nadine said and she jumped into the wagon without bothering to put her shoes on.

The Yellowboy was in the floorboards at their feet, and she

grabbed it and laid it barrel down against the spring seat between them and covered it with her skirt.

"Can you shoot?" she asked the older woman.

"If I'm close enough I hit pretty good, but I don't have a gun with me."

They were now moving towards the road across uneven ground and Nadine didn't want to let the leads get loose in her hands so she simply said. "When we get behind them, I'll give you my Colt."

"You're carrying a pistol?"

"Yes, I have one in my purse," she said back without looking at her friend.

By the time they reached the road, the soldiers were a half a mile ahead and Nadine opened her purse and removed the little revolver. "Here, hide this and let's pray we won't have to use it." Then she slapped the leads on Henry Roosevelt's back and the old horse picked up speed.

When they caught up to the soldiers, she called out, "You boys new in town?" like she had so many times before when troops would arrive in Kansas City during the war.

Immediately the six riders stopped their business and looked back at the approaching white women.

"If you have ever seen a whore in your life Esther, it's time for you to remember how she looked and acted, and do the same," Nadine whispered as she drove among them finally stopping beside a tall blonde officer.

"Well, now, Captain, what on earth are you boys doing so far off the beaten trail?"

"Lieutenant, Ma'am. I'm a Lieutenant not a Captain," he said back.

"Well, you look like you ought a' be a Captain," she replied and leaned forward enough so her ample breasts could be glimpsed by the young officer who sat on the horse beside the wagon.

"Gosh, aw', we're tracking some horse thieves," he said.

"Oh really? Not in our part of the woods, I hope," she said back smiling.

"I'm afraid so, Ma'am," the Lieutenant responded, and then asked, "Where are you two going?"

"Pastor Smith, up the road a few miles, said he needed some money to build a new place to worship, and we thought we would drop by and add a small token to his collection plate. We don't cotton to Sunday morning services, you know," Nadine said back.

The story made sense to the officer, knowing soiled doves often paid well to churches hoping to buy some forgiveness for their transgressions, but he suspected the good pastor was more likely to be paying these two rather than accepting their money.

"I do hope you boys will catch them horse thieves soon, then you can stop by Mary Ann's Boarding House, before you leave the country," she said.

Esther was smiling at a big black sergeant who had moved his mount up on her side of the wagon. "My, you are a big man," she said.

With the white woman breaking the ice, he allowed a huge smile to come across his face, showing a mouth full of pearly teeth.

"I don't think I know this Mary Ann or her house," the Lieutenant replied to Nadine.

"Oh, it's a boarding house up ahead a few miles, we have rooms there ourselves."

"My goodness, I didn't know single ladies lived in this part of the country. However do you make a living?" he said back with a twinkle in his eye.

By now the tracker had come back and was standing in front of Henry Roosevelt, and she knew it would be futile to try and make a break for it and realized she had no choice but to play out the hand she had dealt herself.

"Oh, Miss Mary Ann, she sells a little spirits from time to time and we work for her. Serving the spirits you understand," she said back, smiling.

"Yes, Ma'am, I think I do understand."

"Well, we need to be on our way, and Captain, I do hope you drop in when you finish chasing the horse thieves. It would be so nice to serve you," she paused and then added, "Spirits, I mean."

"Yes, Ma'am I do believe I will do just that," the young officer said as he motioned the tracker out of the way.

Esther looked back at the big sergeant as they pulled off and said. "You will come too won't you, Sergeant?"

"Oh, yes 'um, you bech'a I be's a' coming too," he said, again showing off his huge front teeth.

As soon as they were a hundred yards away from the soldiers Esther looked back and waved and then said, "I don't think I ever been so scared in my life," then quickly asked, "How did I do?"

"Oh, you did just right. You'd make a fine whore, Miss Esther, a fine whore," Nadine said and then both women burst out laughing.

They went around a tight bend where the road cleared a sinkhole and it was then Nadine dropped the whip on Henry Roosevelt's back, and he jumped as if startled and immediately began to trot, but long before they reached the clearing he was winded and had to slow down.

"Damn," Nadine said "I hope that bunch don't decide to give up the chase of the horse thieves too soon and start on a chase after us."

"I wouldn't worry as much about them as I would about what Mary Ann does when she finds out you been telling strange men she runs a house that sell spirits and other works of the flesh," Esther said laughing.

"I don't plan on her finding out," Nadine continued, "You do understand that, don't you?"

This time they both laughed even louder.

Just as they were coming upon the clearing, Nadine saw a large canebrake rattler crossing the road, and she pulled up sharply and grabbed the Winchester and fired. The slug hit him high just behind the head and he rolled over and then turned towards them flipping his wicked tongue in their direction. Henry Roosevelt started dancing about when he smelled the snake. Nadine jumped from the wagon and took careful aim and fired again, this time taking his head off, and then she quickly boarded and again whipped the old horse until he charged right over the dying reptile.

"Those shots will bring the soldiers on at a fast pace," Esther said.

"I hope when they see the dead snake they understand and I also hope it will also alert our men that there is trouble coming," she said as they came around the little curve in the old road and dashed into the clearing as fast as the horse could pull them.

Cliff had immediately recognized the sound as being that of a 44 Henry report, and he called the men to arms. Only moments before the wagon came into view across the large pasture, he had jumped onto a horse and started out in the direction of the shots.

Nadine only yelled as they passed him, "Yankee Cavalry half a mile back."

He pulled up, looked, and then spurred his mount on back after the wagon. Catching up, he yelled. "Did you shoot one of them?"

"No, I shot a snake, mainly to warn you."

Cliff then charged past them and got the men mounted and into the stand of oaks behind the barn.

Israel and Dwayne, who had been outriders keeping the remuda from straying, herded them north into the stand of pine near the river, and when they had the horses contained and being too far to understand what was exchanging between the women and Cliff; they turned back to see what was happening, realizing trouble was obviously in the making.

When the old horse finally made it to the barn, Nadine pulled him around so they were now facing the road they had just come from, and she stood up on the seat and began to wave. Esther did the same.

The soldiers were just coming into the clearing some three hundred yards away, and immediately upon seeing the women waving, the big sergeant spurred his horse and charged in their direction whooping loudly and slapping his horse with his hat. When the other soldiers saw where he was headed, they too charged after him.

The Lieutenant yelled for them to stop, but there was no stopping them once started and the officer found himself in command of only the tracker, who had by now realized that the horse trail he had been following was also headed into the same clearing. He tried to warn the Lieutenant, but the young man had realized that there were six soldiers ahead of him and he didn't know how many whores worked at 'Mary Ann's Boarding House' and he certainly did not want to be grabbing sloppy seconds to a colored man; so he too spurred his mount and galloped off, leaving the lone man afoot.

When they were little more than fifty yards from the wagon, Nadine reached down and grabbed the Winchester.

The sergeant was looking at Esther and he never saw Nadine aiming the carbine at him, until the puff of smoke burst from the muzzle a split second before the heavy slug struck him in the chest and knocked him off the horse backward.

The other men were completely confused at the action and continued on. One did reach for his revolver but made no attempt to slow his horse.

Cliff now came charging with his men from the woods around the barn with revolvers firing and screaming the Rebel Yell as they had done so many times in years past.

Only the Lieutenant, who was behind the others, realized it was a trap in time to stop; but Israel, who had dismounted, took careful aim with an old Chapman musket and sent a mini ball on a true course for the officer.

In less than a minute, the firing had stopped. Several of the soldiers' horses were running in different directions, having been frightened by the sudden and unexpected gunfire.

After the smoke lifted, Nadine realized one man was missing.

"Reb!" she yelled loudly.

He turned towards her.

"The tracker, he's not here."

"What?"

"The one who was doing the tracking was on foot leading his horse. He's not here."

Cliff, realizing the danger, called for Johnny and Sam to follow, and then galloped off in the direction the soldiers had come.

Tracks of a single horse heading east at a fast pace were plain on the road, and they gave chase.

Sam, realizing the two miles of hard galloping had brought all the horses to little more than a fast walk, pulled up and yelled to the others "Go 'head, I think I can see the river crossing from just over there," he said pointing to his left, "I'll try and get a shot." He quickly dismounted; and drawing his Enfield from a saddle scabbard, he ran to a large water oak, whose branches hung out over the river, and began climbing.

He had guessed the man would take the trail of the horse herd rather than going on to the ferry near Belleville.

Sam, being 59 years old, was not a fast climber. Even so, he reached a large limb that gave him the view he was seeking some two hundred yards away, just as the Negro/Shawnee half-breed entered the river.

He would have to be quick but sure, and he cocked the hammer as he brought the stock up and squeezed off a shot.

The horse was scrambling up the other bank when he fired.

Sam felt he had a good sight picture when the hammer dropped, but he did not see the man go down.

The old trail along the west side of the river was as crooked as a snakes track in soft sand, and although it was only a couple hundred yards down the river to the crossing, Cliff had more than twice that distance to travel before reaching the location. When he finally did, there was no sign of the rider or horse, and he knew his mount was spent. Still he pushed the heaving animal into the water and up the other bank.

The next to cross was Johnny, and upon reaching the other bank seeing Cliff's horse rider-less, he pulled up sharply, looking all about him. Finally, he spotted Cliff standing just off the trail looking down at something behind the exposed roots of a big magnolia, and he knew Sam's shot had been true.

Johnny and Cliff had the dead man lying over his saddle when Sam arrived. "I didn't hear you shoot," he said.

"No need fur me to, some old fat man kilt this 'un," Cliff said back, smiling at Sam. "And a mighty good shot he is with that musket."

"That's a relief; I knew I had a good aim on the bastard but I ne'r seen 'im fall."

"He made it up the bank and into the trees yonder, but he was dead all the time and just didn't know it," Johnny added.

Sam gave one sharp nod of his head as if he was telling himself he was satisfied with his performance, and then he pulled on the reins and turned his mare around for the trip back.

When they approached the barn they could hear Esther laughing.

"What's so funny?" Sam asked his wife who just shook her head and continued laughing. Cliff could see the men there had too been laughing but had controlled themselves when the three rode up with the body.

Nadine, too, was laughing but not as uncontrollably as Esther. Finally she caught her breath and tried to tell the men who still sat on their horses. "Esther just got tickled when she was telling about how we acted like a couple a' whores to lure these varmints in here."

"It weren't just that," Esther said between gasps, "It was what you called this place. I can't wait to see the expression on her face."

"Who's face?" Sam asked.

"Alright, what did you call this place?" Cliff asked.

"She told 'em it was known here 'bouts as 'Mary Ann's Boarding House' and that, among other interesting delights, she sold spirits to the local men," Esther finally got it all out.

Sam and Johnny also saw the humor in it, but Cliff knew that it might bring more friction between Mary Ann and Nadine, and he realized more than any of them, the powder was already there and only needed the fuse to be lit to set off a local war, which was the last thing they needed, all living so close together as they now were.

"Alright, let's gather up all these bodies and get rid a' them 'afor someone finds out what happened here."

"What will we do with 'em?" Dwayne asked.

"Dump 'em in the river," Israel suggested, "Gators got 'a eat too."

"No, someone might find them," Cliff said, "I guess we will have to bury them somewhar'."

"Why not start a cemetery here?" Sam suggested.

Thinking on it a minute, Cliff said, "I think you are right Sam, but I like this idea better. Lay off say a half-acre, yonder on that little slope; it's far enough from the river. We'll bury them around the outskirts of "Our Cemetery" and then plant a small tree over each grave."

"What fur you planting trees___?" Dwayne asked.

"These ole boys a' be good fertilizer for the trees to grow, and in time, no one will be able to dig up any evidence," Johnny told him.

Dwayne began smiling when he realized Cliff's thoughts and added, "I like it, too."

The women returning from church saw little evidence of the battle that had taken place there an hour before. In fact, none realized anything had occurred until Addie questioned why the men were digging in the field rather than working on the roof. "After all, that is the excuse you gave for not attending the Lord's services, ain't it?" When no one answered her, she left in a huff and went inside the barn to change from her best dress.

Johnny Gaston had gathered up all the weapons and ammunition from the dead men and any that could be found on their horses, and was separating it as to weapon type and correct ammo. Then he set about cleaning each of the captured guns that had been fired.

"Miss Nadine," he asked, "Will you boil a pot a' water fur me to use 'a cleaning these guns?"

"Sure I will, Johnny," she replied. "Do you need some help?"

"Oh no, Ma'am. I like doing it. A man can't be too careful with his guns."

"Well, if you like it, how about cleaning mine, too?" she asked him.

"Oh, sure Ma'am, it would be a pure pleasure to clean yourn', Miss Nadine."

Cliff's mother returned just in time to over hear this exchange and again she challenged them, "You men been shooting on the Lord's Day?" she asked with a frown crossing her forehead.

"Mama," Cliff said. "Look yonder at what Dwayne and Israel are doing."

She raised her hand and shaded her eyes as she gazed at the men two hundred yards away. "I can't see what they are doing other than digging holes fur something."

"They're digging graves, Mama."

"Who died?" she suddenly turned and looked around not expecting to see Marty but he was there sitting in a chair in front of his new home.

"We wus attacked, while you women-folk were gone. There will be eight graves over there when they're through," Cliff said. "It were the ole devil he-self, what came a-courting, while you women were gone."

"Lord, have mercy!" she exclaimed then quickly looked at him and then Nadine and then asked, "Any a' our people hurt?"

"No, Mama," Nadine said to her. "We're all alright."

"Praise the Lord," Addie said then asked in the same breath "Did you get 'em all?"

"Yes, Ma'am, thanks to Miss Nadine's quick thinking, we did," Johnny injected.

"I see," she said back and then added, "It is a blessing, that's fur shor'."

The drive to the church house is a full hour trip, and save some leftover biscuits the children ate, no one had enjoyed breakfast; and now the women were busying themselves with a hearty noon dinner.

The normal custom was when a meal was ready the children ate first, then were sent off to play. The women served the men next and while they were eating, they cleaned the plates the children had used so there would be some for them to use, but this time Marty asked to be brought over where he could speak to everyone. "Today, I want the women to clean up the children's plates 'fore we begin and us all et' together. I think we need to realize som'pin and that will take some talking and thinking from everybody here."

The meal was mostly consumed in silence as everyone was thinking, trying to figure out what Marty had in mind with the talk he had proposed to them.

When it appeared most were finished he cleared his throat and said, "I been a-thinking on what words to choose to say what's in my mind and I ain't shor' I got 'em right yet, but here it are. All us men fit' in the war. We knows what killing is all about and there is nothing good about it. Nonetheless, there come times when it be necessary. Like it were here today." He stopped, twisted his neck and took a deep breath before he continued. "You women have been sheltered from most of it, leastwise most a' you have, but here today, right here in our little sanctuary, we was attacked by government troops. Colored men came here fur the purpose a' murdering us men and doing unthinkable things to our women-folk. Thanks to the smarts a' Reb's wife, they lay dead instead a' us."

Again he stopped and gathered his thoughts before continuing. "I think it be time that we realize, every one a' us, that we have as good as declared war on the government and they will mount a campaign to hunt us down and kill us all. They got a', to keep us from talking, and stirring up a fracas." He stopped long enough for what he had said to settle on everyone's mind, and then he continued. "The only way to fight a military campaign is to conduct one ourselves, and that will take us looking at our own selves and seeing what we need to do to protect our home place and when and whar' to strike 'em, whar' it will hurt them the most."

Once more he paused. "Reb yonder is the best at leading in the field a' battle, but whipping 'em in the field don't mean squat," he said and then spit. "Why we done did that, ten year ago, but we lost the war cause we wus out-supplied, and that's the simple truth a' it." Again he stopped, cleared his throat, and took a breath. "We need to learn from our own mistakes. We need to plan everything we do around this here idea. When we raid, we raid to get supplies or the Yankee dollars to buy 'em with. Just like Reb said, we don't never hurt homefolk if it can be helped. We hit union trains, union banks, union stores. We don't attack the army if it can be helped or unless it is as a reprisal. When one a' the homefolk is taken away, like they done Reb's brother, then we find out which soldiers it were and we take care a' them and no others lessen they attack us."

"I also figure we need to get a newspaper a-writing 'bout us, so the folks in Washington a' hear 'bout what's happening around here. Right now all they read 'bout is what the Yankee papers tell them and that ain't even half-truths and you's all know it." Marty stopped and took another breath. "I say the first thing we need to do is make us into a better outfit. We is fit'ing with a military unit, then we need to be a military outfit ourselves, and that means everyone will have responsibilities and will be expected to keep them up. Each man will be given a job, and the women-folk too. Even young'uns' old enough will have a job that's suited fur his learning age. It be the only way we can survive. That ought to be plain enough after what happened here today." Marty again spat into the white sand before continuing, "Well, that ain't all I have to say, but I reckon it's all I can think a' right now."

Again there was a long silence, and finally Cliff spoke "Marty's one hundred percent right. We be damn lucky that we ain't up thar' on the hill burying our own or gettin' buried ourselves. I think Tillie and Nadine should get together and come up with a list a' things needed to be done here everyday, and assign them to us. Mary Ann, if you and Esther will get together and work out things the children can do, we will start a list a' chores and assignments among the men fur ourselves. Everybody work on this, and we will report tomorrow night at supper what we come up with."

And so it began, the next day each of the three older children were given the duties of watching the in-bound trails. Buckshot went east down to where Sam shot the fleeing tracker, Freckles went over to Granny Keeling's house, and Sissy was assigned to go up to the beach and watch to make sure no one came down the river.

Two days later, the morning was half over when suddenly Freckles saw a mounted man approaching from the west and she took off down the little dim trail that cut through the woods to where several of the men were sawing down some red oak trees.

"Uncle J! Uncle J!" she called out when she could see him.

"What is it, child?"

"A man's a-coming. A big man on a big horse. Down yonder to Granny's house."

J. M. and Johnny each picked up a rifle and headed back the way she had come. Cliff and Sam went back towards the barn with their guns.

"If it's just one man we'll have him sure," Sam said "but if he's a scout, J. M. and Johnny might be walking into a nest a' hornets."

"We'll just have to see; we got a' warn the others," Cliff said back.

When the man rode into the clearing they saw he was not nearly as large as Freckles had described him. In fact he was about the size of Stan May.

"I liked to never found that trail this side a' the river," he said as he swung his right leg over the saddle horn.

"What brings you down this way in the middle a' the day?" Cliff asked.

"News, brother, news," Stan replied and reached back and pulled a folded paper from his saddlebag and pitched it to Cliff.

"Why hello, Mr. May," Nadine said coming out of the barn and seeing him.

"Please, Ma'am, don't call me Mister."

"Alright, but remember that means you got to call me Nadine."

"Yes, Ma'am," Stan said back as he dismounted. "If 'n that big fellow you married don't mind, I sure don't."

"He don't mind anything I say," she replied and winked at Stan and gave him a sly grin.

Cliff opened the paper and saw it was the front page of *The South Georgia Pioneer* dated December 11, 1870. The headline in big print just below the date read:

RENEGADES RUN RAMPANT

"What do it say, Reb?" Sam asked.

Cliff began to read aloud, the first column.

> Renegades who are believed to be hiding in the swamps north of the Florida State Line on the Alapaha River are terrorizing the community. Last month they held up a train east of town and stole not only the money and most of the prized possessions of the passengers but also the United States mail, which contained the payroll for the troops guarding our town. If your business is not turning a profit this month, it is because the poor soldiers assigned here have no money to spend in your stores. This past week, these ruthless riders rustled a herd of horses that was intended for the army. Friday past, Colonel Northrup sent out a squad of soldiers being guided by a half-breed Shawnee Indian brought all the way from Atlanta, who has a reputation as an excellent tracker, to guide them in search of these desperadoes. They were to return last night and are overdue several hours now. None of these brave men have been heard from. Their fate is known only to God above.

When he finished reading, he looked at the shorter man and nodded his head, "I'm obliged to you Stan. We need to know what is happening in town and we need to know what they are saying about us. Any time you could get us a paper it will be well received."

"How is Eleanor?" Nadine asked.

"She is not well. She has consumption. At least that's what Doc Ashley said."

"Oh, I'm so sorry. I do hope you can bring her down to see us sometime."

"I will if she's able to travel this far," he answered knowing that it would most likely never happen.

"Have you been bothered, Stan?" Cliff asked.

"Not no more," he said removing his hat and rubbing his thinning hair.

Nadine could see strains of sandy color among the premature gray.

"They come to my work after the train hold-up, but Darcy, my boss, swore I was there all the time and I think they have decided I ain't one a' you."

"I hope you're right, Stan," Cliff said.

"Come on in the barn here, Mr. May." Addie called out when she saw him. "Got some grits still on the coals here keeping them warm for the young-uns' when they come in fur a dinner break."

"No, thank you, Ma'am, I done 'et 'a'for I come down. Mr. Watson sent me down to deliver some dry goods to the widow Robards and I just came on down looking fur you. Is Marty here too?"

"Yes, and he's recuperating as good as can be expected considering that they left him for dead," Addie said.

"Come on, Stan, I'll walk you over to his new house. It's just a good stone's throw through the woods yonder," Cliff told him.

"Good, I got this here letter fur him," he replied lifting an envelope from the pocket in his overalls.

The short walk to the Gunter's house gave Cliff and Stan a little time to talk out of the hearing of others. "Is there any good news in town, Stan?"

"Not much, and I'm afraid this here letter will bring more bad."

"Oh, really? Why is that?"

"Come on. I'll explain it to Marty and then I won't have to tell it twice," he said as they approached the house.

After small talk, Stan handed the letter to Marty. "I wus passing your old store today and I see'd this young woman on the front porch peering in a window. She was right purty too, so I stopped and ask her if 'n I could be of assistance, and she said she wus looking fur you, that she had a message from her father for you."

"I told her you had moved away after them blame nigger soldiers had beat you up and all, and she seemed to get downright sick at hearing the news. So I told her I might be seeing you sometime, and she then sat right down and wrote this here letter and asked fur me to give it to you, when I see'd you again. So, I brung it right down in case it might be important."

Marty opened the envelope and took out a single sheet of paper. After reading it, he handed it to Cliff.

"Is it important?" asked Stan.

Cliff handed him the letter, but when he took it he said, "I went to primmer fur three seasons and I can read some, but I don't read so good."

"It says," Cliff began:

> My father was shot in Savannah by unknown assailants and has passed on, but before he did, he asked me to get certain information to you. I have that information. Can you meet me somewhere soon?

"It is signed J.C. Smith, MD."

"What do MD mean?" Stan asked.

"Well, I reckon it means she is a doctor," Cliff answered.

"No way, not that purty little thing," Stan said. "Besides, she are a girl."

"I knew a woman Judge in Wyoming," Cliff said.

"No way."

"Sure did."

"Stan, did she tell you where she could be contacted?" Marty asked.

"She never said nothing about it, but I suppose she is staying with her mother in Valdosta."

"Sure, that's whar' she is. Do you know where that is?"

"Yeah, over off Ashley Street."

"Reb, do you think you could get into town and meet up with her, without getting caught?"

"I think so, Marty, if I go after dark."

"Do you know whar' the Smith house is?"

"No, not exactly."

"Stan, meet Reb tonight after dark som'ers and take him over and introduce 'im to 'er."

"Sure whar' do you want a' meet, Reb?"

"Let's make it the First Methodist Church on Central Street."

"Alright, 'bout what time?"

"It gets dark early but I don't want to run into any drunk soldiers roaming about town, so say nine o'clock."

"Can do."

"You had better get to the woman first, and tell 'er I'm sending Reb," Marty said.

"Alright. I'd better be a-moving if 'n I'm gon'a get all that done," Stan said and stretched forth his hand. "It's good to see you doing so well, Marty. I thought you wus a goner fur sure."

"Yeah, me too, Stan."

When he mounted, Nadine called out, "Be sure to tell your wife we send our greetings."

"I will, I surely will, and I thank ya', Ma'am."

Cliff lifted Freckles up and sat her behind Stan's saddle. "Will you drop her off at Granny Keeling's on your way?"

"Why, shor'."

Cliff spent the rest of the afternoon breaking a red horse he had spotted the first day they bought them from the Barber bunch. He had been working with him, but this was the first time he had mounted him and it was a long, hard afternoon, but finally a little before sundown the gelding gave up and stopped bucking.

That night, he decided to give him a try and he rode him to town. Nadine was furious for him doing such a foolish thing and told him so, but he left atop the sorrel anyway.

They took their time. Cliff turned east at Gunter's old store and cut across the fields where his father had the run in with the soldiers that night which seemed so long in the past. Then swung up and around the west side of Loch Laurel swamp to Brown's Lake and passed the saw mill his Pa used to own, before hitting the road that went from Valdosta to Jennings Station down in Florida, and entered town from that direction.

'As long as they think we are camped out on the Alapaha, might as well not give them any new ideas should anybody spot me coming in.' he thought.

The clock atop the court house was clanging out nine times as he rode past. He arrived at the back of the church building five minutes later and found Stan waiting.

"I told her you wus coming."

"Good, let's leave our horses here and go on foot," Cliff suggested.

Before they had reached the Smith house, Stan was dragging behind and Cliff realized it was a long walk for a man in his fifties. He was sorry he had suggested it. Stopping, he let Stan catch up.

"I took a hit in the leg when I wus at Fort Fisher in North Carolina."

"You were in the navy then, Stan?" Cliff replied.

"Yes, sir, I were, and damn proud o' it to. I wus a cook, the chief cook aboard The CSS Arctic. A good battery, she were. I nigh on lost this here leg there at the Fort, but a Yankee Doctor at Wilmington saved it fur me and I spent the rest or' the war there in a hospital."

For the remaining two hundred yards, Cliff deliberately let Stan set the pace.

When they arrived, a woman in her fifties greeted them and let them in. The house was a two story affair that showed a good deal of planning in its construction and Cliff was quite surprised that such a fine home would not have been taken over by Carpetbaggers.

They waited in a small but well-furnished room until the young woman appeared.

"Mr. Brown?"

"Yes, Ma'am," Cliff answered.

"My father was very specific that I was to give this information to only Mr. Martin Gunter. I know he has sent you and I know he has been injured but I am not sure I should disobey my father. It was his dying wish."

"I understand, Ma'am. If you wish I could take you to see Mr.

Gunter but, he cannot come here. He has lost the sight in one of his eyes and both of his legs were broken and have not healed well. He cannot walk or sit a horse."

"I did not realize it was that bad," she said and turned away and dropped her head in thought.

After several seconds she raised her head and turning to him she said very straightforwardly, "I will go with you. That way I can deliver the message and not disobey my father, but I suggest we leave now as this message has a time factor."

Cliff took a deep breath and held it before blowing it out. "Ma'am, I will take you, but it is not an easy journey at night and I dare not come to town in the daylight hours these days. I have no wagon or buggy with me or extra horse."

Stan stepped forward and made a suggestion. "I live not too far away. I have a one horse wagon we use for getting our supplies. I could get it and drive you there and back."

"That would be splendid," she replied.

When he was gone, Cliff asked about her father.

"I really don't know who shot him or why, but I suspect it had something to do with what I must tell Mr. Gunter. All I know is he had asked me to get certain information for him, which I was able to do. He then left to return here, and he was shot in the back with a revolver near Richmond Hill and left for dead. Finally, some good people came past where he lay and gave him assistance, but he refused to be taken to a doctor who was nearby. Instead, he insisted he be brought to me. By the time he arrived, he had lost so much blood he died in less than an hour," she said. Then taking her hands and placing them to her mouth she added, "He said to deliver the information to Mr. Martin Gunter and not to anyone else as there was a spy in the bunch."

"I think he was right about that, Ma'am," Cliff said to her.

An hour later a wagon pulled up in front of the house with Cliff's sorrel tied behind.

"Come, we must go quickly as I need to be back before morning for work and it will take a good part of the night to make this here trip," Stan said.

Cliff helped the young woman up on the wagon and then untied his new sorrel, who seemed to be glad to see him.

They arrived after the midnight hour and Mary Ann made no bones about being upset for having to wake up her husband at such an hour, but she did it anyway.

"Mr. Gunter?" Dr. Smith asked.

"Yes."

"Mr. Martin Gunter?"

"Yeah, I'm Marty Gunter," he answered again.

"Alright, I'm sorry about this late hour, but my father was specific in his instructions as to who was to hear this information."

Marty nodded his head and asked Mary Ann to fix some coffee. She did not appreciate that either, realizing it was his way of getting her out of the room. Stan was greasing a wheel that had started squealing after they crossed the river, so Cliff was the only other person there. "I'll wait outside," he said turning and walking out of the room.

Cliff could hear conversation taking place, but he could not understand it until he heard, "Wait a minute." Then Marty called out, "Reb!"

"Yep?"

"Come on back in, this lady has brought good and bad news,"he said as he sat in the straight back, wooden chair with his legs extended onto a wooden crate. "First, Aaron was bringing us news that a train is suppose to arrive in Savannah on December the eleventh. That were today, 'err yesterday. Anyway, this here train will have a hundred kegs a powder and three thousand percussion caps on it."

Cliff digested the information and then offered, "It will most likely be going out today, or tomorrow at the latest."

"How are we gon' a know which?" Marty asked.

"If there is an eastbound today, I can go back on it and I'll send mother a telegram when it will leave, if it has not already gone," Doc Smith said.

"How you gon' a find that out?" Marty asked.

"Just like I did for Father, and that is all you need to know," she said.

"All right, let's just hope it don't run today."

Cliff escorted her out and back to the wagon. "Stan, she has to be on the eastbound this morning."

"It don't run until afternoon. It leaves Pensacola in the early morning and gets here around noon."

"What about a westbound?"

"Naw, they's only got one train on this run. It goes from Savannah to Pensacola and then back. It'll come through here this morning eastbound."

"That sounds good, maybe we have made it," Cliff said.

The wagon was soon lost in the darkness of a new moon andCliff then walked back inside to help Marty.

"Can I help you get back in bed, Marty?"

"Naw, not just yet. I got to ponder on som'pin first."

"The bad news?"

"Yep. The bad news," Marty said "That li'l gal said she was a doctor."

"That is what she said, and I remember Aaron saying she was in Savannah studying fur that."

"Well, Doc Jean Smith said both my legs had to be broken all over and set proper like or I will never walk again."

Cliff cleared his throat at that news.

"You think she knows what she's talking about?"

"I doe'no," Cliff replied shaking his head.

"Me neither."

Late the next day, Jerry rode up and handed Cliff a small folded yellow paper.

Opening it, Cliff read the telegram:

TO MRS. A. SMITH, VALDOSTA GEORGIA.

MOTHER I WILL BE ARRIVING ON THE FIFTEENTH
BY TRAIN
                    STOP

PLEASE ADVISE BROTHERS TO MEET ME
THE PACKAGES I WILL BRING ARE TOO LARGE
FOR ME TO CARRY
                    STOP

YOUR LOVING DAUGHTER, JEAN

                    END

"The train we want is the westbound, Friday," Cliff said and then turned to Esther and handed her the wire and asked, "Mrs. Brooks will you take this over to Marty's house and see he gets it?"

"Marty," she repeated realizing he indicated Marty alone.

"That's right. Just Marty. Do you think you can manage that?"

"It might be a tall order, but I'll manage it."

"Thank you," Cliff said to her. When she turned he had to admire her figure. Cliff assumed she was some ten years older than he, but still she carried herself quite well, and was most appealing *'Were it not for the salt-and-pepper hair, she could be taken for a much youngerwoman'*, he thought. *'Sam's a lucky man, to be sleeping next to her, come these cold winter nights.'* How little did he know, she was twenty-five years old when he was born.

The little group of families came to the agreement that Martin Gunter would be the overseer of the group as a whole. J. M. Gunter would organize all supplies and staples. Reb Brown would be in command of all military functions. Israel and Dwayne would be in charge of all horses and vehicles. Robert Maycomber would be responsible for all gun powder, percussion caps and lead for making balls. John Gaston would be responsible for seeing all weapons were properly cleaned and oiled after each firing. Presley Gunter would take care of the chickens. Freckles, Buckshot and Sissy Gunter would be on watch post. Sam Brooks was to hunt for game. Mary Ann and Tillie would do the cooking of the main meals. Esther would bake the bread and pies when available, and Nadine would be in charge of coffee and all the cleaning of the camp site.

Cliff was up two hours before daybreak and had a pot of coffee boiling on the small campfire when Johnny arrived.

"All the guns ready?"

"You bech-um' bossman, and I took special care a' yourn' too."

"Johnny, you don't know how much it helps just knowing everybody's guns will work when called on. I sure can't say I saw that during the war."

"I like seeing to it. I like guns. They's the best tool a man ever come up with and when Colonel Colt thought up the revolver, it put a stop to the bullies a-ruling the world; now even a man my size can say his piece without fear of being bullied by some big no account."

"I hope we can put a stop to them here in Lowndes County."

"We will, Reb, just you wait and see."

"I hope so," Cliff replied before taking a sip of the hot brew.

Robert, who had slept over in the back side of Brown's barn came out stretching and yawning. "You boys done right. The smell a' this here mud a' biling done pulled me right ought' a' the sack."

Cliff poured some in a blue porcelain cup and handed it to him. "I was just asking Johnny about his guns. What can you tell me about the powder and caps?"

"We's in fine shape on powder right now, but caps is another thing. I do hope that train is carrying some."

"Well, if our information is good, it will be."

"I do hope so," the tall man said again nodding his head, as if agreeing with himself. His old slouch hat still carried the red cord of the artillery unit he once served with and moved up and down as he moved his head.

"What kind a cannon you had during the war?" Johnny asked.

"The outfit mostly had twelve pound Napoleons, but I was assigned to a Brooks Gun," the lanky man replied.

"That used to scare me. When I heard them big guns thundering, I'd start a-praying," Johnny said as he became lost in memories.

One by one the other raiders came to the little fire and began to check over their gear.

"There being no moon, we'll have to wait 'til near dawn before we head out," Cliff said looking at the eastern sky for any sign of purple, and seeing none he then added, "The women folk made up some corn-dodgers fur us to carry, so get what you need to hold you over till we get back." He paused and then said, "And that is likely to be late in the day."

Each picked up a few of the little round bread balls and stuffed them in one place or another, and in doing so each secretly realized that these could be the last earthly food they might eat, should things go wrong this day.

The north wind had picked up after midnight and the temperature was dropping steadily.

Cliff had earlier, at the first signs of cold weather, asked Nadine to cut a slit in an old wool blanket and sew it so as to prevent unraveling around the neck hole. This made a fine poncho, not unlike the one he had been issued while wintering in the mud huts in Dalton, Georgia back in January of '64. Several of the other men had done likewise to their blankets, but all had not enjoyed the craftsmanship of a good seamstress, and some of the neck holes were ever so slowly becoming larger as the winter moved on.

"Boys, better bring your blankets with ya', it looks to be turning into a cold one," Cliff said.

Two of the men who had not thought to bring theirs, left the fire, to do as told.

Just as they prepared to get underway, the women came out one by one to give a parting farewell to their man, all realizing some may not return.

A light mist began that quickly wet the robes they wore, and soon the women had to return to shelter. Nadine hated this part of the affair more so than the long hours of waiting. Tears began to fill her eyes as the single column of six mounted men, each leading a spare horse, disappeared into the darkness.

They made their way east and then south along the river bank to Sam's crossing, as the place where he had shot the tracker had become known. There they crossed the Withlacoochee and moved east avoiding Belleville. After a mile they cut back to the old stage road where it wound around a swamp. It was a true winding road, as its engineers simply followed old Indian trails who had followed game trails. It made curves around them rather than cutting down the large trees or filling in sinkholes. They would wind around a big oak and then past another sink and so on, but none the less, the route was steadily bearing east.

Good light found them in a stand of tall pines where Cliff stopped and rested the horses. There had never been a sunup, as the low clouds raced by headed into Florida at a high rate of speed, leaving them with a steady drizzle of cold biting rain.

"There are many ways a man finds misery in this old world, and cold rain rates right up there with the best a' them," Sam said as a steady stream of water ran from the brim of his slouch hat in front of his face.

"I'll take cold rain to hot steel any day," Robert replied as he rubbed the old wound he had received in his leg, when a Yankee Hotchkiss canister exploded against the limber from which he was removing shells. That had been in Tennessee, and he had escaped capture by playing 'possum when the blue coats came by gathering prisoners after the battle. For nearly eleven hours he had laid conscious with a two-inch piece of steel in his thigh without making a sound. Finally, he passed out from the loss of blood and when he awoke, he was in the back of a farm wagon being taken to a local man's home to heal. It was two months before he was well enoughto slip through the lines and get back with his outfit. A script had already been sent to his mother saying he was dead and the Provost Marshall had listed him as a deserter when he didn't show up for the muster roll call a week after the battle. Such was the life of a soldier in gray during those days.

Upon reaching the Jennings Station Road, they turned north into the wind. The rain now was hitting them in the face and each man pulled his hat down as low as he could to stop the stinging water from cutting into his skin.

Skirting the east side of the village of Melrose they turned due east again on an old Indian trail that Cliff and his father had used long ago to log out a large cypress swamp for the mill.

When they reached the new railroad bed that the Atlantic & Western Railroad was laying between Live Oak, Florida and Lawton, Georgia, they turned back to the northeast on the spur, which allowed them to pick up a little speed in their drive.

Four hours later, they could see the DuPont Station ahead and here they left the roadbed and slipped into the lowlands on the east bank of Suwannoochee Creek, and then up to the tracks just west of the DuPont Station. It was there they waited under the trestle.

The rain was now steady and not an inch of their clothing was dry. The winds had picked up and was at times gusting to the point that no one could see more than a few yards in front of them.

Finally, at twelve minutes after two, they heard the train whistle sound off in the distance announcing its arrival to the attendant at DuPont.

Robert, who had planted a keg of powder under the ties at the east end of the trestle, waited while the other five men removed their slouch hats and replaced them with the blue kepis that matched the blouses they wore. It was here they had to drop their blankets, but by now these had become only heavy water soaked wool coverings.

Robert watched the men ride up the steep bank and down the tracks towards the sound of the locomotive. He kept a cigar lit under his blanket just in case he had to blow the bridge. It was also his responsibility to make sure the horses they had left behind did not wander off in the rain.

Cliff approached the engineer and fireman who were just finishing filling the engine with water. There were also two men on the ground who were preparing to load a fresh cord on the woodcar.

"I'm mighty glad I reached you in time," Cliff said to the engineer.

"What's the trouble, Lieutenant?" he asked, seeing the shoulder bars Cliff had taken from the dead officer's tunic a week before.

"Storm has taken out two of the supports on the bridge over the Alapaha River. We tried to wire you, but the lines are down back a ways," Cliff said trying hard not to allow his drawl to be too evident. "I left some of my men there to try and get them back up."

"You will need to either remain here," which he knew they would never do, "Or at least leave your heavy cars behind."

"Hell, Lieutenant, the engine is the heaviest car we got."

"I realize that and if you have enough speed up you can probably get it and maybe one or two more cars across, but if you try to bring this whole train across, the bridge will surely collapse," Cliff said back, then asked, "Are you carrying passengers?"

"Yes we have two passenger cars."

"Well, I would suggest you drop them until the bridge is fixed. I sure wouldn't want to be responsible for killing a bunch a' passengers."

"We can't do that, there is a military freight car and a caboose behind the passenger cars."

"Well, I have told you of the danger. If you go on and get a bunch a' innocent people killed, I'll have to be a witness against you at your trial."

The engineer began to rub his chin with the palm of his hand. "It's fifteen miles to that bridge; I can leave the cars at the Stockton Station just before I get to that bridge. I don't understand why I have to leave them here."

"Here, there is a place for them to stay overnight. Don't you know the hotel in Stockton burned t'other night?"

"No, I haven't heard that."

"Well, it did," Cliff said sternly and then finally added, "It's up to you as to what you do with your train and passengers, but the freight belonging to the army goes no further than here."

"I'll have to drop my caboose then and I need that caboose."

"Alright then, help me unload the freight belonging to the army and you can be on your merry way to do your murder, if you are of a mind to, but you ain't going to destroy government property. If I have to put a ball in your stubborn head, I will. Now what is it to be?"

The man wanted no part of the labor unloading such a cargoinvolved, but he realized the young officer was set on keeping it there, finally he said, "All right, Jones, you and Mills go on back and uncouple the last two cars. I think I can get up enough speed to cross that bridge with this here engine and three."

During the uncoupling of the cars Jean Smith watched from the train window as the Lieutenant was giving instructions to one of his men, and she smiled at Clifford.

Cliff had told Israel to slip back and let Robert know to let the train pass.

An hour later they had Jones, the station attendant, and Virgil Koons, who had stayed with the caboose, tied up in the depot and were using the railroad's luggage wagon, to carry off the load of munitions.

Engineer Meigs, upon stopping at the Stockton Station to take on wood and water asked about the condition of the bridge. The attendant looked at him as if he were crazy. "We ain't had no storm through here," he said. "Just a few hours a' rain like this."

With a questioning expression he turned and looked at the hotel, which was standing as strong as the last time he had taken on water and fuel here.

When the boys reached Tom's Creek, they unloaded the contraband from the wagon and placed it on the pack animals they had brought with them, pushed the wagon off into the creek, then headed south into Florida before turning west towards home.

It was the next morning before pursuit was underway and the rain from the day before had erased all tracks. The soldiers didn't even find the wagon in the creek.

It was full dark when the tired men rode into the clearing of their camp. The flickering of the small fire was the only signal they had in the black air, and even while riding across the open field they did not see the other horses until they were a few yards away from them.

J. M. was riding night herd and they passed within fifty yards of him and neither saw the other.

"Halloo, the camp," Cliff called out when they were a hundred yards out.

"Come ahead if you love Dixie," he heard Nadine call back.

She ran out to meet him and walking back alongside his horse she asked, "How did it go?"

"Unbelievable. Just like clockwork. Even this stinking rain worked to our advantage."

"You got the caps then?"

"We got the caps, powder, a thousand 58 caliber mini balls and never fired a shot."

"Yee-haw!" she yelled.

The rain stopped before they had finished unloading the pack animals and while they were sitting around the fire eating Pileau, Cliff said, "You know, when I was in the Rockies I wanted Pileau something fierce, but right now I'm getting mighty tired of chicken anything. Too bad the Yanks ain't got no cattle to steal."

"The Yanks don't, but there is a fair size herd being raised down to Madison," Johnny said. "I see'd it when I went thar' to see my Ma last week."

"You know who owns them?"

"No, but I can find out."

"All right, tomorrow, we'll go down there and see if we can buy a few head," Cliff said.

Tillie said, "Hey, I could use some salt and flour and beans and a lot of stuff."

"Yes," Esther agreed, "we all need a few things."

"Alright, we'll make it a day. Everybody make a list a' what is needed and we'll go," Cliff said to everyone's delight, except Mary Ann.

"I'll have to stay here and watch over Marty," her voice was depressed even when she added; "I'll get Tillie to get what I need."

No one offered a suggestion otherwise. A day without her complaining would be welcomed by the other women.

The fifteen miles to Madison took almost six hours as they traveled on very unimproved roads and trails, used mainly by men on horseback, save when the pickin' season was in full bloom.

The town was a square with the various merchant shops surrounding it and the big court house on one corner. The main east-west corridor was the Old Spanish Trail or Base Street as it was sometimes called in the town. The main north-south street was Range and it was the road that went to the old Spanish Mission of San Pedro.

Tillie and Esther wanted to go directly to Inglis General Store which was down by the tracks on Second Avenue, but J. M. thought they should first take the wagon over to Beasley's Blacksmith Shop and have the axle looked at.

Nadine went to Steven Brown's Boot Shop to have repairs made to the riding boots that she used extensively while they were coming to Georgia.

Harris' Store had a small, wooden rifle shingle hanging from the porch roof signaling he sold firearms, and that is where Sam, Cliff and Johnny headed.

While there, they ran into Sheriff Montgomery, a mulatto who Johnny knew since he was appointed to the office.

"Hello, Johnny Boy," the sheriff said.

"Hi, Sheriff David, I see you were appointed again," Johnny said back.

Cliff and Sam moved away from the two.

"Yeah, nobody else wanted the job," the large man said, "I heard about your Pa. That was sad news."

"It were at that," Johnny agreed.

Harris' Store on South Range Street
Madison Florida 1870

The two continued with the small talk for several minutes. Cliff noticed the lawman giving him glances from time to time while they talked.

Cliff and Sam walked over and spoke to a man who had been arranging cans on a shelf, "Do you have shells for the Henry?"

**Portrait Of Sheriff David Montgomery In Early 1870'S
Known Locally As The Carpetbag Sheriff,
Originally From Long Island, N.Y. Appointed To Madison, Florida
By The Reconstruction Government**

The man, who looked to be in his middle, perhaps early fifties, with a balding head and long turned down mustache, nodded his head before answering. "Yep, we do, but can't sell them to ya."

"Why is that?" Cliff asked immediately not liking the attitude of the man.

"Got us in a new Smith and Wesson made revolver what shoots the Henry Cartridge, and we will only sell them with the gun," he replied and then turned away.

"Well, let me see the gun."

"The new Smith and Wesson sells for $19.25," he said without turning back towards Cliff.

"I'd like to see it," Cliff said strongly.

A moan came from the man who obviously was annoyed by Cliff's request but he stopped what he was doing.

"Alright, but please be careful with it," the clerk said lifting a box from behind the counter and carefully setting it down before removing the top. "People who buy firearms new don't like to have them all scratched up."

Cliff who had been looking at the gun raised his head and eyes back up at the man. His facial expression was stern and contained a stare that caused a cold chill to run up the older man's spine. When satisfied he had made his point, Cliff looked back at the revolver. The frame was larger than his Colt and the barrel as long, but it had a fine balance and he thought '*The stocks are rather crudely shaped and its general appearance is purty ugly, still,*' he held it and took aim, and was impressed with the way it felt in his hand.

"You say it takes the same round as the Henry?"

"Yes, sir, it does."

Seeing no loading gate he asked, "Where do you load it?"

"It opens at the top, there with the hinge," he man said pointing to the pin.

Cliff lifted the hinge pin and the barrel immediately fell downward exposing the fully open cylinder.

"It is very fast on loading and unloading," the man said as the salesmanship suddenly overcame his arrogance.

"How many boxes a' shells do you have?" Cliff asked as he laid the revolver back into the hard paper box.

"Only four," the clerk replied.

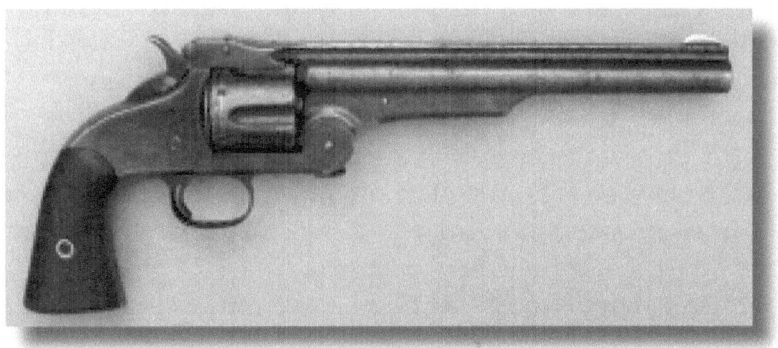

**Smith & Wesson Model 3 Single Action Revolver
Chambered in Henry's 44RF Cartridge**

"I'll take 'um, along with the revolver," Cliff said.

"Oh sir, I'm sorry, I can only sell this for cash, Union cash, no confederate."

"You got a holster fur it?" Cliff asked ignoring his statement.

"Well, no we have only some used military leather that the soldiers trade in."

"No matter," Cliff said. "Figure it up and order me ten boxes a' Henry rounds. I'll be back in a month or so to pick 'um up."

"But, sir, with the ammunition this bill will come to over twenty-five dollars."

Cliff laid two twenty dollar redbacks on the counter, "I'll take my change in cash," he said and paused while the man stared at the paper money, then added, "Union cash, no Confederate."

The clerk, looking at the two bills, swallowed hard. He had not seen anyone with that much cash in over ten years, except for Mr. Inglis of course. "Ugh, yes, sir. I think I can find that much in change."

When they left, the sheriff walked over to him and asked, "What did he buy?"

"That new revolving pistol, and he paid fur it with cash!"

"Let me see the money."

The clerk handed him the two twenty dollar bills.

David Montgomery looked at the bills printed by the Bank of San Francisco. Satisfied they were not greenbacks, he returned them to the clerk.

"Is there something wrong with the money?"

"Not that I can tell," Montgomery replied without looking at

Harris. He eased over to the window and watched Johnny walk down the street toward the barbershop, while the other two headed towards their horses. "Wonder where he did get that money?" he asked himself just above a whisper.

Cliff placed the boxes of cartridges and the new gun in his saddle bags, then they mounted and rode on south to Inglis' store.

"I was surprised you paid cash money fur a gun when we got so many off them dead soldiers," Sam said.

"I like handguns what shoot the same round as my rifles, and besides, that clerk needed taking down a notch or two."

"Well, Barney Harris has always been a stuck up rascal, ever since his uncle reopened the store," Sam said. "I always wondered where he got the money to do that."

"You know him, then."

"Yeah, I been knowin' 'im fur a long time," Sam replied, remembering how Barney had tried to court Esther after her first husband had been killed. "Never had much use fur 'im though."

Jerry Homer had been one of the first young doctors to come and settle in the area, long before it became known as Cotton King Country, and was well liked by most of the people around. His pretty bride was barely seventeen when they moved to San Pedro in 1833. During the Indian uprising three years later, their cabin had been attacked. She had been shot in the lower back with an arrow, a wound that would forever make her childless, and Jerry had been hit in the head with a war club. Both were left for dead, lying outside their burning cabin. Sometime later, Homer awakened, and mustering all his strength, he tended to her wound and then carried her to first one neighbor and then to another, only to find them also burned out. Finally he realized the peril they were in, and headed north to the only house made of stone block on the Old Spanish Trail, some seven miles away, collapsing within twenty feet of the house. When they were found she was still unconscious, having lost considerable blood, and he was dead.

There had been rumors during the years after his death that Doctor Homer had left a large sum of money. It had been reasoned since he came from a wealthy family in South Carolina and he had bought a full section of land when he first moved there, he surely had money, and since none was found on his body, it must be either buried or she had it. In less than a year after his murder, Esther had several young men callers. Some intrigued by her beautiful face surrounded by long brown hair, and others more interested in her supposed fortune. Sam had always thought Barney Harris had been one of the latter. Barney was only a teenager at the time and five years younger than she, and he had always seemed to shy away from honest work. At least Sam had thought so.

When Sam, a small farmer from Georgia, won her heart three years later, no one understood what became of the fortune.

Nadine and Esther were near the side window looking at a roll of linen cloth that had little yellow flowers printed on it, when their men entered the store. Cliff thought of how much they had bonded in the last few weeks. *'I guess the experience they had with the squad a' soldiers must 'a given 'em a feeling of partnership,'* he thought and then let his eyes move from one to the other. *'Strange, except for the age difference they sure look a lot alike. Both about the same height and weight and both carried their figures so well. They could be mistaken fur sisters.'*

"Well now, what have you two been up to?" Sam asked.

"I got my boots repaired," Nadine replied holding up the petite brown shoes.

"I was just looking at this fabric," Esther said "Isn't it so pretty?"

Sam looked at it unable to visualize it as anything other than a roll of cloth, but replied "Sure is, Honey. Do you want some of it?"

"Oh, don't be so foolish. You know very well, Sam Brooks, we can't afford such. I was just admiring it."

Florida, like Georgia, was under martial law and no truly free elections were allowed by Congress. All positions normally held by persons selected by the people, were appointed by the Governor, who was appointed by the President. A Freedman, or a white man, who could prove he had been loyal to the Union during the war, could be elected to an office, but of course there were very few whites in Madison County that could prove such, or dared to do so if they could.

Madison, however, did not have soldiers stationed there as in Valdosta; the nearest were in Tallahassee some fifty miles west.

Although it was about the same size as Valdosta, it had much less crime and rebellion, and the absence of Colored Troops was the reason most gave for this statistic. The majority of the land of any great value had been taken shortly after the war and occupied by rich investors from the north. Only the dirt farmers were left in the county to dig out a living from the soil, and because of these small facts, it was a much better place to get supplies than towns in Georgia.

An exception to the poor farmer was Captain John Inglis, an English born Scotsman, who had offered his services to the Confederacy and who had used his knowledge and enormous business sense to rise from the poverty of a defeated people to that of a successful businessman in a few short years.

Sam had never heard a good southerner ever say a harsh word about Captain Inglis and all were proud of his accomplishments.

While the women continued to purchase staples and order other necessities not found along the wilds of the Withlacoochee River, the men headed south to look at the cattle.

They stayed over that night, camping by the small lake just east of town, and early the next morning headed north with the three wagons now being pulled by newly purchased mule teams. The men herded two white bulls, sixteen cows, one boar and two fat sows; and in one of the wagons were a dozen more chickens for Presley Griffin.

Sheriff Montgomery had questioned Johnny about where they were now living, but Johnny only told him, "Still in Georgia, near Valdosta."

Christmas Eve found the men burning several logs in a shallow pit that had been dug for this purpose. When the logs were down to amber coals they placed a blanket of wet palm fronds over them; a small steer was wrapped in wet burlap before being lowered into the pit, and then once more a covering of palm fronds before they filled the pit over with sand.

Christmas Day dawned bright and sunny, and before noon the temperature had reached the high sixties.

Robert Maycomber had gone up to Albany to put some flowers on his father's grave, and it was just after the noon hour when he returned with news, "The Freedman's Bureau has opened an office in Albany."

"What's that?" asked Mary Ann.

"It's a new bunch a' Yankee Carpetbaggers who the Federals have sent down to see that darkies get all our jobs. If you even got a job today, which most don't, they's taking it away and giving it to the niggers, and they outnumber whites 4 to 1 in Dougherty County."

"When is it ever gon' a stop?" Tillie asked shaking her head. "I never owned a slave in my life and neither did any a' my family, but we are the ones who are being punished for something rich folks done."

"Both North and South," Sam added.

"Yes, both North and South," Tillie agreed, "I went to Philadelphia once and I saw several rich Yankees with slaves they owned to do their housework."

Nadine looked at them and said, "I grew up in Missouri and there were slaves there. Not many, but some, but I never knew folks up north had slaves, too. I thought it was just down here on the plantations."

"Not so. Many a slave was bought and sent north to work, just as they were here, but you'd never know it from the Yankee newspapers," Cliff agreed.

"I got 'a say you're right, Reb. When I was young I used to go down to St. Augustine, Florida with my Pa, and they would unload blacks there to sell at the auction. I never saw a single ship unloading them that was from the south. It was always a sailing ship from New York or Boston Harbor that brung 'um in, but you never hear about that anymore."

"This Freedman's Bureau being so close could be a bad thing for what's left of our way to make a living," J. M. said.

"Well, I know this is bad news, but it is Christmas and I think we should think on better things," Esther said standing and brushing off her apron with her palms, then she turned to her husband and said, "Sam, quit your grumbling and dig up that beef and let's see if it's done yet."

That night after supper and the children had gone to bed, the men gathered around the fire while the women cleaned and washed the cooking utensils.

"I been thinking about what Robert said," Marty began. "If it is as bad as I understand, maybe we ought a' pay them a visit."

"What do you got in mind?" Israel asked.

"I been thinking if 'n their building wus to catch a fire up thar, it would take a while longer for them to get organized, and that would let homefolk keep their jobs a mite longer."

"That sounds good to me," Robert said.

"Wait a minute," Cliff interrupted. "I know Albany has a special meaning to Robert here, 'cause it were his home and all. Several a' us wus sent there to take the oath after the war, which still is a bitter pill to swallow for some, but Albany is nigh on a hundred miles from here. We don't know the roads as well. We don't know the hiding spots, we don't know who can be trusted and who might be willing to turn us in fur a reward, should we be needing hiding," he said. "I don't like it. I think we got plenty a' work right here in this area that needs a-tending to."

Suddenly they heard the echo of Granny Keeling's hound barking and the sound wasn't his ordinary bark.

"I think somebody's a' coming," Sam said.

"You are right," Johnny agreed. "Ole Tatter don't bay like that lessen he's got a coon a-treed, or a stranger is about."

Israel ran towards the water bucket, but Cliff stopped him. "No time to put out the fire. They done smelled it. Get your gun and go stay with the women. They'll need help if things go wrong out here."

Cliff laid his Henry down out of sight beside the old log they had been sitting on near the fire, and put his new revolver next to it. Then he turned to Sam and said, "Stay here with Marty and me and look natural."

"Unless there's a passel a' them, we'll be able to handle 'em, I think."

Minutes crawled by that seemed like hours as they waited wanting to look but daring not to.

Marty, who was sitting in the chair that they had brought out for him, was facing the trail that lead to Granny Keeling's house. Cliff and Sam sat with their backs in the direction the intruder was coming and both had their hands on revolvers under their coats.

"Two riders coming in slow," Marty said. "One big fellow and a smaller one."

Still, they waited another hour long minute with their backs to the possible death riding their way.

Cliff heard a lever cycle and knew Nadine had the Winchester now aimed at one of them. *'I just hope everyone ain't aiming at the same fellow,'* he thought.

"You still see just two?" Sam asked.

"Yep, two's all that's out in the open."

"Seems ta' me these jaspers would have something better to do on Christmas night," Cliff said, knowing conversation was somewhat of a nerve dampener compared to silence in a situation like this.

Finally, a voice called out, "Halloo the camp."

Immediately, Cliff recognized it and stood and turned. "Damn, Stan. You had us a might jumpy there," Cliff said looking past his friend at the smaller rider. Then he asked, "Is that you, Miss Smith?"

"Yes, Mr. Brown, it is," she replied.

When the two dismounted and walked into the light, she removed her hat and shook her hair loose. It was then Nadine realized she had her sites on a woman, and she lowered the carbine.

"Who is that?" Addie asked.

"I'm not sure but it's a lady with Stan May, I think."

"No lady would ride astride a horse. It's downright indecent," Addie snapped back and suddenly Nadine knew what her mother-in-law had held against her these many months.

When the light of the fire fully revealed their faces, Cliff could see Stan was most stressed.

"What is the matter, Stan?"

"Eleanor, she's dead."

"What?" Nadine said as she approached.

"She's dead. She's gone."

"Oh, you poor dear," she said.

"Tell us what happened, Stan," Sam said as he handed him a cup of coffee.

"No, thank you, I don't much hanker to coffee, but I will take a snort 'a 'shine l brung with me if 'n it won't offend."

"Of course not," Nadine said. "You just sit down and take that drink. It'll do you some good."

"I come in on Friday," he began, "from my post, expecting to get my pay. I had it coming. I needed some money fur a Christmas chicken for us," he said and they could see tears building in his eyes but he fought them back and rubbed his nose with the back of his hand.

"Well, Darcy, he's the foreman, he told me I had been replaced and fur me not to come back Saturday," he paused to rub his nose, "I wus shocked. I done them a good job thar'. Well, anyway, Darcy said Roosevelt Jones wus replacing me." He coughed and spit into the sand and rubbed it in with his boot toe before continuing. "I couldn't believe it. Roosevelt Jones is a darkie that can't read or write. I ain't big educated and all, but I can read and write some and you need that with my job. I mean myself, I ain't so good at reading a' loud." Again he paused and this time he took a long swallow from his jug and then he wiped his mouth with the back of his hand. "Anyway I got so mad at that damn Yankee when he grinned at me, I just hauled off and busted his front teeth plum out, and then I run out a' there."

"It wus a' hour a'for I remembered I didn't get my money owed me. So, I went back but Johnny Messer told me I had better get, as they had a warrant out fur me for assault on a government man."

"I was so mad that I went down to that little Tiger behind Miller's Store and commenced to get drunk. I didn't want to go home and have to tell her I lost my job and here it were right at Christmas."

By now 'most everyone had come out from where they had laid ready to ambush the intruders, and were standing around the man in a circle listening to his story.

"I finally went home, and when I got there, the house was burned slap down and my dog was dead, laying there in front in the sand, shot in the face, and when I looked around I found Eleanor out back. She had a bad wound to her back and she wus coughing up blood so bad. I just held her, and she keep saying "Stan, I can't breathe," and I didn't know what to do, but hold her. Finally, I thought of Doc Smith and I carried her there, but when I got her there, she was gone."

"She had been stabbed in the back," the doctor said, "I think with a needle bayonet."

"Bastards!" Sam said harshly.

"I thought it best if I accompany him here. He's really more upset than he's letting on," Doc Smith said and then turning to Marty added, "and it's about time for me to be looking after your legs too, Mr. Gunter."

Marty grunted but gave her no other answer. Instead he said, "I reckon, it's the same here as in Albany. We need to hit this Freedman's Bureau and hit them hard."

"That's the name Darcy used," Stan said suddenly looking up at him. "'Freedman's Bureau.' He said, The Freedman's Bureau done ordered me to be replaced."

"I'd say we got work right here at home," Cliff agreed.

That night Doc Jean Smith stayed in the barn with the Browns. The next day when the men rode out she began to work on Marty.

The four men waited until Darcy left the building and was on his way home. Just before he turned onto Center Street, Cliff stepped out from behind a large mulberry bush. He was wearing one of the frock coats he had taken from the Union officer and had the collar turned up and his hat pulled down low over his forehead. "Got a Lucifer?" he asked, startling the man.

"Err no, I don't smoke." But it was by then too late for him to escape as Cliff was within arm's length and he quickly stuck the long barrel of his revolver in the man's stomach causing him to cry out at the sudden pain.

"You attract attention, Yankee Boy, and they will be notifying your widow a' the funeral date."

"Ugh, ugh, what do you want?"

"Move," Cliff said pushing the revolver deeper into his middle causing him to step backward off the street.

As soon as they were out of sight of passers-by, Cliff stopped and Darcy began to threaten him, "Do you know who I am? I can have you shot for this."

"I know full well who you are, Yankee Boy, that's why I picked you out."

Suddenly Darcy's courage fled him and he felt weak in the knees. "I have some money in my billfold here."

"Put your hand in your coat again, and you're a dead man," Cliff replied cocking the 44.

"I, I, I don't know what you want."

At that moment, Sam dropped a croaker sack over the man'shead and whispered into his ear, "You make another sound and I'll escort your widow to the funeral."

It was then Drake Darcy's bladder failed him.

They tied a rope around his neck securing the sack and then lead him off to a waiting wagon. Two miles out of town just off the railroad tracks they stopped and placed him on horseback and then moved west along the tracks for half an hour before easing into the timber. The moon, being almost full, gave a wonderful silver glow to the forest floor as they moved in deeper, finally stopping at a large white oak.

They removed the rope and lifted the sack almost off his head leaving just enough to keep him from seeing anything except what was below him.

When his eyes adjusted to the moonlight, he saw a long single barrel shotgun pointed at him.

"What do you aim to do?"

No one answered him.

Cliff moved in behind the frightened man and slipped the noose over his head again and slowly pulled the sack off.

Everyone else had moved into the shadows where their presence could be seen, but not recognized.

If you turn around, I'll slap this horse," Cliff said sternly.

"What do you want?" again Darcy asked.

"Last Friday, you and your pals burned Stan May's house and bayoneted his wife to death. I want to know who was with you."

"I, err, I, I had nothing to do with that."

"That is what I told you he'd say," Sam called out. "Why we fooling around, we know he done it. Let's just hang him and get on home. I want some a' them cold catfish Ma was a-frying when we left."

"No, no, I really didn't have nothing to do with it."

"Who did, then?"

"I can't tell you. They will kill me if I do."

"Come on, Reb, let's get it over with," Johnny said getting into the spirit of the scare, not realizing he had used Cliff's name.

"Well, I guess it has to be. It don't look like he's gon'a talk," Cliff said after gritting his teeth over what his friend had revealed.

"No. No, I'll tell you what I know," Darcy said.

"I reported the beating Stan May gave me to Colonel Northrop's command."

"You trying to tell us soldiers killed the woman?"

"Well, I don't know. You see Northrop sent me over to the Civilian Department at the court house."

"The Civilian Department?"

"Yeah, that's right. Mr. Tidwell's office."

"John Tidwell?"

"Yes, John Tidwell."

"Now, that's better," Cliff said, pleased that his old enemy was mixed up in another murder, then he added, "Someone had to show them where the May house was," Cliff realized that was not necessarily so, but hoped it would cause Darcy to expose himself. It did.

"I err, I did show them where he lived, but then I left. I don't know what they did. That is, I didn't know until the next day."

"Well, you might have just saved your life Darcy," Cliff said "How you answer this next question will determine whether you swing here tonight or not."

"Oh, my God. Please, anything. I'll tell you anything."

"Who rode with you to May's house?"

"A Corporal Bacon and four of his men."

"Then it was the army."

"Well, no, not really."

"Either they are or they aren't," Sam said.

All this time Stan had been pointing the shotgun at the man on horseback and Cliff saw he was now raising it up to his shoulder taking aim.

Cliff moved between Stan and Darcy before he said, "Speak quickly, Darcy. I can't keep them from killing you much longer; your only chance is to come straight with us."

"I am. I am. What I mean is them soldiers are not under the army as such. They have been assigned directly to The Civilian Department. They take orders from Mr. Tidwell not the Colonel."

"I want their names."

"Oh God, I don't know. Ugh, ugh, one was called Moses. I heard the sergeant call him that. I never heard no other names."

Cliff then slapped the horse on the rump and he took off with Darcy screaming at the top of his lungs. Only when he fell several yards away, did he realize the rope had not been tied on the other end. Cliff quickly caught the mount and they soon were on their way back to Valdosta.

"How we gon' a find this Corporal Bacon and Moses?" Johnny asked.

"If we can't find them tonight, we will soon enough, since you told Darcy my name was Reb."

"I never said___"

"Yes, you did," Sam disagreed.

"No, way."

"Yes, Johnny, you did," Stan confirmed.

"Well, I didn't mean to."

"I know, Dwayne did the same thing back at the depot in Stockton."

"Why didn't you hang him?" Stan asked changing the subject.

"I should have, but it just didn't feel right. Not tonight. We got what we came for," Cliff said and then they all stopped talking about it, but Stan did not stop thinking on it.

When the courthouse clock was striking two o'clock, Cliff Brown was searching through the desk in John Tidwell's office. He did not find what he was looking for, but he did find several papers that were most interesting and he took them.

It was breaking day when they rode back into camp.

The following Saturday was the 31st and being the last Saturday of the month, the sworn band gathered at 9:30 a.m. for the scheduled meeting.

Marty had planned after the prayer to begin the meeting by having Cliff read the letters he had found in Tidwell's office, but Stan May had slipped into Valdosta after midnight and placed flowers on the spot where Eleanor had fallen. While in town, he had caught a boy selling copies of *'The South Georgia Pioneer'* and paid him the three cents for one. When he opened the paper, the headlines read:

Renegades Kidnap Official

This then became the topic that was being heavily discussed before the meeting began and it only seemed fitting to continue with it.

"It do appear we are beginning to attract the attention of the authorities around these parts, don't it?" he suggested before asking Stan to share it with the others.

"I read purty good to myself, but not to others. How about having Reb do it," Stan said aloud.

"Reb, will you?" Tillie asked.

Cliff took the two pages of news and looking down for a quick scan; he then cleared his throat and began:

> Renegade Riders, who have for several months terrified the decent people of this community, have struck again. This time by kidnapping Drake Darcy the foreman at the Valdosta Turpentine Mill on Hill Ave. Mr. Darcy was taken by twenty armed men to a swamp on the Withlacoochee River in Brooks County and there hung. Had it not been for the hand of God reaching down from the heavens and snapping the rope just in time, Mr. Darcy would today be receiving his just reward, walking the streets of gold with his heavenly father. This is not the first time our good people of Lowndes County have been terrorized by this bunch of cut-throats. A week past they robbed The Express at DuPont Junction killing two soldiers and making off with arms and munitions to further their raids on the innocent. It was believed they are hiding out in the

wilds along the Alapaha River, but now seem to have moved west into Brooks County and are working from swamps that often border the Withlacoochee River. These men are so hideous in their crimes that no decent woman is safe outside her home after dark. Several people including our own troops have simply disappeared after coming face to face with these hoodlums. Mr. Tidwell, Local Commander of the Civilian Department of our Federal Government has asked Governor Bullock for more soldiers to be assigned to his ranks to enforce the laws against these "Withlacoochee Renegades."

"Hey, I like that," Sam said. "We're the Withlacoochee Renegades. It kind a' has a nice ring to it, don't it?"

Johnny laughed and nodded his head. When he did, the old bobcat skin hat he wore slid forward on his head and covered his face, and several of the others now laughed at him.

"If we only could get a paper to print the truth about what's going on around here maybe we could get some justice," Robert added.

"No newspaper will print the truth," J. M. argued.

"I don't know," Sam said. "The paper in Madison blasted Florida Governor Harrison Reed until he was almost impeached."

"What do impeached mean?" Robert Maycomber asked.

"Throwed out a' office," Marty replied.

Robert pushed out his lower lip and nodded his head in approval.

"Sam, do you know any folk with that paper?" Marty asked.

"I know 'em, but it's Esther who is the one what can do us the most good. The Balough's[14], who own the paper, wus good friends with Doc Homer before he was kilt. They thought the world of him and Esther."

"I do think it would be a good thing if you two could go back into Madison and see what you can find out about where his loyalties lay."

"I can do that, but I sure would like to get the roof on our new house 'afore I leave for overnight trips."

"I think we can all pitch in and mostly finish it for you this week,

---

[14] Balough: French pronunciation; Ba-lue, Pronunciation in the Deep South; Blue.

Sam," Cliff said. "Besides with your cabin down there near the road, passers-by will not be wondering about the stock grazing yonder in our fields. Ever since you asked for that place, I have believed it will benefit us all to have you there."

"Thank you, Reb," Sam said. "And we would be happy to go see what we can about the paper."

"Now, Reb, will you share with the others what you have found out from the letters that recently came into your possession?" Marty requested.

Cliff reached into his trouser pocket and pulled out three folded pieces of paper. He put his right foot up behind him and locked his boot heel on the edge of the big log he had been sitting on, and he swayed there perched on only his left foot as he began to read the papers. "The first one, don't really mean a whole lot except it do mention the name Faux as being a helpful assistant."

"I knowed that damn Danny Faux was a no good scalawag," Johnny said stomping his moccasin covered foot on the sandy soil.

"It don't say Dan Faux. I do wish it were clearer, but it ain't, so we got strong suspicion, but no more at this time," Cliff said.

"The next one is a little more interesting," he said, clearing his throat again. "The letter is addressed to Rufus Bullock, Governor, Atlanta, Georgia, and without reading it, I'll just tell you the subject is asking for more soldiers to be removed from direct command of the army and assigned to his Civilian Department as police to enforce the law." Cliff paused then and took a deep breath and swallowed before continuing, "It do seem we are getting the attention of some people in higher places. Listen to this, though. I will read you this part directly as it is written so you can see what we are up against.

Be proud of what we are doing but do so with a sober heart. Cause this ain't sweet," Cliff added before he began reading from the letter.

> "Sir, I have obtained from reliable sources the names of this renegade gang who is freely robbing from the Federal Government payrolls and supplies.
> They are:

Martin Gunter and his brother Joab Munroe Gunter Jr. both, store owners, Lowndes County

John Gaston, farmer, Lowndes County

Jerry Chamblin, carpenter, Lowndes County

Stan May teamster for The Valdosta Turpentine Mill and his brother Robert May, a school teacher in Pelham

Israel Henley, employment unknown

Jason Hufsterler and his brother Chase, both carpenters for a Lowndes County company

Robert Maycomber, employed at a local pulpwood mill

William Fourakres, pig farmer in Lowndes County

Wayne Flanders, employed by the Savannah Pensacola Railroad

Louis Brown farmer Lowndes County and his son Clifford also known as Reb Brown who is wanted for the murder of a Freedman

Dillon Zipper, laborer Lowndes County

Aaron Smith, unemployed merchant."

"I'll be a coon dog in hell," Jerry said, "It's the very people who attended that first meeting at the mill."

"Not quite," Marty said, "Danny Faux and Jay Shaw's names ain't on that list."

"He's right," Johnny said. "I told you it were that damn Danny Faux."

"It do look that way, but we have to have better proof and then we will act," Cliff said.

"What more proof you want?"

"I want proof, not suspicion, before I go and hang a man I once went fishing with," Cliff said strongly.

"How we gon'a get that kind a' proof?" Robert asked.

"I'll work on it," Cliff said. "But there's more here you need to know about," opening the letter again he added, "Here beside these names is written, 'Deceased'."

Aaron Smith, Robert May, William Fourakres, Chase Hufsterler, Jason Hufsterler, Louis Brown, Wayne Flanders.

"I didn't know William was dead, for shor'," Johnny said kicking his toe in the sand.

"And the Hufsterler brothers were supposed to be only arrested," J. M. added.

"Well, the way I see it, there ain't no question but what they were murdered by this bunch," Cliff said, "And this is the kind of evidence I like."

"What do you plan, Reb?" Sam asked.

"This here third letter is addressed to Colonel Northrop and it details a plan to place a flat bottom boat in the Withlacoochee at Valdosta, and another twenty soldiers shadowing it from the bank. They are planning to search the river from there to where it enters the Suwannee. The only thing they are waiting on is a few days of good rain to bring up the river a foot or so."

"Damn, that could be bad fur us."

"I doubt it," Marty said. "The soldiers will most likely stay on t'uther side and I doubt they will even slow down when they pass here," he said, then continued "Besides, Reb don't plan to have them get this far."

"What we gon'a do, Reb?"

"First, we got 'a know when they are coming, and for that I think it would be good if we could get in touch with the folks who still live near Gunter's Mill, like the Clyatt's, or the Yeoman's, as well as any who lives farther north along the river, who can be trusted."

"You remember the woman who we gave the money to on the Quitman Road that day we took Darcy, Reb?"

"Yes, I remember her."

"Well," Sam continued "Her son and his wife live south of Valdosta on The Withlacoochee a mile or so up from whar' the Nankin Road crosses it. I know they will help us after what you done fur his mother."

"Can you contact them?"

"I believe I can."

"I do think it would not be wise for any a' us who was named in that letter to go back to Valdosta alone. When we go, we need to go as a body of well-armed men, and fur a purpose," Cliff said.

There was some soft conversation among the attendants, most of whom were nodding their heads.

Stan May spit into the fire and said "I'm gon'a go and tend to Eleanor as often as I can and to hell with their warrants."

"Stan, you are one of us and you took an oath to do as told for the good of everybody," Marty reminded him. "I give you no order not to go, Stan. I suspect I'd feel a mighty strong will to do as you if 'n it were my wife what got kilt, but I do urge you to wait and go as a group and not let them single you out."

"That's right, Stan. They's sure to be watching for something like that after what happened to Darcy," Sam added.

Stan May kicked the white sand the river had left there hundreds of years before during a time of extreme flood conditions, he looked down as his boot unearthed some of it, but did not answer one way or the other.

"Stan we realize you have lost your brother and your wife in only a few months. I, too, lost family, both brothers and father, to this same bunch, as well as our home property and Pa's sawmill, my good name, and I got a murder charge on my head that I never done. There is no one on this list what hasn't lost folk or property, but we got 'a stick together or the bastards will win," Cliff pointed out.

Stan still did not look up.

The next night being New Year's Eve caused Johnny to bring a jug his Granny Keeling had sent for them to celebrate with, but it being the Lord's Day, Addie protested strongly and there was no tapping the brew until she had retired. The three-quarters moon was as bright as most full moons are, due to the exceptionally clear skies. There had been a stiff wind from the southwest until sundown, and then it became totally calm. The wind had completely cleared all the smoke from the many coal and wood fireplaces in Valdosta that would often drift south this time of year. Soon the cloudless skies drew up what warmth the sun had left, and the night air turned off cold with the temperature dropping below freezing before midnight.

First Nadine, and then Esther finally stopped the jug as it was being passed from one man to the next and took a swig themselves. In no time the two were giggling and this encouraged Tillie to join the fun. Mary Ann looked at her old lover and then her maimed husband and stood up and made an unpleasant comment about the actions of some women and stomped off to her cabin.

Cliff was relieved when she did, for he feared had she become tight, she might make a fool of herself towards him. Marty too, seemed to be most pleased, with her departure.

Now as the small group of men and women sat around enjoying each other's company and allowing the strong drink to sweep away the worries and stress of the times, all prayed for a better year in 1871.

"I see'd in the newspaper advertisement taken out by Mr. Griffiss' Store in Valdosta that Colt now offers a revolver that shoots the Henry cartridge, just like the one you got, Reb," Jerry said. "I wus thinking of maybe getting me one and a rifle to go with it. Kind a' a Christmas present to myself. What a' you think?"

"I do like mine. I have always favored a revolver what shot the same round as my rifle. I now got me two pistols and two rifles that shoot the Henry self-contained cartridge but I got 'a tell ya' it ain't always easy to find shells fur 'em." Clearing his throat before continuing, "Still, I think it would be good if we all were to arm ourselves with repeating rifles and cartridge revolvers. We'd be a far more fearsome force to deal with, but I'd order 'em from Madison not Valdosta."

"He lies," Nadine said and then turning and looking at Esther she giggled a little before finishing. "He's got one rifle. The '66 is mine."

"Yes. I guess that's true," Cliff admitted.

"I got a Yellowboy and a Root Side-hammer and this," Nadine said and reaching into her bosom, she pulled out the little Sharps she kept there, and in doing so almost lifted one of her large breasts with it. "Whoops!" she said and stuffed herself back into the cover of the day dress she had on under the union coat.

"I think it's about time we take you to bed, too," Cliff said.

"What'd you think I been wanting you to do," she replied and again turned to Esther and this time both girls giggled.

The men turned their heads away, surprised at such vulgar talk coming from a lady.

Cliff stood and in a swoop of his arm, took her and lifted her over his shoulder and said to all, "I'll see you in the morning, if I'm able."

While he was walking towards the barn, Nadine raised up from his shoulder and waved to the group who were still sitting around the fire.

No one stayed up long enough to see the light snowflakes that fell that night, but several were still awake after having heard the screams coming from the barn, especially Mary Ann, who twisted her hair around her fingers and cursed Nadine under her breath as she listened to Marty snore.

New Year's morning dawned cold and still. No one was too eager to rise except Addie, who had not taken any drink the night before. She had a pot of coffee boiling soon after sunup and had the smell of bacon frying in the pan drifting over the small village of log homes before the children were even up. The light snow that had fallen during the night had not stuck and there was little sign it had even happened.

January the third was cloudy, and by ten in the morning a cold drizzle began that lasted most of the day.

Tillie and Mary Ann had gone back to their store to retrieve some wool blankets they had left in the attic. Tillie, although substantially larger than her sister-in-law, had been the one who climbed up the flimsy ladder to get them, while Mary Ann went down the road to talk to neighbors she had not seen for several weeks. It was while she was gone they came.

There were six of them. They had been assigned to keep an eye on the old Gunter Store just in case someone should return.

If that happened, their orders were to follow at a safe distance and locate the new hideout of the gang. The Sergeant was a big man standing well over six feet tall. He had been a turpentine worker for the Rhett Plantation in South Carolina before the war and had joined the First North Carolina Colored Infantry at New Berne when it was organized, had fought with great courage at Olustee, but at Honey Hill several months later he had run, and as a result, several of the men in his squad were captured. Only he and those captured men knew he had been a 'coward' that day, and he was greatly relieved when he learned they all had perished at Camp Sumter[15] before Sherman's troops reached that part of Georgia. At war's end he had been chosen to remain in the army due to his record and now Sergeant Benjamin Franklin Pike was assigned as the top noncom in Mr. Tidwell's Civilian Department of Military Police, a position he was most proud of.

Ben Frank, as his men called him, had been directly under Sergeant Major Pepper Durham for almost two years and had learned his job well, but Durham had been killed while burning some of the Sessess' homes several months before. Ben Frank had

---

[15] Camp Sumter: A Confederate prison located near Andersonville Georgia during the war.

no intention of letting a Georgia farmer hang him. He had no doubts it would be he who hung Pepper Durham's assassin.

Corporal Bacon had seen the two women enter the store from his position behind the abandoned chicken house, and he went immediately and informed Sergeant Ben Frank of his discovery. The rest of the squad were down on the riverbank trying to slip up on a good size cooter[16] that had come to bask in the rays of the sun, a warming sun that had finally come out from hiding behind the cloud layer to the west. The turtle's perch, a downed cypress log, was not two feet from the bank, just above the water.

A Green-Necked Cooter On A Downed Cypress Log

When Bacon told Pike of two white women who had entered the store through the back door and that they appeared to be alone, the men immediately dropped all thought of the striped-necked turtle and began to think of cooter of a different color.

"Come on, let's see what dem' white bitches will tells us." Ben Frank said turning and heading up the dim animal trail towards the closed store.

Tillie was just starting out the back door with the blankets in hand when she saw the big sergeant come hurrying around the large azalea bush. She screamed and dropped her load and rushed back into the store, but they were there before she could drop the hewn timber that was used to bolt the door. She again screamed as they burst through the tight opening of the door frame.

Tillie tried to flee into the main room, but Pike pushed hard on

---

[16] Cooter: Pseudemys is a genus of pond turtles also known as cooter turtles. In Georgia, the word also is slang for a woman's vagina.

her back and she lost her balance and fell on her face, bruising her cheek and causing her left arm to go numb. Turning over, she stared in terror as the six men encircled her.

"Bacon, you's and Abuck go fines de oter' on' and brought 'err in 'ear'. Wes' gwine to have us'n a party."

As they entered the other room mumbling, Abuck cursed Pike just above a whisper for having to take the last ride on the captured woman.

"Dis here ober one is not so fat." Bacon said. "We's get to be firsts wib 'err and she be the best looker anyways."

"What you mean fat? Yous fat yous-self."

"Dat don' mean I lik's fat cooter," Bacon said and smiled widely.

They searched everywhere, but could not find any trace of the second woman.

When they were satisfied she was not on the property, they returned to take their turn on Tillie.

"Where be de' ot'er on'? Pike asked.

"I doe'no, Sergeant. She be gone, I 'spec."

"We need to finds her," Pike said pulling up his white suspenders.

When they left, each of them had violated Tillie and she lay bleeding profusely on the plank floor of what had once been Mary Ann's bedroom.

The man sitting on the porch of the Crossroads Store had been watching the young man approaching on a dapple gray horse from the north, when his attention was suddenly interupted by the squad of soldiers riding hard in his direction from the south. The distraction caused him to frown with both disgust and yet curiosity as to why they were charging at him with such speed.

The Crossroads Store, also being the home of Lynch and Phoebe Yeoman, was where Mary Ann had gone to express her woes to her old friends.

Lynch was ramming the last strokes of the ramrod in the right barrel of a shotgun he had used a few minutes earlier to dispatch a cat squirrel he planned for dinner. Now upon seeing the soldiers approaching, he raised the hammer and slid a fresh percussion cap over the nipple and pushed it down hard with his thumb. He did not lower the hammer afterward.

The sight of a shotgun in the hands of a man who looked like he knew how to use it is an intimidating thing. This, along with the pearl grips of the revolvers on the young rider's pommel, gave Sergeant Pike enough concern to think before he spoke. "We's looking fur da' woman what came from da' store' back yonder."

"What do you want her for?" Holliday asked.

"I needs ta' question 'err."

"Only women here, live here," Yeoman said. "That store is abandoned anyways."

"There wus two women's dar' a while back, I see'd 'em," Bacon said.

"Only women there was my wife and her sister, who went there to get a blanket," Yeoman replied, remembering what Mary Ann had said when she arrived.

This news brought a whole new prospect on the situation for Pike. There would be no way they could take these two well-armed men without some of them being shot in the process, and they had now shown their hand about knowing of the two women being there. If the women truly were from this place, and not part of the Withlacoochee gang, he and his men had put themselves in a bad position. Realizing it would only be a matter of time before the woman they left in the store was found, he made a quick decision, *'Let Mr. Tidwell figure out how to deal with it'.*

"Come on, men," he said and led the soldiers back north on the Valdosta Road.

When they had gone, Yeoman spoke to the young rider. "Welcome friend, your presence here may have swung the pendulum against the sergeant. I'm Lynch Yeoman."

"Mr. Yeoman, I'm John Henry Holliday, and it is always a pleasure, I assure you, when one has the opportunity to put a nigger in his place. However, I was rather hoping they would cause trouble."

"I was hoping they would not," Yeoman admitted, then asked "What can I do fur' you, son?"

"Well Sur, I'm not so sure you can, but I was hoping I could get word to a Mr. Brown, Reb Brown. I have information I believe he would be interested in."

"Never heard of him," Yeoman lied.

"I understand, sir. I was hoping word might reach him of my need to speak with him. I do believe he would want to meet with me. I have been of benefit to him in the past."

Before Lynch could answer, Mary Ann and Phoebe came out of the house, "What did the soldiers want?"

"They were asking about you."

"Me! Whatever for?"

"I don't know, but they said two women were seen going into the back of your store and they were looking for you."

Suddenly, they all realized what that meant.

"Tillie!" Mary Ann screamed.

Holliday immediately spurred his horse and galloped off towards the store. By the time the others arrived, he had Tillie on the mattressless bed, and he was trying to stop her hemorrhaging by applying bandages he had made from an old cotton window curtain.

She had been beaten about the face so badly, Mary Ann hardly recognized her. "Oh my God."

"She needs a doctor badly," John Henry said, "or she will bleed to death."

"We can take her to Valdosta but that is ten miles. It will take two hours or more if the mules hold out."

"I don't think she can be bounced around in a wagon for two hours, I will go myself and bring a doctor back," John Henry said.

"No, wait," Mary Ann said. "I know where there's a doctor, half that distance."

"Out here?" Lynch questioned.

"Doc Smith is in camp, tending to my husband."

"Where is this?" Holliday asked.

"Across the river. Come, I'll show you," Mary Ann said then she turned to the Yeomans' and asked, "Will you stay with her?"

"Of course, dear. Go get the doctor," Phoebe told her.

She whipped the pair of horses without mercy towards the river, but when she crashed into the water they were going so fast that Buck, the chestnut gelding, lost his footing and slipped on the steep bank and immediately the wagon over-turned. Mary Ann was thrown clear, but soaked through as she landed spread eagle in the dark brown water.

Immediately, the young man was off his horse and in the cold water to rescue her.

She now was sobbing almost to the point he couldn't understand her words, but with the more injured woman behind them, he helped her to his horse and they continued on, riding double.

It was past sundown when they came into camp on a horse that would never again be able to run.

There was a great commotion as the story was told and the people of this community immediately began to make the necessary preparations for the trip back to the Gunter Store.

Addie and Esther took Mary Ann to her house and added new wood to the fireplace. Cliff showed Holliday where some of his clothes were but it soon was obvious to them both, that John Henry was much too small a man to wear Cliff's pants.

"I'll have Johnny bring you some of his when I pass his house," he told Holliday. "In the meantime, just cover yourself with some blankets and sit by the fire."

"I do thank you, sir."

J. M. had already left with Doc Jean on horseback, and soon Nadine and Cliff were ready to ride, each carrying unlit torches for light should they be needed.

When they got to the river crossing, Cliff saw the overturned wagon with the one horse still hitched. The chestnut was on the south bank standing there patiently waiting for his teammate to be rescued.

Cliff unhitched the buckskin and led him over to his partner, then he tossed a rope over the wagon wheel and had Little Red upright it. After pulling it up the north bank it was obvious the tongue had been broken and until repaired, the horses could not be hitched again.

"I don't want to leave it. Should anyone come along and see it here, it would be easy to find the trail to our camp. I think we should take the horses back and then return and pull the wagon back to the store. It will take some time, but I don't see we have any alternative," he said to Nadine.

"Can Little Red pull it by himself?"

"If I take it slow."

"Then you go ahead and I'll lead the horses back to camp," she said.

"You sure you can find your way in the dark?"

"I'm sure, but give me a kiss first," she said and leaned over in her saddle towards him.

She had only traveled a little over a mile when she came upon Johnny Gaston and young Mr. Holliday.

Explaining what had happened with the wagon, Johnny agreed to take the horses on and she, along with John Henry, turned back for the river. When they arrived at the Gunter Store it was obvious great gloom was upon the folks there.

"She's dead," Cliff told her. "The Doc worked on her, but she had lost so much blood she just couldn't keep her strength up."

"I'll go to J. M.," she said and entered the store.

Fog had set in before they returned home and following the dim trail was impossible, so Cliff tied the reins together and laid them over the horn and let the horse find his way. It took a little longer but no one was really in a hurry.

That night John Henry stayed over with them and as soon as everyone else had gone to bed, Cliff asked Nadine to boil a fresh pot of coffee. "I'm just not ready to turn in and I would like to talk to Mr. Holliday for a spell."

She understood well his concerns of this relative stranger finding the location of their camp and set about making the coffee without question, or suggestion of the late hour.

"Well tell me, Mr. Holliday, what brings you so far south? You won't find any pianos down here."

"I realize I have created a considerable problem for you, Mr. Brown. I assure you I had no intention of doing so," the young man said.

Cliff was impressed with the obvious education of this man, born and raised in the Deep South; in these hard times, few men could read the language and very few could speak it with accuracy.

Cliff knew full well, he himself had let the influence of his peers trash his education of correct English; a course that he had with such great difficulties passed while attending Law School at Cumberland University, before the war.

Today, few who listened to him speak would have suspected he had higher learning, and here was a young man who, much like himself, was in the constant pool of the uneducated, and yet he had not fallen into its use of slang.

"What is your intention, Sur?"

"I have knowledge that I thought might be of use to you, sir."

"Knowledge is always something I can use," Cliff replied waiting.

"May I speak freely," he paused before adding, "in front of Mrs. Brown?"

"I do."

"Very well, sir. I have the pleasure of spending time occasionally, let us say, entertaining a lady in Valdosta," he paused again and cleared his throat. "I have been commissioned to expose her son to the ivory keys," he said looking down at the almost white sand beneath him. "It seems the lad was being schooled in this classic art in the past by his father. The lad does seem to have an ear for the arts; I suppose from his father, for surely his mother possesses no such talent. That was before the man lost a couple of his fingers somehow, and___,"there Holliday stopped as he suddenly began the most awful coughing spell. Finally, after almost a minute, he reached into his coat pocket and retrieved a small silver flask. Nodding his head as if asking permission, he took a long swallow, after which he gasped for his breath for several more seconds until he was finally able to speak again. "I lost my mother and older brother to this dreadful illness, and now I am afraid it has come to claim me also," he took another long draw on the flask and then started again with his story, "Well anyway, let me continue. This lady of whom I mentioned is the wife of one John Tidwell; I assume you know him."

"I do," Cliff said, now more than ever concerned with the presence of John Henry Holliday, although the thought of Tidwell no longer being able to play the piano was pleasing news to him. Especially since Cliff was one of the few who knew how he lost his fingers."[17]

"It just so happens that this very day, while I was at the Tidwell home, one of his oriental servants led me into Mrs. Tidwell's sitting room, where the piano is located. While I was waiting on the lad to come down for his lesson, I," he paused, "let us say, overheard something. It just so happens this room is connected by a thin wall and sliding doors to Mr. Tidwell's study, and while there, I heard him telling someone to be ready to begin the march tomorrow morning. I could not see either; however the other man answered with a most definite Negroid speech and then asked a question concerning a certain flat boat; at which time Mr. Tidwell replied, "It is ready and will shove off at daybreak."

"This is news I can use," Cliff admitted.

"I was trying to have a message relayed to you; hoping to meet with you on this matter, when I came in contact with the murderers of Mrs. Gunter."

"You saw them?"

"Why yes, as did Mr. Yeoman."

---

[17] Tidwell's lost fingers: See the *Owl Hoot Trail Book One Gold in the Red Desert* page 21

"Will you be able to identify them?"

"Perhaps not all, there were some six, I believe, but I will know that big Sergeant and the one he called Bacon without question, perhaps one or two others."

"Mr. Holliday, I do very much appreciate your information," Cliff said and took a deep breath before continuing, "But I must have you stay here until after we verify this. I realize you helped us in the past, but now that we are posted as outlaws, the location of our new homes would be priceless to certain people on the other side. You do understand my position?"

"In other words, I am your prisoner," the man replied.

"Guest, very welcome guest," Cliff said back.

"I see no harm in that, Mr. Brown, if you would take a drink of brandy with me to seal the friendship."

"Without intent to offend, I prefer the jug," Cliff replied, and reached for the brown ceramic container at his feet, "To your health, Mr. Holliday."

"To the success of your mission, Mr. Brown."

Late that night while Cliff was sitting by the fire working on his plans for the coming day, John Henry slipped off into the fog, and locating his horse, disappeared into the night. It was shortly before dawn, while Cliff was awakening the others, that he discovered Holliday missing.

It was during the pre-dawn breakfast that he told them of what he had learned.

"Can we trust him?" Robert asked.

"I don't know. Especially now, with him slipping off like that, but I don't see how we can ignore it, either," Cliff said back "If he is telling the truth, we need to take them before they reach here."

"Of course, it is possible it is all a trap and they will be waiting for you along the trail," Marty said.

"True enough and then there is also the possibility that he has informed of our location and they are just waiting for us to move out and then come in and take the camp while most of us are gone."

"It do present a problem," Marty said.

J. M., who Cliff had not awakened, appeared from out of the fog. "I suppose you think you will ride out of here without me."

"It's not that, J. M. It's just we thought you might want some time to think."

"Let's go kill some of the bastards and then I'll come back and bury the mother of my children," he said.

"I sure wish Sam was here to ride with us," Cliff said. "He's a fair shot with a rifle."

"He should be back today," Robert said.

"Yeah, but we can't wait on him."

"I'll move on out now and get Johnny. You fellows get mounted up and catch up with us," Cliff said standing and pouring the last of his coffee into the edge of the fire. "Be sure to bring plenty of powder and balls."

He reached Granny Keeling's house and awoke the dog first, which soon woke Johnny. The younger man came out with rifle in hand wearing his buckskin pants and fur hat but without shirt or coat. "What's up?"

"Get yourself dressed for a long day 'a hunting Yankees," Cliff replied.

"Yes, sir," Johnny said raising his eyebrows.

And hunt they did. The remainder of the group arrived just as they were pulling out from Granny's.

The riders slipped almost silently through the fog along the dim trail to the river. There Cliff turned west along its south bank and continued on through the stand of pine.

Johnny watched a good size leaf that had fallen from a red oak float atop the black water, some twenty feet below the bank. It was moving very slowly on to its destiny in the Gulf of Mexico, and he wished he could somehow catch a ride on it.

Before the war, his father had taken him down to Mr. Summerlin's camp near Fanning Springs. From there they had taken one of his boats out into the Gulf and on a sandbar had gathered scallops. That was the first time Johnny had eaten scallops and he dearly loved the taste of the little critters, once he learned the knack of getting the shells open. Thinking of it, made him remember he had not eaten anything before he left this morning and he had been in such a hurry he had failed to pick up any of the biscuits Granny Keeling had baked the night before.

Two hours later, they came to Rocky Ford Crossing and Cliff reined up.

"This will be a good place to wait fur them," he said as he slowly stretched his back before dismounting.

The group of men gathered around a small fire and warmed

themselves. Cliff sent Dwayne upriver a mile to a place where he could spot anything coming down by water. Should Dwayne see such a boat, he would be able to give them plenty of time to get ready.

The fog was still very thick and Cliff reached for a pocket watch. *'Ten past ten,'* he thought, *'fog should a' lifted by now.'*

Another hour passed and it began to sprinkle. Soon this turned into a drizzle, and within twenty minutes it was pouring down with a vengeance. By two o'clock, everything they had was drenched including the powder and caps of the percussion guns. Cliff groaned and turned to Johnny. "Will you go get Dwayne? It's raining so hard we couldn't fight with them if they did come."

When the two men returned, everyone had loaded up and were more than happy to get back to shelter.

The cold rain continued for four days. Someone had righted an old wooden barrel they had previously placed upside down near the campfire to be used in lieu of a chair, and when the rain stopped it had fourteen inches of water in the bottom. The temperature had turned off much colder once the rain stopped, and the early morning risers had to crack the thin layer of ice to get water for the coffee.

Sam and Esther had returned from Madison before the rain set in. They brought good news, more supplies, and more things to worry about.

Mr. Balough had been very interested in using *The Madison Trace* to mount a counter-campaign against the newspaper in Valdosta.

He also told Sam about a conversation he had the day before with Captain J. L. Inglis. The Captain had mentioned in the course of the conversation, he had recently made a bid on surplus Henry rifles that the government was selling off.

With a recommendation from Balough, Sam had been able to get Inglis to agree, should he win the bid, not to place them on display or even to advertise them, until he got back to him on the subject.

However, the most stressful news was Sam and Esther had been offered a chance at the franchise for a stage stop along the new stage line that was soon to be running from the railhead at Jennings Station in Florida to the depot in Quitman, Georgia.

"It's already a done deal," Sam told the group. "They showed me the route and it's coming straight down the trail we took with the horse herd. Crossing the river yonder," he said pointing east where he had shot the fleeing soldier, "on over to the ferry at Belleville when the river's too high to ford, and taking up the road here on past Rocky Ford where it cuts the Nankin Road, west to Nankin and then up to Quitman."

"There's even talk of building a ferry across the river yonder," he said pointing to the east, "or maybe a bridge so the stage would not be held up when the river is at flood." He paused, then twisted his neck as if what he was about to say would not be pleasant to him. "Belleville already has a ferry and I can see them choosing it as a stage stop, but it is a mite too far from Jennings Station, and too close if they build a stop at the normal distance of 15 miles. Should they take the rules seriously, then we are just the right distance for the next station. Mr. Balough also said old man Powell's son, Lewis, was one of those hung for the killing of Lincoln, and Powell still lives at Belleville, so there is little love from the Yankee Government towards Belleville and this stage will carry US Mail. Besides, old James Bell has caused considerable discomfort among some of the officials with the stage line, and he is in partners with Bass on the ferry there." He paused again and then smiling he said, "We may just have a chance."

Everyone could see Sam's enthusiasm, but the news did little to cause them cheer. In fact, this indeed caused considerable uneasiness among the folks who had so recently made this remote location their new home.

Cliff studied on it for several minutes while the others talked about this shocking news.

Finally, he said, "Hell, there ain't nothing we can do about it anyway. The road is coming this way and that is a fact. It will be much better if Sam and Esther had a stage stop than somebody else around these parts. At least we will know what's going on, and Sam can always tell inquiring folk that this barn and what stock might be seen, belongs to him or the stage line," Cliff said.

"True, and should anyone see humans in these parts, Sam can say they's his hired hands," Marty offered.

"I guess, Sam, you are about to be in the stage business," Cliff said.

"What are you gon'a call the stop, Sam?" Nadine asked nudging Esther with her elbow.

"Well, I wus thinking, if we get it, we ain't yet, a' calling it *Estherbrook*," he said not looking up.

"I think that is a wonderful name," Nadine said joyfully, enjoying the obvious affection still growing that her friends shared, after so many years together.

'When we are that age, I hope we are just like them,' she thought and smiled at Cliff.

"I do think we need to act immediately on securing that load a' Henry rifles. I suggest we send Captain Inglis a hundred dollar deposit to hold them fur us," Cliff suggested.

There was a low mutter of voices and nodding of heads, but Marty spoke contrary to the idea.

"I don't see no need to be sending money to Captain Inglis, he don't even know if 'n he got the blame bid yet."

Marty had seen his authority erode slowly since his accident. No one had defied him or showed the slightest lack of respect when speaking to him, but it was Reb Brown that led them when their lives were in jeopardy, and it was Reb Brown they turned to for advice. Only Reb himself, still gave him the respect he had in the beginning.

"We got plenty a' powder and now plenty a' caps. I don't see the need to be spending our money on a bunch a' guns what shoot cartridges that can't be reloaded. What if 'n we run out a' them copper shells? We can't reload them. We'd be sitting ducks."

"I can tell ya' from experience, Nadine and I took on four Arapaho warriors who had recently killed a prospector, a man what carried a muzzle loader. I never would a' tried that with a single shot. It were that sixty-six yonder that gave me the confidence to take them on," Cliff said. Then, raising his arm and moving it slowly above the ground as if he were sweeping the area of some unclean or unwanted substance, he added. "I saw too, during the war, whar' a handful a' Bluebellies cut ta' pieces a company a' good cavalrymen. Men that I knew to be good fighting men. Men who had done just the same to other Yankees who were equipped with muskets, but when them Indiana boys got there with their yellow rifles and them Blakeslee Boxes, they were spitting lead like rain and the roar of them Henrys was like a steam train coming down a long straight grade." He stopped and let what he had just said sink in. Looking over at his friend he began again before Marty could object, "I say we need these repeaters. Marty has a good point; we do now have a right good supply of caps and plenty a powder too. Nobody's saying to throw them away. They could be used as back-up, should we run low on the copper shells, and in the meantime, we would be a fighting force to reckon with."

A Blakeslee Box for the Henry Rifle
It was carried strapped over right shoulder riding
along the left side connected to the revolver belt.
Each of the six tubes contained 15 copper 44 RF cartridges.

"What be a Blakely Box?" Johnny asked.

"It's Blakeslee Box, a wooden container covered with leather." Cliff began to explain, using his hands as well as words, "about a foot and a half long. Inside there are six removable tin tubes. Each tube can be loaded with fifteen or sixteen cartridges. With a Henry Rifle, when a fellow runs empty, he just opens the loading tube and sticks one of the tin tubes in, and into the rifle slides a full load a' cartridges and he is ready to shoot again, from empty to fully-loaded in about five seconds clean. A man with a Henry and a Blakeslee Box can lay down more 'n' a hundred shots in less than two minutes."

Again he paused and watched closely, just as Marty opened his mouth to speak, Cliff continued, "I also believe we need to replace our cap & ball revolvers with new ones that fire the same round as the rifles. I did this myself two year ago, and have never regretted it for one minute." The whole time he was talking, his hands were moving around making motions, visual descriptions, and keeping time with his head, which was nodding as if it was agreeing with what his voice was saying.

"This here new Smith & Wesson is a dandy gun. It loads fast and kicks the empties out even faster. I don't know how many we can get a' these but I do know we can send our old cap & balls back to the factories and get them converted. I strongly recommend we do both."

The men were obviously in full agreement with Reb. This was clear to Marty, and with a heavy sigh he said. "Well, if that's what you men want, I'll go along, but I do think it's a waste a' money. Money we might not have an opportunity to get again."

"Hell, Marty, we got more n' a thousand Yankee dollars fur such," Dwayne said.

"We got 'a be careful where we spend them greenbacks too," Marty said back strongly.

"Marty's right," Cliff agreed. "We need to be real careful about that."

"There's another thing," Sam said as if he had been waiting to drop a real load on them.

"What now?" Robert asked.

"Mr. Balough suggested this," Sam said as if in defense before he spoke. "Mr. Balough said that since the newspaper in Valdosta had printed some of our names it would be better if we took on some sort a' alias."

"What's a alias?" Dwayne asked.

"You know, change your name," Nadine said.

"Hell, Dwayne, you already got a' alias," Johnny said laughing.

"I do? What is it?"

"Dwayne, that's what it are," Johnny said and slapped his leg.

"Oh, yeah, I do, don't I?"

"Mr. Balough said it would be good for him when he writes the contradictions about the works we are doing."

"I don't understand what's the need," Mary Ann said sharply.

"Well, you won't have to use one, Mary Ann. You won't be mentioned in the papers anyway," Esther said in just as sharp a tone.

"Well!" Mary Ann said, "I guess my opinion is not needed here."

When no one spoke to the contrary she stood up and yelled over her shoulder. "Don't you be too long, Marty," as she stomped off in the direction of their cabin.

"I think it will be a good idea to do as Balough suggested," Marty offered. "It will just be a little confusing for a while."

"If we do this, I think we should start calling each other by the new name at all times, unless it's important to do otherwise. That way we will learn the names better and should we make a mistake and speak out in front of someone at the wrong time, it wouldn't do us so much harm," Cliff said.

Suddenly everyone turned and looked at Johnny and he realized that the comment had been directed at him. "Hell, Reb, I didn't mean to give you up."

"That's exactly what I mean."

"Reb's right," Marty said. "Everybody think on it and come up with an alias fur yourselves."

"Hey, Dwayne," John Gaston called.

"Yeah?"

"You can be called Dwayne," he said laughing at his friend.

Cliff had brought an alcohol thermometer back with him from Wyoming and had hung it on a nail on the outside of the barn where the shade of the big oaks never let the sun through. The next morning when he came out, he carried the lantern around to the south side of the barn and checked; it read sixteen degrees. He had wanted to put on two pairs of socks, but knew he would never be able to get his old brown boots on over them. Now, as he looked at the thermometer, he knew why he had felt the need.

Before the coffee had boiled enough to properly transfer the flavor from the crushed beans to the water, Robert rode up, dismounted, walked up to the small fire, and began warming his hands over the open flames.

"The river is nigh on spilling its banks," he said dryly.

"That ain't good," Cliff replied shaking his head.

He had assigned Stan May to leave every morning just after breakfast and head to the crossing near Gunter's Grits Mill, just in case the Yankees that the Holliday boy had warned them about materialized. This morning he had planned to send him on up to Rocky Ford, but with the river that high, a boat would be moving faster with the current than a man could ride through that forest.

Even though all of their homes now had either cook stoves or a fireplace where the women could prepare meals, from the beginning they had always gathered as a group and had some sort of meeting along with their meals, and it had not changed with the building of the cabins.

This morning, as soon as they had finished their morning meal, Cliff turned to Marty, "Robert said the river's up. I think we should head up to Rocky Ford and wait, just in case that Holliday boy was right about Tidwell sending a bunch a' soldiers downriver in a boat."

Marty knew Cliff had already decided to do this and was only making this conversation in front of the men so he could save face. Nodding his head he said, "I think that is a good idea, Reb; do it."

No one liked the sound of moving out to spend long hours along the cold river bank on a day like this, but they also were quite aware that should the authorities find their new homes, their lives would be much worse.

"I'll go across to the other side and wait fur them," Stan May said. He had been staying with Dwayne and Robert in a small one-room log cabin they had quickly erected on the north side of the two-holer.

"No need to cross the river when it's this high, Stan; it's too dangerous, that current will be flowing a mile a minute."

"Somebody needs to be over there," Stan said back gruffly. "What if they see our crossing?"

"With the river like this there ain't no crossing fur them to see," Robert mentioned.

"And they won't be able to cross either," Cliff replied.

Stan saw the logic to these words but still wanted to get over to the other side and lay in wait for them.

"Dwayne, mount up and go tell Johnny what we got in mind. That boy is too warm snuggled up there in Granny's quilts while we are freezing out here; time he joined us."

"Be a pure___, it surely will," Dwayne said, tossing the remainder of his coffee from the cup and heading for the corral to get his horse.

By full light, the column of seven mounted men rode slowly westward along the dim trail that all too soon would become a stage road once again. When they arrived at the river crossing, where only a few days before he had pulled the overturned wagon up the bank, they could now see no bank. The river was, at this point, out of its banks and into the timber over a hundred feet on either side from its normal narrow path. Cliff instructed everyone to vary their tracks into the planted pines so as not to create a trail in the wet ground. The heavy layer of pine needles would not show the tracks of one or perhaps two horses, but for seven to follow in tandem would definitely leave a scar that anyone could follow.

The dark, almost black water that usually moved so slowly it was hard to see a current at all, was now obviously brown, not black, with large barrages of white bubbles that floated like islands along until they collided with a fallen tree or rock formation where upon they would break into thousands of water droplets flying in huge clouds of spray. The silence of this beautiful river had also been stolen by the rains of the past week and was now corrupted into a constant roar. Not loud like a waterfall, or even that of rapids, but the sound of a mighty force that could and would tear away anything that happened to be in its new path.

When they arrived at Rocky Ford, Cliff knew that no horse or wagon would cross here for several days.

He was just about to send Johnny ahead to keep watch when Stan May asked, "You want I should go ahead and keep watch?"

"Alright, I'll send relief in a couple hours," Cliff said and watched the man ride off. Cliff did not feel good about Stan. He had taken the death of his wife far more deeply than anyone had expected. He almost seemed to have a death wish of his own on his face; a condition Cliff had seen during the war when a man felt he had just taken all he intended to take.

They built a fire under a big sweet gum tree, where its huge branches would disperse the smoke, and gathered around trying to keep warm.

Cliff had given Sam his Henry that morning, and he had taken the Winchester; a move that did not set well with Nadine but she understood the reasoning; she just wondered what she would do should the Yankees come from the east rather than the west. Finally, she took five of the captured muskets, loaded them, and leaned them all against the old log by the campfire.

At ten, Cliff sent Robert to relieve Stan, but he returned explaining Stan would have none of it and wanted to stay on point.

Less than ten minutes later, they heard a distant report come from the north. Almost immediately, there were several more shots and everybody grabbed their weapons and headed for the river. In what seemed like no time at all, a good size boat appeared from around the bend, with twelve or more men on board, headed their way at the speed of the raging river.

Cliff could see they were attending to something in the bottom of the boat and not looking out.

He held up his arm to keep his men from firing too early, and then just when the men in the boat were fully exposed, he could see the object that had their attention was the body of a man, he swung down his arm and began firing into the men on board. There was a sudden roar as the others with him also fired and then only the sound of the two repeaters blasting away and a few reports from the men in the boat. The helmsman swung the craft towards the north bank in an effort to escape the murderous fire coming from the other side of the river; this maneuver became his fatal mistake. Had he just dropped down and let the river take them on by, they would soon have been out of range, but by trying this manuever he caused the boat to turn broadside to the current, and almost immediately it rolled over spilling her dead and dying along with the one soldier who had not been hit.

Cliff took a careful bead on this wire-haired man now fighting desperately not to drown, and squeezed the trigger. The conical struck the water an inch behind his head and ricocheted into his brain stem.

It was then Cliff heard the sound of a horse coming at a hard run, and he turned to see Stan May at full gallop, headed for the river.

"Stan! No!" he yelled but the man either didn't hear or paid no mind to him and plunged straight into the raging waters.

As soon as the horse could, he dislodged his rider and they watched as their friend was swept away around the bend, still firing his revolver at the helmsman, the last man alive from the boat.

There were two snaps as the caps fired but failed to ignite the powder, and then a distance boom of a sure fire. They heard no more.

Following the river eastward two miles, they saw Stan's horse standing on the opposite side but there was no sign of its rider. Near the old crossing, they could see the wreckage of the boat lodged into the paddle wheel of the grits mill. It had jammed the wheel and the power of the water had torn away several pieces of the big wheel.

Directly across the river on the south side in the shallows, hung up among a cluster of cypress trees, was a blue-clad body still clinching a Spencer Rifle.

"Get his gun and ammo box." Cliff said to Robert. "No need of letting them have it back," he paused and then added, "and drag him up here and let's bury him."

"Hell, let the turtles have him. Turtles got 'a e't too," Johnny Gaston said.

"No, I don't want anything found on this side of the river." Cliff replied and then he remembered, turning first to Sam and then thinking of his age he looked over at Gaston and said. "Johnny, I just thought of it; will you go back and pick up any spent shells from these repeaters and anything else we might a' left there, that could be found later?"

He could tell the lad was not pleased at being selected for this, but he obeyed without question, so Cliff added, "Dwayne will you go with him?"

When they arrived at the edge of the big pasture, Nadine could see they were three men short. It was a quarter mile from where she stood to the line of horses and she could not make out who was missing. Soon she sensed someone beside her and then heard the voice of her mother-in-law, "Who's missing?"

That night there was a considerable amount of recalling going on around the fire but one thing was said over and over "Had it not been for the repeaters of Reb and Sam, the main body of soldiers would have been swept right past us while we were reloading."

Early the next day, while they were waiting for the grits to come to full boil, Marty said, "I brung a hundred dollars with me, Johnny Gaston can take it to Captain Inglis and see to him holding them repeating rifles fur us."

CHAPTER FIVE

Aliases

The next morning while having breakfast, Sam made an announcement. "I've been studying it over and I remember when I was a little tot my Ma said I wus always hungry as a bear and there for a while they teased me by calling me The Hungry Little Bear so that is what I think my alias will be. 'The Hungry Bear'."

"That sounds good," Nadine said then turned to Esther and asked "What about you Esther?"

"I don't think Mr. Balough said anything about the women needing aliases," Cliff said.

"I don't see why not," Nadine countered. "We have reputations too, remember Alabama."

Cliff really had rather Alabama had not been brought up, as no one here knew anything about it, and none needed to know; so he just stopped arguing with her and raised up his hands.

"Alright, now that that's settled, what have you come up with Esther?"

"Well," she started to reply a little embarrassed as to what the others might think and then continued "I thought of "Feeds the Bear, but later decided against that and chose 'The Bear Lady'." She turned to Nadine and asked, "What do you think?"

"I think it's vulgar," Addie said.

"I think it's divine," Nadine said, not even giving her mother-in-law's comment a second thought.

"I'll of course spell it B-e-a-r, not B-a-r-e," Esther was quick to point out.

Nadine turned to Cliff before Addie could add to her earlier statement and asked, "And you, my darling, have you come up with something?"

"Well, I was thinking about The Georgia Rebel or maybe The Valdosta Rebel."

Nadine looked and shook her head with her lips poked out in the front, showing her disapproval. "No, too common."

"What then?" he asked.

"Maybe 'The Wyoming Rebel,' you sure as the devil was that."

"I think I have heard enough," Addie said and she got up and headed back inside the barn.

"I know what I am gon'a use," Robert Maycomber said.

"Well, tell us Robert," Nadine replied enthusiastically.

"You are really getting into this, aren't you?" Cliff said to her.

"You bet. I think it's great fun," she said back without even looking at him.

"Well, I wus in the Artillery you know, and the officers were sometimes referred to as Art Men so that's what I'm gon'a' use, Artillery Mann spelled with two n's. That way you guys will know me as Art Mann."

"Sounds good, how about you, Mary Ann?" Nadine asked the other woman.

"I'm kind a' like Addie, I don't see no need fur us women folk to change our names."

"Suit yourself, if you don't want to be part of the fun."

With that, the red-headed woman burst into tears and shouted, "There ain't nothing fun about any of this. I've been uprooted, my husband is a cripple, I was almost raped, and now I live down here in the middle of God-only-knows-where. I don't see nothing fun here." She grabbed the hem of her apron and covered her eyes just before she ran back toward her cabin.

"I guess we could name her ourselves," Nadine said.

"Nadine," Cliff scolded.

"Alright," Nadine replied looking over at Marty. "I'm sorry Marty, I didn't mean no harm."

"I know, it's just Mary Ann ain't taken to all a' this as the rest of you ladies have."

"Alright then, Marty, how about you? Have you come up with a good one?" she asked.

"Well, I don't know how good it is, but I was thinking of "Store Keep," he paused and looked down at the ground then added, "But I don't know."

"'Store Keep'" just fits you," Nadine said and walked over and slapped him lightly on the arm.

"Alright, Nadine, you been after all 'a us, now it's your turn. Who are you going to be?" Esther asked.

"I guess I'm gon'a' be known as Deadwood's Daughter."

"Really," Esther said "Your Dad was called Deadwood?"

"Yep, he was known as 'The Deadwood Kid'."

"I can feel a story coming on here," Esther said. "Tell us."

"My Dad was called Deadwood, because of where he was found," she said raising her arms as if to illustrate a lifting. "He was just a little boy, about three years old or so, when some folk, who were headed west, found him. His folks had been killed by some Indians. Nobody ever knew why he wasn't kilt too. Anyway, the valley they found him in was a place where there had been a fire a year or two before and all the trees were dead; the valley was known as The Deadwood Valley by locals, so they called him The Deadwood Kid after that; cause he was too young to tell them his real name, so___"

"Good idea," Esther said, "I like that."

"Was that in Missouri?"

"No. Jackson, Tennessee. The people who found him took him on to Missouri with them, when no one could say who he was."

"Alright so far we got, 'The Hungry Bear', 'The Bear Lady', 'Store Keep', 'Art Mann', 'Deadwood's Daughter', 'The Wyoming Rebel'."

"I don't know," Cliff said. "I don't really like that, I wus only in Wyoming a couple a' years."

"Well what, then?" Nadine said.

"I don't know. I'll let you know tomorrow maybe," Cliff said and tossed his coffee into the edge of the fire before he started off towards the horse corral.

The temperature stayed below freezing for several more nights before a wind began to blow from the southwest and cloud cover hid the stars at night.

The morning of the twentieth day of the new year found most of the able bodied men working, building Sam & Esther's house down near the road. At first, Sam had thought of just adding on another room, but Esther had convinced him to build a new two-story house and use the old one as a kitchen house. "That way if we get over-nighters we will have rooms to rent out," she had said. It made sense and he decided to do that very thing.

About ten o'clock, a lone rider was seen approaching from the west.

"Look!" Sam said pointing towards the man.

Cliff was atop the structure placing cut boards on the new roof. He stopped and watched a few seconds and then came down the ladder and picked up the Henry that he had leaned against the west wall of the old cabin.

The stranger, who was some three hundred yards away, stopped and turned towards the area of the barn and other homes, although from where he was they were hidden by the dense oak hammock; but instead of going in their direction, he reined his horse to the right and proceeded towards the Brooks' cabin.

The others had also stopped their work and each either belted on a revolver or moved close to where a long gun was located. When the rider had covered half the distance between the edge of the clearing and the house, Cliff recognized him as the Holliday boy.

He was dressed in dark trousers and a white linen shirt with vest and a black frock coat for warmth. Atop his head was a black flat brimmed hat that was obviously made of fine beaver. He was attempting to grow a mustache, which at this time was only a thin line of sparse sandy colored hairs. One would never describe his expressions as hard or mean, neither could one who took notice of such things remember him smiling.

"Gentlemen," he said when he stopped a few feet away.

"Mr. Holliday," Cliff replied.

"I see, from this garbage printed by the appointed editor of *The South Georgia Pioneer*, you were able to put my information to good use," he said and then tossed the folded paper to him.

Opening the newspaper, Cliff saw the headlines:

Twelve Soldiers Slaughtered

"What do it say, Reb?" Dwayne asked.

Cliff read the column silently and then spoke aloud. "It says:

> A squad of select soldiers was ambushed while helplessly conducting training maneuvers on the Withlacoochee River."

He paused and took a deep breath before continuing, "Says here,

> they weren't even armed and were bushwhacked and slaughtered by the murderous gang of renegades who hide out in the swamps of the Withlacoochee north of Rocky Ford crossing. These outlaws are led by the wanted murderer Reb Brown,"

Cliff said and then added, "It also says a special request to Governor Bullock has been made for more soldiers to stomp out this gang of murderers."

"They do like that word murder, don't they?" Sam said as Cliff handed the paper to him before turning back to Holliday.

"They do." Johnny agreed.

"I guess we do owe you a word of thanks, Mr. Holliday," Cliff said.

"I did not come all this distance for gratitude."

"Well then, what have you come for?"

"For one thing to bring that paper and another to inform you of a train that will leave Valdosta enroute to Pensacola on Friday," he replied before coughing vigorously, followed by the clearing of his throat. "My apologies," he said and wiped his mouth with the white linen, he carried for that purpose, before he continued, "This train will contain three soldiers who are to board a steamer at Fort Pickens, for an unknown port, far away from Georgia," he paused. "It seems that Mr. Tidwell has come to the conclusion they would better serve the cause far away from the scene of the crime."

"What crime is this?"

"The rape and murder of Mrs. Gunter," Holliday said.

"Are you sure?"

"I told you before; I witnessed the culprits as they were fleeing the scene. I had the good fortune to be in a place where I was able to overhear the reason for their transfer. I then made it a personal objective to observe their black faces again. I assure you sir, they are the same men."

"We got 'a get 'em 'afor they get away," J. M. said.

"They won't get away," Cliff assured him without looking away from the mounted lad. "It seems we are again indebted to you, Mr. Holliday."

"Neither do I bring you such news to acquire indebtedness."

"Just why do you help us?"

The young man straightened himself and stretched his back before speaking, "You see, sir, I knew very little of Georgia before the war," he said, lifting his arms and turning a quarter turn in the saddle and then back again. "I simply was too young to remember much of those days. I do observe a glimpse from time to time, from deep within my memory, usually a view of some happening in which my mother played a role, or maybe of my cousin, Melanie, who has always been such a pleasure to me, as we both grew from childhood. So you see it is not for the love of that lost cause that I help you. I have, on the other hand, seen the unjustness that is upon this state, and upon the entire south, in these times," he paused as he again coughed.

"I have read with great admiration Mr. Jefferson's constitution for the original United States, and I see here a government that knows no constitution, a government gone wild with power and greed using the term, 'Reconstruction,' as a means to justify their lust for the property of others. I see you few people as a thorn in the side of this wicked element that is scarring the image our forefathers fought so bravely to win from the Crown. And that, sir, is why I offer these tiny bits of information."

"Mr. Holliday, we are about to break for a light dinner, will you join us?" Cliff asked, as he cradled his rifle in the crook of his arm.

The women had a noon meal ready when they arrived at the barn and Nadine was smiling as usual when they walked up. "Well if it is not the mysterious Mr. Holliday," she said. "Will you join us for a bite to eat?"

"Nothing would pleasure me more, Mrs. Brown," the young sandy-haired man replied as he lifted his hat slightly from his head for a moment before letting it once again drop, and then as a final gesture he tapped the top of it with the extended four fingers of his right hand.

Nadine watched him closely as he dismounted. He stood no taller she, and his body would have easily fit into her clothing, had he tried to wear them. In fact he was downright frail in her opinion, even with the new growth on his upper lip, which caused her to smile slightly; he reminded her of a boy and not a man at all.

The women had prepared a pot of collard greens with the fat of a hog for flavoring and boiled potatoes, the hungry men devoured the noon meal with gusto.

"I do envy you gentlemen," Holliday said. "My father has such meals prepared at the farm, but when I moved into town and left Sophie's cooking on the home place___," he paused and shook his head slowly. "It seems today I must endure with the inspirations of the Romanian cook employed by Louis' Bar and Grill on Center Street; with exceptions on Sundays when the good Christians of the Northeast Methodist congregation have their dinner on the ground and church all around. The ladies do serve some fine cold chicken."

Short Sandy Haired and Frail
John Henry Holliday about 19 years of age

"So you live in Valdosta, Mr. Holliday?" Nadine confirmed.

"Yes, Father procured a small cottage on East Savannah some years back so I could be near The Institute and receive instruction in the arts. I have stayed there," he paused a moment before adding, "since my mother died."

"I see you are not wet, Mr. Holliday. Has the river gone down that much?" Esther asked.

"Unfortunately, no Ma'am. I happened to be at the farm yesterday noon and crossed the river on the old Skipper Bridge."

"Where is your farm?" Nadine asked.

"North of Valdosta near the Bemiss plantation," he replied. "A most lovely portion of the county."

"Do you miss living on the farm, Mr. Holliday?" Esther asked. "I gather that from your tone of voice when you speak of it."

"I do miss the clean air and the wonderful cooking of my Mammy Sophie, but I must admit, I too, enjoy the money I earn teaching the arts. You see, I have developed a passion for the game of poker. Without the funds I receive from the good folks on Sunday and that paid by Mr. Tidwell and his lovely wife, Amaritte, I would have no funds to lose during the week."

"Poker, Mr. Holliday, is most often played in smoky bar rooms and that is no place for a young man with the illness you obviously have contracted," Nadine said.

"If I didn't know better, Mrs. Brown, I would have to say you speak from experience."

Nadine immediately realized he had somehow recognized her for what she was. How or what she might have said or done to give herself away, she had no idea, but he knew, she knew he knew, and she felt suddenly weak and nauseous.

"We have all heard about those places, Mr. Holliday," Esther said back quickly when she noticed the color had gone from her friend's face.

"Of course, I never meant to infer you actually have been in such a den of iniquity," he quickly corrected. "I was only teasing a bit."

Cliff also recognized the panic in his wife's expression and quickly began preparations for the matter at hand, "J. M., Johnny, Sam, and Robert, each of you, be prepared to leave here tomorrow, first light. I want every man to pick two of the best horses you can find out of our remuda and Sam, if you will, I want you to bring along two extra ones for Nadine. She will accompany us on the return trip."

"What are we going to do?" John Henry asked.

Cliff turned to Holliday and said, "Mr. Holliday, the last time you brought us news I asked you to remain here until the encounter was over; instead you snuck off in the night. Are you going to remain here or should we await your departure before discussing our plans?"

"I did not sneak off in the night. I do not, however, cotton to being ordered to do anything by anyone. I gave you good information, which you put to good use, and I in no way exposed you to the authorities as you obviously were frightened of. This time you may do as you please. I must be back in Valdosta before services begin Wednesday night, so I bid you all a farewell and thank you for a most delicious dinner." He stood and nodded to the ladies before he returned his flat hat to his head upon which he tapped the top with his hand and turned to his pony that was scratching at the brown grass a short distance away.

CHAPTER SIX

Raid of The Renegades

As soon as Holliday was out of hearing Cliff began, "Dwayne, you will drive a wagon into Madison. Take with you Miss Nadine, Miss Esther, and Miss Mary Ann if she wants to go. Put Miss Nadine on the train and get a load of supplies while you're there," he said looking at the dark-haired man. "Nadine will board a train in Madison Thursday and go to Tallahassee."

Then turning to Esther, he added, "Miss Esther, if you can, find out if there is any news on those Henry Rifles from Capt. Inglis and take Mr. Balough this paper." He handed her the folded newspaper. "And also give him a list of our aliases while you are there."

Turning back to the small group of men he continued, "We will ride cross-country to Quincy and be there when the train comes in Friday night. It not only takes on water and wood, it also boards passengers in Quincy. Nadine will have located where the three nigger soldiers are by then and point them out to us. There may be more than those three, so we need to know which three they are."

"How am I going to find that out?"

"I leave that up to you," he said sternly without expression or turning in her direction.

"As soon as the train stops again for water, we will take them and all leave the train together," Cliff said and then turning and looking at each in the small group he added, "Any questions?"

After a short pause, he then looked at Gaston and said, "Johnny, I want you to check every man's weapons before we leave. Make sure they are good and clean, lightly oiled, and ready, I'm counting on you."

The young man who was dressed in all buckskin with his bobcat hat, looked up and with a burst of pride building within him replied, "Sure, Reb."

Cliff looked back at his loyal friend and asked, "Have you come up with an alias yet?"

"No, just can't figure one out."

"Alright, until you do, we'll call you Jeremiah Johnny."

"Hey, I like that," the young man said smiling.

Dwayne Zipper turned to Cliff and said, "Reb I been thinking and I ___. You think you could find ___. Get me one I will like."

"Well, Dwayne, right now the only thing I can think of when I look at you is Dizzy."

They all laughed and Dwayne laughed the loudest. "I like that. I will ___. Thank you, Reb."

And from that moment on Dwayne Zipper ceased to exist and 'Dizzy' arrived on the scene.

When the crowd broke up, Nadine went to the barn and began to gather what she would need for this trip. First came her revolver and the Sharps. *'I will take these to Johnny first thing,'* she thought. *'I know they are in good shape as Reb never lets our guns go any length of time without cleaning them, but he told Johnny to check all guns and I will do as the others must do.'*

Nadine then packed a pair of her riding overalls, a heavy cotton shirt she had found in one of the stores in Arkansas, the old floppy hat, and one of Cliff's wool shirts, then rolled and tied them in a blanket. "Be sure to bring these with you," she said to Cliff. "I don't aim to be riding back here bare-bottom in a dress."

He looked at her and let a slight smile come to his lips. "I'll remember," he replied.

The weather slowly began to warm as the cloud cover came

once again and kept the earth's heat in at night. When they boarded the wagon two hours before sunup Nadine was pleased to find the temperature above freezing for the first time in several mornings. She was wearing a pale gray daydress that had small yellow daisies spattered about and a matching bonnet she had made. After careful study, she had decided against wearing underwear. Plain cotton long johns on the bottom would have to suffice for both this dress and her overalls, but not for what she knew she would have to wear on the train. These would have to be pantaloons of some sort, and none she had ever seen would wear well under her overalls. She also suspected that she would have very little time to change after leaving the train, so the decision was made to wear nothing under her dress. *'What would Addie think, if she knew?'* Nadine laughed to herself. Covering all this was one of the heavy woolen coats that had been removed from the dead Yankee cavalrymen who had attacked their home months before.

It was not uncommon to see civilians wearing bits and pieces of uniforms. Many of the soldiers who mustered out kept the clothes they were wearing at the time, and also many who had not yet left the services stole from the warehouses and sold items on the civilian market, often as a payment for a gambling debt, especially shortly after the war when everything was so scarce to the whites in the south.

Nadine had mended the single hole to its left breast where the ball had entered, removed the union buttons, and replaced them with some made of bone Johnny had brought her; no one would question the coat, she was sure.

Dizzy had the team hitched long before Nadine came out. He had chosen Ananias and Sapphira, two large, deep red colored mules that pulled together well. He made sure they were watered and he gave each a sack of grain in which he had added a small amount of sorghum molasses. He was feeling quite proud that Reb had entrusted him with the responsibility of caring for his wife.

Under the wagon seat he had placed his double-barrel shotgun in addition to a Remington revolver he wore cross-draw, hidden by his coat.

When she came out she handed Cliff the bed roll and watched

with interest as he tied it to one of the horse's saddles. "Don't you lose that or I'll be in a hell of a spot," she said to him. Then she took the Sharps from Johnny and hung its long gold chain around her neck and shifted her shoulders around so her large breast would move, giving the small gun a chance to pass between them and rest in a spot where it would not irritate her or be detected by others.

Johnny turned his head when he saw her breast moving. Not that he didn't enjoy the thought of what was taking place under the cotton dress, but he somehow felt it was Reb's right to know of such, and not his.

She then held out her hand to him and he gave her the 32 which she slipped into her small hand bag; a bag she had made from a cap that Tillie had given her. Nadine had taken the bonnet and cut slots around the base and threaded a ribbon in them for a drawstring and carrier; it worked very well as a purse and concealed the small revolver completely.

Cliff watched the wagon move towards the Brooks' house a half mile away. They had not discussed her duties on this trip at all. He had given the instruction that she was to find out who the bad guys were and how she was to do this was left entirely up to her.

He was a little disappointed, though not surprised, that Mary Ann had refused to go to town with them. She had become more and more depressed after Tillie had been killed. Marty had steadily recovered to a point and then his progress had stopped, and it was becoming more and more obvious he would get no better. He could ride now if someone helped him on the horse and he could walk short distances with a cane, but he would never be able to work again; not like he had once done. His knees simply no longer had the strength to carry the weight of anything more than his body and then only for a short time. The idea of him lifting sacks of flour, grain, or sugar was out of the question. If he ever again kept a store, it would be with the help of another strong man, and Cliff realized this, too, was a source of Mary Ann's hopelessness. J. M. on the other hand, who could be just the help Marty needed, was so embedded in hate, that he obviously thought of little other than revenge.

Cliff had become increasingly worried about being able to control J. M. Allowing him to become enraged in front of the wrong people might jeopardize the safety and purpose of a raid, which it was his responsibility to execute properly, but in what they were doing this week, no man could have stopped J. M. from going along, and none should. This Cliff realized well, nonetheless, he knew he must find a time in which to caution him about the importance of following orders when they were given.

Esther was ready when the team pulled up. Sam helped her aboard and then turned to his horse and mounted. "You take care, old woman," he said to her.

Smiling, she replied, "It is you that needs to take care, old man."

He touched the front brim of his hat and said "Ladies." and then turned his horse and rode towards the barn.

The women both watched him gradually disappear into the light fog.

'The moon will be full in two or three nights,' Nadine thought *'that will be good if we have to travel after dark on our way home.'*

Dizzy dropped the reins on the backs of the mules and whistled lightly once, "On Ananias, on Sapphira," he called to them as if they were old friends.

The wagon moved off with a small jerk that bounced them around on the spring seat, and then they settled into a regular rock back and forth as the animals slowly crept along.

When they passed Granny Keeling's house, Nadine saw there was a light on inside and she pictured the old skinny woman moving about behind the logs. *'Johnny would have built a fire before he left and now maybe she was up putting more wood on it, or maybe she was taking a cup of coffee?'* The images of all this ran through her mind as they slowly moved off into the darkness. The trees along the road canopied the area so that only small strands of the moon's silver light were able to fight their way through to the road below, but it was of no consequence, as the mules knew the way as well as the man, and had no thoughts other than the task at hand.

Esther was her joyful self, and by the time they passed Mt. Horeb Church, the girls were in constant conversation about one thing and then another. Dizzy tried to listen for a while, but they talked too fast for him to keep up and they found things to laugh at that he didn't find any humor in at all, so soon he was deep in his own thoughts and no longer hearing anything they were saying. In time and with the rising of the sun, the thin layer of fog began to lift and form light clouds a few hundred feet above the ground. Suddenly, Sapphira lifted her tail and dropped several patties on the road. As if not to be outdone, Ananias followed a few moments later. This brought Dizzy back to the present. He felt terribly embarrassed that such a thing would happen while he was so near two ladies, but he didn't know what to do or say about it, so he said nothing, which of course was exactly the right thing to do. The incident, however, did nothing to interrupt the conversation taking place to his left.

The five riders departed an hour after the wagon. Each man led an extra horse, and there was one more whose reins were tied to the tail of the last in line. They too passed Granny Keeling's house, but instead of turning south on the road that led to Madison, they continued west following the trail towards Rocky Ford and on to Nankin. Cliff cautioned once again for them to vary their tracks so as not to leave too conspicuous a trail.

In less than an hour, the men had passed the grits mill and were entering the swampy area east of Rocky Ford. It was this area that would give them the greatest security should the federals come looking for their hideout. Only locals could successfully maneuver though this knee-deep water without plunging into the many bogs of quicksand that were scattered throughout the swamp.

Cliff knew an experienced tracker would be able to locate the disturbed leaves that blanketed the sand at the bottom of the acid stained water, but there were few good trackers around. Some of the darkies were good at it, but they mostly were afraid of the gators and cottonmouths that called this swamp home, and the homefolk by now knew the reason for their resistance and would offer little help to the invaders of their land. *'That is, except perhaps Dan Faux or Jay Shaw,'* Cliff thought.

He knew it was his responsibility to determine if both these men were truly scalawags, or just one of them, and if so, which one. *'I will have to figure out a trap for them when I get back.'*

That night they camped a mile north of the tracks on a hill of red clay seven miles from Tallahassee. Sitting by the fire, Cliff wondered how Nadine was doing.

It had taken the wagon seven hours to reach Madison. Esther had brought several biscuits with her that she had made that morning, along with a small jar of honey she had gotten when they were in town a month before. These had been wonderful delights as they traveled, and Dizzy thought he had surely been given the choicest of duties on this raid. However, as they were approaching the square, the bell of the Presbyterian Church could be heard ringing out the mid-day hour as it did every day, except Sundays. On Sundays no one dared to interrupt Reverend James' sermon, which was only beginning to warm up by noon.

The sound, however, made the trio forget all about the basket of biscuits they had devoured that morning, and instead caused Esther to instruct in a commanding voice, "Dwayne, stop over there by Albritton's Restaurant and we'll have a bite or two for dinner."

"Yas, Ma'am," he replied and turned the team towards the small building next to the three-story Merchant's Hotel.

**Range Street, Madison, Florida 1870 looking north.
The Merchant's Hotel is on the left.**

Nadine and Esther ordered a bacon sandwich each and Dizzy ordered a bowl of stew that was the special of the day. The room was quite warm, as the heat from the kitchen and the large pot-bellied stove made a joint venture to stomp out the cold air that crept in around the door and windows.

"It feels so good in here," Esther said rubbing the knuckles of first one hand and then the other. "I'm getting to where the cold bothers me more and more all the time."

"Yes, I know what you mean, even though the temperature here is never as low as it would be this time of the year in Wyoming, nonetheless, it feels just as cold. It really cuts you to the bone," Nadine replied.

"I can't even imagine Wyoming," Esther said. "What is it like?"

"Oh, I don't know, nothing like this."

"Tell me," Esther said very enthusiastically.

"Well, most of it is a desert. The only water is in the two or three rivers that cut through the big open, that's what the plains are called there. In South Pass where I met Reb, it is just a huge open valley mostly dotted with sage brush. South Pass City is a little higher up and there are trees there. Scattered trees, where the snow doesn't melt until full summer, nothing like here. There are more trees in Madison County than the whole state of Wyoming."

"Really?" Dizzy asked. "I can't understand that, Wyoming ain't very big, huh?"

"Dizzy, there are more trees in Madison County than all the prairie put together, from Texas all the way to Canada, and Wyoming is bigger than Florida, Georgia and Alabama combined. It seldom rains there, and unless you are high where the snow stays, or along a river bank, there is just not enough water for them to grow."

"Oh," he replied still not being able to visualize it. "I wus in The Shenandoah during the war. There weren't many trees there, least not after the armies cut them all down fur firewood."

"It must be something to be able to see so far," Esther said.

"Yes, that was something I had to get used to all over again," Nadine admitted. "I was so accustomed to finding my way by looking at a mountain that might be fifty miles away, now I seldom can see a few hundred yards, but at least there's no snow."

"It snows here sometimes,", Dizzy said. "I remember back in the winter a' fifty-eight it snowed nigh on two inches."

"Well, in South Pass back in the winter of fifty-eight it snowed forty feet," Nadine said.

Dizzy immediately opened his eyes and mouth as wide as they would go at the thought of such. "Did you see it?"

"No, Dwayne. I was still in Missouri in fifty-eight but it snows forty feet every winter in the Rockies."

With his eyes still open as wide as possible he replied, "It do? Well, I'll be!"

At that moment a girl dressed in a very unladylike garment came through a door at the back of the room and sat four mugs of beer on a table where several gentlemen were sitting. Nadine watched her as she took payment and then quickly vanished back through the door.

Esther saw the interest her friend showed and said "There is a saloon in the rear of the hotel next door. Most men who want spirits enter from the old Saint Augustine Road, but those gents over there happen to be some of the cream of Governor Reed's appointed politicians and they would not lower themselves to enter the saloon in the light of day, so Mrs. Albritton must put up with them eating in here and sending for their beverages," Esther paused and exhaled a long breath before adding, "She has to, or that bunch would take this little business away from her."

"Who is the girl?" Nadine asked.

"I don't know. She is new to me."

"Her name is Vicky," Dizzy said, then added "She's a whore." Immediately he realized what he said and rushed his palm over his mouth. "Oh, I'm sorry Ma'am. I didn't mean no___. I just wus answer___."

"It's quite all right, Dwayne," Esther said "I'm sure we're both fully aware what a whore is."

"Yeah, it's a girl down on her luck," Nadine added without looking away from the door the girl had disappeared through.

After they had finished their meal they walked out and paused where the mules were tied.

"Dwayne, will you drive over to Mr. Parramore's store and wait there for us. It's such a lovely day I think we will walk," Nadine said.

"Yas' 'um," he replied and untied the leads.

As the two women crossed the road Esther commented, "This here road was called The Old Spanish Trail back when I first came here, and now The Saint Augustine Road, because it runs from Saint Augustine to Pensacola. Although west of Tallahassee they called it the Military Road." She thought a moment and then added, "Everywhere else it's called The Bellamy Road, but as the good book says, a king is not recognized in his home land; here in Madison no one gives our own Mr. Bellamy credit for building the road."

Esther questioned as she looked overhead at the thick clouds that now hid the sun, "This is your idea of a lovely day?"

"Sure, don't you think so?"

Shaking her head before answering, she replied, "No. I do not."

They went first into Sue Livingston's Dress Shop and Nadine began looking through what was on display and then at the rolls of cloth that were stacked on a wooden table, running her fingers over the material.

Esther had immediately struck up a conversation with Sue and they sounded like sisters who had not seen each other for years.

'There simply is not anything here I can use.' Nadine thought. She really hadn't expected she would find what she needed in Madison, but hoped she might find something she could quickly modify. That simply was not the case. Finally, she walked over to where the two women were talking.

"Did you find anything?" Esther asked.

"No, I did not."

"Well, we have all sorts of pretty daydresses and some really nice Sunday things. The textile industry in the Carolinas is back in full swing once again, and with our long leaf cotton being sent there, we are getting some really wonderful things."

"I didn't see what I wanted."

"Perhaps if you tell me what you are looking for, I can help."

"No, I guess not just now," she replied trying to be as polite to Esther's friend as she could.

"Something for Sunday, perhaps?"

"No," Nadine said and starting for the door she stopped and turned back. "I'll be back another day."

"If you tell me what you want, I can have it made for you and you can pick it up the next time you are in town."

Shaking her head and wanting to escape, she simply said "Not right now," and continued for the door.

Esther said her goodbyes and quickly followed her friend out to the boardwalk where she was standing.

"I'm sorry; I hope my talking with Sue didn't offend you."

"No, not at all, I'm just worried about the men, that's all," she lied and turned away so Esther would not see her eyes.

"They will be all right. Reb and Sam are good leaders. They won't let J. M. get them into trouble."

"I know," Nadine replied still looking away. Finally she said, "Look why don't you go ahead and get the supplies you need and I'll go back and get us a couple of rooms for the night."

"Well, alright, if you had rather."

"Yes, I think I need to lie down for a little while. I feel a little light-headed."

"You need me to walk back with you?"

"No, of course not; I just want to rest away from that blamed old wagon for a while. Do what you have to do and I'll be ready for supper when you return."

"Alright," Esther said as she tapped Nadine's hand with hers. "I won't be too long."

"Take your time. Do what you have to do. I'll take a nap and be fresh as a daisy when you get back," Nadine said, then turned and immediately headed back towards the hotel before her friend could say anymore.

Nadine walked north under the store canopies for a few minutes and then stopped and looked into the window of Van Priest's Store. After a few moments she glanced back and saw Esther was also gazing into store windows a block behind her.

Finally her friend continued walking up Range Street to Parramore's Store where the wagon was parked, but there was no sign of Dwayne Zipper.

Entering the store, Esther immediately saw Barney Harris who was already headed towards her.

"Hello, Esther."

"Hello, Barney, I didn't know you were working here."

"Yes, for a few weeks anyway; can I help you find something?"

"Why yes, Barney," she said, "I need a barrel of sixteen-penny nails."

He immediately grew a sour look. A barrel of sixteen-penny nails would weigh far more than he cared to load, even for a strikingly handsome lady like the former Mrs. Homer. "Uh, do you have a man with you?"

"Yes, I do, but I seem to have misplaced him at the moment, so you just go ahead and load it in my wagon," she said snickering to herself, without showing the slightest appearance that she realized what a burden she had asked of the thin man.

Fifteen minutes later, when he returned inside she asked, "What do I owe you?"

"That's all you need?"

"Yes, that's all." The truth was she didn't need them, but realized that they would not be a waste with so much building going on around the stage stop.

He looked at her in total surprise.

"Well, anyway, whatever it is, put it on our bill and Sam will pay you when he is in town."

"He's not with you?"

"Heavens no, he's building our new home. I came with Dwayne Zipper."

Barney looked to the back door where Dwayne was playing a game of checkers and said, "You are here with Dwayne?"

"Yes, do you know where he is?"

"Yes, I think I do," he said and wiping the sweat from his brow, turned and fully opened the door that lead to the back room. "Dwayne, Mrs. Brooks is here."

"Oh, got 'a go, see you the____. Be careful and don't let them Yankees get you," he said as he jumped up from the chair.

"Are you ready, Mrs. Brooks?"

"Yes, I now need to go to the newspaper office."

"Yas, 'um," he said as he helped her into the wagon then looking about, he questioned, "Miss Nadine?"

"She's waiting on us."

"Oh," he replied and nodded his head wondering *'How could that be?'*

Nadine watched from the shade of the big live oak in front of the hotel until she saw their wagon start south on Range towards the newspaper office a couple of miles away, then she too turned and headed south on Range Street towards its intersection with Dade.

On their trip down, Cliff had taken his old holster belt with the small snake-buckle that he had used to carry his Colt Army revolver during the war, and had it cut down to fit Nadine's small waist. It made a good strap for her to carry her short Arkansas Toothpick when she was in her overalls. On this day, she had brought it with her along with a drawing she had made, and took both to Bevin's Livery. Handing the belt and her drawing to Mr. Bevin, she began explaining what she wanted. He looked more shocked than surprised at her as she described the contraption she wanted him to make.

"You see, I want you to cut me a strap of soft leather and sew it to the belt here. I will be wearing it with the buckle in the back, and under my dress of course. This here strap runs down my left leg past this and on to this loop, which of course will be around my leg just above the knee. This other one will be around my upper thigh. You must also make me a holster; this too from soft leather that will enclose this,"she said handing him her Root revolver. "The holster will be sewed between these two loops and that way I can carry my revolver unseen between my legs."

When she looked back up at him hoping he had a good understanding of her wants, all she saw was the older man with his mouth and eyes fully open.

"Mr. Bevin, don't be so much of a prude; I'm not going to require you to fit it on me, I just need you to make it. Today. I'm going on the train tomorrow and a lady traveling alone needs protection these days."

Bevin nodded his head and looked from her pretty face back to the sketch. "You are going to wear a pistol under your understuff?"

"No, just under my dress so I can get to it should I need to, and in a hurry too," she said back.

"Uh-huh, you want it to be next to your leg?"

"Yes, this strap will run down from the belt past the first loop which I will have my leg through, high on my thigh and on down to the other loop which also will fit around my leg just above the knee, and the holster will be sewn between the two loops on the other side and fit tightly against my other leg. Now you must make sure the holster fits tight and doesn't flop around while I'm walking. You do understand don't you?"

"Uh-huh, I think so. And you want this today?"

"Yes, I'll pick it up just before you close this evening or first thing in the morning at the latest," Nadine said and then handed him a folded twenty-dollar red note.

Upon seeing this, his eyes became even larger than they had when she first began explaining her desires.

The Madison Trace was located in an old warehouse that had been used to store lumber before the war. In those days the Balough family had made a good living selling the cypress timber located in the nearby swamps and had at one time owned a large sawmill, but that had been taken over when the first occupational troops arrived in Madison County in '66. Later, it mysteriously burned to the ground. A Robert Walker, who had come from Maryville,

Pennsylvania, had invested all his money in the mill, and after the fire, left town with far less wealth than when he arrived.

Horace Balough had scraped together enough money to pay the back taxes on the warehouse, but he didn't have the money to rebuild the mill. However, he was glad he could take his family back home. It had been the right decision. Eventually the family moved into the warehouse and closed off a second story area as living quarters. They rented out most of the ground floor to the new politicians, who had been sent to govern Madison, as a place to store their buggies and surreys while they were in the north during the summer months. Balough, being a man of astute business sense, made good use of these Yankee dollars, and soon had purchased an old printing press that had belonged to the Carter family in Perry, before their property had been taken away. Simon Carter had hid the press in an old abandoned slave shack that had long since been surrounded by new growth and could not be seen from the road.

From that worn press, Horace began "*The Trace*," and it gradually became a paper known to print more truth than propaganda, a policy that didn't always sit well with the appointed few.

Three years after he began the new business, his warehouse caught fire late one night. Thankfully, the Balough family was in Tallahassee at the time. The blaze was brought under control before the building was consumed; however, the press was a total loss. But the greatest loss proved to have been to a young darkie who worked as a delivery boy for the paper, and who slept in a back room at night.

Doc Sinnott reported the smoke from the ink had been so strong, the boy had been killed by poisonous gasses, and not the blaze.

Later, it was proven that the fire had been deliberately set and was obviously an act to hurt the Balough business. Even papers in surrounding areas that were not normally in sympathy with Balough and his editorials made big headlines of the arson of a newspaper office. After the fire, the main header on the front page of *The Tallahassee Democrat* read:

Murder Pure and Simple

In an Attempt to Destroy the Printing Press of the Madison Trace, Unknown Nighthawks Murdered a Young Freedman During Their Cowardly Act of Arson

It was not that the people with the Tallahassee paper were that aligned to Balough, rather the attack on a newspaper, any newspaper, was an unforgivable sin and one they would not let go of. Thus they did not letup printing similar articles for several weeks, until Governor Reed arranged for a newer printing press, that the army had abandoned, to be given to Balough in an effort to stop the blasting in the headlines.

When their wagon arrived in front of the old warehouse, Esther took notice of the two buggies in front of the large building. One, an older black vehicle with a gray horse hitched to it and the second, a new burgundy colored 'Doctor's Buggy,' that a tall, thin darkie, dressed in a black suit, stood by rubbing down the bay horse with a curry comb.

"Mr. Balough is in his office," the young lady said when Esther inquired. "He is with a customer right now, if you care to wait," indicating a single straight back chair constructed from round stakes approximately two inches in diameter taken from the small trees that abound on Balough's property.

"I'll wait," Esther said, before turning to Dwayne. "Looks like this might take a while, if you had rather wait outside, it will be all right."

Nodding thankfully, Dizzy returned his hat to his head and left the small room.

Ten minutes passed and Esther was thinking she had gotten the worst end of her deal with Dizzy, as the chair dug painfully into her bottom and back, but soon she saw Balough and another man, who was overdressed for the area, come down the stairs. Although she could hear them talking, she could not understand their words through the large window. When the tall man turned to leave, Balough saw her there and immediately entered the room.

"Esther, I didn't know you were here. Please come up to my office."

"Thank you. I was about to declare war on that chair."

"Oh, goodness! There is supposed to be a pillow on that seat," he looked around and then ask the lady there, "Molly, do you know what happened to the pillow that goes in the chair?"

"No!" she said back, shaking her head quickly.

"Well, we must find it. I suppose that is terrible punishment, isn't it?" he said to Esther as he took her by the elbow and guided her out of the room to the stairs.

As soon as Molly heard the door close above, she jumped up and took the pillow from her seat and slid it over behind the wooden chair, hoping he would think had been there all along.

"What brings you to town? Is Sam with you?" he asked as they entered the office.

"No, he's working on the new house we are building, hoping for the stage stop contract. If we get it we want to be ready."

"That's great. I know you will make a go of it there, and don't worry, if I have anything to do with it, the contract will be yours."

"Thank you. This could be God-sent in these hard times," she said before turning her attention to more serious questions.

"Mr. Balough, I have here a paper from Valdosta," she said, handing the folded sheets to him. "And here is our version of the same incident," she added, also passing to him a folded sheet of brown paper. "As you will see, there is a substantial difference. I can assure you, ours is the truth."

He took the second paper and quickly glanced first at one and then the other. "This is just as I thought. I will make good use of this," he said with a deep expression of genuine concern.

"There is something else you need to be aware of," she said and then she told him of what had happened to Tillie Gunter.

When she finished, he sat there with his head bowed moving it slowly back and forth. "This so-called Reconstruction is the biggest farce I have ever heard of. I pray someday soon it will come to an end," he said. "But I'm afraid that will not happen as long as we retain Grant as President[18]"

"I do expect there will be justice served on the murderers," she said, preparing him for what was to come.

"As well as should be, but I don't know how, they being occupational soldiers with strong backing of this Tidwell's political arm. You know, he's tied directly in with Governor Bullock," Balough offered.

"Yes, we have heard that, but surely Bullock will someday fall; won't he Mr. Balough?"

"Yes, child, I'm sure he will."

It had been a long time since anyone had called her "Child" and she immediately felt a warm glow deep inside her chest.

---

[18] Present President: Ulysses Simpson Grant the Hero of Appomattox served as president of the United States from 1869 to 1877 today Presidential experts typically rank Grant in the lowest quartile of U.S. presidents, for his tolerance of corruption.

"Here is something else Sam asked me to bring," she said, handing him the list of names and aliases.

"He suggested you burn this after you had a chance to memorize it."

Looking at the paper he nodded his head and agreed, "That's good thinking on his part."

"Are you staying over tonight?"

"Yes, my friend and I are staying at the new Merchant's Hotel in town. We have Dwayne Zipper to drive us."

"Nonsense, you ladies will stay with us, here as our guests. Opal would have a fit if she knew you were staying in that hotel without Sam."

Immediately she realized the dilemma she was in. Reb had made it plain that no one was to know of Nadine's departure on the train Friday morning, and yet it would be near impossible for them to be in their home and the Balough's not learn of the trip.

"I don't know. We have already rented our rooms."

"Nonsense, you just go and un-rent them. We'll expect you for supper, say around five."

She simply didn't know how to get out of it so she reluctantly said, "Alright, I still have to get supplies from Captain Ingles' store."

"You can get that in the morning before you head home. You don't want them left in a wagon all night anyway."

"Alright, I'll go and get Nadine. Dwayne can bring us back by five."

When Esther told her of what had happened a look of concern came over her friend's face. Finally Nadine said, "Alright, I'll go with you tonight, but do not let anyone know I'll be staying over tomorrow night. It is imperative that the Balough's think I am returning with you tomorrow."

"There's something you're not telling me, Nadine."

"Yes there is, and I am not going to tell you, Reb said as few people as knew of the plans, the better off we would all be, and that is how it must be."

This hurt her friend and she saw tears building in Esther's eyes before she spoke, "You don't trust me?"

"Of course I do, but Reb made it clear not to tell anyone about this part of the plan, and I must do as he instructed. Believe me it's best for you and all of us that you and Dwayne not know," she replied placing her arms around her friend and giving her a hug.

"If you say so," Esther finally said, not satisfied with the answer, but smart enough to realize that was the way it was going to be.

Gathering her composure she said, "Come on, we had better go if we are going to make it there by five."

When they passed the clerk at the bottom of the stairs Nadine stopped and paid the man while Esther waited a short distance away. "We'll need both rooms tonight but our driver will not be staying tomorrow night, so that room can go back."

"Very well, Madam."

Retrieving her change from the five-dollar bill she had given him, she added, "I'll also need a buggy to take me to the train station Friday morning," she said.

The man nodded his head and recounted her change, laying seventy-seven cents on the countertop. "Please give us thirty minutes notice before you need the buggy."

"Have the buggy here, ready at three o'clock sharp," she said, and she handed him a sealed envelope that had the name Vickie printed on it. "Also, see this is delivered tonight." She turned away after dropping the coins into a small snap purse and then deposited that into Tillie's old bonnet.

"Very well, Madam," the clerk said a little taken aback by her sternness. When she was out of sight, he held the envelope up to the light but could see nothing of its contents.

The evening was quite entertaining with a large supper prepared by a hugely overweight darkie Mr. Balough referred to as Eldora. The food was delicious, but Nadine somehow had a hard time eating. Dizzy, who ate with the hands in the kitchen, had no such problems and was feeling quite stuffed when he ask if it was alright for him to go back to the hotel.

"Sure, Dwayne," Esther told him. "Just be sure you are here early. We have a lot to do in the morning before we head back."

"Yes, Ma'am."

"Breakfast is served here at seven sharp," Horace Balough said to him and smiled, "If you want some, don't be late."

"Oh, I'll be here alright, you can count on that if 'n I ha___you bet," he replied, just before he disappeared from the dining room.

The next two hours were filled with talk of everything except what was on Nadine's mind. Finally, they got around to talking about Wyoming. "What ever possessed you to go to the wilds of Wyoming?" Mrs. Balough asked.

Nadine looked at their hostess keenly for the first time and seeing her deep blue eyes knew immediately why she had been named Opal. She was an attractive woman about the same age as Nadine's mother had been when she passed. Her dress and mannerisms showed she had been well educated, both in the customs and etiquette of the antebellum south, as well as the necessities of school requirements. This night one would have never known so recently the lady had suffered, along with her family, the cruelties of the post war south.

"That's where my husband took me," she said and then seeing the expression on their faces she added, "My first husband."

"Oh," Mrs. Balough replied with her head lowered slightly.

Nadine realized she was in the presence of another strong-willed church go'er who obviously considered divorce akin to horse stealing, so she added. "Poor Brady was killed working his claim."

"Oh, you poor thing," immediately Opal Balough replied, with a most sincere sympathy. "How ever did you survive?"

Nadine took a deep breath and thought *'I ought to say I was the best damn whore in the territory, but I won't. The old girl would have a stroke right here and we'd lose our connection with the paper.'* Letting the breath out slowly she said, "I worked for the local Judge. I had saved enough money to get me back to Missouri when this tall, dark, handsome man with a deep Georgia drawl asked me to marry him and I couldn't refuse."

"Oh, that's so romantic," her hostess said, before asking, "Had you known him long?"

'You nosey old biddy,' she thought, but what she replied was "Yes, he and my husband had been best friends ever since he arrived," she lied again and then added a touch of truth to her story, "In fact, I met Reb the very day he arrived in town."

"That's just wonderful." she said smiling and then continued with her questions, "What ever did you do with yourself while your husband was away digging in those awful mines?"

"As I said, I worked for the Judge there. Judge Esther Morris."

"I never! A woman judge, why what will come next?" Balough said suddenly.

"The right to vote, I suspect," Nadine replied.

"Maybe in the wild west, but that will never happen here," Horace Balough quickly injected.

"Maybe you're right, Mr. Balough," Nadine said; then she turned to his wife and asked, "And you, Ma'am, what did you do before you became a publisher?"

"Me? Why Horace is the publisher. I'm just a housewife. I ___," Nadine could hear her speaking but no longer listened to the words, her mind was on the plan she was working out for the next two days.

An hour later they were shown to their room and they saw it was somewhat larger than the one at the hotel, but not by much. There was a big featherbed and a pee-pot sitting in a convenient little chair made just for it beside the armoire where they hung their clothes before retiring. There was also a cherry table with a large mirror attached to the top and a pitcher of water with two glasses close by.

Earlier, Nadine had cursed herself for not thinking ahead about the sleeping arrangements before she left home, but at the time she could only think of her task with total uneasiness.

During her hour stay at the hotel room alone, her plan had begun to materialize in her mind; her first step had been to return to Sue Livingston's, where she bought a nice dress, two sizes too small for her, explaining it was for her niece, and a pair of pantaloons, as well as a nightgown for sleeping in. The next step was the envelope she had given the desk clerk.

The two women made small talk, but Nadine could tell there was still a little hurt in Esther over her secrecy and she was sorry about that; but she had no intention of sharing her plan with her friend, or anyone else she knew, not even Reb Brown. She was relieved when Esther suggested they turn down the lamp and get some sleep.

For a long time after she heard her friend begin deep breathing, which soon resulted in a soft snore, Nadine stared at the moonlight reflecting off the mirror to the ceiling overhead. Over and over she rehearsed her plan until she finally fell asleep, and the sound of the rooster's crow was all too quickly heard.

The women dressed without many words spoken between them. Esther was not her usual cheerful self that morning at the breakfast table, and only Nadine knew why.

"I do hope you were warm enough last night," Opal said and then continued talking without giving either a chance to answer.

When they had finished and the dishes had been removed,

Dizzy had still not arrived, and both women began to worry that something might have happened to him.

Nadine realized he was very loyal to the group, but also knew he was not the brightest man that ever walked the streets, and it was possible sharp individuals might be able to trick him into revealing information that could damage their cause.

It was past nine when they heard a wagon approaching at a fast speed. Looking out, Nadine saw the mules lathered up from trotting the two miles from town.

"It's about time," Esther scolded him when he stopped in front of the building.

"Yas, Ma'am," he said lowering his head.

Nadine saw the redness in his eyes and slump to his shoulders and knew he was experiencing a terrible hangover. *'It's a wonder he made it here at all,'* she thought.

When they had said their goodbyes and expressed their gratitude to their host and hostess, they mounted the wagon, with the assistance of Mr. Balough. When seated on the spring seat, Esther suddenly turned to Dizzy and said quite loudly, "Lord above, Dwayne, you smell like a whiskey still."

"Yas, Ma'am," was all he could say in reply.

He stopped twice between the newspaper office and Inglis' store, leaping from the wagon and running around behind, so the women would not see him up-chucking.

Nadine instructed him to stop at the depot where she went in and checked the departure schedules and then quickly returned before either of her companions dismounted the wagon. Arriving at Inglis' Store, which was located just across the tracks from Madison's Depot, Nadine took notice of the single axle cart drawn by a healthy mule and the darkies who made no pretence about their staring at the two ladies who were sitting on the spring seat. Even though she had never felt any animosity toward the African people before, she suddenly found herself having a sour taste for the Freedmen who so often treated white women rudely, when their men folk were not around. Under her breath she said, "I never knew what a nigger was until I came to the south."

Esther talked with the Captain while Nadine supervised the loading of the supplies in the wagon. When finished, she returned inside the store. Esther motioned her to come in the office. "Captain,

Jacksonville, Pensacola & Mobile
RAIL ROAD.

On and after Sunday, July 2, 1871,
PASSENGER TRAINS ON THESE ROADS
will run as follows, every day, except Sundays :

Trains Going East :

Leave Quincy	8.40 A. M.
Arrive at Tallahassee	10.30 "
Leave Tallahassee	10.50 "
Leave Monticello	12.18 P. M.
Leave Madison	3.20 "
Leave Live Oak	5.35 "
Arrive at Savannah	6.25 A. M.
Leave Lake City	7.14 P. M.
Leave Baldwin	10.11 "
Arrive at Jacksonville	11.27 "

Trains Going West :

Leave Jacksonville	6.30 A. M.
Leave Baldwin	8.10 "
Leave Lake City	11.18 "
Leave Live Oak	1.16 P. M.
Leave Madison	3.30 "
Leave Monticello	5.02 "
Arrive at Tallahassee	7.50 "
Leave Tallahassee	8.20 "
Arrive at Quincy	10.00 "

Passenger Train Going East :

Leave Savannah	10.15 P. M.
Leave Live Oak	10.00 A. M.
Leave Lake City	11.18 "
Leave Baldwin	1.85 P. M.
Arrive at Jacksonville	2.35 "

Passenger Train Going West :

Leave Jacksonville	4.00 P. M.
Leave Baldwin	5.10 "

this is Mrs. Brown. It is her husband who is supplying the money for the rifles."

She was quite surprised upon seeing Inglis, having assumed he would be much older considering all she had heard about his accomplishments, yet before her was a man in his early thirties. His light hair and sharp blue eyes matched his fair skin perfectly. He was a reserved man and although moved with an obvious limp, he did it with such poise normally one simply did not notice. *'Not tall like Reb, but still trim, and not bad looking either,'* she thought.

She could not help but notice how he spoke with a slow deliberate speech, as if every word was carefully selected from a vast vault where his vocabulary was stored. He also seemed to always keep a pleasant expression on his face, smiling often as he spoke. One thing she was sure of, once met, John Inglis was a man that would never be forgotten.

"Mrs. Brown, I'm so glad to finally meet you," he said, immediately admiring her fine figure and strikingly handsome face. "I must admit though, I am a little uneasy about this request for so many of these repeating rifles."

Captain John Inglis' General Store
Across the tracks from the Madison Depot

"Captain Inglis, I hope I am not running afoul good judgment, but Esther has told me of your outstanding war record and I hope you still entertain some of the same beliefs that were so important in those days," she began.

"Mrs. Brown, I fought for my state against an invading army. I did not necessarily believe in all the reasons others fought for. For myself, I fought for principal, justice, and the constitutional right to self-government."

"Captain, do you believe this so called 'Reconstruction' is a just movement for all?"

"I certainly do not."

"Do you believe it to be constitutional?"

"It is by all means, unlawful under the Constitution," he said sternly.

"My husband is fighting the unjustness being exercised on homefolk by the occupational forces in Valdosta, as are our entire group, both men and women. We are deeply committed to doing the right thing and only what is right. I will not lie to you and say we never break the laws of the land of this day and time, but we never do an unjust act to anyone; be they southern, northern, black, or white. We do however, try to punish those who do unjust things to homefolk; and we need those rifles badly."

The man stared long and hard at her before saying a word; finally he spoke. "How much ammunition do you need with the rifles?"

She released a tense breath she had been holding before saying another word. "Reb never has given me a number, but in my judgment, all you can let us have."

"How do you plan to pay for all this?"

"We made a fair sum of money in the gold fields of Wyoming during the previous years, and converted that to redbacks on the Bank of San Francisco which we could use, but we also have some greenbacks that we had rather turn with somebody who would not be spending them locally."

Captain John Inglis about 1870

"I see," he replied and again looked her over, from the top of the little pink straw hat to as low as he could see of what was not hidden by the desk that separated them.

"I will tell you, I did receive the bid on the rifles, and with it, I am able to acquire five thousand rounds of ammunition. I would like to meet with your husband and discuss exactly what his needs are before we go any further."

"I believe he will be coming to town within a week."

"I will tell no one else of the purchase until I have had a chance to talk to him."

"I do thank you, Captain," Nadine said standing and extending her gloved hand.

Although Nadine thought of Esther as her dearest friend, she was greatly relieved when she watched their wagon finally move off to the north and out of sight from her hotel window.

It was exactly 10:30 a.m. when the soft knock was heard at the door. "Yes."

"It's me, Vickie. You sent me a note."

Nadine opened the door and let the girl enter. She quickly looked outside into the hallway before closing the door.

Looking around the small room and seeing no one else there, she said, "I a', I don't do ladies, normally. I a', well, it will be extra."

"Cool your britches," Nadine said. "I don't do ladies either, even for extra," she said, walking up and looking the girl over, and then moving around and looking at her backside.

"I'm glad you wore the red dress, like I asked."

"I did, but I don't understand."

"Well, here is the deal. My husband used to be a whoring man, before he met me, that is; and every so often he gets the urge to have him one again. So to keep him home where he belongs, I dress the part and play a game with him and he gets his kicks and I don't catch nothing that he brings home."

"Oh my, if more wives did that, I'd be out of business!" Vickie said looking astonished.

"What do you charge for all night?"

"Depends on who wants it," she said. "If it are a home boy, I get one dollar, but if 'n it is one a them Yankee officials, I get five dollars."

"Alright, I'll give you five dollars for the red dress and another dollar for you not to remember selling it to me."

"Gee, that would be great, but what will I wear?"

"I have a new one here for you," Nadine said, removing the new dress she had bought at Sue Livingston's.

"Well, alright," Vickie said touching the light blue garment with boney and frail looking hands.

"Let's have the dress."

The girl began to remove her outer clothing, as did Nadine saying, "You are going to have to help me get into this before you leave. I never will get it buttoned up by myself."

"Sure, ma'am."

Nadine stripped down to the red bloomers she had already put on, and then tried to get Vickie's corset on and laced up but it was just impossible. Finally, after spending twenty minutes trying, Vickie said, "Ma'am, you just got too much bosom to stuff into this here corset."

"I guess you're right," Nadine agreed and slung the white torture chamber on the bed. "I'll just have to bounce all the way home."

"Boy o' boy, if I had your tits, I could make enough in one year to get out a' this business," Vickie said admiring the naked melons that now swung freely from Nadine's chest.

"It takes more than tits to get out of the business, I assure you," Nadine replied, slipping the red dress over her head and pulling it down over her hips.

"Here, button it up for me," she said turning her back to the girl.

Vickie pulled the sides tightly and slowly got all the buttons through their eyes. Then she walked around and looked at Nadine from the front. "You know, ma'am, you are a real knockout. If you ever want to make some extra money, there are some special parties given up to the Mansion at Tallahassee what pays really good."

Nadine thought back to the party that John Morris had given his wife's legislator friends and gritted her teeth before answering, "No, these days the most I can handle is that man I married."

"I know what you mean. My Joe was much of a man. Even when I was pregnant he wanted a poke 'most every night."

"You have children?" Nadine asked.

"A little girl."

"Where is she?"

"My Ma is keeping her, only till I get enough money saved up to get a start."

"And your man?"

"Oh, Joe, he's buried up in Kentucky som'ers. He never came home from the war."

"That's tough," Nadine said remembering her own life only a year before.

"It's all right. They all said he was a very brave man. He picked up the flag after the man what regularly took it was kilt, and carried it straight into them Yankee lines 'afor he was hit," she said and then her voice began to tremble. "They all said he were a very brave man."

Nadine stepped over and placed her arm around the shorter girl's shoulder. "I'm sorry you lost your husband. I know how it feels. My first husband was shot and killed, too."

"Really?"

"Really."

"I'm glad you found you another man. A lady like you deserves one. A whore like me will never find another husband."

"Oh, I don't know. The Lord moves in mysterious ways, His wonders to perform," Nadine reassured her.

"You think so?"

"I know so," she answered and smiled. "Now help me get this cape on over this outfit so I can go out on the street without being arrested."

Vickie chuckled slightly and then helped her with the cape.

"Here, you can have this," Nadine said tossing her the dress she had worn to town the day before. "You might want to go to church sometime. Of course you might have to take it up a little."

"Ha, me going to church. Them straight-laced ladies would have a hissy were I to go walking into their world."

"You never know," Nadine said back in a knowing manner.

Just as they were about to start down the stairs, Vickie stopped and turned around and spoke, "Ma'am, I want to ask you something."

"Go ahead and ask."

"Just how much are you going to charge your husband?"

"Oh, believe me he is going to pay plenty for what I'm going to do for him today."

Vickie snickered and then said, "I wish I could see that. I bet you will get him good."

Nadine just winked at her and then Vickie turned and headed down the stairs. Nadine waited until she heard the side door open and close before she began slipping on her new purchase. Her descent down the stairs was an awakening and she soon realized she would have to get used to having the Root located where it now rested.

The night had been exceptionally warm for this time of year, and for the first time in several months, mosquitoes had awakened from their long sleep and were buzzing about everyone's heads. Only the smoke produced by the small fire protected the men from the pesky little fliers.

When the dawn broke, he saw fast moving dark clouds just above the tops of the big oaks and he knew another winter storm was headed their way, *'Better enjoy it, this warm snap will be short lived.'*

Before noon, a light drizzle began, followed an hour later by steady rain.

Cliff, Sam, Johnny, and Robert were now on foot awaiting the train at the Quincy Station. J. M. had taken the horses and continued on to the next water stop fifteen miles west.

The westbound had not even left the Madison station when Nadine saw through the open train window the first drops of moisture collecting on the boardwalk between the small building and the tracks.

She could see Captain Inglis' store on the opposite side of the train from the depot and she wondered *'What would he think if he saw me in Vickie's dress?'*

Then her thoughts changed to a more personal tone. *'I hope Reb doesn't catch his death in this.'*

The train consisted of an engine, a wood car, three passenger cars, two freight cars, and a caboose.

Seeing no soldiers in the third passenger car, she had taken a seat near the front to await the conductor. After he had punched her ticket, he moved forward to the next car. She waited five minutes and followed.

Here in the light of the oil burning lamps, she saw three soldiers among the ten passengers riding in this car, but they were all white men. She moved on.

Stopping on the platform between the rocking cars, she gazed through the glass at what lay ahead. She could see eight passengers, all in blue uniforms; the white men sat near the rear, the five colored soldiers were all bunched near the small pot belly stove at the front of the car.

She also saw all wore the light blue ribbon running down their pant legs, declaring them to be uniforms of Mounted Infantry.

'Five colored soldiers. But I only want three.' she thought. *'How am I going to find out which three killed Tillie?'*

Returning to the car she had just left, she waited until the train had taken on water and passengers at Tallahassee; then she again stood and thought before she moved forward, *'Two years ago I would have not even considered this a chore, but that was then and this is now.'* Pressing her upper teeth down over her bottom lip she squeezed slightly. This was one task she wanted to flee from, but she knew she had no escape. Finally she took a deep breath and spoke to herself in a stern but quite voice, "This is for you, Tillie," and then she moved forward to the next car.

Immediately most of the men turned to look at who had opened the door and allowed the most unpleasant air to come rushing in upon them. Once inside, she dropped the heavy coat and stepped forward a single pace. No one turned back after they saw the sight of her.

Nadine walked straight forward, stopping only momentarily to smile at the three men who sat near the rear. She knew her breasts were having a terrible time staying in Vicki's dress and she was not sure if either of her nipples were exposed, but she dared not look down to see; proceeding right past the colored solders, she stopped at the small stove and then turned around and bent forward so as to warm her posterior and then she spoke. "My, it's getting nippy today. My fanny feels like an iceberg."

Her raven hair, contrasting sharply against her white skin and bright red dress, seemed to add color to her face, but the bulging eyes and direct stares of the men who sat there left no doubt that her large breasts were on display as long as she stayed in this position.

The white soldiers now moved up and took the seats just behind the others.

"Are you guys all bound for Pensacola too?" she asked.

"We is," one answered

"You wouldn't happen to have something a gal could take a nip from, to warm her insides, would you?" she said as she untied the cape that covered her shoulders and handed it to one of the men in front of her.

The four men entered the last of the three newly painted yellow cars and took seats. Cliff and Sam occupied one seat near the rear, and four seats ahead Johnny was sitting just behind Robert.

The conductor was slow in coming forward to punch their tickets and Cliff was beginning to think he might be caught up in the melee that had to take place before the next stop for water.

Finally the short stocky man entered from their rear and yelled, "Tickets! All persons boarding at Quincy get out your tickets!"

His lack of a drawl and sharp tone brought a nasty taste in Cliff's mouth. *'Another foreigner sent down here by the government to take jobs away from homefolk,'* he surmised, as he held up his hand with the ticket in it.

The man took the ticket and punched it and placed it back in his hand without speaking another word.

'Maybe he ought to get caught up in this ruckus,' Cliff thought as the chubby little man continued forward.

It is customary for the engineer to announce his approach two miles out with three sharp blasts, and then begin reducing the power for the stop ahead. In this rain it was doubtful if anyone at the water tank heard the whistle, but some ten minutes after the conductor had left the car, those who had just boarded heard it as the signal for them to move, and that they did.

Robert dropped down between the first and second passenger cars where he could pull the connecting pin on the hitch as soon as there was enough forward pressure from the rear cars to give slack. At that moment, the conductor opened the door from the forwardmost passenger car and stood there with an astonished expression on his face.

Cliff quickly thumped him on the little flat hat he wore, and gave him a gentle push; and in an instant he was over the side disappearing before he could give alarm.

Shortly thereafter, the train bucked forward once and Robert pulled the pin free. Immediately, Sam began turning the brake wheel to produce a drag and then they both leaped forward as the back cars began to drift away.

Entering, Cliff could see everyone was gathered in a bunch at the front of the car but he could not see Nadine. Still he had no doubts of what had their attention.

He bent over and retrieved Nadine's coat that he saw laying there beside the door and laid it over the back of a seat, just as the other Renegades moved into the car.

This time no one turned to check on the cold wind that came rushing in.

Cliff side-slapped the first soldier he came to with his Smith & Wesson just as Sam used the butt of his revolver on the man standing next to him. Both fell without giving alarm but the head wounds were spilling a considerable amount of blood on the deck of the car.

They then pushed the next soldier forward and he fell into the others. He cursed at his friends to take it easy, before he turned around and saw the men with neckerchiefs covering most of their faces.

It was then that Nadine was first seen. The big black sergeant was standing behind her with his arms around her shoulders and each hand cupping one of her breasts that no longer were hidden by the red garment. His black skin contrasted sharply with her pearly white breast and Cliff felt a sudden moment of shame that he had exposed her to this task.

"What da' hell?" the black sergeant suddenly said and immediately the chubby Corporal swung around and realized he was staring into the very large bore of a handgun.

"It's about time!" Nadine bitterly shouted at her husband as she pulled the blue-coated arms apart and stepped forward.

Johnny's eyes grew as big as silver dollars when he saw her standing there with her breasts fully exposed and he cocked his revolver and pointed it straight into the sergeant's face.

"You know which ones we are after?" Cliff asked.

"These two are getting off in Marianna but Sergeant Butterball and his pals are headed for Pensacola," she replied as she pulled up her dress and stuffed her breasts back inside.

"Alright, tie them to the seats and gag them," he said motioning to the other soldiers. "Tie these three's hands behind them and bring them to the back of the car," Cliff ordered, and then he took Nadine by the arm and led her back to where he had left her coat.

The small group jumped from the slow moving train a hundred yards east of the Mount Pleasant water tank. Just as they did, a bolt of lightning lit the eastern sky and the boy operating the spout saw them, but gave no alarm.

J. M. had been watching from the nearby trees and was soon upon them with their mounts.

They immediately headed north away from the tracks and then turned west to get ahead of the train.

When they had gone two miles the locomotive was heard passing them, so they reasoned the engineer had not realized he no longer carried the last five cars.

However, what had actually occurred, was one of the soldiers that had been knocked unconscious awakened and released the others, but rather than returning for the other cars, they demanded that the engineer continue ahead with all steam to the next stop at Chattahoochee. He knew there was a Company of Cavalry stationed there and they would be the only chance of them catching the abductors.

The Lieutenant in command of the company was only too happy to assist. He had been stationed there immediately after graduation from "The Point," Class of '68, and had only small civil duties to perform up until this opportunity suddenly appeared in his career.

They waited fifteen minutes until an animal car could be connected, and then were backing full steam eastward towards Mount Pleasant.

The men on horseback had used the time to make sure they had the right three and had gotten Corporal Bacon to confess and identify Sergeant Ben Frank as the actual man who led the assault on Tillie Gunter.

They then moved back to the tracks along which the telegraph wires paralleled.

J. M. had just thrown the first rope over the telegraph pole cross-member when they heard the sound of the approaching train.

Hiding in the brush, the condemned men watched as their last hope raced by at twenty-five miles an hour.

Lieutenant Barber quickly dismounted his animals and had his men in pursuit eastward. When they encountered the soldiers and passengers of the disconnected cars who were walking west along the tracks, Corporal Watson informed him that no one had come east since they had begun their hike, and it was then a fast gallop back to Mount Pleasant.

After wandering about with no commanding action, someone thought to ask the water boy if he had seen anything.

When Barber finally located their trail, his horses were spent from their gallop back to the water tank and they had to rest them before again giving pursuit.

The six riders moved north from the tracks into Georgia and then west.

Nadine had removed her hideout rig and replaced the Root into her handbag when she changed from Vicki's red dress into the riding clothes Cliff had brought her before they left Mount Pleasant. To anyone fifty yards away, they were six men leading three horses.

They crossed Judge Spooner's farm some ten miles south of Bainbridge and then took the stage road southeast, finally cutting due south and fording the Ochlocknee River just north of Tallahassee to the makeshift corral where they changed mounts. With fresh horses, early the next day they rode through Nankin only two miles north of the Florida line and some ten miles west of Clyatt's sawmill.

Lieutenant Barber searched around for most of the night but never found a clear trail and finally headed his men back to Chattahoochee.

The next day while the Renegades were changing horses at the corral, the passengers on the east bound were horrified to see three naked bodies swinging from a single telegraph pole. To the largely overweight body in the middle, was pinned a sign that read:

THESE MEN RAPED AND MURDERED
A WHITE WOMAN.
THIS SAME FATE WILL BEFALL OTHERS
WHO COMMIT SUCH CRIMES.

THE WITHLACOOCHEE RENEGADES

There had been some disagreement about Cliff's signing of the note, but he argued that it was time they came out and became known publicly; they were a force there to fight evil and wrong doings. Finally Sam agreed, but still thought better of it.

On the following Monday, Cliff, Nadine, Sam, and Esther took the wagon into Madison. Sam and Esther went to *The Madison Trace* and Cliff and Nadine to John Inglis' store, Sam, to turn over a prepared script of what had happened to the three colored soldiers for Balough to use as he saw fit; Cliff to confirm the deal on the arms and ammunition.

"Just how many rifles do you want?"

"I will buy 50 Henry rifles and all five thousand rounds of ammunition, if you will accept payment in Yankee Greenbacks," Cliff replied.

John took a lead pencil from his desk drawer and did some

scribbling on a small note pad of yellow paper. Looking over his figures he leaned back in his chair and placed the non-sharpened end of the pencil in his mouth and twisted it around for a few seconds and then returned it to his pad. Finally satisfied with his work, he tossed his pad to the desk and replied. "You understand this is old-issue ammunition. I'm not sure if it is less than ten years old."

"We understand," Nadine said.

"And these rifles were formerly used by the 10th Illinois during their invasion."

"I very well may have been shot at by some of these rifles," Cliff replied.

Again Inglis placed the pencil in his mouth and twisted it around several times before saying, "I must have twelve dollars apiece for the rifles and a cent a round for the ammunition. That comes to $600 for the Henrys and another $200 for the cartridges."

"In greenbacks," Cliff said.

"In greenbacks," Inglis agreed.

"When do you want the money?"

"When the rifles arrive. In about one week, I would say," Inglis replied, and then looking over the couple seated there in his office, he suddenly knew he was doing the right thing.

"Captain," Cliff said as he stood and stretched forth his hand.

"Mr. Brown," John Inglis replied, as he clasped the out stretched hand and shook it.

"There is one favor I will ask of you."

"Captain?"

"There is a boat that is supposed to be offshore near Dead Man's Bay one week from next Tuesday. It will be off-loading cargo for me, among which are a few special items that I cherish. I need an armed escort to rendezvous with my wagons before we arrive there and ride back with us. The Union Rangers have a camp in Gulf Hammock somewhere and often prey on freight wagons that pass that way."

"I don't think I'm familiar with the Union Rangers," Nadine said.

"They are a well-organized bunch of cutthroats. They began as Yellow Jackets[19] and Union deserters during the last years of the late

---

[19] Yellow Jackets: A term given to Confederate deserters.

conflict, but now have within their ranks several other outlaws who have joined their forces over the last few years.

No one is sure of the identity of their present Commander and Lieutenants who command anywhere from thirty to fifty men. It is rumored they own the town of Leno down near the Santa Fe sink and have another bunch there in Gulf Hammock. Some have reported they even have a large encampment near Tampa. They are a force to be reckoned with, I must admit."

"How many men do you want us to bring?"

"A dozen men armed with repeaters should be sufficient," Inglis replied.

"What route will you be takin'?"

"My wagons will leave here and go south through the San Pedro ruins down the old Indian trail to Bill Day's at Brewer Lake and on south until we hit the road from Gainesville and turn east to Mayo; from there we'll take the cut on to Dead Man's Bay," he said as he pointed to a map of Florida on his wall.

"If we were to meet you here," Cliff replied as he pointed to Brewer Lake, "would it be all right?"

"That will be fine, the Day farm is near there and they are good loyal people; we'll meet there. But on the return trip I need you to stay with the wagons all the way back to Madison."

"Can do," Cliff agreed.

After leaving Inglis' and before they met up with the Brooks', Nadine made Cliff take the red dress back to Vickie.

CHAPTER SEVEN

Dead Man's Bay

John Inglis had given them enough information to have a trip planned to Madison for supplies. Due to the fact that the cargo they would be returning with was of such value to their cause, Cliff decided it should be another group event. Of course, no one save Nadine, Sam, and Esther knew the real purpose of the trip.

Wednesday morning broke with light frost, but all the women were more than anxious to get on their way.

Life is less than pleasant for men on the Owl Hoot Trail. Even less for the women, and the fact you are the good guys does little to reduce this burden. Boredom, fear, and the lack of necessary daily comforts are but a few of the hardships these people must endure. When given a chance to break this routine, most were more than ready for the adventure of a visit to town.

Addie stayed home, as did the older children who still had look-out posts to cover along the river and trail.

There were four wagons on this trip, all pulled by a good team of mules. Dizzy drove the wagon that Esther and Nadine rode in, and unlike the others, it was pulled by a team of six. The men who were not driving wagons rode horses alongside.

Today Sam hoped to receive the final approval of his contract on the stage stop and he was quite anxious for that assurance. The first stage run was scheduled to begin in early April.

The town visit was routine to all concerned except for the activity at John Inglis' warehouse a short distance from his store, where wooden crates were loaded in the big wagon Dizzy was driving.

Cliff made all the arrangements and Dizzy simply pulled around back and waited as the darkies, who worked for Mr. Inglis, loaded the crates.

John Inglis' warehouse Madison, Florida late 1800's

Dizzy paid no attention to their complaining about the weight of each. He was accustomed to the sound of darkies complaining.

When he moved out, he did notice that the wagon seemed to pull heavy and decided that he must re-grease the axle and wheels before they came to town again.

That night when they arrived back home, Cliff was as anxious to check his purchase as the women had been to go to town.

The rifles he found were actually better than he had expected, but he was a little disappointed in the first two cases of ammunition. They were the semi-pointed 216 gr. bullet design that had only been used during the first few years of production and he was not sure of their reliability. However, case three contained all rounds of the newer 200 gr. flat nose type. The next crate he opened had no cartridges in it at all rather it contained twelve of the cartridge canisters for the men to carry loaded magazine tubes in. He well remembered these Blakeslee Boxes, and was overjoyed and considered them a prize, one he had not counted on. *'I must express my gratitude for these and now ask the Captain to work on getting us some revolvers that shoot the Henry cartridge.'*

The next two days were filled with continuous test-firing of the rifles. By two in the afternoon, all 50 had been shot and only three found to malfunction. One with broken firing pins, and the other two with magazine tubes bent to the point cartridges could not move through them. Each could be repaired.

They were ready for war with long guns. His next concern was: could they come up with enough revolvers so every man could carry two?

'I must have Captain John work on that right away.' he thought.

The next Monday, the moon came up at eleven o'clock and just after midnight the eight men moved out.

Riding with Reb were The Hungry Bear, Art Mann, Cactus Jac, The Store Keeper, Coup, Bubba, The Tallokas Kid, and Dizzy.

It was near three o'clock when they approached the Methodist Church at Hickory Grove, about seven miles south of their camp. There, Jeremiah Johnny joined them. He had been visiting his Blair cousins who lived nearby.

Dawn found them at the small church at Norton Creek the locals dubbed "The Stonewall" because of its construction. Here they stopped for an hour to give the horses a rest and grain.

Sam, now known as 'The Hungry Bear', built a small fire and fried some bacon while Jeremiah Johnny boiled a pot of Arbuckles.

From the yard of a cracker house across the road, two young boys, one white and one black, came by rolling a steel tire down the hard packed trail with a stick and stopped long enough to admire Sam's horse, before they were off again.

Cracker House near Norton Creek

Noon found them at Day's farm, ahead of Inglis and his wagons.

Mr. Day was out working his cotton field that lay between his house and the Suwannee River but Mrs. Day, a woman of some forty years, was home and had been expecting the wagons for an hour.

However, in the note she had received, the Captain had failed to mention the rendezvous with Reb and his men, and she showed signs of alarm when such a large body of riders came upon the place from the north.

After Cliff explained they were there to give the Inglis wagons escort, she seemed to sway a bit before she said. "Oh Lord above, you gave me the fright. I thought sure you wus them Union Rangers a' coming upon us. A party a' them passed here yesterde', late of the evening. I just could make them out, but I knowed 'um all right. I see'd that no account John Story[20] a leadin' 'um."

"Which way were they headed?" Cliff asked.

"Yonder ways," she replied, pointing south.

Inglis' wagons didn't arrive until shortly before three and 'The Captain' decided to wait and get an early start rather than trying to make camp in a few short hours.

---

[20] John Story: For more on John Story and The Union Rangers read "Man of The Tide" The Glory Years chapter on 1882

That night Cliff met Johnny Gaston's uncle, whom he was named for, and also Uncle Robert Keeling, who had three sons with him as teamsters. Another wagon was driven by a young man introduced as Michael Powers, who was employed by old man Bill Hollinsworth, a man that Cliff had known since he was a small boy.

They stayed up until after nine, talking and taking nips from a jug that Hollinsworth had with him. Every sentence Hollinsworth spoke, he began with, "Praise the Lord." It was: "Praise the Lord, we made it." "Praise the Lord, I remembered the jug," "Praise the Lord, we have enough guns."

Cliff was glad to learn that all the teamsters were armed with new Smith & Wesson[21] shotguns, which used brass shells.

The moon rose late, arriving large and quite bright, which gave them more light than they needed when they pulled out at four the next morning. Cliff could see Mrs. Day busying herself in the kitchen as he rode past the only window of her house.

They reached The Hog Town Road[22], as the stage road that ran from Gainesville to Perry was called, arriving there just as the sun was peeking over the tops of the moss covered oaks that lined the old trail. Both the Captain and Cliff saw what appeared to be a rider, perhaps two, a half mile up this road; however, the large, round, orange ball produced so much glare neither could be sure and the figures, if they truly were figures, almost immediately disappeared.

They were some eight or nine miles west of Mayo and Captain Inglis warned them that he had information The Union Rangers had spies in the little community, so instead of turning towards the main road that ran south from the village he lead them to the southwest on a miserable excuse for a wagon road. "I have decided to keep going straight rather than turning to Mayo; and boys keep alert, the next thirty some miles will be our greatest danger as this trail passes through a good size portion of Gulf Hammock[23], the home of John Story's boys.

It seemed to Cliff that every mile he would see a body moving behind a tree, only to arrive close enough to find hanging moss stirring in the breeze or a patch of haw[24] dancing around. They

---

[21] Smith & Wesson Shotguns: The forerunners of the Parker Brothers Shotguns

[22] The Hog Town Road: Hog Town was the original name for Gainesville Florida.

[23] Gulf Hammock: A large uninhabited sandy area filled with thickets and numerous swamps

[24] Haw: A small fruit used in making jelly that grows on a short bushy tree or bush near water.

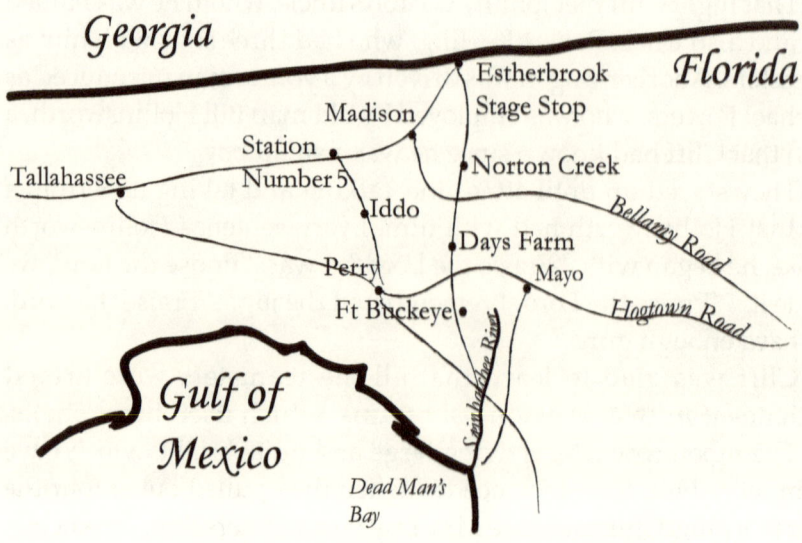

Map of the Trip to Dead Man's Bay

skirted the ruins of old Fort Buckeye, but soon returned to the root-plagued trace towards their impending rendezvous with whom he did not know.

By noon, they had reached a little stream called the Steinhatchee River. Cliff knew it was the same that the Indians call Man's River, and it would be their compass straight to the bay. He surmised years before it had once been called Dead Man's River, as it empted into Dead Man's Bay but the first word had been lost in the contamination from the Creek language to the English.

Sunset found them at a junction with the stage road that ran from Tampa to Tallahassee and there they stopped under the shade of a big sweet gum and two water oaks to rest the animals and have a bite to eat.

"Praise the Lord; this has been a beautiful day."

"That it is, Pa," his oldest son replied as he spit a plug from his mouth.

"Praise the Lord, Little Paul, you need to be a helping with the mules," he said to his youngest just as he slapped him with a gentle hand on his backside.

Cliff reasoned Little Paul might be twelve, not more than fourteen, but he had to admire the way the lad handled his team. Rags, the oldest Hollinsworth boy, on the other hand seemed to have a touch of lazy in him. *'I can't really judge him badly for that I guess,'* Cliff thought *'I got the same failings in me.'*

John Inglis, he observed, was never still. Cliff watched him from a short distance and thought of his own father. *'He's just like Pa, always seeming to have more energy bottled up inside him than his body can hold, and that's what causes him to be fidgeting with first this and then that.'*

Finally Cliff walked over to the Inglis wagon and spoke. "Everything all right, Captain?"

"Oh," the man replied as he looked up at who had spoken to him, "Yes, yes; quite fine."

Cliff had not noticed it before, but now he surmised something more than nervous energy was troubling the Captain.

"Something seems to be on your mind," he said.

"Well, Mr. Brown. I know John Story has spies all over the place and I thought I saw a rider back when we cut the Hog Town Road, even if I was wrong, one of them could have spotted our tracks where we crossed that road. I expected to be hit as we came through the Hammock."

"You were not wrong; I saw him, too, me'bee two of them," Cliff replied, looking around at the ample thickets from which an ambush could be launched. "Me'bee they saw how many we are and decided agin' it."

"I am glad you also saw him; at least I think I'm glad and maybe you are right about seeing how numerous we are, but I doubt it. He's got forty or more men somewhere there in Gulf Hammock," the man said looking at their back-trail, "No, I suspect he's waiting to hit us on our way back."

"I'll remind my boys to keep a sharp lookout," Cliff said and then turned and walked away.

"Obliged," was all Inglis said in return.

It was after three the next day when Cliff noticed the air having a new smell and ten minutes later he saw the gray still waters of the Gulf of Mexico.

He also saw a fair-size schooner lying at anchor some half-mile out in Dead Man's Bay.

Sampala Slim, a close friend of John Inglis who was driving one of the wagons, mentioned the Captain of the ship was Henry Titus, a man John Inglis had known for many years. "He was a blockade runner during the war," the tall lanky man said looking out on the calm waters at the two-mast boat before he added, "Some say he still is."

Cliff took this to mean Captain Titus was perhaps not always working within the parameters of present day maritime law.

Captain Inglis signaled the schooner with the proper code, and almost immediately a longboat was seen being loaded with what appeared to be large wooden crates by means of a block and tackle attached to an overhead beam. When it finally arrived at the shore, the men, both sailor and teamster, struggled in transferring these crates to the wagons. Actually, the seamen moved them onto the beach and then returned for another boatload; leaving the task of moving them through the soft sand to the landlubbers.

The transfers took the remainder of the daylight hours, but had to be stopped when darkness fell upon them, due to the lack of an early moon.

When the last boat of the day came in, one of the seaman spoke out, "Captain Inglis, Captain Titus requests your presence aboard to sup with him this evening."

It was now almost full dark, and the moon had not yet risen; and it was very difficult to see more of the men in the boat than figures, but Cliff knew that voice. "Stan, Stan May, is that you?"

The sailor stepped forward, and then in a quickened pace moved closer to the familiar voice who had beckoned him, "Yeah, it's me. Is that you, Reb?"

The two old friends first stretched forth their hands, but Cliff could not contain himself and quickly threw his arms around his old comrade and drew him close. "We all thought you dead."

"I almost wus."

Other Renegades came forward now realizing who the sailor was and shook his hand. Unfortunately, the Captain needed to go out to the schooner and they had to cut the reunion short. Everyone who had known Stan watched him, as he pulled on the long oars moving the boat away from the beach, with a warm glow in their hearts.

As soon as he could no longer see his friend, Cliff moved over to the campfire and stood in the smoke to ward off some of the sand gnats and mosquitoes.

Most swamps in the south were filled with the pesky little critters, but he had never experienced them as plentiful as here along the Gulf coast. He was thankful that the night turned out cool, as he had already decided to wear everything he could get on to keep them from destroying his sleep.

All were up long before daylight and again the moon was bright, but a high cloud cover had moved in from the north during their sleep and they could not see nearly as well as the morning before. Captain Titus chose not to continue the offloading until there was better light.

Captain Inglis had spent the night aboard the "Smyrna Witch" with Titus, and when the longboat brought him ashore, Cliff was sorry to see Stan was not among those who powered it; there was, however, a heavy chest he helped to load into Inglis' wagon.

Cliff knew quite well from his days in South Pass City that only gold or lead would weigh that much, and he suspected Inglis would not be carrying lead in such a well-made locked box. 'No, I suspect this is filled with Spanish doubloons.'

Now he understood why Inglis had not been overly concerned about taking payment with stolen greenbacks. Titus would exchange them in another port far away from Valdosta, Georgia, and no one would be the wiser.

It was eleven o'clock when the last rowboat started back to the ship. These good-sized longboats had hauled ashore several sacks of flour, rice, and rolls of dry goods; there also were bags of sugar that had been hand-loaded in Havana, where Titus had exchanged his unholy cargo[25], but most of what had been bought was salt-water fish and some hundred pound blocks of pure salt that they had picked up at Cedar Key, a few miles south of where they now stood. Much to Cliff's sorrow, his old friend did not make any of these trips ashore.

John Inglis raised his hand in a long farewell gesture to his friend, as did the men of The Withlacoochee Renegades to theirs, before turning to their caravan.

"Men, I suspect that the Union Rangers will be waiting for us somewhere between here and Mr. Day's farm. Probably in Gulf Hammock, as it is where they have an encampment." The Captain paused before turning again and looking to the gray water, he cleared his throat, "I plan to turn north on the stage road to Tallahassee and deny them that pleasure. Still, we are heavily loaded with goods, and our progress will be slow. It is well that every man stay alert at all times as danger might be behind any tree."

When finished, he spoke not another word; rather climbed

---

[25] Unholy Cargo: Many suspected some of those Freedmen who simply disappeared after the war were captured and sent south to once again assume the status of slaves.

straight into the spring seat of the lead wagon, took the reins from Rags, and gave a little whistle as he slapped them against the mules' backs. His fine bay horse turned and followed as faithfully as the Hollinsworth hounds were doing.

At a point some three miles from where the Steinhatchee crossed the stage road, the river was barely more than a ditch some ten feet wide on the south side of the dike, with a large cypress swamp to the north.

Moments before the sun was completely hidden by huge white clouds, a 58 caliber mini ball passed two inches in front of John Inglis' face and took off most of Rags Hollinsworth's head. Neither of them heard the report of the musket, but the blue-gray smoke appeared to his left and Inglis knew the attack he had feared was upon them. Within ten seconds the cypress swamp on the north side of the road was hidden from view by a cloud of gun smoke filling the heavy air.

Men were yelling, horses were bucking, and mules were screaming. Cliff could tell from the number of smoke puffs there were at least ten men firing at them from the swamp. He also could tell from the time between shots they were using muzzle-loading rifles.

He quickly called his men together around Inglis' wagon and ordered them not to return fire except with their handguns. Cliff was certain a well-trained outfit would not have attempted this type of ambush, and from all he had heard of The Union Rangers, they were a well-trained and reasonably disciplined outfit, therefore he concluded, this was not the main force and he didn't want to let the ambushers know of the firepower he and his men possessed.

He could hear the report of the shotguns the Gaston boys were shooting but doubted if the balls were very lethal at the distance to their intended targets.

When two well-placed shots downed the mules on Inglis' wagon, their fate was sealed; with him being the lead wagon the road was now blocked, since there was not room to turn a wagon and team around on the narrow dike there, they were trapped.

It was at that moment Cliff noticed one of Hollinsworth hounds growling with up-turned lips, and not at the swamp, rather at the thicket ahead of them on the south side of the road.

Moments later, the sounds from by-gone years filled his ears and he recognized them as many horses moving fast on the other side of the river, exactly where the dog had pointed.

Still he saw no one.

Looking earnestly into the heavy brush after turning full around, finally he spotted coming from the trees on the south side of the road, twenty mounted men.

They had to cross the little river, which was waist deep on a man at that point, and this slowed them considerably. Had it not, the Rangers would have overrun the caravan before he could have gotten his men in position.

Cliff thought, 'That little river is God-sent,' and he quickly moved the boys around to face the real danger.

"Hold your fire. Let them all cross the river. Hold it, hold it!" Cliff was speaking as calmly as if they were watching a bobber on a catfish line. He noticed the last horse was a beautiful black and white pinto and it reminded him of Treasure. As soon as this pony had established his hind feet on the sandy bank, Cliff lowered his hand in command form and said loud enough for them to hear him. "Show them no mercy, boys."

The wall of 44 caliber lead bullets that suddenly filled the air was more than any Dragoon could stand and the raiders fell from their mounts as fast as they appeared through the smoke. Cliff finally saw the last rider turning and trying to retreat back across the river. He took careful aim and put a conical ball just under his right armpit. The rider lunged to his left, but was able to stay mounted and he spurred the pony, which now jumped the river, but lost his footing when the south bank began to slide away under the weight of man and animal. This was all the time Cliff needed; and this time he placed the bullet in the man's right ear.

Several of the ambushers who had first fired from the swamp had moved ahead on foot, expecting the horsemen to sweep through the little resistance that had been coming from the wagons. Now these highwaymen were caught out in the open, in knee deep water.

Turning and attempting to flee was at best pitiful. The Gaston boys now had them in range and the new shotguns went to work, cutting the bushwhackers down as they screamed and tried to escape.

Mike Powers, standing next to the Gaston's, also was pouring lead into the Raiders with the brace of Navy Colts he had worn in belt holsters.

As soon as the shooting was over Cliff stood and moved forward.

There were several horses of the fallen men still milling around frightened and not knowing what to do, and he called out to Dizzy and Robert to catch as many of them as they could, and then he turned to Sam and Johnny. "We need to make sure these boys can't do us no more harm." Sam nodded his head and he pulled his ten-round LeMat from the old brown flap-holster and cocked it. Johnny, seeing this, realized Cliff's meaning and he, too, set his Henry against the wagon and stepped alongside Sam with a Remington in one hand and his Griswold in the other. They walked among the dead and dying and placed a pistol ball into the head of each.

Cliff, on the other hand, had kept his eye on the pinto and he moved forward and eased into the river, where the horse now stood moving his ears forward and then backward and then twitching one of them. His rider had been knocked from the saddle by Cliff's last shot but the man's boot was caught in the left stirrup and in a small way had anchored the pony there.

Cliff slowly placed his hand on the animal's nose and rubbing it, spoke to him softly, reassuring him that everything was now over and he had nothing more to fear. Finally, when he thought the horse was calm enough, he moved around and twisted the man's leg from the boot and let him fall into the water. Cliff then slipped the nearly new stovepipe boot from the stirrup and reached for the reins. The pony raised his head in a slight protest as if to say "You are not my master," but resisted no more, and let Cliff lead him up the north bank and back to the wagons.

John Inglis had assisted Old Man Hollinsworth in lowering his son's body from the wagon. They laid him on the sandy road beside the big wheel. John removed his brown coat and laid it gently over the boy's upper body and then walked away to allow the family members to gather around.

"How bad did we get hit?" Cliff asked the captain as he approached.

"Not too bad, I guess. Hollinsworth's oldest boy is dead. A bullet that I'm sure was meant for me," he replied and paused before continuing. "One of the Gaston boys has a hole in his leg but it doesn't seem to have hit the bone. My man Stevie," he began pointing to a small darkie who was now bending over the boy, "is tending to him, how about your men?"

Cliff knelt down, placed one knee in the white sand and began scratching the ears of the blue tic hound that had given him the warning. "The Tallokas Kid was hit right off. He has a bad leg wound, otherwise no other injuries," Cliff replied.

"Lord above, had you not seen them coming, they would have run right over us."

"I kind a' figured they would do something like that," Cliff said, then with the palm of his hand turned down he moved his arm in a short arc in front of him. "That's why I had my men not give away how well armed we were until they had showed their hand."

"That was mighty good thinking," Inglis acknowledged.

"I think we have whipped the passel of them. I doubt they will bother us no more."

"You are probably right, Mr. Brown, but still as soon as we can cut these dead mules clear, I think we had better get out of here," Inglis replied looking around at the downed animals still reined to his wagon.

Cliff fully agreed and nodded his head before he spoke to Sam. "How many of the horses could we save?"

"Eight, with no injuries."

"Well, let the others go and use some of the good ones to pull these dead mules off the road and see if you can hitch a couple a' them to Inglis' wagon," Cliff said then added, "At least until we get to the stage road, where there will be room to maneuver around."

Sam nodded his head and began his work.

"Robert, I'd like you and the other men not doing nothing, to pick up all the spent Henry rounds you can find. No need a-telling the rest a' these varmints what happened to their buddies."

"Right," Art Mann said and motioned for Cactus Jac to help.

Parker had been the last man to leave the cypress trees and quickly saw they had run into a passel of hornets as his buddies began to fall in front of him. A 36 caliber ball from one of the shotguns struck him in the left arm just above the elbow and he had lost his grip on his rifle. Quickly he dropped down behind a large cypress knee, and with one eye exposed, watched as the men ahead of him, one by one, were torn apart by the deadly shotgun fire. The blackwater around him now was dark red and he dared not move. After the firing had stopped, he thought he might just make it if he was very still; until the men from the road began moving forward and shooting the downed bodies, and then his heart sank.

When one of them started out into the water headed in his

direction, he thought he was a goner for sure. He had no place to run and his only gun lay a foot under water with powder and cap soaked through. Suddenly a large cottonmouth moved across the water between him and the shooter, and with great relief he watched Michael Powers look at the snake and then return to the road.

He laid there in the cold water for a full hour until the wagons were out of sight, then he slipped over to the road and found a horse that wasn't too badly hurt, and mounting him he eased off the dike into the thicket and soon found the trail they had come on. The buzzards were already circling overhead as he left the scene.

Parker reached the Tallahassee Road two hours ahead of the Inglis train. There he turned right and moved out as fast as the horse could go.

The big chestnut had belonged to Cotton Olens, an older member of the gang. Cotton had been a Third Sergeant in the Fourth Georgia Cavalry, but decided to ease out of Savannah two nights before Sherman's troops arrived. Somehow Jeff Davis' war and the cause, no longer meant anything to him. He was almost caught by Dickison's men, near Montgomery's farm west of Jacksonville, but by lying in a swamp all day, he managed to escape their detection and slipped by them after dark.

He had killed a man over possession of this very animal in Lake City in the summer of '66 and it was that conflict that caused him to be recruited by John Story.

Story had finally promoted him, and it was Cotton who had been the leader on this raid.

Six miles south of the Steinhatchee River the chestnut played out from loss of blood and Parker abandoned him near a small farm, but not before he took the Remington Beals from the saddle bags and headed for the farm. He approached the little cracker house with the revolver drawn and cocked.

Finding no one in the house, he looked around and saw a man in the field to his left, plowing behind a mule.

Moving around to the small corral he found no other animals; however, it was then she saw him.

Mrs. Woods was a woman in her late fifties. Her long hair had turned gray many years before and she now wore it in a tight bun on the back of her head. Standing barely five feet tall she was as round as a waterbarrel.

Remington Beals Revolver

She had been cooking in the kitchen house, and when she went to the window to throw out the contents of her dishpan, there he was.

Fanny pushed open the wooden door that served as a window cover in cold weather and yelled to Parker. "What chu' want here?"

Parker jerked around, startled by her voice.

It was then she saw the gun.

"Chu' got no business here White Trash, now get!" Fanny bit her lower lip after she spoke, but she knew not what else to do. She had already given herself away before she realized he had a gun, and she reasoned being strong was her only defense. Henry had a long gun that he brought home from his fighting with the Yankees years ago, but it was uncapped in the bedroom of the house and she knew she would never be able to get to it before the man could get to her.

Parker slowly walked around to the open door of the kitchen house and carefully looked in before he entered.

"Call your man," he commanded.

"I'll do no such," she replied and reached for the long-bladed knife she had been using to slice the pork belly.

Parker pulled his Bowie from his left boot and slowly lowered the hammer on the Beals and stuffed it into his trousers. "You call him like I said and I won't use this on you."

"No! You got the look of the devil in your eyes and I ain't gon a' do no such thing," Fanny spat back. She was trying to be strong as she swung the knife across in front of her when she spoke, but inside she was trembling and she felt weak at the knees.

Parker saw that he was getting nowhere with this and he moved a pace closer where he was sure of his distance and then with a mighty swing of his arm, he threw the big knife at the chubby little woman. It hit her high over her left breast and she staggered backward and gave him a blank look, then she screamed and started running straight at Parker.

He side-stepped as she got to him and she continued out the door screaming with all her might. The single six-by-six step was too much for her to manage and she fell forward. When she hit the ground, the force of her weight pushed the knife on through and Parker saw it come out the back of her dress. Still, she was not finished and she quickly jumped up and began running towards the field where Henry was, screaming with each step.

The farmer suddenly heard her and threw the leads from around his shoulders and started running to meet his wife.

"Fanny, what are the matter?"

When she was twenty feet from him he saw the large red stain on the front of her dress and then recognized the wooden handle of the knife protruding from her chest.

"Fanny!"

She fell just as they reached one another and all she could say was, "White Nigger," before she started to scream again.

Henry Woods pulled the Bowie from his wife and slowly laid her down on the ground. His gaze went immediately to the buildings ahead.

"Henry don't leave me," Fanny said but he arose and started off.

"I'll be back Fanny, as soon as I take care of this trash."

"No, don't leave me!"

He did not answer or turn back, keeping his concentration on the log buildings ahead.

Henry Woods had come to Florida with the army back in '36 to fight the Seminoles. When his six-month enlistment was up he refused to re-enlist and General Taylor refused him passage on a ship back to Charleston, so he stayed.

In the spring of '42 he was working as a carpenter at the boat works in Palatka, and Fanny arrived from Jacksonville aboard one of James Burt's steamboats. Her father had promised to show her the wonderful springs at the headwaters of the Silver River and it was an adventure she had dreamed of since he had come home from the army some five years before.

Henry was a tall, lanky fellow who had developed a great physique from his handling of the heavy wood planks needed for the boats they built and repaired there. Fanny, on the other hand, was a foot shorter than him and barely weighted 100 pounds. Her very black hair and dancing blue eyes mesmerized him. When she returned a week later from her trip to the Silver Springs, he was so relieved; he had thought of little else since she had left.

It took Henry a year to earn enough money to make the trip to Baltimore to see her. When he returned a month later, he was bringing a 20 year old bride with him.

Henry Woods was a strong and willing worker and had enough brains to get ahead. By the fall of 1860, there were three boats that moved goods from Jacksonville to Palatka bearing his ownership.

Fanny bore three children, two sons and a daughter. Little Lois had died at age three of a fever.

When war broke out, their sons enlisted in the Marion Light Artillery, and died side-by-side at Richmond, Kentucky, in the summer of '62.

Henry had remained home and kept his boats running salt, niter, and other supplies up and down the Saint John's, a duty needed far more than what he could have done on any battlefield. Henry had renamed his three steamers in honor of predominate people of his state. A year later 'The Governor Milton' was captured by Federals, and Henry sent word to Captain John Dickison who was camped at Sweetwater, a small creek north west of Palatka. Dickison with great haste pursued the captured steamer and arrived near a high bluff a short distance south of Devil's Elbow. Upon hearing the whistle of the approaching boat, Dickison had his men wade out into the river which was spattered here with cypress trees and knees, and there lay in wait.

The Union Captain, seeing the high bluffs along the east side of the river and realizing that it would be an excellent position for Rebel sharpshooters to ambush them, steered the stolen *Governor Milton* over to the opposite side of the river, straight into Dickison's surprise attack.

The men opened fire with their Enfield's and riddled the

pilothouse, killing a large number of Federals, and the craft began to wander about the wide river aimlessly. Finally, Henry watched helplessly as his boat drifted around the bend at Devil's Elbow and was lost forever to the enemy.

That year he also saw his other two boats shelled and sunk when Union troops moved into Palatka.

Henry had built a house for Fanny and the boys on Olive Street, however, upon learning who it belonged to, the Federals burned it to the ground.

Henry took Fanny to Gainesville for the remainder of the war and offered his services to Captain Dickison.

After the surrender, they had tried to regain ownership of the property their house had been located on; it was near the main road and not far from the docks and a valuable piece of land, but this was refused because they were listed as secessionist.

In 1868, he tried to file for farmland under the Homestead Act, but again was refused. It was then he moved Fanny to the westcoast which the invaders had little interest in, and cut out this sixty-acre patch of land for them to live on.

That day, some two years later, when Henry reached the house, he saw Parker coming out the backdoor with his Enfield and immediately he lunged for the man.

Henry Woods was ten years senior to Parker but he had worked hard all his life and was strong as an ox. He quickly twisted the rifle from the younger man's hands, but seeing it still had no percussion cap on the nipple, he dropped it and went for his wife's attacker's throat with both hands.

The wound to Parker's left arm now started bleeding again and he quickly realized he was no match for this old man. Struggling with his feet barely touching the sandy ground, he finally managed to get his hand on the Remington and get it cocked. The first 31 caliber ball burned deep into Henry's lower abdomen but had little effect on stopping him from the job he had set his mind to doing. The second time Parker was able to fire, he had the short barrel pointed higher and this time the little ball entered just above the bellybutton and passed through the left side of the old man's heart.

Henry knew now his life was short, but still he continued to hold tight on the man's throat, pressing as hard as he could with his thumbs on the Adam's apple.

Parker had tried to cock the pistol again but a spent cap had lodged between the cylinder and the pistol's frame successfully jamming the revolver. Finally his hands became numb and he felt the gun slip away.

'*This old man is going to kill me,*' he thought as he danced around struggling for air.

Unfortunately the loss of blood caused Henry to loosen his grip and both he and Parker passed out at the same time.

He didn't know how long he had been unconscious, but finally after experiencing a horrible dream, Parker shook violently awake. The old man's hands were still around his neck but were cold now. With great effort he pulled them loose and struggled to stand.

His left arm was bleeding and he staggered inside the house and tore away a window curtain to make a bandage. Then he rummaged through the house and finally found a tin of percussion caps and a bag of balls that hung beside a powder flask on the bedroom wall. At the foot of the bed was a chest that contained several thousand Confederate dollars and a single five dollar goldpiece. Stuffing the coin into the watchpocket of his trousers, he staggered back outside and spit on his adversary's body before entering the kitchen house.

There he found the pork belly Fanny had cut up and seeing there were still hot coals in the fireplace, he stirred them into a blaze and fried the pork.

While eating and drinking some buttermilk, he decided on a plan.

First he headed out to where the mule still stood attached to the plow. Releasing him from his burden, Parker lead him back to where the woman lay and tied the leads to her feet and had the mule drag her back to the house. Then with great effort, he pulled both bodies into the kitchen house and scattered the hot coals around on the plank floor.

After retrieving his Bowie from where Henry had dropped it along with the Enfield, he led the mule out to the road where he had cached Cotton's saddle.

The mule didn't take to the saddle at all, but he finally bucked him down and they headed into Gulf Hammock as the roof of the kitchen house fell into the flames below.

Three hours later, Coleville rushed into John Story's cabin. "Captain, you better come quick."

"What is it?"

"Gator, Gator's back!"

"Gator?"

"Yeah, just Gator Parker."

"Alright, Parker where are the rest of my men?" Story demanded.

"Dead, Captain. All dead."

"You mean to tell me the thirty a' you couldn't take that bunch a' teamsters?"

"It weren't just them teamsters, Captain. That there John Inglis had a whole group of gunmen hidden in the wagons. They were all armed with them repeating rifles and there was morn' fifty a 'em."

"Fifty men in the wagons? Hell, if there had been fifty men in the wagons there wouldn't been no room for the supplies you were suppose to bring back," Story yelled at him.

"I tell you, Captain, there were fifty or near it."

"All of the men are dead. You sure?"

"Yeah, I seen 'em. Them bastards even walked around and shot 'um in the head after it were over, just to make sure."

"How come you ain't dead then?"

"I wus just lucky I reckon. I got hit right off and fell in the swamp and they never came out far enough to shoot me a second time," Parker said back, holding up his left arm showing Story the bloody bandage.

"Well, you better be glad you were shot or I would shoot you myself for a coward."

"No sur, Captain, I was hit right off."

Turning to the other men he loudly commanded, "Elisworth, take the rest of the men and get them wagons before they get to Mayo."

When he was satisfied his orders would be carried out, he yelled loudly, "Shit! Shit! Shit!" and then turned and stomped back into the cabin.

John Inglis had indeed turned north on the Tallahassee Road and the caravan pushed on until they reached the little community of Perry near midnight. There he stopped and camped until first light.

Early the next morning, Michael Powers found Archer cold when he attempted to wake him. Apparently his leg had begun bleeding again during the night and he simply gave up the ghost in his sleep.

It was a bitter pill for Cliff, as Jim Archer had been a friend for a little less than a year, and had only been one of them a few months; but during that time had proven to be one of the most liked members of The Renegades. Later, upon hearing of his loss, Nadine lowered her head and said, "What a shame, he was such a pleasant young man, and he made the best Short Bread I have ever eaten."

With Jim's death, Cliff felt he needed to even the score a little more with the Union Rangers and he sent Michael Powers to the town of Leno to learn as much about their operation there as he could.

Powers had expressed the enjoyment he found in cards and claimed to be a better than average gambler; he played the guitar and had a fine singing voice. It seemed like a good plan providing he didn't go and get himself killed.

John Inglis bought four mules from Jacob Summerlin's foreman when they passed his spread in Taylor County and from there they took another dim trail to Iddo skirting to the west of the big Sampala swamp and on to intersect the tracks at Station Number Five, where they turned due east on Mr. Bellamy's road to Madison.

While in town, Cliff picked up the latest edition of *The Madison Trace*. The news was again about them, only this time in a little different light. The headlines read:

HOMEFOLK AVENGE MURDER OF
WHITE WOMAN
BY COLORED SOLDIERS

Mr. Balough went on telling of the false report that a certain newspaper in a nearby Georgia town had printed, and then told the story as it had happened beginning with the rape and death of Tillie Gunter, including the mysterious witness who later positively identified the culprits as they were being slipped out of the area by the authorities in Valdosta. He even went so far as to report this is the same paper that named these few boys who refuse to be subjects, The Withlacoochee Renegades, I fully agree that they are truly renegades; renegades from the unjust Occupational Government of Georgia.

On the same page further down was another article that clearly showed the difference between the telling of a tale truthfully and not so. It was headlined:

The Hamburg Riot

I write to you the particulars of a great difficulty that occurred in this county just last week. It seems that after the performance of Grady's Circus Troop, the notorious Negro known as King Phillip came south from his refuge of protection by The US Troops stationed in Valdosta and began preaching his revolutionary cause to the freedmen of Hamburg, Florida. His speech was professed as to be the need to encourage the Freedman to vote in all elections, which may or may not be in the best interest of these people, is still entirely within the laws of the so called New South. Up to that time not a great deal of attention was paid to this inciter, but he soon began to indulge in a most furious and abusive tirade against white people shouting unjust and untruths against several local and well regarded Gentlemen of this county. Adding and I quote from his own words "They only are allowed to continue their deeds against (our people) by protection of those murderous outlaws who hide in the swamps of the Withlacoochee. Men and women so despicable as to be ashamed to show their faces in front of (Our People)." King Phillip continued this including the calling of names of fine and outstanding men who have for years stood against unlawfulness in our community. Finally three young men, two Leland brothers and Patrick Pence who had heard enough of these blasphemous assaults remarked that he was telling a pack of lies. Upon this, Terry Page present Radical Representative from this county, (formerly from Lancaster Pennsylvania), commenced cursing the young men furiously, and threatening their lives being followed by a large crowd of armed and excited Negroes. Messrs. Mike Woodham and Seaborn Palmer went to the three and taking Pence by the arm led them away from the crowd, telling them not to have difficulty as it was obvious that these people had been sent here for the purpose of inciting a riot, but Page and his confederate King Philip seeing their opportunity being ushered away gathered a crowd of some sixty freedmen and began following them shouting and throwing rocks. Seeing this was not working and without other provocation by word or act, Page pulled a long barreled Government issued revolver from his frock and sent a ball into the back of Mr. Charles Leland who fell mortally wounded. While he was down with his brother watching his life's blood flow from his body several more shots were fired from the crowd, driving the men from their fallen comrade's body. It was then, as witnessed by this writer, a Negro by the name of Prince Albert did pounce upon the dying boy's body and stab him twice in the back with a rusty knife. Not less than a dozen shots had been fired and seeing the brutal murder of their friend and brother was more than any mortal man could be asked to endure. Morey Leland did pull the Colt from the belt holster worn by Woodham and fired a shot back at the murderer. This shot struck Page, who was standing beside Albert, in the chest and dropped him to his knees. Very soon thereafter the Negros and their leaders took refuge behind several farm wagons and a long water trough and firing became general from both parties, but the skill of those who had served their state during the northern aggression served them well and the three remaining defenders, who were now trying desperately to save their very lives, dropped King Philip with a well placed shot in his arm shattering it to the shoulder joint and another negro, name unknown, with a ball through the lungs. Finally several other white men ran to the assistance of the three defenders and the riotous attackers each fell back. It is reported King Philip will lose his right arm. Page, though not dead at this time, his personal physicians entertain no hopes of his recovery and will soon meet his reward down under. Two other Negros were wounded, but not seriously. Not one man or woman who witnessed this outrage of treachery being provided under the pretence of voter recruiting, had anything short of high praise for the conduct of Messrs. Leland, Pence, Woodham and Webster, who were remarkably cool and gallant, being surrounded by a group of infuriated Negros led on by determined and desperate white men, they stood their ground until their revolvers were empty and only then made their escape from the mob. Several of the demons were seen to gather around the body of young Leland and reloading their pistols fired repeatedly into this lad's lifeless body. This was a most cold-blooded, unprovoked, fiendish assault that had thus far been made in this county upon innocent men. There were no more than a dozen white men in Hamburg that day. It is obvious the Radicals came south from Lowndes County for the purpose of inciting trouble and seeing their opportunity to intimidate the southern Democrats, who were there with their family's to enjoy the circus, acted in a manner that shows their true color. These are the same type actions that kept Democrats from the polls at the election in their county a few weeks past so these constitution haters could carry the election without opposition. King Philip had abused and vilified the whites in his speech, and told the local freedmen they should arise and drive all whites from the county. Leland, Pence, Woodham and Webster did not flee the county as they expected after escaping from the mob but are now at Madison, the most public place in the county and will surrender themselves to the sheriff as soon as he shows himself again. The 'Rads' have now returned to Georgia and have sent letters showing their extreme anxiousness to compromise and have proposed that no warrants be issued on either side. This writer and witnesses hopefully wish to see the men responsible for the murder of young Mr. Leland be brought to justice, however under the present Appointed Officials in our homeland little hope of this can be expected.

Balough would have been hard pressed to print this a year or two before, but now after the fire and the support he had received from the other newspapers in Tallahassee and the surrounding area, such could be put in print. Also, the fact that the Radical Republicans were losing their grip on congress and that even northern immigrants, who were not part of the tide of carpetbaggers, and had settled in the deep south after the war, had taken notice of the treatment of southerners as less than second class citizens by the government officials.

All these things added to the power Balough now exercised. Of course it also helped that the Occupational Government he was bashing, was for the most part in another state.

Cliff folded the paper and handed it to Sam as they walked toward their horses.

"You might want to read this later."

John Inglis suggested they take all of the extra horses that had become spoils, which Cliff had intended to do anyway, especially the pretty pinto.

Sam had also picked up all the necessary papers and the license for the stage stop. With the exception of the loss of Archer, it had been a good trip, a needed trip. Most of the men had served in the war, they were not new to fighting, dying, or killing, but a man loses his sharpness, his tuned edge, his acute mind and awareness, when he is away from the battlefield too long. Of course they had a few younger boys that experienced their first combat on this trip. Bubba had been one of them, as had Michael Powers and Coup. Now they were no longer green. They had tasted battle and had not been found wanting, a young man's greatest fear.

When Nadine saw the pinto she felt a warm glow sweep over her. He was a gelding, where Treasure had been a mare, but he was only slightly taller and his markings were so nearly the same. She knew at once, when she saw Cliff ride up leading him, that he was a gift for her and a smile as wide as her mouth could produce, swept over her face.

It would have been a most happy occasion had it not been for bad news she must share with him.

"Clifford," she began.

He knew something was very wrong for her to call him by that name.

"What is the matter?"

"It's Addie. She was there yesterday sitting with us all and suddenly she yelled and grabbed her side and then fell over," his wife explained, "I think her heart gave out."

Cliff had always had the ability in times of crisis, to slip into a state of calmness and it was so now. "Where is she?"

"Yonder, in the barn. I didn't want to do anything until you came back."

"You did right."

Mary Ann came up to him as he started for the barn. "Oh Reb, I'm so sorry."

He just nodded his head and walked on past her.

That night he and Nadine along with Sam and Esther loaded his mother in a wagon and the two women drove while the men side rode them. It was late and the moon was high in the sky when they reached the old farm. Sam and Cliff took turns digging the hole in the hard red clay.

They were crossing the Withlacoochee at Rocky Ford when the sun began to slip through the trees.

A week later as Sergeant Moses Washington was leading a line of twelve men across the Brown farm, Corporal Wilson called to him. "Hey Sarge, thar' twernt but one grave here, were thar'?"

The sergeant held up his hand and looked at the two wooden headstones. One obviously had been there for some time as the cypress headboard was now silver; the other was still quite yellow.

He looked at the epitaph and worked on the writing carved there for several seconds.

"Can you tells what the scrip say Sarge?"

"No, I neber' lernt', but I will tells' the Captum' when wes' gots' back," with that they rode on off and let the two graves rest in peace. The new marker read:

ADDIE BROWN
BORN SAINT JOHN'S COUNTY FLORIDA
JULY 6, 1814
DIED OF A BROKEN HEART
MARCH 18, 1871

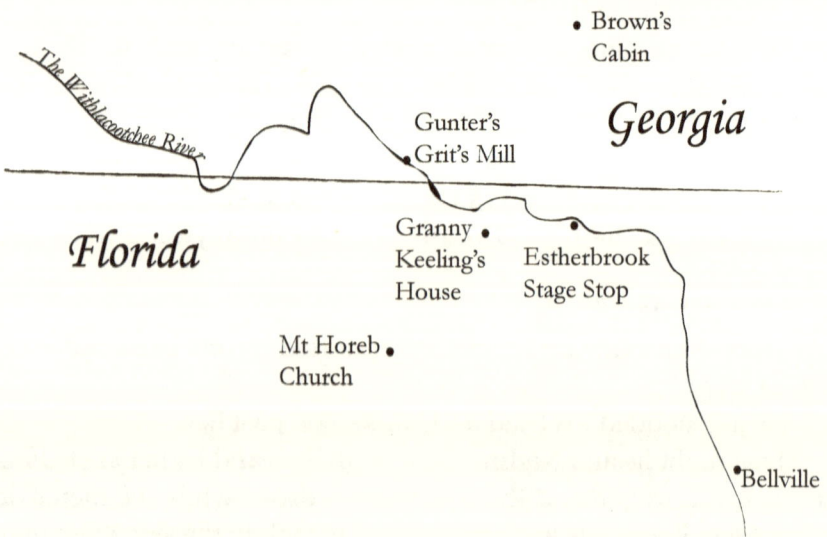

CHAPTER EIGHT

Sam Colt's Open Tops

Within a week of the printing of the article in *The Madison Trace* about the help The Withlacoochee Renegades had given a wagon train of supplies belonging to a local merchant, several connected incidents occurred. The editor of *The Tallahassee Democrat* contacted Balough about the boys with concerned interest, three men from Lowndes County Georgia rode all the way from Valdosta down to Madison asking to be put in touch with The Withlacoochee Renegades, and Balough received a letter from the editor of *The South Georgia Pioneer* in which he threatened a lawsuit if *The Madison Trace* did not retract it's statements about the Renegades.

Balough assured *The Tallahassee Democrat* he would share all his news with them, he left a message at Captain Inglis' store for Reb Brown, indicating he needed to speak to him about the men who tried to contact 'The Renegades', a Ken Nielson, David Clark and Danny Faux all from Valdosta. It was a week before Cliff received the message.

Balough also sent *The South Georgia Pioneer* a single sentence: *You'll never win a suit against a man for telling the truth.* From that point on it was war between the two papers.

The Tallahassee Democrat on the other hand began to add short versions of Balough's stories, which helped in the area, and soon the Renegades were local heroes.

Dizzy had been sent to town for supplies; Sam was in need of more nails and some cut planks for the porch roof and Mary Ann wanted 100 pounds of flour. Nadine said she had forgotten to buy coffee when she was last there and Esther wanted some baking power for the corn pone she planned to serve with the meal for the first stage that was to arrive noon Friday. When Dizzy returned, he handed a sealed envelope to Cliff.

Looking it over carefully, he took a deep breath half expecting bad news, and opened it.

Mr. Brown,

   Just a note to let you know I have good news about a source of the type iron you have shown an interest in.
   Also Mr. Balough has news for you.

Gratefully Yours John Inglis

Cliff was both curious and happy. He was not sure he understood the message, but it did sound like the Captain had come by some cartridge revolvers; what Horace Balough wanted, he had no idea. The next morning, daybreak found Art Mann, Cactus Jac, and Reb southbound on the now familiar trail that lead to Madison. He really hated taking the men from their duties, but he knew well enough that it was not wise to travel alone when there is a price on your head; and Sam, who was the closest man to him, was busy finishing the front porch. Johnny's grandmother was under the weather and he needed to be close. Both Art Mann and Cactus Jac had shown an interest in going to town as neither had been able to pick up anything after the ride to the Gulf. They had earned the trip and Dizzy could look after the stock in their absence.

Without the need to stay close to mule driven wagons they were able to reach the outer limits of the small town in time to hear the whistle announcing the arrival of the morning train, and Cliff headed straight for the rear of Inglis' store, while the other two broke off and eased into town in a meandering route that ended at Gwynn Blair's Saloon and Billiard Hall behind the hotel where Esther and Nadine had stayed a few weeks earlier.

John Inglis looked up from a stack of papers he had his attention buried in when Cliff knocked on the window glass of his office door. A smile swept across his face and he stood and motioned Cliff in. "It is good to see you. I'm pleased you wasted no time. That is good."

"You have my interest and I was in a position to break away."

"Ah yes, I suppose I do at that," Inglis said as he returned to the high back wooden chair behind his desk. "Please sit," he said as he swept his arm across the top of the highly figured wood that covered the desk, and gestured to the chair in front of it.

"I dispatched a wire to a friend of mine, a man who served us well a decade ago. He is a seaman extraordinaire. He has several merchant ships that frequent both New York and Boston harbors, as well as Charleston and Jacksonville."

John reached into a highly carved box that sat on his desk and opening it, offered Cliff a cigar which was declined, then took one for himself. "You don't mind? You are not allergic?" he quickly inquired when Cliff refused.

"No Sur'. You go right ahead," Cliff lied. He enjoyed rolling a smoke for himself but never got the hang of the strong tobacco that cigar smokers seemed to enjoy. Still his respect for John Inglis was too great for him to deny the man his pleasure.

"Ah," Inglis replied and then taking several strong but quick puffs to ensure the log was well lit, he continued. "It is my understanding Colt was overconfident in regards to the new military contract for a self-contained metallic cartridge revolver. My friend informs me that he has information the Ordnance Department has rejected Sam Colt's new revolver and that there is a large number to be had," pausing taking another long draw from the Cuban weed, then he added, "in 44 rim fire."

"It seems the people at Colt are scrambling to gather quick cash so they can pursue their next version without delay, before Smith & Wesson or Remington secures the military contract."

"How many can we get?"

"My friend says there are over one hundred assembled and ready to ship from the factory."

"I don't need a hundred but could use sixty if the price is right," Cliff replied.

"I can let you have them at $16 apiece delivered to Jacksonville."

"Greenbacks?"

**Colt's First Production Cartridge Revolver
The 1871-72 Model in 44 Henry Rim Fire**

"If you are sure they fire the Henry Cartridge, I'll take them."

Cliff nodded his head, satisfied that he now had the firepower to handle anything the 103rd threw at them.

Both men stood and shook hands.

"I'll get a wire off to New York today and he should have your order with him when he sails this week," Inglis said as he placed his arm around Cliff's shoulder and walked him out into the store area. "Is there anything else I can do for you?"

"I have a list of supplies, mostly staples the women folk wanted. I left it with your man at the counter."

"I'll see if it's ready."

"No need, I must still go over to *The Trace* and see what Mr. Balough wants. I'll pick them up just 'afore I leave town."

"As you wish."

Cliff mounted his horse and rode towards the newspaper office.

'The day is turning out to be lovely,' he thought as he passed Bevin's Livery. He waved at the man who was leading two fine mules from the stables to a corral next door.

Cliff truly was enjoying the 65 degree sun and light northwesterly breeze. *'Too bad this time of year doesn't stay with us.'*

Horace Balough was having his lunch when Cliff arrived. The young lady rose from the red cushion when he entered the small office and as she adjusted the strands of hair that had fallen since she last touched it, she spoke, "May I help you, sur?"

"My name is Brown. Mr. Balough sent for me."

"Mr. Balough is busy at the moment." Then turning to the small girl who had been busying herself with a homemade doll she said, "Sapphire, run tell your father a Mr. Brown is here to see him."

"Yas Ma'am."

"Good, now hurry," she said and then turned her attention back, looking the tall man over.

'He is quite handsome and so slim, with such broad shoulders. I wonder why such a man would feel the need to carry a revolver in town?' she mused.

Cliff was amused at the girl's name but it stood to reason a man named Balough would have a daughter named a shade of blue, of course he had no idea her mother was named Opal.

He, too, was a little amused when he heard the sound of the child's shoes descending the steps. Upon entering the room she said, "Daddy will see you right away," not looking at him as she hurried past and picked up her doll once again.

"You may go right up," the young lady said, again touching the back of her head in search of the unknown misplaced strand of hair.

Balough was finishing a large bowl of cornbread covered with mustard greens, as Cliff entered. The stout man had juice from the greens dripping from his chin and he used the palm of his hand to clean his face before he wiped the hand dry on his trouser leg and extended it to Cliff. "Mr. Brown."

The cigar smell was just as annoying the instant he entered Gwynn's Saloon as it had been in Inglis' office, nonetheless, he quickly saw his two companions standing with elbows on the rough bar top and a mug of beer in each of their right hands. *'I see I must give them a much needed lesson,'* he thought as he approached.

"You two get your shopping done?" he asked knowing full well they had not left where they now stood since entering two hours before.

"Well, Reb," Robert began, "you see, there is the cutest little whore old Gwynn has working out a' here and we wus kind a' thinking a' having us a poke before we head back."

"Takes you two hours to talk a whore into selling you a poke?"

"Well, no," Cactus Jac began, "You see, she also works as the dinner server and she couldn't take off until after the noon rush."

"Look, here she comes now," he added pointing behind Cliff.

Looking in the rectangular mirror over the bar, Cliff saw her enter the room from a side door. *'She is wearing the same red dress Nadine wore on the train, only Vickie doesn't have the bosom to do the dress justice or maybe then again, she might have just the right figure for it. Nadine could barely keep her melons in it,'* he remembered.

'Strange,' he thought, *'neither one of us has since spoken a word about that day.'*

"I'll tell you what. If either of you can get your guns out before I can pull mine, I'll pay for your poke with Vickie. If not, it's time to leave."

They looked at each other and immediately realized before they could think of pulling their revolvers, they would have to drop their beer, and by then he would have them dead to rights.

Art Mann nodded his head and then finished the mug and sat it down on the bar.

"Let this be a lesson. Never occupy your gun hand with anything else when you're maybe gon'a have to use it. Now let's go," Cliff said.

Jerry quickly finished his also and sat it beside the other. Then leaning close to Robert whispered, "How do you suppose he knows her name is Vickie?"

"Doe-no," Robert replied lifting his shoulders.

They left by the north door that opened to a hitching post where their three horses were tied.

Suddenly from around the trunk of a huge white oak, they saw several uniformed men, all mounted on bay horses.

Cliff quickly looked for an escape route and saw none.

He let his hand drop to the butt of his Smith & Wesson, which he was carrying in a cross-draw holster on a belt about his waist, but the soldiers continued past the saloon and onto the Spanish Trail.

Cliff felt his lungs once again begin their labor at the same moment Art Mann said. "Boy, I thought we wus in fur it."

The first coach to arrive at *Estherbrook* Stage Stop showed up two hours late and Esther was in tears by the time she heard it approaching.

She had prepared a fine meal of fried chicken and potatoes, corn pone and sweet tea, but the potatoes had boiled into a watery mush, the cured butter she had set out was a runny mess from the afternoon heat, and the chicken was cold. To top it all off, there was only one passenger on board anyway: a skinny little man named Quinlan in a striped suit, who pronounced house, 'hoos', and was quick to inform them he was enroute to Quitman to set up a Freedman's Collation Store there.

After the stage had pulled out, Esther turned to Nadine and said "Well, I guess I have learned one lesson today."

"What's that?"

"From now on when that stage arrives, there will be a warm stew and little more," she said as she once again put on her cotton apron to begin the clean up.

Two days later, the stage returned headed eastbound. This time it had three passengers: a man who looked as though he had spent his last nickel for the fare, a lady with a beautiful bonnet and matching sky blue dress, and a freedman.

The white man, a Buster Cunningham, mentioned that the darkie was headed for a good job working on the docks over on the Saint John's. It was obvious to all Cunningham was bitter about this. The Freedman said very little and took his meal outside away from the others.

Esther tried to make conversation with the lady but her actions quickly made it plain, she considered herself in a class above the wife of a stage stop attendant.

One week to the day of the first stage, Scooter Jones, the teamster who usually drove the stage, arrived on time; it was a memorable day as it was the first time since they had opened this had happened. Scooter also had a letter addressed: Station Master, *Estherbrook* Stage Stop. After the fresh horses had been hitched, he said, "I almost forgot this here letter, it was at the station in Jennings when I got there," he said surrendering it.

Sam opened it and quickly read the short note:

Sam,

Please inform Mr. Brown his shipment should arrive in Jacksonville Saturday. Perhaps here Tuesday, by rail.

John Inglis

"Thank you, Scooter. I'll see to this personally," Sam said as he folded the yellow paper, giving the impression the contents were meant for him.

The arrival of the shipment of new Colt Model 1871 revolvers was indeed a time of joy for Clifford Brown. He carefully removed and inspected each himself before turning them over to Johnny.

They had eight-inch barrels, which seemed long on these guns, but the bright blue finish on the metalworks and case hardened frames were rich in color and they made very handsome additions to the arsenal of the Renegades. Cliff took one that had a fine trigger pull and retired his old 1860 conversion, a gun that had saved his life a dozen or more times for almost ten years. He placed it on a small table beside their bed, where though it was no longer used daily, it still would be available should a need arise late in the night.

After Johnny had test fired each of the new Colts, every man there was issued two, with instructions to become as friendly with them as they were with a jug of corn spirits.

Cliff also gave Buckshot the duty of picking up all spent cases after the men practiced; should uninvited guests come snooping around, he wanted little evidence of their true works to be found here.

CHAPTER NINE

Confederate Memorial Day

On the morning of April 26, 1871, the sun rose to see a thick blanket of fog covering the land of South Georgia from Tifton to the Withlacoochee and into Middle Florida as far south as Gainesville. Heavy cloudcover from an approaching front soon gave ole man sun no chance of heating the ground enough to cause these earth-locked clouds to lift.

Esther was quite disappointed; she had hoped so that they would be able to slip past the troops at Valdosta and go to a gathering John Holliday had invited them to on his father's farm, in celebration of Confederate Memorial Day.

The stage was scheduled to arrive at ten o'clock which would give them sufficient time to make it to Bemis by three, provided nothing interfered.

Nadine, too, was anxious, as this would be her first opportunity to see the celebration. Mary Ann had told her about it and seemed so enthused, that she also had become like a little girl waiting for a Sunday ride.

For several days the women had been making plans and much food had been prepared. The men likewise had polished their saddles, combed their best horses and checked and rechecked their guns. Nadine had Mr. Bevin, who owned one of the carriage and harness shops in Madison, make a pommel rig for Cliff that attached over his horse's back just in front of the saddle. This was a combination of two small leather bags and two Slim-Jim type holsters. Each holster had a narrow hammer strap to retain the revolvers while the horse was at a gallop. Tom Bevin had displayed his talents with leather by adding floral engraving on the rig, and it was quite eye-catching, just the thing for this afternoon's celebration ride. In this, Cliff had slipped two of the new Colts; but the stage never arrived.

A pommel bag with internal holster

Finally, when the two o'clock hour came and passed, Sam turned to Cliff and said, "I'd like to take a couple men and go see if she is broken down somewhere."

"I think we should take more than a couple," Cliff replied and turned to the men who were nearby. "Dizzy, will you go and tell Nadine we are heading out to look for the stage?"

"If the rest of you want, mount up and let's see what has gone wrong." His words were that of a question but everyone including Dizzy understood it as a command.

The six men rode east towards Sam's Crossing, where he had shot the Yankee tracker. The mud there showed no signs of any activity for some time. It had been a dry month with almost no rain, and the Withlacoochee was quite low because of this. The normal brown water was seen to be almost clear with a bluish tint, revealing that what was now flowing slowly past had come strictly from springs and not from any rain runoff.

Four miles after they crossed the river, Sam noticed three big black birds circling high above.

The road here entered a deep hammock and was almost completely canopied with over-hanging limbs, and soon after entering this darkened stretch, they rounded a short curve and came upon the coach. Two buzzards laboriously lifted on long wings and slowly rose between the branches and disappeared above.

Sam wondered how they could have seen the sight through all those thick trees, but somehow they had.

One of the horses lay dead, still harnessed to the drawbar. The others were nowhere to be seen.

They could see a single, sleeved arm hanging loosely from the drivers boot.

"Check that, Johnny," Cliff said pointing his Colt's barrel at the limp appendage.

Sam quickly dismounted, and with revolver in hand opened the door to the coach, stood back up straight, and then reached in after something. A few seconds later he closed it again and looked at Cliff.

"It's Ole Scooter," Johnny said. "He's been shot dead. Looks like a scatter gun."

"Here, too," Sam added "two more dead inside."

"What you got there?" Cliff asked nodding his head at Sam.

"It's a purse, a woman's purse," he said and then walked over to where his friend still sat mounted on the sorrel gelding.

'It is a purse alright, a pretty dark-blue purse,' Cliff thought as he took it from Sam's outstretched hand.

The blue bag had a little drawstring made up of a braided material that caused it to look like a small rope. Inside was a leather coin bag with a gold snap. Inside this he found a dime and three pennies and a small piece of paper that had been torn from a larger sheet. Opening the folded paper, Cliff could see 112 Oak Street had been written there with a lead pencil, nothing more.

Cliff returned the Colt to its holster and looked about studying the men, finally he spoke. "Israel Henley, I want you to go back to *Estherbrook* and tell everyone what has happened here, and then," he hesitated and shook his head before continuing, "then you get a fresh mount and head to Jennings Station and wire the Sheriff of Hamilton County. His office is in Jasper. Tell him what has happened. Here is some money for the wire," Cliff said handing him three two-bit coins.

"Yas, sur," the youngster replied and pulled on his reins without any question.

"Israel," Cliff stopped him, "I don't want no law to go snooping around our place, so you make sure the women folk know to have the place cleaned up before you get back."

"Yas, sur."

"Tell J. M., no, ask Marty to keep everybody out of sight; he can tell J. M.

"Israel, I'm sorry to have to send you alone, it might be dangerous, but I need the rest of the men with me."

"Yas, sur, I'll keep a good look-see," the twenty-year old boy said just before he spurred his roan pony.

"Sam, I reckon you and Johnny are the best trackers we have here, scout out and see what you can find."

Sam nodded his head.

Johnny slid from Midnight, Granny Keeling's stallion, he had borrowed for the ride to Beemis, and immediately began easing into the woods to the north side of the road.

Five minutes later they were back.

"Well, I ain't got much injun in me, but looks to me there was three or maybe four a' them. One a' them laid here in ambush," Sam said pointing to the overhanging limb of the largest oak there, "and shot that lead horse first, then Ole Scooter. Others come a-running from the brush on the side yonder and shot them inside. They dragged the woman out and loaded her on one of the team horses and all cut through the thicket to the north."

Johnny was nodding his head in agreement, then added "I see where one was over yonder to the 't'uther side and let the coach pass him. I reckon he didn't want to be in the line a' fire, but still, he had that side covered should a body make it out that door." Johnny spit and then added, "It were him what dragged the woman out."

Cliff eased his horse off the road and into the dense woods and the others followed.

The ground was totally blanketed with a thick layer of dead and dying leaves which were soft enough to give with the weight of the horses and leave little trail, but one of the horses had a tendency to drag the left rear shoe every so often and this would turn over a dry leaf revealing the dampness that was still trapped beneath. This offending shoe left just enough sign to keep them on the trail through this heavily wooded hammock. Finally after some forty minutes of slow moving, they broke out into an area that had been burned two or three years before. Here the tracks were plain and the going was easy.

"These are a bad bunch, boys. Murderers they are and they have a four hour or more head start on us, but they don't seem to be moving in no great hurry," Sam said.

"Me'bee the draft horses are slowing them down a little?" Cliff replied and then wondered. 'Me'bee the woman?'

It appeared the fire had been started by a strike of lightening and with a southwind, had run to the northeast. Cliff judged there was perhaps two thousand acres burned here, but the knee-high saplings of long needle pine were taking hold on the burnout and looked to be turning what had once been a dense oak hammock into a pine forest.

Again Sam noticed the circling buzzards ahead of them and pointed to the big black birds soaring high above. Cliff nodded his head.

A mile ahead they came upon another dead horse, a saddle horse.

Johnny slid from his mount and checked him. He removed his hat and wiped the sweat from his brow with the sleeve of his buckskin shirt and then used the hat to shade his eyes while he looked up at Cliff. "The way I see it, this here fellow wandered off a little and got his horse tangled up in that downed tree yonder, whar the brush has all grown over. He's got a broken hind leg and his head is shot near off."

Cliff turned and looked at his men. "Keep this in mind; we don't have extra horses should you cripple yours."

"I'm sure relieved, Reb," Sam said leaning over closer to Cliff. "I were a'feared it would be the woman."

"Me, too," Cliff replied and then touched his heels to the horse's belly and they moved out again.

The burn ended at the shores of a fair size lake where the fire had run out of fuel. There along the bank it was plain; the men they were after had stopped and rested their own mounts. The sand around a little beach, where the waterweeds had not grown thick, showed signs of much recent activity.

"Look at this," Robert said holding a short jacket made of the same material as the purse.

"Where did you find that?"

"Yonder," he said pointing a little distance from the beach.

Cliff and Sam followed him through broom sage to where Robert stopped and nodded.

Here, the tall ragweed had been crushed down in an uneven circle. There was much disturbance to the sand as well.

"You thinking what I'm a' thinking?" Sam asked.

"I am," replied Cliff.

When they got back to the others, Johnny said "Looks like they stayed here some time. I see they didn't build no fire though."

"It'll be dark in an hour or so. I reckon they plan to be where they're a' aiming by then, or have a special place in mind to camp fur the night," Cliff replied, then with a sigh he added, "I know these animals are about played out, but if we keep moving we might just catch them 'afor they do anymore harm to the woman."

"Let's keep moving," Sam said.

Everyone slowly mounted and continued their task without complaint.

As dusk began to surround them, following the tracks became more of a chore and this slowed their pace.

"Let's dismount and walk the horses," Cliff suggested as he swung his leg over the saddle. "We'll be able to see their trail better down there."

When total darkness fell upon them and the moon had not yet risen, the idea of continuing seemed to be folly.

'I can't see five feet in front of me,' Cliff thought, *'and I ain't got no idea where I'm placing my feet.'* Taking a deep breath he stopped and turned around just as Robert bumped into the rear of Little Red. After shaking his head a couple of times as he realized it was a wonder the sorrel had not kicked the offender, Cliff reluctantly said, "We'll wait here for the moon," and he turned to his horse and began removing the saddle. Soon he could hear the others doing the same.

Sam scrounged around and found a small limb, wrapped Spanish moss around it and stuck a Lucifer[26] to it, making a quick burning torch.

Moss burns brightly for only a few seconds and then it is all used up. It was enough for them to locate one another and get a quick picture of what was around them, then darkness was upon

---

[26] Lucifer: The brand name of the most popular stick match in the 1870's

them again, even darker than before as their eyes now needed to once again adjust to the lack of light.

"Man, it's blacker than a hundred midnights down in a cypress swamp," Jerry said.

"You ain't wrong there," Johnny agreed, then he turned to where Cliff had been standing and asked, "Should we build a small fire? I'm a hankering fur some coffee."

"Not yet," Cliff replied. "When the moon comes up me'bee. Light of a fire can be seen mighty far on a dark night like this and so far I don't believe they know we are following."

Johnny made no more mention of it; rather settled down on the red clay and leaned against his saddle.

In a little over an hour a great ball of deep orange began to glow through the tall trees to the east. It was at the same time the wind picked up.

Cliff knew the moon would be nearly full when it did rise, and when it came, they were able to get a good view of their surroundings for less than ten minutes. Sadly it also revealed just where the cold front had gotten to by the southbound cloud layer, and soon the ole man in the moon hid behind this, giving them only a little more visibility than before it rose. However, even though the moon had not become their friend, the wind had.

Wind is not correct, the front was not close enough to push a wind, but there was defiantly a breeze coming out of the north.

"I want some coffee so bad I can taste it right now," Johnny said as he took a stick and began flicking small clumps of clay ahead of it.

Sam raised his head up straight.

Cliff did likewise for a moment or two, and then he stood. "You ain't tasting it Johnny boy, you are smelling it," he said turning around in a circle slowly and then he stopped facing northwest.

"Yep," Sam agreed. "There's coffee a-boiling out there and it ain't too far off neither."

They all stood and tuned their noses in the direction of the familiar smell.

"Saddle up," Cliff said then added, "Quietly."

Sam thought of the little torch he had lit, and was grateful it had burned out so quickly, lest their adversaries might have seen it.

Looking about, making sure they were all ready, Cliff said "Let's move easy-like."

He led the way walking ahead of his horse with the reins in his left hand and his Smith & Wesson in his right.

Each step was made with caution and every nerve was at full alert wondering if they would be seen approaching the highwaymen. The going was slow and stressful, but after a little over a mile, the dull glow of a campfire became visible ahead through trees. From that moment on they walked with even greater caution.

Gradually the sounds of voices came drifting through the forest and Cliff stopped.

Turning and looking behind him he saw in line Sam, Johnny, Robert, and Jerry.

"Johnny, ease up here," he whispered and gave him a quick wave beckoning the short man forward.

The young man dropped Midnight's reins and moved forward quickly.

"We are going to wait here for ten minutes. I want you to slip around and see if you can locate where they have their horses and wait there for us."

Johnny did not answer, rather nodded his head, and returning to his mount, removed the Henry from its scabbard, and then disappeared into the night.

"Just rest easy," he said to Sam, who passed it back down the line.

Cliff could not see his watch in this darkness and he had no way of telling the elapsed time, but figured it would be better to give Johnny too much than too little.

Finally after what seemed like two hours to the tensed-up men, Cliff rose from where he had squatted and waved Sam ahead.

Again the men walked in single file for a hundred yards before they came upon a strong-built fence beyond which was a large well-kept grove of pecan trees[27]. Immediately Cliff knew where he was. Mr. Dasher had planted this grove right after the major introduced them to South Georgia a few years before, he and his brothers had hunted squirrels in it.

The glow that had been their beacon now was seen clearly to be a small campfire, although they still could see no one.

Cliff remembered that in the center of this grove there was a half-acre pond that kept water year-round, save on the few times

---

[27] Pecans were introduced to this area by the Holliday family.

when severe drought plagued South Georgia, and he surmised the drought was not that bad this year. *'It will be there the killers have made their camp.'*

"Leave the horses here," he said softy, and with great care climbed over the split-rail fence and advanced slowly in a crouched posture.

When they were a hundred feet from the fire he stood upright and slipped behind one of the mature trees.

There were two men squatted around the fire. Another was lying in a bed roll not far away. His boots were at his side and to his ankle was tied a rope. The rope lay stretched out some twenty feet and there they saw that its other end was tied to the ankle of the woman.

She lay on her back, both feet drawn up so her knees were high in the air. Her arms were out-stretched behind her and her wrists were tied also by a coarse rope around one of the pecan trees. Her dress and undergarments lay scattered about. It was obvious they had tired of having their pleasure with her and were now making friends with the jug one of them held on his upper arm.

Cliff remembered Sam saying there were three, maybe four. *'If there were four, where is the fourth one?'* he looked everywhere but saw nothing. The horses were picketed out of sight so he couldn't get a count of them.

The remembrance of Johnny adding to Sam's statement that one had let the stage pass and was on the other side of the road, kept pricking his mind like a thornbush would do to your ribs when you got too close, but he could not see anything more or anyone else.

Finally the man with the brown jug took a long draw and then spat a little from his mouth as the strong brew began to burn the tender gums. "I think I can get me up another boner," he slurred and pitched the jug to the other man, who simply laughed out.

It was obvious these two were drunk and Cliff guessed the other one was also or he would have not been bedded down so early. This would be to their advantage.

Cliff hesitated again feeling that prick in his mind, but knew he had to stop him before that bastard harmed the woman any more.

Looking about at his own men, he saw each had followed his lead and found a good-sized tree to give them cover, so he cocked the revolver just before he yelled out, "Nobody move or it'll be your last move."

The two men jerked around and reached for the revolvers hanging from their belts.

Cliff stepped from behind his tree just enough for them to see him and added. "Drop them irons or you'll die were you stand."

"Yonder he is, Pike," the man with the jug yelled as he pointed with his Remington.

"I said drop them guns!" Cliff again yelled out this time much louder than before.

"You see any more?" Pike asked without taking his stare from Cliff.

"No, I don't," his partner replied.

"Get up, Rome," Pike yelled and the man in the bedroll stirred some but fell back into deep slumber.

"Drop 'um!" Cliff commanded once more, "Last chance."

"Like hell!" Pike screamed and fired his pistol. The ball passed over Cliff's head and he calmly took careful aim and squeezed the trigger.

Suddenly the grove was alive with gunfire.

The man with the jug didn't get a chance to drop it or fire his weapon before two 44 slugs struck him above the waist.

Cliff's bullet had hit Pike full in the left breast but whether it killed him or not will never be known as Jerry stepped from behind his cover and began whipping the lever on his Henry. Before Pike fell backwards he had four more holes in his chest.

Rome had been blasted from his sleep by the thunder going on around him, and upon seeing his buddies being riddled with lead took off on all fours into the pond and tried to dive under but the two-foot deep pond didn't give him the cover he wanted and finally he just raised both hands, turned and sat down, and then he began to sob, "Don't shoot me no more. Don't shoot me no more."

"Hell boy, we ain't shot you the first time," Sam said and then followed it up with, "Yet."

His quick scramble for a safe haven had pulled the loop of rope from around his foot and the woman looked at it with big round eyes rather than at the men so near.

The scene suddenly became very quiet as everyone looked about at each other, but the silence was short-lived because another shot rang out and Cliff felt the prick again.

The shot was followed by the sound of crashing limbs and the heavy thud of a large body that fell just on the edge of the circle of light. A few seconds later, Johnny stepped into view and kicked the lifeless man.

"I knew he was there, but couldn't get a bead on him until he leaned forward to take aim at you."

Cliff nodded his head and gave Johnny a big smile. It was more than adequate as a thank you.

Turning, he said to Jerry and Robert. "Get that bastard out of there and see what you can get out of him." Then he added loud enough that he was sure the man heard him "If he fails to talk, start cutting off his fingers one at a time, until he gives you the answers you want."

"I'll talk, I'll talk. I'll tell you everything I know."

Sam had cut the woman loose and was gathering her dress for her. Cliff waited until she was again clothed before his approach. When he saw her clearly, he stood up straight and swallowed hard.

'She is just a child, thirteen or fourteen at the most, but she sure seems to be a trooper, holding up so well,' He thought as he watched her talking to Sam with a clear head.

Cliff handed her a canteen of water he had found near the fire and she took a long swallow and thanked him.

Sam turned and stood. "She says her name is Mattie Farall and she was headed to Quitman with-her father and uncle. That was them we found back at the stage. Says she lives on a farm a few miles north a' town," he said and then cleared his throat before adding, "Says the rest a' her family is there."

"Can she travel?"

"I don't know. She had a rough time of it, but she's holding out pretty good."

"I wonder what will happen when the shock wears off," Cliff said.

"Reb, there is something else."

Cliff stopped and looked first at her and then back at Sam.

"She says there was another one at the holdup, a man with yeller hair. Says she couldn't understand what they called him. Say's he split off from them right after they moved out."

"Must a' been in the thicket. We could a missed his tracks there for sure," Cliff replied.

"Mister!" Mattie called out.

Cliff removed his hat and stood close to her. "Ma'am?"

"You kill them all?"

"There is still one alive, yonder," he replied. "The one what was tied to you."

'*She is just a little bit of a thing,*' he thought as she looked up at him with big wide round eyes and asked, "When you shoot him, can I watch?"

Cliff moved his tongue around inside his mouth trying to moisten the dry spots before replying "You can watch when I hang him."

Moving far enough away so she could not hear, Cliff turned to Sam and said "You know this don't make no sense. That stage weren't carrying nothing a' value. There ain't more'n six dollars on all four a' them. Why you reckon they robbed it?"

"Maybe they thought there would be money on it."

"Me'bee."

After finishing their work at the pond he sent Sam and Johnny back to *Estherbrook* with the extra horses, knowing it would be good for Sam to be the one who told the law about the capture and rescue.

The only thing Henry "Rome" Abram told them of any value was Pike had hired him for what he had called '*an assignment.*' He agreed that another tall thin blonde man had been at the holdup scene and told them it looked like Pike took orders from him.

"Rome is from Waycross and has fallen in with a bad bunch. He probably would have never done such things otherwise," Robert said.

"I don't doubt that, but that don't change what he done, none," Cliff said back and walked off.

They moved out at first light.

Jerry made a travois for Mattie to ride on, and as they left the grove, she watched the four bodies swinging slowly first one direction and then the other as the north wind picked up.

The three riders delivered Mattie to her family explaining what had happened and assured them they would bury the bodies of her kin in the *Estherbrook* Cemetery, and Jerry assured them he would make strong coffins from cypress, should they want to transfer them later.

It was late Friday evening when they rode up on *Estherbrook,* as the whole property had now become known among them.

Sheriff Lawrence had left word for them to come to Jasper when they got back.

"How did he take it?" Cliff asked.

"Well, he's appointed by that bunch in Tallahassee you know, so he's got 'a lean their way, but the facts are pretty much clear here and he knows it."

"Did he suspect anything?" Cliff asked motioning with his arm slowly in a semi-circle, pointing at the overall village they had there.

"No, the women were here at the stage stop making soap as was Marty; J. M. stayed out of sight. He didn't seem to pay much attention to anything but the stage. He spent half an hour at the scene."

"Alright, we'll go to Jasper tomorrow. I want to put an end to this as soon as possible, so as not to attract too much attention to the place."

The next morning each of the men who had been with Cliff saddled up and rode east. About half-way there, Johnny spoke, "If we are gon'a' be a riding to some settlement ever three or four days, I'd as soon move closer."

"We should not have to do this much more," Sam answered back. "My guess is, now that Reb has the arms he wants, we will be riding north mostly from now on," Cliff over heard their conversation but decided not to get into it.

They stayed there only a few minutes before they learned Sheriff Lawrence had gone to Madison on some business, so they headed south to cut the St. Augustine Road west of Live Oak.

It was well past noon when they rode down off the little hill into the east end of Madison. After having lived in the west as long as Cliff had, the big oaks and the lovely Southern homes were warming to his heart. *'Not to say there ain't beautiful country out there, for surely there is.'* He had to admit to himself, he found times when the call of the mountains stabbed at his mind. He also knew there was no place that touched the innermost areas of his very being, as did the Deep South. Even in these awful hard times, he was home and he knew it, and this little town of Madison was a fine symbol of the very feeling he held true and warm deep within his heart.

They passed the hotel and headed straight to Sheriff Montgomery's office in the basement of the Court House; it was there they found Lawrence.

Each of the men told their stories one at a time, some to one Sheriff and some to the other. Montgomery had learned one thing while in office. Never let one person tell a story in front of another who intends to tell the same story.

"Of course they had plenty of time to get together and get their stories straight," he said to Lawrence, "but they all told the same story differently and it matched what we done already heard from the Henley boy."

"I reckon they are telling the truth all right," Lawrence agreed.

"I tell you Mr. Brooks, you are damn lucky. Those bastards could have come after you and your Missis."

"I got a' say something that Cliff said," he was careful not to call his friend Reb in front of the lawmen, but was not so sure the others had used the same caution. "This whole thing don't make no sense. That stage weren't carrying nothing worth stealing."

"Maybe it were the girl, they were after," Lawrence suggested.

"Me'bee, but somehow I don't think so. Naw, it were too well planned out."

"Time will tell Mr. Brooks, time will tell," Montgomery said then added. "You all can go on back. If either a' us have a need to question you more, I'll send fur ya'."

When they left, Cliff told the others to go ahead and get any supplies they might need and he would meet them at Gwynn's Saloon when he was ready to head back, knowing full well that was where they would go straight to anyway.

"Sam, will you come with me?"

The two men rode south to the newspaper office.

"I think this is the kind of story Mr. Balough was talking about," he said to Sam. His friend nodded his head in agreement.

When they had repeated their story to the newspaper man, he seemed to fill with enthusiasm, not unlike a kid who was just given a new rifle as a present.

"Oh man, you have no idea what I can do with this," he said jumping up and calling to the printer to hold the front page for a new headline.

On their way out, Balough asked, "Have you had a chance to see the men who sent word they wanted to talk to you?"

"No, need to do that," Cliff replied, nodding his head.

The headlines read in large bold print:

Withlacoochee Renegades Catch Stage Robbers
Rescue Kidnapped Child

The article went into great detail describing the holdup and murders and the intensive and difficult trailing done by the dedicated home boys. It even told of the fire fight but left out the part about the bodies they left swinging in the breeze.

CHAPTER TEN

The Scalawag

The next day Cliff took Johnny, Robert, and Jerry with him and headed north to arrange a rendezvous with the three men who had contacted Balough.

Jerry was more familiar with the happenings going on in Valdosta lately, as he had been the last of them to move from town to *Estherbrook*. He dare not go by Major Day's shop, but he did venture to the Methodist Church on Central Avenue and asked Pastor Goodwire to let John Holliday know they wanted to talk to him.

That afternoon in a stand of magnolias, Holliday came to them not far from the ferry that crossed the Withlacoochee a few miles west of Valdosta.

"Mr. Holliday," Cliff began, "We seem to need your services again."

"Do tell?" the overly thin man replied as if he had been expecting the request.

Cliff explained that these three had sent word that they wanted to contact him and was wondering if Holliday could arrange it.

"I see, I suppose I could send Ezzard to fetch them," he replied, "Is this all you need me for?"

"I realize you are quite busy, sur, but I don't think it would be wise to show our faces in too many places here."

"I think you are very correct, especially right now."

"What does that mean?" Cliff asked.

"I suppose you have not seen the *South Georgia Pioneer,*" he replied unfolding a newspaper he had in his coat pocket and handing it to Cliff. "I assumed this meeting I was summoned to was in reference to this:"

Withlacoochee Renegades Rob Stage Coach Murder Three and Kidnap Young Girl

Cliff read the headline. The story contained details about the robbery and kidnapping but nothing about the tracking and eventual rescue of the girl.

"I don't understand how these people can make up such lies," Cliff said as he read on:

> Reb Brown, known leader of cutthroats, shot-gunned the driver to death and then raped a woman passenger on the scene as she had to stare into the dead eyes of the poor teamster. Her father and another passenger were forced to watch as Brown and his men repeatedly defiled this poor unfortunate woman before being murdered themselves.

"This is all Yankee lies," he said.

"I suspected they would have had you in jail in Madison by now," Holliday said. "This has been on the lips of everyone for the past two days.

Cliff shook his head. "Something just isn't right. I can't believe they would go so far as___, Wait a minute, what did you say?"

He then looked at the date above the letterhead: April 27, 1871.

"April 27th? Hell, we had not even reported the holdup when this was printed."

"What?" Holliday asked.

"That's right. The robbery took place on Memorial Day; we were waiting for Sam and Esther to finish with their duties and then we all were planning to come up to enjoy your invitation. Nobody knew about the robbery before us, we found it and sent word to Sheriff Lawrence late on the 26th. He didn't tell anyone until after he had questioned us and we told the newspaper in Madison ourselves after noon on the 28th. No way the paper here in Valdosta could have found out about it until late on the 28th, that was yesterday."

"Unless someone at the scene told them," John Henry suggested.

"Mattie said there was one who got away," Cliff offered.

"Who is Mattie?"

"Mattie Farall. The girl they kidnapped."

"You know who she is?"

"Sure, we rescued her and took her home."

"Tell me everything," Holliday said in a commanding voice.

Cliff explained the entire day and night including the hanging of one live man and three dead ones.

"You know I was assisting little Jimmy Tidwell with his piano lesson on the morning of the 27th when a man came to the Tidwell home and demanded to speak with Mr. Tidwell immediately; I have seen him before but do not know his name. I could hear them talking in the library, but could not understand any of the conversation. Soon after, they both left in great haste. I could tell that whatever this man had told Tidwell, it pleased him very much," Holliday said and then added. "Lucky for me he left when he did, as Mrs. Tidwell needed me to assist her also."

"I'm sure you were more than willing to oblige her," Cliff replied without emotion.

"Someone needs to. Certainly her husband has no time for her."

"Can you recognize this man again if you were to see him?"

"Of course," Holliday replied. "I will see if I can find out his name."

"That will be great," Cliff said.

Holliday turned and placed a foot in the stirrup of the gelding and then said, "I don't suppose you still want me to find those chaps for you now, do you?"

"Yes, we are up here, we might as well try and make the rendezvous."

"Is that wise?"

"I don't know what is wise anymore John Henry, but we'll give a go at it anyway."

"I'll see what I can do and get back to you, here," he said and after nodding his head he added, "Before four this afternoon."

"Thank you."

Looking back at the paper, the whole question on motive suddenly burst out to him plain as day. "You know, this whole thing was pulled just to have a story that would paint a bad picture in the minds of homefolk about us."

"You think so?" Jerry asked.

"Sure, they can't catch us because the homefolk will never tell on us. We are their heroes, but nobody would look up to a thief who commits murder on innocent passengers and rapes women. Don't you see, they had to break down our image to our friends?"

"That one Mattie told us about, the one who cut away from the others soon after the robbery, went straight and told someone the plan had been successful, maybe the newspaper, maybe Tidwell, maybe both, but printing this so early means only someone who was actually there could have brought the news to them, and that will be their undoing," Cliff said slapping the paper against his leg. "The greedy bastards should a' waited one more day to print this."

It was a little before four when a colored man was seen approaching on a well-kept mule. His appearance gave one to think he had once been owned by a well-to-do family. His hair was cut short, what part one could see protruding from the bottom of the black, short top hat he wore. His coat was of flannel material and the color of a white tail deer. His trousers were jet black and obviously made for him alone.

The three men stayed behind the cover of old growth azalea bushes until he had passed them. Shortly thereafter, he stopped and looked all around and finally called out in not-so-loud a voice. "Misser Brown?"

Cliff did not answer him.

A few moments later he spoke again, "Misser Brown," and waited then added "Misser John Henry sent me. I's Ezzard."

Cliff slowly stood and stepped out in clear view to the rear of the mule.

"What do you want, Boy?"

The man jumped as if he had been struck with a whip.

"Lard, Lard, you shouldn't put a fear in a man like that," he said and removed his hat, and with an oversized red handkerchief wiped his brow and then his whole face.

"Misser John Henry sent me. He says them men you are looking fur will be a-waiting come sundown near the Nub Riber Ferry's."

"Get down if you are a' mind to," Cliff said. He could see the Darkey was uneasy and wanted him to know he was among friends.

The man swung one leg over the animal's back, but stopped there with it sticking straight back when he saw the others step out around him.

"You knows, I's should otta be a-getting on back, casen' he needs me," he said still holding the leg straight out over the mule's back.

"Where is Mister John Henry? Why did he send you?" Cliff asked. He could see this man was in his late forties and very large. Cliff was sure he would stand taller than even his own 74 inches and he appeared to be in excellent physical condition.

"Misser John Henry doesaunt' tell me whys he do's things."

"You one of Major Holliday's people, before the war?"

"Yas' sur. I still is. The Major treats a man fair."

"That sounds like the Major," Cliff replied, even though he had never met the man, he had heard of his good deeds.

"If you had rather, you do not have to get down," Cliff said.

"I thanks ya' sur," the Negro said and slowly returned his leg back and slipped his polished boot into the stirrup.

"Tell Mr. Holliday I thank him for his troubles," Cliff said and began reaching into his pocket for a coin as he added "And you, too."

The colored man stopped him, "Sur, I don ass fur nutton. The Major, he's takes good care ob' Ezzard."

"Very well," Cliff said, "I'm indebted to you then," and he touched the front brim of his hat.

The colored man slowly turned his mule and started off in the direction he had come.

"We need to move on to make that appointment," Cliff said to the others as he started towards the big magnolia where he had left his horse.

The New River is a tributary of the Little Withlacoochee, which in itself, is a tributary of the Suwannee; it cuts the road to Moultrie some three miles west of Valdosta. There had been a bridge there before the war, but the Valdosta Guard had destroyed it when the Federals approached their town. After the war, a Yankee by the name of Bresnahan came down from somewhere in New York and set up a ferry at the old bridge site and charged a dollar to cross a wagon and two-bits for every animal. Folks accompanying their animals stayed dry for free; all and all, not a bad deal for either.

At this location, the river had cut a deep slice in the clay which left high banks in dry season and overflowed them when at flood stage. Late April 1871 found it low.

They saw three men standing on the east bank of the river as they approached through the woods. Cliff could tell the tallest one was Dan Faux. The other two he studied for some time before deciding he had not seen either before.

He motioned back to the others and Johnny eased forward. "Do you know these hombres?"

Johnny studied them for a few seconds before whispering "That big guy there with the white horse," he paused.

Cliff nodded his head.

"He's Ken Nielson. I see'd him over to a sheriff's sale in '61."

"He's homefolk then?"

"Don't know him personally but he is from somers' around these parts."

"The other one?"

"Never seen him 'afore."

Cliff turned his head where he could see Jerry and Robert's faces and both slowly shook their heads.

"Well, Faux knows us all but the others don't," Cliff said, then he looked at Johnny and asked "Do you think Nielson knows you?"

"Doe-no', he might."

Robert had brought his Robinson Sharps with him. Although it was a single-shot, it did fire a considerably larger ball than the Henry and was accurate to a much greater distance. In a firefight, he would not be much help, but at the range they were from these men, the Sharps would be much more likely to find its intended target than would the Henrys.

"Robert, take a bead on Dan with your cannon. If anything goes wrong, send him to hell."

"Can do," Art Mann replied as he slipped off his mount, and reaching with his right hand pulled the carbine from its leather scabbard.

The tall lad eased over to where he had a good clear shot at them before cocking the massive hammer.

"Johnny go out and meet them and if everything seems alright, bring them back."

The younger man nodded his head and without hesitation he leaned his rifle against a tree and headed off to their right through the timber.

"Johnny!" Cliff called to him.

The man stopped and turned back around.

"If anything, anything at all doesn't look right, drop to the ground and we will cut them down before they can harm you."

The man raised his hand in reply and then turned again and slipped through the timber.

**Art Mann Taking Aim at Dan Faux
with his Robinson Sharps**

He came out onto the road two hundred feet west of where his friends were, knowing should there be an ambush waiting, the attention would be at that point, not where Cliff and the others really were.

The buckskinned lad moved swiftly on short legs down the road towards the three men.

Finally the one he had called Nielson noticed him approaching and motioned to the others. They turned and then all three started walking to meet him.

'A positive move,' Cliff thought.

Johnny talked with them for a few short minutes and then turned and headed back to where he had left the woods. The three men, now leading horses, followed a little behind him.

"Keep your bead on Faux," Cliff said, "I don't trust him." Then he turned and said to Jerry, "Watch the bank, just in case there are others that should come sneaking along in a minute or two."

Jerry nodded his head.

Cliff then moved ahead to intercept them when they entered the forest.

All three were big men. Faux was an inch taller than Cliff and both Nielson and the other man were over six-feet. Nielson was also broad shouldered and barrel-chested. He wore a black hat with a large brim. Cliff remembered a lot of Texicans had worn such a hat during the war. The other man wore a straw hat of the planter's style.

Johnny, on the other hand, was a foot shorter than any of them, but his knowledge of the woods made him have to take a back seat to no man in these swamps.

"This here is Ken Nielson and David Clark," he said swinging his arm back as an introduction when they reached the location where Cliff was waiting, "You already know Dan."

"Yes I do," Cliff said and then stretched forth his left hand to shake their extended rights.

Cliff had seen a man shot to death in Cheyenne, when he allowed another to clasp his gun hand in a shake. His killer had held a tight grasp on it and then pulled a hide-a-way with his left hand and blasted him point blank as he struggled to free his strong hand.

Thereafter, when Cliff was shaking an unknown or unsure hand, he used his left if at all possible.

The group moved deeper into the woods until they were a couple hundred feet from the road, and only then began their conversation.

Dan Faux started off with, "Several homefolk have heard of the good deeds you are doing, especially in your fight against the Occupational Forces sent by the President," he paused, and then continued. "And these men want to join up and help in your struggle." He cleared his throat and then, as if in an afterthought he added, "and I do, too. We all do."

"You had your chance 'afore my Pa was murdered and didn't see the need."

Dan again cleared his throat and twisted his head around in his collar as if he were trying to exercise the muscles in his neck, before he replied "I know. I should have then, but I was foolish. I thought you were just a radical bunch and it would all go nowhere, but I was wrong."

"Yep," was all Cliff said in reply.

"Look, sur," Dave Clark said. "I have no military experience, but my father was a graduate of the VMI[28] and served his country well in the war with Mexico. When Georgia seceded, he immediately resigned his commission and offered his services to his home state. Unfortunately, we lost him only four months later at Manassas Junction. My only two brothers also gave their lives for their state during the invasion. I, too, would have, save for my age."

Cliff judged him to be in his early twenties and what he said could very well have been true. There were boys in their early teens that had fought in Gray, but it was the exception rather than the rule. Most males under fifteen were needed at home to tend to the farm work.

"I now see an opportunity to serve, against perhaps not as great a foe, but surely as dreadful a' one to honest folk," Clark continued. "And I can shoot and ride as well as any man."

"I too, am fair with a piece," Nielson said. "I was an armorer at Fort Morgan until we lost her and I was captured. Spent the rest a' the war at Camp Chase near Columbus, Ohio. That's where I met Dan here."

28 VMI: Virginia Military Institute

Cliff turned to Faux. "I didn't know you were in the army, Dan."

"He wasn't a Reb prisoner," Nielson said. "He was sent there because he was considered "A Disloyal Citizen" by the authorities."

"That right?"

"Yep, I had expressed my belief that the south should be allowed to go its own way and we should end the fighting, but when a certain daughter of the local tax collector seemed to enjoy my company, I was suddenly arrested and placed in Camp Chase."

"You remained there for the rest of the fighting?" Cliff asked, trying to catch a flaw in the man's story.

"No," Dan said, again twisting the cramps in his neck, "I was able to escape in late '64 by way of Ontario. I didn't get back to Georgia until '66."

"Oh, then Georgia was your home to begin with," Cliff replied.

"Sure, I was born in Savannah," Dan explained.

"How did you find yourself in Ohio in the middle of a war your birth state was heavily involved in then?"

"My father was a sea-going man and he had taken my mother and me up the Mississippi, and then we went up the Ohio and the Wabash. I was in Indiana when hostilities broke out."

"Alright," Cliff cut him short, seeing the man had an answer for any of his questions, whether true or well thought out ahead, he was not sure, "What can we do for you?"

"We want to join up with you," Clark said quickly. "And fight the ones who are enforcing this hostile and foreign bayonet rule imposed by Grant and his phonies over our folks."

"That's about the size of it, Reb," Ken Nielson agreed.

"I'll think on it and get back to you. It ain't just up to me."

"Ah. We can't just go back into Valdosta," Clark said.

"That's right, Reb," Faux said. "These two jumped four colored soldiers who were harassing a lady and ruffed them up a bit. They have warrants out on their heads."

Cliff turned around looking away from them. He run his tongue around in his mouth trying to moisten it, it had been a habit of his since the war, he often did it when he was about to do something he didn't want to do.

"Shit," he said just above a whisper.

"Alright," he said. "I'll take you with us."

Immediately, Johnny cleared his throat allowing all to know he didn't agree with the last statement.

Cliff led them down the little game trail they had taken to where Robert and Jerry were. He knew Faux already knew them, but he surmised the other two didn't. "This is Art Mann and Cactus Jac," he said.

Dan extended his hand and said, "Hello, Jerry."

Immediately Cliff stopped him. "We only use our alias among ourselves. You three be thinking of what yours will be as we ride."

"Sure, Reb," Faux said lowering his hand.

"By the way Danny, whatever happened to Ray Shaw?"

The question seemed to suddenly trouble Faux for a moment, but he quickly regained his composure and answered, "Ray Shaw, gee, I haven't seen him in nearly a year."

Johnny, who was behind them, noticed the funny look Nielson and Clark gave each other and he decided to tell Reb about it as soon as they were alone.

When they reached the grits mill where he had last seen Dan Faux, he halted the little caravan.

"Cactus Jac, I want you to stay here with these new men until I return," he said without further explanation.

Jerry nodded his head and turned his horse into the little garden of ferns that Tillie had planted two years before.

That night Cliff discussed with the others about the three men and their wants. Johnny was adamant against letting them in.

Sam reminded everyone that they had lost several members and would be better able to withstand an attack with more men.

Normally when business of the Renegades was discussed, it was kept within the men folk, but when it involved the women also, they were asked to sit in and give their opinion.

This night, Mary Ann had sat with her husband and his brother and not even looked up while the idea was brought up, instead she had her knitting needles in hand and she occupied herself making a new bonnet for one of her girls. To everyone's surprise she suddenly said. "I think we should let them in."

The entire group, including Marty, looked at her and then he looked around at the others and then back at her.

"Just like Sam said, we need new blood," she added, still working the long needles with her hands.

Johnny told of the strange look exchanged between Nielson and Clark when Faux had made the statement about Shaw.

"I do think we need to watch Mr. Faux carefully," Cliff said, "In fact I believe we should put them all to a test before we bring them here."

"What kind of test?" Esther asked.

"Oh, I don't know right off the top of my head," Cliff replied as he reached for the big coffee pot that was sitting on the edge of the small fire in the center of the circle of people. "I'll think of something to tell them that will sound very important and then see if it gets out?"

"They will have to be free to come and go, if that is to work," J. M. added.

"True, I'll work on it," Cliff said.

Then, as a cool breeze began moving the leaves around on the trees, Nadine said, "I'm getting cold. You men decide and I'll go along." She then rose and lifted a shawl from around her back to her shoulders and headed for the barn.

"I have a suggestion," Marty said. "Let Reb here test them and if they pass the test, we'll take them in under close watch. If they fail then____," he lifted his shoulders as if all knew what the punishment of failing would be.

"That sounds reasonable," Robert agreed.

It was put to a vote and all except Johnny agreed. Standing, he expressed his doubts. "I don't know; I don't trust that Danny Faux no further than I can throw him, and that ain't very far."

The next morning Cliff was up early. He had thought on it for sometime before going to sleep, and had come up with a plan.

As soon as breakfast was over, he asked Israel Henley, J. M., and Robert to accompany him today.

The morning sun was just drying the dew from the green grass in the big pasture when they finished gathering what they would need for the mission, and had caught and saddled their horses.

Just then, Buckshot came running through the hammock yelling quite loudly.

"Mr. Reb! Mr. Reb!"

"What is it, son?"

"Three riders coming," he said pointing west. "T'other side a' Granny's house."

"Good boy. Now go and tell Miss Nadine to give you your biscuits and don't let her not give you that honey for them, too."

"I won't, Mr. Reb. I'll tell her you said she should."

Cliff nodded his head at the boy and then looked at the men who stood by.

"Israel, tell Marty and the women folk we have unexpected guests and then high tail it down and let Sam and Esther know."

He could tell the lad was disappointed he was again being used as an errand boy, but he didn't argue. Instead he turned and headed for the Gunter cabin on a run.

'I got a' show him I know he's a man,' Cliff thought just before he turned his attention to the uninvited trio. "Let's ride to the edge of the pasture and slip into the timber there and wait fur them," he said as he threw one leg over the horse's back.

Cliff had strapped on his Smith & Wesson and also placed the pommel rig with the two Colts in front of his saddle; with a Henry in his scabbard, he was ready to take on the local cavalry should they be encountered.

When the three horses came into view, he and his men charged out of the trees each with a revolver in hand.

The women screamed.

Doc Jean riding in front of the other two ladies yelled her protest. "Dear God, man, are you trying to scare us to death, or do we look that dangerous to you?"

Cliff dropped his head and returned his revolver to the holster. "Morning, Ladies."

"Good morning, yourself," she shot back, slowly regaining her composure.

Then raising her head high on her neck she cleared her throat before speaking again. "I have brought with me these two ladies who need a place where they can be safe for a while." After a moment, giving the information time to sink in, she added, "This is Maybell Knight." She lifted her hand that held the reins and pointed at the short blonde woman in her early twenties. "She arrived in Lowndes County only a few days ago from the west and has been staying with her good friends, the Slades." Then shifting her hand much to her horse's displeasure, she pointed to the dark haired woman, who was taller and ten years the blonde's senior. "This is Jim Slade's wife, Michelle, err' should I say, his widow. Jim was killed last week in Valdosta while playing cards in Jason's Saloon. He was gunned down for stating *The South Georgia Pioneer* made up lies, and over some other disputed facts between the paper there and *The Madison Trace*. One witness swore Jim was not armed, but now several have come forward and swear he was caring a silver sawed-off shotgun under his coat."

"My husband never owned such a gun," the lady in black responded angrily.

"The shooter," Jean added, "is an employee of the Civil Department; and the witnesses, the new witnesses, all seem to in some way have connections there, too; anyway, these ladies are being harassed by the local authorities and need to be looked after."

Cliff nodded his head. '*A little late to tell her don't bring them here.*' he thought, and knowing there was little else to do, he replied. "Take them on up to my place and explain to Nadine, and while you are there, send Israel Henley on."

"Yes, sir," she replied coldly; obviously displeased with his commanding voice, she saluted him sharply.

Cliff knew she was a valuable asset to their little community. She was the only Doctor that he trusted with the knowledge she had about them, and he believed she was totally loyal to their cause, still she was most arrogant, and often showed lack of respect for anyone in authority.

Israel Henley caught up with them before they left Granny Keeling's home.

Cliff had gone inside to talk to Johnny and the others had stayed outside. He could tell Johnny was a little hurt that he had not been asked to go.

"I can't leave the place with Marty or Dizzy in charge. I need some men I can count on to be here. While I'm on this, you and Sam are my best men, but Sam has his own work that can't be put off now, with the stage stop and all. They will have a new driver today and I don't want him getting suspicious about anything. We don't know who it will be or where his loyalties will lie. So Sam must be there all the time. That just leaves you and Robert to cover the whole place. I need you here."

When Cliff had put it to him that way, Johnny didn't have any more objections. He had never questioned anything Cliff had done, but he too wanted to be in on this test as he was sure Danny Faux would fail and he knew when that happened, were he with them, Faux would not escape.

"I won't let you down," Johnny said.

Cliff slapped him lightly on his back and replied, "I knew that all along."

"Just you watch that Danny Faux. He's a no good scalawag, just you wait and see."

"You might just be right," Cliff agreed.

The cabin smelled of fresh baked goods and he hated having to leave without the pleasure of enjoying some of Granny's hot buttermilk biscuits.

When he walked outside, he saw he was the only one who had missed out on them, as she was giving the last one from her basket to Israel.

The other men were stuffing the white bread into their mouths as fast as they could find room for it.

"Always like to send my boys off with a full stomach," she said to Cliff. "Makes 'em 'member what they is fighting fur."

"That is mighty kindly a' you, Granny," Cliff said as he mounted and turned west without a bite.

When they reached the mill, Cliff had everyone surround the place and watch for some time before he moved in alone.

Jerry was on the top floor, in the little room where they had their first meeting, keeping watch from the window. He had spotted Cliff when he first emerged from the trees to the south west and gave him a wave.

The others were around the other side of the mill boiling coffee over a small fire. This had been built out in the open which allowed a thin trail of smoke to rise straight as an arrow.

He dismounted and walked over. "Morning. Got enough a' that for me a cup?" he asked.

"Sure," David replied and gave him his cup.

Cliff took the blue porcelain covered tin and refilled it, then standing, he poured the remainder on the fire.

There was a hissing as the hot coals began to drown, as well as surprised expressions on the faces of the three men.

"We need to be going," he said and no one questioned him.

When they had moved out, he led them cross country through the timber on a game trail to the Nankin Road. His other men followed a mile behind, out of sight.

Two hours later, while they had stopped to rest the horses, he was able to get Jerry far enough away to ask him about the night.

"How inquisitive were they?

"Well, Nielson fell asleep right away," he said and then thought back. "Faux and Clark stayed up and talked awhile. Both seemed interested in what we did. Faux asked a lot of questions, but then so did David. They both seemed interested."

Cliff nodded his head and looked at the three men before he asked his next question, "Who built the fire this morning?"

"I don't know. They did that after I went up to watch and being they wus on the 't'uther side a' the mill, I didn't even know they had a fire until I came down and saw you putting it out."

Again Cliff just nodded his head.

He had hoped Jerry would have been able to pick up some tid-bit of information that would do him some good in making a decision on these three, but it just hadn't worked out that way.

A few more hours in the saddle found them in Brooks County, south of Quitman some five miles on The Johnson Short.

Cliff pulled up in a little grove of oaks and rested the animals.

"I want you, David, to go on into town and see if the sheriff is around. Now, don't let him see you, just ease around and find out and come back here."

"Yes, sir," the young man said.

"Ken, I want you to go north of town on the Tallokas Road to the Farall farm. It's on what's left of the Gaulden Plantation. Only a few miles north a' town, first farmhouse you can see from the road. Check and see how little Mattie is doing. She is the girl that got taken from the stage holdup t'other' day," Cliff said and then turning as if not concerned, he added. "I'm not sure if she will live or not."

Danny Faux spoke immediately. "I know where that is, I can go with him and show him the way."

"No, Nielson can handle it. I have another important run that must be made."

"I want you to take this message to a woman who lives east of town on the Maryville Road. Her house is three miles out and there is an old red barn to the side that is mostly fallen down," Cliff told him as he handed him the sealed envelope. "Her name is Jo Ann Turner. She should give you an answer; bring it back here as fast as you can. It might be important."

"Well, Ken can take this and I can go to the Farall house, since I already know where it is."

"No, in this outfit you do as told," Cliff said back with a hard look.

"Sure," Faux replied and reached for the envelope. "Three miles out on Maryville Road, old red barn, can't be that hard to find."

"Not hard at all," he agreed then added, "Jerry and I got a' see a loyal family that lives west a' here some three or four miles. We'll probably be back before you all can return, but if we are not, wait here for us," Cliff said and then mounting the gelding, he rode off without looking back.

"That loyal family, might be the Johnson's?" Dan asked in a rather straight statement.

"Information you ain't yet earned the right to know," Jerry said and then heeling his horse he followed Cliff.

On the way to the river that morning, Cliff had instructed his men what to look for. Israel Henley and Jerry were to follow David Clark and see if in fact he tried to find out about the sheriff or tried to contact him, J. M. and Robert were to follow Nielson, and he intended to watch Faux.

He was especially interested in Faux now that he had made such a fuss over Mattie. '*I wonder why he wanted so to go there.*' Cliff thought.

The three men were riding together for the first few miles, and then Clark moved on ahead of the others.

Cliff hoped this didn't present a problem with Jerry and Israel keeping him in sight without being seen themselves.

Just before Nielson and Faux entered the town of Quitman, they stopped and seemed to be arguing. Nielson kept shaking his head and finally he pulled his revolver and pointed it at Faux.

They watched the tall man slap his hat on the rump of his horse and ride east. Nielson then returned his Remington to his belt holster and continued into town.

"Wonder what that was all about?" Robert said.

"We'll find out later," Cliff replied and there he split with them and followed Faux.

He had not gone a mile when he came to the top of a rise and pulled up short; there only a hundred yards ahead was Faux.

Immediately Cliff felt better than he had in weeks. Finally, as if by the will of God, a great weight suddenly was being lifted from his shoulders while he watched the rider ahead reading the letter he had sent to the fictitious Jo Ann Turner. Actually, she was not truly fictitious. She had been his girl friend when he was a child in the academy school, but her parents had moved down to somewhere in South Florida and he had not heard from her since '53. There was a farm house there on the Maryville Road as he described, but he knew no one was living there now and Cliff smiled slightly, knowing what Dan Faux had seen when he opened the envelope was:

Mrs. Council Turner

I do hope this finds you in good health. I can assure you your husband is fine and carrying out his duties to my greatest expectations. If all goes well with this raid I feel sure he will be able to join you very soon.

We have information the westbound, day after tomorrow, will be carrying the pay roll for the troops *in Pensacola; over a thousand in greenbacks. It is our intention to hit it between Valdosta and Thomasville at the same water tank we spoke of before.*

What I need to know from you is can you find out if Mr. John Griffiss can again exchange the greenbacks for gold. We are in dire need of the gold, our limited funds are almost depleted and it is impossible for us to spend the greenbacks for fear of being caught. We will once more accept his two-for-one terms.

The man who has delivered this will bring me your answer.

Please be swift.

Your Servant, Reb Brown.

Faux returned the letter to the envelope, and then looked off into the eastern sky for several seconds before mounting his horse and cutting a trail towards Quitman.

Cliff turned back the way he had come and kicked his horse into a fast gallop for more than a mile before allowing the animal to slow.

He needed to be ahead of Faux and he had to make sure the rascal didn't overtake J. M. and Robert as they followed Nielson. If that happened, he would quickly figure out they were trailing Nielson and then surmise he too had been followed.

The sleepy little town of Quitman had little going for it other than the railroad depot and a fair-size general store. The Quitman Factory was under construction but not yet completed. *'When operational, it should bring much needed revenue into the area,'* Cliff thought.

Quitman, being the county seat of Brooks County, enjoyed the courthouse being located there along with other county offices, but little else.

He overtook J. M. and Robert just as they were approaching the tracks and quickly motioned them aside.

By the time Cliff had told them to keep out of sight, they saw Faux approaching from the south.

He went straight to the railroad depot.

"What's he going a' do, take a train back to Valdosta?" J. M. asked.

"No," Cliff said, "He's sending a telegram back to Valdosta. He probably has military authority and the railroad telegrapher will do it fur him."

"Som' bitch," J. M. replied "I'll cut his cods off."

"Not yet. Everyone who wants to see it will get to watch his execution."

"Come on and slip around town and check to see if Nielson does as told. I'll stay on Faux," Cliff said.

The two men were gone before the tall blonde man came out of the depot. He mounted his horse and started into town and then pulled up as if he had changed his mind and then he headed east towards the Maryville Road.

'He almost went to Mattie's house, but thought better of it and decided to go and check to see if there really was a farm with a red barn falling down,' Cliff thought as he watched the man, and again he wondered, *'Why is he so interested in Mattie?'*

Cliff headed on back to the rendezvous point and waited.

It was near four when David Clark returned and almost an hour later they saw Faux and Nielson approaching together.

When they all had gotten back, he told them to unsaddle and rest up the horses.

"Was Mattie alright?" He asked of Nielson.

"Yes, she seemed to be. Her mother looked worse off than the little girl."

"How about her Uncle Jim?"

"I didn't see no men there, just Mattie, her mother, and another older woman. I don't know who she was," Ken Nielson replied.

"And the sheriff?"

"He was there, I think," Clark replied. "I never actually seen him, but I asked a little nigger boy and he said the big blue roan tied in back of the court house wus the sheriff's. You said not to let him see me."

"You did right," Cliff assured him.

"And Jo Ann Turner, did you see her?"

"Yes, sir. She was down next to the road when I came up. I gave her your letter."

"Didn't she send me a reply?" Cliff asked.

"Yeah, sure, she didn't write nothing' but she read your letter and said to tell you she would take care of it and let you know. Whatever that means."

"I see," Cliff replied and then added, "I thank you all. My men are known on sight in Quitman, and I couldn't take the chance of letting them be seen. You have been a big help."

Then he said, "One of you build us a small fire and we'll boil some coffee while we wait. Others are supposed to meet us here."

David already had his saddle off before the other two had returned, so he began to gather some wood for the fire. By the time he had enough, the others were also finished with their task.

Clark dropped the load of small dry wood next to his horse and began looking in his saddle bags for some Lucifers.

"Here, I have some," Dan Faux said and produced two of the sulfur and flint tipped sticks.

David arranged the wood in a small circle stacking the smaller ones carefully on the bottom and the larger ones in a dome above the others, and then Dan struck one of the matches against his britches leg.

"Wait a minute," Cliff said.

They looked at him in question.

"You make the fire this morning?" he asked, looking at David.

"Ah, no, Dan did. Why?'

"When you're on the Owl Hoot Trail you never build a fire in the open. You always build it near a tree, so the branches will disperse the smoke.

"Oh," David replied and moved everything over next to a tree with low hanging branches.

"You should have known that, Dan," Cliff said.

"Never heard of it," he said back, not looking at Cliff.

Thirty minutes after the coffee was ready, the men began to ride in.

Cliff gave each of them a knowing glance and then told his little bunch to saddle up. "We have a big assignment first thing tomorrow."

He led the pack and the others followed in a loose column of twos.

J. M. and Robert brought up the rear. Cliff had made no mention of what he had learned.

It was well after dark when they arrived at Granny Keeling's house, but Cliff stopped anyway. They had listened to the slow but deliberate howls of her blue-tic[29] for two minutes, announcing their arrival.

Johnny had been behind a tree with his Henry long before they pulled up. No one saw him in the darkness until he stepped out.

"Everything go alright today?" Cliff asked.

"Yeah, Reb, everything's quiet. How about with you?"

"Better than I expected," Cliff replied. "Get dressed and come on down to the barn as soon as you can."

"Will do!" Johnny replied and headed for the porch in a flash.

"Johnny, can I get you to go by Sam's and get him and Esther, too?" Cliff saw the disappointment sweep over the young man's face.

"Don't worry, we won't start without you."

"Can do," Johnny answered.

The men rode into the camp and dismounted in front of the big barn. Small boys seemed to appear from out of the darkness to lead their horses out to the corral.

Cliff fetched a handful of pine needles that had been piled close by for the purpose and kindled a small blaze in the big circle of rocks they used to contain the campfire when there was a large group gathered together. Pulling his Smith & Wesson, he fired it once in the air to make sure everyone was awake and then he handed the revolver to Johnny.

Turning to the new men he said. "Johnny is our armorer. It is his job to check every weapon when we return from a mission and make sure they are in good working order and properly cleaned before we go out again. So, everyone who was out with me today give him your guns, he will check them over and return them to you, ready for action the next time.

The other men immediately pulled their revolvers from their holsters and handed them to Johnny, and then they took their Henrys and leaned them in a row against the big log.

Cliff watched the three new men.

---

[29] Blue-Tic: A breed of hound common in the south.

David Clark made no hesitation but followed suit and relinquished his Remington and then stacked his Enfield beside the Henrys.

Ken Nielson and Dan Faux seemed hesitant to turn over their guns.

Johnny had put all the others in the buckboard he had driven up in, and walked over to Nielson. "Your revolvers," he said.

"I don't want to be a sore thumb, but I feel qualified to check my own guns. After all, I was in charge of the whole garrison at Fort Morgan."

"Fort Morgan was overrun, too," Robert said.

"Not because of any of my guns not working properly."

"Me'bee, Me'bee not," Johnny said.

"If you feel Johnny ain't as good as you, then you check them again after he gives them back to you. Here, we all turn them in when we come from a mission. If you can't live with that you can't live," Robert said, paused and then added, "here."

"Alright," Nielson replied, "but as you said, I will check them myself later."

"Suit yourself," Johnny said as he reached for the two revolvers.

Dan Faux had already seen it was fruitless to argue so he handed Johnny his Colt Navy but he did not reveal he had a Philadelphia derringer in his boot.

By the time the fire was going good and coffee was boiling, a dozen or more people had appeared from the darkness.

Most were men but Dan could also see six women. He recognized Mary Ann and nodded his head at her and she smiled, but the other women he had never seen before.

He also noticed the men who were coming all wore their revolvers, but seeing the ones who had been with him today made no attempt to retrieve theirs, he concluded, *'I guess it is alright.'*

Finally, Cliff stood and addressed the crowd. "As you all now know we left here this morning to see about these three men who wanted to join our family. I gave each of them an assignment. Each carried it out, except one," he paused without looking at the three men.

"I instructed David Clark to go into Quitman and find out if the sheriff was there. I sent Jerry and Israel to follow him. What did he do?" he asked turning to Cactus Jac.

"He went in and looked for the sheriff just as you sent him to do," Israel replied and Jerry nodded his head in approval.

"I sent Ken Nielson to check on little Mattie Farall. Had J. M. and Robert follow him." Still not looking at any of them he asked, "What did he do?"

Robert stood up from the squatted position he had been in and said, "He went straight to the Farall farm and stayed about half an hour and then left."

"Now we come to Mr. Faux," Cliff looked hard at him before continuing, "Dan, I got a' tell you that Johnny has said all along you were a no good scallywag, and today you proved it."

"No, it ain't so! I don't know who told you stuff on me, but it is a pack of lies!"

"I am the one who followed you, Dan," Cliff said and now all eyes were on the tall man.

Faux knew he was in trouble and he wasn't sure how to get out of it.

Cliff looked at Nielson, "Ken, just before you and Faux split up, you two had an argument."

"Yeah, we did. He wanted to trade assignments with me and I told him no. You were very clear about following orders. I even had to pull my pistol on him to get him to shut up and leave me alone."

"That's right, you did. We were watching you," Cliff said.

Robert and J. M. looked at each other and nodded in agreement.

"Then Dan went just over the hill and opened my letter to Jo Ann Turner, my girlfriend from the fifth grade," Cliff said.

Cliff told the rest of them what was in the letter and then added about Faux going into the depot where the railroad had a telegraph. "What you want to bet that westbound tomorrow will have a company of nigger soldiers on it, and Mr. John Griffiss will be in jail in Valdosta?"

Faux suddenly dropped to his knees and grabbed the little pistol he kept hidden there, but he never was able to raise it.

Johnny's tomahawk hit him in the wrist and destroyed his left hand. The small pistol dropped harmlessly to the ground in front of him as he grabbed his wrist with his good hand, screaming.

Ten minutes later, Doc Jean had the bleeding mostly stopped, but she knew he would never use that hand again. When she stood and shook her head looking at Cliff, he walked up in front of the group and began.

"It's you," Cliff said sweeping his right arm in a big flat semi- circle, "all of us, this man is trying to destroy. There is no doubt now it was him that turned us in after the first meeting and got us all listed as wanted by name. It was his actions that got Chase and Jason arrested and kilt. It very well was his action, although possibly indirectly, that resulted in the soldiers going to your store, which we all know ended up with Tillie being killed. My Pa, and my Ma, Stan May's wife, his brother and his brother's wife, and God only knows how many more, so it will be up to you, as to what we are to do with him," Cliff said.

"Kill him, that's what to do to him," Johnny said. "A little at a time. I can take off his other hand."

"No, he is the reason my wife was murdered. I'll do the killing," J. M. said.

Dan Faux was in such great pain from the hatchet wound that had almost severed his hand; he really didn't fear their talk. He only spat at them and lashed back with words. "You ignorant bunch of turncoats. You all will be wiped out. You are the ones who will be killed, every last one of you. Your whores, your seed, and all, will be wiped off the face of the earth." His eyes were wild. His blonde hair tossed about in total disarray. His mustache coated with blood, where he had brought his hand to his mouth as if he could suck the pain away. "You dirty white trash," he shouted again.

"Yes, kill him," Marty said, "Kill him for Tillie."

"Oh, there is no doubt he will be killed," Cliff reassured them, "What I was leaving up to you was how we kill him."

"We ought a' nail his balls to a stump and push him off backwards," J. M. shouted.

Esther looked at Nadine and snickered at the last statement.

"We got a lot a' hog fat, we could bile it and fry 'im a little at a time. The Creeks used to do a man that a' way," Johnny suggested. "I got Creek blood in me you know and I heard my Grandpa Keeling tell of it."

"I think we should hang him slow," Robert said.

"No, hanging is too good for him, too fast," Johnny protested.

"Not if we do it slowly," Robert argued, and then he slipped a coarse hemp rope around Dan's neck and eased the loose knot down. He had tied a simple granny knot and a loop in the rope, not the traditional hangman's noose that almost always caused the neck to snap.

There was suddenly a rush to the rope's end as several of the group began to pull on it.

Dan Faux fell over backwards and grabbed at the rough braided hemp squeezing around his neck, but the strength of the mass was simply too much, and he was dragged along to the edge of the light; there they stopped next to a big sweet gum tree, and tossed the end over a limb. J. M. and Robert were the first to pull on the rope; then as he began to struggle and choke, Israel Henley and Dizzy joined in.

Dan's feet were lifted an inch off the ground just enough, so when he danced and struggled, his toes would touch and he would gain a moment of hope and then the rope would tighten again and once more, he would begin choking and struggling to free himself with his one good hand. Finally, they pulled him a foot off the sandy ground and tied off the rope. Everyone came around and watched him dance in the air trying desperately to again touch the ground with his toes but failing by only inches.

Cliff decided that enough was enough, and he walked over to the log and picked up his Henry and shot Dan Faux in the chest.

Normally a man being hit from so short a range with so large a piece of lead would die, if not immediately, very soon after being hit, but not so Faux. Still his legs danced and struggled in search of the ground.

Nadine took the rifle from her husband and also shot the man. Then as if being commanded to do so, each member of the Renegades took a turn and shot him, everyone save Mary Ann.

After the third shot, the smoke was so thick that no one there noticed when Faux stopped dancing, but when the rifle was again leaned back against the log, it was obvious to all the man was dead. His body now slowly turned back and forth on the tight rope.

"I think we should take him into Valdosta and hang his worthless carcass from the Courthouse Veranda," Jerry said.

"Yeah, let them all know what happens to scalawags," Johnny agreed. "Might give that no account Shaw a moment of panic."

"No, not this time," Cliff said. "We'll take him out and dump him in the swamp. Gators will rid us of his body."

"Hell, I think the lousy bastards should see what happens to them that help murder," J. M. argued.

"Right now, the Federals are moving on information he sent them. If we let them know we killed him, they might stop and do a wait and see routine. No, it is better that they take out Mr. John Griffiss."

"Who is he, Reb"? Israel asked.

"He is one of Governor Bullock's men these days, but he was born in Troupville[30] so it will make sense to them that he could be one of us working undercover."

"Oh, that's good," Robert said nodding his head as a big smile came across his face.

---

[30] Troupville: The original county seat of Lowndes that was abandoned after the railroad went through Valdosta.

CHAPTER ELEVEN

The Swimming Hole Incident

Dawn found Cliff, Robert, and Jerry saddling their horses. There was already a mule with a load securely tied over its back. Wrapped in a canvas, was the body of Dan Faux.

Ken Nielson and David Clark approached Cliff. They explained it had been the first opportunity they had had to catch him alone. They told him that they both had seen Dan Faux and Bob Shaw together earlier that week in a Valdosta tavern, and that they were surprised when Faux had told them he had not seen Shaw for a long time. Both of these men were somewhat concerned about their own safety. They had seemingly passed Cliff's test, but still no one had told them they were being accepted into the group.

They had witnessed the hanging of Faux and had no doubt, if they ever questioned it before, they were among a very violent group who would snap out a man's life with as much forethought as one would use to blow out a lamp.

Cliff could see their uneasiness, but he had not yet made up his mind on them, so he said nothing more than, "I appreciate your information. I wish you had decided to share it with me before I wrote that note to Mrs. Turner. I could have included Shaw's name in it."

"Well, we should have, but at the time we did not realize the importance of it," Nielson said.

Cliff nodded his head in reply and then added "You two stay close, help with the work here. I will talk to you more when I get back."

Their conversation was interrupted by the shouting of Buckshot as he ran through the hammock on his now well worn trail. "Rider coming! Rider coming!"

He was almost out of breath, and he gasped when he stopped next to Cliff.

"Catch your breath, son," Cliff told him. "Just one?"

"Yas sur," he said gasping and then got out, "I think it could be Mr. Holliday."

"You're a good scout, Buckshot. I'll have to teach you how to track one of these days. You will be good at that too, I 'spec," Cliff said as he placed his arm around the boy's shoulder. "Get you a biscuit and a good drink a' cold water and then get back to your post."

"Can I have some coffee?" the boy asked.

Cliff looked down at the seven year old and nodded his head "If you are of a mind to."

"I am."

Cliff turned to his men and said, "Wait here for me," then he turned his attention to Nielson and Clark and said, "Gentlemen," and rode off towards the stage road.

John Henry was startled, but not surprised when he turned into the big pasture and rode straight into Clifford Brown. Pulling up sharply, he patted his horse who also had been startled.

"Mr. Brown," he said touching the front brim of his short tophat.

"Mr. Holliday."

"I'm glad I caught you. I have some very disturbing news."

"You always bring us news, Mr. Holliday."

The small sandy haired rider lifted his left hand and wiped the moisture from his mustache before speaking. "The man, Daniel Faux. I sent him to meet with you yesterday."

"Yes," Cliff replied.

"Well, I do hope you did not bring him down here."

"As a matter of fact, I did."

"Curse it."

"What are you trying to tell me, Mr. Holliday?"

"The man I saw, the man who reported to John Tidwell about the stage hold up___."

"Yes."

"Well sur, they are one in the same."

"I see," Cliff replied turning and looking off into the woods to the north of the barn. "Are you sure of this?"

"Indeed I am; Mrs. Tidwell herself informed me."

"That confirms why he was so anxious to go and check on Mattie."

"Yes, he would try to get to her. She is the only one who could place him at the scene of the crime," Holliday said. "We must stop him."

"Come with me," Cliff told the man as he turned and rode toward the barn.

When there, John Henry dismounted and followed him past the old log structure.

Cliff led him up a dim path west of Marty's cabin to where Art Mann and Cactus Jac were waiting with the horses.

"Art Mann."

"Yas sur."

"Show Mr. Holliday our luggage."

Robert shot a quick look at Jerry but said nothing. He walked over to the mule and untied one end of the load; pulling back the canvas, he grabbed a hand full of blonde hair and lifted the head of the dead man for Holliday to see.

Holliday stared at the twisted expression on the face of Faux and then nodded his head. "I see I am too late."

"What about Nielson and Clark?" Cliff asked.

"I have nothing to report on them. As far as I know they are just who they say they are," Holliday replied, and then suddenly he began coughing. It had become a common thing for his conversation to be interrupted by this and most people who knew him treated him somewhat like one does a man who stammers his speech. However, this time the coughing did not stop in a few seconds or even a minute.

Cliff could see the man was becoming weak from lack of oxygen and appeared about to pass out, so he placed his arm under the arm pit of the shorter man and helped him over to the stump of an old oak fall.

Holliday continued to cough and finally began to gasp for breath and then began the coughing all over again.

"Come on; help me get him back to the barn where he can lay down."

Art Mann and Reb placed his arms over their shoulders and

literally lifted him off the ground and carried him back to the barn that Cliff and Nadine called home.

"Keep him here," Cliff said to her.

"What if he don't want to be kept?"

"I know you can charm him into staying," he said back to her and smiled.

She smiled back before replying, "I'll do my best."

"That will be enough," he said and then turned and walked away.

The three riders had been gone over an hour when Esther walked over to the barn.

Holliday was sitting outside on the big log that had become the most common piece of furniture for socializing around the campfire. Nadine had just poured him a cup of coffee when she saw her friend approaching.

"Morning," she said and then added, "You look as happy as the sunshine this morning."

"I am feeling good, for an Old Gal," Esther replied and then turning her attention, she added, "And a good morning to you Mr. Holliday; I did not know you were here."

Standing quickly, he almost spilled his drink. "Mrs. Brooks. I only arrived this morning."

"I do hope you stay awhile," Esther said back, and then looking over at Nadine, she added, "It looks like it is going to turn into such a nice warm day, I was wondering if you would like to go up to the river and take a swim."

Nadine thought a moment and then looked around as if trying to see anything that would prohibit it, then looked back and said, "I'd love to!" and giggled.

"Good, let's see if the other ladies want to go, too."

"Alright," Nadine said and then she turned back to their guest.

"Mr. Holliday, my husband asked me to keep you here until he got back. I do hope you won't get me in trouble by leaving while we girls indulge ourselves in a little fun."

"Mrs. Brown, no gentleman would dare get such a lovely lady in trouble. If you wish me to stay, I will be here when you return."

"Thank you, sir," she said and then headed off with Esther towards Mary Ann's cabin.

The Withlacoochee River is typical of so many black water streams that cut through the Deep South. It was as crooked as the track a snail leaves in soft sand. Cliff had once said that a crow could fly three miles in a straight line and be at the same spot down river that a man in a boat would have traveled ten miles. At the north edge of the property they had bought from Granny Keeling, the river made a sharp bend and this created a natural sand bar or little beach of beautiful white sand where the kids loved to go swimming.

Estherbrook **Swimming Hole on the Withlacoochee River**

When the river was not high, this beach was some less than an eighth of an acre and it was the perfect place to sun oneself dry after a dip in the cold water. Three bald cypress trees grew there giving just enough shade to allow one not to overheat.

This day, the six women had instructed Freckles to stay up on the high bank and keep watch. They didn't want to have the men who were supposed to be working back at the stage stop or helping with the livestock, to come upon them. No one actually expected any of the Renegades to be peeping toms, but Nadine did not know about the two new men that had arrived yesterday.

The little girl didn't mind; she had "Sally," a doll that had become her best friend and constant companion since her mother had died and her father had become so withdrawn.

The women began to remove their clothes and hang them on the waist high brush that grew along the bank.

The two new girls looked at one another when the other ladies stripped to their pearly white skin and then at Doc Jean.

She just smiled and said, "This is the way we swim here," and then she also began removing her dress.

Mae, being the youngest, giggled and then slipped her long dress over her head; Michelle soon followed.

Nadine had brought two large cotton sheets that she spread out over the sand for them to lay on when they came out.

Then the six naked women, one by one, walked into the water. Each squealed when the 72 degree water covered their bodies.

Splashing and giggling, they appreciated the wonderful time of joy and freedom they were having, if only for a few minutes. A time when only such a luxury as this could totally overshadow the heavy weight they all shared with the constant danger they and their men were in, here on the Owl Hoot Trail.

Nadine was pleased to once again see that Mary Ann's breasts were sagging far lower than her own. In fact, Esther's were even more firm and nicer in appearance than Cliff's old girlfriend, and Esther was thirty years her senior which brought a slight smile to Nadine's lips, but she said nothing.

Esther caught the expression and asked. "What are you snickering to yourself about?"

Nadine kicked her legs in the brown water until she was standing waist deep next to her friend and then said just above a whisper. "I'll tell you later."

The women enjoyed themselves for almost an hour before Nadine and Esther walked up on the beach and lay on their stomachs on one of the sheets. Soon the new girl, Mae, also came up and asked if she could join them.

"Of course," Esther replied.

"I have been wanting to talk to you ever since we got here but just couldn't find the right time," she said looking at Nadine.

"Well, here we don't let things get in the way of girls talking," Nadine replied.

"Esther told me you were from Wyoming."

"No, I am from Missouri; I was living in Wyoming when I met my husband," Nadine corrected.

"I see. The reason I ask is that I, too, have recently come from Wyoming myself."

A lump suddenly rushed into Nadine's throat. '*Oh God, does she know about my past?*'

The younger girl looked at Nadine, seeing the strange expression suddenly appear on her face she asked, "Is everything all right?"

"Yes, of course. I just felt a little sick there for a moment. Must a' been something I ate."

Esther looked at her and knew that what had made her feel sick was not something she ate.

Taking a deep breath, Nadine asked, "Is Wyoming your home? What part?"

"No, I wish it was," the girl replied.

Nadine looked at her as she began to speak. '*She can't be over twenty-one or twenty-two. Such a pretty little thing with her flaxen hair and fair skin.*' Nadine thought.

"I was born in New Jersey very near the Susquehanna River. My Pa was a blacksmith by trade, but mostly he had to hire out as a farmer through necessity. I have one brother and three sisters, so my mother through necessity, was a homemaker," the young girl said rolling over onto her back and looking up at the white puffs that were slowly moving to the northeast a few hundred feet above. She seemed lost in another time and Esther and Nadine just looked at her and smiled within themselves, remembering when they also were too young to have worries nagging at them almost every waking moment.

Mae began telling them her story, "My Grandpa Dailey went out to Montana Territory years ago, when the gold rush was on; made a pretty good load I suppose. He bought a ranch in Wyoming and he sent for Grams to come out, oh some twelve years back."

She sighed and stopped for a moment, then continued, "My brother and sisters were so different from me. My brother always enjoyed planting, and received so much pleasure from watching his toil burst to life. Whether it was corn, beans, potatoes, it didn't seem to matter to him, and the girls fell into the routine of helping Ma with the household chores, but not me. I loved to watch Pa when he would shoe the horses and I even got him to teach me to sew the leather harnesses. Would have become a smith myself had I stayed, or so I always told myself, but when Grams began to pack for the long trip west, all I could think about was the wide open spaces I had read about in the dime novels. I wanted to ride and rope and carry a six-gun on my hip.

"I had read everything I could about the west, and that great land filled with mystery. I knew all about the history of the mountain men, too. It seemed to be such a' untamed land, just like I felt I was. I still read all of General Custer's recent articles in the monthly magazine, *The Galaxy*; he is such a wonderful writer.

"So____, when Grams headed out, I stowed away in her belongings. Had she found me the first few days she would have made arrangements to send me back, but I stayed hid behind her big trunk and a hundred pound sack a' flour. I got so thirsty there in the daytime I thought my tongue was going ta' swell up and choke me ta' death, but at night when I heard Grams snoring under the wagon I would slip out and drink my fill and eat the cold leftovers from the stew pot they usually left out for the men who kept watch over the wagons at night.

"There were six wagons from New Jersey and two more joined us in Allentown, Pennsylvania.

"I was lucky all the way until we reached Pittsburgh. There they had to unload some of the wagons to get them on the big boat that was to take us to Saint Louis. That unloading of Grams' wagon was the undoing of me.

"Grams whaled me good and I was so sore that I had to write my folks a letter standing up.

"Of course she helped me with it. I know now how important it was to let them know where I was and that I was all right. Back then I was too young to understand all that, I only cared that we were too far for her to send me back."

Mae now rolled back over and lay on her stomach like her audience. "Where in Wyoming did you meet your husband?" she asked.

Nadine knew this was already known by most of the folks that called *Estherbrook* their home, so she replied. "I was working fur Judge Esther Morris." When she said this, she nodded her head and smiled at her friend Esther. "Over in the Sweetwater Region."

"I heard a' her!" the young girl said excitedly "She is the first woman judge anywhere."

"Was," Nadine agreed, "She has been replaced now."

"Really? Must a' been them men politicians scared she would outshine them."

"Oh, I think she was ready to move on with her life," Nadine replied. "The last official act she did as a Judge was to marry Reb and me."

"Oh, that's so romantic, but me, I don't aim to get married," Mae said.

"You are so young and pretty," Esther injected. "I believe the right man just hasn't come along yet."

"Nope, I done seen what men want from women and I ain't interested, besides I can do anything a man can, and do it better than most."

"You seem a tad bitter."

"Well, it took Grams and me nigh on six months a-bouncing in that old wagon after we joined up with the train in Saint Jo 'afor we reached Fort Caspar. Of course, it weren't called that yet. The soldiers were still building on it then and the Cheyenne were attacking nearly every week.

"We got held up there because of them Cheyenne, and then the Sioux shut down the Bozeman Trail and there we sat. Finally some mail came from Montana and Gram's got word that Grandpa Dailey had been killed. We thought it was by Indians at first, but later learned it 'twernt, just white men after his gold."

"I know about Indians," Esther said, "I lost my first husband to them."

"Really, I didn't know Sam weren't your first," Mae remarked.

"No, Sam came later," Esther replied.

"Well, you done had two, so you have equaled it out, 'cause I ain't going to have none."

"What makes you so bitter?" Nadine asked thinking she might have been raped as a child.

"I just know men. After we heard about Grandpa being killed, we were sort a' lost as to what to do. We were in a strange land with most a' her money already spent, and nowhere to turn," the girl continued, "Grams took a job at the fort, washing the soldier's clothes, but I didn't like that much," she said shaking her head. "There had been a scout on the wagon train named "Black Hawk," he was a half-breed. His mother was Osage and his Pa had been a trapper. He kind a' took a liking to me I guess. I was always pestering him about learning me stuff. You know, like how to track animals and how to set snares, although I had already learned that back in Jersey, but not the way he taught me," she stopped and looked back at the other women splashing around in the river.

"You always go in naked?"

"Only if the men folk ain't around," Esther said back and smiled.

"I should say so. I ain't hankering to have no man see me naked."

"That may change in time," Esther replied.

Nadine thought a moment and then added "You're right, Esther, I love for my man to look at me and get all stirred up."

"Not me," Mae sternly said.

"In time, in time," Esther repeated.

"Nope, not me. I had some men see me down to the Platte one day when Grams and me were washing. Of course the water is too cold to get in, but Grams used to have me strip down and she would have a big wash tub there she used to scrub the uniforms in and she would bathe me in it too, when I was still little. Well these two men came down there with news that a band of Cheyenne had been seen a mile or so north of the fort, and there I was stark naked, and I didn't like it at all."

"How old were you then?"

"Oh I reckon around ten, I guess. It was the same day we heard 'bout the Indians done killed young Caspar Collins," she said then added, "It were him they named the fort after. He was the Lieutenant there."

"I remember about that," Nadine replied, feeling much better about this girl. She apparently knew nothing of South Pass City.

"Black Hawk had made me a long shirt and a pair of shoeing britches out of some deer and antelope skins he had soft tanned, and I loved them. Used to wear them almost every day, but I tell you right now," Mae said and laughed "They ain't something a body can slip into quick like, not over wet skin any ways, but I was a' trying when them men came down and saw me naked" she stopped for a few seconds and then added "That's why they call me Buckskin Mae out west."

"What are shoeing britches?" Nadine asked.

"Oh, they are what folks out west call chaps but my Pa always referred to them as shoeing britches."

At that moment, a yell came from across the river some two hundred feet away. "Yell is not quite correct; a war hoop would better describe it," Esther later said.

They all looked up in the direction from where the voice had come. In a split second, three colored soldiers appeared on the opposite bank.

The women who were still in the river immediately dropped down so the dark brown water covered their nakedness, but Esther, Nadine, and Mae were completely exposed to the men who by now had shed their leather and were running down the steep bank.

Nadine's first thought was *'Well Mae, you've been caught without your Buckskins again.'*

Mary Ann was the farthest from the south bank and it was her they first reached. She screamed as the big black arm reached around her shoulder and grabbed a handful of white breast.

The other two men were close behind Jean and Michelle, who by now were in waist deep water and making high splashes as they rushed toward the south shore.

"Freckles, Freckles, go get help!" Esther screamed as she scrambled in the soft sand of the beach, and then on hands and knees she tried to climb to the top of the 8-foot high bank, but a huge black hand grabbed her ankle just as she thought she had made it, and pulled her back down.

He suddenly let go of her, as Mae leaped high on his back and started clobbering him frantically about the head with her fists.

Nadine had found an oak branch that had fallen from one of the trees on the bank, and even though it was really too long for the purpose she intended, began to beat him as hard as she could on his back just below Mae's fanny. Finally he turned and she got him a good strike across the face and he screamed.

Mae's fists were now bloody where she had torn the skin from her knuckles, and she stopped hitting him and began scratching him as fast as she could about the already bloody face. Soon he was able to get a hand up and grabbed a good grip on her blonde locks, and with a mighty pull, sent her flying over his head.

Nadine saw this opportunity to again send a full swing with the limb striking him exactly where Mae had been scratching. Immediately he collapsed, slapping his torn and bloody face into the white sand.

Nadine looked up to see Esther disappear over the bank and knew if they could hold them off for a few minutes, help would come.

She then turned to see how the others were doing.

Doc Jean was almost to the beach, but Mary Ann was completely controlled by the huge man who stood a foot taller than her, and the other soldier had Michelle by the back of her head with a fistfull of hair, and was ducking her head under and holding it there, only lifting it just before she ingested her lungs full of river water.

Nadine started towards the river with her limb, but at that moment, Mae flashed past her and dove into the water and headed for him.

At the same instant the man who had his face buried in the sand, rose onto his outstretched hands and began cursing, so Nadine returned and clubbed him once more, this time breaking the limb over his back, and he went down and out.

She turned back and watched for a moment the scene in the river.

'My club is broken, what should I do?' she asked herself, but before she could gather an answer, a loud explosion erupted above her.

Looking up, she saw Mr. Holliday cocking the hammer on a short barreled revolver. Smoke was slowly rising from the muzzle and twisting in a strange sort of way as it sometimes does after a pistol is fired.

Looking back towards where his gaze was fixed, she saw the man who had been assaulting Michelle was now face-down in the river. Red liquid was oozing from his back and quickly diluting itself in the brown water.

The other man had let go of Mary Ann and had both of his hands high in the air. He had been able to get her almost to the opposite bank and was now standing in the shallow water there exposing himself above the knees. It was obvious to all who wanted to see that any thoughts of a sexual nature had fled him.

Holliday had the side-hammer Colt cocked and was standing as straight as Nadine had ever seen him. His arm was outstretched and the little blue piece of steel seemed to be simply an extension of his wrist and hand. The barrel was pointed straight at the colored man across the river.

At that moment, the one who Nadine had knocked out began to stir and this interrupted Holliday's attention, looking down onto the beach where the man lay, he brought the revolver down to engage the new danger if need be.

This was interrupted by a loud splash and when he looked back, the other soldier had disappeared.

"Oh, thank you, Mr. Holliday," Esther said as she stood behind him still buck naked.

He turned slightly and caught a glimpse of her and suddenly felt very embarrassed himself. He quickly turned the pistol back to the man on the beach and said. "You have one minute to get across that river, and if you ever bother these women again, I will personally hunt you down and shoot both of your eyes out."

The man quickly gathered his strength and scrambled on hands and knees back into the river and swam across.

Holliday watched until he had disappeared into the brush on the far bank and then turned away.

Mary Ann was screaming. She had not stopped screaming from the first moment the men had shown themselves, but she was at least now out of the water, and covering herself with one of Nadine's sheets.

Mae was still helping Michelle in the waist deep water. Her friend had not regained her strength sufficiently to walk and the shorter girl was holding her up and keeping her from falling forward into the same depths her attacker had disappeared.

Nadine, too, rushed back into the river, and the two of them helped Michelle to the bank. When she looked back up to where Holliday had been, he was gone, but she knew it wasn't far as she could hear him coughing.

Just then, two heavy revolvers began firing from the far bank immediately followed by the lighter report of Mr. Holliday's pocket pistol.

No one was hit by the last exchange of gunfire, but as John Henry reloaded his revolver he called back to the women. "As soon as you are all decent, I will escort you back."

'Save that time in Annie Sue's brothel, never before have I been in the company of six so beautiful and totally naked women, he thought *'and not since I was a child, have I been so embarrassed.'*

Cliff and the others were just returning when they heard the last of the gunshots, and heeling his horse he led on in the direction of the reports.

The men, who had been alerted by the little red-haired girl, the same who had told John Holliday first, were also on horseback at full gallop through the herd of cattle towards the river, some three quarters of a mile away.

That afternoon they all went to the stage stop for a late dinner.

The stage was scheduled to arrive at one, but with a new driver, Sam was not surprised when it did not show on time.

Esther had to cook the noon meal for any passengers that might be aboard so she invited all to come over and eat with them. "Besides," she had said, "I can use the help with the cooking." It seemed a fitting gesture after the ordeal they had been through that morning.

Everyone was deeply appreciative to John Henry and each, in their own way, personally found an opportunity to thank him.

Mary Ann approached him saying, "Mr. Holliday, I do wish to again thank you for appearing at the most perfect time. I have convinced myself were it not for you, I would this day share my dear sister-in-law's fate."

"Mrs. Gunter, I too, am so thankful I happened to be in the right place with the right equipment."

"I do hope you were not recognized," Cliff offered.

"I doubt the two that got away remember anything of me other than the report of my revolver," he replied.

"Well, let's hope so," Esther added.

Nadine suddenly remembered Esther had thanked him on the riverbank and had called him by name while the one man was still only ten feet away. Whether or not he had heard it or would remember it was a question certainly, but she suddenly experienced a queer feeling when the incident was remembered; she made no mention of Esther's slip to anyone though.

John Henry Holliday, too, had realized her mistake when she made it, but knew at the time to make notice of it would only worsen the situation and to mention it now would only serve to trouble Mrs. Brooks. He too said nothing of it.

When the stage did arrive a little before two, it rode on a wheel that had lost its tire crossing the rocky bank just up from the ferry.

The new driver who introduced himself as Coleman, had retrieved the steel tire and having no passengers, carried it inside the coach.

This new driver was tall and solidly built. His dark mustache mostly hid the straight white teeth that peeked from behind it when he looked at Mae and smiled.

Esther noticed how quickly the young girl had smiled back, and she elbowed Nadine in the ribs.

Mae quickly assured Sam she was quite at home in a blacksmith's shop and was soon pounding away at the bent tire with a two-pound hammer that looked completely out of place in her small hands.

Coleman was holding the big steel rim and she was talking away at him. Finally Sam decided he was in their way and left to tend to the team.

That night, they moved the quarter mile from the stage stop to the big old log by the campfire in front of Cliff and Nadine's home, and J. M. brought out a two gallon brown jug and passed it around.

The liquor was strong but smooth, and soon the men had relaxed from all the tension that the day had brought upon them and were talking freely. Nadine was jealous that the jug was not offered to the ladies. *'After all they had had the worst of it, had they not?'* she reasoned.

Sam turned and handed the jug to the new driver who had been invited to join them, a move Cliff was uneasy with, but he had said nothing, and in reality was helpless to do so without creating a greater concern when Nadine had extended the invitation.

"You certainly don't talk American," Sam said when the man lowered the light brown container. "But I reckon it ain't polite to ask where do you hail from?"

The man took a deep breath to regain his ability to talk after the warm liquid had scarred his throat. "I don't know what you call American in these parts, but I was born in a land that is no more, within sight of old Fort Ticonderoga, near the pristine waters of Lake Champlain."

"That north a' Atlanta?" Johnny asked.

"Yes, some north of it," the man replied, looking strangely at the small man who had presented such a question.

"What brings you so far south, Mr. Coleman, the war?" Esther asked. It seemed to her every Yankee she had met in the last fifteen years had come south because of being sent here as a soldier or as a carpetbagger, and she hoped this nice man was not the latter.

"Darktower, Coleman Darktower, and no Madam," he replied "I was not in the war."

"Now, that had to take some maneuvering," Sam replied.

"Not so much, I was in China and the far east during those years."

"Really?" Mae replied enthusiastically. "I have always wanted to go to China."

"It is very beautiful in some places and too very ugly in others."

"Were you a seaman then?" Jerry asked.

"I was a navigator aboard a British merchant ship, a navigator and the only man with any medical knowledge on board. The Captain was weak in both skills, but one of the best traders when it came to the orient. I have never known a man who better understood the mind of an easterner."

"How did a New York Yankee get aboard a British ship?" Sam inquired.

"My father was murdered by what we thought was his best friend, I have been on his trail ever since."

"And this trail brings you to Middle Florida?" Sam inquired.

"Yes, in a 'round-about way. I know the bastard was in Jacksonville three years ago. He traded much silk and other fine linen for several horses there," and then as an afterthought Coleman added, "and a piano."

He had been squatting when he had taken the drink and began his story, but the pressure now began to work on the old knee injury, and the man stood.

Cliff noticed the stranger stood every bit as high as he, and much larger in the chest, as large as Sam, only much taller.

"I was told there he lived somewhere in these parts," the man added.

Mae now moved closer to him and tilting her head back so she could still look into his face, she asked, "Will you tell us something of the Orient?"

"If you are really interested," he replied looking back down at the delightful face that was shinning as it stared up at him.

"Oh, I am," she said.

Later when they were all preparing to turn in, Esther moved over close to Nadine and whispered. "Have you told Reb yet?"

"Told him what?"

"Look little sister, I saw that bulge just beginning to show in your belly and it weren't there the last time we went swimming."

Nadine immediately sucked in her stomach.

"That ain't gon'a' help what ails you," Esther said and snickered.

"What are you two conjuring up here?" Sam asked as he approached the two women.

"Nothing men need to know about," Esther said and then laying her palm on her friend's shoulder, she whispered. "I'm happy for you," before she turned and left with her husband.

"What was that all about?" Sam inquired.

"In due time, Mr. Brooks, in due time," Esther said back to her man.

The next morning as John Holliday prepared to leave, Cliff informed David Clark and Ken Nielson they could go with him. He was sure they knew full well the fate of anyone who informed on the Renegades, after watching the death of Dan Faux and even though he was not one hundred percent convinced they were for the cause, he doubted they would betray it.

"We really would like to become a part of your organization," Nielson said. "We even have several other men who are very much appreciative of what you are doing and most likely will want to join also."

"I'll talk it over with the group and send you word," Cliff said.

John Henry had told Cliff that Michelle Slade had asked if he would escort her to the train depot. The experience she had suffered apparently was more than she could handle along with the loss of her husband, and she wanted to be away from the whole area as soon as she could.

"I have an aunt who lives in Washington and I intend to go there and start over," she had told him.

Cliff was relieved. The last thing he needed was another woman who could not handle what they must endure here. He knew Mary Ann was here to stay, at least as long as Marty was alive, and even though she had become a thorn in the side of all The Renegades, he also knew they would have to put up with her, but not so a new whiner.

Doc Jean was also ready to return to Valdosta. She kept a small house on Ashley Street and practiced her trade there one or two days a week. It gave her an income of her own and Cliff valued the information she often provided him.

Mae Dailey, on the other hand, had no intention of leaving. She felt like she had found a home here, at least for the time being, and she was totally happy. At the very moment others were saying their goodbyes to Michelle, Mae was once again dressed in buckskin and riding herd on the small bunch of beeves that the little community collectively called theirs.

She renovated a stall in the barn where Sam kept the feed and tack for the stage horses and in no time had a small, but clean, living quarters of her own.

Esther liked the girl; she did more than her share of work around the stage stop, although she was of little help to her. Mae showed her early exposure to the trade and helped with small repairs of leather, the shoeing of the horses, and other chores with the stock. Everytime the stage rolled in, she was there helping with the hitching of the new team and the leading of the tired animals out to pasture. That is, she would turn them out as soon as the stage pulled away. While it was there, she was seldom far from the new stage driver's side.

Remembering only a week before as they lay on the beach Mae's stern conviction she would never let a man see her naked, '*I wonder how long it will be.*' Esther thought as she watched the short blonde girl working diligently beside Coleman Darktower at each of his chores.

CHAPTER TWELVE

Off To Pennsylvania

Saturday June 1, 1871 broke cloudy, and soon after daylight a thick fog began to form. In less than twenty minutes it had thickened so, Cliff could not see the stage stop from the old log in front of the barn.

He never liked foggy days. They had always been a bad omen to him. Even back during the war, it seemed the Bluebellies loved to attack on foggy mornings where they could get in close before opening fire, especially after they were mostly equipped with Spencers which fired the new copper cartridges that were not affected by the humidity like the Enfields, which were so often used by the boys in gray.

He called to the kids, which were scheduled to be on watch this morning, warning of the extra danger and cautioning them to be on full alert, and not to become distracted by their play.

At first they had always sent two children together, but later he realized that two children were a team and a team would often spend more time playing games, than watching. Once he had ridden right up on Freckles and Sissy. They were so involved in a hide and seek game that they did not know he was there until Sissy ran right into him standing in plain sight next to a big oak. After that he changed the policy and sent only one to each post, but had them replaced every three hours so they wouldn't get too bored and go to sleep.

Doc Jean arrived again on Saturday. She had with her a newspaper, and as soon as she stopped her horse in front of Brown's barn, she held up the front page for Cliff to read the headlines:

Four Men Found Lynched in Dasher Grove

She tossed him the two-page edition and then dismounted from her side-saddle and slipped to the ground, her split riding skirt sliding high on her thigh as she did. Both Johnny and Dizzy turned their heads so as not to be thought of as oglers.

Cliff read with interest the column on the finding of the stage robbers he had left in the pecan orchard. The paper went on to say the badly rotting bodies appeared to be white and from their dress, possibility the railroad workers who had disappeared several weeks earlier. The article ended with:

> Evidence found at the scene proved beyond any doubt this was the work of the ruthless outlaw band known as The Withlacoochee Renegades, who now have committed such dastardly crimes in the area, all honest residents of South Georgia fear for their lives, when not enjoying a Government escort. It is high time for Governor Bullock to send more troops here for the protection of God fearing people.

"Took them long enough to find the bastards," Cliff said.

"Let me see," Nadine said reaching for the paper. She quickly read the article and then turned to the back side of the second sheet where small advisements of new fashions were sometimes printed. Today though, instead of these, all she saw was a short article with a small header.

Fire Destroys Home

> Some may remember the family of one time Lowndes County resident Rubin Robards and his widow, Mary, who moved to Thomasville after his death in 1863. It has been reported they were living on a small farm in Thomas County northeast of the village when fire began in the kitchen house and then because of unusually high winds spread to the living quarts and that structure burned also. No injuries are reported but the structures are a total loss.

"Did you know a Rubin Robards, Honey?" she asked Cliff.

"Yes, I knew Lieutenant Robards," he replied as he reached for the old blue speckled coffee pot that was staying warm just off the now dying coals of the breakfast fire. "He was killed at Perryville Kentucky, if I remember correctly."

"Well, his family's home burned to the ground over near Thomasville," she said folding the yellow paper and handing him the not too obvious article.

"His wife was a nice lady. I remember she helped Ma with the canning one year."

"I think she could use some help herself now," Nadine said. The manner she spoke was not that of a person making a statement nor was it as a casual comment. She had just dropped a hint. Long before, she had learned it was often better for men to believe they came up with a good idea than to be told one.

Today she was wearing the light blue gingham dress he admired her in and she knew if something did not trouble him too much, he would take notice of what she said to him, whether he would remember it was her that dropped the seed or not, she neither knew nor cared.

Before noon, he saddled his sorrel and rode over to Sam and Esther's. The need to ride the short distance was not there, but he liked to keep his mounts accustomed to having his weight on their backs and besides, he knew animals felt loyalty to the humans that often showed affection to them.

Sam was out back of the stage stop repairing a corral fence one of the horses had apparently kicked through during the night. The high fence had been constructed quickly to accommodate the first bunch of horses the stage company sent, and thereby had been made of soft pine. The fact much of it was easily busted with such a blow had not seemed as important as the time. Even then, they both knew that these poles would have to be replaced with "heart pine" within a year or two, when no schedule was bearing down on Sam.

The girl, Mae, was there helping him. She was dressed as usual in buckskin shirt and latigo chaps. He had known women before who seemed they had to prove they were as good as a man, while doing a man's work. Usually he considered them to have less desire for men-folk than they did for their own sex, but this little blonde offered a contrasting view to that idea. She most definitely wanted to let everyone around know she could and would carry her own weight in a man's world, but she had also flipped head over heels for the new teamster. That was very obvious to all around, even though when Nadine casually mentioned him, she would reply "Who?" as if she didn't remember Coleman at all.

"Morning, Sam, ma'am," Cliff said and touched the front brim of his big hat.

"Reb," Sam returned and stopped what he was doing to straighten his torso, looking very grateful for the break in the bending the repair was requiring of him.

'Sam is showing his age at times.' Cliff thought. *'His weight has increased noticeably in the time since I met him and what little dark hair he had a year ago is now mostly gray.'*

"I think I will be heading down to Madison come morning. I want to show Mr. Balough this paper," he said tossing it to his friend.

Sam opened the folded sheets and began reading.

The girl came over and though standing back a little, also read the headlines.

"Yes, I think he needs to print a rebuttal to this."

"Sam, you being from down Florida, you may not remember Captain Robards."

"I do remember the name but___?"

"He was a Captain in the Valdosta Guard. Got himself killed near Perryville, Kentucky, back in '62. He was the first Mayor of Valdosta, back when they formed the town."

"Yes, I remember him," his friend replied not really sure just how much he remembered.

"Well, if you look on the back page there," Cliff said nodding at the paper Sam still held in his gloved hand, "You will see his family had moved to Thomasville and 't'uther day their place burned down."

Sam turned the paper over and quickly read the small article.

"Well, I aim to go over there and see what I can do to help. I know you need to be here with the stage stop and all, but I like to feel you will watch the place while I'm away. Marty just keeps slipping more all the time, and his brother is so e't up with revenge ___."

"I understand, don't you fret none; I'll keep a close eye on everything," Sam said feeling quite honored at the thought. "Who you aim ta' take with you?"

"I was thinking of taking the Henley boy and Johnny, maybe Robert if you don't need 'em."

"Robert is riding herd today, but Dizzy is with him. Israel is trying to catch some catfish fur supper, down at the river. I don't know where Johnny is, probably at Granny Keeling's," the older man said then spitting and wiping his mouth with the palm of his hand and then his hand on his pants leg he added. "I don't need any of them really. Mae here has been doing more than any two of the men around here anyway."

Cliff looked over at the young girl and watched her posture become a little straighter, as if she subconsciously was suddenly trying to stand up to the compliment just handed her.

"Purtyer', too," Cliff replied and pulled on the reins of his horse turning him.

"That, too," Sam agreed.

The early morning moon was almost full, which gave Cliff and the boys more than enough light to leave by. The trail that had been almost nonexistent less than a year before was now a well used road. The coming and going of the stage two and sometimes three times a week, along with the use the Renegades themselves gave it, had worn well defined ruts in the otherwise blanketed sand.

Cliff had not been pleased with the idea of a stage line suddenly appearing right along the south edge of his property, but there was nothing he could do about it, the road had been there for more years than he had been alive and even though when he bought the place it was abandoned, he could not stop the later use of it. Now as much traffic as they themselves were placing on the old trace, the stage line did serve a purpose should anyone wonder by whom or how the road had suddenly become so well traveled, after all those years of non-use, the stage was a logical answer.

Johnny was on the porch when they arrived. He handed each a warm biscuit that had been dipped in honey, before Cliff explained what he wanted. In no time he was mounting the little white pony he favored so much.

Cliff felt good about Johnny. A more loyal man he did not know, and the little fellow was as good a tracker as he had seen lately.

The bell at the Saint Mary's Episcopal Church was chiming nine beats as they dropped off the green grassy hill just north of Madison.

This little church house had been there for twenty years now and always rang out the daylight hours from six to six, except when the pastor was sick, and on Sundays of course.

Cliff had told them they could do some shopping if they wished while he was tending to his work. This he knew would be done at Gwynn's Saloon however, much to his surprise, this day they elected to go with him. *'The early hour.'* he suspected.

The men rode up to the large wooden structure that housed Balough's paper business and tied up to the hitching rail out front, all that is, except Johnny.

He eased his pony over under some big oaks and waited there. "I just got a queer feeling," he explained.

No one questioned him. Whether his feeling played out or not was immaterial, to criticize such would have been foolish, as at one time or another each had experienced something similar, and too often, the unexplained feeling had proven correct. So the others simply followed Cliff into the building.

Israel had heard Molly Spencer was working there. He saw her once before when he had come to town with Mr. Brown and he was struck with the sight of her big brown eyes and long curls that seem to hang like angel hair around her small shoulders.

Today her hair was parted down the middle and pulled back tightly into a bun at the back of her head. The bright pink dress she had worn before was also nowhere in sight, and although disappointed by the changes, nonetheless, her eyes were captivating to him.

The fact that she was a couple years his senior, and showed much more interest in the older Robert, had no effect on him whatsoever.

'She shor' is purty.' he thought when they entered the office.

Cliff asked them to wait there while he spent his time upstairs with Mr. Balough, a request that was well received by Israel.

Robert on the other hand was a little uncomfortable with it, as the girl seemed to stare at him most of the time. Finally he excused himself and went back outside and stood with Johnny.

He had not been there long when they noticed a single horse come up the long driveway. The rider stopped some fifty yards from the building and dismounted before he led his animal off into a stand of pine to the south side of the drive.

Johnny and Robert both watched from the trees that hid them from this intruder, but he never approached any closer.

Half and hour later when Cliff came out followed by Israel, Robert eased through the timber to the south of the building then around back, and from there he walked out to where his horse was hitched with the others. To anyone watching it would make good sense he had gone around back to use the little house located there. Then as inconspicuously as possible he informed, Cliff of the hidden man.

They mounted and rode on out, leaving Johnny behind.

Later he explained, "The spy was that high yellow no account, Sheriff Montgomery. I followed him as he trailed back a' you into Madison, but he turned off when he got to the town limits and went over past the lake yonder and on to the courthouse, to his office I reckon. Never trusted a man with a badge."

"No, just never trust a man who has been appointed instead of elected," Cliff corrected. They all nodded approval of that thought.

The choice of routes was open. They could head north on Little Cat Creek Road and cross the river at Rocky Ford, or they could go west on the Saint Augustine Road and then turn north where the Coffee Road cut The Saint Augustine, east of Tallahassee. Either way, it would be dark before they reached Thomasville.

Cliff elected to go west from there. If Montgomery intended on following them, they would not give him reason to question their motives by suddenly disappearing on the dim road to Quitman. Besides, the less time Montgomery spent in the north end of the county, the better Cliff liked it.

That night they stayed at the stage stop at Sharps' Store. It was a good place to purchase food and refreshment and old man Sharps allowed them to camp there near the stop, in a field that he had cleared a summer before, but had never gotten enough spilt timber to fence. The wild grass was deep and made good forage for their tired animals as well as a soft pallet for their own bedrolls. The bright moon made for a restless night for Cliff. Years before, Corporal Laing had teased him saying, "It's the night demons that trouble your soul what keeps you awake on moon bright evenings."

This night Cliff remembered his words, he also remembered Laing losing the top of his head to a Yankee shell during the retreat from Columbia, Tennessee. 'Too bad, I liked that boy.' he thought tenderly.

The morning sun found them five miles west of Sharps' Store. The country here was still cleared, mostly. It had been the land of cotton before the war and although there were many new growth scrub trees and heavy brush, no real timber had taken hold yet.

'A man who knows how to work the land could make these hills produce without too much struggle.' Cliff thought then added, *'If he could find anyone to labor for him.'*

They reached Thomasville an hour before noon and Johnny led them to an old wooden structure that had once been a nice home, now it was mostly a memory of days long gone. The porch no longer was connected to the front of the house, and it was the side entrance Johnny's aunt used to come and go.

Mrs. Horne, as she was introduced, was a well-rounded woman in her late sixties. She stood some five feet and two or three inches and carried 160 or more pounds. Her once proud stance had now given way to a bent back and stooped shoulders. Her smile was not tarnished though, and when she recognized Johnny she was overjoyed that her nephew had come to see her.

A breakfast of guinea eggs was fried along with one sweet potato that she found in her kitchen. Her coffee had been boiling for several hours on the kitchen stove when she poured them each a cup. The black liquid seemed thick enough to cut with a bowie knife, but no one complained. Each man realized that the yam they were eating was to have been her supper, but to refuse it would have been an insult she would have felt personally, and no one did.

She told them where the widow Robards was staying now that she had lost her home. She also said that local folk thought the fire to have been the work of arsonists because of her husband's record in the war.

Moments before they left, Cliff gave Johnny five gold eagles for him to discreetly place somewhere she would find them only after they were well away. They both knew that much money would sustain her for the rest of her life and the gesture created just another layer of respect Johnny had deep inside him for the man who had come home to help them.

Aunt Marian had informed them Mrs. Robards was staying in the home of the widow Russell. They found this small home also in need of repair, but not nearly so much as Johnny's aunt's.

Johnny also was given the responsibility to deliver a small package to Mrs. Robards. He asked to speak to her alone, and was reluctantly escorted into what once was a living room, but now was used as a bedroom for her and her children.

Sadie Russell called back through the open door as she left the strange man with her friend. "I'll be right in here if you need me."

"Mrs. Robards, I know you don't remember me but I am John Gaston, Emmett's boy. My Pa knew your husband when he was the Mayor."

"I do remember a' 'Emmett Gaston'," she replied being as polite as the situation allowed.

"Well, Ma'am there are some folks who heard what happened to you recently, losing your home and all, and they sent me here to deliver this package to you. I can't tell you who they are, 'cause they said I shouldn't say their names but the paper in Valdosta says some pretty bad lies about them," he said and then laid the paper open with the headlines up and atop this, a small blue handkerchief tied with one small knot. "Please don't open this until I'm gone a distance, but I tell you the people need to know that that no account Valdosta paper tells lies about these homefolk."

They had been gone ten minutes when Sadie Russell pestered her into opening the handkerchief. There the women stared at two hundred dollars in gold coin.

"Lord, Lord. Why did he give you all that money? Who was that man?" Sadie shot one question after another without waiting for an answer.

Mrs. Robards simply replied "I don't know, but he said it was from folks that this paper told lies about."

"Give me that," Sadie said almost snatching it from her friend's hand.

She read the paper as fast as she could and then turned it over and started on the back of the first page; finally she said, "I don't see nothing in here about nobody except them outlaws, The Withlacoochee Renegades."

"Then it wus them what delivered us from poverty," her friend replied.

That night half of Thomasville knew that 'The Withlacoochee Renegades' had given money to the widows.

A week later, Jack Russell arrived at the front door of Granny Keeling's house.

She met him with a shotgun in hand.

Johnny quickly rode his mare to find Reb and tell him of the newcomer who had suddenly arrived at his place.

Cliff thought on it while Johnny was telling him about Russell. *'He already knows where Johnny lives, and somehow he was able to figure out he was a contact person. We might as well have him here so several can watch, rather than down at Granny's where it would endanger her as well, should he be bait.'*

"Johnny, you did right by leaving him there 'afore coming on, but I think we should bring him here. You go back and get him and I will tell the others to stay alert and out of sight until we figure out what to do with him," Cliff told the young man.

"If you say so, Reb, I just didn't want to bring him here, lessen you said so."

"You did right," Cliff said back to his friend again as he strapped on his belt that carried the Smith & Wesson.

After Johnny had mounted the pony and was headed back, Cliff walked over to Marty's cabin.

There he saw the man, on the front porch, rocking in the chair Johnny had made for him from the branches of a cypress tree that had fallen into the river. Beside the chair was a two gallon ceramic jug. Marty's head was bowed forward to where his chin was almost touching his bare chest. The straps of his overalls that once had rubbed calluses on his shoulders now stood two inches above the skin, and Cliff realized this once proud man was but a shadow of his former self.

His brother, on the other hand, had now moved in with them, and seemed to grow larger and tougher each day, as did his hate.

Cliff worried about J. M., he was the one man in the outfit that only followed the orders he liked, a situation that could be devastating to an organization like theirs.

"Marty," he said softly, not really wanting to wake his friend.

Before he could speak again, Mary Ann came to the open door. Her face was bright and her cheeks rosy, not unlike he remembered them from so many years before. She was covered in a plain cotton dress, but due to the heat, nothing else. When she stopped there framed in the doorway, the light from the opposite window shined easily through the dress, exposing her outline almost as if she were naked. She had been baking something he suspected, as her arms had small traces of flour here and there where she had missed when she cleaned herself with a towel. The sweat of her body had dampened the cotton and the firm outline of her large breasts was unavoidable to the eye.

Cliff knew the last thing he wanted to do was to have sexual contact with her again, still the sight of her standing there caused his blood to move into places that immediately caused him uneasiness.

"Can I help you, Reb?" her voice was soft and pleasing, and he knew there was more of an invitation than a question in her statement.

"I came to tell Marty and J. M. to stay close. There is a stranger approaching and I don't know what he is about, yet."

"I see, and I had the impression perhaps you had come to see me. How foolish that idea was," she replied in a cutting voice. "As you see Marty is asleep. He is always asleep. J. M. went up to the river to fish."

"Well, until I find out more on this fellow, it would be best not to expose our forces too much."

She knew well he meant for her to stay out of sight and to keep the men here. "Keeping Marty here will be no ordeal at all as long as he has his jug, but to keep J. M.'s attention on anything," she paused as if suddenly she had a quick thought and Cliff almost thought he saw a slight upturn to her lips for a split second before she continued, "he don't want, is no more possible than for a man to walk on the moon," she said to him. Then as if she just didn't care about much of anything, she added, "I'll tell them, when I can talk to them again."

Walking back he thought of her. It was obvious she held no loyalty to her marriage vows. He remembered how she had made it plain she was available for his taking before Marty had been hurt, and still even here and now she made such suggestive remarks in front of her sleeping husband, not that he could have heard her anyway.

'I wonder if J. M. is poking her?' he thought. 'Hell, of course he is, if he hasn't let his hate ruin his root; none of my business anyway.'

Jack Russell was a man about his own age, give or take a year or so. He was shorter than Cliff but still well built and in good health. His sandy hair and well trimmed beard gave him the appearance of a Southern Gentleman from a decade past. Even the voice was a pleasant drawl with the flow of the south that had always brought warmth to Cliff's heart.

The one thing that he had found lacking in Nadine was her lack of a drawl. She had an accent, a mixture of her native Missouri and the learned western twang, but it was not southern, at least that was her voice when he met her; now that she had lived here for almost a year, the flow of her words was becoming better all the time. This pleased him.

Jack Russell, on the other hand seemed to have full control of his accent and it was certainly a pleasant one.

Johnny had introduced him and then stepped back and leaned against the big log there by the campfire site.

"Mr. Russell," Cliff offered him the opportunity to explain himself and his uninvited appearance.

"I realize my showing up like this puts me in somewhat of an awkward stance. I knew no other means to contact you. Aunt Sadie told me, well truth be known, she told most everybody in Thomas County about what you fellows did for the Widow Robards and others, and she knew that John Gaston had somehow been involved with the delivery of the money. Anyway I did some scouting on my own and found out about a Granny Keeling living here along the border and that she is kin to the Gaston's by marriage, I understand."

The man looked Cliff straight in the eye while he was explaining himself. Then he dropped his eyes and placed the round toe of his brown boot on a cow-ant that was busily passing, and ground the black and orange insect in the sand. Cliff recognized the boot toe.

The man's trousers were a dark brown with small vertical orange stripes, storebought or more correctly, ordered, the large legs fit loosely over the upper portion of the boots. Cliff had been more interested in the facial expression of the man as he talked, than his attire. He had learned long before it was hard for a man to look you straight in the eye and lie at the same time. When he first enlisted in the army he was under a Sergeant Graham. The man seemed to pleasure himself with making his men as uncomfortable as possible. He would often come up with some screwball line of work for them to do and when they would protest he would look away and say, "The Lieutenant ordered it." Sam Graham could never look a man in the eye when he was lying and the way Cliff remembered him, that gesture was often. Cliff never could say he was sorry when Sergeant Sam succumbed to measles.

Jack Russell had not once looked off while telling his story. The boots, too, told of the man. They were Cavalry, Confederate issue, imported from England sometime after 1862. Cliff remembered when the war first began, black leather was standard, but in early '62 the Confederate government contracted with several English firms to supply uniforms and leather for her armies, and since there was an extra charge to dye leather black, the decision was made in Richmond to save the money for better usage and thereafter all issued leather was natural brown.

"I brung you this," he said, and then after handing the newspaper to Cliff he stepped back and continued with his interview. "The homefolk in Thomas County hold what you men are doing here in high esteem and I came with the hopes that I might be of some use to you. I am a good fighter and I am humble enough to do any work you find fit for a man of my stature to endure."

Cliff had to admit that his first misgivings were no longer sharp; on the contrary, he liked the man right off. "What outfit were you with?"

"I rode with the 12th Alabama," he said proudly.

"You from Alabama?"

"Naw, I'm from Thomasville, but I was in Saint Clair when Major Bennett organized his command and I figured it were as good a place as any to fight the invaders."

"Where'd you fight?"

"Murfreesboro, Chickamauga, I was hit at Dalton but was back in the saddle by Campbellsville. I was still wearing butternut, what I had left to wear, when we had to end it on April 25th. There weren't but 125 a' us left, but we disbanded and never surrendered."

"Murfreesboro, huh? I was there with Forrest," Cliff said nodding his head, as in agreement that only men who had experienced terrible happenings together could understand.

"Yeah, ole Stones River wus running red by the second day."

"Glad to say most of the red had seeped through blue tunics," Cliff offered.

Johnny could see these two were now bonded and there would be no doubt this man Russell would be accepted into the group. Bonded by by-gone times and by-gone fears that he could not himself be a part of, and this saddened him some.

The two men talked on for another hour and finally Nadine, having finished her crocheting and grown weary of the darkness inside their home, came out. "Just who is this that has stolen so much of your attention?" she asked.

The man stood and immediately removed his hat. Her beauty

had caught his breath. He had not expected such a lady to be found in so remote a place as this. Her long flowing raven hair rested softly on her shoulders and the smile of her cheerful face was like a breath of sunshine to him.

"Nadine, this is Jack Russell. A fellow warrior from days gone by," then turning he said with much pride of his own. "This is my bride."

"Mrs. Brown, it is my pleasure."

She liked the man too. His mannerisms were not unlike she remembered the men of her youth having possessed. Her father had always had gentlemen around him, and seldom those who were not. She had lost contact with such men when she had to fare on her own, but now, she once again recognized it and cherished it.

That night Cliff called for a general meeting of the Renegades. His first order of business was to show everyone the newspaper headlines of *The Thomasville Times*.

The Withlacoochee Renegades
Robin Hoods of the South

The paper went on to tell of the beliefs that the fire that had destroyed the Robard's home was arson set by people who resented the respect the Captain had earned during the war, and that the very men being condemned in the Valdosta papers were the saviors of defenseless women. It was a long article revealing several other unexplained fires and other crimes that had fallen upon veterans and their families during the years since the war. It closed with:

> Finally, we have someone who is taking care
> of the real sufferers of this nation.

They also made mention of the kidnapping of little Mattie and the rescue and return of her by these brave men.

Cliff passed the paper around and then motioned for Jack to step forward. "I want you to know Jack Russell. It was he who brung that paper to us and he has offered his services to us in any way we can use him. I realize it is up to the group to allow a new man in, but I tell you I accept him as my friend and offer him to you for consideration."

With an introduction like that from the undisputed leader of the gang, there was little doubt but that he would be accepted. Only the Gunter brothers questioned him and Marty finally said, "Well, if Reb says you are his friend, you are mine, too."

J. M. was not so easy and grunted and groaned and offered several comments about accepting unknowns into the fold, but when the vote was cast his and Mary Ann's were the only negative ones of the group.

Most there believed she had so cast in support of the man she obviously now considered her keeper.

Cliff knew better, she did it more to defy him because he had not shown her more affection earlier that day.

"Come on, Marty," she spat then stood, turned and walked off into the darkness without offering help to her ailing husband.

Dizzy helped Marty up and his brother assisted him in returning to the cabin. The little log structure was just far enough away, that on a still night conversation could be heard but not understood.

"Jack, you will stay with us tonight," Cliff said not leaving room for protest from anybody. "Tomorrow, I will talk to you more on the operations here."

He really didn't expect to wait until the next day, but it was a polite way to adjourn the meeting without saying he wanted the rest to leave.

Jack entered the big wooden structure and looked about in amazement. The exterior gave no hint of what the interior contained. Cliff had cut a walk-in door in the north side that could not be seen unless right upon it. He and Nadine had divided the interior into private living quarters in one corner, and next to that along the south wall, was a full armory complete with stacked rifles, revolvers, shelves of ammunition boxes, powder flasks, percussion cap tins, formed lead balls, stacks of pure lead logs, and powder kegs of various sizes. Forward of that were closets full of uniforms, cleaned and patched. There was a large shelf where black boots of several sizes and other uniform accouterments were stored, below that were poles where McClellan saddles hung, and yellow and blue stripped saddle blankets lay on a shelf beside them. All of this was hidden behind large planked doors that were outlined with iron reinforcements that could be bolted and locked in an instant. Beyond these, along the east wall where the large doors were, was an area set aside for guests. Not as one would think of a guest house, rather set up as a bunk house. The area was walled well, giving insulation from the cold and heated by a small iron stove. There were twelve bunks there and each was so constructed that another could be set above it should the need be. The remainder of the barn was just that. There were stalls for horses and an area where other stock could be gotten in out of the weather, or prying eyes should the need be. The open area had a short loft where hay was kept and also a window on both ends to let in cooler air in the summer months to keep the fire hazard down. The windows were situated in such a manner as to allow keen observation of the dim trail that led the children to their lookout post to the west, and most of the three hundred acres to the east.

Jack was amazed that the whole structure, inside and out, seemed to be made of bald cypress, a wood which he knew resisted insects and would not rot in a thousand years. It also was far less of a fire trap than heart pine, which was the hardwood of choice for house construction in the area.

"Jack," Cliff said as Nadine brought them a jug of smooth shine that Johnny had given them a few months before. "I have a' unpleasant burden resting on my mind," he turned and offered a drink of the jug to the new man. After receiving it back, he laid it over his left bicep and took a long swig himself. He swallowed the mouthful of clear liquid and then waited for several seconds before trying to speak again.

Nadine had poured herself half a mug full before bringing it out to where the men sat. She did not drink much anymore. The days past when it was as much a part of her work as other unpleasant happenings had given her a taste for the fiery liquid, but the pleasure of not having to drink it had also been pleasing to her, she seldom touched the stuff anymore. Only in the dead of winter when it helped fight the biting cold and sometimes when she wanted to feel a buzz around her friends, such was her reason tonight. She wanted to be a part of everything that gave Cliff pleasure and this man obviously did just that, still it was too unladylike to drink from a jug, so she used the same mug she always enjoyed her morning coffee in and she doubted Jack Russell realized she was not having coffee at the moment.

"Not long ago we had a' unfortunate happening here at *Estherbrook*. The women were up to the river for a cooling swim when three nigger soldiers from Valdosta happened upon them.

There were assaults, but luckily before anything damaging was accomplished, one of our members came to their rescue. Shots were exchanged and one of the darkies was killed, another injured, but unfortunately he and another got away," Cliff said, then offered the jug again to Russell, who lifted his hand in a' gesture of saying no thanks, but did offer, "Most unfortunate."

"The really unfortunate part is, these two know of our location. We have stationed lookouts across the river along the trails they would most likely come," he stopped and took another swig and then after taking a deep breath, he continued. "That is the reason you were able to make it to Granny Keeling's without us knowing it. We have pulled the children from there to watch the trail that runs along the north side of the river. I don't know what they told their commanders when they returned without one of their own, but I expected some activity before now from Valdosta."

"Where is the state line here?" Jack asked.

"The road you came in on, the stage road, I think. It was in Georgia for shor and t'other side, Florida. However, some say the line has been moved to the river. We rightly don't know which state we live in."

"We get along fairly well with the sheriff in Madison County with caution; he is a mulatto and a carpetbagger and we all know it, but there are no troops stationed there. Tallahassee is the closest fur them in Florida. However, as you know, we are branded murderers and thieves, among other things, in Lowndes County."

Jack shifted his weight and looked around before speaking. "I see your problem. May I suggest something?"

"I wish you would speak freely," Cliff said back.

Nadine was surprised at how soon Reb had taken this man into his confidence. It was not at all like him and she hoped dearly he had not made a mistake.

"I'm not known in Valdosta, haven't been there morn' three times in the last five years. I could go an' hang around and keep ma' ears open and mouth mostly shut," he paused, "See if' I can pick up anything."

"That is what I wanted to hear," Cliff admitted.

Nadine finished her mug and begging forgiveness, retired after taking fresh cotton linens to one of the bunks.

The men stayed up for another hour, during which time Cliff explained the supremacy they had over their opponents by the use of the same cartridge in both repeating rifle and revolver. He also stressed the fact they never took anything or did harm to anyone that was not Federal or working against homefolk for the Federals.

Jack could see he had found what had been missing in his life since the surrender six years past, a chance to right a small portion of the wrong swept upon his nation by an unconstitutional war and the persecution of civilians just because they were loyal to their home state.

He had experienced a gnawing in his gut since the fall of Atlanta. It was then he realized the obvious end to the hostilities would not be in favor of the Confederacy. Still, he fought on, hoping against hope that some sort of honorable peace could be worked out. No one had any thought that a more devastating future was in store for them after the war than during, or they would have never given in. The promises offered by the Yankee Generals in order to obtain the surrender, were never lived up to. He sometimes wondered if they were ever intended to be honored by those who gave them, especially Grant who had offered the most and then after becoming President allowed his administration to run rampant with greed and corruption.

Most everyone agreed that the death of Lincoln was the greatest blow the South endured during the war, but he had come to believe it only served as an excuse to the Yankee congress to rob, murder, and steal, which was their intention when they pushed and pushed the southern states to fight, or shamefully bow to their demands of a mighty central government controlled by the Radical Republican Party.

'Now here is a tiny group of men and women who resisted Carpet-bag Government and Martial Law imposed by the lawless. Here, I could perhaps regain my pride, my self-respect, and right some wrong or assist in striking out against the very ideas that degrade our homeland.'

That night as he ingested the many things that were told to him, he made up his mind he would hit that lick, or die trying. At last he had found a way to wipe clean, the shame he felt clouding him for so long, a self inflicted shame because he stopped fighting, and allowed this terrible flood of death and disgrace to cover his land, and most of the south.

He would be a Renegade, not in the usual meaning of the word, rather as a man who turned away from shame and disgrace and ran head on into the fight against a foe who used their power for the oldest sin of all, GREED.

Jack Russell did indeed fit right into the mainstream of Valdosta nightlife, the only time or place one could find information not asked for.

Two nights later, a little after nine, just as the twilight was giving command to the evening darkness and the heat of southern Georgia dropped down to a more pleasant 80 degrees, the young man located the saloon he had been directed to. The Baseball Tavern sat only ten feet distance from Tom Griffin's Store, around the corner on Hill Street.

Griffin did not like a 'den of the devils brew' located so close to his business, but he dared not complain. So far, he had managed to retain ownership of his store, which was something not everyone in Valdosta could say, probably because he allowed his building to be used as their stockade. He too was fully aware of the significance of the name of the tavern. Baseball was a game that had risen from the streets of New York and spread throughout the Union Army with the rush of a prairie fire. It had been encouraged by the generals as an inexpensive morale booster for the soldiers in blue during the war, and a symbol of loyalty to the Union after the war. Until a former Confederate State could even seek statehood once again, it had to have a State Baseball Team. It was a badge of The New South along with a declaration showing they no longer supported the ideas of states' rights, slavery, or Christianity above that of a powerful central government. Baseball became a shining symbol proclaiming the people of a state fully understood The Old South and its values were gone forever.

Tom Griffin was not a college-educated man, but he did use the brain God had given him and he knew, all too well, that to complain about anything with the word baseball in its name was a sure sign someone else would soon own his property and business.

The Baseball Tavern was little more than a caretaker's shack that had once belonged to Doc Ashley. It was a slab board building an anonymous being had taken some care in applying a coat of yellow paint with white trim to, so many years past. Enough of the wash still was visible so that some folks tagged it The Yellow Dive, with more of a snicker towards the people who frequented it, than its paint.

Jack entered and sat with his back to the wall. The room was filled with a dozen other men being served by one barmaid. She was at least forty and looked as if she had earned every one of the wrinkles she wore on her forehead. He tried to picture her ten years younger, but it was hard to do. She was neither tall nor overweight, on the contrary, a little too thin. Her hair had been combed before she began work that day, he assumed, but now had lost its part and was stringing loose and often falling forward over her face when she bent her head. Her shape most likely at one time had been desirable, but no more. What little fat she had been able to store was located in an obvious pot where a flat belly had once surely been. Her breasts swayed freely under the loose fitting garment that he assumed had once contained fifty pounds of flour, but they were flat breasts with small nipples, positioned so that when she put just the right strain on the garment, poked against its underside, pointing downward. There was a poorly rolled cigarette hanging from her lips and it pumped up and down with each movement of her mouth. The ash had become half an inch in length and Jack watched her speak, wondering when it would fall, and upon who or what it would land.

"Hey Good Looking, you're new in here," she said when she finally got to him.

"Yes, a friend told me this was a good place to enjoy a cool beer on a hot summers evening, and to watch lovely ladies going about their task."

"Oh my, ain't you a smooth one," she said back as he watched the ash fall, striking the toe of his left boot. "Beer you say?"

"Beer would be great."

She was off with a whirl and he noticed a twinkle in her eye and a slight upturn at the corners of her lips. '*I believe she actually appreciated the comment.*' he thought.

Some three minutes passed before she was back with the dark brew. She slammed the tall mug down hard on the table and spilled a small amount.

It was then he noticed the table she had just abused appeared to be made of rich mahogany, down underneath a quarter-inch of dirt and grime that had been ground into its surface.

'*This undoubtedly had been in someone's sitting room or perhaps a den or fine living room at one time. Now it is disgraced to be no more than a shelf where upon bottles and mugs of brew are often slammed.*' He could picture in his mind, the gentleness with which petite hands had carefully set objects on its highly polished top. '*No more will it be so tenderly appreciated or treated.*'

"Two bits," she said straight forwardly.

"Two bits for the beer, and another two for the lady," Jack said as he reached forward and took her hand turning it palm upward and dropping a silver coin there, before he gently closed her fingers around it. "What's your name?"

"Judy," she answered almost shyly.

"Hi Judy, I'm Jack."

This time when she left the table there was definitely a smile on her once pretty face.

For the next three hours he was never without attention for very long, even when the small room filled with men of all sizes and smells. One thing he did notice common among them, all the accents were strangely sharp and foreign to this land, New York and New Jersey mostly, he surmised.

Around midnight he heard the name Holliday used by a fellow who was standing at the bar, a man who had been there less than ten minutes, and who had bullied himself into the tight crowd, a man who stood six feet tall and wore a light colored shirt that had the sleeves rolled up exposing oversized forearms. Jack noticed when he lifted his shot glass there were three fingers missing from his left hand. He also was covered in a light coating of soot. *'A sure sign of a railroad worker.'*

Despite the tall ceiling, there was much noise in the room from the many drunks that now were raising their voices just a little higher than what their buddy had done a moment before.

The man who had his attention pushed a smaller man aside and the little man yelled back "Hey, I was here first."

The bigger man glanced at him, and then turned away looking once again at the fellow to whom he was talking on his left.

"I say, hey, you over-grown baboon," the little man yelled.

Again the bigger man looked at him and said nothing verbally, but spoke plainly by moving his large hips to his right, completely covering the space the smaller man had occupied only moments before.

"You big ox," the man yelled and picked up a chair from the table where Jack was sitting and started to swing it over his head at the back of the larger man.

It didn't work though; his intended victim either saw it, sensed it, or guessed it was coming, and suddenly and with purpose, he placed his right hand on the chair and with his left, he jabbed the flat area left by the departed fingers straight into the man's Adam's apple, collapsing him with the single blow.

The small man slowly coiled downward into a pile of flesh on the floor and jerked around as he fought for breath. Finally, another who he had been talking to picked him up and carried him outside into the night air.'

Jack wondered if it would be enough.

The assaulter simply returned to his loud conversation, "I heard 'em say they wus getting a warrant fur Holliday for shooting that nigger," he smiled and then added, "That'll teach 'em high and mighty Copperheads a thing or two 'bout messing with our nigger troops around here."

When Judy came by with his refill he moved his finger, beckoning her close. She leaned forward and her dress top fell forward but he chose not to peek. "Who is the bully?"

She turned and looked at where he had nodded. "Oh, that son-a'-bitch calls himself Teehold. I don't think it's his real name though. He is a bull for the railroad, used to be a switchman till he got his hand caught between the cars."

"He is a mean one alright," Jack agreed.

"Only on men half his size and helpless women," she said then lowered the edge of her dress exposing a deep crevice in her shoulder, then threw her thumb towards Teehold. "Bastard," was all she said on that subject.

Jack listened as well as he could to the conversation until the bully ran out of money, and finding no one who would buy him another round he left staggering out into the street.

Jack had heard enough to believe this man was speaking truth as well as he knew it.

He didn't want to be too obvious in his quest for information but he made a decision.

There was a half-empty bottle of whiskey on the table next to him and both occupants were turned talking to others at the table beyond.

He rose and slipped the bottle in his hand and turned so it was hidden by his arm, and with his other hand saluted Judy a smiling good bye and was out the door.

He saw a sharp expression of disappointment sweep over her face when he did so.

Teehold was staggering slowly down Hill Street when suddenly he stopped and began fingering the buttons on his pants.

This gave Jack the time to catch up, and he was just passing the man as he finished his business and began a feeble attempt to button his fly.

"Hey man, you know where a fellow can go and enjoy a bottle without being bothered by them nigger soldiers?"

"You got a bottle?"

Jack staggered himself at about the same sway he had witnessed his opponent doing a minute before, and then lifted the dark brown bottle and took a swig.

'This is awful-tasting whiskey. Some of the worst I have ever swallowed, including the stuff they made during the war. My God, how can they get men to pay for this?' he thought as he cleared his throat before replying "Shor' do."

"I know a spot."

"Good, will you show me?"

"Come on," Teehold replied and started off into the night between two houses.

Gradually the man worked his way around to where he was behind Jack, and then when he thought they were far enough away so as not to be heard, he raised his clasped hands high over his head.

There was a light coming from a coal oil lamp in a nearby window that gave a faint glow to the side of a house they were passing at the time, and both their shadows were dimly, though plainly, projected there.

Jack had been waiting for just such a move and when he turned suddenly, he had the butt of his big Remington facing forward as he held to the cylinder. The cracking sound was sharp when the grip strap struck Teehold's forehead, and his lights went out before his eyes rolled back.

Jack hoped he had not killed him, and was relieved to find him breathing heavily when he slowly let him to the ground.

Then, looking about making sure no one had observed his actions, he hurried back and retrieved the horse he had tied at The Baseball Tavern. He also led away another horse that some drunk had tied to the same hitching post before he returned to pick up his trophy. When he left town on the Clyattville Road, Teehold was tied across the saddle of the stolen horse.

They were still five miles from the ford when the sun climbed over the tall pine. Jack stopped and rested the animals and there removed the dark blue neckerchief Teehold had stuffed in his back pocket and made a hood of it for his head, effectively denying the man sight of anything except what lay directly below the stirrup to which his hands were bound with a piece of rawhide.

His feet were also bound to the other stirrup, and both stirrups were connected by a piece of rope beneath the animal's belly.

Crossing the river aroused Teehold when the horse's side went below the water, carrying his head with it.

Gasping and shaking his head, he began to yell "What the hell?"

"Calm down or I will have to clobber you again," Jack said calmly.

"Oh shit, what are you doing? Where are you taking me? I'll kill you for this. Untie me this instant. Do you know who I am?"

Jack did not dignify him with an answer to any of his questions and worried little about his threats.

It was after 9:00 when he approached the camp.

Buckshot, who had been assigned watch this day west of Granny Keeling's, had already alerted Cliff of the situation.

When they arrived, Cliff walked around and looked at the hooded man. "What's this?"

"Knows something you would like to hear I believe."

"Wait here."

Cliff went into the barn and shortly returned with a croaker sack that had stored corn at one time. Slipping this over the man's head to better blind him, they removed him from the horse and sat him on the ground before tying his hands behind him with the same rawhide that had held him so securely to the horse.

He groaned loudly when his stomach muscles were moved to a different position than they had been in for the last several hours. The moaning did not stop quickly either.

Leaving him there near the campfire area they walked away far enough to speak freely without his hearing.

Dizzy had come up to see what was going on and sat by smiling at the sight before him on the ground.

Once, when Teehold attempted to get up, Dizzy kicked him in the shin and sent him sprawling back into the sand face-down. When he stopped moaning from the pain to his shin, he heard the soft chuckle of his assailant. "You bastard, I'll get you."

Dizzy giggled and kicked him again.

Returning from the short conference, Cliff motioned for Dizzy to help them raise their captive and forced him to stand on an old wooden chair that had long since lost its sturdiness. Quickly they slipped a knotted rope around his neck and tossing it across the overhead oak limb, Cliff pulled it tight until the man had no doubts as to what was happening. Then rather than tying it off, he handed the end to Dizzy and winked. The man immediately understood and kept the rope taut.

"Why are you doing this to me? I never hurt nobody. I'm a God-fearing man."

"You killed a man with your stub last night in the tavern. He was my brother," Jack lied.

"No, I didn't do it, it was Johnson."

"It were you I saw____," Dizzy said back.

"No it was an accident. Please."

"You work for the railroad, don't you?" Cliff said.

"Yes. Yes, I do."

"Last night you were bragging about over hearing something on Mr. Holliday."

Suddenly, he froze stiff. "I don't know nothing about no man named Holliday."

"Too bad, that might have been the one thing that would have saved you. We are after Holliday ourselves," Cliff said then added. "Go ahead and kick the chair out from under him."

"No. No, I do remember something."

They could see his head moving back and forth under the coarse cloth as if he could somehow remove the noose with such actions.

"Where can we find Holliday?"

"I don't know. I____"

"Shit, he's lying," Cliff said.

"No, No, I ain't."

Just then Nadine came out of the barn and saw the happenings. Dizzy moved one hand from his grip on the rope and put his finger to his mouth as if to tell her to be quiet, the wrong thing to do to Nadine.

"My God man, you ain't gon'a hang another one. That's the third one this week," she said in a spiteful voice.

"Oh, God," came the utterance from under the sack as they watched the chair swivel about and thought he was about to turn it over. Quickly, Jack lunged forward and added support until the man again got control of his balance.

"That damn graveyard will be full a' these scum if'n you all don't quit a' bring 'um here to hang."

They saw his knees again weaken when she said that.

"I gave him a chance to tell us something we needed to know, but he refused," Cliff said.

"Well, go ahead and hang him then, but next time you do it back in the swamp. I'm tired a' cleaning up where they mess in their britches when they strangle and kick," she said almost giggling this time.

Jack also smiled broadly when she said it.

"No, no I'll tell you. I'll tell you all I know."

"Talk then and be quick about it; I got breakfast to e't," Cliff said.

"I, I overheard Mister Tidwell tell Mr. Munden, he's my boss, that one of the colored soldiers had overheard a lady call out Mr. Holliday's name just as he murdered another soldier." He paused a moment and then when the chair began to tilt as the legs on one side began to dig into the sand, he quickly continued, "I, err', they had this man, the soldier, watch the Holliday family home until he saw Mr. John Holliday come out a' the house, and then he recognized him as the murderer."

"When did this happen?"

"I don't know for sure. I heard it today, I mean yesterday. Now, you ain't gon'a hang me are you?" the man asked almost in a weep. Moments later they could tell he was crying under the hood.

"I don't know. We got a' check out your story. If you are lying or if we find out you ain't telling us all, then I can promise you for shor' you will never see another sunrise," Cliff replied in as strong a voice as he could muster.

Louder sounds of sobbing were now emitted from behind the coarse woven sack that covered his head; "I ain't lying, I ain't a'tall."

Cliff looked towards Dizzy and said. "Take him to the barn and tie him good," pointing towards his own home, then added "and if he gets loose I 'm gon'a hang you."

Dizzy smiled at Cliff's remark and released the tension on the rope.

Teehold felt the tightness go from the noose around his neck and he breathed easier until Dizzy kicked the wiggly chair and he fell to the sandy soil with a scream.

He was then lead away into the barn and bound tightly to an end post at the gate to one of the horse stalls. Later that night, Dizzy came with a mirrored lantern and removed his hood and blindfold, fed him, and gave him drink, and then replaced both blindfold and hood after securing his hands and feet again. This time he was tied where he was lying instead of sitting against the post.

Cliff and Robert headed out into the pasture and picked up Israel Henley, who was helping with the calving; then they headed north towards Bemiss.

The area of Bemiss is located some ten miles north of Valdosta, a farming area before the war and still showing much of the same render of the land in areas where field workers could be found. The Holliday plantation was now only a myth savored by the few family members who could remember what had existed ten years before. It was old man Holliday that had first planted pecans in this part of Georgia and had once enjoyed over a thousand acres of the neatly groomed orchards on his plantation. The Major had been able to hold on to his father's main house, where most of what was left of the Holliday's and Harden's lived. The once three thousand acre holdings had been divided into 160 acre homesteads now owned by Freedmen. The Holliday's themselves farmed 40 acres. It was enough to feed them during the harvest and with what could be canned, but during many of the months, the women of the once proud family took in wash and sewing for the ladies who had come south with their men after hostilities had ended. It was obvious the family had lost most of their worldly possessions, but little of their dignity.

Cliff recognized the colored man there in the front of the faded white house. He was pushing a small girl with long blonde curls in a swing that hung from the limb of a dying pecan tree.

"Good morning," he said "I do believe you are Ezzard."

"That I am, sur," the man answered and pushed again on the wooden seat that quickly flew forward.

"I'm looking for Mr. Holliday," Cliff said and then thought he should introduce himself. "I'm Reb Brown."

"I's member ya', sur'. Would you's be seeking the Major or young Mr. Holliday?" the black-skinned man replied before turning and nodding towards a run of trees that snaked though the nearby field.

"Young Holliday. I don't think I've had the pleasure of meeting the Major, but I did know his father. My father and he did some business together before the war."

"Yas sur, Poppa Holliday was my Master and a fine gentleman, rest his soul. I believes' you'll find Young Mr. Holliday yonder to the rib'er."

The man then reached forward and stopped the swing and held it fast in his big hands "Shod' I goe's aon' fetch 'um?"

"No, you have a most important job there. I'll be able to find him," Cliff said and then touched the front of his wide brimmed Stetson.

"'Bye," the little girl of five said waving to the men as they started towards the river.

"Good-bye, Ma'am," Cliff said back and again touched his brim.

Suzzi McMae looked up at Ezzard and said. "He called me ma'am."

"Yas ma'am, he did."

Cliff saw the fresh tracks made less than an hour before, headed east. Along with these tracks were some of a light wagon that had traveled the same direction earlier in the day. Cliff followed them. Twenty minutes later they heard the sound of female voices and the splashing of water. Shortly thereafter they came upon a spot where the New River widened and there in a little pool some forty feet across, were four girls having the time of their life on this hot summer day. The oldest girl might have been twelve or thirteen and the youngest perhaps eight or nine.

The buckboard was seen on the west bank stopped under the limbs of a huge water oak. Leaning their backs against the large ribbed bark of its trunk were two men.

One was John Henry Holliday, the other Cliff did not know.

They were deep in conversation about some faraway place or time and had not noticed the arrival of the three riders until the horse harnessed to the wagon spoke to the new members of his kind.

Cliff had always appreciated the communication animals of the same kind could have with one another, and especially the way horses seemed to appreciate the presence of another horse nearby.

Holliday jumped to his feet upon seeing them, but the other man rose slowly. He was considerably larger than Holliday and his cotton work shirt showed much wear and stain, so unlike his companion.

Cliff noticed Holliday's hand slowly slip out of his dark coat where obviously a weapon was concealed.

"Gentleman," he said "You gave us quite a start."

"Tell me John Henry. Do you always watch over ladies while they bathe?"

"Swim, Mr. Brown, swim. These young ladies are kinfolk and it is a mortal sin to gaze upon naked kin. As you may observe, they are all fully covered with proper swimming attire."

Cliff smiled, "Yes well, I guess down where we come from swimming attire isn't the fashion yet."

John Henry cleared his throat and turning to the blond man at his side, he said, "Gentlemen, this is my cousin James Swain[31]." Then with hand extended and pointing at Cliff, he added, "and this, James, is the much renowned Reb Brown, who has *The South Georgia Hypocrite*[32] in such turmoil."

Cliff nodded his head, and his companions also waved at the men.

"John I need to speak with you."

"I certainly did not consider you had traveled this distance to assist me in protecting my kin."

"Can we talk alone?"

"Certainly, but I suspect anything you say would be well protected with my cousin."

"I'm sure," Cliff replied just before he turned and walked a few steps away. Holliday followed showing a frown on his overly thin face.

Turning again to him, Cliff noticed a lock of thick hair had fallen from the top of John's head and now hung across his forehead, *'It looks so out of place, so un-John Henry Holliday hanging there.'* he thought and wanted to reach forward and guide it back where it belonged on this almost perfectly dressed man, but he didn't.

"John, I have come into the possession of disturbing news. I'm afraid one of the ladies must a' spoke your name the day you saved our women at the swimming hole."

"Yas, that is true; she did," Holliday said looking down at the red clay at the toe of his small highly polished brown boot.

"Well, you have been identified by one a' the niggers that got away, and there is a murder warrant out for you."

"There was no murder. I simply stopped him from murdering the lady with the long dark hair."

---

[31] James Swain: an alias for John Wesley Harden, a cousin of the Hollidays and an infamous gunman in his own right from Texas

[32] South Georgia Hypocrite: Slang for *the South Georgia Pioneer* newspaper.

"Yas, I know this and everyone there knows this, but that don't change the facts none. Tidwell has a warrant out for you."

"Oh, that impotent bastard. Amaritte said he was becoming suspicious."

"He aims to see you hung."

The thin man turned around and looked across the river at a man who was plowing behind a mule. The red earth was slowly being turned and he could see the left hand was dropping invisible seeds into the fresh clay as man and beast seemingly strolled along.

"There will be squash there before fall," he said and then lifting his arm and moving in a half circle he added, "Once, as far as one could see, were pecan trees, Holliday pecans."

Before he could speak again, a coughing spell descended upon him and he was doubled up by the time it cleared. Weak from the exertion, he reached for Cliff's hand to steady himself. Finally he spoke again. "I have a cousin, one Robert Holliday, who founded the Pennsylvania College of Dental Surgery. It was my intention to become a dentist at one time, but then," he paused and took a short breath, "this damned consumption arose again, only much worse than before so I had given up the idea. Now, I doubt I could come up with enough money for a train fare___" he let the sentence slide off into his thoughts.

Cliff waited until the man was standing strong again before he spoke. "The Renegades have redirected several hundred greenbacks from the payroll of the 103rd to be used in assisting home folk. I know of no man who deserves more of it than you."

The thin man looked off again into the far distance and let his thoughts go deep in his complex mind. For a long minute, he said nothing and Cliff was wondering, *'Have I made a mistake offering. Had this somehow been the ultimate insult to so proud a family?'*

The young man slowly came back to the present and replied. "Greenbacks will be difficult to exchange around here."

"I have a few redbacks on the bank of California for use around here; you can use the greenbacks in Pennsylvania."

Holliday attempted to clear his throat with only some success and then adjusted his short black beaver hat before he stretched and twisted his neck. "I do believe Mr. Brown, I will take you up on your kind offer," he said, and then walked away.

Two days later, six Renegades escorted John Henry Holliday to the depot in Thomasville; from there he rode the train back through Valdosta, where he did not disembark, and on to Savannah. From there he enjoyed a three day sea voyage north to Chesapeake, and then another train delivered him to his relatives in Pennsylvania.

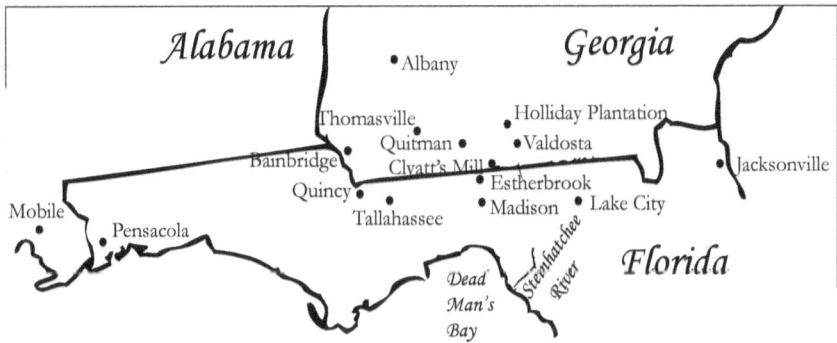

Renegade Country

CHAPTER THIRTEEN

The Renegades Come To Life

"Several mounted men headed this way," Robert answered as he turned and pointed south down the clay road he had just come from. "Just over the hill yonder."

They quickly exited Bemiss road and galloped over the rise to the west.

When Cliff heard the rumble of many horses' hooves slamming hard on the clay, he eased forward just enough for his head to rise above the recently overturned earth.

A line of eight soldiers were following two white men, one Cliff didn't know, the other he recognized as Robert Shaw.

They stayed hidden until the squad was out of sight and then followed at a safe distance.

The line of blue riders went straight to the Holliday house. There was a loud exchange of words between the Lieutenant and the man who was sitting in a rocker on the verandah, but Cliff could not hear what was being said. Next, he witnessed the soldiers dismount and rush past those on the once proud porch into the house.

Ezzard attempted to stop them and received a rifle butt to his head for his efforts.

More screaming immediately came from the Holliday home.

Major Holliday[33], unlike his son, was a man of great stature. He stood near six feet with broad shoulders and large chest, and was still as healthy as a man of fifty-two could be, save the bad leg wound he had received in the Mexican War. He had been skewed by a lance in the upper left thigh during the battle for Chapultepec Castle. Captain Robert E. Lee and Henry Holliday were to share the same ambulance that day.

Fifteen years and fifty-five days later at Fort Walker, a Yankee shell fragment ripped open the old wound and removed a portion of the bone. Henry Holliday would never fully regain his ability to walk after that dark November afternoon in South Carolina, and on this day he was barely able to stand in resistance to the invaders of his home.

"Dem' som-bitches" Robert said in his slow steady drawl, when they watched the man in civilian dress push the older man down after he tried to stop him from entering his home.

The women and children were escorted and dragged out to the front porch. Finally, when it became obvious the person or object they were after was not to be found, the Lieutenant removed his Hardee hat as a salute to them and then mounted and turned once again in the direction of Valdosta.

When they passed where the Renegades were hidden, Cliff could see Ezzard with them. His hands were bound behind him, and his mule was being led by one of the soldiers.

"What you reckon they took him fur?" Israel asked.

"They don't much cotton to darkies who don't rebel against their former owners," Cliff said back.

He thought about an ambush on the column but decided against it. *'It is unlikely they will harm him much, and we could just get Ezzard or one of us killed in a rescue attempt,'* he thought. *'Besides, the authorities knew they were coming to the Holliday house, and killing them surely would bring more reprisals on this family.'*

After checking back with the Major, they learned that indeed the men had come to arrest young John Henry, and Cliff felt good he had been able to get his friend out of the area in time.

They cut a westerly course, skirting around the village of Valdosta before turning south; as he rode, Cliff began forming a plan in his mind to take care of the scalawag Robert Shaw.

---

[33] Major Holliday: Henry Burroughs Holliday in later years twice was elected the mayor of Valdosta

When they arrived at the New River Ferry, Israel left them heading west. His mission was to locate Ken Nielson and deliver a letter to him before returning to *Estherbrook*.

Nielson lived with his wife, two daughters, and three grandchildren in a little cracker house made of slab board construction some three miles west of the ferry. He had been out of work ever since the railroad had replaced him with W. P. Spikes, an immigrant from Pittsburgh. Now he fed his family by hunting and growing a small vegetable garden at the rear of his house.

When Israel arrived, he saw Ken out back tending to a fire he had going, trying to burn out a huge stump that was a sore in the middle of his planted field. The smoke was so thick that the big man didn't see the rider until Israel was upon him. Startled, he grabbed for the old Enfield that was lying close by, but in turning he was caught up in his own legs and tripped himself, losing his grip on the rifle, and it flew forward into the fire.

"Hold on!" Israel yelled and quickly dismounted. "I'm Israel Henley; I got a letter fur ya."

Assisting Ken Nielson to his feet, they both grabbed for the rifle before the fire could destroy it.

Ken looked at the long musket as he held it in his hands like one might a wounded child. The stock had a sizeable crack behind the lock, above the trigger guard. It was repairable but it would take some doing. "Damn. Busted my gun," he said.

"Sorry, I meant no harm."

"What it were you said you wanted, boy?"

"I have here a letter fur you," Israel said stretching forth his arm.

"A letter, you say?" Nielson replied taking the brown folded paper and looking at it then stuffing it into a pocket of his overalls.

"Well, ain't you gon'a read it?" Israel asked. "I got 'a take back me an answer."

"Boy, I can fix this here gun I busted, I can repair might 'n nary any damn thing what goes wrong with a steam engine locomotive. I can grow corn taller than your horse there. I can do anything, but read. Never learned to read," he said back and then pointing with rifle barrel towards the house he added, "My woman yonder, she can read."

Israel could smell the strong scent of smoke on the man as they walked the fifty yards back to the little house.

There he saw at the back of the house a skinny boy, some ten years old, sharpening a butcher knife on a large wheel stone. A pearl-gray guinea hen kept pecking at the carpenter ants that were marching out of a hole in the earth from an unknown work location under the house.

"Boy, take this here gun in fur me and fetch your Grandma," he said handing the Enfield to the youngster.

When he disappeared through the back door Nielson looked sadly in the direction the boy had gone. "Ain't been the same, that boy, since his Pa was arrested."

"His Pa was arrested? What fur?" Israel questioned thinking that it might be something Reb would want to look into.

"Oh nutten' really. He were down to Clark's Store and got into an argument with some blame ignorant som-bitch' over the war, and the next thing we knew six a' them colored troops came and arrested him. Said he assaulted some-on'. Tweren't so," the older man added. "Anyways, they said he escaped by jumping into the river from the ferry. Tweren't so neither"

Ken spit a long stream of dark juice from his mouth that landed squarely on the ant hole. The reddish black creatures immediately went into a frenzy rushing here and there over the small mound of clay.

A woman soon appeared at the door. "What you want, Ken?"

She looked several years younger than her husband. Her hair was dark with only a few strands of gray showing. Israel thought she had a very pleasant face, not at all as he expected.

"Here," her husband said handing her the folded paper.

She opened it carefully and then read it silently to herself before speaking. "Ken, you don't want to go and get yourself mixed-up in no such as this. You remember what happened to Jimmy," she said sternly.

"How 'm I a gon'a know what I don't want to get mixed-up in, if'n you don't read the paper to me?" he shot back.

She looked down at him. Israel noticed the pleasant face now was frowning and had taken on a hateful expression. "You gon'a' end up floating down the New River just like Jimmy."

"Read the damn letter, woman!" he commanded.

"It says," she began as she again opened the folded paper and looked at it:

Mr. Nielson,

We are in need of having one Robert Shaw of Valdosta, brought to Clyatt's mill tomorrow near dusk. I believe you know of him.

You will find him most willing to accompany Israel, were you to tell him the boy had made arrangements to join up with us and wondered if he wanted to do so too.

Very important he doesn't get a chance to tell others of this rendezvous.

She stopped, and with a heavy sigh added, "It are signed Reb Brown."

Finishing, she looked back at Ken and then threw the paper at his face and said before she turned and stomped away, "Go ahead and get yourself kilt. We don't need ya' around here no ways."

"Damn women. Don't understand anything," the older man said and then wiped his mouth with his palm.

"I know Shaw, he worked fur the railroad with me, good man with a' engine, but I hear he left the railroad, gone to work keeping the steam engine what powers the works at The Valdosta Institute[34]. I don't know much about that place."

"You know Professor Floyd, Grandpa?" a little girl about the same age as the skinny boy suddenly spoke.

Israel was taken back. He had not heard her approach and she surprised him.

"Yes, I know Professor Floyd, fixed his gun a couple a' times," Nielson said as he scratched his whiskers.

Israel went with Nielson into Valdosta in search of Floyd at the school off Oak Street. It did not appear to be much of a school where formal education would be taught, but it was noted as being advanced in languages and mathematics. The three wooden buildings which made up the Institute sat on a slight rise a few yards

---

[34] The Valdosta Institute: A school of higher learning in Valdosta Georgia where Samuel McWhir Varnedoe presided as headmaster assuring all his graduates were well educated in the arts as well as masters of Latin, Greek and the English language.

off River Street. The larger building, a two story affair with a white board fence around it, at first gave one the impression it was a fine home or at least it had been before the war; however, when suddenly a bell began ringing and soon twenty or more youngsters began to spill from its front door, some as young as ten or twelve and others as old as Israel himself, he decided it truly was a school.

Nielson found Floyd in the side building. He was a Professor of Mathematics and renowned in his field having completed his higher education at John Emory's College in Atlanta some twenty-five years before. He was a large man, standing over six feet and weighing more than three hundred pounds. Israel judged him to be about the same age as Nielson.

When asked about Shaw, Floyd answered, "Yes, I know the scoundrel."

"This is Israel Henley," Ken said introducing his companion.

"Sur," the Professor said nodding his head.

"Howdy," Israel said back and nodded his head also.

"He has a message for Shaw."

"You are not employed by the government are you?"

"Naw sir, I surely ain't."

"Alright, but I tell you to watch yourself around him, boy," the big man said lifting one heavy eyebrow.

"Yas sur, I will," Israel replied and then turned and headed for the door.

The Professor pointed to the building in the rear of the larger one and said, "That structure in need of a good whitewash, contains the boiler; Shaw can usually be found asleep in the boiler room in the heat of the day. That is, when he's not playing kissy with one of the scalawags over at the Civilian Department." Then with a scoff he added, "Civilian Department, ha, what a joke."

Israel was glad to head out. There was something about a man with so much education that made the hair on the back of his neck want to stand up. *'Wonder what a man with all them brains thinks about?'* he considered as he crossed the cut grass lawn towards the big white building.

Bob Shaw was indeed asleep under the shade cast by the big steamboiler, which was used to run the many power tools as well as to provide heat for the buildings in the winter months. Today the boiler was cold; in fact Shaw had not been told to build it up in almost a week, as most of the classes that would use it were not in session at the time and the daily temperatures in no way suggested the need for additional heat.

Israel knew Shaw; he had met him once before the first meeting at Clyatt's Mill and twice afterward. He was a tall man, perhaps as tall as Henley and somewhat thinner, his sandy hair always seemed to be out of place and he was very negative about everything. Israel remembered once they were sitting together eating fried chicken that Mrs. Gunter had prepared, and Israel had been thinking how wonderful it tasted when at that very moment Shaw had made the comment, "I don't know why they always got 'a fry their chicken down here. My Ma would have baked this and it would have been much better."

After awakening Shaw, they talked a few minutes about old times and about a girl they both knew and then Israel made the statement "Well, I got 'a go, Bob. I'm joining up with the Renegades today and I don't want to be late."

"I didn't know you still run with them," Shaw replied sitting up straighter.

"I haven't been; but I heard they were needing to replace some men that got killed and I got the word to meet with them."

"I'd like to go, too. Do you think they would take me back?"

"I don'-know," Israel said looking out the small window. "They took Danny Faux back but then he got himself drowned."

"He did?" Shaw questioned "I didn't know that."

"Yeah, I was there. He fell off his horse trying to climb the bank and hit his head on some rocks there and just went under. We all looked fur him for two hours and never did find his body. I reckon he ended up in one a' them big holes in the New River and them catfish ate him."

Shaw thought about what he had just heard and then said, "I'd be obliged to go with ya' if'n you don't mind, but first I got 'a go and get my stuff at the house."

"I don't mind you a-riding with me, but I can't be late. You know how mad Reb gets when a fellow shows up late. You want to go with me you got a' come on now."

Shaw thought a few seconds on this. *'I don't want to go without letting someone know where I am, but I don't want to let this opportunity slip by either. Mr. Tidwell will pay well for the location of the outlaw camp.'*

He was in a bind all right but finally greed overcame his caution and he grabbed his hat and followed after Israel Henley.

Nielson and Floyd watched as the two younger men mounted up and headed into downtown Valdosta.

The Valdosta Institute

"I hope that boy is not getting himself into trouble with that no good rascal," Floyd said.

"He came to me with a note from Reb Brown. I think it might be Shaw that's getting himself into trouble."

"Couldn't happen to a better scalawag," Floyd replied as he watched the two men vanish from sight over the hill.

Cliff and seven of the Renegades were watching their back trail when Henley and Shaw crossed the river. They waited until the two men were out of sight and then Cliff moved out following them. He left Dizzy and Johnny there to continue watching until dark, just in case the two had been followed from a distance.

When they finally rode into camp near nine-thirty, Shaw was sitting on the big log with a coffee cup in his hand. Several of the others were milling around.

Nadine prepared a plate of collards and corn pone and sat a clear gallon of water in front of them to drink. "Sorry boys, I run out a' tea and will have to boil some."

"No, ma'am, no need," Johnny said back looking at his friend's wife. "This here well-water is fine."

"All right," she replied. "If you are sure," then she added, "I'll have some sun tea made up tomorrow and I'll make sure you boys get some."

"That's kindly of ___I do___you," Dizzy said nodding his head and looking up from the pewter plate, to the woman standing there in the light of the fire.

Robert Shaw was carefully making mental notes of who was there and the layout of the place. He had seen them bring Marty from a dim trail in the hammock and planned to slip down it later and find out how many buildings were there.

He had been apprehensive on the trip down. He wanted desperately to leave word where he was going, but to have done so would possibly have caused suspicion on the part of Henley, so he didn't push the issue and this worried him until Reb Brown arrived. He was pleasantly surprised at the welcome Reb had given him and was sure that indeed they were in need of recruits.

However, slowly as the evening progressed, more and more men and women appeared around the fire. Most he knew, but some were new to him. After supper, the arrival of Johnny Gaston brought the group number to twenty adults and half a dozen children, a larger gang than he had realized the outlaws still had.

He too wondered about the women. Mary Ann Gunter of course was there because of her husband, but the young Doctor was a surprise. He had never heard of a woman doctor before, and the cute little blonde in buckskins was worth perhaps helping out when he returned with the troops, and the beautiful woman with the shining black hair that tended to the serving of the meal was a knockout, he thought. *'I wonder who she is? Nadine, I think I heard Reb call her.'* His gaze followed her as she moved about around the campfire adjusting the location of the coffee pot alongside the coals so it would remain warm, but no longer boil. He liked the way she moved, sort of an all-knowing, no-nonsense movement. He liked too, the way her legs and hips were outlined in the white cotton dress when she squatted to tend to the coffee. He would like to get to know her better, but was fully aware this was not the time for such things. He could do nothing to spoil the self-imposed mission he was on. A thousand dollars awaited him and he would put it to good use.

Turning, he saw Mary Ann smile and he returned her warm gesture. *'She is not bad-looking either for a red-head.'* He had never been attracted to women with red hair. The freckles were scarring in his opinion, but even though he could not see well in the dim light offered by the campfire, he remembered Mary Ann had few freckles, compared to most red-heads.

'I wonder if she would like to go to Ohio?' he thought.

With the thousand dollars Mr. Tidwell was offering for the location of this hideout he would be able to go back and could afford to take a handsome woman with him. He had been born there near the town of Toledo and had lived there until age twelve, when his father had moved to Milledgeville, Georgia. He had hated the move but could do nothing about it. Then, a year later when Georgia seceded, his father moved to the newly formed village of Valdosta, hoping that by leaving the Capital he could avoid the war. All of Bob Shaw's friends thought he was from Milledgeville and none knew he was really from Ohio. *'Dumb Crackers,'* he thought as he looked around at Dizzy and Johnny.

The sound of horses approaching on the road interrupted everyone's thoughts and suddenly Mae jumped up and looked off into the darkness towards the stage stop. "It's Cole!" she exclaimed and immediately forgot about the conversation she had been having with Nadine. "I better get over there and see if Sam needs help changing the team."

"Yes, you had better go help Sam," Nadine said smiling at the young girl.

Cliff had been waiting for the stage to come and go so Sam and Esther could be a part of what must take place tonight, and he was relieved that Darktower had finally gotten there. *'Another twenty minutes and we can get this over with,'* he thought.

Half an hour passed and he did not hear the coach pull out. Finally Esther and Mae arrived in the buckboard and explained the delay. "Broken king pin," Esther said.

"Yes, it is a wonder that Cole even got it this far. He was able to slip the barrel of his pistol in the hole or he would have been stranded back at the ford," Mae added.

"Is Sam going to be tied up long?" Cliff asked.

"I don't think they can fix it tonight," Mae answered.

"I'm not sure," Esther said, "He knows you are waiting on him, but there is this new problem," she nodded towards the stage stop.

"Alright," Cliff said back. He didn't want to wait until the morrow on this thing for fear Shaw would slip off in the night, and yet he didn't want to do anything without Sam there. His older friend had become as much a leader as most anyone among them, except Cliff himself, but neither did Cliff want to let Darktower know about what was going to happen to Shaw. The man had shown nothing short of friendship, but he really knew nothing of their true reason for being there; and besides Cliff knew very little about him.

The moon was now rising over the stand of pine that lined the east side of the big pasture. It would be a half-moon in a cloudless sky. *'Plenty of light for one to slip off in, and not enough to track by, unless the pursued was careless.'* And Cliff didn't figure Shaw would be careless. Finally he said, "Miss Mae, will you go back and tell Sam we will go ahead and have the meeting without him, but we won't tie anything up until he is able to join us."

"Sure, but I think they can come on right away," Mae said.

"Well, just tell Sam what I said if you will, and I'll be obliged."

"Sure," she answered and took off at a fast walk towards the stage stop.

'Oh for the energy of youth,' Nadine thought watching the girl disappear into the night, and then looking up at her husband she saw his nod and knew her role.

"Mr. Shaw, can I bring you more coffee?" she said and headed towards him with the old gray pot.

"Thank you," he replied and lifted his cup.

She moved in front of him and began to pour the black liquid into his tin.

Bob Shaw was looking at the pretty face standing above him and failed to realize that the men also had moved. When she finished, she looked up from his cup and gave him a harsh expression which he didn't understand.

Her moving away revealed the group of men who now encircled him.

He looked up at those in front and then twisting his neck he saw there were three to his rear. "Hey, what is this?" Shaw burst out as he quickly stood.

"Tell him, Robert," Cliff said.

"This is for what you did to Major Holliday," the tall boy from Albany said, and he shoved Shaw hard with both hands on his chest.

The action had caught him off guard; he had not fully gotten his stance yet and the blow of Robert's large hands sent him falling backwards to the ground.

"What is this? I don't know what you are talking about." There was a sternness in his voice as he spoke, but when he finished, the left side of his mouth where the lips join was quivering, exposing the fear that had suddenly swept over him.

"You don't, huh'?" Robert asked. "I'm talking about the way you shoved the Major down on his front porch 'tother day."

"No, you got it wrong. I was at The Institute every day this week."

"You are a cold liar," Israel said stepping forward. "We see'd ya'."

"You're wrong, it must a' been someone else. You are mistaken."

"No mistake, it were you alright," Cliff injected, "I just want to know what happened to Ezzard."

"I don', I don't know no Ezzard."

"He's the Darkey ya'll took away from the Holliday farm," Cliff said back as he lifted the big Smith & Wesson from its holster and pointed it at Shaw's head.

"That was Lieutenant Jarvis' doing. I had nothing to____,"
Suddenly he realized what he had just done and panic plunged over him like a breaking wave on the Atlantic shore. Springing to his feet he twisted to run, but Johnny Gaston was behind him, the shorter man body-blocked him and they fell together.

Mary Ann screamed and backed up several steps placing the back of her hand over her mouth. "You ain't gon'a' hang another one are you?"

Shaw, hearing her, became desperate to escape and he grabbed at Gaston's new Colt, but the little man had a slip of rawhide over the hammer and Shaw couldn't remove it rapidly enough.

Johnny pulled the long thin knife from the other side of his gunbelt and slashed out at the man who was now over him. The blade of the Bowie went through Shaw's shirtsleeve like a warm knife going through butter and the man cried out when it stopped against the bone of his upper arm. The bicep was no longer a muscle but rather two pieces of hard meat that had once been a powerful asset to the man.

The pain was blinding and he loosened his grip on the stock of the Colt and grabbed instead the bloody arm with his right hand.

Israel was the next to get to him, grabbing a handful of the stringy hair and pulling his head backward.

Shaw twisted and tried to break free, but he was hurt too bad to resist much, and Henley had a tight hold and was pulling him off of Johnny. In doing so, Shaw's right hand slipped away and blood flew out from the wound onto Mary Ann's dress and again she screamed, this time much louder, and she turned and ran towards her cabin holding both hands over her face.

Johnny jumped to his feet and now turned the sharp knife at Shaw's neck.

The man's eyes were locked on the cold steel that was coming towards his throat even though his head was pulled back hard against his upper back. "No!" he screamed.

Cliff stepped forward now and slapped Shaw across the side of the head with the heavy revolver and his lights went out and he slumped down.

Slowly, Israel released his grip of hair and Johnny stepped back and wiped the blood from his knife on Shaw's pant leg before he returned it to his scabbard.

Cliff turned to Jean Smith who had stayed back with the other three women and watched. "Can you stop the bleeding, Doc?"

"I don't know," she answered honestly as she stepped forward to examine the wound.

Just as she was finishing with the bandage, Shaw began to awaken.

The gun had struck him in the temple and cheek and had ripped his ear but otherwise it had not caused greater harm than a terrible headache and some swelling and bruises.

"He'll live, at least long enough," she said standing and wiping her hands off with a strip of white cloth that had been the bottom of her petticoat.

Just then, they heard the sound of a couple of horses coming hard and many eyes turned to search the dark pasture.

Mae was the first to arrive and she jumped from the draft horse she had ridden bareback from the corral. Seconds later, Coleman Darktower appeared with a scattergun across the back of his mount.

"We heard a woman's screams!" the girl yelled.

"It's all over now," Cliff said.

Darktower drew his eye tight and focused on the man with the bloody bandaged arm. Slowly he swung his right leg forward and slipped off the big horse keeping the shotgun pointed ahead.

Robert had noticed his move and stepped back out of the firelight, lifted his revolver, and then let it settle back in the holster a little higher than before.

A queer quietness suddenly settled over the group. Eyes moved back and forth, from one to another as if everyone was waiting for someone to make a move and stop the spell.

It was the sound of Sam approaching on another horse that broke the silence. When he arrived, he looked at Shaw and then Cliff before he spoke.

"Sorry, they suddenly took off, I couldn't stop them."

"What's going on here?" Darktower asked still holding the shotgun in his right hand. He was not pointing it at anyone but he was not pointing it at the ground either.

"Hell!" Cliff finally said. "We have here a scalawag," pointing at Shaw.

"A who?" Mae asked.

"A traitor," Nadine said stepping forward towards Mae. Her move had been carefully calculated from the second she had thought of it. She now was also standing between Cliff and the teamster. There would be no way Darktower could shoot without hitting her, and she did not think such was his plan.

"Oh," replied Mae, "We heard screaming, we didn't know, thought it was a woman."

"It's all right," Nadine assured her. "We just didn't want to involve Mr. Darktower in our dirty business."

"What 'e do?" Coleman asked.

"He used to be one of us," Johnny said, "But then he started selling out information on us."

"He tried to have Mr. Holliday arrested," Israel added.

Coleman Darktower began to realize that perhaps these people were not the quiet farmers they had appeared to be. He had noticed before, everyone was well-armed and with the latest equipment which was unusual for southerners in these times; but had dismissed it with the thought they had brought home the Henrys from the war. The Colt open tops didn't look any different than an 1860 Model when in a holster so he had not given them any thought. Now he could see each man had a new cartridge Colt in his hand except for Brown himself, and he was toting the fast loading top break.

'*Am I in the midst of a pack of thieves?*' he wondered.

"It was Mr. Holliday that saved us women from the Negros," Mae offered.

Sam walked up behind Darktower and laid his arm around the big man's back, resting his hand on his shoulder. He had sensed the strain, the tension, and the questions that were now flowing through this man's mind. His gesture had broken the spell, temporarily.

"I'm afraid we must clue this man in on what's going on here," Sam said not liking it himself. The big stage driver had the sharp speech of a New Englander and that most likely placed him as having been a union soldier even though he had said otherwise. Today, as surely as ten years before, Union Soldiers were their enemy; not because either of these people wished it that way, but their desires changed the facts none. The Yankee Congress had placed martial law over the Confederate states and was using Union soldiers to enforce their unconstitutional laws. Right or wrong, like it or not, the Union Army was the enemy. Sam just hoped they wouldn't have to hang Darktower too. He had begun to like the man.

Cliff, not pleased with it either, spoke to Robert and Israel, "Tie him up," he said nodding to Shaw. Then he turned back and looked at the three standing just out of the circle.

"Nadine, move out of the way."

She did not like it, but she did as told.

"Come on in here and sit with us and have some coffee," Cliff told them, more as a friendly order than as a welcoming gesture.

Darktower looked the situation over quickly and decided to lower the scattergun, realizing he was far outnumbered should he try to use it. He then stepped forward and sat on the old log and leaned the double-barrel there beside him, where it was not imposing, but still not out of reach.

Mae quickly came up and sat beside him, and Sam took a seat beside her.

"You said you didn't fit in the war Mr. Darktower?" Cliff said.

"No, I was mostly in China during those years."

"China, huh?" Cliff replied suddenly remembering he had said that before.

"Yes, he's been all over the world," Mae added.

"Well, we didn't start what we have here," Cliff began, "we didn't want it neither, but we did end up fighting back, and now we are on the Owl Hoot Trail."

For the next forty minutes he told the northerner of the atrocities that had fallen on the homefolk of South Georgia and North Florida since the war ended. "My father's business was stolen, a' unjust murder charge was levied on me, my whole family has been murdered in one way or another, Ma grieved herself to death after Pa was murdered, and my two brothers were arrested and then murdered, even the little farm we were able to save from the taxes was burned, as was Johnny's and Jerry's and more. Everyone here has lost nearly all their possessions, either in death of loved ones, or in burning, or having been legally stolen by this Occupational Government and their troops. There are as many Jennison Monuments[35] here in South Georgia as there are in Missouri. J.M.'s wife was raped repeatedly until she bled to death. Doc Jean's father was murdered because he befriended us. Not one of us here has not suffered great loss from this Occupational Government; and more so, The Civilian Department, run by John Tidwell."

Suddenly Bob Shaw, who had been sitting quietly listening, spat out in a disgusted voice. "Mr. John Tidwell to you trash; Mr. John Mouton Tidwell and it will be him that hangs you all."

Darktower immediately turned his attention to the injured man. Anytime the name Mouton was mentioned he took notice. It had been a man named Mouton who had been his father's good friend. The man who, after seducing his mother, had killed his father. John Mouton, the man he has searched for since he was but sixteen years old, a search that had taken him all over the country as well as several ports abroad. He spent five years in the Orient following leads on Mouton, finally discovering his prey had slipped away only the day before on a steamer for Spain; that was in 1865. The next ship he could find that was headed in the right direction was a Portuguese Clipper bound for Cape Verde loaded with spices and silk. Coleman had hired on as a navigator and was well out in the Indian Ocean before he learned the currency for their goods was men, prisoners

---

[35] Jennison Monuments: Charles Jennison was the commander of the Kansas Jayhawkers and he and his men were responsible for burning almost every southern sympathizer's home in Missouri, leaving only the scarred chimney as evidence there had once been a farm there. These blackened brick chimneys were known as Jennison Monuments.

captured by the Nigerians in their war with neighboring Niger, a war that had lasted for centuries.

From Brava, Port Verde, he had found work as a ship's carpenter on the 'The Raposa do Mar', a Portuguese Steamer carrying 12 passengers. She stopped in Lisbon to take on more passengers before departing for Boston, and it was there that Coleman departed the ship's company and headed for Seville, a hard journey of two weeks, only to find Mouton had left for Savannah, Georgia. Six months later, he was headed south from Savannah to Mayport near Jacksonville, where he learned Mouton had gone inland; perhaps Tallahassee, perhaps Valdosta, perhaps somewhere beyond. It was such leads that had found Coleman Darktower a teamster traveling weekly between Jennings, Florida and Quitman, Georgia.

He fully realized on a stagecoach a man could learn much by asking a few questions and listening to a lot of travelers. 'Could this John Mouton Tidwell be my Mouton?' he wondered.

Suddenly he remembered, 'John Mouton's grandparents in Albany were named something like that. Yes, I believe it was Tidwell,' he thought, 'This is really a lead,' and Coleman Darktower left no lead unturned.

"This man," Brown continued, "was one of us, then he split away; we have suspected him for some time of being an informer, but had no proof until a few days ago. Then we saw with our own eyes, him riding with a detachment of occupational troops to a friend's door," Cliff paused and then after spitting he continued, "There he led the party that ransacked the home of innocent folk and took away a servant who dared to defend his old master."

"He must die!" J. M. said, almost in a rage.

"How you punish your traitor is no concern of mine," Darktower replied realizing he also was suspect for no other reason than he was not from here. "I am interested though in this man Mouton Tidwell. I would like to talk to him before you make that impossible," Darktower said nodding to their prisoner.

Shaw did not know the new man who came up with Brooks, but he recognized his accent and thought, 'If I am to survive this, the big Yank is my only escape route.'

Cliff nodded his head and stepped back. It was not just a gesture; everyone realized it was his way of giving a command and each of the Renegades also stepped back a few paces to give Darktower room. J. M. was reluctant to do so, but after he looked into the blue-green eyes of the big man staring at him a few seconds, he too stepped back.

Darktower squatted down in front of Shaw and talked with him for twenty minutes. Their conversation was low, too low for the others to make it out. Finally he stood and turned and looking at Cliff nodded his head as a sign of gratitude before he began walking toward the campfire. On his second step, the world seem to explode and he turned instantly into the sound. One second the big man was walking away, and the next he had turned completely around and was on one knee with a cocked Dragoon in his hand.

What he saw was J. M. standing over Shaw with a smoking Colt in his hand. The heavy lead had entered the skull two-thirds of the way back from his forehead and passed downward into his throat and exited below the Adam's apple. Shaw was still sitting there with his hand holding tightly to his cut arm; there was no sign of a wound in his sandy hair only now the chin had fallen down, hiding the exit wound. Had it not been for the brains and blood that had been splattered on his pant legs and between them on the sand, one might not have realized he had been hit.

When Darktower realized the armed man did not appear to pose a threat to him, he stood and slowly lowered the hammer before returning the big revolver to its holster.

Buckskin Mae stood looking at the dead man with her mouth open.

Cliff just shook his head and walked off into the night.

Less than a week after the execution of Shaw, a letter was received by stage from Jack Russell requesting a meeting. He indicated that there were several men whom he had met at the Masonic Hall in Tallahassee who were very interested in the cause and would like to be considered for membership. Cliff returned a letter agreeing to meet them at the Farall farm north of Quitman.

He had no intention of allowing several unknown men to come riding into *Estherbrook* and he likewise had no intention of riding to meet several unknown men alone, so he would have to take five or six Renegades with him. They had already arranged for there to be a house building day at the Farall Farm Sunday next, and many local homefolk would be there assisting in the rebuilding of the house. The home had come to some damage when a mysterious fire had broken out in the main house and caused some of the roof to drop. Cliff knew their presence in force would not be noticed at a house building so it was then and there he agreed to meet with Russell and his recruits.

When the Saturday morning sun began to peek over the stand of long-needle pine, Sam's Studebaker buckboard was already loaded with several baskets of food for the noon dinner as well as eight Henry rifles and three fully loaded Blakeslee Boxes.

Dizzy drove the wagon and The Bear Lady and Deadwood's Daughter sat beside him.

Riding along in front in a loose column of twos were Reb, The Hungry Bear, followed by Jeremiah Johnny, and Art Mann.

Following in the other wagon was J. M. and Mary Ann. Their schooner was loaded with several cypress planks and behind them, bringing up the rear, were Shaky and Cactus Jac.

Marty was not up to a trip of this nature, but Mary Ann put on a show about wanting to get away for a couple days. She made a coon pileau for him to eat while she was away, so he agreed she could go along with his brother.

Buckskin Mae had volunteered to stay behind and take care of the stage stop while they were gone. She had given several reasons as to why she did not want to go, from having a headache to a pain in her lower back, and it was all unneeded. Everyone knew the stage was scheduled to arrive Monday noon and Coleman would be driving.

The cute little blonde was obviously infatuated with the big man and Nadine thought they made a great pair, but Esther was not so sure.

"He is at least ten years her senior; who knows for sure, I really can't tell just how old he is," she pointed out as Dizzy laid the heavy leather leads gently over the mules backs.

"Yeah, that's true. Sometimes I think he's around thirty or so and then he will say something with full knowledge on the subject and that will make me think, jeepers he would have to be fifty to know that," Nadine said.

"Watch it___ fifty ain't old," Esther said back in almost a command, and then laid the palm of her hand on Nadine's shoulder and laughed.

Soon both girls were giggling their heads off, and Dizzy didn't have the slightest notion of what they found so funny; so other than a smile occasionally, he ignored their conversation and crept into his own thoughts.

The Withlacoochee River meandered its way around Valdosta, coming from the northeast and passing west of the village in its journey to join with the Suwannee many miles to the south. The river crossing known as Rocky Ford was located in a flat shallow bend where the river turned almost due east for a few miles. Here at Rocky Ford the old trail forked. Folks headed for Valdosta took the right fork and crossed the river and then traveled north-northeast, but it was also here the stage road took the left fork and by-passed the river's bend, heading west to Nankin before turning almost due north into Quitman. It was the left fork they would take that day.

The little group arrived at the Farall farm two hours before dark and seeing a spring wagon in front of the house, suspected some locals had already arrived. They set up camp in a small cove

The Farall Farm on the Tallokas Road north of Quitman

shaded by some live oaks and a couple of sweet gums. The men were all accustomed to such, as it had became second nature to them for several years, less than a decade before. The two wagons were pulled into a 'V' before unhitching the mules.

Mattie had been the first to see them coming and was as joyful as any child her age could be when company was observed approaching. Cliff was amazed she showed no signs of the ordeal that she had endured only a few months before, and that night Nadine could not help but smile at the child who was often found sitting between them gazing in awe at her rescuer, while they all gathered around the campfire until quite late, appreciating the camaraderie shared by folks with a common bond.

The next day everyone present went with the Farall family to The Primitive Baptist Church on the Moultrie Road three miles away, and immediately after the services they returned with the thirty members of the congregation for a quick dinner on the ground before the work began.

Cliff had the cypress planks cut to size so they could build Mattie a room of her own off to the side of the house. She had not been told of this and was like a child under a Christmas tree when she learned the new room was for her.

During the noon meal Jack Russell arrived with six other men who pitched in and helped with the construction and repairs as if they were locals.

After the work was finished, Jack gathered his men and approached the small fire by the Renegades' wagons. "I would like to introduce you to these men" he said to Cliff. "I know them all; they are good Masons and are true to their word. If they tell you they will follow you, you can take it to the bank."

Cliff nodded his head. He had accepted Russell and believed in him and he believed Russell was sincere in what he said about his friends. Still, to accept so many new men unknown to him or the other long time members of the group, was scary at best. Should there be a spy among them or worse yet, they might all have fooled Jack Russell; so many could be disastrous to the group he so carefully led. Had it been six months before he would not have even considered accepting them, but they had lost this many men and were in need of more to give the homefolk of the area the protection he wanted, so he listened as Jack introduced them.

"This is Ed Buist, George Murrel, and this Bill Donavon, Melvin Dixon here, the big red-head is Max Kohnke and that skinny fellow is Mark Mominger, and lastly Seaborn Palmer.

Cliff looked them over, carefully staring straight into the eyes of each when he shook hands with them. George Murrel was young, but a large well-built man about as tall as Cliff. He had a good, strong handshake and a firm grip; Melvin Dixon was slight of meat on his bones and was considerably shorter than Murrel, but he had a big smile on his otherwise drawn face and walked with a definite limp, a war wound that had twisted his left foot considerably. Cliff later learned he had received the injury while repeatedly rescuing wounded men from the battlefield and was one of a select and very few men to receive a Medal for Bravery from the Confederate Government. Cliff knew it would be hard not to like him. The biggest man of the bunch stepped forward suddenly and stretched forth his hand. "I'm Max, some call me Big Max but my friends use Red Max."

He was truly a big man. He even caused the six-foot-two-inch Cliff Brown to look up, but his height seemed lost in his overall appearance as his broadness was overpowering to one's view. His shoulders were a good yard across and the rest of his body seemed to just follow them down to his hips. Cliff judged his weight to be 350 pounds, perhaps more. Somehow his bright red hair and smiling face seemed to make one think of "Little John" in the story of the Nottingham bandits. Although Max seemed never to stop talking, Cliff knew right away he was going to like this big fellow, and when he replied to him he said, "I hope I am among those who call you Red Max."

Next, he shook hands with Bill Donavon, and Cliff immediately knew this man was not from Dixie. His accent was sharp rather than smooth, not in the quick tone of Coleman Darktower but still that of a Yankee. "Do I detect a northern accent?" Cliff questioned.

"You do," The man replied. "I was born and raised in southern Illinois but don't let that alarm you. There were as many from the north who believed in states' rights, as there were southerners who wore blue. I am very proud to say I hail from one of the eighteen counties in southern Illinois who attempted to secede and form the state of South Illinois. We figured if Ole Abe could tear off a part of Virginia and make it a northern state we could break away and become a southern state. Unfortunately it never happened. I ended up serving with the Fourth Tennessee, sir."

Cliff studied his eyes and face. The blue eyes were straight, he never once glanced away while telling his tale and Cliff liked the manner in which he had spoken. *'I will watch him closely, but for now I have to say I can't find anything, other than his accent, to doubt him on.'* Cliff thought a moment and then said, "Glad you chose the right side Mr. Donavon, but there is something funny about your speech. I had no doubts you were not from the south, but I fought with the 89th Illinois morn' once and we captured a passel of them at Murfreesboro, I never heard any of them that sounded like you do."

"Perhaps you are noticing a slight influence of Arizona here. I have been in Tucson since the summer of sixty-five, until less than a year ago."

Cliff judged this man to be five years his senior and indeed it was a western twang that he had noticed but not recognized. "That is surely it, Mr. Donavon," Cliff said and then looked at the slight man to his left. "Is it Mark?"

"Yes, sur, Mark Mominger at your service," the man replied.

Cliff noticed this man was wearing a wide belt with holsters which had the unmistakable grip of Colt revolvers extending from them; the only one of the group that was wearing exposed weapons. Also, from his left boot pipe, the grip of a long-bladed knife could be seen. This man, who appeared to be about Cliff's age, give or take a year or two, was clean-shaven and well-dressed. His shirt was store-bought and boiled; his trousers were black and fit him tightly. His tall black boots were highly polished. He gave every appearance of a military man and he most likely had been an officer. "You cause me to think of a major I once served under," Cliff replied as he shook the man's hand.

"Major, sur? No, I was a Third Lieutenant with the Marian Artillery Battery; wounded in August of '64 at Marietta and was unable to continue in the struggle."

"That's not entirely true," Jack Russell interjected. "Mark perhaps was mustered out after losing his leg, but he got him a wooden one and caused considerable discomfort to the occupational soldiers at Pensacola until the end of the hostilities."

"I would like to cause them some more discomfort if you will allow me, sur," he said to Cliff with a sternness, yet almost plea in his voice.

"I, too, enjoy causing them discomfort," Cliff said back and nodded his head then looked at the smallest man Russell had brought. "I'm sorry; I don't remember your name.'

"Seaborn Palmer, sur," the man replied.

Seaborn Palmer appeared to be ten years younger than himself, and Cliff doubted he had been old enough to have been in the war. The young man had long flowing black hair and was so skinny he looked almost sickly.

"I was with the 29th Battalion, Georgia Cavalry, sur; I too was wounded, at Wolf's Island, over to Darien."

"You must have been mighty young, Seaborn," Cliff replied. For the first time today he doubted the story he had been told.

"I was, sur; I was fourteen at the time, but I could blow a bugle and Captain Hunter liked the way I played. I got 'a' tell ya,' sur. I ain't a-feared to say I sure wus mighty scared the day I wus hit, had been awful sick fur nigh on two weeks 'afor dat Yankee shell knocked me plum off my horse and killed him right off. Had 'na been fur some fine ladies thar what nursed me back to health, I would 'a died too."

"There weren't a day in that awful war I weren't scared, Seaborn, taint nothing to be ashamed of," Cliff said back, now a little ashamed he had doubted the lad. "Do you still play the horn?"

"No, sur, I hain't had none since I lost mine, when I got hit."

"Well, maybe we'll find you one."

The boy's chest swelled and his head came up straight when he realized what had just been said. "Yas, sur!" he replied to Cliff.

Turning now to the last of Russell's band, Cliff extended his hand, "Good day, sur."

"And to you, sir. I'm Edward Lucius Buist, but due to a slight limp, my friends call me Lucius Leadbottom."

Cliff appreciated the self-imposed joke and chuckled slightly before remarking, "Another strange accent?"

"A man has no choice in where he is born or who his parents are. Mine were German, my father an officer in the Prussian Army. I was born December 25, 1845 in Newark, New Jersey; but I have kin all over the Carolinas and as a young man came south to find some of my Pa's people; finally on to North Florida back in '59 to help a friend in his arms business. When the War broke out, there was no doubt in my mind which side was in the right, and being in Tallahassee at the time, I immediately signed on with the 2nd

Florida Volunteer Infantry Regiment. I was lucky enough to be chosen as the Sharpshooter for Company D and perhaps that is why I survived some of the war's major engagements. After the General surrendered, I returned to Tallahassee and have tried a number of jobs to make ends meet during these very hard times."

The man paused and Cliff looked him hard in the eyes and found no flaw in them or what he had said. "Why are you here today?"

"I heard there was a group of southern patriots who had formed a vigilante band and they just might understand some northern born are true believers in the cause also. I myself am one such person. I maintain the Southern Confederacy was right, and for those who doubt it, I will be quick to point out the mess our country is in now-a-days because of too much power in a central government. So if your goal is to end Yankee oppression and restore the south's pride and dignity, I will offer my services, my blood, and my soul to your command. Given my shooting skills and experience in arms dealing, I am convinced I have something to offer keepers of the flame, and that's why I rode up here today."

"2nd Florida Volunteer Infantry, huh," Cliff replied, "Then you were at Seven Pines, if I remember correctly?"

"Yes, sir, I still have a Yankee splinter in my thigh I picked up that May morning, a little south of the Chickahominy River."

Cliff liked this man right from the get-go and had already accepted him in his mind before he said, "Well, it ain't up to me, our people as a whole makes the decision on who we bring in and who we don't."

Turning slightly so he was facing the group of new volunteers as a whole and no one in particular, he continued, "I will tell you all this, if you are accepted and you fail us, your death will be sure and painful."

And then he turned and looked to his wife. "Nadine, will you see these men have something to drink their coffee from?"

That night, after Russell and his boys had gone, they sat around the fire and discussed the newcomers. No one really had any objections except J. M., but his reasons were weak. Later, when Cliff and Nadine were alone, he confided in her he was not so sure about the man who was from Illinois. "I just can't quite accept him, I mean; I lost friends to the fire of Illinois Militia."

"Didn't he say he fought with the south?" she reminded him.

"Yes, he said that," Cliff replied acting as though he somehow did not fully believe it. "It's hard for me to believe a Yankee about anything."

"You believed in Bruce Whitticur," she said.

The heavy load he was now carrying and the constant struggle with the government forces he had been engaged in ever since he had returned home, had tainted his views and he realized it suddenly.

'It is the cold truth; Bruce Whitticur[36] is a big Yank if there ever was one; and a close friend who was extremely helpful to me in Wyoming. Plain stupid of me to have forgotten.'

"You are right, I did. I will give Mr. Donavon a chance to prove himself," he said nodding his head. "Thank you."

"And I bet you he does, too," Nadine added.

The next day he addressed a letter to Russell, telling him to bring his men to *Estherbrook* as soon as he could, and mailed it at the Post Office in Quitman when they passed through the small town on their way home.

Robert had asked Cliff if he could go home for a few days since they were already twenty miles in that direction. When he returned three days later, he had with him one Elvis Dennis.

Dennis had served with the 8th Texas Cavalry, Company C, Shannon's Scouts, one of the only Confederate units during the war to be completely armed with repeaters of both personally purchased Henrys and captured Spencers. Dennis had been friends with Robert when they both had worked for the Littleton Wagon Works in Albany before the war. Dennis' father had been arrested for striking a darkey who had been given ownership of their small farm, and sentenced to twelve years for the crime. He was bludgeoned to death by guards, less than a month after he arrived at the prison in Atlanta. The official report was he had attacked the man and was about to overpower him and the guard only defended himself. No one really believed the sixty-six year old man with consumption had over-powered a guard, but there was nothing else that could be done at the time. Now Dennis wanted to even the score. He believed, from what he had read about these Withlacoochee Renegades and from what Robert had told him, he had found just such a way.

"You realize you must come up with an alias."

"Yes, Robert, err' Art Mann, told me that, and I must say I thought hard on the subject as we rode down. This might not be what you are looking for, I mean considering the times, but I have

---

[36] Bruce Whitticur : See *The Owl Hoot Trail Book One Gold In The Red Desert* for more on Bruce Whitticur

always admired Mr. Cooper's writings and especially *"The Last of the Mohicans,"* Dennis paused and then added, "I think I would like to be called La Longue Carabine," before looking up at Cliff through gold-rimmed glasses.

"I admire Mr. Cooper myself," Cliff replied, "I think that would be a great alias."

"Welcome Longue Carabine," Nadine said smiling.

"Thank you Ma'am," he said, "and to whom do I have the pleasure of addressing?"

"Deadwood's Daughter," she replied, "When I'm not Mrs. Reb Brown."

"May I be so bold as to say, Deadwood had a lovely daughter," Dennis said and bowed deeply removing his Hardee hat in a wide swinging gesture.

"My, My," she replied and curtsied. "I haven't seen such gallantry in quite a spell."

The Russell party arrived the next day. Sam and Cliff spent two hours showing Jack's men the lay of the land and informing them of the operation that took place here. Next, Johnny took them into the armory in Cliff's barn and issued each man a rifle, two new Colts, and ten boxes of cartridges. He then took them out to the cut on the north end of the property where the river overflowed at flood stage and set up empty bottles for them to shoot at while they became accustomed to the new guns. The Henrys were a snap to load once the knack of it was learned and with the three Blakeslee boxes, they were unbelievably fast. Everyone was impressed.

Cliff took the paper he had written down the aliases Russell had given him and made out a new list of all of the Renegades now there:

Storekeep.................................Marty Gunter
Red Rose..............................Mary Ann Gunter
Grits..J. M. Gunter
Reb...Cliff Brown
Deadwood's Daughter..................Nadine Brown
The Hungry Bear......................... Sam Brooks
The Bear Lady..........................Esther Brooks
Jeremiah Johnny...........................John Gaston
Art Mann............................Robert Maycomber
Cactus Jac...........................Jerry Chamblin
Dizzy...................................Dwayne Zipper
Shaky....................................Israel Henley
Buckskin Mae...........................Maybell Dailey
Doc Jean....................................Jean Lathrop
Alabama Jack..............................Jack Russell
Arizona Bill...............................Bill Donavan
Red Max.................................Maxwell Kohnke
Dixie Outlaw..............................Marvin Dixon
The Sunshine Bandit...........Terry Gittemeier
The Singing Ranger................Michael Powers
Armorer...................................Ken Nielson
Dapper Dave.................................David Clark
Longue Carabine............................Elvis Dennis
Cheat N' Charlie..........................Charles Russo
Whiskey George...........................George Murrell
Bugle Boy....................................Seaborn Palmer
Lucius Leadbottom..............................Ed Buist

They were twenty-seven strong now and with the reviews the Florida newspapers and even some of the Georgia papers were giving them, their popularity was growing weekly.

"You know, I somehow feel like we have a void in the list," Cliff said to Nadine.

"What do you mean?"

"Stan, Stan May. I know he is at sea and very likely will never return to us, but I still feel he is one of us."

"Look, if you feel that strongly about him, add him to the list. What difference would it make to Balough?"

"Yeah, it would make no mind to him and I'd feel a might better about it."

"Then add him."

Cliff sent Johnny and Jerry to Madison to deliver the list to Mr. Balough and to see if John Inglis could order another five thousand rounds of 44 rim fire cartridges and more Blakeslee Boxes. The additional name of Stan May with the alias of Stew Burner was now on the list. Stan had been kidded many times about it being his cooking that had caused *The CSS Arctic* to burn in the Cape Fear River near Wilmington in '65, and now he was the chief cook on *'The Smyrna Witch'*, the addition just seemed right.

When Jerry returned, he gave Cliff two notes; one from Inglis confirming the order, and another from Balough. The editor wanted to send one of his reporters out to stay with them and keep a running account of the activities that took place there.

Cliff didn't like the idea. There were times when things had to be done; like taking care of Shaw and Faux, that were not what he wanted printed in the papers, but Balough seemed bound on the idea and he was also sure he did not want to do anything to harm the relationship between 'The Renegades' and the paper. It was just one more weight to the yoke about his shoulders.

The note said Jack Gillie was to arrive in two days. When they agreed to accept Russell and his men into the group, they had decided to build another bunkhouse back in the hammock west of Marty's cabin. He hoped it would be ready soon. *'At least I can put the paper-boy in there and not have to nursemaid him in the barn.'* he thought.

That day he also sent word by Israel to Michael Powers, to have him return to *Estherbrook*. He now realized his stay at Leno had produced nothing, and had been a waste of manpower.

When Jack Gillie arrived at the stage stop, Sam sent word immediately to Cliff; twenty minutes later they arrived at the barn.

Everyone there was looking in amazement at the size of the man.

'Big Jack Gillie would have been more appropriate,' Nadine thought.

Cliff was relieved when he saw the size of the man. He would not be a burden in a scrap should one arise when he was around. The only problem was, he brought a woman with him.

"Good morning, Cliff," Sam said "I want you to meet the reporter Mr. Balough sent us, Jackie Gillie and her husband, Jim."

Cliff just stood there for a few seconds. He felt like a tub of wash water had been thrown into his face. Not only must they have a newsreporter with them, but a woman reporter. Who ever heard of such a thing?

"Ah, I, ah, I, I am glad to meet you ma'am and you too, sur," he said tipping his hat to her and then extending his hand to the big man.

Nadine saw Mrs. Gillie was somewhat offended by Cliff's welcome and she stepped around him, took Jackie's arm and started talking as she led the woman towards the coffee pot. "I'm so glad to have you with us, Jackie. You just don't know how lonely we women get with all these men around talking business and such. Won't you join us in a cup of coffee?"

Jackie Gillie was a slender woman with very dark hair and a pretty face. The fitted suit she wore left little doubt she had a very nice figure hidden beneath.

Nadine didn't give the woman a chance to reply; rather she poured a blue cup full of the steaming black liquid and lifted it to her. "Tell me, how long have you been in the newspaper business?"

'Thank God for good wives.' Cliff thought, but he was not alone. Sam had just muttered almost the same thing himself under his breath.

"Well, Jim, I am glad to make your acquaintance," Cliff said. "Are you in the paper business also?"

"No, I am a lawyer."

'I'll have to think on that one a while.' Cliff thought. *'Might be good, might not.'*

"Can you stay over, or must you head on back?"

"Oh, no, I always stay with Jackie wherever she goes. The business of law can wait on justice."

"Good," Cliff replied, nodding his head while he thought *'Now where in the hell am I going to put up a married couple for an extended period of time?'*

CHAPTER FOURTEEN

Darktower

His great-grandfather came to Canada as a soldier in the French army. He had been one of Villier's Three Hundred and had fought well and proved his courage over and over. He too, found love for the new land that offered so much promise, but had disagreed strongly with his commanding officer over the release of so many captive British soldiers. To argue with an Officer in 1757 was as sure a sentence of death as was desertion, so during the assault on Monroe's men by the Hurons that August morning, Adrian Mouton slipped off into the woodlands and became one of the "missing" casualties of the French Indian War.

Jean Mouton was born October 10, 1825, the third child and first son to Charlemagne Mouton and Mary Marlene Tidwell Mouton, in the beautiful land to the east of Saratoga Springs. Jean grew up working and playing around his father's lumber mill, but realized he possessed more of a tendency to favor the many books he was privileged to read than the arduous labor with Mouton's Timber Company.

Mary Marlene's parents both were scholars. Her father, Robert Tidwell, a learned English professor at the University in Albany, and Elizabeth, a teacher of the languages at Queen Ann's, the most prestigious school for young ladies in all New York State.

The genes from his mother's side of the family were somewhat dominate in most matters where Jean needed to use his brain. The arts and music were in his veins, and his hands moved over the keys of a piano with such rhythmical grace, many, much older, would sit for long recitals listening as he played. Likewise, languages were a simple matter to him. Having a French father and an English mother exposed him from birth to both languages, but all languages to him were a simple matter, and came quite naturally. By the time he was a dozen years old he spoke and read six languages quite well, and was the pride of his mother's eye. She envisioned him Professor of Language at some predominate University and thereby mending the bridge that had been burned so deeply by her elopement with The Frenchman, as her parents referred to her husband; a race of people looked upon in this part of the United States not unlike the way Negroes were looked upon in the south.

However, one should not consider young Jean to be a mama's boy, quite the contrary. He was a healthy spirited individual who loved the times spent with his father afield. He would beg Charles Mouton to tell him stories of his own youth, a time when a young man often made his livelihood using his expertise with a gun. "The ability to hunt is part of being a man, not particularly to his credit if he has it, but something lacking if he hasn't," his father would often say. A skill, young Jean would hone to a sharp edge.

He was half an inch shy of six feet in height, and at eighteen he carried a well-proportioned 160 pound frame. His hair was so black, it at times seemed to shine; and his skin, darkened from much exposure to the sun, contrasted sharply with his bright blue eyes, eyes that seemed to see right through a body.

It was the summer of '43 that came to change forever the direction of young Jean's life. For several months he had been enjoying the occasional friendship of one Jewell Hood, a spirited sixteen year old blonde who lived on a small farm whose borders touched the river that connected the lakes. Widower Jacob Hood had made a bad business deal in the purchasing of his farmland and worked very hard eking out a living from his 120 acres and thus had little time to watch over his children; a responsibility he considered to be woman's work, anyway.

Jewell had become totally infatuated with the handsome young boy whose father was the rich man who owned the lumber company. She dreamed of becoming Mrs. Jean Mouton and living in the large stone house that sat high on the hill overlooking the big lake. Her older brother, who had been the one who had watched over the younger children, had now taken an apprenticeship to a silversmith in Victory Mills, some thirteen miles away, and she was suddenly the oldest of the children at home, a position of authority Jewell greatly enjoyed.

It had taken her much thought and several nights of planning along with advice from her friend Hydee, to devise her plan. She knew Jean often hunted the thick woodlands west of the river for squirrel. From her father's east field she had seen him many times in the late afternoon enter the timber. Her plan required her to wait until he disappeared into the woods, then she would go down to the river for a swim, and in doing so make enough noise to attract his attention. When she was sure he was close by, she would pretend to be drowning and he would come to her rescue. Then when he helped her out and upon seeing she was naked, he would be unable to resist her beauty and have his way with her, after which, he would have to marry her and she would fulfill her dream. It was a simple plan and both Hydee and she were sure it would work, although Hydee did call her wicked for even thinking about actually doing it.

On the last Wednesday of August in the year 1843, she saw young Jean slip into the woods near the river. She knew the moon would be only a sliver, not giving enough light for him to find his way out of the forest should he wait out the last of the wily bushy tails. No, he would not go deep into the forest on this afternoon and she should move quickly if her plan was to work. Jewell had ordered her sister Arleen to take their two younger brothers back to the house and to stay there and watch over them. When she saw Arleen was apparently doing just that, she eased over the stone fence and headed out across the cleared field for the river.

A moment of indecision swept over her as she began to remove the last of her clothing, but she took a deep breath and slipped them down and then walked out into the freezing water.

She walked slowly until the cold water touched her triangle and then she plunged forward covering her body with the crystal clear liquid. It was both breathtaking and rejuvenating at the same time. She surfaced and began laughing loudly. Finally when this no longer seemed natural she began singing.

It had been more than ten minutes since she entered the cold water and she was beginning to doubt her plan. There had been no sign of him and the cold was chilling her to the bone. She started swimming back to the shallow water to leave when she saw a willow branch move along the bank. She turned and swam back, not looking directly at the branch but keeping her eyes in that general direction. Finally she lowered herself underwater and waited half a minute before surfacing again. When she did, she was looking straight at the place she knew he must be, and sure enough, she now saw a brown pant leg below the branch. It was then she began to scream and splash around. Within seconds he was out of hiding and charging into the river to her rescue.

Her plan had worked. When he saw she was totally naked he almost fainted, but a rush of blood filled his manhood with such force he thought it would burst.

Pulling her to the bank he laid her on the soft grass then retrieved her dress to cover her with, but she reached for the back of his neck instead and pulled him down to her parted lips. *'Everything is working perfectly,'* she told herself. Minutes later when he entered her, she gritted her teeth at the initial pain but soon began enjoying the coupling.

Only everything had not been so perfect after all. Arleen had grown to despise Jewell's bossing of her after their brother had gone away, and she often rebelled at Jewell's orders. Today had been one of those times and as soon as she had sent the two younger boys on their way, she had quickly turned back and followed her sister to the river. She watched in astonishment while Jewell stripped and entered the water.

Arleen knew now she had what she needed on Jewell to break her sister's rule over them. As soon as Jewell came out of the water, she intended to approach her and let her know that if she didn't want their father to know of her disgraceful actions this day, she had better stop bullying her around. Only Jewell started to drown before she had the chance to tell her, and Arleen ran as fast as she could to get help. She found it in her father, who was plowing behind King George just over the next hill.

Jacob Hood, a large God-fearing man who had worked with his hands and his back all of his life, arrived while the couple was engaging in the second act of their new found pleasure.

He had feared he might find the death of his blonde baby girl, instead he found her in the act of fornication with the son of the very man who had cheated him in his purchase of his land. The shock was more than he could stand and Jacob went into a fit, ripping them apart and lashing out at the boy who had caused his precious little girl to condemn herself to hell. He struck Jean with mighty up-swinging blows of his right hand, while his left held tightly to the boy's black hair. Again and again he struck the lad until Jewell was unsure if her lover was still alive. Finally she picked up a rock and hurled it at her father, striking him in the back of the head and bringing him from the trance he had been in, back to reality. He turned and looked at her and then back to the bloody mess that had been so handsome a face only minutes before. He then dropped the boy in the water at the river's edge, and grabbed his daughter's forearm.

The sudden immersion into the cold water shocked Jean back to consciousness. He heard the man screaming at Jewell, and then when the two began walking away he slowly raised himself on outstretched arms and finally straightened his elbows.

Jacob Hood had gathered all of Jewell's clothes, flung them at her, and turned his back as she began putting them back on.

When satisfied she had time to be properly dressed, he turned; and with his strong right hand he again clenched tightly around her small forearm before leading her towards the bank where Arleen had watched in horror at what she would surely be blamed for causing.

The father and daughter had progressed some fifty yards when Jean yelled out. She turned first and then screamed, "No!"

Releasing her arm when she screamed, Jacob Hood turned to see what had so terrified his daughter. They both watched the small puff of blue smoke appear when the flint ignited the finely grained powder in the frizzen pan.

It all seemed so unreal to her. The man she loved was pointing his squirrel rifle at them and very slowly the smoke was rising first from its side and then from its barrel.

The 31 caliber round ball struck Jacob in the throat and he staggered backward as he lifted his hands to cover the entrance hole. Then slowly he sank to his knees; and finally the big man fell face-down onto the newly turned soil.

Arleen ran up and said only one word as she watched the dirt change color under his neck. "Papa!"

It was late when Charles Mouton sent his son off into the night. His only advice was "Change your name and go west."

That was precisely what Jean intended to do. He decided as he rode the big bay horse westward he would take on the English spelling of his name. No one would know him then. He would go to Ohio or Kentucky and become a famous Indian fighter and then he could send for Jewell and they would make their life away from all this trouble that suddenly fell upon him.

Jean Mouton, now John Martin, rode all night and well into the morning before he stopped. When he did, he found himself on a high bank overlooking a sizeable body of water.

It was there he ate from the leather bag his mother had given him only moments before she burst into tears and ran back into their home. A lean piece of cured pork and a loaf of hard bread were the first things he touched when he opened the bag and they seemed just right for the occasion. He reached for the waterbag that was strapped to the rear of his saddle only to find it had snagged on something in the night and the skin was now only damp.

"Damn," he said aloud. "I must go down there and refill this."

He looked again in the belongings that had been hastily prepared for his escape and finally found the needle and thread he was sure his mother would not have forgotten. Sitting there beside "Dane," his father's favorite horse, he sewed the bottle back together. When satisfied it would once again hold water he mounted and eased off the hill towards the lake.

There was a dim road that ran along the east side a few feet from the water and he turned south along it looking for a good spot to fill the bottle. It was then he saw two men walking his way along the path.

He had traveled for eight hours, only stopping to rest Dane from time to time. He was certain he had out-traveled any news of the killing that might be heading in this direction. He wasn't really worried about anyone looking for him around here. His father had told him he would let the word slip out he was headed for Albany in hopes his grandparents there would assist him in escaping to the sea. His father was a very convincing man and John was sure that would be the direction any pursuit would go, when it did go. He was not worried that these approaching men might be looking for him.

They actually paid him little mind as the trio came upon one another. Only one of them even bothered to nod, the other didn't even raise his head; but the moment they had passed, the two jumped back and dragged him from his horse and clubbed him with his own rifle before tossing him into the lake.

For the second time in as many days, cold water revived him and kept him from drowning.

As he struggled to get himself out of the water, he saw them riding off on Dane with all his provisions, including his rifle, in the direction they had been traveling in the first place.

Now the back of his head was throbbing as bad as was the front. Well, almost as bad.

Slowly John Martin began to drag one foot after another back up to the dim road and then in pursuit of his robbers.

As he stumbled along between the intervals of the pounding taking place in his head, he kept hearing his father say: "A theft cannot go unpunished." He had first heard that when he was some six years of age and they had caught a Negro stealing potatoes from the root cellar. Charles Mouton had tied the black man to the outhouse and proceeded to beat him with a buggy whip until the man passed out. Between each stroke his father would repeat the message. Not unlike what was happening now, between each pounding of pain in his head was his father saying with a strong French accent "A theft can no go unpunished."

After what seemed like half a day to him, but in reality was only some twenty minutes, he saw the hind quarters of Dane ahead just rounding a small bend in the road. He could also hear the two men talking and laughing.

John slipped up the bank with new-found strength and eased through the brush to where he was only a few yards from the pair. They were conversing in French about their good fortune and speculating at how much Dane would bring at Saratoga Springs.

John slipped closer until he could see them through the thick undergrowth. He watched while they ate the last of the pork his mother had packed for him, and there reaching for his boot-knife, he waited until finally, the man who held his rifle stood.

Using all the strength his legs could muster he leaped upon the back of the tall man and slit his throat.

The man dropped the rifle and threw both hands up high into he air as he if was surrendering before he fell.

The other man had a large piece of pork in his mouth and he began to choke as he stumbled backward before he cut and run, this time going south on the dim road.

John grabbed the rifle and fired off a quick shot but the priming powder had mostly spilled from the fission and the main charge did not ignite. By the time John found his horn, the other thief was out of sight.

Satisfied with what he had accomplished, he turned back and gathered what belongings were left of his poke, and then he pilfered the pockets of the dead Frenchman. There he found a Dix note[37]. Looking at it John wondered, *'Why would a man with so much money, reduce himself to robbery?'*

He finally refilled his water bottle before mounting Dane and heading on his way.

After traveling for two months, taking first one job and then another, he finally came to Ticonderoga. There he happened upon a man who ran a blacksmith shop, a man with a pleasant smile and a joyful personality, a man who reminded him somewhat of his grandfather Tidwell.

Dane needed all of his shoes replaced but John only had enough money left for one. The blacksmith, Frank Coleman, offered to let him work off the remainder of the expense. Six years later he was still happily working for Coleman.

Now twenty-four years of age and a fine specimen of the male species, he no longer gave the impression of a boy on the run. The years laboring as a blacksmith with Frank had hardened his muscles, and the discipline of hard work had shaped his character into a well-defined young man who gave the impression to all around him that he was self-confident and dedicated to becoming a strong and important citizen of the community. However, John Martin had one secret fault that he kept hidden well inside him, that being he possessed a burning desire to have the lovely Diane, Frank's wife.

Not once had he spoken of the two men he had killed and never had anyone here connected the fine up-standing young John Martin of English descent to the French boy Jean Mouton who had murdered a farmer over a girl, some fifty miles to the south.

He also had become somewhat of an idol to the young Michael Coleman, Frank and Diane's sixteen year old son.

John would have left the first week had it not been for the beauty of Diane Coleman. Although she was twice his age at the time, he was totally captivated by her. She, like Jewell, had a full head of hair the color of corn silk and eyes so green he imagined it was the true color of the emerald stones. Her skin was smooth and

---

[37] A Dix Note: Paper currency the equivalent of ten dollars in gold.

blemish free. She was tall and lean and every movement she made oozed the image of a woman at her finest. If there was a fault in Diane Coleman, as far as John Martin was concerned, it was her fine character.

She had felt his desire immediately upon his arrival and she admitted to herself she considered it quite flattering, and knew she should have encouraged Frank to help him and then have him move on, but she hadn't. Her husband was in every way the perfect husband, at least on the outside. He was a hard worker and good provider. He raised his child to be honest and God-fearing, and he set a fine example for the lad; but Frank had never had a strong drive for private times. He was always off to work early and given out by the time he made it home. Never once did Frank not show her the utmost respect and admiration, it was affection that he was short on.

There was another man who worked at times for Frank Coleman; a man known only as Cap' Burgess, a man some years older than her husband.

Michael also idolized Cap' Burgess. It was Cap' Burgess who had taken the time to show him the skills necessary to become a fine soldier, which was exactly what he himself had been for thirty years. Cap' Burgess was a direct descendant of a McKnight of King Arthur's time, a prize of his ancestry he never failed to reveal after getting to know a body. Not that he was a bragger, rather the contrary; but he carried such pride over this fact he made certain all who knew him, knew this also.

Cap' Burgess had spent as much time in the raising of young Michael as had Frank and Diane combined, and he disapproved of John Martin and the time Martin spent with Michael.

"That lad is no good. He will bring shame to this house if he is allowed to remain here," he had said to Frank, a month after John had arrived, but Frank felt he was plenty good enough to judge a man's character and he scoffed off Cap' Burgess' accusation as a silly form of jealousy because the boy seemed to share his admiration with them both where before John's arrival Cap' had enjoyed it all.

John also sensed Diane's affection for him and believed he would be able to persuade her to share her bed with him, were it not for Cap' Burgess. The man was forever putting small stumbling blocks in the way of his progress. It seemed every plan he would work out for an accidental rendezvous with the fair Mrs. Coleman, Cap' Burgess would see through it and in some way interfere.

Finally during the fall of 1849, Cap' Burgess had given Michael a challenge; something he often did as a means to develop the lad's mind and hunting skills. This time he was to take only a knife, a loaf of bread, and a bottle of water and was to work his way over the mountain to a certain pond; it was a pond the two had spent many days together at over so many years, so locating it would not be a problem for the lad. Once there, he would find necessary provisions cached for the return trip, a journey totaling some seven days. On the third day Cap' Burgess had left on horseback to oversee the boy's progress without his knowledge.

His parents had no concern; Cap' Burgess was always coming up with new challenges to train the boy in one skill or another. Diane at first worried about these challenges, but as the years passed and she began to learn that Cap' Burgess was never very far from her son when he was away; gradually she stopped her worries and was always proud of him in his accomplishments at the completion of each challenge.

On the fifth day of Michael's journey, Frank was called by the local magistrate to assist in the repair of the foundry at The Pavilion[38] beside the old fort, a job that would take at least two, possibly three days to complete.

The night before he was called away, Diane had made a special dinner for him and adorned in her best dress, hoped he would be inclined to take care of some needs she had herself. Frank instead came home late and went straight to bed.

John had watched her from a window as she sat and wept.

The scene was set and he knew the time was right. He would have her before Frank returned or he would never have her.

The next morning before he left, Frank had asked of him, "Son will you take care of everything that needs tending to until I return?"

"You can count on me," John answered.

"I should be back in two or three days, so not to worry. You know the trade as well as me. I'm confident to leave it all in your

---

[38] The Pavilion: in 1820 William Ferris Pell, a wealthy New York merchant bought the land of old Fort Ticonderoga and built a large house there naming it The Pavilion and opened it as a hotel catering to the growing tourist trade coming to see the ruins of the famous Fort.

very capable hands," and with that he dropped the leads on the back of his mule and was off to The Pavilion.

John removed his shirt; even though there was a cool wind slipping in from Canada, he had seen the looks of admiration Diane had given him before, when she would suddenly appear unannounced at the shop and catch the men there bare-chested. Today he would be bare-chested if the thermometer dropped to zero.

'Perhaps I will see you bare-chested this very night, Mrs. Coleman.' he thought.

Snow had begun to fall early that morning high in the mountains and Michael struggled to make it through the pass before it closed. It was early for deep snow, but early storms were not out of the question in this part of the Adirondacks.

That day John worked very hard finishing most of the chores Frank had left for him to do in his absence.

A little past the one o'clock hour, she came to the shop with a small tray of food.

She was clean and had every strand of blonde hair in place, her dress was fresh and he knew she had changed it after she had made the bread. Usually when she brought them lunch there would be a large pitcher of cool water to quench their thirst, and he would often tease and say men needed red wine to keep up their strength. Frank would also go along with the joke as everyone knew he never touched the fruit of the vine, except when taking communion, of course. Today there was a small clay jar and no pitcher.

"What have we here?" he asked, and she blushed.

The taste of the sweet wine was indeed rejuvenating and he offered her a sip, but she declined saying, "Oh no, what if somebody were to see me drinking of the devil's brew with a half-naked man, while my husband was away."

"They would be so jealous," he quickly replied.

"You are probably so right," she said and giggled slightly.

Diane stayed a little longer than she usually did, but a very little. When she left by the back door she paused and took one more look at him and then slipped out of sight.

The blacksmith shop bordered King George Street and Frank Coleman owned four acres of land there. Behind the shop, some one hundred feet away, was the three room home he had built for his family twenty years before, soon after he had married the sixteen year old Diane. To the left of their home, near the east property line, was the small one room cabin that Frank had lived in before they had married; John Martin had stayed there ever since the first night he had arrived with his bay horse. Across the yard on the west side was a small corral where draft animals and Dane were now kept. It also served as a pen for customer's animals for short periods of time.

John closed the shop at precisely five o'clock and went straight to his cabin and heated himself water to wash with. It was not uncommon for Frank to invite him to sup with them, but Frank was not there and she had not returned since she had brought lunch. As he bathed, he wondered what she was doing at that very moment. *'Is she baking? Is she cleaning? Is she sewing? Is she bathing?'* The very thought brought an immediately reaction to his manhood.

John had not forgotten the first time he had enjoyed a woman. He had been ill-prepared for the occasion and he spent himself almost immediately. Luckily he had been young at the time, so he was again ready before Jewell became disinterested. He vowed never to let that happen again with a woman. He realized it had been his inexperience that had caused the quickness of his performance and after making his goal in life the seduction of Diane Coleman, he visited a whore weekly until he had total control over his physical self. Today___ tonight he would be ready.

The sun had gone down minutes before he closed the shop, and with the heavy cloudcover, the sliver of moon that had been seen the night before was totally absent. Only the pale yellow glow of a coal oil lamp escaping from the window gave any light at all when John stepped through the door of the little cabin. He looked about, but nothing was noticeable save the gentle shadow of a branch that the breeze was blowing to and fro. His horse neighed, telling him that he had been seen by the big animal, but that too was the only sound to be heard close by.

Far off down the road, faint sounds of laughter came from the tavern where he often spent his time; the same tavern where Honey Vee worked.

Tonight he had far greater ambitions than to pay for a woman's body.

John eased to the window and peered inside. He could see the table and four chairs where he often had taken sup, there too was the lamp. Beyond the circle of light given off by the globe and the flickering of light dancing along the back wall which told of a small blaze in the fireplace, all was dim. The door to the room Michael slept in was closed, but the other was slightly open. He was not sure, but he thought there was a flicker of light in there too. Diane Coleman could not be seen anywhere but he knew she was there.

Moving cautiously, as if any unnecessary motion or sound would expose him to horrors untold, he slipped past the window to the only entrance into the cabin.

At the time the first cabin was built here, there was still the real threat of Indian attacks; and any orifice was a breach of security as well as a robber of structural strength. Frank Coleman would never consider lowering the integrity of anything he built for mere conveniences. It had taken a real fight on Diane's part to get a single window placed in each room. Two doors were out of the question. The fact that there were really no longer any serious problems with the Indians was of no consequence, not to this blacksmith.

John placed his hand on the wooden dowel and slid it backwards to its wrought iron stop.

Now the next movement would tell him if he had read the expressions of Diane Coleman correctly, or was he simply a foolish young man inflicted with a terrible case of over-confidence. The door moved open with his gentle push. She had not locked it. He had not read her wrong.

John was not so foolish not to realize, even though he now was certain she wanted him as he did her, the manner in which he proceeded from this point could be critical to the results of his seduction.

For weeks he had thought of little else than Diane Coleman and what she would find pleasurable in her private chambers. *'Does she like it gentle, does she like it slow? Would she like to be loved in her bed or taken on the table? Does she want me to undress her or had she rather undress herself for me, or does she want her dress ripped from her in a wild swift downward grasp?'* He had wondered all these things and then tried each one with Honey Vee until he felt he had perfected them all. All, that is, but ripping her garments away. Honey Vee seldom wore anything, once behind her closed doors; and he was not sure he would be able to pay her price should he rip her clothing. That he had denied himself the practice of, but all the techniques of the act itself had been tried and refined. He would not have a repeat of the Jewell experience.

Moving slowly into the cabin he watched the shadow his form made against the wall. When it crossed the partially open door he heard a noise come from inside; a human noise. Not a normal sound; rather a gasp. *'Yes that was it, a very faint gasp.'*

Slowly, he continued to the door and when there he pushed it open gently.

Diane was standing there with a frightened expression on her face. In her hand was a small candle. Her beautiful blonde hair was now down and flowing off her shoulders disappearing along her back. She was wearing a cotton night shirt that exposed her small ankles and feet but little more. It was more than enough. Immediately all his reservations fled from him and his blood surged into his manhood.

She had been looking at his face but now she let her eyes lower to the open blouse that exposed his hairy chest, then on down to the huge bulge in his loose fitting trousers.

"We should not do this," she said quickly looking back at his face.

John moved closer to her.

"I am a married woman."

Closer he came.

"I love my husband."

Now he was so close she felt his hot breath showering down on her as she gazed up at him. "You must go!"

John eased his left arm around her back and pulled her to him.

"No! Don't!" were the last words she said before he crushed her mouth with his big soft lips. A moment later she felt his tongue shoot into her mouth and she felt panicky. Never had anyone done this; never had Frank. *'This must stop. This must soon stop,'* she thought as she melted into his embrace.

The kiss was long and moist and finally she knew she no longer had any resistance to use against this devil-man.

'Oh Frank. Why did you let this happen?' she cried to herself as she dropped the candle.

"Not on the bed," was her last bid to be the lady.

He lifted her in his arms and carried her back into the big room. When he let her stand he reached forward and grasped the front of her nightshirt and in one swift jerk ripped it from her. The action bumped the table and the oil lamp fell to the hard packed floor and spilled. Immediately a small fire started and

John, without thought, dropped the shirt from his hand onto it and swiftly smothered it with his foot.

The flickering flames in the fireplace were now their only source of light and it bathed her beautifully. Her breasts were small and tight and her nipples stood straight and proud from two-inch wide puffy areolas; more perfect than he had imagined. Her slim body and very tiny waist gave way to narrow but round hips. The whiteness of her long legs was only disturbed by the silky flaxen triangle at their intersection.

She was now pulling back at his blouse trying to slip it from his shoulders, but it would not go.

Not removing his eyes from her he stepped back and pulled it over his head and reached for his trousers, but she stopped him.

"No, I want to do this," she said and then she tugged at his waist hem and suddenly the pants fell to the floor. His member now stood straight ahead and she looked down and grasped it with both hands as if it were a present she had dreamed of.

He then pushed her gently until he was able to lower her back to the table. Her feet were still touching the cold earth and she slowly spread her legs a little. It was an invitation he did not miss and almost immediately he was in her.

Their sex was furious and before they both were spent, Diane had begged him to do things to her that she had never uttered before in her life.

Later he carried her to bed and they continued their feasting until neither hungered anymore; at least not until some sleep could be gotten.

The next morning he wanted to continue, but she strongly refused.

"The shop must be opened on time. There are people who will pass and will know of Frank's being away," she said. "Now go before the sun rises."

John moved into the outer room and fumbled over to the fireplace where he found an iron poker and stirred the coals until they were again glowing. Enough light now revealed split wood nearby and he placed small pieces of tender on the coals followed by two larger pieces of wood.

Then he found his clothes on the dirt floor, dressed quickly, and left just as the east began to show purple light.

Again Diane spoke as he set a bare foot into the inch deep snow, "Hurry!"

The first snow of the fall; he had always loved the first snow. It was so appropriate that it should come the night he had waited six long years to happen.

Diane was slow to move this morning. She was sore in places she had not been in twenty years. She also suddenly had a horrible thought. *'This man has hammered more of his seed in me in the last few hours than my husband has in the last sixteen years. What if I conceived last night?'* Suddenly she felt weak and her stomach turned.

She up-righted the chair they had knocked over and quickly sat down. For several seconds she gazed blankly at the fire. Finally she decided, *'As soon as Frank comes home I must make him take me. I must, no matter how tired he is. No matter how he tries to get out of it.'*

Cap' Burgess had seen the storm clouds building before sundown and made every effort to locate the lad. When he did, he was pleased. Michael had also recognized the danger and had already built a lean-to and was chopping small branches for a fire with his large bladed knife; a knife that he had forged himself with the guiding hands of both Cap' Burgess and his father.

The teacher watched the pupil for a long time and finally realized the lad had already passed the challenge. There was little need to wait longer.

Mounting, he moved closer through the tall trees until the boy saw him.

"Do you think you might share that fine shelter you have there with an old man?"

"Cap' Burgess, were you watching me?"

"I only thought the drifts might be enough to cause frostbite. You did not take proper shoes for snow."

"I should have thought of that, shouldn't I?"

"It is always well to be prepared for the unexpected."

"But how can I take everything, to be prepared for everything? I mean I would not be able to carry the burden."

"The wise ones observe before they pack and only take what might be needed at the time and place. Warmer shoes would have been appropriate this time. Now as soon as you get that fire going, we can put it to use," he said producing a large hare that he had killed with a thrown rock an hour before.

The two rode the horse off the mountain, and once they had reached the rolling hills below, Cap' Burgess let Michael down. The sun now had melted most of the snow that had fallen at the lower altitude and it would be no danger for the lad to walk the remainder of his journey.

"It is best for a man to return alone from a challenge. We will not speak of our meeting on the mountain."

Cap' Burgess was very surprised when he learned of Frank Coleman's absence from the shop. He immediately looked from John to the cabin in back where she would be. He knew well the lust this wicked young man held for his friend's wife, and he doubted there was much John Martin would not do to satisfy his hunger.

He would have killed him long ago had not Frank and Michael put such stock in him. Once, two years before, he had happened upon Martin as the man was gazing at Mrs. Coleman. The lust in his expression was as plain as the blue of a clear morning sky. He had almost killed him that very day, but Michael had said something in admiration of the older lad, and he decided to wait and let Michael learn for himself the truth of John Martin.

As soon as he could, he found an excuse to approach her; her safety being an utmost concern to him suddenly. When he did, he found her in better spirits than he had seen her in quite a long time and this confused him. Surely she had worried about what this man was capable of. Women have a sense that alerts them when a man desires them, and he had never doubted Mrs. Coleman was well aware of the lust oozing from this boy's black heart.

Frank did indeed return earlier than he had thought. The boiler at The Pavilion would need more work than could be done there. He had to return to his own shop and make the necessary pieces, and take them back in a few days to finish the repairs. Mr. Pell's own men, working with Frank, had made sufficient repairs to temporarily put them back in action but it truly was temporary; their repair would last two weeks at the most. He would have to work fast with little interruption and John would simply have to take care of any local emergencies that came up.

That night in spite of his fatigue, Diane practically raped him. 'It is nice she loves me so,' Frank thought as he dropped off to sleep.

The next few weeks were almost as much hell for John as before. Now he had tasted the fruit and wanted more, much more; however, she was not encouraging and that damn Cap' Burgess never seemed to leave anymore. When Frank went back to finish his work at The Pavilion, Cap' Burgess stayed and bunked in the shop.

John had only once been able to get her alone for a few minutes and stole a long kiss, but she refused to leave her door unlocked. "Not while Cap' Burgess is around," she had said sternly and he knew she meant it.

Something had to be done. He was now loping his mule nightly thinking of her. Even Honey Vee did not excite him anymore.

Late December turned off unusually warm and the snow had all melted. Cap' Burgess had two final challenges for Michael to overcome. He knew the boy possessed only two real internal fears; that of height and total darkness, and both must be conquered before he became a full grown man.

Michael was not afraid of darkness provided there was some light, a moon, a fire, a lantern and all was well; but from a small child total darkness terrified the lad, as did the fear of falling.

This was a great problem, but they had worked on it for two years now; and for the most part he had learned to overcome anything with raw courage. He now could climb trees, climb over large rocks, and even walk along the roof's eaves, but Cap' Burgess could tell the terror had not been conquered, and that must be accomplished. So he set out planning the last challenge, and this Indian-Summer would be the perfect time.

Cap' Burgess also knew time was short. He had for some time endured the extreme pain that would suddenly appear in his chest and arms. He was no fool. He had seen his own father suffer such an ordeal, and was sure it too would be his fate. He refused to share this knowledge with anyone and especially his friends; but he was determined to finish his work with Michael and also to expose John Martin for what he was, before he left this world.

December twenty-second broke clear again with a warm wind coming from the south, but Cap' Burgess had long ago learned to smell weather, it had been one of the teachings his father had concentrated so strongly on; but more trustworthy even than this, was the stone arrowhead that rested against the large bone in his left thigh. When a storm was approaching, the arrow point turned cold; it mattered little, be it a summer storm, or one like what was headed their way arriving sometime in the next twenty-four hours.

Tonight Michael must conquer both his fears. To take on both at the same time would be his greatest challenge of all.

By the noon hour, thick clouds were rapidly approaching from Ontario and Cap' Burgess knew, even though there was a quarter-moon, it would be well hidden by the cloudcover. This night was the night.

Frank had once again invited Cap' Burgess to sup with them; he did every day he was there and Cap' Burgess usually refused, knowing Mrs. Coleman had enough work to do without a fifth mouth to supply food for, but this night he accepted and he could see his friend was pleased.

She had prepared a shepherd's pie that he considered to be one of the finest meals he had enjoyed in months. Just as they were sitting down, he turned to Michael and said calmly, but sternly, "Immediately after eating, Michael, you must adorn your hiking shoes and follow me."

Everyone there realized a new challenge was about to be placed on the boy. Both Frank and Diane had become very much in favor of these tests. They were tests of manhood, and both were proud of their son's accomplishments; too they trusted Cap' Burgess to be there in case Michael needed him.

As they stepped from the home of Frank Coleman, the older man pointed and spoke, "The Episcopal Church that sits yonder," indicating the ghostly building some two hundred yards to the north almost to the top of the rise, "The pastor always delays his sleep to read from the good book, in his study. Anyone could enter the building and climb the staircase to the belltower without his knowledge, but only a true warrior could obtain that same vantage point from the outside of the building, without his knowledge."

Michael looked at the church house. It was not a large structure, only the two rooms. But the roof was covered with copper sheeting he knew quite well; his own father had helped to roof it. A man had slipped and fallen to his death while they were doing so, and the steeple where the bell was located stood another whole story above the steep roof. It would be impossible to obtain at night from the outside, and the belltower had only a small floor around a very large hole where the big bell had been hoisted.

The Episcopal Church of Ticonderoga

'It would be pitch-dark in that tower. No, he could not do it. This was too much. This time Cap' Burgess had asked too much of him,' he thought but the man simply began walking in the direction of the church with his arm around the boy's shoulder.

'I really do not have a choice. I cannot let Cap' Burgess down. If I am to die this night, I will not let this man who has spent so much of his time with me, who has shared so much of his knowledge with me, who has been my second father, know of this fear____. When I die I will do so as bravely as I can; and when I fall, I will not scream out,' he told himself over and over as they walked towards the stone building.

They reached the church a little before the pastor rang eight bells. He would ring them once more before he retired for the night.

Michael knew to be in that tower when the bell chimed nine times would deafen him for life. He had to make it there and back within the hour.

Cap' Burgess removed a Melvin file from his clothing and ruffed up the soles of Michael's leather shoes and then without any words of instruction, he turned and walked away.

It was now up to him and him alone, but Michael knew he must try.

In truth, Cap' Burgess had only disappeared a short distance into the darkness of the night, but Michael did not know this. The wind was picking up, and the air was turning colder by the minute. Cap' hoped the temperature would not drop enough to cause a thin layer of ice to stick to the metal roof; also he had not counted on the freezing wind to arrive so soon. Still he had confidence in the boy, and did not want to put a stop to the exercise yet.

While he waited staring at the dark building, he rested against the trunk of a large hickory tree. Fifteen minutes had passed and he could just barely see the boy working his way up the side of the west roof. *'He is making good time,'* Cap' Burgess thought. *'He will be up and over with plenty of time to spare.'*

It was then his thoughts were interrupted by the passing of two men on the near side of the pike. He peered into the darkness at the figures, and finally recognized them as Frank Coleman and Pell's foreman.

'Something must have gone wrong at the fort and he has been summoned.'

He started to call out to them, but then he saw the third shadow following them. This one too, seemed familiar. Finally he realized, *'This one is no other than Martin himself, sneaking along behind them. What does he hope to gain? What is his devilish plan?'*

Cap' Burgess had confidence in Michael's ability to finish his task; he had no confidence in Frank Coleman realizing his danger. He would follow Martin.

The road soon took a sharp turn around the barn of Christian Stuckey, and then again headed northeast towards old Fort Ticonderoga.

Michael had just reached the tower when a huge hole came in the cloudcover and the quarter-moon shone brightly through, lighting the countryside nearby. He turned and looked for Cap' Burgess, but could not find him. He looked everywhere and then finally he saw what looked like his old friend passing Stuckey's barn. *'It cannot be. Cap' Burgess would not leave me; not in this hour of my greatest ordeal. It was just a body that walks like Cap' Burgess.'*

It was at that time he saw also the dark figure hiding behind a neatly stacked pile of cut firewood.

'What is the man doing?' he wondered. *'Has he been stealing something and the passing stranger disturbed his felony? He certainly is acting as if he is up to no good.'*

At that moment, Michael witnessed the figure lunge out and strike at the man, at Cap' Burgess! He thought, *'No it's not Cap' Burgess. It's somebody that walks like Cap' Burgess.'*

There was some struggle and loud voices, but the wind was now strong enough to carry away the words long before he could understand them.

The fight raged on for almost a minute and then one of the dark figures slumped, and the other stepped back from him. The staggering man fell forward with his arms under him, and he suddenly stopped all movement.

'I think I have just witnessed a murder!' the boy thought. *'I must get down from here and tell Cap' Burgess so he can summon help before the murderer escapes!'* but when he moved, his foot missed the narrow platform and he fell into the dark hole below the large bell. The coarse rope burned his face as he passed it, and his heart was in his throat. *'I must not scream!'* he thought to himself. *'Cap' Burgess must not hear me scream!'*

Time has a funny way of being translated within the human mind. Sometimes it is real time, sometimes it is fast time and sometimes it is slow time. The span of time for when he lost his footing began in very slow motion, and Michael suddenly was witnessing his life passing before him. *'He saw the time he had first gone fishing with his father, and the big catfish they had caught. He saw the rifle Cap' Burgess had used to teach him to shoot, and the big cumbersome pistol he had had so much trouble finding how to manipulate in order to obtain accuracy. He saw his mother when she had brought him recently picked blueberries. They were swimming in fresh cream and she smiled so beautifully, so pure, when she handed the cup to him. He saw each of Cap' Burgess' challenges. Each endurance he had been able to conquer; one by one they passed by ever so slowly; and he saw the two men struggling there in the cold windy night while the moon played a funny trick on the storm clouds, and he remembered not to scream.* Suddenly, his hands struck the platform on the opposite side of the tower and instinctively he clasped tightly to the cold wooden planks while his legs swung back and forth in the dark hole.

He had known fear before. He had always conquered fear before, but now it was not fear he experienced; not at this moment when the clouds moved past and once again the valley was as dark as death itself; no, this moment Michael Coleman knew not fear, rather he experienced terror. Real terror, as no man had experienced before. He was swinging from a narrow platform sixty feet above the hard plank floor of the bell tower, in the blackest darkness he had ever experienced. Swinging with the smallest grip a body could have and still cling to the rough boards.

His fingers were like nails though, pinning his hands to the plank. Again time stopped, and he was alone in the dark tower; alone with himself and his fears. Alone as few men have experienced the emotion.

John had full intentions of killing Cap' Burgess. He heard the old man approaching from behind, and when the moon was shining its brightest, he caught a quick glance behind, and clearly saw who it was that followed.

He had intended only to follow long enough to be sure Frank was indeed going all the way to the Fort; but when he saw Cap' Burgess following, he seized the opportunity and darted past the barn and around just as his pursuer was passing.

The small thin blade he always kept in his boot would be just the needed weapon, but when he lunged at the old man his foot slipped and he missed with the knife.

He very soon was surprised at the strength and fighting ability of a man three times his age. Cap' Burgess had within seconds forced him to drop the knife, and then it had been brute strength and knowledge defeating his youth. In short order, John Martin realized he had truly bitten off more than he could chew, as the smaller man slowly overpowered him; but suddenly as if by some strange predestined fate, Cap' Burgess had cried out, "No!" and stopped the struggle, releasing his tight grip and slapping his balled fist to his chest before falling face down in the muddy road, beside the pale blue barn.

He had no time to follow Frank further; he must return to Diane immediately. '*She will know if Frank would be gone all night or not*', he thought, '*we have so few opportunities to be together I cannot let this one pass.*'

Frank had stopped in his tracks. The distant cry had cut through the wind and pierced his ears. He waited for another sound but none came.

"What be the matter?" Robin Bauer asked.

"I'm not sure. I heard something."

"The wind, the wind cries out on a night like this."

"No, it was not the wind," Frank said looking at their back track for several seconds.

The silver light that had for a spell been such a blessing was now gone, and only darkness filled the valley. He suddenly knew he must go back; he must find and help the poor soul who had cried so mournfully a few moments before.

"You go on Mr. Bauer; I'll be there directly."

"But Mr. Coleman, Mr. Pell, he said to bring you promptly. They need you."

"Directly!" was the only word he replied as he started walking back.

He had not taken three steps before the first flake landed on his cheek and melted almost immediately allowing a tiny stream of water to run down his face.

By the time he reached Stuckey's barn, the snow was thick and he had difficulty staying on the road. The mud below his feet was now freezing and it made tiny crunching noises as he walked upon it. If the noise stopped he knew he had left the road and was able to retrace his trail by sound rather than sight.

Frank had now raised the heavy wool collar of his overcoat and closed the front, covering most of his face. He had pulled the stocking cap down as low as he could and still have any sight. In reality he was walking blind, save for the crunching of the muddy crystals below his boots.

He almost walked into Stuckey's barn before he saw it; and did indeed stumble over the body lying in the road.

Turning the man over, Frank was horrified to find it was his dearest friend and he immediately picked the little man up and began carrying him towards where Stuckey's house should be.

Luck was smiling on Frank this night, or so he thought. The brother-in-law of Christian Stuckey was Doctor Sanders, and he had come to sup with the Stuckey family only to be caught by the sudden storm.

The Doctor immediately recognized the problem and began to bleed the injured Cap' Burgess. Some twenty minutes after being brought there, the little old man opened his eyes and saw above him the face of his best friend and he smiled.

Frank was so relieved, he almost burst into tears; but restrained himself.

A few moments passed, and suddenly a heavy frown swept across Cap' Burgess' forehead and he tried to raise his head but had not the strength.

Frank leaned forward to gently push his friend back so he could rest, but Cap' Burgess did not want to rest. He knew better than any of them his rest was but moments away, and he reached deep within himself for strength and pulled the knife from where he had slipped it as he lay there in the road.

After Martin had left him for dead and he was lying on the knife, he knew it was the only evidence that could connect the man to the scene, and he had with great difficulty gotten the blade inside the pocket of his trousers.

Now handing it up to Frank, he said "Martin," then with great difficulty he added "You find Martin," and then he gave up the ghost.

Frank was devastated. He had just witnessed the one true friend in his life die, and he really did not understand what he had been trying to tell him. Suddenly, he thought, *'Martin is in trouble.'* Frank rose with the knife in hand. *'He must be in trouble and that is what Cap' Burgess was doing out there on the road instead of being with Michael. He was trying to overtake me and tell me Martin was about to engage in some act that would endanger him.'*

"I must go. I will be back in the morning to take my friend, but now I must go," he said and before anyone could question him he was out of the house and struggling against the blinding snow that was soon to be known in these parts as the terrible blizzard of '49.

Frank didn't really know where to look, but first he went and looked all about in the drifts near where he had found Cap' Burgess, next he went to the Black Mountain Tavern. He knew Martin frequented the place. Inside he saw many men he knew but no Martin, and no one there had seen him this night. He checked at the small shack in the back the whore kept, but her customer this hour was not young John. Among other things she yelled at him, was that she had not seen John Martin in three weeks. This surprised Frank. He knew of John's appetite for the sinful works of the flesh. He too had been stricken with them at the lad's age, but after his marriage he no longer frequented such women. He had given his life to the Lord and thereafter used his desires for the very purpose God had given them to him to begin with, to father children.

It would be foolish to say that he did not still lust after the flesh of a woman, but he was a strong man both in body and in mind and he could overpower most obstructions that came his way.

When their son had been born, Diane had a very bad time in childbearing and Doc Sanders had told them she should never again give birth. It had been a bitter thing to swallow, but Frank was strong and if this was God's way of testing him, he would prove faithful in the end. That is not to say there weren't times after Michael had come to them he had not given into his lust, after all Diane had the body only the devil himself would have created. He had gone a year fighting his desire before he gave in and as he grew older the power of the demon was not as strong as it had been in his youth. Here in his forty-eighth year he had only succumbed once. A restraint any God-fearing man could be proud of.

Not finding John at the tavern he wondered, '*Where would he be?*'

Finally he realized there was a good chance the boy was at home. '*After all, if he were in trouble or injured where else would he go, but to his family.*'

She rested beside her lover. He had spent himself and now his breathing had become steady and heavy. She knew he was asleep. '*I should send him on, but I just want to feel his wonderfully wicked, naked body beside me a few minutes more.*'

Their sex had been fast and furious at first and then slow and long. She had almost lost her mind several times, and then when she felt him send his seed deep within her bowls for the second time, she almost passed out. Even in the cold night air after the fire had burned down, they both were wet with sweat. Her long blonde hair felt damp, and after awhile she arose to find something to dry it with. She had kept the candle lit as she received great pleasure from looking at his body, and now she allowed herself to feast on the sight of him a few more seconds before she covered him with a heavy blanket.

Taking the candle she started out to stir the embers in hopes of rekindling the fire. She reached for her nightshirt but remembered how much he liked to gaze upon her body, and she left it on the peg beside the bed.

Michael had lost track of time. Time was something in a different world than he was at this moment. This very moment, as he hung 60 feet above the hard planks that made up the floor at the bottom of the bell tower, he had no knowledge of time. Terror was now in control of his brain. He thought of nothing. His mind was a blank. His arms no longer hurt. He felt nothing. He knew soon he would be no more. *'It is all right. It will be over in a moment.'* Then suddenly he realized if he could envision these things, cultivate these thoughts, he still had a brain. He still could think. If he could think, he could act in some way. Looking upward, all he could see was the dim outline of the dark tower. Looking down was nothing but black air, *'So funny, so hilarious; the two things I fear most, heights and total darkness, and here I will die surrounded by each of them.'*

He again began to feel pain in his arms. *'It will not be long now.'* he thought, *'all I have to do is let go and all these problems will be over, gone forever. No more fears, no more pain, no more challenges that I must conquer.'*

There in the blackness he began to remember all the challenges Cap' Burgess had made him do. They seemed to have all been stupid things to someone about to die. *'What good will they do me in the afterlife. Cap' Burgess was preparing me for life in this world, not the next.'*

He suddenly remembered his mother bringing him blueberries she had picked for him and how they looked so dark swimming in the cream. He remembered how she had smiled when she watched him eat them. *'How old was I then, six, seven?'*

'Mother, so beautiful, so pure, so perfect a mother.'

'I hope my death does not bring you too much grief, Mother. Maybe you will have another son. You are still young. Younger than Mrs. Joyce and Mrs. Joyce had a baby just last month.'

He then thought of his father and the first time he had taken him fishing, the only time he had taken him fishing. His father had taught him all of his own skills. Michael was today as good a blacksmith as Robin Bauer at The Pavilion. He had heard his father say that to Cap' Burgess, but his father had so little time to do anything except work. Had it not been for Cap' Burgess, he would have learned almost nothing of the woods, of life outside of the blacksmith shop.

'Mother of course had seen that I learned to do my letters and now I can read most books.' He even read the Good Book to his father, although he didn't like reading it much. It had too many difficult words; words

no one used anymore. He could only read it aloud if his mother was there to help him over the difficult words.

'*Cap' Burgess has really been my tutor in all other knowledge. Cap' Burgess, oh Cap' Burgess will be so disappointed in me for not completing this challenge. I hope Cap' Burgess will not blame himself for my death.*'

'*What was it Cap' Burgess had said? "A man can overcome any obstacle when he puts his mind to it."*'

'*That is good advice.*' he nodded his head in approval, '*I will have to always remember that.*'

Suddenly he realized what he had just said to himself. '*If I am to remember that, I must live. If truly a man can overcome all obstacles when he puts his mind to it, then why could I not pull myself up from here and live to remember that for a long time?*'

His arms now began to pain him greatly. '*During the time before, the time when I was in another world, they did not hurt. Now they hurt greatly, but I can overcome this obstacle. I can overcome any obstacle. I will not let Cap' Burgess down.*'

With extreme difficulty, Michael strained tired muscles until he was up high enough to lock his elbows straight. Then he swung one leg up onto the narrow platform, followed by the other and suddenly he was lying on his back looking at the dim insides of the dark bell tower dome.

'*Truly Cap' Burgess was right; I can overcome any obstacle, any fear, if I want to bad enough.*'

After a few minutes of laying there resting and regaining some of his strength, he rolled over against the wall and began to move on his hands and knees until he found the stair opening.

'*Cap' Burgess had wanted me to come up one side and down the other but I believe when he finds out that I witnessed a murder, he will approve of me using my time in notifying the authorities rather than creeping down that slick roof.*'

Michael headed down the dark stairs and exited the front door just as Pastor Webb came from his little room in the back of the building to pull the long rope nine times.

Michael heard the bell chime out and was astonished that the ordeal had taken place in less than an hour. Of course he also realized had he still been hanging by his hands from the platform when the bell began, he not only would be dead now, but very possibly Pastor

Webb would too; for surely he would have crushed him when he fell down that dark hole.

Cap' Burgess was not by the tree where he had expected to find him. Michael stopped and thought a moment.

He remembered, before the clouds once again snuffed out the light of the moon, seeing a silver reflection in the hand of the assailant; a knife no doubt. He also knew that most often a body takes a long time to lose enough blood to succumb to a stabbing. *'So it may be possible that I can save the man, were I to get to him and stop his bleeding.'*

He remembered how the victim had stopped struggling and cried out just before he grabbed his chest and fell forward.

'Yes he certainly looked like he had just been stabbed.' Michael thought.

Turning up the road, he headed for Stuckey's barn. The snow was now blowing fiercely and when he reached the barn he could find nothing; no body, no blood, nothing.

'Maybe he was able to stagger off and is buried there someplace,' he wondered and began to run here and there looking, but finally came to the realization that if he was going to find the man he would need help; and help was home.

Frank, unable to see in the dark shop, lit a lantern and hung it on the wall. *'No one in here'* he thought, *'I must look in John's cabin.'*

Again he lit a lamp, but the boy was not there either; and then he realized, *'If John is hurt he would be in our house, where Diane could look after him.'*

He walked in and pushed the door closed behind him but the worn latch didn't catch fully. Turning, he removed his snow-covered coat and laid it on the table and then looked up at the faint light.

She was standing there in front of the door to the bedroom holding a candle.

At first it did not register with him, but suddenly he focused on her naked body; the pale glow from the candle haloing her beautiful form. Frank swallowed hard. He had not seen her totally naked since Michael was born sixteen years previous. *'She is beautiful, but why is she naked on a cold night like this?'*

Suddenly the latch slipped, and the door blew open and a rush of freezing air poured in.

"For God's sake, sweet woman, close the damn door."

Frank now began to grasp the situation, slowly. The voice was that of John Martin. *'Why is he calling Mrs. Coleman sweet woman? Why is she coming from their bedroom stark naked?'*

At that moment, John himself came forward; and reaching out, ran his hand over the soft skin of her backside and then he said. "Never mind, I'll get the door."

Her expression was so strange. *'What is the matter with you?'* John wondered; and he looked where she was staring, and then he too was looking straight into the frozen beard on Frank Coleman's face. He only saw it for a moment. The next instant Frank had turned his huge body and was reaching for the long rifle he kept hanging over the door.

A new blast of wind snuffed out the flame from her candle, but she still held to it, not moving. Life as she knew it had disappeared in that moment. No matter what occurred in the next few minutes, her life as Mrs. Frank Coleman, mother of Michael Coleman, lead singer in the choir at The Episcopal Church of Ticonderoga, New York State, was over forever.

Frank had always kept the rifle loaded; he would shoot it occasionally to clear it, and then clean and reload it. He had once killed a Huron with it long before he married, but otherwise it had never drawn blood; not even animal blood.

This night, he knew the priming powder would be spilled but that was an easy matter. In a swift motion, he had the small horn that contained the finely ground powder in his hand and even though in his haste he spilled most of it, the fission was primed and he was bringing the long barrel up to eliminate this vermin that had entered his house.

John knew in a moment his life would be history. He watched as the long gun began to rise and the huge black hole that held his eternity now pointed at his face. He knew he could not reach the man or the gun in time, and he looked desperately for a weapon, any weapon. There beyond Diane beside the fireplace, hanging from an iron dowel that Frank had forged with his very own hands and driven into the stone, there hanging from a rawhide string, was a poker; a long round iron poker with a wicket barb forged there to snag logs.

He lunged behind her for the weapon just as the explosion occurred; before the smoke had fully filled the room he had his weapon.

Frank was now silhouetted by the light coming through the door from the lantern that he had left in the shop across the courtyard. He was moving with unreal speed at reloading the rifle.

John lifted the poker and swung it hard. He heard the sound of the rifle fall, but then the man was on him. A strong right hand clasped his neck and suddenly he was lifted so his feet merely danced in the air.

The strength of the blacksmith was incredible. He had been amazed at the strength of Cap' Burgess but this man possessed twice that.

With his one good arm, Frank lifted John up to his eye-level staring into his face, and then showed his gritted teeth as if his next act would be to bite off the lad's face.

John was slowly choking. The huge hand had trapped his last breath inside and denied him another. Also the big thumb was now pressing hard against the side of his neck and he began to feel faint from the lack of blood to the brain.

'Surely if I don't do something soon I will be dead.'

He had tried a second swing, but that was impossible with the way the huge man held him. Finally he thought of something.

Using both hands he lunged the poker upward and drove it into Frank's lower stomach, there was a faint groan from the big man but still he held on to John's throat.

He tried to pull it back out to do another puncture, but the nasty barb held it tight and refused to allow it to be pulled out.

Next he tried to twist it, but by now the blood gushing from Frank's groin was so great, that his hands simply slipped on the black iron.

John realized he was being killed by the man he was killing. *'This has become such a comical irony,'* he thought.

Just then, Frank staggered and fell against the table but he still held to Martin's throat and tightened his grip.

John thrashed about, no longer holding on to the poker. Suddenly, a hand found the snow-covered coat laying on the table and a second later, there protruding from one of the pockets, was the tang of his knife.

With a bloody hand, he pulled it free and lashed out with all the strength he could muster at the big man's head.

Frank sensed the threat coming and pulled his head backward, but in doing so exposed his most vulnerable body part. The thin blade sliced into his neck. Martin had used such force in his last effort to survive; the knife cut Frank's head half off.

A queer expression suddenly crossed Frank's face and then he slowly slumped to the floor.

Coughing and gagging, John rolled around in the blood, and finally, by accident a hand found the coal oil lamp that had miraculously stayed on the table during the whole affair. He then dragged it to the fireplace, where he began digging in the coals until he finally found one that burned his hands. Pulling it free he began to blow, between coughs, until it began to glow and he had to drop it. Next, he located a small sliver of wood and laid it on the coal and again blew. When the flame burst to life, he lit the lamp and then fell backwards coughing uncontrollably.

Michael first entered the shop and seeing no one there, headed immediately for the open door of his home.

Entering, he saw the sick figure of his friend's nude body as he coughed between gasps for breath. Next he looked at his mother where she lay.

She was naked. He had no conscious remembrance of ever seeing her naked before. She was beautiful as always, except for the red spot below her neck perfectly aligned with her shoulder blades where the large ball, meant for John Martin, had entered her body.

'Why is she naked?'

He caught a quick glimpse of the motion to his left a moment before John crashed the hard wooden chair over his head.

It was three days before he regained consciousness. When he did, Doc Stanley told him of the death of his parents, and that he had had his skull split open, and they had really not expected him to ever open his eyes again.

The next day, he told his story to the sheriff. It was almost as if they had already surmised it from the evidence. Only Michael had not known before that day the figure on the road that had reminded him of Cap' Burgess was indeed Cap' Burgess.

His parents had already been buried when he awoke, but as the storm raged on the grave diggers begged for a reprieve on the body of Cap' Burgess until a thaw.

Michael made certain Cap' Burgess' remains would be laid to rest beside his parents. *'After all, Cap' was family.'*

He then sold all the belongings that had been left him, and he began the pursuit of his former friend.

John Martin had hurriedly packed all his worldly possessions and the gold coins he knew Frank Coleman kept hidden in his shop. He traveled east until he came upon a squad of soldiers who were moving a Six Pound Napoleon with Caisson to the fort.

He deliberately stopped and talked to them, inquiring of the direction to the ferry where he could cross to the Rutland Road. After receiving his directions, he rode east on Dane into the stormy night and disappeared from the New York countryside, as far as the sheriff's posse could find.

Most of the good people in the valley thought the storm had swallowed him. Michael never considered it a possibility and it took him two months of hard riding in bitter weather before he uncovered enough evidence to learn that in fact, John Martin had moved east from the view of the soldiers only long enough to be certain the fast falling snow would cover his tracks, and then he simply eased off the road a few yards and waited for them to pass. He then turned westward to the Hudson River, and followed it south to Albany. There he left Dane with his grandparents and hired on a southbound barge bound for New York City.

Michael learned from the hostler of a livery not more than a mile from the large Tidwell home, that John Martin had indeed been there; in fact, as the man had no love for the Tidwell's, he showed him where Dane was kept. He also informed Michael that Mr. Tidwell had given him two-bits for any information of a Michael Coleman or anyone else who might be asking about the horse or his grandson.

Michael thanked him with a nod of his head and handing him the reins of his mule he said, "He should be worth more than two-bits; he's yours, my friend."

Feeling good about what he had learned and done for the man who had helped him, he smiled as he walked to the Hudson River to continue his pursuit. He also, after some reflection of what he had just heard, decided to change his name. Several came to mind and he at one time chose Burgess, but finally decided he would retain his father's name, only use it as his Christian name in his honor, and as a given name he would choose Darktower. It had been the dark tower of that church steeple, where he had overcome the last of his great fears___.

That day he signed on as deck-hand aboard *'The Kinderhook'* as Coleman Darktower, and for the remainder of his life, so would he be called.

'The Kinderhook'

CHAPTER FIFTEEN

The Destruction of the Renegades

John Tidwell was no fool, he knew well the prime time for profit was over in Georgia, and it would only be a matter of months before the political climate would change.

He and others who had profited so greatly from the Federal Reconstruction Laws would be called upon the carpet in various courts around the country, especially here in the Deep South.

He also realized the adverse publicity Occupational Forces in general, and The Civilian Department in particular, had been receiving in the last few months, would eventually be a wound that would kill them, if something was not done, and done soon.

The stage coach hold-up had been just as big a blunder, as not having done a better background on young John Holliday before he allowed his wife to hire him.

'There is no telling how much that fancy pants found out while he was sneaking around here,' he thought more than once after finding out Holliday's true colors.

His years in China had been very good for him. He had formed a trading company and found the exportation of opium very profitable. Also in less than six years he had arranged for over three thousand Chinese to be imported into the United States; with a profit, after all his expenses were deducted, amounting to more than two hundred U. S. dollars in gold, per man.

He perhaps would have stayed in the East, had the Hung Hsiu-ch'uan not begun to lose favor. John had allied early with the revolutionist and his association of God worshipers. They had come close in overturning the government in Shanghai; but the attack had failed and Mouton escaped with his head, by only a few hours.

In the early years when he lived in New York, he had been the supplier of women for all of the parties the extremely wealthy Bullock family had put on, entertaining their political friends. He even had become personal friends with Rufus Bullock, and on many occasions spent time at his beach home on the Connecticut shore only a day's journey from the city.

It had been Bullock who had originally steered him to Senator Thad Stevens and thus into the training schools for Reconstruction Administrators, when he returned from China.

A few years later, the favor had been repaid when John Tidwell was able to offer political support in the appointment of Bullock as Governor of Georgia.

He had twice before sent wires to Atlanta asking for more troops to rid the area of these renegades who swarmed out of the swamps south of Valdosta and reigned havoc on his people there, but no additional soldiers were sent.

Today he was going to Atlanta himself. He would spend a few days with his old friend. If he could not get enough support to wipe out this bunch before they became local saints, it would never happen.

Time was becoming critical. He must move before the election or they would probably lose most of their friends to past sympathizers who were again becoming less afraid of the powers that be. If that happened, he would need to be gone before the courts could get at him.

Darktower had been steadily working at his job as teamster. He didn't want to lose this position, it offered him too many contacts; nonetheless, he was anxious to find out more about this John Mouton Tidwell.

Not once in the long years had he faltered in his desire to destroy Mouton. Still, there had been frustrations when everything seemed to be headed in the right direction; only to find it had been a false trail, or he had arrived just a little late to trap his prey.

Remembering back, he did hear the name Tidwell while he was in China. There was a Tidwell shipping concern in Shanghai right on the Huangpu River. The company operated dozens of junks up and down the river and even had docks on the Yangtze near the East China Sea. They were heavy into the opium trade, as he remembered it.

Three weeks after he had learned about this John Mouton Tidwell in Valdosta, a passenger on his coach had in idle conversation mentioned he was going to travel to the Governor's Mansion in Atlanta with Mr. Tidwell.

Darktower did not ask questions of the man, rather made it his next goal to find out more about this journey.

John Tidwell had tried hard to have the north/south rail line brought to Valdosta; but it had stopped at Macon and would not go farther due south, rather turning southwest. It was one of his great failures and he knew it. Still, he calculated, he had time to gather a lot more assets before he would have to move on.

The election coming in a few weeks would be a huge disappointment should it not go their way. Still there was no great concern among any of them, why should it not go their way? Grant was almost a sure shoe-in and with him would be his people, one of which was Governor Rufus Bullock of Georgia.

Still, one never can rest until the polls have reported in. This business with these renegades in Lowndes County was a festering thorn in his side. Many of the papers were now showing sympathy for the cutthroats, especially that damn Reb Brown. One paper in Florida was even calling him a modern day Robin Hood.

'I should have hung him four years ago,' Tidwell thought as he touched his top hat with the crown of his walking stick, a parting gesture to Captain Jarvis just as the train jerked hard when the cars began to catch up to their couplings.

The ride to Thomasville had been unpleasant. September in South Georgia could be nasty cold or unpleasantly hot, and this day had proven to be hot. His wife had complained the entire journey from Valdosta. The sun was too hot, the road too dusty, the soldiers too smelly. He dearly wished he had left her home. Little Marty had been no better. After awaking shortly after sunrise, he had whined most of the first hour. '*Perhaps I should have waited for the train on Thursday,*' he thought but then confident with his ability to make the correct decisions he concluded, '*No I need to be there tomorrow, not on Friday. Rufus is always a little inebriated by noon on Fridays.'*

Finally John stopped the carriage and placed the lad on Captain Jarvis' saddle; a move that stopped the aggravation to the Tidwell's, but only irritated the Captain.

Rodger Jarvis did not like the move one bit; in fact he did not like Little Marty one bit. He did not like any children that were poorly disciplined. *'I am a soldier, a professional, not a mammy.'*

Jarvis did not like being here. He did not like escorting a civilian around when there were military matters that needed his attention. He did not like his company being assigned to The Civilian Department. He did not like John Tidwell or his political position. On top of all that, he did not like Georgia; and he especially did not like being in command of colored troops in Georgia.

Captain Rodger Jarvis had been Brevetted Major General during the war. He volunteered with his home company, the 92nd Indiana in '62, and was elected Second Lieutenant of Company H. By the time they moved into Hoover's Gap, he had made First Lieutenant, and as attrition raised its ugly head, Rodger Jarvis rose with it. In April of '65 he had just received the promotion to Major General, in time to see Forrest receive his only defeat of the war near Selma Alabama.

The war had been good to him but the post war 'War Department' was not so generous. He had lost his stars before Johnson surrendered, and by the time his outfit was being disbanded, he was back to First Lieutenant and glad to get the job with the Capital Guards. That position only lasted until '68 when the Pinkertons took over, and he was again about to be mustered out when he was offered this position as Captain of the 103rd Colored, in Valdosta. He gladly accepted it to stay in the army. He had no other trade, no other options. This day, former Brevet General Rodger Jarvis was babysitting a spoiled brat in a hot, dusty, miserable land, filled with hostile residents who thought of him as an invader.

John Tidwell knew very well Jarvis considered himself above his position and that was the very reason he had chosen his horse rather than that of someone of lesser rank. *'It will do him good to be put in his place.'* Tidwell thought.

However, once they were on the train moving out of Thomasville and Jarvis was returning to Valdosta, John had no one to place the little brat with except his wife, and she was hardly in any mood to control the child. After what seemed like two days, they jerked into Albany. There they would take on more coal, water, and passengers; and there John Tidwell would stretch his legs.

Cliff did not know where Darktower had come by his information, he really didn't care; but the man had approached him with news that was quite interesting and he felt like they should move on it.

'*It seems John Tidwell is enroute to Atlanta to see his buddy Rufus, and will be traveling by train from Thomasville through Albany, enroute to the new Capital,*' Cliff thought.

Darktower had said his escort would leave him when he boarded the train and he would be without protection save his personal bodyguard Butch Espie, a half-breed Chinaman who lived on the Tidwell property and oversaw the other oriental workers. Espie was a powerfully built man who was not to be taken lightly.

However as good as this news was, the real reason he had readily agreed to go on this lead was Darktower had also told him Tidwell was moving a large amount of his personal funds from the Bank of Valdosta north to Atlanta; supposedly some eighty pounds of gold amounting to about twenty-five thousand dollars.

'*This is almost too good to be true,*' Cliff thought. '*Should I trust this big Yank? This could be a trap with some sweet smelling bait.*'

However, when Darktower had insisted the girl Buckskin Mae come along, he decided it must be for real. Darktower knew how she had become one of the girls around the stage stop, and he would not want her to see him betray her friends. '*No, this must be good information; at least he believes it's good.*'

There would be eleven of them altogether. Alabama Jack had boarded the train in Thomasville with Arizona Bill, Red Max, and Whiskey George. Darktower and Buckskin Mae had also gotten on there but sat in a separate car. Art Mann, Deadwood's Daughter, and Reb had been waiting in Albany.

Art Mann boarded immediately as the train pulled to a stop, and walked forward to locate Tidwell. Darktower nodded him towards the car directly in front of where he and the girl sat. He had spotted Tidwell earlier and was convinced at long last he had found Mouton. In fact, when after all these years at last he saw the man he held responsible for the death of his parents and Cap' Burgess, he had almost charged forward and strangled him with his bare hands; but finally thought better of it and decided to stay with the plan. It was a good plan and he was sure it would work out for the best in the long run.

Cliff and Nadine waited until just before the train was to pull out before boarding. Cliff knew Tidwell would recognize him if he saw his face and he didn't want that to happen while the train was at the depot. The only flaw in his plan was no one had seen Tidwell detrain.

John Tidwell had indeed stepped from the train to use the water closet behind the depot. When he emerged, he immediately saw a dark-haired woman come from the depot and walk towards the train. She was so striking he could not help but admire her, with her shiny black hair flowing easily over the shoulders of her smart gray cape.

'*She has the face of an angel and the body of a she-devil. I must find out more about her before we get to Atl___*' His thoughts were suddenly and rudely interrupted when the tall thin man walked to her side and taking her arm, led her to the train.

Tidwell stopped and quickly turned back where he could hide behind the yellow slab board wall of the depot.

'*I haven't any idea who she is, but that bastard is Reb Brown.*' He looked towards the small town only a hundred yards away. '*I must get the sheriff.*'

He started in the direction of the town's main street, but just as he stepped out, he looked back at the train and saw Reb Brown looking out a window of the car directly behind the one his wife was in. Quickly he jerked back behind the protection of the yellow wall, and there he stayed until the train had moved away.

"The Sheriff's gone over to Dosaga to serve a paper; he ain't likely to be back 'for dark," the old man who was sweeping the office with a straw broom told him.

"Well, where are his deputies?

"Only got one, Charlie. Had two, but Ben got bit right here," the old man said pointing to the back of his leg behind the knee, "A big ole diamondback struck him, right here. Sheriff Arnold done told him a thousand times not to step over no down log. You see you got 'a' step up on top a' them and then kind 'a jump off so them durn rattlers won't a'strike you," he explained before he looked back down at the small pile of red dust he had accumulated and shook his head, Ole Ben, he never learned that. Dead, he wus' dead as a doornail when Sheriff Arnold got him back to town."

"Well, where is this Deputy Charlie?"

"Oh, he went to Dosaga with the sheriff. Them Putnam boys ain't nobody to fool with alone," the old man said before he began sweeping the same pile of dirt again. "No they ain't. You know, them boys dun told on they own kin, to the Yankees 'bout where they had mules hid. Them damn Yankees come through here a while back with papers to take all the horses and mules what home folk had. Sheriff Arnold, he was a Yankee, too, in the war, but he don't hold to no stealing and he say them Yankee soldiers were stealing them animals. Legal maybe, but stealing them, anyhow."

John Tidwell could see he would get no help from the local law; so in desperation he began to run back towards the depot, where the clerk, who also was a telegrapher, could send a wire north.

"Where is your next depot?" he demanded

"There is one in Americus."

"How far is that?"

"Oh, 'bout a hour," he clerk said rubbing his chin with his thumb and fingers as if it helped him think.

"All right, that's good. Send a wire there to the post commander."

"Can't."

"Can't? Why not?" John asked with wide eyes.

"The telegrapher there is sick with the measles. I talked to him yesterdee, said he wouldn't be there fur a week or so. His wife is running the station so as he won't lose his job, but she don't know Morse[39]."

"Shit," Tidwell said and turned and looked out the dirty window for a few long seconds before he turned back. "Listen, I'm John Tidwell, the Commander of the Civilian Department for South Georgia. I just saw the bandit Reb Brown board the train that just pulled out of here. They are planning to rob that train; now how are we going to stop them?"

"Oh!" the little man said in surprise and then he shook his head and said. "There ain't nothing on that train fur him to rob sep' a few broke folk who don't have enough money to rub together for a prayer."

"There is gold on that train, you idiot. My gold. Now are we going to help me or not?"

---

[39] Morse: Morse Code the language of telegraphers.

"Gold! Well, you never declared it. The railroad can't be held for no undeclared gold."

John reached into his coat with his left hand and when it appeared again he was holding a thin shiny knife. "I don't have time to squabble with you, you little weasel, but if you don't come up with some answers to our problem real soon this knife will draw blood," he paused before he added, "again."

The clerk looked at the silver blade and then back at the man before swallowing hard. "We could send a wire to Fort Valley. They got um' a' army post there, if's that's okey?"

"OK?" Tidwell questioned.

"Oh, I'm sorry, that's code for 'alright' or 'all korrect.' Only telegraphers know what okey means," the little man said adjusting his cap. "Some say it was a Choctaw word."

"I thought you said you didn't know code?"

"Naw, I said the telegrapher in Americus was sick and his wife don't know code, I never said I didn't know it, but I ain't the telegrapher and I don't get paid to send no wires."

"Send the wire," Tidwell said, pointing his knife at the man.

Cliff had Nadine go forward to find a seat behind the Tidwell's and he turned to the car where his men were.

Coleman Darktower was seated with Buckskin Mae near the front of the car, behind them were three rows of civilian passengers, and then four soldiers sitting two abreast on either side of the isle playing a game of cards on a make-shift table of some sort with a gray wool blanket over it. Behind them Art Mann had found a seat.

In the next car, Cliff saw Arizona Bill and Red Max on one side and Alabama Jack and Whiskey George on the opposite side one row back; behind them were the lawyer Gillie and his wife the newswoman. At first Cliff didn't want her along, but slowly gave in, thinking she might be an asset to correct any wrongs *The South Georgia Pioneer* might print.

Darktower walked back with a large unlit cigar in his mouth. He passed them all and went out onto the landing between the last two cars where he lit the tobacco. Cliff followed. Neither man looked at the other, rather at the timber and rolling farm land that was flying past at thirty miles an hour.

"Have you seen him?

"Yes, he's in the front car where your wife went. He is there with his wife and son and a Chinaman who apparently works for him. There were no others in that car before we arrived in Albany. I haven't been up there since we pulled out."

"Where is the gold?"

"Haven't seen it, but probably with him; I somehow doubt he would bank it in the caboose."

"We'll check both places."

"When do we take him?"

"Johnny and Dizzy are waiting for us at the Flint River trestle. They have a flat boat that will take us back down river to where we have the horses corralled. Won't leave any tracks that way."

"I don't know where this Flint River is."

"It's on up the road a good piece. I'll let you know when we are fifteen minutes or so away."

Darktower nodded his head then spoke. "When we take him, I'll be the one who kills him."

Cliff looked at the big man for the first time since he had followed him outside. He really didn't care who killed Tidwell; he surely had reason to do so himself, but so did several of the others; what he did not like was the way Darktower had said it. He had spoken as if giving an order, and in this outfit Cliff gave the orders. He thought a minute on it and then said. "Alright, you kill him but don't make a mistake and let him get away."

"I assure you I will make no mistake about his death."

Cliff didn't know what had brought on the obvious hate this man held for Tidwell, but it was surely strong and that usually surfaced in a situation like this.

'Still I must watch him,' Cliff thought.

Johnny had made contact with Robert's cousin at Oglethorpe the night before. Near there they had constructed a makeshift corral to hold the livestock, then Johnny and Dizzy had poled on up the Flint to the high trestle where the railroad tracks crossed the river and began fishing.

Sergeant Livingston had received the telegram but had no idea who John Tidwell was. He sent a wire to Macon to Company Headquarters relaying the information he had received about 'The Withlacoochee Renegades' planning on robbing the northbound out of Albany, but that didn't make sense because it was reported to not be carrying anything of value. Two hours later, he received a return wire explaining John Tidwell's credentials, and was advised to assist him in any way he could. With that, he set up perimeters around the depot with two squads of men and had the Artillery Officer move a 12 pound Napoleon onto the tracks as a definite deterrent to the train's failure to stop when flagged.

When Cliff figured they were some five miles south of Oglethorpe, he gave the motion to move forward with the plan.

Darktower and the girl, both with neckerchiefs over their faces, moved into the forward car with guns drawn. "Everybody reach high!" she yelled.

Nadine did as ordered immediately, but the other woman and the Chinaman looked dumbfounded at the two masked robbers.

Darktower cocked the hammers on the big Colt Dragoons he carried, and pointed one directly into the face of the Chinaman. Slowly he raised his hands like he had seen the woman do.

At that point Mrs. Tidwell, realizing what was happening, stood and screamed loudly and placed her hands over her mouth.

The boy ran behind his mother's leg and peered around at the two armed bandits.

"Where's Tidwell?" Mae asked just above a whisper.

"He was in here," Darktower replied.

They then both looked at Nadine who very slowly shook her head slightly.

"Keep them covered," he said to Mae. "If any of them moves don't hesitate to shoot immediately," then he turned and started back to the next car.

Arizona Bill and Red Max had their Colts out covering the tying of the four soldiers by Whisky George. Alabama Jack was standing on the platform to the rear talking with Cliff.

He pushed past them and out the door.

"Tidwell is not up front."

"What!" Cliff shot back sharply, "You said he was in the first car."

"He was. I saw him there when we pulled into Albany."

Cliff looked around. So far, they had not bothered the men in the caboose. He had rather they didn't; but now it seemed that would have to be done to find their target. "Did you see the gold?"

"No, I was looking for him."

Cliff gritted his teeth and then moved into the car. When he reached Alabama Jack he stopped and whispered to him. "Tidwell is loose, keep an eye out."

Jack nodded his head.

Cliff moved on forward, just as he opened the door, he heard a shot come from the front car. Charging forward, he saw the young girl with a thin trail of smoke rising from the revolver she held with both hands.

The Chinaman lay face down, bleeding on the floor, a few steps in front of her.

"What happened?"

"He wouldn't sit down," Mae said.

Nadine could see the strain in her husband's eyes. She knew he had wanted no one to be hurt except Tidwell. Still she knew that Mae had done the only thing she could when the man started moving towards her. Nadine herself had already reached into her draw bag for the Root, but Mae had fired before she had to expose it.

Mrs. Tidwell was now hysterically screaming. The boy too, was bawling his head off. The whole car seemed to be louder than the rumble of the steam engine that was only a few yards ahead of them.

Cliff moved forward and turned the man over; he was conscious. His eyes seemed to dart about from one thing to another. There was a badly burned patch on the front of his light blue vest where the powder had started a small fire just after the bullet punched through it. Blood was squirting out a foot from his body every time his heart pounded, and Cliff knew that would not be much longer in this world. 'There is no more fight in this man', he thought. 'I wonder where he came from. How long had been his journey, only to rendezvous with death in middle Georgia?'

He stepped over the man and went to the woman. Placing his arm around her shoulder, he squeezed slightly before saying. "I'm sorry Ma'am. I never had intention to see killing here."

The woman suddenly stopped her screaming and slowly began sniffing her nose. She even reached back and took her child and pulled him close and hushed at him.

She herself did not understand why, but she believed this strange man and she no longer felt afraid.

When Cliff released her, he stepped back and looked around.

There where the Chinaman had been sitting, he saw a heavily constructed leather bag.

"Are you Mrs. Tidwell?"

"Yes," she said nodding her head and wiping her nose with a small laced handkerchief.

"Where is your husband?" he asked softly.

"I don't know. I haven't seen him since he left to stretch his legs. I assume he's back with the other men," she said nodding towards the rear of the train. "He does so love to gamble."

"How long ago did he go to stretch his legs?"

"Oh, long ago; when we were stopped in Albany," she said.

"Did he leave the train?"

"I, I don't think so," she answered shaking her head.

"Does this bag belong to the Chinaman?" he asked reaching for the leather bag. When he tried to lift it he knew what it contained.

"No, that's my husband's; Butch was only carrying it for us," she said again wiping her nose with the white cloth.

Cliff returned his Smith & Wesson to the belt holster and with both hands, lifted the bag and then slung its wide strap over his shoulder and moved towards the back of the car.

When he got to where Nadine sat, he said loudly, "Ma'am you had better come with us; we may need a hostage, and this poor woman has suffered enough here."

She stood and quickly, turned, and led them out of the car.

It was at that time they heard another report; this time from the rear car. Cliff set the heavy bag down and again pulled his top break. "Keep your eye on that," he said to Nadine before he headed through the door.

Arizona Bill shook his head as Cliff gave him a questioning gaze.

"Came from back there," Red Max said pointing to the car behind them.

When Cliff entered, he saw Coleman Darktower standing over a very dead conductor.

"We had to kill him, too?" Cliff asked.

"I had to," Jim Gillie said "He came slipping in from behind and almost struck Coleman on the back of the head with that hammer."

Cliff looked at the lawyer, who he now saw was holding a Navy Colt that someone had shortened the barrel by some three inches; then he looked at Darktower and finally at the dead man there on the deck.

'True enough, he is holding a small-headed hammer in his hand,' Cliff thought.

"Did anyone else see this?"

"Just her," Coleman said motioning with his head at the woman sitting behind them.

Cliff nodded his head and then said. "We'll check the caboose for Tidwell, but I suspect he got off the train at Albany."

"You think he saw what was happening?"

"Don't figure; if he had, he would have sent a wire and there would have been a posse waiting when we got to Americus," Cliff replied shaking his head.

"He's either back there," he motioned towards the caboose, "or he got off the train for some reason and failed to get back on."

"You think he planned it that way just in case?"

"No, he would have never left his gold here if he meant to travel on another train."

"You found it, then?"

"Yeah, his Chinaman had it."

They very slowly opened the door to the caboose and entered. The lantern was high and the little room was well lit. The signal man was asleep on a cot and no one else was in there. Darktower even climbed up and looked forward from the crow's nest to make sure he was not on top of the cars.

Cliff knew they had missed him.

When they got back to the car where the Gillie's were he said, "It's still best for you two to stay on board and act as if you were nothing but passengers. I would reload that revolver though, and give it to her just in case they want to search you."

"I'll do as you say, but they had better not attempt to search me. I'll have them in court so fast they won't know what hit them," he said back.

Cliff had to admit to himself, he was beginning to like this couple.

Robert climbed over the coal car and stuck his pistol barrel in the engineer's back.

The train stopped some fifty yards beyond the trestle, and they dismounted and watched it chug away before turning for the river.

When the train reached Fort Valley there was no need for the Napoleon. The engineer had no thoughts other than stopping to report the robbery in which two men had been killed and a woman kidnapped.

Sergeant Livingston took the report and immediately sent a wire to Headquarters, and waited for further orders. An hour later, he received one back that instructed him to pursue and capture with great haste.

While he was reading the wire, The Renegades were moving east along the old military road through Dooly County. They had taken the flatboats south on the Flint to the rendezvous point, and then moved east on foot for over a mile to the corral. Before moving out they had disassembled it, leaving little evidence anyone had even been in these parts lately.

Robert's cousins had taken the two boats on south, down the Flint to Turkey Creek and then west into Montgomeryville, and tying up there, began selling the catfish and brim they had caught along the way.

The Renegades spent the night in a barn that was located in the back pasture of a large farm. They did not know whose land it was; but mostly it was in cotton, save this three hundred acre field that had been hayed recently. The barn was full of the fresh cut grass, and Nadine sneezed most of the night awaking every hour with a splitting headache.

The next morning they turned due south, and by noon, cut a new road about three miles from Isabella that the Brunswick & Albany Railroad was putting through. The bed had been cut, but the ties and rails had not yet come this far. It presented a clear and fast route east towards the headwaters of the Withlacoochee. From there, they followed its banks home, skirting west of Valdosta.

Jim and Jackie Gillie continued on to Macon where they stayed for two days before returning by rail to Thomasville; there Dizzy met them with a buckboard and with Johnny riding behind on Granny's black stallion, escorted them into Madison.

It had been both successful and a failure as far as the Renegades were concerned. They had taken Tidwell's gold alright, which amounted to near eighty-two pounds, a worthy sum; but the fact Tidwell had escaped dampened the whole affair, especially for Coleman Darktower and Cliff Brown.

Darktower took it only as a minor setback. He had come close so many times over the years, when something like this happened, he just stored it in his memory pack and planned not to let it happen again in this manner. What was most important to him was he now knew where his old enemy was and that was not far away.

Cliff was a little more disappointed. He had thought he would be able to once and for all have the means to erase the only witness to the old murder charge Tidwell had falsely placed on him years before, but it was not to be, not yet anyway.

Sergeant Livingston found no trace of anyone or anything having been around the location where the engineer had told him the robbers had departed the train.

Returning to Fort Valley, he had to withstand the wrath of one John M. Tidwell who had just lost almost $33,000 dollars worth of gold; gold that he had painstakingly smuggled out of China and into the United States.

Two days later at the Governor's Mansion in Atlanta, he was like a caged panther pacing back and forth, slamming his fist down on tables and cursing loudly.

Rufus Bullock had never seen his friend in such a state. He had his own problems with the election coming up and so many of the newspapers once again in the hands of people he couldn't control. It had all started with that little insignificant *"Madison Trace,"* in Middle Florida. That damn editor was a bulldog. The bastard had gotten his teeth locked onto them and he wouldn't let go. Now a dozen or more papers were calling for his resignation. There were even calls for his impeachment and prosecution on corruption, and even conspiracy to murder.

"I'll tell you right now, John; I can't do anything that will give these vultures a chance to get at my throat. They are even threatening to indict me, 'Me', the Governor of this miserable piece of real estate. Hell, them damn darkies can keep it. I'm tired of the whole mess. I'm ready to go back to New York."

"That's exactly what you can't do. You leave now, and it will be an admission of guilt. I tell you, send me the troops I asked for and place them all under my command and I will wipe out this bunch of renegades in a week."

"Renegades, ha! That is what you said six months ago and you haven't done one damn thing, but lose your gold and get me more bad press."

"I can't work with my hands tied," Tidwell said reaching for the glass of Port the colored servant set before them. "Northrop is such a pussy he won't launch any attacks. Hell, he's happy with things as they are; he's getting more and more of the land the darkies are selling for next to nothing, and with all the payoffs, now even the secessionists are paying him to open back up their businesses. Hellfire, Northrop is more one of them than one of us; and Jarvis is worse. He is so dumb and filled with himself, he can't even see the profits that he could be making."

"Now John, we all counted on the darkies not having enough of a human brain to operate without being told what to do. Northrop is only doing what you and I, and everyone else, are doing," the governor sighed, "Jarvis is only a Captain, surely you can handle him."

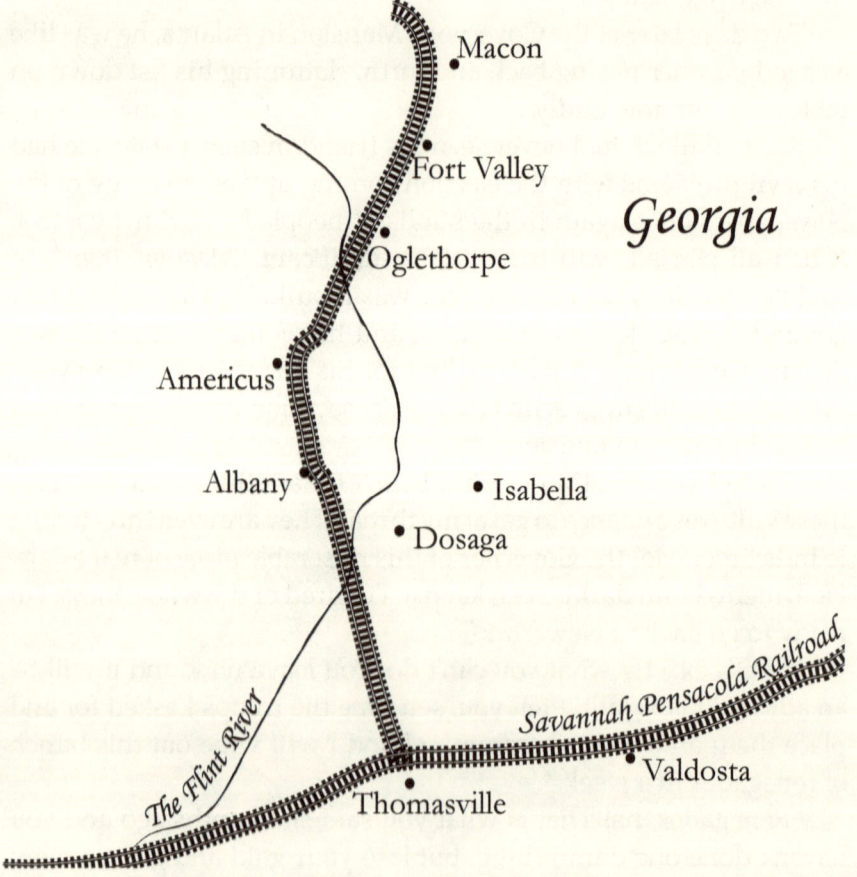

"He could cooperate a little more. He allows me to use his troops when it suits him; not when, or in the strength, I need them."

"Colonel Northrop is in the army, not the state militia. We are civilians, me as well as you. There is just so much I can get away with, or Washington will be on my ass, too."

"Damn it, Grant is your friend; he appointed you. Send him a wire. Tell him of Northrop's incompetence. Give me a full company of good white troopers and I'll bring destruction to these renegades. Then the papers won't have anyone to call their Robin Hood."

"I could use some relief there," Bullock admitted as he pulled back the heavy wine colored drapes and looked out the window.

As far as the Governor could see there were buildings under construction. *'Atlanta will soon have no trace Sherman's army ever came anywhere near here'*, he thought.

"There is a detachment of infantry that has been dealing with some white slavery down in a little trashy village called Smyrna or New Smyrna," he paused and took a sip of the wine, "Down somewhere in Florida; they are being relieved next week and are returning to Ohio to muster out. Since they are coming through here, I received a wire from Stanton to have them stay in Atlanta for two weeks until some red tape in Washington can be cleared up. I might be able to have them diverted to Valdosta for those two weeks."

"Well, infantry cannot do half what Dragoons[40] can, but I will take them, if I can get them," Tidwell said rising from the chair he had just sat down in. "I must be in command though."

"I'll see what I can do. You had better get back on tomorrow's southbound and be ready if Grant approves this."

Tidwell was already headed for the door.

"And John," Bullock said stopping him just before he reached the door, "don't foul this one up. My future," he paused, "and yours could be at stake here."

Tidwell did not like being chastised by a man he had helped get as far politically as Bullock had, but he knew what Rufus had said was true.

The South Georgia Pioneer's headlines were:

Two Murdered by the Withlacoochee Renegades In Daring Train Holdup

---

[40] Dragoons: Another name for Cavalrymen

The Madison Trace covered the same story and the headlines there were:

WOMAN MUST DEFEND HERSELF AGAINST ATTACK BY JOHN TIDWELL'S PERSONAL SERVANT

> The Trace's own reporter 'Jackie Gillie' was an Eye Witness to Assault on a Woman Passenger by the Chinese Servant of John Tidwell, the same John Tidwell who is Director of Valdosta's Civilian Department of Reconstruction. Had it not been for the daring rescue of the defenseless woman by homefolk she maybe dead or at the very least assaulted, by the oriental.

The Trace made no mention of the conductor Jim Gillie had shot, and neither paper had anything about gold or other goods stolen.

For a few days the story from Valdosta spread, but before long what an eyewitness had reported seemed to hold more weight, and soon even the papers in Atlanta and Washington were running Jackie's account.

Bullock rolled his paper into a bat and began slapping himself in the leg with it. "Good God above, this is all we need," he shouted at John Washington. The old colored man just nodded his head and replied softly "Yas, sur, dis am all we needs," as he poured another glass of Port for the Governor.

Grant had agreed with Bullock's request to use the 23rd Infantry in quelling the uprising of southern renegades that were resisting the Reconstruction Plan. He had also cautioned the governor about future sour publicity on the manner in which Reconstruction was being implemented; a note Rufus Bullock did not fail to understand.

"Obviously these headlines had not reached Washington when Grant gave me the 23rd," he said aloud.

John Washington nodded his head once again in agreement.

Major O. C. Scott had been greatly relieved that he and his men were finally going home. The assignment of stopping the slavery that was moving out of the little port of New Smyrna was a difficult one. There was truth in the accusations that Freedman, both male and female, and even a few white women who had shown sympathy towards the Union during the rebellion, had disappeared in Volusia and surrounding counties. There was even some evidence they had been loaded aboard a schooner at New Smyrna and taken to Cuba where the men were sold as slaves to work in the sugarcane fields and the colored women were forced into prostitution, but there was no trace of the white women who were also reported to have been taken from that area. Scott believed the white women were being transported much farther south into the Caribbean Islands or maybe even to Mexico or South America. There had been a lot of unconfirmed rumors that 'The Smyrna Witch' was the offending vessel; however, in the two years he had been stationed at Port Orange, a small village that had been started strictly as a Freedman's community only a few miles north of New Smyrna, he had not been able to confirm any of the reports or make a single arrest.

His men were tired; they needed a change. Most had overstayed their enlistment and were ready to muster out. Those who still had time to serve would be assigned to other outfits and the 23rd would be phased out altogether. It had been organized during the fourth year of the war, consisting mostly of men from and around Cincinnati.

Ozzie Scott had been a Second Lieutenant then; fresh out of the Point with the Class of '64. He had risen rapidly in rank and since the 23rd was not a militia, he had retained the rank when the conflict ended. Now, almost eight years later, his beloved 23rd was being dissolved. He, of course, would remain in the Army. He knew nothing else, never wanted anything else; but he knew also most of the men would be glad to return to civilian life. Eighty percent of them had joined just before or just after the surrender, and had come to the 23rd as replacements for war casualties. They had been so full of patriotism at the time; but most never saw a single battle. Some had been in on the final days in Carolina before Joe Johnson finally gave up the fight, but had not engaged anyone or fired a shot from their new Spencers in anger. This detour to Valdosta had been a blow to the morale of the men; but from the information he had received it was simply a mopping up of a few Secessionists that did not understand the war was lost. He had been assured it would be less than two weeks delay, and then they would once again be northern bound.

Reporting immediately to Colonel Northrop as his orders had instructed, Scott was astonished to learn he would be directly under the command of a civilian.

"I don't know what to tell you. My orders came from Washington instructing me to assist Governor Bullock in the extermination of this bunch of renegades that operate out of the swamps along the Withlacoochee River south of town. Bullock wires me that you will arrive and be assigned to John Tidwell, who is the Director of The Civilian Department of Reconstruction.

"This Tidwell is well entrenched in Grant's administration and a close personal friend of Governor Bullock," Northrop stood and placing his hands behind his back strolled over to the window as he continued. "I have tried to stay clear of him, as much as I can. It's not that he is not a capable man or leader for that matter; but he seems to be driven by personal ambitions or perhaps demons, and often his escapades result in bad publicity. The newspaper down in Madison, Florida, has taken on the cause of these rebels and made them into local heroes," he paused and then turned back and once again faced Scott, "No one thought much of it at first. Our local paper, at least the main one, is owned by a man who was sent for that purpose, as are most in the region; but this *Trace* in Madison has a following now, and is beginning to be more than a thorn in our side, actually Tidwell's side, and Bullock's too."

"Why don't you put a stop to it?" Scott asked.

"Not that easy. Madison is in Florida. My authority stops at the state line, unless of course we are in pursuit or something like that. The big papers in Tallahassee and Jacksonville now support this *Trace*. Even papers in Atlanta and Washington are beginning to show some sympathy. They have this woman reporter who supposedly is riding with these outlaws and writes flowing reports of their side of everything, as an eyewitness. It is becoming a problem for sure. They recently have started a campaign to have Governor Bullock indicted on charges of conspiracy to murder; Tidwell, too," the Colonel said turning back to the window. "Washington sent me a Company of colored soldiers to police the region. Some idiot thought that would really rub salt in the wounds of the defeated rebels, and it has too; only it has made them a tighter group and very hard to get any cooperation from. The only times I have gotten anywhere with the locals is in the last few months, when I started letting a few of them begin doing business again. This, of course, is against what Washington wants; but it eases tension here somewhat, and we need that."

"Are your men well trained? Will they follow orders?" Scott inquired.

"Oh, yes, they are good soldiers. Of course, we have white officers to do the thinking for them. The non-comms are colored, but they are good leaders," he paused then added, "For the most part. We, of course, have had a few incidents where the boys have gotten a little out of hand. It's very hard for a man to be taken from a life of being told when to spit and when to shit, and then give them absolute power over the very ones who at one time did the telling. On occasion there has been some abuse of power by the colored boys, but those times are mostly blown out of proportion. It is the same with all occupational armies throughout time. It's just when the soldiers are colored and some Secessionist woman cries rape, or some prisoner has to be shot while escaping; the whole community turns out with a hue and cry. If I had white troops under my command, this whole affair would have been different."

Ozzie Scott tried to digest all this. This little detour could become a hornet's nest, if it was not already one. He was not pleased and prayed that the two weeks would pass without incident so none of his men would be hurt.

John Tidwell arrived within minutes of Scott's conversation with Colonel Northrop.

Tidwell looked the young Major over and liked what he saw; he liked the fact he was shorter than himself. He also liked that he was younger; although surprised that so young an officer had obtained such rank when many older and more experienced officers were being cut or booted out altogether. His youth also gave Tidwell greater confidence that the Major would follow his command, but he was somewhat suspicious of his possible political connections.

"What we have here is pure and simple, a rebellion on a small scale, and must be dealt with as we would any other insurrection. No quarter will be given to anyone who opposes us," he said as he walked over to the large map of south central Georgia. "We are here. We know they have an encampment somewhere in these swamps," he pointed to the low area marked Brown's Pond, "or here in the Loch Laurel swamp some eight to ten miles south of Valdosta. The river runs south of here and will be to their backs. I think it best if we skirt the old Alcyone Plantation, because there are a few darkies still living in the outbuildings whose loyalty is in question. They just might give an alarm; although I surely don't know why.

"I want your mounted Infantry to come south to Loch Laurel Road and there split into two sections. Colonel, you lead the column on the west and Captain Jarvis will____"

"Hold on just a minute," Colonel Northrop interrupted. "I have been ordered to assist you with my men; I have not been ordered to assist you with my person. This hurrah will be yours alone, Mr. Tidwell."

John looked up. He was shocked that the Colonel would take such a stand given the orders that had come directly from Grant's Staff in Washington, but he could see Northrop was steadfast in his position and he didn't have the time to have his position countermanded; besides he was unsure if he could have that done anyway. Standing straight and looking rather hatefully at the older man he replied, "Very well, Colonel, if you do not wish to be a part of crushing Georgia's only real opposition to the President's Reconstruction Plan, then you will not enjoy any of the spoils when it is publicized in all the Washington papers."

"That I will have to live with," Northrop said and then reaching for his hat he added, "Gentlemen, I have a luncheon engagement; please feel free to use my office."

"Well, I for one am glad that is taken care of," Tidwell said. "Now back to our strategy for this campaign. Major, I will send your infantry by rail over to the Jasper spur here," he said pointing to the map. "You will ride south until you get to this location; from there you will follow an old trail that cuts through the timber to the stage road about here, then taking that west until you come to Belleville. There you will divide your forces, sending one squad across the river and keeping three on this side," he stopped and looked at Scott. "Captain Jarvis will be moving east from the mill road and should flush them. When they retreat, you will be waiting in ambush. Should any escape over the river, your other squad will be there to pick them off," Tidwell finished and clasping his hands behind his back, he looked over again at the Major, expecting praise for his plan.

Scott took a deep breath before speaking. "How will we know where we are to depart the train?"

"I will have a good tracker going with you. He knows the way."

Scott nodded his head "And you are certain they are on this side of the river."

"Absolutely, I have good information they have moved their main camp into this swamp. Their leader, a diehard Rebel, was raised on this land. The saw mill here was built by his father," Tidwell said pointing to a mark on the map.

"Do they still operate the mill?"

"Well, no. Actually I own it at this time," Tidwell said and then he turned and walked back to Northrop's desk where he took a cigar from the finely polished cherry wood box that had once sat on the desk in Mr. Dasher's law office.

"I seem to get the impression you do not intend to arrest these people," Scott injected.

"Arrest?" Tidwell said throwing the Lucifer onto the hardwood floor. "These renegades won't be arrested. They will fight to the death. If you try to arrest them, they will trick you and end up killing just that many more of your men."

"Aren't there women and children with them?"

"Yes, some, but don't let them fool you either. One of the women killed a soldier who was just funning with her. Shot him dead right in front of several witnesses," he replied and then stopped and turned again and stared directly into Scott's eyes and sternly said, "And one of those fine ladies is a reporter who has caused me much heartburn. I saw her at Thomasville and I will recognize her when I see her again," he now looked up towards where the wall met the ceiling as if he could see her as he spoke and added, "She is a beautiful, raven haired, woman; about thirty, carries herself very well; but there is a banshee living in that body. If you find her, I want her brought to me," he turned and looked again at Scott. "Is that understood?"

"Yes, sir. I understand she is not to be killed; rather brought to you."

"That's right, but watch her every minute; don't let her escape."

"When do you expect all of this to take place?"

"You and your men will be ready to leave at 0400 hrs, day after tomorrow. I will introduce you to Captain Jarvis at dinner tonight."

"Very well, sir. Is that all?"

"Yes, for now. Major, you are dismissed."

Ozzie walked out and closed the door and rolled his eyes and slowly shook his head. He headed straight for the officers' quarters looking for Colonel Northrop.

Northrop wasn't there, but he did finally see him walking on Ashley Street towards Central. "Colonel, may I speak to you?"

Northrop stopped and waited until the Major caught up to him.

Scott explained what Tidwell had laid out. "This man is a lunatic. He plans for us to slaughter all those people; women, and children too. He wants no one arrested, except one, how did he describe her, a beautiful raven haired banshee; he wants me to bring her to him."

"I'm not surprised," Northrop replied, "That is why I left. I want to know nothing of his plans," the Colonel said as he began walking again. "I can't be held accountable for things I knew nothing about."

"But sir, this ain't no war; these people need arresting maybe, but not murdered."

"Major Scott, I don't know where you have been for the past eight years but we have been murdering them as long as I have been in the south. That is what Washington's Reconstruction is all about. Steal their land; if they resist arrest, eliminate. Then we give the land to the Freedman, and then," he raised his voice and waved his hands in the air, "when he finds he can't make it work without help, we buy it back from him for pennies of its true value. My God, Major, don't you realize by now that's what the whole damn war was about to begin with?"

"I know that goes on. That's politics. I'm a soldier. This civilian is ordering me to kill people that I'm not sure has even done anything wrong."

"Oh, they've done wrong alright. They stole Tidwell's gold and he's mad about it, and they were born wrong. Born in a land that lost a war and now the victors are reaping their spoils. Surely you are not so naive as to think we are really here to help the poor coloreds, Major."

"Colonel, I protest this assignment."

Northrop looked at him and then said, "Put it in writing and I will see that it is processed up the channels; might do you some good at your court-martial, if you live through this skirmish."

"I can't ask my men to do this."

"Major, you are under orders, I am under orders, both our orders came from the President of these United States, and those orders are for you to follow John M. Tidwell. He is your commanding officer until further notice."

Northrop looked at the stunned and confused young officer and then shook his head and added just before he walked off leaving him there, "You are not the first officer that was given an assignment he didn't like, being a good soldier is sometimes a rotten job; we can't help that." He paused, then finished with, "Son, do your duty, as best as you can."

That night the Major met Captain Jarvis and they both agreed John Tidwell was on a mission of revenge; but they also both knew if they wanted to stay in the Army they must do as ordered. Before departing, Scott said, "I will not tell my men to shoot down anyone who is not resisting."

"I understand, Major, I too feel the same way. Let Tidwell do his own murder."

"I have never heard of a civilian leading an army attack before; what is going on here?" Scott asked as if there were someone who could give him a logical answer.

"Tidwell has Governor Bullock's full support, and I understand Grant is a personal friend."

"What about Sheridan; does he know about this?"

"Must, he sent the orders didn't he?"

"I guess so," Scott said shaking his head.

Charles Gillie, Jim's brother, a telegrapher for the railroad, intercepted the wire reassigning the 23rd to Valdosta for two weeks. He sent one himself to his brother at Station Number Three.

YOUR SURPRISE BIRTHDAY PACKAGE
WRAPPED IN BLUE WILL ARRIVE VALDOSTA
TWO DAYS HENCE
STOP

YOU WILL HAVE TWO WEEKS TO ENJOY IT
BEFORE YOU MUST SEND IT ON TO MOTHER IN
OHIO
END

It was signed, THE CRIPPLE CREEK DRIFTER

Jim brought it straight to Cliff.

"What do you make of it?" Jim asked.

"How much does he know about what we are doing here?" Cliff questioned.

"Jackie sends Donna a copy of all the papers that she has articles in; I guess he has a pretty good idea."

"I would say he is telling us there is a new bunch of Bluebellies, headed for Valdosta."

"That's what I made of it, but I don't understand the two weeks."

Cliff thought a long time and then removed his foot from the log and turned looking across the pasture he rubbed the palm of his hand on the butt of his revolver before speaking again. "Could be they are planning something and need more men," he nodded his head as if he agreed with his last statement, "Could be Tidwell wants his gold back."

"Maybe, I don't know; but I thought you should know about this wire."

"Thank you, Jim, I did need to know."

It was the first time Cliff had not referred to him as Mr. Gillie, and it pleased the lawyer to know he had been accepted by this man.

"I know it's a long ride up here and if you hear anything else, send a wire to Darktower at the Jennings Station and he can get it to me when he comes through," Cliff said.

"That might take too long. If I think it's important I will bring it myself," the lawyer said, "Not only are you doing what's right and what has needed to be done a long time ago, but it's getting to be fun."

Cliff looked at the big man and squinted his eyes, '*I never thought I'd like him so much.*'

In the cool late evening hours of Thursday, September the 14th, 1871, under a new moon, the 23rd Infantry boarded the special train in Valdosta for their last mission as a unit. Major O. C. Scott looked on as his men boarded the cars by lantern.

Twice he had patted the small bulge on his left breast where he had placed, in the inner pocket of his blouse, the folded orders he had demanded be put in writing before he would move his men. Now he had no choice. They had to go, and he had to lead them.

The train moved east for some less than an hour before they switched to the Jasper spur. Their travel southward was in total darkness. The night air was heavy and damp as they moved past numerous small cypress swamps that pocked the landscape. The farming area had mostly been in cotton before the war; but being left idle, nature had begun to reclaim it, and now much former cultivated acreage supported scattered pines and the small tender water oaks that had been able to struggle to life.

The train slowed to a stop just as Ozzie's watch ticked away at the midnight hour. The unloading in the dark was slow, but without incident save Private Mark Bauer, one of Lieutenant Yingling's men, who twisted his ankle and had to return by rail.

Four hours later, Captain Jarvis had his troops mounted and began moving out of Valdosta. Their orders were to push south on the pike past Clyatt's mill and then turn east keeping the river to their right and cutting slowly back to the northeast coming to Loch Laurel Swamp. It seemed easy enough, but Jarvis had a bad feeling; especially when they passed the Valdosta courthouse and he saw John Tidwell there mounted on a black stallion, two of his remaining Chinamen were with him.

Dawn found them within sight of the big saw mill. Tidwell had always wanted to take over that mill. It was the only competition to the one he owned on the north end of Brown's Lake, but the Clyatt brothers had stashed away hundreds of dollars worth of coin before the war and had not given so freely as most in these parts had for "The Cause," so when the tax man came around in sixty-six, they paid their "War Taxes" and continued to operate.

The column skirted the mill, because Tidwell knew well there were many Renegade sympathizers working there.

Darktower had pulled out of Jennings at six sharp. He had only one passenger, a banker returning home to Quitman.

Thirty minutes after sunup, the low fast moving clouds opened up, and a steady drizzle came pouring forth just as he rounded a curve where the winding road came out of a thick hammock into a long stretch of mostly clear ground. He arrived just in time to see the last of Ozzie Scott's men cross the road and enter a thick patch of pine a quarter mile ahead.

"Do you think they saw us?" Lieutenant Yingling asked, wiping the rain from his face with the palm of his hand.

"I don't know; doubt it," the Major answered, "I was watching the teamster when he passed and he never once looked our way."

As soon as the stage was out of sight, the men returned to the road and continued west in what was rapidly becoming a muddy trail; still, the going here was much better than it had been between the railroad tracks and where they cut this road, and they were making up for some lost time. Ozzie figured they would make the ferry by nine as planned.

The river was low. August had not produced the rains it usually did. Two days before, the ferry had been just above bottoming out when heavily loaded. So Coleman took a chance and bypassed it and charged on off the bank at the old crossing. He looked hard at the dark water ahead and saw, with relief, sand only a couple of feet below the surface.

The splashing was fierce and Charley Pitcher once again bounced out of his seat. This was the third time in the last half hour. "That damn driver is gone plain mad," he said with no one to hear him.

With the steady pattering of rain on the corrugated tin roof, Frosty Bass was still asleep in his little shack until he heard the commotion of the stage crossing the river at speed. Coming out, he rubbed his balding head in wonder as the coach disappeared in a cloud of flying mud and rain.

He went behind the shack and relieved himself before checking his trot line. By the time he had removed the two catfish and was back sitting in the shack, Coleman had covered the three miles to the stage stop.

Sam knew something was up by the way he had come charging in. "What's up, Coleman?"

"Where's Mae?"

"In the house, she will be out in a minute."

"Need her now," he said to Sam and then turned and yelled to his passenger. "Be here a spell, go inside and get something to eat."

Jumping from the coach, he took Sam by the arm and led him around the building where Pitcher couldn't hear. "Big bunch of soldiers coming this way on foot. Be here in an hour, no more."

Sam looked at Buckskin Mae as she came out the backdoor. She was fixing her hair; she had not expected Cole for another thirty minutes, and was still prepping herself when she heard the team come up; smiling, she walked towards the sound.

"Get a horse and go get Reb. Quick, girl," Sam told her in a stern voice.

Her smile vanished and she looked at her lover.

He motioned her to get on with it and she, though not understanding why, obeyed immediately by jumping on a lineback dun and dashing away across the pasture bareback.

"Something's wrong!" she yelled as she approached where several were sitting around under the branches of a cluster of white oaks, not far from the fire, drinking their morning brew.

"What is it?"

"I don't know, Cole just came in, in a big rush, and Sam told me to come get Reb as fast as I could."

Cliff didn't wait for anymore questions. He likewise jumped on the back of his horse and the two dashed toward *Estherbrook Stage Stop*.

The weather was gathering in the Gulf of Mexico and flowing straight for Savannah, replenishing the Okefenokee with much needed water. *Estherbrook* lies some sixty miles northeast of the Gulf, as the crow flies, and directly in the path of this two-day storm.

The boy they all called Buckshot, had left an hour earlier for his post at Sam's crossing. From there, one had a clear view of both sides of the river and was only two miles from *Estherbrook's* back pasture.

He found lookout duty exciting at first, but now after months of almost no one coming around, he had begun to hate it. His father kept a short rifle behind the door in the kitchen house to shoot snakes or other pests, and today Buckshot had slipped the 1869 Remington out with him when he left for his morning duty. The seventeen-inch barrel and skeleton stock made the little 22 just the right size for a six year old boy. He only had the one shell, but he pretended he had hundreds and he would save the family from an attack of hostile Creek Indians. After an hour of play, shooting one imaginary Indian after another, he climbed into the fork of a large magnolia tree and there fell fast asleep until the rain awakened him, or perhaps it was the sound of a metal canteen bouncing off a slung rifle. Even to a mere boy, the sound of metal to metal in these woods could mean only one thing, man, or in this case, men.

Buckshot flattened himself on the big limb and held his breath as Yingling's squad marched loosely by, passing directly beneath his perch.

He thought of shooting, but quickly decided against it. He had but one cartridge and was not supposed to have that, so he stayed still and counted the blue-coated men. Finally they were all out of sight save one, who had stopped to relieve himself and had not caught up.

Buckshot knew his duty was to warn the camp of danger and he also was ashamed he had fallen asleep and let these intruders get so close before he saw them.

'Should a' seen them when they wus crossing the river.' he thought, *'I let Pa and Reb, and everybody else down.'*

Slowly he eased his little Remington into the fork of the tree where the limb split from the trunk, and placing the front bead on the back of the straggler's head he jerked off a shot.

His aim had been good, but the jerked trigger had moved the end of the barrel a fraction of an inch and the little bullet hit high and to the right of his planed location, striking Colin Littleton's skull above and behind his right ear.

Buckshot immediately dropped down behind the big trunk and pulled in his arms and legs as tightly as he could.

The drizzle wisked away the tell-tale twist of gunsmoke, and by the time his friend, Larry Turner returned, he found Littleton leaning against a big oak. There was no trace of where the shot had come from.

Two others came back, and after a minute of scanning the heavy woods without a sight of anything, they lifted the wounded man and carried him forward.

The muffled sound of the shot was heard by Ozzie Scott who was a half mile to the east of Yingling's men on the opposite side of the river and also very faintly by a few of the men who were now hurriedly gathering their equipment at *Estherbrook*.

"Did you hear a shot?" Nadine asked.

"Yeah, I think I did," Cliff replied.

Art Mann looked off to the east and then at Cliff, "I think I heard a shot yonder."

"Me, too," Cliff agreed before turning to Marty and asking, "Which one of the children went east this morning?"

Colin Littleton Falling from Buckshot's Bullet

"Little Buckshot," Marty replied with a worried expression on his face.

"Does he have a gun?"

"Not supposed to, but you know him."

"That shot came from about where he is supposed to be," Nadine added, also looking to the timber line half a mile east.

Cliff was ready now as were half a dozen others and they headed across the pasture at speed past the stage stop, and eastward on the road to the ferry.

Lieutenant Yingling, following orders, had kept close to the river expecting the Rebels to be fleeing across it, and due to the thick timber between him and the stage road, failed to see the mounted men as they passed behind him.

A heavy clap of thunder followed by a fierce blowing rain had drowned out the sounds of the horse's hooves pounding on the now muddy road.

Cliff headed straight up the road towards the ferry and seeing it was still on the other side, turned and headed for Sam's crossing where the boy was supposed to be.

Buckshot saw the riders coming and at first stayed drawn up as small as he could; but finally recognizing his hero in the lead, he rose and waved.

"You shoot?"

"Yas, sur," the boy said and then turning he pointed in the direction the men had disappeared and added "Bluebellies; thirteen of them."

Cliff smiled and said something to Johnny and then heard the boy yell again. "I got one of them."

Cliff thought, *'He's a little rascal but I sure am proud of that boy this day.'* and then waved at him before leading his men forward after the intruders at as fast a trot as they could manage through the timber and scrub.

Johnny stopped and helped the boy from the tree limb to his horse and slipped him around behind his saddle.

The Withlacoochee, after winding west of Valdosta, cuts east for about three or four miles and then makes a sharp turn to the south and heads for its junction with the Suwannee some twenty miles away. Before making this abrupt turn, as it meanders eastward it passes *Estherbrook's* northernmost boundaries.

Yingling was now unknowingly headed west following its banks. Major Scott, no longer in sight of the river, continued north not realizing the stream made such a sharp turn and was steadily moving farther away from his Lieutenant.

The first of Yingling's squad came out of the forest almost directly across the pasture from Marty's cabin, but they did not see the structure as it was set back from the clearing some seventy feet with a big sweet gum half way between the porch and the pasture. The rain also helped camouflage all the west side of the clearing, but the people who were there in waiting did not failed to see the dark figures slowly moving from the tree line into their pasture.

Marty had seven men with him, as well as Mary Ann and Nadine. This was the first time he had been able to exercise his authority since his accident, and he suddenly felt the pride and weight of the responsibility.

"Wait, give them time to get much closer," he ordered just above a whisper, "Wait, let them all get out in the open," he held up his hand and looked at his ambushers laying on the ground behind the conference log, and standing behind various trees on either side of him. "Wait; let them get better than half-way across the pasture, then none of the bastards will be able to make it back to cover before we cut them down."

Yingling was leading his men across the big field. They were almost halfway across when some motion caught his eye and he looked south. Several head of scrub cattle were milling around as were more horses than would normally be found around one of these cracker farms. He stopped and studied the area more closely. Finally he made out the outline of the stage stop and the corral there. He could see the dim outline of the coach and several people moving around the buildings and felt relief. *'For a moment I thought we might have walked straight into the headquarters of these renegades, but the stage station explains the unusual number of animals and the well kept pasture.'* Bringing his gaze back he now focused on the dark spot that slowly took on the shape of a large barn some two hundred yards away through the now heavy rain. Suddenly he came upon the thought, *'We'll take shelter in that barn and wait out this thunderstorm there.'* Motioning his men to follow he turned slightly to his left and headed straight for the log behind which Nadine lay repeating over and over to herself the words she remembered her husband say so many times when he was teaching her marksmanship, "Site, picture, squeeze; site, picture, squeeze."

She had taken Cliff's large brimmed Stetson from the peg where he hung it as soon as the rain had begun with all intention of bringing it to him, but he suddenly darted off with Buckskin Mae before she could give it to him. Now she was glad, as it kept the rain out of her eyes while she focused on the sights of her carbine.

"Wait!" Marty ordered again.

Lieutenant Yingling was less than forty yards from the barn when he saw the man step from behind the tree and a cold chill ran up the length of his spine. He held up his hand and his whole world suddenly went into slow-motion. From out of his rain-swept vision, suddenly, seemingly from nowhere, armed men were pointing long guns at him.

There in that moment in time when he knew he had walked into a deadly trap, his only clear thought was, *'I have found their main camp.'*

He was glad his men were equipped with Spencers in this awful storm. *'We would have many misfires in this rain had we been equipped with muskets,'* he thought.

His next thought was to tell them to fire once and run for cover, but even in the slow time everything was happening, he never got it out.

Nadine had recognized the different blouse the one blue soldier was wearing, and immediately surmised he was the officer. It was on his chest she had placed the front site and she did not fail to squeeze the trigger when she saw his defensive movements.

The little carbine slammed against her collarbone, but she did not feel the recoil.

Her shot had been the first, but in less than ten seconds a volley erupted from her left side that shredded the ranks of the oncoming men.

When the smoke cleared, there were a few men who were still moving arms or legs and groaning, but all ten who had entered the field were hit, and hit hard.

Suddenly the rain stopped and only a very fine mist replaced it.

Bart Rogman and Larry Turner, who were carrying the dying Littleton, had not reached the clearing at the same time as the others, and they had only been a short distance from the treeline when the firing started. Immediately they dropped Littleton and threw themselves to the ground. Slowly they crawled back into the cover of the trees behind them.

Cliff and his mounted men came upon the two just as they re-entered the pines. Both men immediately surrendered.

Jeremiah Johnny let Buckshot slide off his mount as he himself dismounted. Johnny pointed his revolver at the two prisoners and little Buckshot followed suit, with his unloaded 22.

Moving forward they walked through the ranks of the dead and dying, removing all weapons and other useable gear and placing these spoils on Johnny's horse. When they reached the Lieutenant, Johnny turned to the others and called out to Cliff. "Here be the Officer, Reb. You want I should search him?"

Cliff nodded his approval and rode up beside the young man. He looked so peaceful, his blue eyes were staring into the fast moving clouds above and there was a slight upward turn to his lips as if he were smiling.

"Shouldn't ought a' sneak up on a man's home," Cliff said to the dead man, who's only real wish had been to return to Ohio.

"Here's som'pin" Johnny said and passed the letter Jessie Yingling had only recently finished to his girlfriend back in Cincinnati.

August 7, 1871

Dearest Sophie,

We have been relieved and are expecting to return home before the month has pasted, Praise Jehovah.

You will never know how much I long to see your face and feel your heart beating against my breast. These long years of separation have been very difficult for me but the hardest part was not being near you.

I plan to see your father as soon as I am home and ask him to release you for my bride.

I am being reassigned and the rumors have it both Major Scott and I will be headed to the frontier. Perhaps Wyoming Territory or Montana. I will know I'm sure, by the time I reach your arms.

Must go now, will write later.
All my love Jessie

September 10, 1871

Dearest Love,

Unhappy to report we are still in Dixie. We were relieved almost a week ago but problems of train passage for all the men presented itself. About half of the outfit could have left on the second, and others coming two days later, but Major Scott refused to leave a single man behind. So we all waited for a train to Jacksonville. I thought we would go by ship from there as it has a fine port with much sea travel, but after an overnight stay, we boarded a train and headed west to a small town called Lake City. I have no idea how it got its name as I never saw one lake there. Then we changed trains and once again headed north. The rumor was to Atlanta but somehow we detrained in a tiny town in southern Georgia called Valdosta. Don't try to find it on your map as I'm sure it is not listed.

There is a Company of Mounted Infantry (Colored) stationed here and they have been having trouble with a band of renegade ex-rebels who don't know they lost the war. Anyway, we must help these coloreds clean out the nest. Shouldn't take more than a day or two, I would surmise, but Major Scott is in a bad way about this. I overheard him talking with another officer and the Major said that the whole affair is a mess mostly caused by the incompetence of a man named Tidwell. He is a political big wig and is in charge of the Civilian Division of Reconstruction, and according to Scott, is leading this raid.

Anyway it will be over in a day or two, and we will once again be headed home.

September 15

Just a note to you, Sophie,

I am on a train southbound into Florida again where we are supposed to come upon the rebels from the rear should any escape the attacks he has planned. Scott has decided to send me and my squad on one side of the river so we can catch any of them that try to escape by swimming across. The Major has the remainder of the men and will attack them from the east, while the Cavalry (Mounted Infantry) attacks them from the west. It does sound like a good plan but I was somewhat disappointed in my assignment. I doubt I will see any action and before I leave Dixie. I would like to kill at least one secessionist to pay for my brother John.

Got to go now, we are stopping and will be detraining very shortly.

Hopefully will finally get this posted later today or tomorrow.

All my love,
Jessie

Cliff folded the letter and stuffed it in his pants pocket and then called out to Art Mann, "Robert as soon as you can finish here, have all the men who can travel come to the stage stop."

The tall lanky man nodded his head and looked skyward as the rain began to fall again.

Doc Jean was tending to the wounds of the two men who were still alive. "This is crazy, ten minutes ago I was trying to kill them and now I am trying to save their lives," she said.

Cliff told the others of what he had learned in the letter found on the dead Lieutenant.

"Looks like Tidwell is making a big show; trying to wipe us out in one big push," Sam said.

"That it does," Cliff agreed, then turning to Darktower. "Did you give Alabama Jack the message I sent day before yesterday?"

The big man nodded his head and added, "Saw him at the Flint Diner and handed it to him personally."

"Good, that might be our ace in the hole," Cliff said then turning to Israel Henley, he asked, "Shaky, I need you to go as fast as you can and try and intercept Alabama Jack. He is on his way here with his regular men and some new ones he has recruited. Find him and give him this," Cliff said as he touched the pencil to his tongue to moisten the lead before scribbling a note on the small piece of paper. "If you are caught, eat this, boy. If Tidwell finds it on you he will hang you for it and it will probably get the rest of us killed."

"Not to worry, I'll find him," the young lad said and then he was gone, headed toward his horse.

"This bunch of Ohio boys were all armed with Spencers. We'll try and avoid a fight with them. Instead, we will cut around them and set an ambush for Tidwell. The 103rd are still armed with their Springfields and my guess half of them won't fire in this rain."

He stopped and looked around waiting for questions, but when none came he said, "Alright, boys, make sure everyone is carrying two revolvers and a fully loaded Blakeslee Box. Now let's go find the bastards!"

The men mounted and followed him back to his barn where they waited as Johnny passed out the weapons and ammunition.

When he handed two of the Open Top Colts to Coleman, the big man shook his head and replied. "No thanks, I am used to these," he said and patted the stocks of the Dragoons.

"Them ain't no good in the rain," Johnny said still holding out the cartridge revolvers.

"They have served me well for over twenty years. I know how to keep them dry," the big man replied.

Johnny did not think it would go well with Reb, but didn't say anything more. Instead, he handed the two Colts to the girl who was next to Darktower, along with a Blakeslee Box.

"I aim to go with you, Mr. Brown," Jackie Gillie said sternly.

"Due respect, ma'am, we are going to be riding hard."

"I see your wife is going, and her, too," she nodded her head at Mae, "I will not be left behind on what may be the most important battle of this whole ordeal."

"I'll see she keeps up," her husband interjected as he accepted his pair of Colts.

"Alright," Cliff replied, not liking it, but he had little time to argue the point. Besides, he looked over at Nadine on her paint, and Mae on her dun, *'Perhaps she is right.'* he thought.

He turned to Johnny and said. "As soon as you are finished here, I want you to backtrack these Bluebellies and see where they split off from their company. Locate the main force if you can; and then get back to me and let me know where they are. We will be going over at the deer crossing yonder," he nodded to the northeast, where they all knew whitetail often crossed the river, "and then head straight north for a mile before cutting west on Ross' Trail. My guess, that's the route Tidwell will be coming on."

Johnny nodded his head and hurried along with his responsibility of arming the men.

Cliff rode up beside Jean Lathrop. "Can you leave them? I would like you to be with us. We'll probably need your services before this day is over."

She looked at him and then back to the men who were seriously wounded, both with rounds in their stomachs. "I can't help them much anyway. They need to be in a hospital," she replied and started gathering the supplies she would need to tend more gunshot wounds.

Cliff stopped at the top of the bank and looked around; a quick count gave him eighteen riders. Not a third of what they would surely face, but he would not trade places with Tidwell for any amount of money.

Darktower rode up beside him and said, "Remember, if we find Tidwell, he's mine. You let me kill him."

Cliff looked at him a few moments and then replied, "I did it your way last time and he got away," then without looking again at Coleman he spoke to the group. "Men, today we are going against the strongest force we have ever had to deal with. I ain't gon'a' lie to you and say it's gon'a' be a piece a' cake. We do have the advantage of better arms and with the rain, that is even better odds than at other times. These people have come here on our land and destroyed our homes and burned our food and killed our families, all so their politicians can steal our property for a song. These poor darkies we are gon'a' kill today probably don't even know they are being used as pawns in this here stealing, but they are the very ones who did the killing and the burning, even if they were under orders from the Government, and I don't think even the Government ordered them to rape our women. Kill them as you did the other blue coats during the war and do it with a clear conscience. I don't think God holds with the kind of men who we are opposing this day."

He looked about him and then pulled on the left rein and turned his horse towards the steep river bank.

The others followed single file.

Ozzie Scott had not heard anymore gunshots since the first muffled boom an hour and a half before. He had since heard several distant rumbles of thunder and was beginning to think it had been thunder and not a gunshot at all. *'Surely if Yingling had engaged anyone there would have been more than one shot.'*

His line of march had continued north for several miles and now he had ordered a rest. He had not found any trace of the hideout camp of these raiders, nor had he come upon the large swamp Tidwell had shown him on his map.

'It's a good thing I studied his map well, the one he gave me is useless after getting soaked.'

Scott had sent out two scouts; one in advance, hoping to find the Loch Laurel swamp or the 103rd, and one to his left to make contact with Yingling and his men.

At the very moment Scott had ordered his men to stop for the rest, Bart Rogman and Larry Turner were wrestling with the rough hemp that bound their hands behind them. Each was sitting on the rain-soaked sand facing the barn with their backs against the big log. Only Marty, Esther, and Mary Ann were left to guard the prisoners and most of their time had been spent trying to ease the suffering of the two wounded men.

"I think I can get my hands free shortly," Turner whispered.

"Yeah this drizzle is helping; mine are not cutting as much as when that big fellow tied me."

"That red-head yonder seems addicted to coffee, she done come twice to refill her cup. If I can get free I'll stay here until she comes again for the pot and then jump her."

"That sounds good, otherwise that tall lanky fellow will sure kill us when he gets back, we know too much."

"Yeah, that's my thinking, too," Turner agreed. "There was a lot of hate in all of their eyes."

Ten minutes later he said, "Bart, I'm free."

"Good boy, I seen that little fellow come from the barn with guns, there could be more in there. What we gon'a do with these three?"

"I reckon we'll have to kill 'em or they might summon help. Ain't no telling how many of these Crackers there are in these woods," Turner replied.

"Yeah, after we get us some of that pussy."

Turner smiled and then added, "Well, we might have just enough time for a couple of quick ones. I kind'a fancy the one with the big tits."

"That's alright with me, touther one is the purdiest and besides, once we're done we can swap and have another round before we have to leave."

"Yeah. Look out, here comes Miss Big Tits for more coffee."

The moment Mary Ann bent over to pick up the pot, Turner made his move, and in an instant she was on her stomach with Turner on her back, his hands at the back of her head grinding her face in the sand.

She had screamed out when she first felt him push her, but it was at the same time one of the wounded men gave up the Ghost also with a loud yell, and neither Marty nor Esther realized Mary Ann had also screamed.

A couple of seconds later, Turner had twisted her around and struck her hard on the left jaw with a mighty balled fist and Mary Ann stopped struggling; although she was not unconscious, she was addled to the point she didn't understand what was happening or where she was.

Immediately, he jumped from her and began to free the hands of his comrade. Once done, they both crouched and studied their situation. "That old man in the chair is armed, but the woman ain't. At least I ain't seen no gun on her."

"You want to wait until I check the barn?" Bart asked.

"Naw, this here bitch might come to first and cry out. Let's both cut a shuck for that big tree while they got their backs to us. From there you can get to the barn and I can slip up on them. That way, if they realize something is amiss, we can make it to the woods yonder and get away."

"Sounds good, Turner," Bart said just before he shot towards the tree that Dan Faux had been hung from and then slapped his back against its hard bark. A second later, Larry Turner was beside him.

After taking a quick glance around the big trunk Turner said, "They are still there, go ahead to the barn."

Esther was using Sam's folding knife to cut another bandage from her petticoat, when suddenly a strong hand clasped her wrist tightly causing her to drop the knife as she gave a startled scream.

Marty immediately tried to get to the revolver he carried in a belt holster, but the stock caught in the crudely formed chairback and he just wasn't agile enough to swing free before the man buried the short knife in his chest. A moment later they all heard a report from the barn and Turner thought, *'I guess Rogman found another one a' them in the barn.'*

Ten seconds later as he stood and turned back towards where his friend was, he was shocked to see a small boy stepping from the barn doors with a rifle in hand and pointed straight at his face. "Look here, boy; put that down."

"You put down the knife," Buckshot shouted as he continued walking closer.

Turner looked at the bloody blade in his left hand and then over at the dark haired woman. *'If only I can get to her before he shoots.'*

Buckshot saw the man's expression change and he then took deliberate aim and squeezed the trigger, just like Reb had taught him.

The little 22 bullet struck Turner's middle finger right at the knuckle and ricocheted into the palm of his hand causing him to fling Sam's knife away. It was all she needed, and without hesitation Esther rolled Marty over and grabbed his Colt.

A second later, realizing the boy's rifle was a single shot, Turner also turned for the revolver, but he was too late and found only the sight of burning powder as it pushed the heavy 44 slug from the barrel and into his upper chest. He staggered back grasping at his wound; and suddenly, as he dropped to his knees and then on to the sandy ground, he wondered if it was raining in Cincinnati this morning.

Tidwell had moved east several miles after skirting Clyatt's Mill. They had covered much timber and hilly country that was spattered with cypress swamps but none the size he was looking for. He now had stopped, awaiting the artillery piece to catch up.

First Lieutenant Ervin Spats had taken the position in this dirty little post, in order to stay in the army. He had commanded an Artillery battalion in Maryland and Northern Virginia, but now was demoted to Lieutenant and hating every minute of it.

He hated the south. He hated the locals in the south; other than the hookers, the women wanted nothing to do with him or his men. He hated the food. He hated the humidity. He hated being in command of colored troops. Still he wanted to stay in the army and considered this just one of the distasteful stepping stones in his military career.

Valdosta only had a six-pound piece and that was used mostly for parades on Independence Day when he arrived, but he located a ten-pound Brooke the Confederates had abandoned near Macon and had finally convinced Northrop to allow him to bring it to the garrison in Valdosta. He had replaced the Brooke timing fuse with a standard nipple and percussion cap arrangement and had twice now fired it with good success, although they were not firing at anything in anger.

The gun was really too large to be pulled around by horses, but he knew this was most likely the only time he would be able to put it to use against a hostile enemy, and had convinced Tidwell to let him bring it instead of the six-pounder.

Even though he had harnessed eight mules to the big gun, they could not keep up with the main force and were falling farther and farther behind.

Tidwell too had sent out scouts looking for the same objectives as Scott. His man reported back first.

Chad Clayton had moved his family away from the town and town people soon after the first carpetbagger arrived in Valdosta. He had no use for town people and less use for the new town people who came with the war's end. Clayton was fifty years old when the war broke out and had been a poor dirt farmer all his life. He considered the conflict a rich man's war and wanted no part of it, and became quite bitter when six of his eight boys joined in Jeff Davis' fight; two of them never came home. His two daughters had married boys who also went away, and one of them did not return from a prison somewhere in Illinois.

Now he wanted only to be left alone and he did mostly the same to others. This rainy morning he, his children, and his two remaining sons-in-law, had headed into the swamp country to kill off a few gators for their tasty white meat and tough hides. They were riding their mules along the ridge that runs south from Valdosta past the west side of Loch Laurel to the big swamp.

Buff Mims had been a slave in South Mississippi when the war came through the area. He was taken prisoner by Union Troops and then released by conscript to join in the conflict against his former master.

Buff didn't really know what it meant to be free. He had been trained by Misser Oliver as a tracker, because he was one of the few coloreds who was not afraid of the gators, and when they would go down river to the big bayou country, he would get in the swamps and locate their dens. He didn't especially dislike Misser Oliver, but then he couldn't say he liked him either. The army had shown him little more than he had known all his life. Some white man was always telling him what to do and he had better do it. He found the food not as good as at the plantation, but the clothes were substantially better and the way he figured it, now he had a little money to buy a woman once a month and that wus more than he had been able to do before.

The rain was again falling in sheets when Buff saw the line of mounted men traveling south along the ridge. They didn't look much like military men but they all were armed with long guns and seemed to be commanded by a single leader. The big black man turned back and made haste to report his discovery.

Spats had finally arrived with his gun and was just beginning to unhitch his animals for a much needed rest, when Buff came racing on the scene. The artillery man watched the colored go straight to Captain Jarvis, who immediately headed for Tidwell's hastily erected lean-to.

Tidwell obviously pleased about the news, came rushing out into the rain slapping his hands together.

'Shit!' Spats thought, *'He looks like he thinks he's a General, a' spitting out orders just like he knew a blame thing, which he don't. Hellfire, most a' the Generals don't neither.'*

"Lieutenant Spats, how far will that piece you have dragged all the way here, accurately shoot?"

"I think some 2000 yards."

"A mile?" Tidwell confirmed.

"A mile, a little more," Spats answered, hoping he was correct. He had never fired this gun for extreme range but he knew of its design and had investigated it thoroughly. It was a well-made piece much like the Parrott Guns he had commanded in Virginia. *'Actually a little stronger.'* he thought.

"Good; we have located the enemy about three miles ahead on a ridge. The mounted men will move forward and pin them down and I want you to bring that thing forward and obliterate them," Tidwell said.

When he received no reply he asked, "Do you understand?"

Spats looked at Captain Jarvis for an answer, but Jarvis only raised his eyebrows.

Finally Spats replied, "Yes, sir. Obliterate them."

"That's right. Use canister."

Blanche had remained a widow for seven years, finally her cousin Gippy Clanton convinced her of the folly to do so any longer, and they had been married the first day of the new year. Her sister Audrey had been against the marriage and made the lives of the newlyweds as miserable as she could; at every opportunity she found. Blanche's husband knew the reason. Audrey had come to him on several occasions while her husband was away fighting the Yankees and she still gave him longing glances when no one else could see. She was giving him just such a look when the first mini-ball crashed into the pack on the mule she was walking beside; it had passed through her pretty neck a split second before. The last thing she saw in this world was the man she would never again have.

Chad Clayton had heard the boom of the musket at about the time he heard Blanche scream. Audrey never uttered a sound.

Several more shots rained down on them as they tried to pull their mules off the exposed ridge. Finally they let go of the reins and took cover in the pine timber east of the ridge.

Blanche stayed with her fallen sister until Gippy and Charlie could carry her out of the line of fire.

The Clayton clan began returning fire as best as they could. For the most part, their powder and caps were too wet to ignite, and there were as many snaps as combustion from their guns. Still they were getting off enough to keep the unknown bushwhackers pinned down until the first heavy report of Spat's Brooke thundered through the rainy morning.

Chad didn't know what the sound meant; but his sons did, and they immediately dove for cover.

The canister shell exploded a hundred yards behind them high in the trees. The raining shrapnel cut through the mules and killed or scattered them all. Chad Clayton, seeing his favorite mule, Nell, go down stood and yelled at the top of his lungs at the murderers. A second later, he was struck by two mini-balls and he fell backward dead.

For the next ten minutes, Lieutenant Spats lobbed shell after shell at them, as the alligator hunters hugged the back side of the little ridge and prayed.

Ozzie Scott was three miles south when he heard the cannon reports, and he hurried his men on with caution. "Men, keep a sharp eye. These outlaws will be fleeing and Captain Jarvis will be driving them our way."

Cliff and his mounted men also heard the booming of the heavy gun. He had moved in a large clockwise semi-circle after crossing the river, and was now west of the cannon.

"That big gun is close," Sam said.

"Yeah," Cliff agreed," but what are they shooting at?"

"Doe-no'. We're too far north for them to be shelling the stage stop."

Cliff moved forward cautiously until he could see the artillery piece ahead in a small clearing. There he motioned for all to dismount.

They moved in on foot closing to within forty yards, and there he pointed for them to take cover behind the trees in the skirts of the clearing.

Still he waited, unsure what they were shooting at and why.

The gun finally stopped and the artillery men were now standing around awaiting orders from their officer, who stood before them looking ahead with field glasses.

Finally, a colored sergeant rode up and shouted "Mr. Tidwell wants to know why you have stopped shooting."

Cliff heard the sergeant's question and thought, *'Tidwell huh', well that settles the question for me.'*

They heard the Lieutenant reply that he only had three more canister shells left and was keeping them in reserve.

The sergeant turned his mount and headed east again.

"Robert."

The tall lanky boy slipped up beside him. "Yeah."

"Think you can operate that gun?"

He looked at it closely and then replied with a smile. "Them Bluebellies have done stole um' a Brooke. Sure I can. Hell fire, I can shoot the balls off a squirrel half a mile away with that."

"No squirrels today, but maybe a rat," Cliff said and then motioned for several others to come close so he could speak to them.

Nadine was one of the ones who came forward.

"I want you to spread out, two of us to every one of them, and when I shoot, be sure you kill them with the first volley."

He then turned to his wife and said "You wait here. I don't want to be worrying about you instead of doing my job."

His words were firm, but not demeaning and she understood how she could be just such a burden on him at a time like this.

Cliff moved around where he had a clear shot at the officer and then taking careful aim with Teachman's[41] Henry, he squeezed the trigger.

There followed almost instantly a roar of shots, sounding almost as one.

Scott and Jarvis both heard it, but Tidwell paid no attention. His mind was glued on the ridge ahead of him.

[41] Teachman: See Book One Gold in the Red Desert of The Owl Hoot Trail

About that time, Sergeant Tucker arrived and reported Spats' information.

Tidwell turned and cursed and was just about to send the sergeant back to order more shelling, when one of the men shouted and pointed at a blue-uniformed figure near the ridge.

"Cease fire!" Captain Jarvis yelled as he stood waving his arms.

Soon the woods to the south of where the butchered trees lay scattered about, was filling with Scott's men.

There was no return fire from the ridge.

Tidwell stood now and smiled. "Tell the men, good work," he said looking about, "Good work men. I think we have wiped them out."

He returned to where he had tied his horse and prepared to mount when there came several shouts from the short ridge. Turning, he could see it was Major Scott who was doing the most shouting.

"Whatever is the matter with him?" he said to the soldier who had been holding the horses.

Then suddenly, Scott came running as a madman towards where they were.

When he was twenty-five yards away he began cursing Tidwell at the top of his lungs. "You idiot, you blooming idiot! You have just wiped out a whole family of people and not one of them looks to be your renegades."

Tidwell was visibly shaken by the accusations. '*It could not be,*' he thought. "The scout reported he had found them. We were only doing what we came to do."

"That's right you idiot. Murder! That's what you were doing; and that's what you came here to do."

"You're wrong. These Renegades don't dress in uniforms. They look like everyday people. We got the right ones, I tell you."

"Women. That is what you just shelled, women and old men, and a few mules; just ordinary people who were armed with shotguns for hunting alligators."

"You're wrong!"

"I'm taking my men and going back to Valdosta, and when I get there I'm sending a report to Washington immediately."

"You stop that talk now. Do you hear?" Tidwell said "That's an order. I'm in command here!"

"You're damn right you are in command here and that is exactly what I am going to say in my wire. This is one massacre that will not be covered up."

The men were all staring at him. John knew he had to do something and do it immediately. Reaching inside his coat he pulled a revolver. "I'm placing you under arrest, Major; surrender your weapons now."

Ozzie looked around at him and shook his head and turned and stomped off. He had had enough from this political imbecile. "Lieutenant, send a runner back for Yingling and his men, we are marching for Valdosta."

He turned and pointed a finger at Tidwell to tell him one more thing, but never got the words out.

John Tidwell dropped the hammer of his revolver as the man was shouting orders at the Lieutenant, but the cap misfired. The second did not, and the 36 caliber ball struck the Major under his out-stretched arm and passed through both lungs, before stopping against a rib on his other side.

Everyone stood in shock. No one could believe what they had just witnessed.

Captain Jarvis rushed forward and helped the stricken Major down, as his knees began to buckle. The young man looked into Ozzie's eyes as the rain again began to fall and then he gave up the ghost in Jarvis' arms.

Jarvis now realized what he must do. Slowly he stood and looking about him he called to several of the soldiers that were standing close by and told them to cover him.

"Tidwell, you are a madman. I am relieving you of command this very moment and placing you under arrest."

John laughed and lifted the revolver again; but when he did, he immediately heard the unmistakable sound of carbines being cocked and turning his head slightly he saw four of Major Scott's men pointing their Spencers at him and he knew he was no match for them. Slowly he lowered his revolver before he turned his horse and rode towards Valdosta.

A moment later, the air was once again filled with the sound of gunfire and the deadly whistle of flying lead.

Cliff moved his men forward and had been watching the recent events from a distance. He had seen Tidwell shoot the soldier, but could not see who he was or hear why he had been executed. Before he had given the command to fire, he sent Darktower back to tell Robert to send a round on the ridge that was now filled with blue-clad men milling about.

When he felt enough time had elapsed to pass the word, he ordered general firing at anything in blue.

Robert lived up to his word and placed a shell directly on the ridge where most of Scott's men now were.

Immediately upon seeing this, and realizing the big gun was now in the hands of their adversaries; the horsemen of the 103rd cut and followed Tidwell to the north.

A firefight broke out between the 23rd Ohio and the Renegades.

Finally Cliff was able to regroup his men and head out after Tidwell, leaving the infantry behind.

Art Mann turning it on them

John Tidwell had heard the report of the field piece, and assuming Lieutenant Spats was still in command of the gun, turned and headed back. Several of the Colored Troopers followed him but some continued on towards the north.

Robert had only fired the one shell and then waited further orders from Cliff. Nadine and Buckskin Mae had stayed to help Robert, as did Charlie Russo and Bob Shipp to tend to the loading of the gun.

Tidwell came on them at as fast a gallop as he could manage through the rain and timber. When he saw that those manning the gun were not Spats' men, he pulled up short and hard on his reins almost causing his horse to stumble. Nadine saw the motion, but the others were peering out into the rain ahead, trying to catch a glimpse of someone who might tell them what to do next.

Tidwell also saw Nadine, immediately remembering her from the train depot in Thomasville. "The newspaper woman!" he said aloud.

Nadine, seeing his approach, yelled out, and Coleman Darktower turned and saw his old enemy. It had been over thirty years and finally they would once again meet face to face.

He did not wait another second, instead he drew one of his big revolvers and cocked it, but Tidwell was now moving. He had spurred his horse and was charging through the trees at the raven haired woman.

Nadine lifted her carbine and fired, realizing she had jerked the trigger even before the bullet had left the barrel. The round slammed harmlessly into a tree over Tidwell's head. Desperately she worked the lever but she had mistakenly turned the lever-lock on while they were traveling, and had forgotten to twist it clear again.

The man and the big black stallion were on her before she could clear the lever.

Coleman now had a good clear shot and he squeezed the trigger, but all he heard was a sickening snap as the wet cap failed. Again he cocked the cylinder into position, and again he heard a snap. Instinctively he reached for the other Dragoon, but his chance was gone and Martin now had his arm under Nadine's armpit and was hefting her to his saddle. She was between Darktower and his prey. There was but one thing to do. He charged forward with all his might and reached for the stirrup to dislodge the rider and his captive.

For a moment John Mouton Tidwell looked into the eyes of the man who was trying so desperately to kill him, and then he swung his Colt around and shot point blank at the big man. This cap fired and the 77 grain lead ball struck his old lover's son, Michael Coleman between the eyes an inch above the eyebrows. He fell backward like the falling of a huge log; before his soul departed he saw the face of Cap' Burgess, and then his body struck the ground and he lay still in the muddy clay.

Buckskin Mae screamed at the sight of her lover falling, and immediately began shooting at the horseman.

The first round hit the stallion and he kicked sideways throwing his load. The next shot struck Tidwell in the elbow and he had nothing left to hold Nadine with, and she rolled away.

While rolling, the Sharps she always carried fell free and Tidwell, seeing it fall, grabbed it. When Mae rushed up to send the man who had killed her lover to hell, she was met with a blast from the derringer and the little 22 hit her square in the left breast taking away all of her fight. She dropped her revolver and turned and walked back to where Coleman lay face up with his eyes open. It was there she fell.

Nadine, scrambling to get away, saw Mae's fallen Colt and she dived for it.

Tidwell, realizing her intentions quickly twisted, and sent a tiny ball into her side, just as she reached the Colt.

Robert now had his rifle up, but there were several Colored Soldiers coming into the clearing and he is busy keeping them off himself and Shipp, who was already wounded.

Charlie was now blasting with his Henry from the hip at Tidwell, but the man rolled away and as if by a miracle the bullets struck all around him, but none connected.

Tidwell finally mounted the wounded horse and fled the scene just as one of his men sent a mini-ball into Bob Shipp's chest.

Charlie swung and shot that man, then turned back and tried one last round at the fleeing Tidwell.

Suddenly all was quiet. Robert looked around and saw Darktower and the blonde girl where they lay, and then he saw the arm move of the other body. Rushing over he picked up Nadine and held her for a few moments. Finally she opened her eyes and smiled before asking, "Take me to Reb?"

Robert lifted her in his arms and ran the half mile to where so much shooting had taken place only moments before.

Doc Jean was working on David Clark who had received a nasty hit to his upper-right shoulder blade. When Art Mann arrived, she immediately stopped and rushed to Nadine.

"Someone go get Reb!" Jean Lathrop shouted.

"I'll find him," Dizzy said.

When Reb returned, she was lying in the lean-to that Tidwell had used as camp headquarters twenty minutes before. Her breathing was uneasy and she coughed a lot, but otherwise was resting.

Cliff could hardly keep the tears back.

He had for so long not needed anyone, and then when he realized he never wanted to be without her beside him ever again, he had thought of little else but her.

Now she was here, in this damp field, surrounded by the dead and dying, on a miserable day with her life's blood spilling from her side.

When she realized it was he who had come up, she looked up at him and smiled. She started to tell him about the baby but decided against it. *'No need for him to grieve more.'*

Taking a deep breath she spoke as lovingly as she knew how. "It's been one hell of a picnic, Georgia," and then she closed her eyes and was gone.

He tried but he couldn't stop the flow. The tears streamed down his face and he turned and looked at the others who stood around, both friend and foe. He thought it queer they all seem to be crying too.

Shaky reached Alabama Jack in time to turn him, and his little force intercepted Tidwell and his seven men north of Clyattville.

Red Max caught one of them with his big hand and lifted him from the saddle and strangled him before he let go. All the others save Tidwell, fell in the hail of bullets; but Tidwell had exchanged his wounded stallion for a horse one of the soldiers was riding, and it being less winded than the mounts of the Renegades, he soon out-distanced them. Arizona Bill and Lucius Leadbottom both had ridden hard from the time Shaky met them until the skirmish and their horses were too spent to overtake Tidwell. Even so, they chased him to the village limits; but when several towns people came out to see what the shooting was all about, they had to give it up.

"Sorry, Reb; I'd a' had him if I had my old Whitworth," Lucius said as he shook his head.

Blanche Clayton had lain in the ditch on the east side of the little ridge and watched as her new husband, her father, her sister, her brother-in-law and all her brothers died in the rain of steel and lead that fell on them that day. Two days later she was at the office of *The Madison Trace* telling Balough her horror story.

Jackie had taken good notes and watched most of the fighting between the Renegades and the Blue-Coats, both in the pasture and in the pine forest near the ridge, and she hurried back to Madison to have the type set for her editorial before the next edition of *The Madison Trace* was printed. Her headline was as follows:

Carpetbaggers and Occupation Troops Attack and Murder In Two Separate Incidents

1d instant[42] this reporter had the horrible experience of being at a stage stop on the Jennings to Quitman route near the state line, when men of the 23rd Ohio attacked without cause or warning, the buildings on the station property where several families live. Two brothers were murdered, one while sitting in a wheel chair, by men of this battalion. Local members of the so-called Withlacoochee Renegades were able to counterattack and save the remaining women and children from this cowardly assault. It was learned, from one of the surviving Ohio men, that they had been ordered, by one John Tidwell, who is the Director of The Civilian Division of the Reconstruction Plan in Valdosta and a personal friend of Georgia Governor Bullock, to destroy anyone who might be involved with or have knowledge of these loyal vigilantes, women and children included. Within the same hour, several miles north, a family who had nothing to do whatsoever with The Renegades, were brutally attacked by men of the 103rd, the Colored unit stationed in Valdosta. This bunch of cowards, not being satisfied with simply burning and shooting homefolk had, with great effort, brought a heavy piece of artillery with them through the muddy fields, to attack this family. This large cannon was unleashed on a man who had taken his children, both sons and daughters, on a hunting expedition in search of food in the wilds of a nearby swamp. They were gunned down, first by musket and then by canister. Read elsewhere in this publication the

---

[42] 1d instant: Editorial langage for one day past or more commonly, yesterday.

personal account from the sole surviving member
of this innocent family. This reporter is sad to say,
this man Tidwell personally gunned down two
women who were friends of mine, women who I
have learned to respect and love as sisters, in their
fight against political wrong. Also this same John
Tidwell, a personal friend of Governor Bullock,
with malice aforethought, shot and killed a Major
in the Union Army, who tried to stop his acts of
murder. Let's see how Governor Rufus Bullock
gets his fair haired boy out of this one!

Also on the front page beside Jackie Gillie's article, was another
one entitled:

The Editor Speaks

You have on occasion before seen situations
where something is so disturbing to the very nature
of mankind that you know you must speak out. I feel
I must personally report on this as it is one of those
times. I had the sorrowful experience of interviewing
a young wife who lay in a rain-filled ditch while her
whole family was being massacred under the colors of
the United States Flag. I now share with you unedited
the details of this disgraceful event that summarizes
the ungodly misuse of power by so called enforcers
of Washington's Reconstruction Plan.

The Trace: I understand your name is Blanche
Clayton. Is that right?
Blanche: Yes, that's right.
The Trace: Where do you live Blanche?
Blanche: I live south of Valdosta in Lowndes
County, Georgia.
The Trace: Do you or any members of
your family belong to the group known as The
Withlacoochee Renegades?
Blanche: No, Sur. I never even heard of them
'til yesterday.
The Trace: Blanche, tell me about yesterday.

Here we had to stop for a few moments as the
girl burst out in tears.

The Trace: Blanche, we can wait; you just take
your time.
Blanche: No, it's alright. It needs to be told, sure
enough.

The Trace: Alright then, in your own words tell us.

Blanche: Well, yesterde' morning Pa told us we were to come and go with him to kill us some gators as we's getting low on meat. So me and my husband Gippy and my sister Audrey and her husband and my six brothers took some axes and Pa brung his shotgun and little Roy, he was the youngest, took his squirrel gun, just in case, and we followed Pa over to the big swamp, where there are a might a' gators.

The Trace: Did you walk or ride horses?

Blanche: We rode mules, we ain't got no horses; only my sister Audrey wus walking at the time, anyways we were headed back and I wus' a talking to my sister when all of a sudden her neck just exploded. I didn't know what ailed her till Gippy told me she had been shot. I didn't want to believe him. Why would a body want to shoot Audrey? Why? Suddenly there were several more shots and the mules were a bucking and stomping and Pa wus trying to keep them from running off when he wus shot too. My husband and Audrey's husband helped me pull her off the ridge, there are a trail up on top a' that ridge and we were traveling on it, back to home. Then all at once these big explosions started in the trees over our heads and I heard my brother Zack cry out but my husband lay on top of me and shoved me down in the water where only my face was above it, and then only when I turned my head sideways. These big explosions kept coming for a long time and then it suddenly went quiet. When I told Gippy to let me up he didn't answer me and when I finally got out from under him I saw a big hole in his back. He died for me. You see, were he not laying on me like that, it would a' been my back what had the hole in it. He loved me very much.

The Trace: How many of your family were killed?

Blanche: All of them. I got nobody left now. I ain't been married a year yet. My first husband wus killed in the war and I just remarried.

The Trace: Now let me make a count of this awful incident. Your father, your husband, your sister, her husband and six of your brothers were all killed yesterday? That's ten members of one family murdered by Occupational Troops for no reason. This is The Radical Republican Congress' Plan to help the Freedman, at work.

Blanche: I don't know nothing about that stuff, but it is what happened to me yesterde'.

The Trace: What will you do now?

Blanche: I don't rightly know.
The Trace: Will you go home?
Blanche: Lord no. They might come and get me so I can't testify again 'um. That happens you know.
The Trace: Yes Blanche we know. We know it is not safe for man, woman, or child who was born south of Maryland to be in this land called The New South. A name shoved down our throats by the very people who support these despicable acts of terror on innocent folk.

Balough ended his editorial with the following paragraph:

What will Blanche do?

Only God above and a few loyal citizens who remain anonymous know where she is today. Must she live the rest of her life in hiding, in fear? Only Congress and President Grant can answer that before the next election. Then everyone can have a say in it.

History Does Reveal:

Georgia's Governor, Rufus Bullock did flee the state fearing convictions on conspiracy to murder and other corruption charges.

October 1871 found Benjamin Conley, President of the Senate, Acting Governor of Georgia.

January 12, 1872 Georgia inaugurated James M. Smith Governor.

During the year 1872, United State Forces left the State of Georgia, and ever so slowly lives began to return to normal.

John Mouton Tidwell fled the state before charges could be brought against him.

Being finally cleared of the charge of the murder of Bugger-T Polk, as there were no longer any witnesses to accuse him, Clifford "Reb" Brown buried his wife in the new cemetery at *Estherbrook*, gave his property and most of his possessions to Sam and Esther Brooks, and struck a trail after the man who had murdered his wife.

John Inglis moved farther south and today there is a small town on Florida's west coast named in his honor.

The remaining men and women who had been called 'The Withlacoochee Renegades' slipped silently into the normal activities required to eke out a living in the rural south of the 1870's. Their remaining years being lost to history, save one incident that occurred in the spring of 1928 in the little town of Madison Florida, when a lady stepped from the train, and after seeing the square Confederate battle flag waving proudly on one pole and the American Standard nearby on another, made a loud and harsh exclamation to her companion, "My God, Wesley, look at that, these people down here must still be fighting the Civil War."

A very old man standing nearby, though uninvited, replied to her statement, "No, ma'am, we lost the war fair and square, we ain't still fighting it. It are the hard years after the war that left far greater scars and the bitterness in the minds and hearts of the people of the South. Of course, you most likely never heard of such, being as who wrote the history books."

He then touched the brim of his old gray hat and ended the conversation with, "Ma'am," before he turned and with bent back and weak knees, hobbled away with the assistance of a short cane made from the limb of a sweet gum tree.

**The Withlacoochee Renegades in front of the
Napoleon Hotel & Social Club
Early 1870's**

Don't fail to read the next chapter In Reb Brown's life as he pursues his old enemy on the long trail:

Book Three
of the
Owl Hoot Trail

The Long Trail

After having enjoyed T.H. Bear's *The Owl Hoot Trail, Book 2, The Withlacoochee Renegades,* may we suggest T.H. Bear's *Gold in the Red Desert*? This is the first book of the trilogy that tells the story of Reb Brown's flight from Georgia to Wyoming. Another good one in our roster of westerns is Denny Williams' *Bad Times.* This is a funny cowboy tale, guaranteed to make you laugh out loud. *Honeymoon Vengeance* by Roger Scott is the tale of a cowboy doing right by someone wronged.

Gold in the Red Desert by T. H. Bear
Book One of the *Owl Hoot Trail Trilogy*

T.H. Bear introduces us to Reb Brown, a returning POW from the Federal Prison in Point Lookout, MD. Within months of his homecoming, he is falsely charged with a capital crime and must flee his home state just ahead of a lynch-man's posse.

The Owl Hoot Trail leads him from a murder committed among the cypress and sweet gum trees of South Georgia, to a murder committed among the sage brush and prickly pear on the Red Desert of Central Wyoming, at a time when the cry of 'Gold!' was raging throughout the Sweetwater Region.

Ride along with Reb as he crosses from his home in the Southeast to the Red Desert of Wyoming.

You may order online at www.bluewaterpress.com/gold or by mail:

Bluewater Press LLC
52 Tuscan Way Ste 202-309
Saint Augustine FL 32092

Name: _____

Address: _____

City, State, Zip: _____

Phone number: _____

Email Address: _____
(All information kept in the strictest confidence)

Please send me T.H. Bear's *Gold in the Red Desert*. Cost is $20.95 per copy. Shipping & handling is $3.95 per book for one copy, $6.95 for up to seven of any titles, and $1.15 per book for any combination of more than seven.

Number of books _____ x $20.95 = _____

Shipping and handling = _____

FL residents, please add sales tax for county of residence = _____

Total remitted = _____

We gladly accept payment of your choice: check, money order, or credit card.

Honeymoon Vengeance
by Roger Scott

Scott Mckendree is all cowboy. The real thing. Nothing about the man is false or fake; he is strong, he is a survivor, and he lives by doing the right thing. He does not like it when people take advantage of the weak and his gentle manner always compels him to help those in need when he crosses their path.

One spring day, his path crosses with those of Larin and Lynn Willbright, a young couple from back east, newly married and trying to make their way in the new frontier. Unfortunately, their life together is cut short by men with no conscience and it is up to McKendree to help the young bride.

You may order online at www.bluewaterpress.com/honeymoon or by mail:

BluewaterPress LLC
52 Tuscan Way Ste 202-309
Saint Augustine FL 32092

Name: _____

Address: _____

City, State, Zip: _____

Phone number: _____

Email Address: _____
(All information kept in the strictest confidence)

Please send me Roger Scott's *Honeymoon Vengeance*. Cost is $13.95 per copy. Shipping & handling is $3.95 per book for one copy, $6.95 for up to seven of any titles, and $1.15 per book for any combination of more than seven.

Number of books _____ x $13.95 = _____

Shipping and handling = _____

FL residents, please add sales tax for county of residence = _____

Total remitted = _____

We gladly accept payment of your choice: check, money order, or credit card.

Bad Times by Denny Williams

Jack O'Mally is a decent kind of man. One who has lived his life with integrity, a man who always strived to do the right thing.

In the twilight of his years, he finds himself going west to find a way to live out the rest of his life. He encounters, just as he did when he was a youngster, that life is hard and filled with bad times.

This is not a somber story however. Jack laughs in the face of bad times. Denny Williams brings a richness and wonderful humor to the characters of his western novel, Bad Times.

This is a cowboy tale, a rich, funny, cowboy tale written in a fresh new style that will doubtless leave you laughing out loud for a while. Readers are sure to enjoy each twist and turn in the adventure that is Jack O'Mally's life.

\-

You may order online at www.bluewaterpress.com/badtimes or by mail:

BluewaterPress LLC
52 Tuscan Way Ste 202-309
Saint Augustine FL 32092

Name: _____

Address: _____

City, State, Zip: _____

Phone number: _____

Email Address: _____
(All information kept in the strictest confidence)

Please send me Denny Williams's *Bad Times*. Cost is $15.95 per copy. Shipping & handling is $3.95 per book for one copy, $6.95 for up to seven of any titles, and $1.15 per book for any combination of more than seven.

Number of books _____ x $15.95 = _____

Shipping and handling = _____

FL residents, please add sales tax for county of residence = _____

Total remitted = _____

We gladly accept payment of your choice: check, money order, or credit card.